INSOMNIA

By Stephen King and published by
New English Library

Carrie
'Salem's Lot
The Shining
Night Shift
The Stand

By Stephen King as Richard Bachman

Thinner
The Bachman Books

Published by Hodder & Stoughton

Christine
Pet Sematary
It
Misery
The Tommyknockers
The Dark Half
The Stand: the Complete and Uncut Edition
Four Past Midnight
Needful Things
Gerald's Game
Dolores Claiborne
Nightmares and Dreamscapes

stephen KING

INSOMNIA

BCA

LONDON NEW YORK SYDNEY TORONTO

This edition published 1994
by BCA
by arrangement with Hodder & Stoughton Ltd.

CN 4007

First reprint 1995

Printed and bound in Germany
by Graphischer Großbetrieb Pößneck GmbH
A member of the Mohndruck printing group

For Tabby . . . and for Al Kooper, who knows the playing-field.
No fault of mine.

PROLOGUE

Winding the Deathwatch (I)

Old age is an island surrounded by death.
Juan Montalvo
'On Beauty'

No one – least of all Dr Litchfield – came right out and told Ralph Roberts that his wife was going to die, but there came a time when Ralph understood without needing to be told. The months between March and June were a jangling, screaming time inside his head – a time of conferences with doctors, of evening runs to the hospital with Carolyn, of trips to other hospitals in other states for special tests (Ralph spent much of his travel time on these trips thanking God for Carolyn's Blue Cross/Major Medical coverage), of personal research in the Derry Public Library, at first looking for answers the specialists might have overlooked, later on just looking for hope and grasping at straws.

Those four months were like being dragged drunk through some malign carnival where the people on the rides were really screaming, the people lost in the mirror maze were really lost, and the denizens of Freak Alley looked at you with false smiles on their lips and terror in their eyes. Ralph began to see these things by the middle of May, and as June set in, he began to understand that the pitchmen along the medical midway had only quack remedies to sell, and the cheery quickstep of the calliope could no longer quite hide the fact that the tune spilling out of the loudspeakers was 'The Funeral March'. It was a carnival, all right; the carnival of lost souls.

Ralph continued to deny these terrible images – and the even more terrible idea lurking behind them – all through the early summer of 1992, but as June gave way to July, this finally became impossible. The worst midsummer heatwave since 1971 rolled over central Maine, and Derry simmered in a bath of hazy sun, humidity, and daily temperatures in the mid-nineties. The city – hardly a bustling metropolis at the best of times – fell into a complete stupor, and it was in this hot silence that Ralph Roberts first heard the ticking of the deathwatch and understood that in the passage from June's cool damp greens to the baked stillness of July, Carolyn's slim chances had become no chances at all. She was going to die. Not this summer, probably – the doctors claimed to have quite a few tricks up their sleeves yet, and Ralph was sure they did – but this fall or this winter. His longtime companion, the only woman he had ever loved, was going to die. He tried to deny the idea, scolding himself for being a morbid old fool, but in the gasping silences of those long hot days, Ralph heard that ticking everywhere – it even seemed to be in the walls.

Yet it was loudest from within Carolyn herself, and when she turned her calm white face toward him – perhaps to ask him to turn on the radio so she could listen while she shelled some beans for their supper, or to ask him if he would go across to the Red Apple and get her an ice-cream on a stick – he would see that she heard it, too. He would see it in her dark eyes, at first only when she was straight, but later even when her eyes were hazed by the pain medication she took. By then the ticking had grown very loud, and when Ralph lay in bed beside her on those hot summer nights when even a single sheet seemed to weigh ten pounds and he believed every dog in Derry was barking at the moon, he listened to it, to the deathwatch ticking inside Carolyn, and it seemed to him that his heart would break with sorrow and terror. How much would she be required to suffer before the end came? How much would *he* be required to suffer? And how could he possibly live without her?

It was during this strange, fraught period that Ralph began to go for increasingly long walks through the hot summer afternoons and slow, twilit evenings, returning on many occasions too exhausted to eat. He kept expecting Carolyn to scold him for these outings, to say, *Why don't you stop it, you stupid old man? You'll kill yourself if you keep walking in this heat!* But she never did, and he gradually realized she didn't even know. That he went out, yes – she knew that. But not all the miles he went, or that when he came home he was often trembling with exhaustion and near sunstroke. Once upon a time it had seemed to Ralph she saw everything, even a change of half an inch in where he parted his hair. No more; the tumor in her brain had stolen her powers of observation, as it would soon steal her life.

So he walked, relishing the heat in spite of the way it sometimes made his head swim and his ears ring, relishing it mostly *because* of the way it made his ears ring; sometimes there were whole hours when they rang so loudly and his head pounded so fiercely that he couldn't hear the tick of Carolyn's deathwatch.

He walked over much of Derry that hot July, a narrow-shouldered old man with thinning white hair and big hands that still looked capable of hard work. He walked from Witcham Street to the Barrens, from Kansas Street to Neibolt Street, from Main Street to the Kissing Bridge, but his feet took him most frequently west along Harris Avenue, where the still beautiful and much beloved Carolyn Roberts was now spending her last year in a haze of headaches and morphine, to the Harris Avenue Extension and Derry County Airport. He would walk out the Extension – which was treeless and completely exposed to the pitiless sun – until he felt his legs threatening to cave in beneath him, and then double back.

He often paused to catch his second wind in a shady picnic area close to the airport's service entrance. At night this place was a teenage drinking and makeout spot, alive with the sounds of rap coming from boombox radios, but during the days it was the more-or-less exclusive domain of a group Ralph's friend Bill McGovern called the Harris Avenue Old Crocks. The Old Crocks gathered to play chess, to play gin, or just to shoot the shit. Ralph had known many of them for years (had, in fact, gone to grammar school with Stan Eberly), and was comfortable with them . . . as long as they didn't get too nosy. Most didn't. They were old-school Yankees, for the most part, raised to believe that what a man doesn't choose to talk about is no one's business but his own.

It was on one of these walks that he first became aware that something had gone very wrong with Ed Deepneau, his neighbor from up the street.

2

Ralph had walked much farther out the Harris Avenue Extension than usual that day, possibly because thunderheads had blotted out the sun and a cool, if still sporadic, breeze had begun to blow. He had fallen into a kind of trance, not thinking of anything, not watching anything but the dusty toes of his sneakers, when the four forty-five United Airlines flight from Boston swooped low overhead, startling him back to where he was with the teeth-rattling whine of its jet engines.

He watched it cross above the old GS&WM railroad tracks and the Cyclone fence that marked the edge of the airport, watched it settle toward the runway, marked the blue puffs of smoke as its wheels touched down. Then he glanced at his watch, saw how late it was getting, and looked up with wide eyes at the orange roof of the Howard Johnson's just up the road. He had been in a trance, all right; he had walked more than five miles without the slightest sense of time passing.

Carolyn's time, a voice deep inside his head muttered.

Yes, yes; Carolyn's time. She would be back in the apartment, counting the minutes until she could have another Darvon Complex, and he was out on the far side of the airport . . . halfway to Newport, in fact.

Ralph looked up at the sky and for the first time really saw the bruise-purple thunderheads which were stacking up over the airport. They did not mean rain, not for sure, not yet, but if it *did* rain, he was almost surely going to be caught in it; there was nowhere to shelter between here and the little picnic area back by Runway 3, and there was nothing there but a ratty little gazebo that always smelled faintly of beer.

He took another look at the orange roof, then reached into his right-hand pocket and felt the little sheaf of bills held by the silver money-clip Carolyn had given him for his sixty-fifth. There was nothing to prevent him walking up to HoJo's and calling a cab . . . except maybe for the thought of how the driver might look at him. Stupid old man, the eyes in the rear-view mirror might say. Stupid old man, walked a lot further than you shoulda on a hot day. If you'd been swimming, you woulda drownded.

Paranoid, Ralph, the voice in his head told him, and now

its clucky, slightly patronizing tone reminded him of Bill McGovern.

Well, maybe it was and maybe it wasn't. Either way, he thought he would chance the rain and walk back.

What if it doesn't just rain? Last summer it hailed so hard that one time in August it broke windows all over the west side.

'Let it hail, then,' he said. 'I don't bruise that easy.'

Ralph began to walk slowly back toward town along the shoulder of the Extension, his old high-tops raising small, parched puffs of dust as he went. He could hear the first rumbles of thunder in the west, where the clouds were stacking up. The sun, although blotted out, was refusing to quit without a fight; it edged the thunderheads with bands of brilliant gold and shone through occasional rifts in the clouds like the fragmented beam of some huge movie-projector. Ralph found himself feeling glad he had decided to walk, in spite of the ache in his legs and the steady nagging pain in the small of his back.

One thing, at least, he thought. *I'll sleep tonight. I'll sleep like a damn rock.*

The verge of the airport – acres of dead brown grass with the rusty railroad tracks sunk in them like the remains of some old wreck – was now on his left. Far in the distance beyond the Cyclone fence he could see the United 747, now the size of a child's toy plane, taxiing toward the small terminal which United and Delta shared.

Ralph's gaze was caught by another vehicle, this one a car, leaving the General Aviation terminal, which stood at this end of the airport. It was heading across the tarmac toward the small service entrance which gave on the Harris Avenue Extension. Ralph had watched a lot of vehicles come and go through that entrance just lately; it was only seventy yards or so from the picnic area where the Harris Avenue Old Crocks gathered. As the car approached the gate, Ralph recognized it as Ed and Helen Deepneau's Datsun . . . and it was really moving.

Ralph stopped on the shoulder, unaware that his hands had curled into anxious fists as the small brown car bore down on the closed gate. You needed a key-card to open the gate from the outside; from the inside an electric-eye beam did the job. But the beam was set close to the gate, very close, and at the speed the Datsun was going . . .

At the last moment (or so it seemed to Ralph), the small brown car scrunched to a stop, the tires sending up puffs of blue smoke that made Ralph think of the 747 touching down, and the gate began to trundle slowly open on its track. Ralph's fisted hands relaxed.

An arm emerged from the driver's side window of the Datsun and began to wave up and down, apparently haranguing the gate, urging it to hurry it up. There was something so absurd about this that Ralph began to smile. The smile died before it had exposed even a gleam of teeth, however. The wind was still freshening from the west, where the thunderheads were, and it carried the screaming voice of the Datsun's driver.

'You son of a bitch fucker! You bastard! Eat my cock! Hurry up! Hurry up and lick shit, you fucking asshole cuntlapper! Fucking booger! Ratdick ringmeat! Suckhole!'

'That can't be Ed Deepneau,' Ralph murmured. He began to walk again without realizing it. '*Can't* be.'

Ed was a research chemist at the Hawking Laboratories research facility in Fresh Harbor, one of the kindest, most civil young men Ralph had ever met. Both he and Carolyn were very fond of Ed's wife, Helen, and their new baby, Natalie, as well. A visit from Natalie was one of the few things with the power to lift Carolyn out of her own life these days, and, sensing this, Helen brought her over frequently. Ed never complained. There were men, he knew, who wouldn't have cared to have the missus running to the old folks down the street every time the baby did some new and entrancing thing, especially when the granny-figure in the picture was ill. Ralph had an idea that Ed wouldn't be able to tell someone to go to hell without suffering a sleepless night in consequence, but—

'You fucking whoremaster! Move your sour shit-caked ass, you hear me? Butt-fucker! Cunt-rammer!'

But it sure *sounded* like Ed. Even from two or three hundred yards away, it certainly *sounded* like him.

Now the driver of the Datsun was revving his engine like a kid in a muscle-car waiting for the light to turn green. Clouds of exhaust smoke farted up from the tailpipe. As soon as the gate had retracted enough to allow the Datsun passage, the car leaped forward, squirting through the gap with its engine roaring, and when it did, Ralph got a clear look at the driver. He was close enough now for there to be no doubt: it was Ed, all right.

The Datsun bounced along the short unpaved stretch of lane between the gate and the Harris Street Extension. A horn blared suddenly, and Ralph saw a blue Ford Ranger, heading west on the Extension, swerve to avoid the oncoming Datsun. The driver of the pickup saw the danger too late, and Ed apparently never saw it at all (it was only later that Ralph came to consider Ed might have rammed the Ranger on purpose). There was a brief scream of tires followed by the hollow bang of the Datsun's fender driving into the Ford's sidewall. The pickup was driven halfway across the yellow line. The Datsun's hood crumpled, came unlatched, and popped up a little; headlight glass tinkled into the street. A moment later both vehicles were dead in the middle of the road, tangled together like some weird sculpture.

Ralph stood where he was for the time being, watching as oil spread beneath the Datsun's front end. He had seen several road accidents in his almost-seventy years, most of them minor, one or two serious, and he was always stunned by how quickly they happened and how little drama there was. It wasn't like in the movies, where the camera could slow things down, or on a videotape, where you could watch the car go off the cliff again and again if you so chose; there was usually just a series of converging blurs, followed by that quick and toneless combination of sounds: the cry of the tires, the hollow bang of metal crimping metal, the tinkle of glass. Then, *voilà – tout finis.*

There was even a kind of protocol for this sort of thing: How One Should Behave When Involved in a Low-Speed Collison. Of course there was, Ralph mused. There were probably a dozen two-bit collisions in Derry every day, and maybe twice that number in the wintertime, when there was snow and the roads got slippery. You got out, you met your opposite number at the point where the two vehicles had come together (and where, quite often, they were still entwined), you looked, you shook your heads. Sometimes – often, actually – this phase of the encounter was marked with angry words: fault was assigned (often rashly), driving skills impugned, legal action threatened. Ralph supposed what the drivers were really trying to say without coming right out and saying it was, *Listen, fool, you scared the living hell out of me!*

The final step in this unhappy little dance was the Exchange of the Sacred Insurance Screeds, and it was at this point that the drivers usually began to get control of their galloping emotions . . . always assuming that no one had been hurt, as appeared to be the case here. Sometimes the drivers involved even finished up by shaking hands.

Ralph prepared to watch all this from his vantage point less than a hundred and fifty yards away, but as soon as the driver's door of the Datsun opened he understood that things were going to go differently here – that the accident was maybe not over but still happening. It certainly did not seem that anyone was going to shake at the end of *these* festivities.

The door did not *swing* open; it *flew* open. Ed Deepneau leaped out, then simply stood stock-still beside his car, his slim shoulders squared against a background of deepening clouds. He was wearing faded jeans and a tee-shirt, and Ralph realized he had never seen Ed in a shirt that didn't button up the front. And there was something around his neck: a long white something. A scarf? It *looked* like a scarf, but why would anyone be wearing a scarf on a day as hot as this one had been?

Ed stood beside his wounded car for a moment, seeming to look in every direction but the right one. The fierce little pokes of his narrow head reminded Ralph of the way roosters studied their barnyard turf, looking for invaders and interlopers. Something about that similarity made Ralph feel uneasy. He had never seen Ed look that way before, and he supposed that was part of it, but it wasn't *all* of it. The truth of the matter was simply this: he had never seen *anyone* look exactly like that.

Thunder rumbled in the west, louder now. And closer.

The man getting out of the Ranger would have made two of Ed Deepneau, possibly three. His vast, deep belly hung over the rolled waistband of his green chino workpants; there were sweatstains the size of dinner-plates under the arms of his open-throated white shirt. He tipped back the bill of the West Side Gardeners gimme-cap he was wearing to get a better look at the man who had broadsided him. His heavy-jowled face was dead pale except for bright patches of color like rouge high on his cheekbones, and Ralph thought: *There's a man who's a prime candidate for a heart attack. If I was closer I bet I'd be able to see the creases in his earlobes.*

'Hey!' the heavyset guy yelled at Ed. The voice coming out of that broad chest and deep gut was absurdly thin, almost reedy. 'Where'd you get your license? Fuckin Sears n Roebuck?'

Ed's wandering, jabbing head swung immediately toward the sound of the big man's voice – seemed almost to home in, like a jet guided by radar – and Ralph got his first good look at Ed's eyes. He felt a bolt of alarm light up in his chest and suddenly began to run toward the accident. Ed, meanwhile, had started toward the man in the sweat-soaked white shirt and gimme-cap. He was walking in a stiff-legged, high-shouldered strut that was nothing at all like his usual easygoing amble.

'Ed!' Ralph shouted, but the freshening breeze – cold now with the promise of rain – seemed to snatch the words away before they could even get out of his mouth. Certainly Ed never turned. Ralph made himself run faster, the ache in his legs and the throbbing in the small of his back forgotten. It was murder he had seen in Ed Deepneau's wide, unblinking eyes. He had absolutely no previous experience upon which to base such an assessment, but he didn't think you could mistake such a naked glare; it was the look fighting cocks must wear when they launch themselves at each other, spurs up and slashing. 'Ed! Hey, Ed, hold up! It's Ralph!'

Not so much as a glance around, although Ralph was now so close that Ed must have heard, wind or no wind. Certainly the heavyset man glanced around, and Ralph could see both fear and uncertainty in his look. Then Heavyset turned back to Ed and raised his hands placatingly.

'Look,' he said. 'We can talk—'

That was as far as he got. Ed took another quick step forward, reached up with one slim hand – it was very white in the rapidly darkening day – and slapped Heavyset across his far from inconsiderable jowls. The sound was like the report of a kid's air rifle.

'How many have you killed?' Ed asked.

Heavyset pressed back against the side of his pickup, his mouth open, his eyes wide. Ed's queer, stiff strut never faltered. He walked into the other man and stood belly to belly with him, seemingly oblivious of the fact that the pickup's driver was four inches taller and outweighed him by a hundred pounds or more. Ed reached up and slapped him again. 'Come on! Fess up, brave boy – *how many have you killed?*' His voice rose to a shriek that was lost in the coming storm's first really authoritative clap of thunder.

Heavyset pushed him away – a gesture not of aggression but of simple fright – and Ed went reeling backward against the crumpled nose of his Datsun. He bounced back at once, fists clenched, gathering himself to leap at Heavyset, who was cringing against the side of his truck with his gimme-cap now askew and his shirt untucked in the back and at the sides. A memory flashed across Ralph's mind – a Three Stooges short he'd seen years ago, Larry, Curly, and Moe playing painters without a clue – and he felt a sudden surge of sympathy for Heavyset, who looked absurd as well as scared to death.

Ed Deepneau did not look absurd. With his yanked-back lips and wide, unblinking eyes, Ed looked more like a fighting cock than ever. 'I know what you've been doing,' he whispered to Heavyset. 'What kind of comedy did you think this was? Did you think you and your butcher friends could get away with it forev—'

At that moment Ralph arrived, puffing and gasping like an old carthorse, and put an arm around Ed's shoulders. The heat beneath the thin tee-shirt was unnerving; it was like putting an arm around an oven, and when Ed turned to look at him, Ralph had the momentary (but unforgettable) impression that that was exactly what he was looking into. He had never seen such utter, unreasoning fury in a pair of human eyes; had never even suspected such fury might exist.

Ralph's immediate impulse was to recoil, but he suppressed it and stood firm. He had an idea that if he pulled back, Ed would fall on him like a rogue dog, biting and clawing. It was absurd, of course; Ed was a research chemist, Ed was a member of the Book of the Month Club (the kind who took the twenty-pound histories of the Crimean War they always seemed to offer as alternates to the main selection), Ed was Helen's husband and Natalie's dad. Hell, Ed was a friend.

. . . except this wasn't that Ed, and Ralph knew it.

Instead of pulling back, Ralph leaned forward, grasped Ed's shoulders (so hot under the tee-shirt, so incredibly, throbbingly hot), and moved his face until it blocked Heavyset from Ed's creepy fixed gaze.

'Ed, quit it!' Ralph said. He used the loud but steadily firm voice he assumed one used with people who were having hysterics. 'You're all right! Just quit it!'

For a moment Ed's fixed gaze didn't waver, and then his eyes moved over Ralph's face. It wasn't much, but Ralph felt a small surge of relief just the same.

'What's the matter with him?' Heavyset asked from behind Ralph. 'He crazy, do you think?'

'He's fine, I'm sure,' Ralph said, although he was sure of no such thing. He spoke out of the corner of his mouth, and didn't take his eyes from Ed. He didn't *dare* take his eyes from Ed – that contact felt like the only hold he had over the man, and tenuous at best. 'Just shaken up from the crash. He needs a few seconds to calm d—'

'Ask him what he's got under that tarp!' Ed yelled suddenly, and pointed over Ralph's shoulder. Lightning flashed, and for a moment the pitted scars of Ed's adolescent acne were thrown into sharp relief, like some strange organic treasure map. Thunder rolled. 'Hey, hey, Susan Day!' he chanted in a high, childlike voice that made Ralph's forearms break out in goosebumps. 'How many kids did you kill today?'

'He ain't shook up,' Heavyset said. 'He's crazy. And when the cops get here, I'm gonna see he gets tooken in.'

Ralph glanced around and saw a blue tarpaulin stretched across the bed of the pickup. It had been tied down with bright yellow hanks of rope. Round shapes bulked beneath it.

'Ralph?' a timid voice asked.

He glanced to his left and saw Dorrance Marstellar – at ninety-something easily the oldest of the Harris Avenue Old Crocks – standing just beyond Heavyset's pickup truck. There was a paperback book in his waxy, liver-spotted hands, and Dorrance was bending it anxiously back and forth, giving the spine a real workout. Ralph supposed it was a book of poetry, which was all he had ever seen old Dorrance read. Or maybe he didn't really read at all; maybe he just liked to hold the books and look at the artfully stacked words.

'Ralph, what's wrong? What's happening?'

More lightning flashed overhead, a purple-white snarl of electricity. Dorrance looked up at it as if unsure of where he was, who he was, or what he was seeing. Ralph groaned inside.

'Dorrance –' he began, and then Ed lunged beneath him, like some wild animal which has only lain quiet to regain its strength. Ralph staggered, then pushed Ed back against the crumpled hood of his Datsun. He felt panicky – unsure of what to do next or how to do it. There were too many things going on at once. He could feel the muscles in Ed's arms humming fiercely just below his grip; it was almost as if the man had somehow swallowed a bolt of the lightning now loose in the sky.

'Ralph?' Dorrance asked in that same calm but worried voice. 'I wouldn't touch him anymore, if I were you. I can't see your hands.'

Oh, good. Another lunatic to deal with. Just what he needed.

Ralph glanced down at his hands, then looked at the old man. 'What are you talking about, Dorrance?'

'Your hands,' Dorrance said patiently. 'I can't see your—'

'This is no place for you, Dor – why don't you get lost?'

The old man brightened a little at that. 'Yes!' he said in the tone of one who has just stumbled over a great truth. 'That's just what I oughtta do!' He began to back up, and when the thunder cracked again, he cringed and put his book on top of his head. Ralph was able to read the bright red letters of the title: *Buckdancer's Choice.* 'It's what *you* ought to do, too, Ralph. You don't want to mess in with long-time business. It's a good way to get hurt.'

'What are you—'

But before Ralph could finish, Dorrance turned his back and went lumbering off in the direction of the picnic area with his fringe of white hair – as gossamer as the hair on a new baby's head – rippling in the breeze of the oncoming storm.

One problem solved, but Ralph's relief was short-lived. Ed had been temporarily distracted by Dorrance, but now he was looking daggers at Heavyset again. 'Cuntlicker!' he spat. 'Fucked your mother and licked her cunt!'

Heavyset's enormous brow drew down. *'What?'*

Ed's eyes shifted back to Ralph, whom he now seemed to recognize. 'Ask him what's under that tarp!' he cried. 'Better yet, get the murdering cocksucker to show you!'

Ralph looked at the heavyset man. 'What have you got under there?'

'What's it to you?' Heavyset asked, perhaps trying to sound truculent. He sampled the look in Ed Deepneau's eyes and took two more sidling steps away.

'Nothing to me, something to him,' Ralph said, lifting his chin in Ed's direction. 'Just help me cool him out, okay?'

'You know him?'

'Murderer!' Ed repeated, and this time he lunged hard enough under Ralph's hands to drive him back a step. Yet something was happening, wasn't it? Ralph thought the scary, vacant look was seeping out of Ed's eyes. There seemed to be a little more *Ed* in there than there had been before . . . or perhaps that was only wishful thinking. 'Murderer, *baby* murderer!'

'Jesus, what a loony tune,' Heavyset said, but he went to the rear of the truckbed, yanked one of the ropes free, and peeled back a corner of the tarpaulin. Beneath it were four pressboard barrels, each marked WEED-GO. 'Organic fertilizer,' Heavyset said, his eyes flicking from Ed to Ralph and then back to Ed again. He touched the bill of his West Side Gardeners cap. 'I spent the day workin on a set of new flower-beds outside the Derry Psych Wing . . . where *you* could stand a short vacation, friend.'

'Fertilizer?' Ed asked. It was himself he seemed to be speaking to. His left hand rose slowly to his temple and began to rub there. *'Fertilizer?'* He sounded like a man questioning some simple yet staggering scientific development.

'Fertilizer,' Heavyset agreed. He glanced back at Ralph and said, 'This guy is sick in the head. You know it?'

'He's confused, that's all,' Ralph answered uneasily. He leaned over the side of the truck and rapped a barrel-top. Then he turned back to Ed. 'Barrels of fertilizer,' he said. 'Okay?'

No response. Ed's right hand rose and began to rub at his other temple. He looked like a man sinking into a terrible migraine.

'Okay?' Ralph repeated gently.

Ed closed his eyes for a moment, and when they opened again, Ralph observed a sheen in them he thought was probably tears. Ed's tongue slipped out and dabbed delicately first at one corner of his mouth and then the other. He took the end of his silk scarf and wiped his forehead, and as he did, Ralph saw there were Chinese figures embroidered on it in red, just above the fringe.

'I guess maybe –' he began, and then broke off. His eyes widened again in that look Ralph didn't like. 'Babies!' he rasped. 'You hear me? *Babies!*'

Ralph shoved him back against his car for the third or fourth time – he'd lost count. 'What are you talking about, Ed?' An idea suddenly occurred to him. 'Is it Natalie? Are you worried about Natalie?'

A small, crafty smile touched Ed's lips. He looked past Ralph at the heavyset man. 'Fertilizer, huh? Well, if that's all it is, you won't mind opening one of them, will you?'

Heavyset looked at Ralph uneasily. 'Man needs a doctor,' he said.

'Maybe he does. But he was calming down, I thought . . . *could* you open one of those barrels? It might make him feel better.'

'Yeah, sure, what the heck. In for a penny, in for a pound.'

There was another flash of lightning, another heavy blast of thunder – one that seemed to go rolling all the way across the sky this time – and a cold spackle of rain struck the back of Ralph's sweaty neck. He glanced to his left and saw Dorrance Marstellar standing at the entrance to the picnic area, book in hand, watching the three of them anxiously.

'It's gonna rain a pretty bitch, looks like,' Heavyset said, 'and I can't let this stuff get wet. It starts a chemical reaction. So look fast.' He felt around between one of the barrels and the sidewall of his truck for a moment, then came up with a crowbar. 'I must be as nutty as he is, doin this,' he said to Ralph. 'I mean, I was just goin along home, mindin my business. *He* hit *me.*'

'Go on,' Ralph said. 'It'll only take a second.'

'Yeah,' Heavyset replied sourly, turning and setting the flat end of the crowbar under the lid of the nearest barrel, 'but the memories will last a lifetime.'

Another thunderclap rocked the day just then, and Heavyset did not hear what Ed Deepneau said next. Ralph did, however, and it chilled the pit of his stomach.

'Those barrels are full of dead babies,' Ed said. 'You'll see.'

Heavyset popped the lid on the end barrel, and such was the conviction in Ed's voice that Ralph almost expected to see tangles of arms and legs and bundles of small hairless heads. Instead, he saw a mixture of fine blue crystals and brown stuff. The smell which rose from the barrel was rich and peaty, with a thin chemical undertone.

'See? Satisfied?' Heavyset asked, speaking directly to Ed again. 'I ain't Ray Joubert or that guy Dahmer after all. How 'bout that!'

The look of confusion was back on Ed's face, and when the thunder cracked overhead again, he cringed a little. He leaned over, reached a hand toward the barrel, then looked a question at Heavyset.

The big man nodded to him, almost sympathetically, Ralph thought. 'Sure, touch it, fine by me. But if it rains while you're holdin a fistful, you'll dance like John Travolta. It burns.'

Ed reached into the barrel, grabbed some of the mix, and let it run through his fingers. He shot Ralph a perplexed look (*there was an element of embarrassment in that look as well,* Ralph thought), and then sank his arm into the barrel all the way to the elbow.

'Hey!' Heavyset cried, startled. 'That ain't a box of Cracker Jack!'

For a moment the crafty grin resurfaced on Ed's face – a look that said *I know a trick worth two of that* – and then it subsided into puzzlement again as he found nothing further down but more fertilizer. When he drew his arm out of the barrel, it was dusty and aromatic with the mix. Another flash of lightning exploded above the airport. The thunder which followed was almost deafening.

'Get that off your skin before it rains, I'm warning you,' Heavyset said. He reached through the Ranger's open passenger window and produced a McDonald's take-out sack. He rummaged in it, came out with a couple of napkins, and handed them to Ed, who began to wipe the fertilizer dust from his forearm like a man in a dream. While he did this, Heavyset replaced the lid on the barrel, tamping it into place with one large, freckled fist and taking quick glances up at the darkening sky. When Ed touched the shoulder of his white shirt, the man stiffened and pulled away, looking at Ed warily.

'I think I owe you an apology,' Ed said, and to Ralph his voice sounded completely clear and sane for the first time.

'You're damn tooting,' Heavyset said, but he sounded relieved. He stretched the plastic-coated tarpaulin back into place and tied it in a series of quick, efficient gestures. Watching him, Ralph was struck by what a sly thief time was. Once he could have tied that same sheetbend with that same dextrous ease. Today he could still tie it, but it would take him at least two minutes and maybe three of his best curse-words.

Heavyset patted the tarp and then turned to them, folding his arms across the substantial expanse of his chest. 'Did you see the accident?' he asked Ralph.

'No,' Ralph said at once. He had no idea why he was lying, but the decision to do it was instantaneous. 'I was watching the plane land. The United.'

To his complete surprise, the flushed patches on Heavyset's cheeks began to spread. *You were watching it, too!* Ralph thought suddenly. *And not just watching it land, either, or you wouldn't be blushing like that . . . you were watching it taxi!*

This thought was followed by a complete revelation: Heavyset thought the accident had been his fault, or that the cop or cops who showed up to investigate might read it that way. He had been watching the plane and hadn't seen Ed's reckless charge through the service gate and out to the Extension.

'Look, I'm *really* sorry,' Ed was saying earnestly, but he actually looked more than sorry; he looked dismayed. Ralph suddenly found himself wondering how much he trusted that expression, and if he really had even the slightest idea of

(*Hey, hey, Susan Day*)
what had just happened here . . . and who the hell *was* Susan Day, anyhow?

'I bumped my head on the steering wheel,' Ed was saying, 'and I guess it . . . you know, it rattled my cage pretty good.'

'Yeah, I guess it did,' Heavyset said. He scratched his head, looked up at the dark and convoluted sky, then looked back at Ed again. 'Want to make you a deal, friend.'

'Oh? What deal is that?'

'Let's just exchange names and phone numbers instead of going through all that insurance shit. Then you go your way and I go mine.'

Ed looked uncertainly at Ralph, who shrugged, and then back at the man in the West Side Gardeners cap.

'If we get into it with the cops,' Heavyset went on, 'I'm in for a ration of shit. First thing they're going to find out when they call it in is I had an Operating Under the Influence last winter, and I'm drivin on a provisional license. They're apt to make problems for me even though I was on the main drag and had the right-of-way. See what I mean?'

'Yes,' Ed said, 'I guess so, but the accident was entirely my fault. I was going much too fast—'

'The accident part is maybe not so important,' Heavyset said, then looked mistrustfully around at an approaching panel truck that was pulling over onto the shoulder. He looked back at Ed again and spoke with some urgency. 'You lost some oil, but it's stopped leakin now. I bet you could drive her home . . . if you live here in town. You live here in town?'

'Yes,' Ed said.

'And I'd stand you good on repairs, up to fifty bucks or so.'

Another revelation struck Ralph; it was the only thing he could think of to explain the man's sudden change from truculence to something close to wheedling. An OUI last winter? Yes, probably. But Ralph had never heard of such a thing as a provisional license, and thought it was almost certainly bullshit. Old Mr West Side Gardeners had been driving without a license. What complicated the situation was this: Ed was telling the truth – the accident *had* been entirely his fault.

'If we just drive away and call it good,' Heavyset was going on, 'I don't have to explain all over again about my OUI and *you* don't have to explain why you jumped out of your car and started slapping me and yelling about how I had a truckload of dead bodies.'

'Did I actually say that?' Ed asked, sounding bewildered.

'You know you did,' Heavyset told him grimly.

A voice with a wispy French-Canadian accent asked, 'Everyt'ing okay here, fellers? Nobody urt? . . . Eyyy, Ralph! Dat you?'

The truck which had pulled over had Derry Dry Cleaners printed on the side, and Ralph recognized the driver as one of the Vachon brothers from Old Cape. Probably Trigger, the youngest.

'That's me,' Ralph said, and without knowing or asking himself why – he was operating purely on instinct at this point – he went to Trigger, put an arm around his shoulders, and led him back in the direction of the laundry truck.

'Dem guys okay?'

'Fine, fine,' Ralph said. He glanced back and saw that Ed and Heavyset were standing by the truckbed with their heads together. Another cold spatter of rain fell, drumming on the blue tarpaulin like impatient fingers. 'A little fender-bender, that's all. They're working it out.'

'Beauty, beauty,' Trigger Vachon said complacently. 'Howdat pretty little wife of yours, Ralph?'

Ralph twitched, suddenly feeling like a man who remembers at lunch that he has forgotten to turn off the stove before leaving for work. 'Jesus!' he said, and looked at his watch, hoping for five-fifteen, five-thirty at the latest. Instead he saw it was ten minutes of six. Already twenty minutes past the time Carolyn expected him to bring her a bowl of soup and half a sandwich. She would be worried. In fact, with the lightning and the thunder booming through the empty apartment, she might be downright scared. And if it *did* rain, she would not be able to close the windows; she had almost no strength left in her hands.

'Ralph?' Trigger asked. 'What's wrong?'

'Nothing,' he said. 'It's just that I got walking and lost all track of time. Then this accident happened, and . . . could you give me a ride home, Trig? I'll pay you.'

'No need to pay nuttin,' Trigger said. 'It's on my way. Hop in, Ralph. You t'ink dose guys gonna be all right? Ain't gonna take after each udder or nuttin?'

'No,' Ralph said. 'I don't think so. Just one second.'

'Sure.'

19

Ralph walked over to Ed. 'Are you okay with this? Are you getting it worked out?'

'Yes,' Ed replied. 'We're going to settle it privately. Why not? A little broken glass is all it really comes down to.'

He sounded completely like his old self now, and the big man in the white shirt was looking at him with something that was almost respect. Ralph still felt perplexed and uneasy about what had happened here, but he decided he was going to let it go. He liked Ed Deepneau a lot, but Ed was not his business this July; Carolyn was. Carolyn and the thing which had started ticking in the walls of their bedroom – and inside her – late at night.

'Great,' he told Ed. 'I'm headed home. I make Carolyn her supper these days, and I'm running way late.'

He started to turn away. The heavyset man stopped him with an outstretched hand. 'John Tandy,' he said.

He shook it. 'Ralph Roberts. Pleased to meet you.'

Tandy smiled. 'Under the circumstances, I kinda doubt that . . . but I'm real glad you showed up when you did. For a few seconds there I really thought him and me was gonna tango.'

So did I, Ralph thought but didn't say. He looked at Ed, his troubled eye taking in the unfamiliar tee-shirt clinging to Ed's stalk-thin midriff and the white silk scarf with the Chinese-red figures embroidered on it. He didn't entirely like the look in Ed's eyes when they met his; Ed was perhaps not all the way back after all.

'Sure you're okay?' Ralph asked him. He wanted to go, wanted to get back to Carolyn, and yet he was somehow reluctant. The feeling that this situation was about nine miles from right persisted.

'Yes, fine,' Ed said quickly, and gave him a big smile which did not reach his dark green eyes. They studied Ralph carefully, as if asking how much he had seen . . . and how much

(*hey hey Susan Day*)

he would remember later on.

3

The interior of Trigger Vachon's truck smelled of clean, freshly pressed clothes, an aroma which for some reason always reminded Ralph of fresh bread. There was no passenger seat, so he stood with one hand wrapped around the doorhandle and the other gripping the edge of a Dandux laundry basket.

'Man, dat look like some strange go-on back dere,' Trigger said, glancing into his outside mirror.

'You don't know the half of it,' Ralph replied.

'I know the guy drivin the rice-burner – Deepneau, his name is. He got a pretty little wife, send stuff out sometime. Seem like a nice fella, mos usually.'

'He sure wasn't himself today,' Ralph said.

'Had a bug up his ass, did he?'

'Had a whole damn ant-farm up there, I think.'

Trigger laughed hard at that, pounding the worn black plastic of the big steering wheel. 'Whole damn ant-farm! Beauty! Beauty! I'm savin dat one, me!' Trigger wiped his streaming eyes with a handkerchief almost the size of a tablecloth. 'Look to me like Mr Deepneau come out dat airport service gate, him.'

'That's right, he did.'

'You need a pass to use dat way,' Trigger said. 'How Mr D get a pass, you tink?'

Ralph thought it over, frowning, then shook his head. 'I don't know. It never even occurred to me. I'll have to ask him next time I see him.'

'You do dat,' Trigger said. 'And ask him how dem ants doin.' This stimulated a fresh throe of laughter, which in turn occasioned more flourishes of the comic-opera handkerchief.

As they turned off the Extension and onto Harris Avenue proper, the storm finally broke. There was no hail, but the rain came in an extravagant summer flood, so heavy at first that Trigger had to slow the panel truck to a crawl. 'Wow!' he said respectfully. 'Dis remine me of the big storm back in '85, when haffa downtown fell inna damn Canal! Member dat, Ralph?'

'Yes,' Ralph said. 'Let's hope it doesn't happen again.'

'Nah,' Trigger said, grinning and peering past his extravagantly flapping windshield wipers, 'dey got the drainage system all fixed up now. Beauty!'

The combination of the cold rain and the warm cab caused the bottom half of the windshield to steam up. Without thinking, Ralph reached out a finger and drew a figure in the steam:

'What's dat?' Trigger asked.

'I don't really know. Looks Chinese, doesn't it? It was on the scarf Ed Deepneau was wearing.'

'Look a little familiar to me,' Trigger said, glancing at it again. Then he snorted and flapped a hand. 'Listen to me, wouldja? On'y t'ing I can say in Chinese is *moo-goo-gai-pan!*'

Ralph smiled, but didn't seem to have a laugh in him. It was Carolyn. Now that he had remembered her, he couldn't stop thinking about her – couldn't stop imagining the windows open, and the curtains streaming like Edward Gorey ghost arms as the rain poured in.

'You still live in dat two-storey across from the Red Apple?'

'Yes.'

Trigger pulled in to the curb, the wheels of the truck spraying up big fans of water. The rain was still pouring down in sheets. Lightning raced across the sky; thunder cracked.

'You better stay right here wit me for a little bit,' Trigger said. 'She let up in a minute or two.'

'I'll be all right.' Ralph didn't think anything could keep him in the truck a second longer, not even handcuffs. 'Thanks, Trig.'

'Wait a sec! Let me give you a piece of plastic – you can puddit over your head like a rainhat!'

'No, that's okay, no problem, thanks, I'll just—'

There seemed to be no way of finishing whatever it was he was trying to say, and now what he felt was close to panic. He shoved the truck's passenger door back on its track and jumped out, landing ankle-deep in the cold water racing down the gutter. He gave Trigger a final wave without looking back, then hurried up the walk to the house he and Carolyn shared with Bill McGovern, feeling in his pocket for his latchkey as he went. When he reached the porch steps he saw he wouldn't need it – the door was standing ajar. Bill, who lived downstairs, often forgot to lock it, and Ralph would rather think it had been him than think that Carolyn had wandered out to look for him and been caught in the storm. That was a possibility Ralph did not even want to consider.

He hurried into the shadowy foyer, wincing as thunder banged deafeningly overhead, and crossed to the foot of the stairs. He paused there a moment, hand on the newel post of the banister, listening to rainwater drip from his soaked pants and shirt onto the hardwood floor. Then he started up, wanting to run but no longer able to find the next gear up from a fast walk. His heart was beating hard and fast in his chest, his soaked sneakers were clammy anchors dragging at his feet, and for some reason he kept seeing the way Ed Deepneau's head had moved when he got out of his Datsun – those stiff, quick jabs that made him look like a rooster spoiling for a fight.

The third riser creaked loudly, as it always did, and the sound provoked hurried footsteps from above. They were no relief because they weren't Carolyn's, he knew that at once, and when Bill McGovern leaned over the rail, his face pale and worried beneath his Panama hat, Ralph wasn't really surprised. All the way back from the Extension he had felt that something was wrong, hadn't he? Yes. But under the circumstances, that hardly qualified as precognition. When things reached a certain degree of wrongness, he was discovering, they could no longer be redeemed or turned around; they just kept going wronger and wronger. He supposed that on some level or other he'd always known that. What he had never suspected was how long that wrong road could be.

'Ralph!' Bill called down. 'Thank God! Carolyn's having . . . well, I guess it's some sort of seizure. I just dialed 911, asked them to send an ambulance.'

Ralph discovered he could run up the rest of the stairs, after all.

4

She was lying half in and half out of the kitchen with her hair in her face. Ralph thought there was something particularly horrible about that; it looked sloppy, and if there was one thing Carolyn refused to be, it was sloppy. He knelt beside her and brushed the hair away from her eyes and forehead. The skin beneath his fingers felt as chilly as his feet inside his soaked sneakers.

'I wanted to put her on the couch, but she's too heavy for me,' Bill said nervously. He had taken off his Panama and was fiddling nervously with the band. 'My back, you know—'

'I know, Bill, it's okay,' Ralph said. He slid his arms under Carolyn and picked her up. She did not feel heavy to him at all, but light – almost as light as a milkweed pod which is ready to burst open and disgorge its filaments into the wind. 'Thank God you were here.'

'I almost wasn't,' Bill replied, following Ralph into the living room and still fiddling with his hat. He made Ralph think of old Dorrance Marstellar with his book of poems. *I wouldn't touch him anymore, if I were you,* old Dorrance had said. *I can't see your hands.* 'I was on my way out when I heard a hell of a thud . . . it must have been her falling . . . ' Bill looked around the storm-darkened living room, his face somehow distraught and avid at the same time, his eyes seeming to search for something that wasn't there. Then they brightened. 'The door!' he said. 'I'll bet it's still open! It'll be raining in! I'll be right back, Ralph.'

He hurried out. Ralph barely noticed; the day had taken on the surreal aspects of a nightmare. The ticking was the worst. He could hear it in the walls, so loud now that even the thunder could not blot it out.

He put Carolyn on the couch and knelt beside her. Her respiration was fast and shallow, and her breath was terrible. Ralph did not turn away from it, however. 'Hang in there, sweetheart,' he said. He picked up one of her hands – it was almost as clammy as her brow had been – and kissed it gently. 'You just hang in there. It's fine, everything's fine.'

But it wasn't fine, the ticking sound meant that *nothing* was fine. It wasn't in the walls, either – it had never been in the walls, but only in his wife. In Carolyn. It was in his dear one, she was slipping away from him, and what would he ever do without her?

'You just hang on,' he said. 'Hang on, you hear me?' He kissed her hand again, and held it against his cheek, and when he heard the warble of the approaching ambulance, he began to cry.

5

She came around in the ambulance as it sped across Derry (the sun was already out again, the wet streets steaming), and at first she talked such gibberish that Ralph was sure she had suffered a stroke. Then, just as she began to clear up and speak coherently, a second convulsion struck, and it took both Ralph and one of the paramedics who had answered the call to hold her down.

It wasn't Dr Litchfield who came to see Ralph in the third-floor waiting room early that evening but Dr Jamal, the neurologist. Jamal talked to him in a low, soothing voice, telling him that Carolyn was now stabilized, that they were going to keep her overnight, just to be safe, but that she would be able to go home in the morning. There were going to be some new medications – drugs that were expensive, yes, but also quite wonderful.

'We must not be losing the hope, Mr Roberts,' Dr Jamal said.

'No,' Ralph said, 'I suppose not. Will there be more of these, Dr Jamal?'

Dr Jamal smiled. He spoke in a quiet voice that was rendered somehow even more comforting by his soft Indian accent. And although Dr Jamal did not come right out and tell him that Carolyn was going to die, he came as close as anyone ever did during that long year in which she battled to stay alive. The new medications, Jamal said, would probably prevent any further seizures, but things had reached a stage where all predictions had to be taken 'with the grains of salt'. The tumor was spreading in spite of everything they had tried, unfortunately.

'The motor-control problems may show up next,' Dr Jamal said in his comforting voice. 'And I am seeing some deterioration in the eyesight, I am afraid.'

'Can I spend the night with her?' Ralph asked quietly.

'She'll sleep better if I do.' He paused, then added: 'So will I.'

'Of gorse!' Dr Jamal said, brightening. 'That is a fine idea!'

'Yes,' Ralph said heavily. 'I think so, too.'

6

So he sat beside his sleeping wife, and he listened to the ticking that was not in the walls, and he thought: *Some day soon – maybe this fall, maybe this winter – I will be back in this room with her.* It had the feel not of speculation but of prophecy, and he leaned over and put his head on the white sheet that covered his wife's breast. He didn't want to cry again, but did a little anyway.

That ticking. So loud and so steady.

I'd like to get hold of what's making that sound, he thought. *I'd stamp it until it was so many pieces scattered across the floor. With God as my witness I would.*

He fell asleep in his chair a little after midnight, and when he woke the next morning the air was cooler than it had been in weeks, and Carolyn was wide awake, coherent, and bright-eyed. She seemed, in fact, hardly to be sick at all. Ralph took her home and began the not-inconsiderable job of making her last months as comfortable as possible. It was a long while before he thought of Ed Deepneau again; even after he began to see the bruises on Helen Deepneau's face, it was a long time before he thought of Ed again.

As that summer became fall, and as that fall darkened down toward Carolyn's final winter, Ralph's thoughts were occupied more and more by the deathwatch, which seemed to tick louder and louder even as it slowed down.

But he had no trouble sleeping.

That came later.

PART I

Little Bald Doctors

There is a gulf fixed between those who can sleep and those who cannot. It is one of the great divisions of the human race.

Iris Murdoch
Nuns and Soldiers

Chapter One

1

About a month after the death of his wife, Ralph Roberts began to suffer from insomnia for the first time in his life.

The problem was mild to begin with, but it grew steadily worse. Six months after the first interruptions in his heretofore unremarkable sleep cycle, Ralph had reached a state of misery he could hardly credit, let alone accept. Toward the end of the summer of 1993 he began to wonder what it would be like to spend his remaining years on earth in a starey-eyed daze of wakefulness. *Of course it wouldn't come to that,* he told himself, *it never does.*

But was that true? He didn't really know, that was the devil of it, and the books on the subject Mike Hanlon steered him to down at the Derry Public Library weren't much help. There were several on sleep disorders, but they seemed to contradict one another. Some called insomnia a symptom, others called it a disease, and at least one called it a myth. The problem went further than that, however; so far as Ralph could tell from the books, no one seemed exactly sure what sleep itself was, how it worked, or what it did.

He knew he should quit playing amateur researcher and go to the doctor, but he found that surprisingly hard to do. He supposed he still bore Dr Litchfield a grudge. It was Litchfield, after all, who had originally diagnosed Carolyn's brain tumor as tension headaches (except Ralph had an idea that Litchfield, a lifelong bachelor, might actually have believed that Carolyn was suffering from nothing but a moderate case of the vapors), and Litchfield who had made himself as scarce as medically possible once Carolyn *was* diagnosed. Ralph was positive that if he had asked the man about that point-blank, Litchfield would have said he had handed the case off to Jamal, the specialist . . . all quite proper and aboveboard. Yes. Except Ralph had made it his business to get a good look into Litchfield's eyes on the few occasions he had seen him between Carolyn's first convulsions last July and her death this March, and Ralph thought that what he'd seen in those eyes was a mixture of unease and guilt. It was the look of a man trying very hard to forget he has fucked up. Ralph believed the only reason he could still look at Litchfield without wanting to knock his block off was that Dr Jamal had told him that an earlier diagnosis probably would have made no difference; by the time Carolyn's headaches started, the tumor was already well entrenched, and no doubt sending out little bursts of bad cells to other areas of the brain like malignant CARE packages.

In late April Dr Jamal had left to establish a practice in southern Connecticut, and Ralph missed him. He thought that he could have talked about his sleeplessness to Dr Jamal, and he had an idea that Jamal would have listened in a way Litchfield wouldn't . . . or couldn't.

By late summer Ralph had read enough about insomnia to know that the type with which he was afflicted, while not rare, was a lot less common than the usual slow-sleep insomnia. People unaffected by insomnia are usually in first-stage sleep seven to twenty minutes after turning in. Slow-sleepers, on the other hand, sometimes take as long as three hours to slip below the surface, and while normal sleepers begin to ramp down into third-stage sleep (what some of the old books called theta sleep, Ralph had discovered) forty-five minutes or so after drifting off, slow-sleepers usually took an additional hour or two to get down there . . . and on many nights they did not get all the way down at all. They awoke unrefreshed, sometimes with unfocused memories of unpleasant, tangled dreams, more often with the mistaken impression that they had been awake all night.

Following Carolyn's death, Ralph began to suffer from premature waking. He continued to go to bed most nights following the conclusion of the eleven o'clock news, and he continued to pop off to sleep almost at once, but instead of waking promptly at six-fifty-five, five minutes before the clock-radio alarm buzzed, he began to wake at six. At first he dismissed this as no more than the price of living with a slightly enlarged prostate and a seventy-year-old set of kidneys, but he never seemed to have to go *that* badly when he woke up, and he found it impossible to get back to sleep even after he'd emptied what *had* accumulated. He simply lay in the bed he'd shared with Carolyn for so many years, waiting for it to be five of seven (quarter till, anyway) so he could get up. Eventually he gave up even trying to drop off again; he simply lay there with his long-fingered, slightly swollen hands laced together on his chest and stared up at the shadowy ceiling with eyes that felt as big as doorknobs. Sometimes he thought of Dr Jamal down there in Westport, talking in his soft and comforting Indian accent, building up his little piece of the American dream. Sometimes he thought of places he and Carolyn had gone in the old days, and the one he kept coming back to was a hot afternoon at Sand Beach in Bar Harbor, the two of them sitting at a picnic table in their bathing suits, sitting under a big bright umbrella, eating sweet fried clams and drinking Bud from longneck bottles as they watched the sailboats scudding across the dark-blue ocean. When had that been? 1964? 1967? Did it matter? Probably not.

The alterations in his sleep schedule wouldn't have mattered, either, if they had ended there; Ralph would have adapted to the changes not just with ease but with gratitude. All the books he hunted through that summer seemed to confirm one bit of folk wisdom he'd heard all his life – people slept less as they got older. If losing an hour or so a night was the only fee he had to pay for the dubious pleasure of being 'seventy years young', he would pay it gladly, and consider himself well off.

But it *didn't* end there. By the first week of May, Ralph was waking up to birdsong at 5:15 a.m. He tried earplugs for a few nights, although he doubted from the outset that they would work. It wasn't the newly returned birds that were waking him up, nor the occasional delivery-truck backfire out on Harris Avenue. He had always been the sort of guy who could sleep in the middle of a brass marching band, and he didn't think that had changed. What had changed was inside his head. There was a switch in there, something was turning it on a little earlier every day, and Ralph hadn't the slightest idea of how to keep it from happening.

By June he was popping out of sleep like Jack out of his box at 4:30 a.m., 4:45 at the latest. And by the middle of July – not quite as hot as July of '92, but bad enough, thanks very much – he was snapping to at around four o'clock. It was during those long hot nights, taking up too little of the bed where he and Carolyn had made love on so many hot nights (and cold ones), that he began to consider what a hell his life would become if sleep departed entirely. In daylight he was still able to scoff at the notion, but he was discovering certain dismal truths about F. Scott Fitzgerald's dark night of the soul, and the grand-prize winner was this: at 4:15 a.m., anything seems possible. *Anything*.

During the days he was able to go on telling himself that he was simply experiencing a readjustment of his sleep-cycle, that his body was responding in perfectly normal fashion to a number of big changes in his life, retirement and the loss of his wife being the two biggest. He sometimes used the word 'loneliness' when he thought about his new life, but he shied away from The Dreaded D-Word, stuffing it back into the deep closet of his subconscious whenever it happened to glimmer for a moment in his thoughts. Loneliness was okay. Depression most certainly was not.

Maybe you need to get more exercise, he thought. *Do some walking, like you used to last summer. After all, you've been leading a pretty sedentary life – get up, eat toast, read a book, watch some TV, get a sandwich across the street in the Red Apple for lunch, potter around in the garden a little, maybe go to the library or visit with Helen and the baby if they happen to be out, eat supper, maybe sit on the porch and visit with McGovern or Lois Chasse for a while. Then what? Read a little more, watch a little more TV, wash up, go to bed. Sedentary.* Boring. *No wonder you wake up early.*

Except that was crap. His life *sounded* sedentary, yes, no doubt, but it really wasn't. The garden was a good example. What he did out there was never going to win him any prizes, but it was a hell of a long way from 'pottering around'. Most afternoons he weeded until sweat made a dark tree-shape down the back of his shirt and spread damp circles at his armpits, and he was often trembling with exhaustion by the time he let himself go back inside. 'Punishment' probably would have been closer to the mark than 'pottering', but punishment for what? Waking up before dawn?

Ralph didn't know and didn't care. Working in the garden filled up a large piece of the afternoon, it took his mind off things he didn't really care to think of, and that was enough to justify the aching muscles and the occasional flights of black spots in front of his eyes. He began his extended visits to the garden shortly after the Fourth of July and continued all through August, long after the early crops had been harvested and the later ones had been hopelessly stunted by the lack of rain.

'You ought to quit that,' Bill McGovern told him one night as they sat on the porch, drinking lemonade. This was in mid-August, and Ralph had begun to wake up around three-thirty each morning. 'It's got to be hazardous to your health. Worse, you look like a lunatic.'

'Maybe I *am* a lunatic,' Ralph responded shortly, and either his tone or the look in his eyes must have been convincing, because McGovern changed the subject.

2

He did begin walking again – nothing like the Marathons of '92, but he managed two miles a day if it wasn't raining. His usual route took him down the perversely named Up-Mile Hill, to the Derry Public Library, and then on to Back Pages, a used bookstore and newsstand on the corner of Witcham and Main.

Back Pages stood next to a jumbled junkatorium called Secondhand Rose, Secondhand Clothes, and as he passed this store one day during the August of his discontent, Ralph saw a new poster among the announcements of outdated bean suppers and ancient church socials, placed so it covered roughly half of a yellowing PAT BUCHANAN FOR PRESIDENT placard.

The woman in the two photographs at the top of the poster was a pretty blonde in her late thirties or early forties, but the style of the photos – unsmiling full face on the left, unsmiling profile on the right, plain white background in both – was unsettling enough to stop Ralph in his tracks. The photos made the woman look as if she belonged on a post office wall or in a TV docudrama . . . and that, the poster's printed matter made clear, was no accident.

The photos were what stopped him, but it was the woman's name that held him.

WANTED FOR MURDER
SUSAN EDWINA DAY

was printed across the top in big black letters. And below the simulated mug-shots, in red:

STAY OUT OF OUR CITY!

There was a small line of print at the very bottom of the poster. Ralph's close vision had deteriorated quite a bit since Carolyn's death – gone to hell in a handbasket might actually have been a more accurate way of putting it – and he had to lean forward until his brow was pressed against the dirty show window of Secondhand Rose, Secondhand Clothes before he could decipher it:

Paid for by the Maine LifeWatch Committee

Far down in his mind a voice whispered: *Hey, hey, Susan Day! How many kids did you kill today?*

Susan Day, Ralph recalled, was a political activist from either New York or Washington, the sort of fast-speaking woman who regularly drove taxi-drivers, barbers, and hardhat construction workers into foaming frenzies. Why that particular little jangle of doggerel had come into his mind, however, he couldn't say; it was tagged to some memory that wouldn't quite come. Maybe his tired old brains were just cross-referencing that sixties Vietnam protest chant, the one which had gone *Hey, hey, LBJ! How many kids did you kill today?*

No, that's not it, he thought. *Close, but no cigar. It was—*

Just before his mind could cough up Ed Deepneau's name and face, a voice spoke from almost beside him. 'Earth to Ralph, earth to Ralph, come in, Ralphie-baby!'

Roused out of his thoughts, Ralph turned toward the voice. He was both shocked and amused to find he had almost been asleep on his feet. *Christ,* he thought, *you never know how important sleep is until you miss a little. Then all the floors start to tilt and all the corners on things start to round off.*

It was Hamilton Davenport, the proprietor of Back Pages, who had spoken to him. He was stocking the library cart he kept in front of his shop with brightly jacketed paperbacks. His old corncob pipe – to Ralph it always looked like the stack of a model steamship – jutted from the corner of his mouth, sending little puffs of blue smoke into the hot, bright air. Winston Smith, his old gray tomcat, sat in the open doorway of the shop with his tail curled around his paws. He looked at Ralph with yellow-eyed indifference, as if to say, *You think you know old, my friend? I'm here to testify you don't know* dick *about getting old.*

'Sheesh, Ralph,' Davenport said. 'I must have called your name at least three times.'

'I guess I was woolgathering,' Ralph said. He stepped past the library cart, leaned in the doorway (Winston Smith held his place with regal indifference), and grabbed the two papers he bought every day: a Boston *Globe* and a *USA Today*. The Derry *News* came right to the house, courtesy of Pete the paperboy. Ralph sometimes told people that he was sure one of the three papers was comic relief, but he had never been able to make up his mind which one it was. 'I haven't—'

He broke off as Ed Deepneau's face came into his mind. It was Ed he'd heard that nasty little chant from, last summer, out by the airport, and it really wasn't any wonder it had taken him a little while to retrieve the memory. Ed Deepneau was the last person in the world from whom you'd expect to hear something like that.

'Ralphie?' Davenport said. 'You just shut down on me.'

Ralph blinked. 'Oh, sorry. I haven't been sleeping very well, that's what I started to say.'

'Bummer . . . but there are worse problems. Just drink a glass of warm milk and listen to some quiet music half an hour before bed.'

Ralph had begun to discover this summer that everyone in America apparently had a pet remedy for insomnia, some bit of bedtime magic that had been handed down through the generations like the family Bible.

'Bach's good, also Beethoven, and William Ackerman ain't bad. But the real trick' – Davenport raised one finger impressively to emphasize this – 'is *not to get up from your chair* during that half hour. Not for anything. Don't answer the phone, don't wind up the dog and put out the alarm-clock, don't decide to brush your teeth . . . *nothing*! Then, when you *do* go to bed . . . bam! Out like a light!'

'What if you're sitting there in your favorite easy-chair and all at once you realize you have a call of nature?' Ralph asked. 'These things can come on pretty suddenly when you get to be my age.'

'Do it in your pants,' Davenport said promptly, and burst out laughing. Ralph smiled, but it had a dutiful feel. His insomnia was rapidly losing whatever marginal humor value it might once have had. 'In your *pants*!' Ham chortled. He slapped the library cart and wagged his head back and forth.

Ralph happened to glance down at the cat. Winston Smith

looked blandly back at him, and to Ralph his calm yellow gaze seemed to say, *Yes, that's right, he's a fool, but he's* my *fool.*

'Not bad, huh? Hamilton Davenport, master of the snappy comeback. Do it in your . . .' He snorted laughter, shook his head, then took the two dollar bills Ralph was holding out. He slipped them into the pocket of his short red apron and came out with some change. 'That about right?'

'You bet. Thanks, Ham.'

'Uh-huh. And all joking aside, try the music. It really works. Mellows out your brain-waves, or something.'

'I will.' And the devil of it was, he probably would, as he had already tried Mrs Rapaport's lemon and hot water recipe, and Shawna McClure's advice on how to clear his mind by slowing his respiration and concentrating on the word *cool* (except when Shawna said it, the word came out *cuhhhh-ooooooooooool*). When you were trying to deal with a slow but relentless erosion of your good sleep-time, any folk remedy started to look good.

Ralph began to turn away, then turned back. 'What's with that poster next door?'

Ham Davenport wrinkled his nose. 'Dan Dalton's place? I don't look in there at all, if I can help it. Screws up my appetite. Has he got something new and disgusting in the window?'

'I *guess* it's new – it's not as yellow as the rest of them, and there's a notable lack of flydirt on it. Looks like a wanted poster, only it's Susan Day in the photos.'

'Susan Day on a – son of a bitch!' He cast a dark and humorless look at the shop next door.

'What is she, President of the National Organization of Women, or something?'

'Ex-President and co-founder of Sisters in Arms. Author of *My Mother's Shadow* and *Lilies of the Valley* – that one's a study of battered women and why so many of them refuse to blow the whistle on the men that batter them. She won a Pulitzer Prize for it. Susie Day's one of the three or four most politically influential women in America right now, and she can really write as well as think. That clown *knows* I've got one of her petitions sitting right by my cash register.'

'What petitions?'

'We're trying to get her up here to speak,' Davenport said. 'You know the right-to-lifers tried to firebomb WomanCare last Christmas, right?'

Ralph cast his mind cautiously back into the black pit he'd been living in at the end of 1992 and said, 'Well, I remember that the cops caught some guy in the hospital's long-term parking lot with a can of gasoline, but I didn't know—'

'That was Charlie Pickering. He's a member of Daily Bread, one of the right-to-life groups that keep the pickets marching out there,' Davenport said. 'They put him up to it, too – take my word. This year they're not bothering with gasoline, though; they're going to try to get the City Council to change the zoning regulations and squeeze WomanCare right out of existence. They just might do it, too. You know Derry, Ralph – it's not exactly a hotbed of liberalism.'

'No,' Ralph said with a wan smile. 'It's never been that. And WomanCare *is* an abortion clinic, isn't it?'

Davenport gave him an out-of-patience look and jerked his head in the direction of Secondhand Rose. 'That's what assholes like *him* call it,' he said, 'only they like to use the word *mill* instead of *clinic*. They ignore all the other stuff WomanCare does.' To Ralph, Davenport had begun to sound a little like the TV announcer who hawked run-free pantyhose during the Sunday afternoon movie. 'They're involved in family counselling, they deal with spouse and child abuse, and they run a shelter for abused women over by the Newport town line. They have a rape crisis center at the in-town building by the hospital, and a twenty-four-hour hotline for women who've been raped or beaten. In short, they stand for all the things that make Marlboro Men like Dalton shit bullets.'

'But they *do* perform abortions,' Ralph said. 'That's what the pickets are about, right?'

There had been sign-carrying demonstrators in front of the low-slung, unobtrusive brick building that housed WomanCare for years, it seemed to Ralph. They always looked too pale to him, too intense, too skinny or too fat, too utterly sure that God was on their side. The signs they carried said things like THE UNBORN HAVE RIGHTS, TOO and LIFE, WHAT A BEAUTIFUL CHOICE and that old standby, ABORTION IS MURDER! On several occasions women using the clinic – which was near Derry Home but not actually associated with it, Ralph thought – had been spat upon.

'Yeah, they perform abortions,' Ham said. 'You got a problem with that?'

Ralph thought of all the years he and Carolyn had tried to have a baby – years that had produced nothing but several false alarms and a single messy five-months miscarriage – and shrugged. Suddenly the day seemed too hot and his legs too tired. The thought of his return journey – the Up-Mile Hill leg of it in particular – hung in the back of his mind like something strung from a line of fish-hooks. 'Christ, I don't know,' he said. 'I just wish people didn't have to get so . . . so shrill.'

Davenport grunted, walked over to his neighbor's display window, and peered at the bogus wanted poster. While he was looking at it, a tall, pallid man with a goatee – the absolute antithesis of the Marlboro Man, Ralph would have said – materialized from the gloomy depths of Secondhand Rose like a vaudeville spook that has gotten a bit mouldy around the edges. He saw what Davenport was looking at, and a tiny disdainful smile dimpled the corners of his mouth. Ralph thought it was the kind of smile that could cost a man a couple of teeth, or a broken nose. Especially on a dog-hot day like this one.

Davenport pointed to the poster and shook his head violently.

Dalton's smile deepened. He flapped his hands at Davenport – *Who gives a shit what you think?* the gesture said – and then disappeared back into the depths of his store.

Davenport returned to Ralph, bright spots of color burning in his cheeks. 'That man's picture should be next to the word *prick* in the dictionary,' he said.

Exactly what he thinks about you, I imagine, Ralph thought, but of course did not say.

Davenport stood in front of the library cart full of paperbacks, hands stuffed into his pockets beneath his red change apron, brooding at the poster of

(*hey hey*)

Susan Day.

'Well,' Ralph said, 'I suppose I better—'

Davenport shook himself out of his brown study. 'Don't go yet,' he said. 'Sign my petition first, will you? Put a little shine back on my morning.'

Ralph shifted his feet uncomfortably. 'I usually don't get involved in confrontational stuff like—'

'Come on, Ralph,' Davenport said in a let's-be-reasonable voice. 'We're not talking confrontation here; we're talking about making sure that the fruits and nuts like the ones who run Daily Bread – and political Neanderthals like Dalton – don't shut down a really useful women's resource center. It's not like I'm asking you to endorse testing chemical warfare weapons on dolphins.'

'No,' Ralph said. 'I suppose not.'

'We're hoping to send five thousand signatures to Susan Day by the first of September. Probably won't do any good – Derry's really not much more than a wide place in the road, and she's probably booked into the next century anyhow – but it can't hurt to try.'

Ralph thought about telling Ham that the only petition he wanted to sign was one asking the gods of sleep to give him back the three hours or so of good rest a night they had stolen away, but then he took another look at the man's face and decided against it.

Carolyn would have signed his damned petition, he thought. *She was no fan of abortion, but she was also no fan of men coming home after the bars close and mistaking their wives and kids for soccer balls.*

True enough, but that wouldn't have been her main reason for signing; she would have done it on the off-chance that she might get to hear an authentic firebrand like Susan Day up close and in person. She would have done it out of the ingrained curiosity which had perhaps been her dominating characteristic – something so strong not even the brain tumor had been able to kill it. Two days before she died she had pulled the movie ticket he'd been using as a bookmark out of the paperback novel he'd left on her beside table because she had wanted to know what he'd been to see. It had been *A Few Good Men,* as a matter of fact, and he was both surprised and dismayed to discover how much it hurt to remember that. Even now it hurt like hell.

'Sure,' he told Ham. 'I'll be happy to sign it.'

'My man!' Davenport exclaimed, and clapped him on the shoulder. The broody look was replaced by a grin, but Ralph didn't think the change much of an improvement. The grin was hard and not especially charming. 'Step into my den of iniquity!'

Ralph followed him into the tobacco-smelling shop, which did not seem particularly iniquitous at nine-thirty in the morning. Winston Smith fled before them, pausing just once to look back with his ancient yellow eyes. *He's a fool and you're another,* that parting stare might have said. Under the circumstances, it wasn't a conclusion Ralph felt much inclined to dispute. He tucked his newspapers under his arm, leaned over the ruled sheet on the counter beside the cash register, and signed the petition asking Susan Day to come to Derry and speak in defense of WomanCare.

3

He did better climbing Up-Mile Hill than he had expected, and crossed the X-shaped intersection of Witcham and Jackson thinking, *There, that wasn't so bad, was—*

He suddenly realized that his ears were ringing and his legs had begun to tremble beneath him. He stopped on the far side of Witcham and placed one hand against his shirt. He could feel his heart beating just beneath it, pumping away with a ragged fierceness that was scary. He heard a papery rustle and saw an advertising supplement slip out of the Boston *Globe* and go seesawing down into the gutter. He started to bend over and get it, then stopped.

Not a good idea, Ralph – if you bend over, you're more than likely going to fall over. I suggest you leave that one for the sweeper.

'Yeah, okay, good idea,' he muttered, and straightened up. Black dots surged across his vision like a surreal flock of crows, and for a moment Ralph was almost positive he was going to wind up lying on top of the ad supplement no matter what he did or didn't do.

'Ralph? You all right?'

He looked up cautiously and saw Lois Chasse, who lived on the other side of Harris Avenue and half a block down from the house he shared with Bill McGovern. She was sitting on one of the benches just outside Strawford Park, probably waiting for the Canal Street bus to come along and take her downtown.

'Sure, fine,' he said, and made his legs move. He felt as if he were walking through syrup, but he thought he got over to the bench without looking too bad. He could not, however, suppress a grateful little gasp as he sat down next to her.

Lois Chasse had large dark eyes – the kind that had been called Spanish eyes when Ralph was a kid – and he bet they had danced through the minds of dozens of boys during Lois's high school years. They were still her best feature, but Ralph didn't much care for the worry he saw in them now. It was . . . what? *A little too neighborly for comfort* was the first thought to occur to him, but he wasn't sure it was the *right* thought.

'Fine,' Lois echoed.

'You betcha.' He took his handkerchief from his back pocket, checked to make sure it was clean, and then wiped his brow with it.

'I hope you don't mind me saying it, Ralph, but you don't *look* fine.'

Ralph *did* mind her saying it, but didn't know how to say so.

'You're pale, you're sweating, and you're a litterbug.'

Ralph looked at her, startled.

'Something fell out of your paper. I think it was an ad circular.'

'Did it?'

'You know perfectly well it did. Excuse me a second.'

She got up, crossed the sidewalk, bent (Ralph noticed that, while her hips were fairly broad, her legs were still admirably trim for a woman who had to be sixty-eight), and picked up the circular. She came back to the bench with it and sat down.

'There,' she said. 'Now you're not a litterbug anymore.'

He smiled in spite of himself. 'Thank you.'

'Don't mention it. I can use the Maxwell House coupon, also the Hamburger Helper and the Diet Coke. I've gotten so *fat* since Mr Chasse died.'

'You're not fat, Lois.'

'Thank you, Ralph, you're a perfect gentleman, but let's not change the subject. You had a dizzy spell, didn't you? In fact, you almost passed out.'

'I was just catching my breath,' he said stiffly, and turned to watch a bunch of kids playing scrub baseball just inside the park. They were going at it hard, laughing and grab-assing around. Ralph envied the efficiency of their air-conditioning systems.

'Catching your breath, were you?'

'Yes.'

'Just catching your breath.'

'Lois, you're starting to sound like a broken record.'

'Well, the broken record's going to tell you something, okay? You're *nuts* to be trying Up-Mile Hill in this heat. If you want to walk, why not go out the Extension, where it's flat, like you used to?'

'Because it makes me think of Carolyn,' he said, not liking the stiff, almost rude way that sounded but unable to help it.

'Oh shit,' she said, and touched his hand briefly. 'Sorry.'

'It's okay.'

'No, it's not. I should have known better. But the way you looked just now, that's not okay, either. You're not twenty anymore, Ralph. Not even forty. I don't mean you're not in good shape – anyone can see you're in great shape for a guy your age – but you ought to take better care of yourself. Carolyn would want you to take care of yourself.'

'I know,' he said, 'but I'm really—'

– *all right,* he meant to finish, and then he looked up from his hands, looked into her dark eyes again, and what he saw there made it impossible to finish for a moment. There was a weary sadness in her eyes . . . or was it loneliness? Maybe both. In any case, those were not the only things he saw in them. He also saw himself.

You're being silly, the eyes looking into his said. *Maybe we both are. You're seventy and a widower, Ralph. I'm sixty-eight and a widow. How long are we going to sit on your porch in the evenings with Bill McGovern as the world's oldest chaperone? Not too long, I hope, because neither of us is exactly fresh off the showroom lot.*

'Ralph?' Lois asked, suddenly concerned. 'Are you okay?'

'Yes,' he said, looking down at his hands again. 'Yes, sure.'

'You had a look on your face like . . . well, I don't know.'

Ralph wondered if maybe the combination of the heat and the walk up Up-Mile Hill *had* scrambled his brains a little. Because this was *Lois*, after all, whom McGovern always referred to (with a small, satiric lift of his left eyebrow) as 'Our Lois'. And okay, yes, she was still in good shape – trim legs, nice bust, and those remarkable eyes – and maybe he wouldn't mind taking her to bed, and maybe she wouldn't mind being taken. But what would there be after that? If she happened to see a ticket-stub poking out of the book he was reading, would she pull it out, too curious about what movie he'd been to see to think about how she was losing his place?

Ralph thought not. Lois's eyes were remarkable, and he had found his own eyes wandering down the V of her blouse more than once as the three of them sat on the front porch, drinking iced tea in the cool of the evening, but he had an idea that your little head could get your big head in trouble even at seventy. Getting old was no excuse to get careless.

He got to his feet, aware of Lois looking at him and making an extra effort not to stoop. 'Thanks for your concern,' he said. 'Want to walk an old feller up the street?'

'Thanks, but I'm going downtown. They've got some beautiful rose-colored yarn in at The Sewing Circle, and I'm thinking afghan. Meanwhile, I'll just wait for the bus and gloat over my coupons.'

Ralph grinned. 'You do that.' He glanced over at the kids on the scrub ballfield. As he watched, a boy with an extravagant mop of red hair broke from third, threw himself down in a headfirst slide . . . and fetched up against one of the catcher's shinguards with an audible *thonk*. Ralph winced, envisioning ambulances with flashing lights and screaming sirens, but the carrot-top bounced to his feet laughing.

'Missed the tag, you hoser!' he shouted.

'The hell I did!' the catcher responded indignantly, but then he began to laugh, too.

'Ever wish you were that age again, Ralph?' Lois asked.

He thought it over. 'Sometimes,' he said. 'Mostly it just looks too strenuous. Come on over tonight, Lois – sit with us awhile.'

'I might just do that,' she said, and Ralph started up Harris Avenue, feeling the weight of her remarkable eyes on him and trying hard to keep his back straight. He thought he managed fairly well, but it was hard work. He had never felt so tired in his life.

Chapter Two

1

Ralph made the appointment to see Dr Litchfield less than an hour after his conversation with Lois on the park bench; the receptionist with the cool, sexy voice told him she could fit him in next Tuesday morning at ten, if that was okay, and Ralph told her that was fine as paint. Then he hung up, went into the living room, sat in the wing-chair that overlooked Harris Avenue, and thought about how Dr Litchfield had initially treated his wife's brain tumor with Tylenol-3 and pamphlets explaining various relaxation techniques. From there he moved on to the look he'd seen in Litchfield's eyes after the magnetic resonance imaging tests had confirmed the CAT scan's bad news . . . that look of guilt and unease.

Across the street, a bunch of kids who would soon be back in school came out of the Red Apple armed with candy bars and Slurpies. As Ralph watched them mount their bikes and tear away into the bright eleven o'clock heat, he thought what he always did when the memory of Dr Litchfield's eyes surfaced: that it was most likely a false memory.

The thing is, old buddy, you wanted *Litchfield to look uneasy . . . but even more than that, you wanted him to look guilty.*

Quite possibly true, quite possibly Carl Litchfield was a peach of a guy and a helluva doctor, but Ralph still found himself calling Litchfield's office again half an hour later. He told the receptionist with the sexy voice that he'd just rechecked his calendar and discovered next Tuesday at ten wasn't so fine after all. He'd made an appointment with the podiatrist for that day and forgotten all about it.

'My memory's not what it used to be,' Ralph told her.

The receptionist suggested next Thursday at two.

Ralph countered by promising to call back.

Liar, liar, pants on fire, he thought as he hung up the phone, walked slowly back to the wing-chair, and lowered himself into it. *You're done with him, aren't you?*

He supposed he was. Not that Dr Litchfield was apt to lose any sleep over it; if he thought about Ralph at all, it would be as one less old geezer to fart in his face during the prostate exam.

All right, so what are *you going to do about the insomnia, Ralph?*

'Sit quiet for half an hour before bedtime and listen to classical music,' he said out loud. 'Buy some Depends for those troublesome calls of nature.'

He startled himself by laughing at the image. The laughter had a hysterical edge he didn't much care for – it was damned creepy, as a matter of fact – but it was still a little while before he could make himself stop.

Yet he supposed he would try Hamilton Davenport's suggestion (although he would skip the diapers, thank you), as he had tried most of the folk remedies well-meaning people had passed on to him. This made him think of his first *bona fide* folk remedy, and that raised another grin.

It had been McGovern's idea. He had been sitting on the porch one evening when Ralph came back from the Red Apple with some noodles and spaghetti sauce, had taken one look at his upstairs neighbor and made a *tsk-tsk* sound, shaking his head dolefully.

'What's that supposed to mean?' Ralph asked, taking the seat next to him. A little farther down the street, a little girl in jeans and an oversized white tee-shirt had been skipping rope and chanting in the growing gloom.

'It means you're looking folded, spindled, and mutilated,' McGovern said. He used one thumb to tilt the Panama back on his head and looked more closely at Ralph. 'Still not sleeping?'

'Still not sleeping,' Ralph agreed.

McGovern was quiet for a few seconds. When he spoke again, he did so in a tone of absolute – almost apocalyptic, in fact – finality. 'Whiskey is the answer,' he said.

'I beg your pardon?'

'To your insomnia, Ralph. I don't mean you should take a bath in it – there's no need of that. Just mix a tablespoon of honey with half a shot of whiskey and hook it down fifteen or twenty minutes before you hit the hay.'

'You think?' Ralph had asked hopefully.

'All I can say is it worked for me, and I had some real problems sleeping around the time I turned forty. Looking back on it, I guess that was my midlife crisis – six months of insomnia and a year-long depression over my bald spot.'

Although the books he'd been consulting all said that booze was a vastly overrated cure for sleeplessness – that it often made the problem worse instead of better, in fact – Ralph had tried it just the same. He had never been much of a drinker, so he began by adjusting McGovern's recommended half-shot dosage down to a quarter of a shot, but after a week of no relief he had upped the ante to a full shot . . . then to two. He woke up one morning at four-twenty-two with a nasty little headache to accompany the dull brown taste of Early Times on the roof of his mouth, and realized he was suffering his first hangover in fifteen years.

'Life's too short for this shit,' he had announced to his empty apartment, and that had been the end of the great whiskey experiment.

2

Okay, Ralph thought now as he watched the desultory mid-morning flow of customers in and out of the Red Apple across the street. *Here's the situation: McGovern says you look like shit, you almost fainted at Lois Chasse's feet this morning, and you just cancelled the appointment you made with Ye Olde Family Physician. So what next? Just let it go? Accept the situation and let it go?*

The idea had a certain Oriental charm – fate, karma, and all that – but he was going to need more than charm to get him through the long hours of early morning. The books said there were people in the world, quite a lot of them, who managed very well on no more than three or four hours of sleep a night. There were even some who got along on only two. They were an extremely small minority, but they *did* exist. Ralph Roberts, however, was not among their number.

How he looked wasn't very important to him – he had a feeling that his matinee-idol days were well behind him – but how he felt was, and it was no longer just a matter of not feeling good; he felt horrible. The insomnia had begun to pervade every aspect of his life, the way the smell of frying garlic on the fifth floor will eventually pervade an entire apartment building. The color had started to drain out of things; the world had begun to take on the dull, grainy quality of a newspaper photograph.

Simple decisions – whether to heat up a frozen dinner for his evening meal or grab a sandwich at the Red Apple and go up to the picnic area by Runway 3, for example – had become difficult, almost agonizing. In the last couple of weeks he had found himself coming back to the apartment from Dave's Video Stop empty-handed more and more often, not because there was nothing at Dave's he wanted to watch but because there was too much – he couldn't decide if he wanted one of the *Dirty Harry* movies or a Billy Crystal comedy or maybe a few old *Star Trek* episodes. After a couple of these unsuccessful trips, he had plopped himself down in this very wing-chair, almost crying with frustration . . . and, he supposed, fear.

That creeping sensory numbness and the erosion of his decision-making capabilities were not the only problems he had come to associate with the insomnia; his short-term memory had also begun to slip. It had been his practice to go to the movies at least once and sometimes twice a week ever since his retirement from the printshop where he had finished his working life as the bookkeeper and general supervisor. He had taken Carolyn until last year, when she had gotten too sick to enjoy going out anywhere. After her death he had mostly gone alone, although Helen Deepneau had accompanied him once or twice when Ed was home to mind the baby (Ed himself almost never went, claiming he got headaches at the movies). Ralph had gotten so used to calling the cinema center's answering machine to check showtimes that he had the number by heart. As the summer went on, however, he found himself having to look it up in the Yellow Pages more and more often – he could no longer be sure if the last four digits were 1317 or 1713.

'It's 1713,' he said now. 'I *know* it is.' But *did* he know it? Did he really?

Call Litchfield back. Go on, Ralph – stop sifting through the wreckage. Do something constructive. And if Litchfield really sticks in your craw, call somebody else. The phone book's as full of doctors as it ever was.

Probably true, but seventy was maybe a little old to be picking a new sawbones by the eenie-meenie-minie-moe method. And he wasn't going to call Litchfield back. Period.

Okay, so what's next, you stubborn old goat? A few more folk remedies? I hope not, because at the rate you're going you'll be down to eye of newt and tongue of toad in no time.

The answer that came was like a cool breeze on a hot day . . . and it was an absurdly simple answer. All his book-research this summer had been aimed at understanding the problem rather than finding a solution. When it came to answers, he had relied almost solely on back-fence remedies like whiskey and honey, even when the books had already assured him they probably wouldn't work or would only work for a while. Although the books *did* offer some presumably reliable methods for coping with insomnia, the only one Ralph had actually tried was the simplest and most obvious: going to bed earlier in the evening. That solution hadn't worked – he had simply lain awake until eleven-thirty or so, then dropped off to wake at his new, earlier time – but something else might.

It was worth a try, anyway.

3

Instead of spending the afternoon in his usual frenzy of backyard pottering, Ralph went down to the library and skimmed through some of the books he had already looked at. The general consensus seemed to be that if going to bed earlier didn't work, going later might. Ralph went home (mindful of his previous adventures, he took the bus) filled with cautious hope. It might work. If it didn't, he always had Bach, Beethoven and William Ackerman to fall back on.

His first attempt at this technique, which one of the texts called 'delayed sleep', was comic. He awoke at his now-usual time (3:45 by the digital clock on the living-room mantel) with a sore back, an aching neck, no immediate idea of how he had gotten into the wing-chair by the window, or why the TV was on, broadcasting nothing but snow and a soft, surflike roar of static.

It was only as he allowed his head to roll cautiously back, supporting the nape of his neck with a cupped palm, that he realized what had happened. He had intended to sit up until at least three o'clock and possibly four. He would then stroll off to bed and sleep the sleep of the just. That had been the plan, anyway. Instead, The Incredible Insomniac of Harris Avenue had dropped off during Jay Leno's opening monologue, like a kid who's trying to stay up all night long just to see what it's like. And then, of course, he had finished the adventure by waking up in the damned chair. The problem was the same, Joe Friday might have said; only the location had changed.

Ralph strolled off to bed anyway, hoping against hope, but the urge (if not the need) to sleep had passed. After an hour of lying awake, he had gone back to the wing-chair again, this time with a pillow propped behind his stiff neck and a rueful grin on his face.

4

There was nothing funny about his second try, which took place the following night. Sleepiness began to steal over him at its usual time – eleven-twenty, just as Pete Cherney was giving the following day's weather forecast. This time Ralph fought it successfully, making it all the way through *Whoopi* (although he almost nodded off during Whoopi's conversation with Roseanne Arnold, that evening's guest) and the late-night movie that came on after that. It was an old Audie Murphy flick in which Audie appeared to be winning the war in the Pacific pretty much single-handed. It sometimes seemed to Ralph that there was an unspoken rule among local TV broadcasters which stated that movies telecast in the small hours of the morning could only star Audie Murphy or James Brolin.

After the last Japanese pillbox had been blown up, Channel 2 signed off. Ralph dialed around, looking for another movie, and found nothing but snow. He supposed he could have watched movies all night if he had the cable, like Bill downstairs or Lois down the street; he remembered having put that on his list of things to do in the new year. But then Carolyn had died and cable TV – with or without Home Box Office – had no longer seemed very important.

He found a copy of *Sports Illustrated* and began to slog through an article on women's tennis he'd missed the first time through, glancing up at the clock every now and then as the hands began to close in on 3:00 a.m. He had become all but convinced that this was going to work. His eyelids were so heavy they felt as if they had been dipped in concrete, and although he was reading the tennis article carefully, word for word, he had no idea of what the writer was driving at. Whole sentences zipped across his brain without sticking, like cosmic rays.

I'm going to sleep tonight – I really think I am. For the first time in months the sun is going to have to come up without my help, and that isn't just good, friends and neighbors; that is great.

Then, shortly after three o'clock, that pleasant drowsiness began to disappear. It did not go with a champagne-cork pop but rather seemed to ooze away, like sand through a fine sieve or water down a partially clogged drain. When Ralph realized what was happening, it wasn't panic he felt, but sick dismay. It was a feeling he had come to recognize as the true opposite of hope, and when he slipper-scuffed his way into the bedroom at quarter past three, he couldn't remember a depression as deep as the one which now enveloped him. He felt as if he were suffocating in it.

'Please, God, just forty winks,' he muttered as he turned off the light, but he strongly suspected that this was one prayer which was not going to be answered.

It wasn't. Although he had been awake for twenty-four hours by then, every trace of sleepiness had left his mind and body by quarter of four. He was tired, yes – more deeply and fundamentally tired than he had ever been in his life – but being tired and being sleepy, he had discovered, were sometimes poles apart. Sleep, that undiscriminating friend, humankind's best and most reliable nurse since the dawn of time, had abandoned him again.

By four o'clock Ralph's bed had become hateful to him, as it always did when he realized he could put it to no good use. He swung his feet back onto the floor, scratching the mat of hair – almost entirely gray now – which curled through his mostly unbuttoned pajama top. He slid on his slippers again and scuffed back to the living room, where he dropped into the wing-back chair and looked down at Harris Avenue. It was laid out like a stage set where the only actor currently on view wasn't even human: it was a stray dog moving slowly down Harris Avenue in the direction of Strawford Park and Up-Mile Hill. It held its right rear leg up as much as possible, limping along as best it could on the other three.

'Hi there, Rosalie,' Ralph muttered, and rubbed a hand across his eyes.

It was a Thursday morning, garbage-pickup day on Harris Avenue, so he wasn't surprised to see Rosalie, who'd been a wandering, here-and-there fixture in the neighborhood for the last year or so. She made her way down the street in leisurely fashion, investigating the rows and clusters of cans with the discrimination of a jaded flea-market shopper.

Now Rosalie – who was limping worse than ever this morning, and looked as tired as Ralph felt – found what looked like a good-sized beef bone and trotted away with it in her mouth. Ralph watched her out of sight, then simply sat with his hands folded in his lap, gazing out on the silent neighborhood, where the orange hi-intensity lamps added to the illusion that Harris Avenue was nothing but a stage set standing deserted after the evening performance had ended and the actors had gone home; they shone down like spotlights in a perfect diminishing perspective that was surreal and hallucinatory.

Ralph Roberts sat in the wing-chair where he had spent so many early-morning hours lately and waited for light and movement to invest the lifeless world below him. Finally the first human actor – Pete the paperboy – entered stage right, riding his Raleigh. He biked his way up the street, tossing rolled newspapers from the bag slung over his shoulder and hitting the porches he aimed at with a fair degree of accuracy.

Ralph watched him awhile, then heaved a sigh which felt as if it had come all the way from the basement, and got up to make tea.

'I don't remember *ever* reading about this shit in my horoscope,' he said hollowly, and then turned on the kitchen tap and began to fill the kettle.

5

That long Thursday morning and even longer Thursday afternoon taught Ralph Roberts a valuable lesson: not to sneer at
three or four hours' sleep a night simply because he had spent
his entire life under the mistaken impression that he had a right
to at least six and usually seven. It also served as a hideous
preview: if things didn't improve, he could look forward to
feeling like this most of the time. Hell, *all* of the time. He went
into the bedroom at ten o'clock and again at one, hoping for a
little nap – even a catnap would do, and half an hour would
be a life-saver – but he could not so much as drowse. He was
miserably tired but not in the least bit sleepy.

Around three o'clock he decided to make himself a Lipton
Cup-A-Soup. He filled the teakettle with fresh water, put it
on to boil, and opened the cupboard over the counter where
he kept condiments, spices, and various envelopes containing
foods which only astronauts and old men actually seem to eat
– powders to which the consumer need only add hot water.

He pushed cans and bottles around in aimless fashion and
then simply stared into the cupboard for awhile, as if expecting
the box of soup packets to magically appear in the space he
had made. When they didn't, he repeated the process, only
this time moving things back to their original positions before
staring in again with the look of distant perplexity which was
becoming (Ralph, mercifully, did not know this) his dominant
expression.

When the teakettle shrieked, he put it on one of the rear
burners and went back to staring into the cupboard. It dawned
on him – very, very slowly – that he must have drunk his last
packet of Cup-A-Soup yesterday or the day before, although
he could not for the life of him remember doing so.

'That's a surprise?' he asked the boxes and bottles in the open
cupboard. 'I'm so tired I can't remember my own name.'

Yes, I can, he thought. *It's Leon Redbone. So there!*

It wasn't much of a joke, but he felt a small smile – it
felt as light as a feather – touch his lips. He stepped into
the bathroom, combed his hair, and then went downstairs.
*Here's Audie Murphy, heading out into enemy territory in search
of supplies,* he thought. *Primary target: one box of Lipton Chicken
and Rice Cup-A-Soup packets. If locating and securing this target*

should prove impossible, I'll divert to my secondary: Noodles 'n Beef.
I know this is a risky mission, but—

'– but I work best alone,' he finished as he came out on the porch.

Old Mrs Perrine happened to be passing, and she favored Ralph with a sharp look but said nothing. He waited for her to get a little way up the sidewalk – he did not feel capable of conversation with anyone this afternoon, least of all Mrs Perrine, who at eighty-two could still have found stimulating and useful work among the Marines at Parris Island. He pretended to be examining the spider-plant which hung from the hook under the porch eave until she had reached what he deemed a safe distance, then crossed Harris Avenue to the Red Apple. Which was where the day's real troubles began.

6

He entered the convenience store once again mulling over the spectacular failure of the delayed-sleep experiment and wondering if the advice in the library texts was no more than an uptown version of the folk remedies his acquaintances seemed so eager to press upon him. It was an unpleasant idea, but he thought his mind (or the force below his mind which was actually in charge of this slow torture) had sent him a message which was even more unpleasant: *You have a sleep-window, Ralph. It's not as big as it once was, and it seems to be getting smaller with every passing week, but you better be grateful for what you've got, because a small window is better than no window at all. You see that now, don't you?*

'Yes,' Ralph mumbled as he walked down the center aisle to the bright red Cup-A-Soup boxes. 'I see that very well.'

Sue, the afternoon counter-girl, laughed cheerfully. 'You must have money in the bank, Ralph,' she said.

'Beg pardon?' Ralph didn't turn; he was inventorying the red boxes. Here was onion . . . split pea . . . the beef-and-noodles combo . . . but where the hell was the Chicken and Rice?

'My mom always said people who talk to themselves have *Oh my God!*'

For a moment Ralph thought she had simply made a statement a little too complex for his tired mind to immediately grasp, something about how people who talked to themselves had found God, and then she screamed. He had hunkered down to check the boxes on the bottom shelf, and the scream shot him to his feet so hard and fast that his knees popped. He wheeled toward the front of the store, bumping the top shelf of the soup display with his elbow and knocking half a dozen red boxes into the aisle.

'Sue? What's wrong?'

Sue paid no attention. She was looking out through the door with her fisted hands pressed against her lips and her brown eyes huge above them. 'God, look at the blood!' she cried in a choked voice.

Ralph turned further, knocking a few more Lipton boxes into the aisle, and looked through the Red Apple's dirty show window. What he saw drew a gasp from him, and it took him a space of seconds – five, maybe – to realize that the bloody, beaten woman staggering toward the Red Apple was Helen Deepneau. Ralph had always thought Helen the prettiest woman on the west side of town, but there was nothing pretty about her today. One of her eyes was puffed shut; there was a gash at her left temple that was soon going to be lost in the gaudy swelling of a fresh bruise; her puffy lips and her cheeks were covered with blood. The blood had come from her nose, which was still leaking. She wove through the Red Apple's little parking lot toward the door like a drunk, her one good eye seeming to see nothing; it simply stared.

More frightening than the way she looked was the way she was handling Natalie. She had the squalling, frightened baby slung casually on one hip, carrying her as she might have carried her books to high school ten or twelve years before.

'*Oh Jesus, she's gonna drop the kid!*' Sue screamed, but although she was ten steps closer to the door than he was, she made no move – simply stood where she was with her hands pressed to her mouth and her eyes gobbling up her face.

Ralph didn't feel tired anymore. He sprinted up the aisle, tore open the door, and ran outside. He was just in time to catch Helen by the shoulders as she banged a hip against the ice cabinet – mercifully not the hip with Natalie on it – and went veering off in a new direction.

'Helen!' he yelled. 'Jesus, Helen, what happened?'

'Hun?' she asked, her voice dully curious, totally unlike the voice of the lively young woman who sometimes accompanied him to the movies and moaned over Mel Gibson. Her good eye rolled toward him and he saw that same dull curiosity in it, a look that said she didn't know who she was, let alone where she was, or what had happened, or when. 'Hun? Ral? Wha?'

The baby slipped. Ralph let go of Helen, grabbed for Natalie, and managed to snag one of her jumper straps. Nat screamed, waved her hands, and stared at him with huge dark-blue eyes. He got his other hand between Nat's legs an instant before the strap he was holding tore free. For a moment the howling baby balanced on his hand like a gymnast on a balance beam, and Ralph could feel the damp bulge of her diapers through the overall she was wearing. Then he slipped his other hand around her back and hoisted her up against his chest. His heart was pounding hard, and even with the baby safe in his arms he kept seeing her slip away, kept seeing her head with its cap of fine hair slamming against the butt-littered pavement with a sickening crack.

'Hum? Ar? Ral?' Helen asked. She saw Natalie in Ralph's arms, and some of the dullness went out of her good eye. She raised her hands toward the child, and in Ralph's arms, Natalie mimicked the gesture with her own chubby hands. Then Helen staggered, struck the side of the building, and reeled backward a step. One foot tangled in the other (Ralph saw splatters of blood on her small white sneakers, and it was amazing how bright everything was all of a sudden; the color had come back into the world, at least temporarily), and she would have fallen if Sue hadn't picked that moment to finally venture out. Instead of going down, Helen landed against the opening door and just leaned there, like a drunk against a lamppost.

'Ral?' The expression in her eyes was a little sharper now, and Ralph saw it wasn't so much curiosity as incredulity. She drew in a deep breath and made an effort to force intelligible words past her swelled lips. 'Gih. Gih me my bay-ee. *Bay*-be. Gih me . . . Nah-lie.'

'Not just yet, Helen,' Ralph said. 'You're not too steady on your feet right now.'

Sue was still on the other side of the door, holding it so Helen wouldn't fall. The girl's cheeks and forehead were ashy pale, her eyes filled with tears.

'Get out here,' Ralph told her. 'Hold her up.'

'I can't!' she blubbered. 'She's all bluh-bluh-*bloody*!'

'Oh for God's sake, quit it! It's Helen! Helen Deepneau from up the street!'

And although Sue must have known that, actually hearing the name seemed to turn the trick. She slipped around the open door, and when Helen staggered backward again, Sue curled an arm around her shoulders and braced her firmly. That expression of incredulous surprise remained on Helen's face. Ralph found it harder and harder to look at. It made him feel sick to his stomach.

'Ralph? What happened? Was it an accident?'

He turned his head and saw Bill McGovern standing at the edge of the parking lot. He was wearing one of his natty blue shirts with the iron's creases still in the sleeves and holding one of his long-fingered, oddly delicate hands up to shade his eyes. He looked strange, somehow naked that way, but Ralph had no time to think about why; too much was happening.

'It was no accident,' he said. 'She's been beaten up. Here, take the kid.'

He held Natalie out to McGovern, who at first shrank back and then took the baby. Natalie immediately began to shriek again. McGovern, looking like someone who has just been handed an overfilled airsick bag, held her out at arm's length with her feet dangling. Behind him a small crowd was beginning to gather, many of them teenage kids in baseball uniforms on their way home from an afternoon game at the field around the corner. They were staring at Helen's puffed and bloody face with an unpleasant avidity, and Ralph found himself thinking of the Bible story about the time Noah had gotten drunk – the good sons who had looked away from the naked old man lying in his tent, the bad one who had looked . . .

Gently, he replaced Sue's arm with his own. Helen's good eye rolled back to him. She said his name more clearly this time, more positively, and the gratitude Ralph heard in her blurry voice made him feel like crying.

'Sue – take the baby. Bill doesn't have a clue.'

She did, folding Nat gently and expertly into her arms. McGovern gave her a grateful smile, and Ralph suddenly realized what was wrong with the way he looked. McGovern wasn't wearing the Panama hat which seemed as much a part of him (in the summertime, at least) as the wen on the bridge of his nose.

'Hey, mister, what happened?' one of the baseball kids asked.

'Nothing that's any of your business,' Ralph said.

'Looks like she went a few rounds with Riddick Bowe.'

'Nah, Tyson,' one of the other baseball kids said, and incredibly, there was laughter.

'Get out of here!' Ralph shouted at them, suddenly furious. 'Go peddle your papers! Mind your business!'

They shuffled back a few steps, but no one left. It was blood they were looking at, and not on a movie screen.

'Helen, can you walk?'

'Yeff,' she said. 'Fink . . . *Think* so.'

He led her carefully around the open door and into the Red Apple. She moved slowly, shuffling from foot to foot like an old woman. The smell of sweat and spent adrenaline was baking out of her pores in a sour reek, and Ralph felt his stomach turn over again. It wasn't the smell, not really; it was the effort to reconcile this Helen with the pert and pleasantly sexy woman he had spoken to yesterday while she worked in her flower-beds.

Ralph suddenly remembered something else about yesterday. Helen had been wearing blue shorts, cut quite high, and he had noticed a couple of bruises on her legs – a large yellow blotch far up on the left thigh, a fresher, darker smudge on the right calf.

He walked Helen toward the little office area behind the cash register. He glanced up into the convex anti-theft mirror mounted in the corner and saw McGovern holding the door for Sue.

'Lock the door,' he said over his shoulder.

'Gee, Ralph, I'm not supposed to—'

'Just for a couple of minutes,' Ralph said. 'Please.'

'Well . . . okay. I guess.'

Ralph heard the snick of the bolt being turned as he eased Helen into the hard plastic contour chair behind the littery desk. He picked up the telephone and punched the button marked 911. Before the phone could ring on the other end, a blood-streaked hand reached out and pushed down the gray disconnect button.

'Dough . . . Ral.' She swallowed with an obvious effort, and tried again. '*Don't.*'

'Yes,' Ralph said. 'I'm going to.'

Now it was fear he saw in her one good eye, and nothing dull about it.

'No,' she said. 'Please, Ralph. Don't.' She looked past him and held out her hands again. The humble, pleading look on her beaten face made Ralph wince with dismay.

'Ralph?' Sue asked. 'She wants the baby.'

'I know. Go ahead.'

Sue handed Natalie to Helen, and Ralph watched as the baby – a little over a year old now, he was pretty sure – put her arms around her mother's neck and her face against her mother's shoulder. Helen kissed the top of Nat's head. It clearly hurt her to do this, but she did it again. And then again. Looking down at her, Ralph could see blood grimed into the faint creases on the nape of Helen's neck like dirt. As he looked at this, he felt the anger begin to pulse again.

'It was Ed, wasn't it?' he asked. Of course it was – you didn't hit the cutoff button on the phone when someone tried to call 911 if you had been beaten up by a total stranger – but he had to ask.

'Yes,' she said. Her voice was no more than a whisper, the answer a secret imparted into the fine cloud of her baby daughter's hair. 'Yes, it was Ed. But you can't call the police.' She looked up now, the good eye full of fear and misery. 'Please don't call the police, Ralph. I can't bear to think of Natalie's dad in jail for . . . for . . .'

Helen burst into tears. Natalie goggled at her mother for a moment in comic surprise, and then joined her.

7

'Ralph?' McGovern asked hesitantly. 'Do you want me to get her some Tylenol or something?'

'Better not,' he said. 'We don't know what's wrong with her, how bad she might be hurt.' His eyes shifted to the show window, not wanting to see what was out there, hoping not to, and seeing it anyway: avid faces lined up all the way down to the place where the beer cooler cut off the view. Some of them were cupping their hands to the sides of their faces to cut the glare.

'What should we do, you guys?' Sue asked. She was looking at the gawkers and picking nervously at the hem of the Red Apple duster employees had to wear. 'If the company finds out I locked the door during business hours, I'm apt to lose my job.'

Helen tugged at his hand. 'Please, Ralph,' she repeated, only it came out *Peese, Raff* through her swollen lips. 'Don't call anybody.'

Ralph looked at her uncertainly. He had seen a lot of women

wearing a lot of bruises over the course of his life, and a couple (although not many, in all honesty) who had been beaten much more severely than Helen. It hadn't always seemed this grim, though. His mind and morals had been formed at a time when people believed that what went on between a husband and wife behind the closed doors of their marriage was their business, and that included the man who hit with his fists and the woman who cut with her tongue. You couldn't make people behave, and meddling into their affairs – even with the best of intentions – all too often turned friends into enemies.

But then he thought of the way she had been carrying Natalie as she staggered across the parking lot: held casually on one hip like a textbook. If she had dropped the baby in the lot, or crossing Harris Avenue, she probably wouldn't have known it; Ralph guessed that it was nothing but instinct that had caused Helen to take the baby in the first place. She hadn't wanted to leave Nat in the care of the man who had beaten her so badly she could only see out of one eye and talk in mushy, rounded syllables.

He thought of something else, as well, something that had to do with the days following Carolyn's death earlier in the year. He had been surprised at the depth of his grief – it had been an expected death, after all; he had believed he had taken care of most of his grieving while Carolyn was still alive – and it had rendered him awkward and ineffective about the final arrangements which needed to be made. He had managed the call to the Brookings-Smith funeral home, but it was Helen who had gotten the obit form from the Derry *News* and helped him to fill it out, Helen who had gone with him to pick out a coffin (McGovern, who hated death and the trappings which surrounded it, had made himself scarce), and Helen who had helped him choose a floral centerpiece – the one which said *Beloved Wife*. And it had been Helen, of course, who had orchestrated the little party afterward, providing sandwiches from Frank's Catering and soft drinks and beer from the Red Apple.

These were things Helen had done for him when he could not do them for himself. Did he not have an obligation to repay her kindness, even if Helen might not see it as kindness right now?

'Bill?' he asked. 'What do you think?'

McGovern looked from Ralph to Helen, sitting in the red plastic chair with her battered face lowered, and then back to

Ralph again. He produced a handkerchief and wiped his lips nervously. 'I don't know. I like Helen a lot, and I want to do the right thing – you *know* I do – but something like this . . . who knows what the right thing is?'

Ralph suddenly remembered what Carolyn used to say whenever he started moaning and bitching about some chore he didn't want to do, some errand he didn't want to run, or some duty call he didn't want to make: *It's a long walk back to Eden, sweetheart, so don't sweat the small stuff.*

He reached for the phone again, and this time when Helen reached for his wrist, he pushed it away.

'You have reached the Derry Police Department,' a recorded voice told him. 'Push one for emergency services. Push two for police services. Push three for information.'

Ralph, who suddenly understood he needed all three, hesitated for a second and then pushed two. The telephone buzzed and a woman's voice said, 'This is Police 911, how may I help you?'

He took a deep breath and said, 'This is Ralph Roberts. I'm at the Red Apple Store on Harris Avenue, with my neighbor from up the street. Her name is Helen Deepneau. She's been beaten up pretty badly.' He put his hand gently on the side of Helen's face and she pressed her forehead against his side. He could feel the heat of her skin through his shirt. 'Please come as fast as you can.'

He hung up the telephone, then squatted down next to Helen. Natalie saw him, crowed with delight, and reached out to give his nose a friendly honk. Ralph smiled, kissed her tiny palm, then looked into Helen's face.

'I'm sorry, Helen,' he said, 'but I had to. I couldn't not do it. Do you understand that? I couldn't not do it.'

'I don't understand *anyfing!*' she said. Her nose had stopped bleeding, but when she reached up to swipe at it, she winced back from the touch of her own fingers.

'Helen, why did he do it? Why would Ed beat you up like this?' He found himself remembering the other bruises – a pattern of them, perhaps. If there *had* been a pattern, he had missed it until now. Because of Carolyn's death. And because of the insomnia which had come afterward. In any case, he did not believe this was the first time Ed had put his hands on his wife. Today might have been a drastic escalation, but it hadn't been the first time. He could grasp that idea and admit its logic, but he discovered he still couldn't see Ed *doing* it. He could see Ed's quick grin, his lively eyes, the way his hands moved restlessly when he talked . . . but he couldn't see Ed using those hands to beat the crap out of his wife, no matter how hard he tried.

Then a memory resurfaced, a memory of Ed walking stiff-legged toward the man who had been driving the blue pickup – it had been a Ford Ranger, hadn't it? – and then flicking the flat of his hand across the heavyset man's jowls. Remembering that was like opening the door of Fibber McGee's closet in that old radio show – only what came falling out wasn't an avalanche of old stored junk but a series of vivid images from that day last July. The thunderheads building over the airport. Ed's arm popping out of the Datsun's window and waving up and down, as if he could make the gate slide open faster that way. The scarf with the Chinese symbols on it.

Hey, hey, Susan Day, how many kids did you kill today? Ralph thought, only it was Ed's voice he heard, and he pretty well knew what Helen was going to say before she even opened her mouth.

'So stupid,' she said dully. 'He hit me because I signed a *petition* – that's all it was. They're circulating all over town. Someone pushed it into my face when I was going into the supermarket day before yesterday. He said something about a benefit for WomanCare, and that seemed all right. Besides, the baby was fussing, so I just . . .'

'You just signed it,' Ralph finished softly.

She nodded and began to cry again.

'What petition?' McGovern asked.

'To bring Susan Day to Derry,' Ralph told him. 'She's a feminist—'

'I know who Susan Day is,' McGovern said irritably.

'Anyway, a bunch of people are trying to get her here to speak. On behalf of WomanCare.'

'When Ed came home today he was in a great mood,' Helen said through her tears. 'He almost always is on Thursdays, because it's his half day. He was talking about how he was going to spend the afternoon pretending to read a book and actually just watching the sprinkler go around . . . you know how he is . . .'

'Yes,' Ralph said, remembering how Ed had plunged his arm into one of the heavyset man's barrels, and the crafty grin

(*I know a trick worth two of that*)

on his face. 'Yes, I know how he is.'

'I sent him out to get some baby food . . .' Her voice was rising, becoming fretful and frightened. '*I* didn't know he'd be upset . . . I'd all but forgotten about signing the damned thing, to tell the truth . . . and I still don't know exactly *why* he was so upset . . . but . . . but when he came back . . .' She hugged Natalie to her, trembling.

'Shhh, Helen, take it easy, everything's okay.'

'No, it's *not*!' She looked up at him, tears streaming from one eye and seeping out from beneath the swelled lid of the other. 'It's nuh-nuh-*not*! Why didn't he stop this time? And what's going to happen to me and the baby? Where will we go? I don't have any money except for what's in the joint checking account . . . I don't have a *job* . . . oh Ralph, why did you call the police? You shouldn't have done that!' And she hit his forearm with a strengthless little fist.

'You're going to get through this just fine,' he said. 'You've got a lot of friends in the neighborhood.'

But he barely heard what he was saying and hadn't felt her small punch at all. The anger was thudding away in his chest and at his temples like a second heartbeat.

Not *Why didn't he stop*; that wasn't what she had said. What she had said was *Why didn't he stop this time?*

This time.

'Helen, where's Ed now?'

'Home, I guess,' she said dully.

Ralph patted her on the shoulder, then turned and started for the door.

'Ralph?' Bill McGovern asked. He sounded alarmed. 'Where you going?'

'Lock the door after me,' Ralph told Sue.

'Jeez, I don't know if I can do that.' Sue looked doubtfully at the line of gawkers peering in through the dirty window. There were more of them now.

'You can,' he said, then cocked his head, catching the first faint wail of an approaching siren. 'Hear that?'

'Yes, but—'

'The cops will tell you what to do, and your boss won't be mad at you, either – he'll probably give you a medal for handling everything just right.'

'If he does, I'll split it with you,' she said, then glanced at Helen again. A little color had come back into Sue's cheeks, but not much. 'Jeepers, Ralph, look at her! Did he really beat her up because she signed some stupid paper in the S and S?'

'I guess so,' Ralph said. The conversation made perfect sense to him, but it was coming in long distance. His rage was closer; it had its hot arms locked around his neck, it seemed. He wished he were forty again, even fifty, so he could give Ed a taste of his own medicine. And he had an idea he might try doing that anyway.

He was turning the thumb-bolt of the door when McGovern grabbed his shoulder. 'What do you think you're doing?'

'Going to see Ed.'

'Are you kidding? He'll take you apart if you get in his face. Didn't you see what he did to her?'

'You bet I did,' Ralph replied. The words weren't quite a snarl, but close enough to make McGovern drop his hand.

'You're seventy fucking years old, Ralph, in case you forgot. And Helen needs a friend right now, not some busted-up antique she can visit because his hospital room is three doors down from hers.'

Bill was right, of course, but that only made Ralph angrier. He supposed the insomnia was at work in this, too, stoking his anger and blurring his judgement, but that made no difference. In a way, the anger was a relief. It was better, certainly, than drifting through a world where everything had turned shades of dark gray.

'If he beats me up bad enough, they'll give me some Demerol and I can get a decent night's sleep,' he said. 'Now leave me alone, Bill.'

He crossed the Red Apple parking lot at a brisk walk. A police car was approaching with its blue grille flashers pulsing. Questions – *What happened? She okay?* – were thrown at him, but Ralph ignored them. He paused on the sidewalk, waited for the police car to swing into the parking lot, then crossed Harris Avenue at that same brisk walk with McGovern trailing anxiously after him at a prudent distance.

Chapter Three

1

Ed and Helen Deepneau lived in a small Cape Cod – chocolate brown, whipped-cream trim, the kind of house which older women often call 'darling' – four houses up from the one Ralph and Bill McGovern shared. Carolyn had liked to say the Deepneaus belonged to 'the Church of the Latter-Day Yuppies', although her genuine liking for them had robbed the phrase of any real bite. They were *laissez-faire* vegetarians who considered both fish and dairy products okay, they had worked for Clinton in the last election, and the car in the driveway – not a Datsun now but one of the new mini-vans – was wearing bumper stickers which said SPLIT WOOD, NOT ATOMS and FUR ON ANIMALS, NOT PEOPLE.

The Deepneaus had also apparently kept every album they had ever purchased during the sixties – Carolyn had found this one of their most endearing characteristics – and now, as Ralph approached the Cape Cod with his hands curled into fists at his sides, he heard Grace Slick wailing one of those old San Francisco anthems:

> *One pill makes you bigger,*
> *One pill makes you small,*
> *And the ones that Mother gives you*
> *Don't do anything at all,*
> *Go ask Alice, when she's ten feet tall.*

The music was coming from a boombox on the Cape Cod's postage stamp-sized porch. A sprinkler twirled on the lawn, making a *hisha-hisha-hisha* sound as it cast rainbows in the air and deposited a shiny wet patch on the sidewalk. Ed Deepneau, shirtless, was sitting in a lawn-chair to the left of the concrete walk with his legs crossed, looking up at the sky with the bemused expression of a man trying to decide if the cloud passing overhead looks more like a horse or a unicorn. One bare foot bopped up and down in time to the music. The book lying open and face-down in his lap went perfectly with the music pouring from the boombox: *Even Cowgirls Get the Blues,* by Tom Robbins.

An all but perfect summer vignette; a scene of small-town serenity Norman Rockwell might have painted and then titled *Afternoon Off.* All you had to overlook was the blood on Ed's knuckles and the drop on the left lens of his round John Lennon specs.

'Ralph, for God's sake don't get into a fight with him!' McGovern hissed as Ralph left the sidewalk and cut across the lawn. He walked through the lawn sprinkler's fine cold spray almost without feeling it.

Ed turned, saw him, and broke into a sunny grin. 'Hey, Ralph!' he said. 'Good to see you, man!'

In his mind's eye, Ralph saw himself reaching out and shoving Ed's chair, pushing him over and spilling him onto his lawn. He saw Ed's eyes widen with shock and surprise behind the lenses of his glasses. This vision was so real he even saw the way the sun reflected on the face of Ed's watch as he tried to sit up.

'Grab yourself a beer and drag up a rock,' Ed was saying. 'If you feel like a game of chess—'

'Beer? A game of *chess*? Christ Jesus, Ed, what's wrong with you?'

Ed didn't answer immediately, only looked at Ralph with an expression that was both frightening and infuriating. It was a mixture of amusement and shame, the look of a man who's getting ready to say, *Aw, shit, honey – did I forget to put out the trash* again?

Ralph pointed down the hill, past McGovern, who was standing – he would have been lurking, if there had been something to lurk behind – near the wet patch the sprinkler had put on the sidewalk, watching them nervously. The first police car had been joined by a second, and Ralph could faintly hear the crackle of radio calls through the open windows. The crowd had gotten quite a bit bigger.

'The police are there because of *Helen*!' he said, telling himself not to shout, it would do no good to shout, and shouting anyway. 'They're there because you beat up your *wife,* is that getting through to you?'

'Oh,' Ed said, and rubbed his cheek ruefully. '*That.*'

'Yes, *that,*' Ralph said. He now felt almost stupefied with rage.

Ed peered past him at the police cars, at the crowd standing around the Red Apple . . . and then he saw McGovern.

'Bill!' he cried. McGovern recoiled. Ed either didn't notice or pretended not to. 'Hey, man! Drag up a rock! Want a beer?'

That was when Ralph knew he was going to hit Ed, break his stupid little round-lensed spectacles, drive a splinter of glass into his eye, maybe. He was going to do it, nothing on earth could stop him from doing it, except at the last moment something did. It was Carolyn's voice he heard inside his head most frequently these days – when he wasn't just muttering along to himself, that was – but this wasn't Carolyn's voice; this one, as unlikely as it seemed, belonged to Trigger Vachon, whom he'd seen only once or twice since the day Trig had saved him from the thunderstorm, the day Carolyn had had her first seizure.

Ayy, Ralph! Be damn careful, you! Dis one crazy like a fox! Maybe he want *you to hit im!*

Yes, he decided. Maybe that was *just* what Ed wanted. Why? Who knew? Maybe to muddy the waters up a little bit, maybe just because he was crazy.

'Cut the shit,' he said, dropping his voice almost to a whisper. He was gratified to see Ed's attention snap back to him in a hurry, and even more pleased to see Ed's pleasantly vague expression of rueful amusement disappear. It was replaced by a narrow, watchful expression. *It was,* Ralph thought, *the look of a dangerous animal with its wind up.*

Ralph hunkered down so he could look directly at Ed. 'Was it Susan Day?' he asked in the same soft voice. 'Susan Day and the abortion business? Something about dead babies? Is that why you unloaded on Helen?'

There was another question on his mind – *Who are you really, Ed?* – but before he could ask it, Ed reached out, placed a hand in the center of Ralph's chest, and pushed. Ralph fell backward onto the damp grass, catching himself on his elbows and shoulders. He lay there with his feet flat on the ground and his knees up, watching as Ed suddenly sprang out of his lawn-chair.

'Ralph, don't mess with him!' McGovern called from his place of relative safety on the sidewalk.

Ralph paid no attention. He simply remained where he was, propped on his elbows and looking attentively up at Ed. He was still angry and afraid, but these emotions had begun to be overshadowed by a strange, chilly fascination. This was madness he was looking at – the genuine article. No comicbook super-villain here, no Norman Bates, no Captain Ahab. It was just Ed Deepneau who worked down the coast at Hawking Labs – one of those eggheads, the old guys who played chess at the picnic area out on the Extension would have said, but still a nice enough fella for a Democrat. Now the nice enough fella had gone totally bonkers, and it hadn't just happened this afternoon, when Ed had seen his wife's name on a petition hanging from the Community Bulletin Board in the Shop 'n Save. Ralph now understood that Ed's madness was at least a year old, and that made him wonder what secrets Helen had been keeping behind her normal cheery demeanor and sunny smile, and what small, desperate signals – besides the bruises, that was – he might have missed.

And then there's Natalie, he thought. *What's* she *seen? What's* she *experienced? Besides, of course, being carried across Harris Avenue and the Red Apple parking lot on her staggering, bleeding mother's hip?*

Ralph's arms broke out in goosebumps.

Ed had begun to pace, meanwhile, crossing and recrossing the cement path, trampling the zinnias Helen had planted along it as a border. He had returned to the Ed Ralph had encountered out by the airport the year before, right down to the fierce little pokes of the head and the sharp, jabbing glances at nothing.

This is what the gee-whiz act was supposed to hide, Ralph thought. *He looks the same now as he did when he took after the guy driving that pickup truck. Like a rooster protecting his little piece of the barnyard.*

'None of this is strictly her fault, I admit that.' Ed spoke rapidly, pounding his right fist into his open left palm as he walked through the cloud of spray thrown by the sprinkler. Ralph realized he could see every rib in Ed's chest; the man looked as if he hadn't had a decent meal in months.

'Still, once stupidity reaches a certain level, it becomes hard to live with,' Ed went on. 'She's like the Magi, actually coming to *King Herod* for information. I mean, how dumb can you get? "Where is he that is born King of the Jews?" To *Herod* they say this. I mean, wise men my ass! Right, Ralph?'

Ralph nodded. Sure, Ed. Whatever you say, Ed.

Ed returned the nod and went on tramping back and forth through the spray and the ghostly interlocking rainbows, smacking his fist into his palm. 'It's like that Rolling Stones song – "Look at that, look at that, look at that stupid girl". You probably don't remember that one, do you?' Ed laughed, a jagged little sound that made Ralph think of rats dancing on broken glass.

McGovern knelt beside him. 'Let's get out of here,' he muttered. Ralph shook his head, and when Ed swung back in their direction, McGovern quickly got up and retreated to the sidewalk again.

'She thought she could fool you, is that it?' Ralph asked. He was still lying on the lawn, propped up on his elbows. 'She thought you wouldn't find out she signed the petition.'

Ed leaped over the walk, bent over Ralph, and shook his clenched fists over his head like the bad guy in a silent movie. 'No-no-no-*no!*' he cried.

The Jefferson Airplane had been replaced by the Animals, Eric Burdon growling out the gospel according to John Lee Hooker: Boom-boom-boom-boom, gonna shoot ya right down. McGovern uttered a thin cry, apparently thinking Ed meant to attack Ralph, but instead Ed sank down with the knuckles of his left hand pressed into the grass, assuming the position of a sprinter who waits for the starter's gun to explode him out of the blocks. His face was covered with beads of what Ralph at first took for sweat before remembering the way Ed had paced back and forth through the spray from the sprinkler. Ralph kept looking at the spot of blood on the left lens of Ed's glasses. It had smeared a little, and now the pupil of his left eye looked as if it had filled up with blood.

'Finding out that she signed the petition was fate! Simple fate! Do you mean to tell me you don't see that? Don't insult my intelligence, Ralph! You may be getting on in years, but you're far from stupid. The thing is, I go down to the supermarket to buy baby-food, how's that for irony – and find out she's signed on with the baby-*killers!* The Centurions! With the Crimson King himself! And do you know what? I . . . just . . . saw . . . *red!*'

'The Crimson King, Ed? Who's he?'

'Oh, please.' Ed gave Ralph a cunning look. '"Then Herod, when he saw that he was mocked, was exceeding wroth, and sent forth, and slew all the children that were in Bethlehem, and in all the coasts thereof, from two years old and under, according to the time which he had diligently enquired of the wise men." It's in the Bible, Ralph. Matthew, chapter 2, verse 16. Do you doubt it? Do you have *any fucking question* that it says that?'

'No. If you say so, I believe it.'

Ed nodded. His eyes, a deep and startling shade of green, darted here and there. Then he slowly leaned forward over Ralph, planting one hand on either side of Ralph's arms. It was as if he meant to kiss him. Ralph could smell sweat, and some sort of aftershave that had almost completely faded away now, and something else – something that smelled like old curdled milk. He wondered if it might be the smell of Ed's madness.

An ambulance was coming up Harris Avenue, running its flashers but not its siren. It turned into the Red Apple's parking lot.

'You *better*,' Ed breathed into his face. 'You just *better* believe it.'

His eyes stopped wandering and centered on Ralph's.

'They are killing the babies wholesale,' he said in a low voice which was not quite steady. 'Ripping them from the wombs of their mothers and carrying them out of town in covered trucks. Flatbeds for the most part. Ask yourself this, Ralph: how many times a week do you see one of those big flatbeds tooling down the road? A flatbed with a tarp stretched across the back? Ever ask yourself what those trucks were carrying? Ever wonder what was under most of those tarps?'

Ed grinned. His eyes rolled.

'They burn most of the fetuses over in Newport. The sign says *landfill,* but it's really a crematorium. They send some of them out of state, though. In trucks, in light planes. Because fetal tissue is extremely valuable. I tell you that not just as a concerned citizen, Ralph, but as an employee of Hawking Laboratories. Fetal tissue is . . . more . . . valuable . . . . than gold.'

He turned his head suddenly and stared at Bill McGovern, who had crept a little closer again in order to hear what Ed was saying.

'*YEA, MORE VALUABLE THAN GOLD AND MORE PRECIOUS THAN RUBIES!*' he screamed, and McGovern leaped back, eyes widening in fear and dismay. '*DO YOU KNOW THAT, YOU OLD FAGGOT?*'

'Yes,' McGovern said. 'I . . . I guess I did.' He shot a quick glance down the street, where one of the police cars was now backing out of the Red Apple lot and turning in their direction. 'I might have read it somewhere. In *Scientific American*, perhaps.'

'*Scientific American!*' Ed laughed with gentle contempt and rolled his eyes at Ralph again, as if to say *You see what I have to deal with*. Then his face grew sober again. 'Wholesale murder,' he said, 'just as in the time of Christ. Only now it's the murder of the unborn. Not just here, but all over the world. They've been slaughtering them by their thousands, Ralph, by their *millions*, and do you know why? Do you know why we've re-entered the Court of the Crimson King in this new age of darkness?'

Ralph knew. It wasn't that hard to put together, if you had enough pieces to work with. If you had seen Ed with his arm buried in a barrel of chemical fertilizer, fishing around for the dead babies he had been sure he would find.

'King Herod got a little advance word this time around,' Ralph said. 'That's what you're telling me, isn't it? It's the old Messiah thing, right?'

He sat up, half expecting Ed to shove him down again, almost hoping he would. His anger was coming back. It was surely wrong to critique a madman's delusional fantasies the way you might a play or a movie – maybe even blasphemous – but Ralph found the idea that Helen had been beaten because of such hackneyed old shit as this infuriating.

Ed didn't touch him, merely got to his feet and dusted his hands off in businesslike fashion. He seemed to be cooling down again. Radio calls crackled louder as the police cruiser which had backed out of the Red Apple's lot now glided up to the curb. Ed looked at the cruiser, then back at Ralph, who was getting up himself.

'You can mock, but it's true,' he said quietly. 'It's not King Herod, though – it's the Crimson King. Herod was merely one of his incarnations. The Crimson King jumps from body to body and generation to generation like a kid using stepping-stones to cross a brook, Ralph, always looking for the Messiah. He's always missed him, but this time it could be different. Because *Derry's* different. All lines of force have begun to converge here. I know how difficult that is to believe, but it's true.'

The Crimson King, Ralph thought. *Oh Helen, I'm so sorry. What a sad thing this is.*

Two men – one in uniform, one in streetclothes, both

presumably cops – got out of the police car and approached McGovern. Behind them, down at the store, Ralph spotted two more men, these dressed in white pants and white short-sleeved shirts, coming out of the Red Apple. One had his arm around Helen, who was walking with the fragile care of a post-op patient. The other was holding Natalie.

The paramedics helped Helen into the back of the ambulance. The one with the baby got in after her while the other moved toward the driver's seat. What Ralph sensed in their movements was competency rather than urgency, and he thought that was good news for Helen. Maybe Ed hadn't hurt her too badly . . . this time, at least.

The plainclothes cop – burly, broad-shouldered, and wearing his blond mustache and sideburns in a style Ralph thought of as Early American Singles Bar – had approached McGovern, whom he seemed to recognize. There was a big grin on the plainclothes cop's face.

Ed put an arm over Ralph's shoulders and pulled him a few steps away from the men on the sidewalk. He also dropped his voice to a bare murmur. 'Don't want them to hear us,' he said.

'I'm sure you don't.'

'These creatures . . . Centurions . . . servants of the Crimson King . . . will stop at nothing. They are relentless.'

'I'll bet.' Ralph glanced over his shoulder in time to see McGovern point at Ed. The burly man nodded calmly. His hands were stuffed in the pockets of his chinos. He was still wearing a small, benign smile.

'This isn't just about abortion, don't get that idea! Not anymore. They're taking the unborn from all kinds of mothers, not just the junkies and the whores – eight days, eight weeks, eight months, it's all the same to the Centurions. The harvest goes on day and night. The slaughter. I've seen the corpses of infants on roofs, Ralph . . . under hedges . . . they're in the sewers . . . floating in the sewers and in the Kenduskeag down in the Barrens . . .'

His eyes, huge and green, as bright as trumpery emeralds, stared off into the distance.

'Ralph,' he whispered, 'sometimes the world is full of colors. I've seen them since *he* came and told me. But now all the colors are turning black.'

'Since who came and told you, Ed?'

'We'll talk about it later,' Ed replied, speaking out of the corner of his mouth like a con in a prison movie. Under other circumstances it would have been funny.

A big game-show host grin dawned on his face, banishing the madness as convincingly as sunrise banishes night. The change was almost tropical in its suddenness, and creepy as hell, but Ralph found something comforting about it, just the same. Perhaps they – he, McGovern, Lois, all the others on this little stretch of Harris Avenue who knew Ed – would not have to blame themselves too much for not seeing his madness sooner, after all. Because Ed was good; Ed really had his act down. That grin was an Academy Award winner. Even in a bizarre situation like this, it practically demanded that you respond to it.

'Hey, hi!' he told the two cops. The burly one had finished his conversation with McGovern, and both of them were advancing across the lawn. 'Drag up a rock, you guys!' Ed stepped around Ralph with his hand held out.

The burly plainclothes cop shook it, still smiling his small, benign smile. 'Edward Deepneau?' he asked.

'Right.' Ed shook hands with the uniformed cop, who looked a trifle bemused, and then returned his attention to the burly man.

'I'm Detective Sergeant John Leydecker,' the burly man said. 'This is Officer Chris Nell. Understand you had a little trouble here, sir.'

'Well, yes. I guess that's right. A little trouble. Or, if you want to call a spade a spade, I behaved like a horse's ass.' Ed's embarrassed little chuckle was alarmingly normal. Ralph thought of all the charming psychopaths he'd seen in the movies – George Sanders had always been particularly good at that sort of role – and wondered if it was possible for a smart research chemist to snow a small-city detective who looked as if he had never completely outgrown his *Saturday Night Fever* phase. Ralph was terribly afraid it might be.

'Helen and I got into an argument about a petition she'd signed,' Ed was saying, 'and one thing just led to another. Man, I just can't believe I hit her.'

He flapped his arms, as if to convey how flustered he was – not to mention confused and ashamed. Leydecker smiled in return. Ralph's mind returned to the confrontation last summer between Ed and the man in the blue pickup. Ed had called the heavyset man a murderer, had even stroked him one across the face, and still the guy had ended up looking at Ed almost with respect. It had been like a kind of hypnosis, and Ralph thought he was seeing the same force at work here.

'Things just kinda got out of hand a little, is that what you're telling me?' Leydecker asked sympathetically.

'That's about the size of it, yeah.' Ed had to be at least thirty-two, but his wide eyes and innocent expression made him look barely old enough to buy beer.

'Wait a minute,' Ralph blurted. 'You can't believe him, he's nuts. And dangerous. He just told me—'

'This is Mr Roberts, right?' Leydecker asked McGovern, ignoring Ralph completely.

'Yes,' McGovern said, and to Ralph he sounded insufferably pompous. 'That is Ralph Roberts.'

'Uh-huh.' Leydecker at last looked at Ralph. 'I'll want to speak to you in a couple of minutes, Mr Roberts, but for the time being I'd like you to stand over there beside your friend and keep quiet. Okay?'

'But—'

'*Okay?*'

Angrier than ever, Ralph stalked over to where McGovern was standing. This did not seem to upset Leydecker in the least. He turned to Officer Nell. 'You want to turn off the music, Chris, so we can hear ourselves think?'

'Yo.' The uniformed cop went to the boombox, inspected the various knobs and switches, then killed The Who halfway through the song about the blind pinball wizard.

'I guess I *did* have it cranked a little.' Ed looked sheepish. 'Wonder the neighbors didn't complain.'

'Oh, well, life goes on,' Leydecker said. He tilted his small, serene smile up toward the clouds drifting across the blue summer sky.

Wonderful, Ralph thought. *This guy is a regular Will Rogers.* Ed, however, was nodding as if the detective had produced not just a single pearl of wisdom but a whole string of them.

Leydecker rummaged in his pocket and came out with a little tube of toothpicks. He offered them to Ed, who declined, then shook one out and stuck it in the corner of his mouth. 'So,' he said. 'Little family argument. Is that what I'm hearing?'

Ed nodded eagerly. He was still smiling his sincere, slightly puzzled smile. 'More of a discussion, actually. A political—'

'Uh-huh, uh-huh,' Leydecker said, nodding and smiling, 'but before you go any further, Mr Deepneau—'

'Ed. Please.'

'Before we go any further, Mr Deepneau, I just kind of want to tell you that anything you say could be used against you – you know, in a court of law. Also that you have a right to an attorney.'

Ed's friendly but puzzled smile – *Gosh, what did I do? Can you help me figure it out?* – faltered for a moment. The narrow, appraising look replaced it. Ralph glanced at McGovern, and the relief he saw in Bill's eyes mirrored what he was feeling himself. Leydecker was maybe not such a hick after all.

'What in God's name would I want an attorney for?' Ed asked. He made a half-turn and tried the puzzled smile out on Chris Nell, who was still standing beside the boombox on the porch.

'I don't know, and maybe you don't,' Leydecker said, still smiling. 'I'm just telling you that you can have one. And that if you can't afford one, the City of Derry will provide you with one.'

'But I don't—'

Leydecker was nodding and smiling. 'That's okay, sure, whatever. But those are your rights. Do you understand your rights as I've explained them to you, Mr Deepneau?'

Ed stood stock-still for a moment, his eyes suddenly wide and blank again. To Ralph he looked like a human computer trying to process a huge and complicated wad of input. Then the fact that the snow-job wasn't working seemed to get through to him. His shoulders sagged. The blankness was replaced by a look of unhappiness too real to doubt . . . but Ralph doubted it, anyway. He *had* to doubt it; he had seen the madness on Ed's face before Leydecker and Nell arrived. So had Bill McGovern. Yet doubt was not quite the same as disbelief, and Ralph had an idea that on some level Ed honestly regretted beating Helen up.

Yes, he thought, *just as on some level he honestly believes that these Centurions of his are driving truckloads of fetuses out to the Newport landfill. And that the forces of good and evil are gathering in Derry to play out some drama that's going on in his mind. Call it* Omen V: In the Court of the Crimson King.

Still, he could not help feeling a reluctant sympathy for Ed Deepneau, who had visited Carolyn faithfully three times a week during her final confinement at Derry Home, who always brought flowers, and always kissed her on the cheek when he left. He had continued giving her that kiss even when the smell of death had begun to surround her, and Carolyn had never failed to clasp his hand and give him a smile of gratitude. *Thank you for remembering that I'm still a human being,* that smile had said. *And thank you for treating me like one.* That was the Ed Ralph had thought of as his friend, and he thought – or maybe only hoped – that that Ed was still in there.

'I'm in trouble here, aren't I?' he asked Leydecker softly.

'Well, let's see,' Leydecker said, still smiling. 'You knocked out two of your wife's teeth. Looks like you fractured her cheekbone. I'd bet you my grandfather's watch she's got a concussion. Plus selected short subjects – cuts, bruises, and this funny bare patch over her right temple. What'd you try to do? Snatch her bald-headed?'

Ed was silent, his green eyes fixed on Leydecker's face.

'She's going to spend the night in the hospital under observation because some asshole pounded the hell out of her, and everybody seems in agreement that the asshole was you, Mr Deepneau. I look at the blood on your hands and the blood on your glasses, and I got to say I also think it was probably you. So what do *you* think? You look like a bright guy. Do *you* think you're in trouble?'

'I'm very sorry I hit her,' Ed said. 'I didn't mean to.'

'Uh-huh, and if I had a quarter for every time I've heard that, I'd never have to buy another drink out of my paycheck. I'm arresting you on a charge of second-degree assault, Mr Deepneau, also known as domestic assault. This charge falls under Maine's Domestic Violence law. I'd like you to confirm once more that I've informed you of your rights.'

'Yes.' Ed spoke in a small, unhappy voice. The smile – puzzled or otherwise – was gone. "Yes, you did."

'We're going to take you down to the police station and book you,' Leydecker said. 'Following that, you can make a telephone call and arrange bail. Chris, put him in the car, would you?'

Nell approached Ed. 'Are you going to be a problem, Mr Deepneau?'

'No,' Ed said in that same small voice, and Ralph saw a tear slip from Ed's right eye. He wiped it away absently with the heel of his hand. 'No problem.'

'Great!' Nell said heartily, and walked with him to the cruiser.

Ed glanced at Ralph as he crossed the sidewalk. 'I'm sorry, old boy,' he said, then got into the back of the car. Before

Officer Nell closed the door, Ralph saw there was no handle on the inside of it.

2

'Okay,' Leydecker said, turning to Ralph and holding out his hand. 'I'm sorry if I seemed a little brusque, Mr Roberts, but sometimes these guys can be volatile. I especially worry about the ones who look sober, because you can never tell what they'll do. John Leydecker.'

'I had Johnny as a student when I was teaching at the Community College,' McGovern said. Now that Ed Deepneau was safely tucked away in the back of the cruiser, he sounded almost giddy with relief. 'Good student. Did an excellent term paper on the Children's Crusade.'

'It's a pleasure to meet you,' Ralph said, shaking Leydecker's hand. 'And don't worry. No offense taken.'

'You were insane to come up here and confront him, you know,' Leydecker said cheerfully.

'I was pissed off. I'm *still* pissed off.'

'I can understand that. And you got away with it – that's the important thing.'

'No. *Helen's* the important thing. Helen and the baby.'

'I can ride with that. Tell me what you and Mr Deepneau talked about before we got up here, Mr Roberts . . . or can I call you Ralph?'

'Ralph, please.' He ran through his conversation with Ed, trying to keep it brief. McGovern, who had heard some of it but not all of it, listened in round-eyed silence. Every time Ralph looked at him, he found himself wishing Bill had worn his Panama. He looked older without it. Almost ancient.

'Well, that certainly sounds pretty weird, doesn't it?' Leydecker remarked when Ralph had finished.

'What will happen? Will he go to jail? He shouldn't go to jail; he should be committed.'

'Probably should be,' Leydecker agreed, 'but there's a lot of distance between should be and will be. He won't go to jail, and he isn't going to be carted off to Sunnyvale Sanitarium, either – that sort of thing only happens in old movies. The best we can hope for is some court-ordered therapy.'

'But didn't Helen tell you—'

'The lady didn't tell us anything, and we didn't try to question her in the store. She was in a lot of pain, both physical and emotional.'

'Yes, of course she was,' Ralph said. 'Stupid of me.'

'She might corroborate your stuff later on . . . but she might not. Domestic abuse victims have a way of turning into clams, you know. Luckily, it doesn't really matter one way or the other under the new law. We got him nailed to the wall. You and the lady in the little store down the street can testify to Mrs Deepneau's condition, and to who she said put her in that condition. I can testify to the fact that the victim's husband had blood on his hands. Best of all, he said the magic words: "Man, I just can't believe I hit her." I'd like you to come in – probably tomorrow morning, if that works for you – so I can take a complete statement from you, Ralph, but that's just filling in the blanks. Basically, this one's a done deal.'

Leydecker took the toothpick out of his mouth, broke it, tossed it in the gutter, and produced his tube again. 'Pick?'

'No thanks,' Ralph said, smiling faintly.

'Don't blame you. Lousy habit, but I'm trying to quit smoking, which is an even worse one. The thing about guys like Deepneau is that they're too goddam smart for their own good. They go over the high side, hurt someone . . . and then they pull back. If you get there soon enough after the blow-up – like you did, Ralph – you can almost see them standing there with their heads cocked, listening to the music and trying to get back on the beat.'

'That's just how it was,' Ralph said. '*Exactly* how it was.'

'It's a trick the bright ones manage for quite awhile – they appear remorseful, appalled by their own actions, determined to make amends. They're persuasive, they're charming, and it's often all but impossible to see that underneath the sugar coating they're as nutty as Christmas fruitcakes. Even extreme cases like Ted Bundy sometimes manage to look normal for years. The good news is that there aren't many guys like Ted Bundy out there, in spite of all the psycho-killer books and movies.'

Ralph sighed deeply. 'What a mess.'

'Yeah. But look on the bright side: we're gonna be able to keep him away from her, at least for a while. He'll be out by suppertime on twenty-five dollars bail, but—'

'Twenty-five dollars?' McGovern asked. He sounded simultaneously shocked and cynical. 'That's *all*?'

'Yup,' Leydecker said. 'I gave Deepneau the second-degree

assault stuff because it do sound fearsome, but in the state of Maine, lumping up your wife is only a misdemeanor.'

'Still, there's a nifty new wrinkle in the law,' Chris Nell said, joining them. 'If Deepneau wants bail, he has to agree that he'll have absolutely no contact with his wife until the case is settled in court – he can't come to the house, approach her on the street, or even call her on the phone. If he doesn't agree, he sits in jail.'

'Suppose he agrees and then comes back, anyway?' Ralph asked.

'Then we slam-dunk him,' Nell said, 'because that one *is* a felony . . . or can be, if the district attorney wants to play hardball. In any case, violators of the Domestic Violence bail agreement usually spend a lot more than just the afternoon in jail.'

'And hopefully the spouse he breaks the agreement to visit will still be alive when he comes to trial,' McGovern said.

'Yeah,' Leydecker said heavily. 'Sometimes that's a problem.'

3

Ralph went home and sat staring not at the TV but through it for an hour or so. He got up during a commercial to see if there was a cold Coke in the refrigerator, staggered on his feet, and had to put a hand on the wall to steady himself. He was trembling all over and felt unpleasantly close to vomiting. He understood that this was nothing but delayed reaction, but the weakness and nausea still frightened him.

He sat down again, took a minute's worth of deep breaths with his head down and his eyes closed, then got up and walked slowly into the bathroom. He filled the tub with warm water and soaked until he heard *Night Court*, the first of the afternoon sitcoms, starting up on the TV in the living room. By then the water in the tub had become almost chilly, and Ralph was glad to get out. He dried off, dressed in fresh clothes, and decided that a light supper was at least in the realm of possibility. He called downstairs, thinking McGovern might like to join him for a bite to eat, but there was no answer.

Ralph put on water in which to boil a couple of eggs and called Derry Home Hospital from the phone by the stove.

His call was shunted to a woman in Patient Services who checked her computer and told him yes, he was correct, Helen Deepneau *had* been admitted to the hospital. Her condition was listed as fair. No, she had no idea who was taking care of Mrs Deepneau's baby; all she knew was that she did not have a Natalie Deepneau on her admissions list. No, Ralph could not visit Mrs Deepneau that evening, but not because her doctor had established a no-visitors policy; Mrs Deepneau had left that order herself.

Why would she do that? Ralph started to ask, then didn't bother. The woman in Patient Services would probably tell him she was sorry, she didn't have that information in her computer, but Ralph decided he had it in *his* computer, the one between his giant economy-size ears. Helen didn't want visitors because she was ashamed. None of what had happened was her fault, but Ralph doubted if that changed the way she felt. She had been seen by half of Harris Avenue staggering around like a badly beaten boxer after the ref has stopped the fight, she had been taken to the hospital in an ambulance, and her husband – the father of her daughter – was responsible. Ralph hoped they would give her something that would help her sleep through the night; he had an idea things might look a little better to her in the morning. God knew they couldn't look much worse.

Hell, I wish someone would give me *something to help me sleep through the night,* he thought.

Then go see Dr Litchfield, you idiot, another part of his mind responded immediately.

The woman in Patient Services was asking Ralph if she could do anything else for him. Ralph said no and was starting to thank her when the line clicked in his ear.

'Nice,' Ralph said. 'Very nice.' He hung up himself, got a tablespoon, and gently lowered his eggs into the water. Ten minutes later, as he was sitting down with the boiled eggs sliding around on a plate and looking like the world's biggest pearls, the phone rang. He put his supper on the table and grabbed it off the wall. 'Hello?'

Silence, broken only by breathing.

'Hello?' Ralph repeated.

There was one more breath, this one almost loud enough to be an aspirated sob, and then another click in his ear. Ralph hung up the telephone and stood looking at it for a moment, his frown putting three ascending wave-lines on his brow.

'Come on, Helen,' he said. 'Call me back. Please.' Then he returned to the table, sat down, and began to eat his small bachelor's supper.

4

He was washing up his few dishes fifteen minutes later when the phone rang again. *That won't be her,* he thought, wiping his hands on a dishtowel and then flipping it over his shoulder as he went to the phone. *No way it'll be her. It's probably Lois or Bill.* But another part of him knew differently.

'Hi, Ralph.'

'Hello, Helen.'

'That was me a few minutes ago.' Her voice was husky, as if she had been drinking or crying, and Ralph didn't think they allowed booze in the hospital.

'I kind of figured that.'

'I heard your voice and I . . . I couldn't . . .'

'That's okay. I understand.'

'Do you?' She gave a long, watery sniff.

'I think so, yes.'

'The nurse came by and gave me a pain-pill. I can use it, too – my face really hurts. But I wouldn't let myself take it until I called you again and said what I had to say. Pain sucks, but it's a hell of an incentive.'

'Helen, you don't have to say anything.' But he was afraid that she did, and he was afraid of what it might be . . . afraid of finding out that she had decided to be angry at him because she couldn't be angry with Ed.

'Yes I do. I have to say thank you.'

Ralph leaned against the side of the door and closed his eyes for a moment. He was relieved but unsure how to reply. He had been ready to say *I'm sorry you feel that way, Helen* in the calmest voice he could manage, that was how sure he'd been that she was going to start off by asking him why he couldn't mind his own business.

And, as if she had read his mind and wanted to let him know he wasn't entirely off the hook, Helen said, 'I spent most of the ride here, and the check-in, and the first hour or so in the room, being terribly angry at you. I called Candy Shoemaker, my friend from over on Kansas Street, and she came and got Nat.

She's keeping her for the night. She wanted to know what had happened, but I wouldn't tell her. I just wanted to lie here and be mad that you called 911 even though I told you not to.'

'Helen—'

'Let me finish so I can take my pill and go to sleep. Okay?'

'Okay.'

'Just after Candy left with the baby – Nat didn't cry, thank God, I don't know if I could have handled that – a woman came in. At first I thought she must have gotten the wrong room because I didn't know her from Eve, and when I got it through my head that she was here to see me, I told her I didn't want any visitors. She didn't pay any attention. She closed the door and lifted her skirt up so I could see her left thigh. There was a deep scar running down it, almost all the way from her hip to her knee.

'She said her name was Gretchen Tillbury, that she was a family-abuse counsellor at WomanCare, and that her husband had cut her leg open with a kitchen knife in 1978. She said if the man in the downstairs apartment hadn't gotten a tourniquet on it, she would have bled to death. I said I was very sorry to hear that, but I didn't want to talk about my own situation until I'd had a chance to think it over.' Helen paused and then said, 'But that was a lie, you know. I've had plenty of time to think it over, because Ed first hit me two years ago, just before I got pregnant with Nat. I just kept . . . pushing it away.'

'I can see how a person would do that,' Ralph said.

'This lady . . . well, they must give people like her lessons on how to get through people's defenses.'

Ralph smiled. 'I believe that's about half their training.'

'She said I couldn't put it off, that I had a bad situation on my hands and I had to start dealing with it right away. I said that whatever I did, I didn't have to consult her before I did it, or listen to her line of bullshit just because her husband had cut her once. I almost said he probably did it because she wouldn't shut up and go away and give him some peace, can you believe that? But I was really pissed, Ralph. Hurting . . . confused . . . ashamed . . . but mostly just PO'd.'

'I think that's probably a pretty normal reaction.'

'She asked me how I'd feel about myself – not about Ed but about *myself* – if I went back into the relationship and Ed beat me up again. Then she asked how I'd feel if I went back in and Ed did it to Nat. That made me furious. It *still* makes me furious. Ed has never laid so much as a finger on her, and I said so. She nodded and said, "That doesn't mean he *won't,* Helen. I know you don't want to think about that, but you have to. Still, suppose you're right? Suppose he never so much as slaps her on the wrist? Do you want her to grow up watching him hit *you*? Do you want her to grow up seeing the things she saw today?" And that stopped me. Stopped me cold. I remembered how Ed looked when he came back in . . . how I knew as soon as I saw how white his face was . . . the way his head was moving . . .'

'Like a rooster,' Ralph murmured.

'What?'

'Nothing. Go on.'

'I don't know what set him off . . . I never do anymore, but I knew he was going to start in on me. There's nothing you can do or say to stop it once he gets to a certain point. I ran for the bedroom, but he grabbed me by the hair . . . he pulled out a great big bunch of it . . . I screamed . . . and Natalie was sitting there in her highchair . . . sitting there watching us . . . and when *I* screamed, *she* screamed . . .'

Helen broke down then, crying hard. Ralph waited with his forehead leaning against the side of the doorway between the kitchen and the living room. He used the end of the dishtowel he'd slung over his shoulder to wipe away his own tears almost without thinking about it.

'Anyway,' Helen said when she was capable of speaking again, 'I ended up talking to this woman for almost an hour. It's called Victim Counselling and she does it for a living, can you believe it?'

'Yes,' Ralph said. 'I can. It's a good thing, Helen.'

'I'm going to see her again tomorrow, at WomanCare. It's ironic, you know, that I should be going there. I mean, if I hadn't signed that petition . . .'

'If it hadn't been the petition, it would have been something else.'

She sighed. 'Yes, I guess that might be true. *Is* true. Anyway, Gretchen says I can't solve Ed's problems, but I can start solving some of my own.' Helen started to cry again and then took a deep breath. 'I'm sorry – I've cried so much today I never want to cry again. I told her I loved him. I felt ashamed to say it, and I'm not even sure it's true, but it *feels* true. I said I wanted to give him another chance. She said that meant I was committing Natalie to give him another chance, too, and that made me think of how she looked sitting there in the kitchen, with pureed spinach all over her face, screaming her head off while Ed hit me. God, I hate the way people like her drive you into a corner and won't let you out.'

'She's trying to help, that's all.'

'I hate that, too. I'm very confused, Ralph. Probably you didn't know that, but I am.' A wan chuckle drifted down the telephone line.

'That's okay, Helen. It's natural for you to be confused.'

'Just before she left, she told me about High Ridge. Right now that sounds like just the place for me.'

'What is it?'

'A kind of halfway house – she kept explaining that it was a *house,* not a shelter – for battered women. Which is what I guess I now officially am.' This time the wan chuckle sounded perilously close to a sob. 'I can have Nat with me if I go, and that's a major part of the attraction.'

'Where is this place?'

'In the country. Out toward Newport, I think.'

'Yeah, I guess I knew that.'

Of course he did; Ham Davenport had told him during his WomanCare spiel. *They're involved in family counselling . . . spouse and child abuse . . . they run a shelter for abused women over by the Newport town line.* All at once WomanCare seemed to be everywhere in his life. Ed would undoubtedly have seen sinister implications in this.

'That Gretchen Tillbury is one hard sugarbun,' Helen was saying. 'Just before she left she told me it was all right for me to love Ed – "It *has* to be all right," she said, "because love doesn't come out of a faucet you can turn on and off whenever you want to" – but that I had to remember my love couldn't fix him, that not even Ed's love for Natalie could fix him, and that no amount of love changed my responsibility to take care of my child. I've been lying in bed, thinking about that. I think I liked lying in bed and being mad better. It was certainly easier.'

'Yes,' he said, 'I can see how it might be. Helen, why don't you just take your pill and let it all go for awhile?'

'I will, but first I wanted to say thanks.'

'You know you don't have to do that.'

'I don't think I know any such thing,' she said, and Ralph was glad to hear the flash of emotion in her voice. It meant the essential Helen Deepneau was still there. 'I haven't quit being mad at you, Ralph, but I'm glad you didn't listen when I told you not to call the police. It's just that I was afraid, you know? Afraid.'

'Helen, I –' His voice was thick, close to cracking. He cleared his throat and tried again. 'I just didn't want to see you hurt any more than you already were. When I saw you coming across the parking lot with blood all over your face, I was so afraid . . .'

'Don't talk about that part. Please. I'll cry if you do, and I can't stand to cry anymore.'

'Okay.' He had a thousand questions about Ed, but this was clearly not the time to ask them. 'Can I come see you tomorrow?'

There was a short hesitation and then Helen said, 'I don't think so. Not for a little while. I have a lot of thinking to do, a lot of things to sort out, and it's going to be hard. I'll be in touch, Ralph. Okay?'

'Of course. That's fine. What are you doing about the house?'

'Candy's husband is going to go over and lock it up. I gave him my keys. Gretchen Tillbury said that Ed isn't supposed to go back for anything, not even his checkbook or a change of underwear. If there's stuff he needs, he gives a list and his housekey to a policeman, and the policeman goes to get it. I suppose he'll go to Fresh Harbor. There's plenty of housing there for lab employees. These little cottages. They're actually sort of cute . . .' The brief flash of fire he'd heard in her voice was long gone. Helen now sounded depressed, forlorn, and very, very tired.

'Helen, I'm delighted that you called. And relieved, I won't kid you about that. Now get some sleep.'

'What about you, Ralph?' she asked unexpectedly. 'Are *you* getting any sleep these days?'

The switch in focus startled him into an honesty he might not otherwise have managed. 'Some . . . but maybe not as much as I need. Probably not as much as I need.'

'Well, take care of yourself. You were very brave today, like a knight in a story about King Arthur, but I think even Sir Lancelot had to fall out every now and then.'

He was touched by this, and also amused. A momentary picture, very vivid, arose in his mind: Ralph Roberts dressed in armor and mounted on a snow-white steed while Bill McGovern, his faithful squire, rode behind him on his pony, dressed in a leather jerkin and his snappy Panama hat.

'Thank you, dear,' he said. 'I think that's the sweetest thing anyone's said to me since Lyndon Johnson was President. Have the best night you can, okay?'

'Okay. You too.'

She hung up. Ralph stood looking at the phone thoughtfully for a moment or two, then put it back in its cradle. Perhaps he *would* have a good night. After everything that had happened today, he certainly deserved one. For the time being he thought he might go downstairs, sit on the porch, watch the sun go down, and let later take care of itself.

5

McGovern was back, slouched in his favorite chair on the porch. He was looking at something up the street and didn't immediately turn when his upstairs neighbor stepped outside. Ralph followed his gaze and saw a blue step-van parked at the curb half a block up Harris Avenue, on the Red Apple side of the street. DERRY MEDICAL SERVICES was printed across the rear doors in large white letters.

'Hi, Bill,' Ralph said, and dropped into his own chair. The rocker where Lois Chasse always sat when she came over stood between them. A little twilight breeze had sprung up, delightfully cool after the heat of the afternoon, and the empty rocker moved lazily back and forth at its whim.

'Hi,' McGovern said, glancing over at Ralph. He started to look away, then did a doubletake. 'Man, you better start pinning up the bags under your eyes. You're going to be stepping on them pretty soon if you don't.' Ralph thought this was supposed to come out sounding like one of the caustic little *bons mots* for which McGovern was famous along the street, but the look in his eyes was one of genuine concern.

'It's been a bitch of a day,' he said. He told McGovern about Helen's call, editing out the things he thought she might be uncomfortable with McGovern's knowing. Bill had never been one of her favorite people.

'Glad she's okay,' McGovern said. 'I'll tell you something, Ralph – you impressed me today, marching up the street that way, like Gary Cooper in *High Noon*. Maybe it was insane, but it was also pretty cool.' He paused. 'To tell the truth, I was a little in awe of you.'

This was the second time in fifteen minutes that someone had come close to calling Ralph a hero. It made him uncomfortable. 'I was too mad at him to realize how dumb I was being until later. Where you been, Bill? I tried to call you a little while ago.'

'I took a walk out to the Extension,' McGovern said. 'Trying to cool my engine off a little, I guess. I've felt headachey and sick to my stomach ever since Johnny Leydecker and that other one took Ed away.'

Ralph nodded. 'Me, too.'

'Really?' McGovern looked surprised, and a little skeptical.

'Really,' Ralph said with a faint smile.

'Anyway, Faye Chapin was at the picnic area where those old lags usually hang out during the hot weather, and he coaxed me into a game of chess. What a piece of work that guy is, Ralph – he thinks he's the reincarnation of Ruy López, but he plays chess more like Soupy Sales . . . and he *never* shuts up.'

'Faye's all right, though,' Ralph said quietly.

McGovern seemed not to have heard him. 'And that creepy Dorrance Marstellar was out there,' he went on. 'If we're old, he's a fossil. He just stands there by the fence between the picnic area and the airport with a book of poetry in his hands, watching the planes take off and land. Does he really read those books he carries around, do you think, or are they just props?'

'Good question,' Ralph said, but he was thinking about the word McGovern had employed to describe Dorrance – *creepy*. It wasn't one he would have used himself, but there could be no doubt that old Dor was one of life's originals. He wasn't senile (at least Ralph didn't *think* he was); it was more as if the few things he said were the product of a mind that was slightly skewed and perceptions that were slightly bent.

He remembered that Dorrance had been there that day last summer when Ed ran into the guy in the pickup truck. At the time he'd thought that Dorrance's arrival had added the final screwy touch to the festivities. And Dorrance had said something funny. Ralph tried to recall what it was and couldn't.

McGovern was gazing back up the street, where a whistling young man in a gray coverall had just come out of the house in front of which the Medical Services step-van was parked. This young man, looking all of twenty-four and as if he hadn't needed a single medical service in his entire life, was rolling a dolly with a long green tank strapped to it.

87

'That's the empty,' McGovern said. 'You missed them taking in the full one.'

A second young man, also dressed in a coverall, stepped out through the front door of the small house, which combined yellow paint and deep pink trim in an unfortunate manner. He stood on the stoop for a moment, hand on the doorknob, apparently speaking to someone inside. Then he pulled the door shut and ran lithely down the walk. He was in time to help his colleague lift the dolly, with the tank still strapped to it, into the back of the van.

'Oxygen?' Ralph asked.

McGovern nodded.

'For Mrs Locher?'

McGovern nodded again, watching as the Medical Services workers slammed the doors of the step-van and then stood behind them, talking quietly in the fading light. 'I went to grammar school and junior high with May Locher. Way out in Cardville, home of the brave and land of the cows. There were only five of us in our graduating class. Back in those days she was known as a hot ticket and fellows like me were known as "a wee bit lavender". In that amusingly antique era, gay was how you described your Christmas tree after it was decorated.'

Ralph looked down at his hands, uncomfortable and tongue-tied. Of course he knew that McGovern was a homosexual, had known it for years, but Bill had never spoken of it out loud until this evening. Ralph wished he could have saved it for another day . . . preferably one when Ralph himself wasn't feeling as if most of his brains had been replaced with goosedown.

'That was about a thousand years ago,' McGovern said. 'Who'd've thought we'd both wash up on the shores of Harris Avenue.'

'It's emphysema she has, isn't that right? I think that's what I heard.'

'Yep. One of those diseases that keep on giving. Getting old is certainly no job for sissies, is it?'

'No, it's not,' Ralph said, and then his mind brought the truth of it home with sudden force. It was Carolyn he thought of, and the terror he had felt when he came squelching into the apartment in his soaked sneakers and had seen her lying half in and half out of the kitchen . . . exactly where he had stood during most of his conversation with Helen, in fact. Facing Ed Deepneau had been nothing compared to the terror he had felt at that moment, when he had been sure Carolyn was dead.

'I can remember when they just brought May oxygen once every two weeks or so,' McGovern said. 'Now they come every Monday and Thursday evening, like clockwork. I go over and see her when I can. Sometimes I read to her – the most boring women's magazine bullshit you can imagine – and sometimes we just sit and talk. She says it feels as if her lungs are filling up with seaweed. It won't be long now. They'll come one day, and instead of loading an empty oxy tank into the back of that wagon, they'll load May in. They'll take her off to Derry Home, and that'll be the end.'

'Was it cigarettes?' Ralph asked.

McGovern favored him with a look so alien to that lean, mild face that it took Ralph several moments to realize it was contempt. 'May Perrault never smoked a cigarette in her whole life. What she's paying off is twenty years in the dyehouse at a mill in Corinna and another twenty working the picker at a mill in Newport. It's cotton, wool, and nylon she's trying to breathe through, not seaweed.'

The two young men from Derry Medical Services got into their van and drove away.

'Maine's the north-eastern anchor of Appalachia, Ralph – a lot of people don't realize that, but it's true – and May's dying of an Appalachian disease. The doctors call it Textile Lung.'

'That's a shame. I guess she means a lot to you.'

McGovern laughed ruefully. 'Nah. I visit her because she happens to be the last visible piece of my misspent youth. Sometimes I read to her and I always manage to get down one or two of her dry old oatmeal cookies, but that's about as far as it goes. My concern is safely selfish, I assure you.'

Safely selfish, Ralph thought. *What a really odd phrase. What a really* McGovern *phrase.*

'Never mind May,' McGovern said. 'The question on the lips of Americans everywhere is what we're going to do about *you*, Ralph. The whiskey didn't work, did it?'

'No,' Ralph said. 'I'm afraid it didn't.'

'To make a particularly apropos pun, did you give it a fair shot?'

Ralph nodded.

'Well, you have to do *something* about the bags under your eyes or you'll never land the lovely Lois.' McGovern studied Ralph's facial response to this and sighed. 'Not that funny, huh?'

'Nope. It's been a long day.'

'Sorry.'

'It's okay.'

They sat in companionable silence for a while, watching the comings and goings on their part of Harris Avenue. Three little girls were playing hopscotch in the Red Apple's parking lot across the street. Mrs Perrine stood nearby, straight as a sentry, watching them. A boy with his Red Sox cap turned around backward went past, bopping to the beat of his Walkman headset. Two kids were tossing a Frisbee back and forth in front of Lois's house. A dog barked. Somewhere a woman was yelling for Sam to get his sister and come inside. It was just the usual streetlife serenade, no more and no less, but to Ralph it all seemed strangely false. He supposed it was because he had gotten so used to seeing Harris Avenue empty lately.

He turned to McGovern and said, 'You know what was just about the first thing I thought of when I saw you in the Red Apple parking lot this afternoon? In spite of everything else that was going on?'

McGovern shook his head.

'I wondered where the hell your hat was. The Panama. You looked very strange to me without it. Naked, almost. So come clean – where'd you stash the lid, son?'

McGovern touched the top of his head, where the remaining strands of his baby-fine white hair were combed carefully left to right across his pink skull. 'I don't know,' he said. 'I missed it this morning. I almost always remember to drop it on the table by the front door when I come in, but it's not there. I suppose I put it down somewhere else this time and the exact locale has slipped my mind for the nonce. Give me another few years and I'll be wandering around in my underwear because I can't remember where I left my pants. All part of the wonderful aging experience, right, Ralph?'

Ralph nodded and smiled, thinking to himself that of all the elderly people he knew – and he knew at least three dozen on a casual walk-in-the-park, hi-how-ya-doin basis – Bill McGovern bitched the most about getting on in years. He seemed to regard his vanished youth and recently departed middle age as a general would regard a couple of soldiers who desert on the eve of a big battle. He wasn't about to say such a thing, however. Everyone had their little eccentricities;

being theatrically morbid about growing old was simply one of McGovern's.

'Did I say something funny?' McGovern asked.

'Pardon?'

'You were smiling, so I thought I must have said something funny.' He sounded a bit touchy, especially for a man so fond of ribbing his upstairs neighbor about the pretty widow down the street, but Ralph reminded himself it had been a long day for McGovern, too.

'I wasn't thinking about you at all,' Ralph said. 'I was thinking about how Carolyn used to say practically the same thing – that getting old was like getting a bad dessert at the end of a really fine meal.'

This was at least half a lie. Carolyn *had* made the simile, but she had used it to describe the brain tumor that was killing her, not her life as a senior citizen. She hadn't been all that senior, anyway, just sixty-four when she died, and until the last six or eight weeks of her life, she had claimed to feel only half of that on most days.

Across from them, the three girls who had been playing hopscotch approached the curb, looked both ways for traffic, then joined hands and ran across the street, laughing. For just a moment they looked to him as if they were surrounded by a gray glow – a nimbus that illuminated their cheeks and brows and laughing eyes like some strange, clarifying Saint Elmo's fire. A little frightened, Ralph squeezed his eyes shut and then popped them open again. The gray envelope he'd imagined around the trio of girls was gone, which was a relief, but he *had* to get some sleep soon. He *had* to.

'Ralph?' McGovern's voice seemed to be coming from the far end of the porch, although he hadn't moved. 'You all right?'

'Sure,' Ralph said. 'Thinking about Ed and Helen, that's all. Did you have any idea how screwy he was getting, Bill?'

McGovern shook his head decisively. 'None whatsoever,' he said. 'And although I saw bruises on Helen from time to time, I always believed her stories about them. I don't like to consider myself a tremendously gullible person, but I may have to reassess my thinking on that score.'

'What do you think will happen with them? Any predictions?'

McGovern sighed and touched the top of his head with his fingertips, feeling for the missing Panama without realizing it. 'You know me, Ralph – I'm a cynic from a long line of them.

I think it's very rare for ordinary human conflicts to resolve themselves the way they do on TV. In reality they just keep coming back, turning in diminishing circles until they finally disappear. Except disappearing isn't really what they do; they dry up, like mudpuddles in the sun.' McGovern paused and then added: 'And most of them leave the same scummy residue behind.'

'Jesus,' Ralph said. 'That *is* cynical.'

McGovern shrugged. 'Most retired teachers *are* cynical, Ralph. We see them come in, so young and so strong, so convinced that it's going to be different for them, and we see them make their messes and then paddle around in them, just as their parents and grandparents did. What I think is that Helen will go back to him, and Ed will do okay for awhile, and then he'll beat her up again and she'll leave again. It's like one of those sappy country-western songs they have on the juke out at Nicky's Lunch, and some people have to listen to that song a long, long time before they decide they don't want to hear it anymore. Helen's a bright young woman, though. I think one more verse is all she'll need.'

'One more verse might be all she'll ever get,' Ralph said quietly. 'We're not talking about some drunk husband coming home on Friday night and beating his wife up because he lost his paycheck in a poker game and she dared to bitch about it.'

'I know,' McGovern said, 'but you asked for my opinion and I gave it to you. I think Helen's going to need one more go-round before she can bring herself to call it off. And even then they're apt to keep on bumping up against each other. It's still a pretty small town.' He paused, squinting down the street. 'Oh, look,' he said, hoisting his left brow. 'Our Lois. She walks in beauty, like the night.'

Ralph gave him an impatient look which McGovern either did not see or pretended not to. He got up, once again touching the tips of his fingers to the place where the Panama wasn't, and then went down the steps to meet her on the walk.

'Lois!' McGovern cried, dropping to one knee before her and extending his hands theatrically. 'Would that our lives might be united by the starry bonds of love! Wed your fate to mine and let me whirl you away to climes various in the golden car of my affections!'

'Gee, are you talking about a honeymoon or a one-night stand?' Lois asked, smiling uncertainly.

Ralph poked McGovern in the back. 'Get up, fool,' he said,

and took the small bag Lois was carrying. He looked inside and saw three cans of beer.

McGovern got to his feet. 'Sorry, Lois,' he said. 'It was a combination of summer twilight and your beauty. I plead temporary insanity, in other words.'

Lois smiled at him, then turned to Ralph. 'I just heard what happened,' she said, 'and I hurried over as fast as I could. I was in Ludlow all afternoon, playing nickel-dime poker with the girls.' Ralph didn't have to look at McGovern to know his left eyebrow – the one that said *Poker with the girls! How wonderfully, perfectly Our Lois!* – would be hoisted to its maximum altitude. 'Is Helen all right?'

'Yes,' Ralph said. 'Well, maybe not exactly all right – they're keeping her in the hospital overnight – but she's not in any danger.'

'And the baby?'

'Fine. Staying with a friend of Helen's.'

'Well, come on up on the porch, you two, and tell me all about it.' She linked one arm through McGovern's, the other through Ralph's, and led them back up the walk. They mounted the porch steps that way, like two elderly musketeers with the woman whose affections they had vied for in the days of their youth held safely between them, and as Lois sat down in her rocking chair, the streetlights went on along Harris Avenue, glimmering in the dusk like a double rope of pearls.

6

Ralph fell asleep that night bare instants after his head hit the pillow, and came wide awake again at 3:30 a.m. on Friday morning. He knew immediately there was no question of going back to sleep; he might as well proceed directly to the wing-chair in the living room.

He lay there a moment longer anyway, looking up into the dark and trying to catch the tail of the dream he'd been having. He couldn't do it. He could only remember that Ed had been in it . . . and Helen . . . and Rosalie, the dog he sometimes saw limping up or down Harris Avenue before Pete the paperboy showed up.

Dorrance was in it, too. Don't forget him.

Yes, right. And as if a key had turned in a lock, Ralph

suddenly remembered the strange thing Dorrance had said during the confrontation between Ed and the heavyset man last year . . . the thing Ralph hadn't been able to remember earlier this evening. He, Ralph, had been holding Ed back, trying to keep him pinned against the bent hood of his car long enough for reason to reassert itself, and Dorrance had said

(*I wouldn't*)

that Ralph ought to stop touching him.

'He said he couldn't see my hands anymore,' Ralph muttered, swinging his feet out of bed. 'That was it.'

He sat where he was for a little while, head down, hair frizzed up wildly in back, his fingers laced loosely together between his thighs. At last he stepped into his slippers and shuffled into the living room. It was time to start waiting for the sun to come up.

Chapter Four

1

Although cynics always sounded more plausible than the cockeyed optimists of the world, Ralph's experience had been that they were wrong at least as much of the time, if not more, and he was delighted to find that McGovern was wrong about Helen Deepneau – in her case, a single verse of 'The Beaten Up, Broken-Hearted Blues' seemed to have been enough.

On Wednesday of the following week, just as Ralph was deciding he'd better track down the woman Helen had spoken with in the hospital (Tillbury, her name had been – Gretchen Tillbury) and try to make sure Helen was okay, he received a letter from her. The return address was simple – just *Helen and Nat, High Ridge* – but it was enough to relieve Ralph's mind considerably. He sat down in his chair on the porch, tore the end off the envelope, and shook out two sheets of lined paper crammed with Helen's back-slanted handwriting.

Dear Ralph, [the letter began],
I suppose by now you must be thinking I decided to be mad at you after all, but I really didn't. It's just that we're supposed to stay out of contact with everyone – by phone and letter – for the first few days. Rules of the house. I like this place very much, and so does Nat. Of course she does; there are at least six kids her age to crawl around with. As for me, I am finding more women who know what I've been through than I ever would have believed. I mean, you see the TV shows – Oprah Talks With Women Who Love Men Who Use Them For Punching Bags – but when it happens to you, you can't help feeling that it's happening in a way

it's never happened to anyone else, in a way that's brand-new to the world. The relief of knowing that's not true is the best thing that's happened to me in a long, long time . . .

She talked about the chores to which she had been assigned – working in the garden, helping to repaint an equipment shed, washing the storm windows with vinegar and water – and about Nat's adventures in learning to walk. The rest of the letter was about what had happened and what she intended to do about it, and it was here that Ralph for the first time really sensed the emotional turmoil Helen must be feeling, her worries about the future, and, counterbalancing these things, a formidable determination to do what was right for Nat . . . and for herself, too. Helen seemed to be just discovering that she also had a right to the right thing. Ralph was happy she had found out, but sad when he thought of all the dark times she must have trudged through in order to reach that simple insight.

I'm going to divorce him, [she wrote.] *Part of my mind (it sounds like my mother when it talks) just about howls when I put it that bluntly, but I'm tired of fooling myself about my situation. There's a lot of therapy out here, the kind of thing where people sit around in a circle and use up about four boxes of Kleenex an hour, but it all seems to come back to seeing things plain. In my case, the plain fact is that the man I married has been replaced by a dangerous paranoid. That he can sometimes be loving and sweet isn't the point but a distraction. I need to remember that the man who used to bring me hand-picked flowers now sometimes sits on the porch and talks to someone who isn't there, a man he calls 'the little bald doctor.' Isn't that a beaut? I think I have an idea of how all this started, Ralph, and when I see you I'll tell you, if you really want to hear.*

I should be back at the house on Harris Avenue (for awhile, anyway) by mid-September, if only to look for a job . . . but no more about that now, the whole subject scares me to death! I had a note from Ed – just a paragraph, but a great relief just the same – saying that he was staying at one of the cottages at the Hawking Labs compound in Fresh Harbor, and that he would honor the non-contact clause in the bail agreement. He said he was sorry for everything, but I didn't get any real sense of it, if he was. It's not that I was expecting tear-stains on the letter or a package with his ear in it, but . . . I don't know. It was as if he wasn't really apologizing *at all, but just getting on the record. Does that make sense? He also included a $750 check, which seems to indicate he understands his responsibilities. That's good, but I think I'd have been happier to hear he was getting help with his mental problems. That should be his sentence, you know: eighteen months at hard therapy. I said that in group and several people laughed as if they thought I was joking. I wasn't.*

Sometimes I get these scary pictures in my head when I try to think of the future. I see us standing in line at Manna for a free meal, or me walking into the Third Street homeless shelter with Nat in my arms, wrapped in a blanket. When I think of that stuff I start to shake, and sometimes I cry. I know it's stupid; I've got a graduate degree in Library Science, for God's sake, but I can't help it. And do you know what I hold onto when those bad pictures come? What you said after you took me behind the counter in the Red Apple and sat me down. You told me that I had a lot of friends in the neighborhood, and I was going to get through this. I know I have one friend, at least. One very true friend.

The letter was signed *Love, Helen.*

Ralph wiped tears from the corners of his eyes – he cried at the drop of a hat just lately, it seemed; it probably came from being so goddam tired – and read the PS she had crammed in at the bottom of the sheet and up the right-hand margin:

I'd love to have you come and visit, but men are off limits out here for reasons I'm sure you will understand. They even want us to be quiet about the exact location! H.

Ralph sat for a minute or two with Helen's letter in his lap, looking out over Harris Avenue. It was the tag end of August now, still summer but the leaves of the poplars had begun to gleam silver when the wind stroked them and there was the first touch of coolness in the air. The sign in the window of the Red Apple said SCHOOL SUPPLIES OF ALL TYPES! CHECK HERE FIRST! And, out by the Newport town line, in some big old farmhouse where battered women went to try and start putting their lives back together, Helen Deepneau was washing storm windows, getting them ready for another long winter.

He slid the letter carefully back into its envelope, trying to remember how long Ed and Helen had been married. Six or seven years, he thought. Carolyn would have known for sure.

How much courage does it take to fire up your tractor and plow under a crop you spent six or seven years growing? he asked himself. *How much courage to go on and do that after you've spent all that time finding out how to prepare the soil and when to plant and how much to water and when to reap? How much to just say, 'I have to quit these peas, peas are no good for me, I better try corn or beans.'*

'A lot,' he said, wiping at the corners of his eyes again. 'A damn lot, that's what I think.'

Suddenly he wanted very badly to see Helen, to repeat what she so well remembered hearing and what he could barely remember saying: *You'll be okay, you'll get through this, you have a lot of friends in the neighborhood.*

'Take it to the bank,' Ralph said. Hearing from Helen seemed to have taken a great weight off his shoulders. He got up, put her letter in his back pocket, and started up Harris Avenue toward the picnic area on the Extension. If he was lucky, he could find Faye Chapin or Don Veazie and play a little chess.

2

His relief at hearing from Helen did nothing to alleviate Ralph's insomnia; the premature waking continued, and by Labor Day he was opening his eyes around 2:45 a.m. By the tenth of September – the day when Ed Deepneau was arrested again, this time along with fifteen others – Ralph's average night's sleep had shrunk to roughly three hours and he had begun to feel quite a little bit like something on a slide under a microscope. *Just a lonely l'il protozoa, that's me*, he thought as he sat in the wing-back chair, staring out at Harris Avenue, and wished he could laugh.

His list of sure-fire, never-miss folk remedies continued to grow, and it had occurred to him more than once that he could write an amusing little book on the subject . . . if, that was, he ever got enough sleep to make organized thinking possible again. This late summer he was doing well to slide into matching socks each day, and his mind kept returning to his purgatorial efforts to find a Cup-A-Soup in the kitchen cabinet on the day Helen had been beaten. There had been no return to that level since, because he had managed at least *some* sleep every night, but Ralph was terribly afraid he would arrive there again – and perhaps places beyond there – if things didn't improve. There were times (usually sitting in the wing-back chair at four-thirty in the morning) when he swore he could actually feel his brains draining.

The remedies ranged from the sublime to the ridiculous. The best example of the former was a full-color brochure advertising the wonders of the Minnesota Institute for Sleep Studies in St Paul. A fair example of the latter was the Magic Eye, an all-purpose amulet sold through supermarket tabloids like the *National Enquirer* and *Inside View*. Sue, the counter-girl at the Red Apple, bought one of these and presented it to him one afternoon. Ralph looked down at the badly painted blue eye staring up at him from the medallion (which he believed had probably started life as a poker-chip) and felt wild laughter bubbling up inside him. He somehow managed to suppress it until he had regained the safety of his own upstairs apartment across the street, and for that he was very grateful. The gravity with which Sue had given it to him – and the expensive-looking gold chain she had threaded through the eyelet on top – suggested it had cost her a fair amount of money. She had regarded Ralph with something close to awe since the day the two of them had rescued Helen. This made Ralph uncomfortable, but he had no idea what to do about it. In the meantime, he supposed it didn't hurt to wear the medallion so she could see the shape of it under his shirt. It didn't help him sleep, though.

After taking his statement on Ralph's part in the Deepneaus' domestic problems, Detective John Leydecker had pushed back his desk chair, laced his fingers together behind his not inconsiderable breadth of neck, and said that McGovern had told him Ralph suffered from insomnia. Ralph allowed that he did. Leydecker nodded, rolled his chair forward again, clasped his hands atop the litter of paperwork beneath which the surface of his desk was mostly buried, and looked at Ralph seriously.

'Honeycomb,' he said. His tone of voice reminded Ralph of McGovern's tone when he had suggested that whiskey was the answer, and his reply now was exactly the same.

'I beg your pardon?'

'My grandfather swore by it,' Leydecker said. 'Little piece of honeycomb just before bedtime. Suck the honey out of the comb, chew the wax a little – like you would a wad of gum – then spit it out. Bees secrete some sort of natural sedative when they make honey. Put you right out.'

'No kidding,' Ralph said, simultaneously believing it was

utter crap and believing every word. 'Where would a person get honeycomb, do you think?'

'Nutra – the health food store out at the mall. Try it. By next week this time your troubles are going to be over.'

Ralph enjoyed the experiment – the comb honey was so sweetly powerful it seemed to suffuse his whole being – but he still woke at 3:10 a.m. after the first dosage, at 3:08 after the second, and at 3:07 after the third. By then the small piece of honeycomb he'd purchased was gone, and he went out to Nutra right away for another one. Its value as a sedative might be nil, but it made a wonderful snack; he only wished he had discovered it earlier.

He tried putting his feet in warm water. Lois bought him something called an All-Purpose Gel Wrap from a catalogue – you put it around your neck and it was supposed to take care of your arthritis as well as help you sleep (it did neither for Ralph, but he had only the mildest case of arthritis to begin with). Following a chance meeting with Trigger Vachon at the counter of Nicky's Lunch, he tried camomile tea. 'That cammy's a beaut,' Trig told him. 'You gonna sleep great, Ralphie.' And Ralph did . . . right up until 2:58 a.m., that was.

Those were the folk cures and homeopathic remedies he tried. Ones he didn't included mega-vitamin packages which cost much more than Ralph could afford to spend on his fixed income, a yoga position called The Dreamer (as described by the postman, The Dreamer sounded to Ralph like a fine way to get a look at your own hemorrhoids), and marijuana. Ralph considered this last one very carefully before deciding it would very likely turn out to be an illegal version of the whiskey and honeycomb and the camomile tea. Besides, if McGovern found out Ralph was smoking pot, he would never hear the end of it.

And through all these experiments a voice in his brain kept asking him if he really *was* going to have to get down to eye of newt and tongue of toad before he gave up and went to the doctor. That voice was not so much critical as genuinely curious. Ralph had become fairly curious himself.

On September 10th, the day of the first Friends of Life demonstration at WomanCare, Ralph decided that he would try something from the drugstore . . . but not the Rexall downtown where he'd gotten Carol's prescriptions filled. They knew him down there, knew him well, and he didn't want Paul Durgin, the Rexall druggist, to see him buying sleeping-pills. It was probably stupid – like going across town to buy rubbers – but that didn't change the way he felt. He had never traded at the Rite Aid across from Strawford Park, so that was where he meant to go. And if the drugstore version of newt's eye and toad's tongue didn't work, he really *would* go to the doctor.

Is that true, Ralph? Do you really mean it?

'I do,' he said out loud as he walked slowly down Harris Avenue in the bright September sunshine. 'Be damned if I'll put up with this much longer.'

Big talk, Ralph, the voice replied skeptically.

Bill McGovern and Lois Chasse were standing outside the park, having what looked like an animated discussion. Bill looked up, saw him, and motioned for him to come over. Ralph went, not liking the combination of their expressions: bright-eyed interest on McGovern's face, distress and worry on Lois's.

'Have you heard about the thing out at the hospital?' she asked as Ralph joined them.

'It wasn't at the hospital, and it wasn't a "thing",' McGovern said testily. 'It was a demonstration – that's what they called it, anyway – and it was at WomanCare, which is actually *behind* the hospital. They took a bunch of people to jail – somewhere between six and two dozen, nobody really seems to know yet.'

'One of them was Ed Deepneau!' Lois said breathlessly, and McGovern shot her a disgusted glance. He clearly believed that handling this piece of news had been his job.

'Ed!' Ralph said, startled. 'Ed's in Fresh Harbor!'

'Wrong,' McGovern said. The battered brown fedora he was wearing today gave him a slightly rakish look, like a newspaperman in a forties crime drama. Ralph wondered if the Panama was still lost or had merely been retired for the fall. 'Today he's once more cooling his heels in our picturesque city jail.'

'What exactly happened?'

But neither of them really knew. At that point the story was little more than a rumor which had spread through the park like a contagious headcold, a rumor which was of particular interest in this part of town because Ed Deepneau's name was attached to it. Marie Callan had told Lois that there had been rock-throwing involved, and that was why the demonstrators had been arrested. According to Stan Eberly, who had passed the story on to McGovern shortly before McGovern ran into

Lois, someone – it might have been Ed, but it might well have been one of the others – had Maced a couple of doctors as they used the walkway between WomanCare and the back entrance to the hospital. This walkway was technically public property, and had become a favorite haunt of anti-abortion demonstrators during the seven years that WomanCare had been providing abortions on demand.

The two versions of the story were so vague and conflicting that Ralph felt he could reasonably hope neither was true, that perhaps it was just a case of a few overenthusiastic people who'd been arrested for trespassing, or something. In places like Derry, that kind of thing happened; stories had a way of inflating like beachballs as they were passed from mouth to mouth.

Yet he couldn't shake the feeling that this time it would turn out to be more serious, mostly because both the Bill version and the Lois version included Ed Deepneau, and Ed was not your average anti-abortion protestor. This was, after all, the guy who had pulled a clump of his wife's hair right out of her scalp, rearranged her dental work, and fractured her cheekbone simply because he had seen her name on a petition which mentioned WomanCare. This was the guy who seemed honestly convinced that someone calling himself the Crimson King – *it would be a great name for a pro wrestler,* Ralph thought – was running around Derry, and that his minions were hauling their unborn victims out of town on flatbed trucks (plus a few pickups with the fetuses stuffed into barrels marked WEED-GO). No, he had an idea that if Ed had been there, it had probably not been just a case of someone accidentally bonked on the head with a protest sign.

'Let's go up to my house,' Lois proposed suddenly. 'I'll call Simone Castonguay. Her niece is the day receptionist at WomanCare. If anyone knows exactly what happened up there this morning, it'll be Simone – she'll have called Barbara.'

'I was just on my way down to the supermarket,' Ralph said. It was a lie, of course, but surely a very small one; the market stood next to the Rite Aid in the strip-mall half a block down from the park. 'Why don't I stop in on my way back?'

'All right,' Lois said, smiling at him. 'We'll expect you in a few minutes, won't we, Bill?'

'Yes,' McGovern said, and suddenly swept her into his arms. It was a bit of a reach, but he managed. 'In the meantime, I'll have you all to myself. Oh, Lois, how those sweet minutes will fly!'

Just inside the park, a group of young women with babies in strollers (*a gossip of mothers,* Ralph thought) had been watching them, probably attracted by Lois's gestures, which had a tendency to become grandiose when she was excited. Now, as McGovern bent Lois backward, looking down at her with the counterfeit ardor of a bad actor at the end of a stage tango, one of the mothers spoke to another and both laughed. It was a shrill, unkind sound that made Ralph think of chalk squealing on blackboards and forks dragged across porcelain sinks. *Look at the funny old people,* the laughter said. *Look at the funny old people, pretending to be young again.*

'Stop that, Bill!' Lois said. She was blushing, and maybe not just because Bill was up to his usual tricks. She'd also heard the laughter from the park. McGovern undoubtedly had, too, but McGovern would believe they were laughing with him, not at him. *Sometimes,* Ralph thought wearily, *a slightly inflated ego could be a protection.*

McGovern let her go, then removed his fedora and swept it across his waist as he made an exaggerated bow. Lois was too busy making sure that her silk blouse was still tucked into the waistband of her skirt all the way around to pay him much notice. Her blush was already fading, and Ralph saw she looked rather pale and not particularly well. He hoped she wasn't coming down with something.

'Come by, if you can,' she told Ralph quietly.

'I will, Lois.'

McGovern slipped an arm around her waist, the gesture of affection both friendly and sincere this time, and they started up the street together. Watching them, Ralph was suddenly gripped by a strong sense of *déjà vu,* as if he had seen them like that in some other place. Or some other life. Then, just as McGovern dropped his arm, breaking the illusion, it came to him: Fred Astaire leading a dark-haired and rather plump Ginger Rogers out onto a small-town movie set, where they would dance together to some tune by Jerome Kern or maybe Irving Berlin.

That's weird, he thought, turning back toward the little strip-mall halfway down Up-Mile Hill. *That's very weird, Ralph. Bill McGovern and Lois Chasse are about as far from Fred Astaire and Ginger Rogers as you can g—*

'Ralph?' Lois called, and he turned back. There was one intersection and about a block's worth of distance between them now. Cars zipped back and forth on Elizabeth Street, turning Ralph's view of them into a moderate stutter.

'What?' he called back.

'You look better! More rested! Are you finally getting some sleep?'

'Yes!' he returned, thinking, *Just another small lie, in another good cause.*

'Didn't I say you'd feel better once the seasons changed? See you in a little while!'

Lois wiggled her fingers at him, and Ralph was amazed to see bright blue diagonal lines stream back from the short but carefully shaped nails. They looked like contrails.

What the fuck—?

He shut his eyes tight, then popped them open again. Nothing. Only Bill and Lois once again walking up the street toward Lois's house, their backs to him. No bright blue diagonals in the air, nothing like that—

Ralph's eyes dropped to the sidewalk and he saw that Lois and Bill were leaving tracks behind them on the concrete, tracks that looked exactly like the footprints in the old Arthur Murray learn-to-dance instructions you used to be able to get by mail-order. Lois's were gray. McGovern's – larger but still oddly delicate – were a dark shade of olive green. They glowed on the sidewalk, and Ralph, who was standing on the far side of Elizabeth Street with his jaw hanging almost down to his breastbone, suddenly realized he could see little ribbands of colored smoke rising from them. Or perhaps it was steam.

A city bus bound for Old Cape snored by, momentarily blocking his view, and when it passed the tracks were gone. There was nothing on the sidewalk but a message chalked inside a fading pink heart: SAM + DEANIE 4-EVER.

Those tracks are not gone, Ralph; they were never there in the first place. You know that, don't you?

Yes, he knew. The idea that Bill and Lois looked like Fred Astaire and Ginger Rogers had gotten into his head; progressing from that idea to a hallucination of phantom footprints leading up the sidewalk like tracks in an Arthur Murray dance-diagram had a certain bizarre logic. Still, it was scary. His heart was beating too fast, and when he closed his eyes for a moment to try and calm down, he saw those marks trailing up from Lois's waving fingers like bright blue jet contrails.

I've got to get more sleep, Ralph thought. *I've got to. If I don't, I'm apt to start seeing anything.*

'That's right,' he muttered under his breath as he turned toward the drugstore again. 'Anything at all.'

3

Ten minutes later, Ralph was standing at the front of the Rite Aid Pharmacy and looking at a sign which hung on chains from the ceiling. FEEL BETTER AT RITE AID! it said, seeming to suggest that feeling better was a goal attainable by any reasonable, hard-working consumer. Ralph had his doubts about that.

This, Ralph decided, was retail drug-dealing on a grand scale – it made the Rexall where he usually traded look like a tenement apartment by comparison. The fluorescent-lit aisles seemed as long as bowling alleys and displayed everything from toaster ovens to jigsaw puzzles. After a little study, Ralph decided Aisle 3 contained most of the patent medicines and was probably his best bet. He made his way slowly through the area marked STOMACH REMEDIES, sojourned briefly in the kingdom of ANALGESICS, and quickly crossed the land of LAXATIVES. And there, between LAXATIVES and DECONGESTANTS, he stopped.

This is it, folks – my last shot. After this there's only Dr Litchfield, and if he suggests chewing honeycomb or drinking camomile tea, I'll probably snap and it'll take both nurses and the receptionist to pull me off him.

SLEEPING AIDS, the sign over this section of Aisle 3 read.

Ralph, never much of a patent medicine user (he would otherwise have arrived here much sooner, no doubt), didn't know exactly what he'd expected, but it surely had not been this wild, almost indecent profusion of products. His eye slipped across the boxes (the majority were a soothing blue), reading the names. Most seemed strange and slightly ominous: Compōz, Nytol, Sleepinal, Z-Power, Sominex, Sleepinex, Drow-Zee. There was even a generic brand.

You have to be kidding, he thought. *None of these things are going to work for you. It's time to quit fucking around, don't you know that? When you start to see colored footprints on the sidewalk, it's time to quit fucking around and go to the doctor.*

But on the heels of this he heard Dr Litchfield, heard him so clearly it was as if a tape recorder had turned on in the middle of his head: *Your wife is suffering from tension headaches, Ralph – unpleasant and painful, but not life-threatening. I think we can take care of the problem.*

Unpleasant and painful, but not life-threatening – yes, right, that was what the man had said. And then he had reached for his prescription pad and written out the order for the first bunch of useless pills while the tiny clump of alien cells in Carolyn's head continued to send out its microbursts of destruction, and maybe Dr Jamal had been right, maybe it was too late even then, but maybe Jamal was full of shit, maybe Jamal was just a stranger in a strange land, trying to get along, trying not to make waves. Maybe this and maybe that; Ralph didn't know for sure and never would. All he really knew was that Litchfield hadn't been around when the final two tasks of their marriage had been set before them: her job to die, his job to watch her do it.

Is that what I want to do? Go to Litchfield and watch him reach for his prescription pad again?

Maybe this time it would work, he argued to – *with* – himself. At the same time his hand stole out, seemingly of its own volition, and took a box of Sleepinex from the shelf. He turned it over, held it slightly away from his eyes so he could read the small print on the side panel, and ran his eye slowly down the list of active ingredients. He had no idea of how to pronounce most of the jawbreaking words, and even less of what they were or how they were supposed to help you sleep.

Yes, he answered the voice. *Maybe this time it* would *work. But maybe the real answer would be just to find another doc—*

'Help you?' a voice asked from directly behind Ralph's shoulder.

He was in the act of returning the box of Sleepinex to its place, meaning to take something that sounded a little less like a sinister drug in a Robin Cook novel, when the voice spoke. Ralph jumped and knocked a dozen assorted boxes of synthetic sleep onto the floor.

'Oh, sorry – clumsy!' Ralph said, and looked over his shoulder.

'Not at all. My fault entirely.' And before Ralph could do more than pick up two boxes of Sleepinex and one box of Drow-Zee gel capsules, the man in the white smock who had spoken to him had swept up the rest and was redistributing them with the speed of a riverboat gambler dealing a hand of poker. According to the gold ID bar pinned to his breast, this was JOE WYZER, RITE AID PHARMACIST.

'Now,' Wyzer said, dusting off his hands and turning to Ralph with a friendly grin, 'let's start over. Can I help you? You look a little lost.'

Ralph's initial response – annoyance at being disturbed while having a deep and meaningful conversation with himself – was being replaced with guarded interest. 'Well, I don't know,' he said, and gestured to the array of sleeping potions. 'Do any of these actually work?'

Wyzer's grin widened. He was a tall, middle-aged man with fair skin and thinning brown hair which he parted in the middle. He stuck out his hand, and Ralph had barely begun the polite reciprocatory gesture when his own hand was swallowed. 'I'm Joe,' the pharmacist said, and tapped the gold tunic-pin with his free hand. 'I used to be Joe Wyze, but now I'm older and Wyzer.'

This was almost certainly an ancient joke, but it had lost none of its savor for Joe Wyzer, who laughed uproariously. Ralph smiled a polite little smile with just the smallest touch of anxiety around its edges. The hand which had enfolded his was clearly a strong one, and he was afraid if the pharmacist squeezed hard, his hand might finish the day in a cast. He found himself wishing, at least momentarily, that he'd taken his problem to Paul Durgin downtown after all. Then Wyzer gave his hand two energetic pumps and let go.

'I'm Ralph Roberts. Nice to meet you, Mr Wyzer.'

'Mutual. Now, concerning the efficacy of these fine products. Let me answer your question with one of my own, to wit, does a bear shit in a telephone booth?'

Ralph burst out laughing. 'Rarely, I'd think,' he said when he could say anything again.

'Correct. And I rest my case.' Wyzer glanced at the sleeping aids, a wall done in shades of blue. 'Thank God I'm a pharmacist and not a salesman, Mr Roberts; I'd starve trying to peddle stuff door to door. Are you an insomniac? I'm asking partly because you're investigating the sleeping aids, but mostly because you have that lean and hollow-eyed look.'

Ralph said, 'Mr Wyzer, I'd be the happiest man on earth if I could get five hours' sleep some night, and I'd settle for four.'

'How long's it been going on, Mr Roberts? Or do you prefer Ralph?'

'Ralph's fine.'

'Good. And I'm Joe.'

'It started in April, I think. A month or six weeks after my wife died, anyway.'

'Gee, I'm sorry to hear you lost your wife. My sympathies.'

'Thank you,' Ralph said, then repeated the old formula. 'I miss her a lot, but I was glad when her suffering was over.'

'Except now *you're* suffering. For . . . let's see.' Wyzer counted quickly on his big fingers. 'Going on half a year now.'

Ralph suddenly found himself fascinated by those fingers. No jet contrails this time, but the tip of each one appeared to be wrapped in a bright silvery haze, like tinfoil you could somehow look right through. He suddenly found himself thinking of Carolyn again, and remembering the phantom smells she had sometimes complained of last fall – cloves, sewage, burning ham. Maybe this was the male equivalent, and the onset of his own brain tumor had been signaled not by headaches but by insomnia.

Self-diagnosis is a fool's game, Ralph, so why don't you just quit it?

He moved his eyes resolutely back to Wyzer's big, pleasant face. No silvery haze there; not so much as a hint of a haze. He was almost sure of it.

'That's right,' he said. 'Going on half a year. It seems longer. A lot longer, actually.'

'Any noticeable pattern? There usually is. I mean, do you toss and turn before you go to sleep, or—'

'I'm a premature waker.'

Wyzer's eyebrows went up. 'And read a book or three about the problem too, I deduce.' If Litchfield had made a remark of this sort, Ralph would have read condescension into it. From Joe Wyzer he sensed not condescension but genuine admiration.

'I read what the library had, but there wasn't much, and none of it has helped much.' Ralph paused, then added: 'The truth is none of it has helped at all.'

'Well, let me tell you what I know on the subject, and you just kind of flop your hand when I start heading into territory you've already explored. Who's your doctor, by the way?'

'Litchfield.'

'Uh-huh. And you usually trade at . . . where? The People's Drug out at the mall? The Rexall downtown?'

'The Rexall.'

'You're incognito today, I take it.'

Ralph blushed . . . then grinned. 'Yeah, something like that.'

'Uh-huh. And I don't need to ask if you've been to see Litchfield about your problem, do I? If you had, you wouldn't be exploring the wonderful world of patent medicines.'

'Is that what these are? Patent medicines?'

'Put it this way – I'd feel a helluva lot more comfortable selling most of this crap off the back of a big red wagon with fancy yellow wheels.'

Ralph laughed, and the bright silvery cloud which had been gathering in front of Joe Wyzer's tunic blew away when he did.

'That kind of salesmanship I might be able to get into,' Wyzer said with a misty little grin. 'I'd get a sweet little honeybun to do a dance in a sequined bra and a pair of harem pants . . . call her Little Egypt, like in that old Coasters song . . . she'd be my warm-up act. Plus I'd have a banjo-picker. In my experience, there's nothing like a good dose of banjo music to put people in a buying mood.'

Wyzer looked off past the laxatives and analgesics, enjoying this gaudy daydream. Then he looked back at Ralph again.

'For a premature waker like you, Ralph, this stuff is entirely useless. You'd be better off with a shot of booze or one of those wave machines they sell through the catalogues, and looking at you, I'd guess you probably tried em both.'

'Yes.'

'Along with about two dozen other oldtimer-tested home remedies.'

Ralph laughed again. He was coming to like this guy a lot. 'Try four dozen and you'll be in the ballpark.'

'Well, you're an industrious bugger, I'll give you that,' Wyzer said, and waved a hand at the blue boxes. 'These things are nothing but antihistamines. Essentially they're trading on a side-effect – antihistamines make people sleepy. Check out a box of Comtrex or Benadryl down there in Decongestants and it'll say you shouldn't take it if you're going to be driving or operating heavy machinery. For people who suffer from occasional sleeplessness, a Sominex every now and then may work. It gives them a nudge. But they wouldn't work for you in any case, because your problem isn't *getting* to sleep, it's *staying* asleep . . . correct?'

'Correct.'

'Can I ask you a delicate question?'

'Sure. I guess so.'

'Do you have a problem with Dr Litchfield regarding this? Maybe have some doubts about his ability to understand how really pissy your insomnia is making you feel?'

'Yes,' Ralph said gratefully. 'Do you think I should go see him? Try to explain that to him so he'll understand?' To this question Wyzer would of course respond in the affirmative, and Ralph would finally make the call. And it would be, *should* be Litchfield – he saw that now. It was madness to think of hooking up with a new doctor at his age.

Can you tell Dr Litchfield you're seeing things? Can you tell him about the blue marks you saw shooting up from the tips of Lois Chasse's fingers? The footprints on the sidewalk, like the footprints in an Arthur Murray dance-diagram? The silvery stuff around the tips of Joe Wyzer's fingers? Are you really going to tell Litchfield *that stuff? And if you're not, if you* can't, *why are you going to see him in the first place, no matter what this guy recommends?*

Wyzer, however, surprised him by going in an entirely different direction. 'Are you still dreaming?'

'Yes. Quite a lot, in fact, considering that I'm down to about three hours' sleep a night.'

'Are they coherent dreams – dreams that consist of perceivable events and have some kind of narrative flow, no matter how kooky – or are they just jumbled images?'

Ralph remembered a dream he'd had the night before. He and Helen Deepneau and Bill McGovern had been having a three-sided game of Frisbee in the middle of Harris Avenue. Helen had a pair of huge, clunky saddle shoes on her feet; McGovern was wearing a sweatshirt with a vodka bottle on it. ABSOLUT-LY THE BEST, the sweatshirt proclaimed. The Frisbee had been bright red with fluorescent green stripes. Then Rosalie the dog had shown up. The faded blue bandanna someone had hung around her neck was flapping as she limped toward them. All at once she had leaped into the air, snatched the Frisbee, and gone running off with it in her mouth. Ralph wanted to give chase, but McGovern said, *Relax, Ralph, we're getting a whole case of them for Christmas.* Ralph turned to him, intending to point out that Christmas was over three months away and to ask what the hell they were going to do if they wanted to play Frisbee between then and now, but before he could, the dream had either ended or gone on to some other, less vivid, mind-movie.

'If I understand what you're saying,' Ralph replied, 'my dreams are coherent.'

'Good. I also want to know if they're *lucid* dreams. Lucid dreams fulfill two requirements. First, you know you're dreaming. Second, you can often influence the course the dream takes – you're more than just a passive observer.'

Ralph nodded. 'Sure, I have those, too. In fact, I seem to have a lot of them lately. I was just thinking of one I had last night. In it this stray dog I see on the street from time to time ran off with a Frisbee some friends of mine and I were playing with. I was mad that she broke up the game, and I tried to make her drop the Frisbee just by sending her the thought. Sort of a telepathic command, you know?'

He uttered a small, embarrassed chuckle, but Wyzer only nodded matter-of-factly. 'Did it work?'

'Not this time,' Ralph said, 'but I think I *have* made that sort of thing work in other dreams. Only I can't be sure, because most of the dreams I have seem to fade away almost as soon as I wake up.'

'That's the case with everyone,' Wyzer said. 'The brain treats most dreams as disposable matter, storing them in extreme short-term memory.'

'You know a lot about this, don't you?'

'Insomnia interests me very much. I did two research papers on the link between dreams and sleep disorders when I was in college.' Wyzer glanced at his watch. 'It's my break-time. Would you like to have a cup of coffee and a piece of apple pie with me? There's a place just two doors down, and the pie is fantastic.'

'Sounds good, but maybe I'll settle for an orange soda. I've been trying to cut down on my coffee intake.'

'Understandable but completely useless,' Wyzer said cheerfully. 'Caffeine is not your problem, Ralph.'

'No, I suppose not . . . but what is?' To this point Ralph had been quite successful at keeping the misery out of his voice, but now it crept back in.

Wyzer clapped him on the shoulder and looked at him kindly. 'That,' he said, 'is what we're going to talk about. Come on.'

Chapter Five

1

'Think of it this way,' Wyzer recommenced five minutes later. They were in a New Age-y sort of diner called Day Break, Sun Down. The place was a little too ferny for Ralph, who believed in old-fashioned diners that gleamed with chrome and smelled of grease, but the pie was good, and while the coffee was not up to Lois Chasse's standards – Lois made the best cup he had ever tasted – it was hot and strong.

'Which way is that?' Ralph asked.

'There are certain things mankind – womankind, too – keeps striving for. Not the stuff that gets written up in the history and civics books, either, at least for the most part; I'm talking fundamentals here. A roof to keep the rain out. Three hots and a cot. A decent sex-life. Healthy bowels. But maybe the most fundamental thing of all is what you've been missing, my friend. Because there's really nothing in the world that can measure up to a good night's sleep, is there?'

'Boy, you got that right,' Ralph said.

Wyzer nodded. 'Sleep is the overlooked hero and the poor man's physician. Shakespeare said it's the thread that knits up the ravelled sleeve of care, Napoleon called it the blessed end of night, and Winston Churchill – one of the great insomniacs of the twentieth century – said it was the only relief he ever got from his deep depressions. I put all that stuff in my papers, but what all the quotes come down to is what I just said: nothing in the whole wide world can measure up to a good night's sleep.'

'You've had the problem yourself, haven't you?' Ralph asked suddenly. 'Is that why you . . . well . . . why you're taking me under your wing?'

Joe Wyzer grinned. 'Is that what I'm doing?'

'I think so, yes.'

'Hey, I can live with that. The answer is yes. I've suffered from slow-sleep insomnia ever since I was thirteen. It's why I ended up doing not just one research paper on the subject but two.'

'How are you doing with it these days?'

Wyzer shrugged. 'So far it's been a pretty good year. Not the best, but I'll take it. For a couple of years in my early twenties, the problem was acute – I'd go to bed at ten, fall asleep around four, get up at seven, and drag myself through the day feeling like a bit player in someone else's nightmare.'

This was so familiar to Ralph that his back and upper arms broke out in goosebumps.

'Here comes the most important thing I can tell you, Ralph, so listen up.'

'I am.'

'The thing you have to hang onto is that you're still basically okay, even though you feel like shit a lot of the time. All sleep is not created equal, you see – there's good sleep and bad sleep. If you're still having coherent dreams, and, maybe even more importantly, *lucid* dreams, you're still having good sleep. And because of that, a scrip for sleeping pills could be about the worst thing in the world for you right now. And I know Litchfield. He's a nice enough guy, but he loves that prescription pad.'

'Say it twice,' Ralph told him, thinking of Carolyn.

'If you tell Litchfield what you told me while we were walking down here, he's going to prescribe a benzodiazepine – probably Dalmane or Restoril, maybe Halcion or even Valium. You'll sleep, but you'll pay a price. Benzodiazepines are habit-forming, they're respiratory depressants, and worst of all, for guys like you and me, they significantly reduce REM sleep. Dreaming sleep, in other words.

'How's your pie? I only ask because you've hardly touched it.'

Ralph took a big bite and swallowed it without tasting. 'Good,' he said. 'Now tell me why you have to have dreams to make your sleep good sleep.'

'If I could answer that, I'd retire from the pill-pushing business and go into business as a sleep guru.' Wyzer had finished his pie and was now using the pad of his index finger to pick up the larger crumbs left on his plate. 'REM stands for rapid eye movements, of course, and the terms REM sleep and dreaming sleep have become synonymous in the public mind, but nobody really knows just how the eye movements of sleepers relate to the dreams they are having. It seems unlikely that the eye movements indicate "watching" or "tracking", because sleep researchers see a lot of it even in dreams test subjects later describe as fairly static – dreams of conversations, for instance, like the one we're having now. Similarly, no one really knows why there seems to be a clear relationship between lucid, coherent dreams and overall mental health: the more dreams of that sort a person has, the better off he seems to be, the less he has, the worse. There's a real scale there.'

'Mental health's a pretty general phrase,' Ralph said skeptically.

'Yeah.' Wyzer grinned. 'Makes me think of a bumper sticker I saw a few years back – SUPPORT MENTAL HEALTH OR I'LL KILL YOU. Anyway, we're talking about some basic, measurable components: cognitive ability, problem-solving ability, by both inductive and deductive methods, ability to grasp relationships, memory—'

'My memory is lousy these days,' Ralph said. He was thinking of his inability to remember the number of the cinema complex and his long hunt through the kitchen cabinet for the last Cup-A-Soup envelope.

'Yeah, you're probably suffering some short-term memory loss, but your fly is zipped, your shirt is on right-side out, and I bet if I asked you what your middle name is, you could tell me. I'm not belittling your problem – I'd be the last person in the world to do that – but I *am* asking you to change your point of view for a minute or two. To think of all the areas in your life where you're still perfectly functional.'

'All right. These lucid and coherent dreams – do they just indicate how well you're functioning, like a gas gauge in a car, or do they actually help you function?'

'No one knows for sure, but the most likely answer is a little of both. In the late fifties, around the time the doctors were phasing out the barbiturates – the last really popular one was a fun drug called Thalidomide – a few scientists even tried to suggest that the good sleep we've been beating our gums about and dreams aren't related.'

'And?'

'The tests don't support the hypothesis. People who stop

dreaming or suffer from constant dream interruptions have all sorts of problems, including loss of cognitive ability and emotional stability. They also start to suffer perceptual problems like hyper-reality.'

Beyond Wyzer, at the far end of the counter, sat a fellow reading a copy of the Derry *News*. Only his hands and the top of his head were visible. He was wearing a rather ostentatious pinky-ring on his left hand. The headline at the top of the front page read ABORTION RIGHTS ADVOCATE AGREES TO SPEAK IN DERRY NEXT MONTH. Below it, in slightly smaller type, was a subhead: *Pro-Life Groups Promise Organized Protests.* In the center of the page was a color picture of Susan Day, one that did her much more justice than the flat photographs on the poster he had seen in the window of Secondhand Rose, Secondhand Clothes. In those she had looked ordinary, perhaps even a bit sinister; in this one she was radiant. Her long, honey-blonde hair had been pulled back from her face. Her eyes were dark, intelligent, arresting. Hamilton Davenport's pessimism had been misplaced, it seemed. Susan Day was coming after all.

Then Ralph saw something which made him forget all about Ham Davenport and Susan Day.

A gray-blue aura had begun to gather around the hands of the man reading the newspaper, and around the just-visible crown of his head. It seemed particularly bright around the onyx pinky-ring he wore. It did not obscure but seemed to *clarify,* turning the ringstone into something that looked like an asteroid in a really realistic science-fiction movie—

'What did you say, Ralph?'

'Hmm?' Ralph drew his gaze away from the newspaper reader's pinky-ring with an effort. 'I don't know . . . was I talking? I guess I asked you what hyper-reality is.'

'Heightened sensory awareness,' Wyzer said. 'Like taking an LSD trip without having to ingest any chemicals.'

'Oh,' Ralph said, watching as the bright gray-blue aura began to form complicated, runic patterns on the nail of the finger Wyzer was using to mash up crumbs. At first they looked like letters written in frost . . . then sentences written in fog . . . then odd, gasping faces.

He blinked and they were gone.

'Ralph? You still there?'

'Sure, you bet. But listen, Joe – if the folk remedies don't work and the stuff in Aisle 3 doesn't work and the prescription drugs could actually make things worse instead of better, what does that leave? Nothing, right?'

'You going to eat the rest of that?' Wyzer said, pointing at Ralph's plate. Chilly gray-blue light drifted off the tip of his finger like Arabic letters written in dry ice vapor.

'Nope. I'm full. Be my guest.'

Wyzer pulled Ralph's plate to him. 'Don't give up so fast,' he said. 'I want you to come back to the pharm with me so I can give you a couple of business cards. My advice, as your friendly neighborhood drug-pusher, is that you give these guys a try.'

'What guys?' Ralph watched, fascinated, as Wyzer opened his mouth to receive the last bite of pie. Each of his teeth was lit with a fierce gray glow. The fillings in his molars glowed like tiny suns. The fragments of crust and apple filling on his tongue crawled with

(*lucid Ralph lucid*)

light. Then Wyzer closed his mouth to chew, and the glow was gone.

'James Roy Hong and Anthony Forbes. Hong is an acupuncturist with offices on Kansas Street. Forbes is a hypnotist with a place over on the east side – Hesser Street, I think. And before you yell quack—'

'I'm not going to yell quack,' Ralph said quietly. His hand rose to touch the Magic Eye, which he was still wearing under his shirt. 'Believe me, I'm not.'

'Okay, good. My advice is that you try Hong first. The needles look scary, but they only hurt a little, and he's got something going there. I don't know what the hell it is or how it works, but I do know that when I went through a bad patch two winters ago, he helped me a lot. Forbes is also good – so I've heard – but Hong's my pick. He's busy as hell, but I might be able to help you there. What do you say?'

Ralph saw a bright gray glow, no thicker than a thread, slip from the corner of Wyzer's eye and slide down his cheek like a supernatural tear. It decided him. 'I say let's go.'

Wyzer clapped him on the shoulder. 'Good man! Let's pay up and get out of here.' He produced a quarter. 'Flip you for the check?'

2

Halfway back to the pharmacy, Wyzer stopped to look at a poster which had been put up in the window of an empty storefront between the Rite Aid and the diner. Ralph only glanced at it. He had seen it before, in the window of Secondhand Rose, Secondhand Clothes.

'Wanted for murder,' Wyzer marvelled. 'People have lost all goddam sense of perspective, do you know it?'

'Yes,' Ralph said. 'If we had tails, I think most of us would spend all day chasing them and trying to bite them off.'

'The poster's bad enough,' Wyzer said indignantly, 'but look at this!'

He was pointing at something beside the poster, something which had been written in the dirt which coated the outside of the empty display window. Ralph leaned close to read the short message. KILL THIS CUNT, it said. Below the words was an arrow pointing at the left-hand photo of Susan Day.

'Jesus,' Ralph said quietly.

'Yeah,' Wyzer agreed. He pulled a handkerchief from his back pocket and wiped away the message, leaving in place of the words a bright silvery fan-shape which Ralph knew only he could see.

3

He followed Wyzer to the rear of the pharmacy and stood in the doorway of an office not much bigger than a public-toilet cubicle while Wyzer sat on the only piece of furniture – a high stool that would have looked at home in Ebenezer Scrooge's counting-house – and phoned the office of James Roy Hong, acupuncturist. Wyzer pushed the phone's speaker button so Ralph could follow the conversation.

Hong's receptionist (someone named Audra who seemed to know Wyzer on a basis a good deal warmer than a merely professional one) at first said Dr Hong could not possibly see a new patient until after Thanksgiving. Ralph's shoulders slumped. Wyzer raised an open palm in his direction – *Wait a minute, Ralph* – and then proceeded to talk Audra into finding (or perhaps creating) an opening for Ralph in early October. That was almost a month away, but a lot better than Thanksgiving.

'Thanks, Audra,' Wyzer said. 'We still on for dinner Friday night?'

'Yes,' she said. 'Now turn off the damned speaker, Joe – I have something that's for your ears only.'

Wyzer did it, listened, laughed until tears – to Ralph they looked like gorgeous liquid pearls – stood in his eyes. Then he smooched twice into the phone and hung up.

'You're all set,' he said, handing Ralph a small white card with the time and date of the appointment written on the back. 'October fourth, not great, but really the best she could do. Audra's good people.'

'It's fine.'

'Here's Anthony Forbes's card, in case you want to call him in the interim.'

'Thanks,' Ralph said, taking the second card. 'I owe you.'

'The only thing you owe me is a return visit so I can find out how it went. I'm concerned. There are doctors who won't prescribe *anything* for insomnia, you know. They like to say that no one ever died from lack of sleep, but I'm here to tell you that's crap.'

Ralph supposed this news should have frightened him, but he felt pretty steady, at least for the time being. The auras had gone away – the bright gray gleams in Wyzer's eyes as he'd laughed at whatever Hong's receptionist had said had been the last. He was starting to think they had just been a mental fugue brought on by a combination of extreme tiredness and Wyzer's mention of hyper-reality. There was another reason for feeling good – he now had an appointment with a man who had helped *this* man through a similar bad patch. Ralph thought he'd let Hong stick needles into him until he looked like a porcupine, if the treatment allowed him to sleep until the sun came up.

And there was a third thing: the gray auras hadn't actually been *scary*. They had been sort of . . . interesting.

'People die from lack of sleep all the time,' Wyzer was saying, 'although the medical examiner usually ends up writing *suicide* on the cause-of-death line, rather than *insomnia*. Insomnia and alcoholism have a lot in common, but the major thing is this: they're both diseases of the heart and mind, and when they're allowed to run their course they usually gut the spirit long before they're able to destroy the body. So yeah – people *do* die from lack of sleep. This is a dangerous time for you, and you have to take care of yourself. If you start to feel really wonky, *call Litchfield*. Do you hear me? Don't stand on ceremony.'

Ralph grimaced. 'I think I'd be more apt to call you.'

Wyzer nodded as if he had absolutely expected this. 'The number under Hong's is mine,' he said.

Surprised, Ralph looked down at the card again. There *was* a second number there, marked J.W.

'Day or night,' Wyzer said. 'Really. You won't disturb my wife; we've been divorced since 1983.'

Ralph tried to speak and found he couldn't. All that came out was a choked, meaningless little sound. He swallowed hard, trying to clear the obstruction in his throat.

Wyzer saw he was struggling and clapped him on the back. 'No bawling in the store, Ralph – it scares away the big spenders. You want a Kleenex?'

'No, I'm okay.' His voice was slightly watery, but audible and mostly under control.

Wyzer cast a critical eye on him. 'Not yet, but you will be.' Wyzer's big hand swallowed Ralph's once more, and this time Ralph didn't worry about it. 'For the time being, try to relax. And remember to be grateful for the sleep you *do* get.'

'Okay. Thanks again.'

Wyzer nodded and walked back to the prescription counter.

4

Ralph walked back down Aisle 3, turned left at the formidable condom display, and went out through a door with THANK YOU FOR SHOPPING AT RITE AID decaled above the push-bar. At first he thought there was nothing unusual about the fierce brightness that made him squint his eyes almost shut – it was midday, after all, and perhaps the drugstore had been a little darker than he had realized. Then he opened his eyes wide again, and his breath came to a dead stop in his throat.

A look of thunderstruck amazement spread over his face. It was the expression an explorer might wear when, after pushing his way through just one more nondescript tangle of bushes, he finds himself looking at some fabulous lost city or brain-busting geological feature – a cliff of diamonds, perhaps, or a spiral waterfall.

Ralph shrank back against the blue mailbox standing to one side of the drugstore's entrance, still not breathing, his eyes shuttling jerkily from left to right as the brain behind them tried to understand the wonderful and terrible news it was receiving.

The auras were back, but that was a little like saying Hawaii was a place where you didn't have to wear your overcoat. This time the light was everywhere, fierce and flowing, strange and beautiful.

Ralph had had only one experience in his entire life which was remotely similar to this. During the summer of 1941, the year he'd turned eighteen, he'd been riding his thumb from Derry to his uncle's place in Poughkeepsie, New York, a distance of about four hundred miles. An early evening thunderstorm at the end of his second day on the road had sent him scurrying for the nearest available shelter – a decrepit barn swaying drunkenly at the end of a long hayfield. He had spent more of that day walking than riding, and had fallen soundly asleep in one of the barn's long-abandoned horse stalls even before the thunder had stopped blasting the sky overhead.

He'd awakened at mid-morning the next day after a solid fourteen hours of sleep and had looked around in utter wonder, not even sure, in those first few moments, where he was. He only knew it was some dark, sweet-smelling place, and that the world above and on all sides of him had been split open with brilliant seams of light. Then he had remembered taking shelter in the barn, and it came to him that this strange vision had been caused by the cracks in the barn's walls and roof combined with the bright summer sunlight . . . only that, and nothing more. Yet he'd sat there in mute wonder for at least five minutes just the same, a wide-eyed teenage boy with hay in his hair and his arms dusted with chaff; he sat there looking up at the tidal gold of dust-motes spinning lazily in the slanting, crosshatching rays of the sun. He remembered thinking it had been like being in church.

This was that experience to the tenth power. And the hell of it was simply this: he could not describe exactly what had happened, and how the world had changed, to make it so wonderful. Things and people, particularly the people, had auras, yes, but that was only where this amazing phenomenon began. Things had never been so *brilliant,* so utterly and completely *there*. The cars, the telephone poles, the shopping carts in the Kart Korral in front of the supermarket, the frame apartment buildings across the street – all these things seemed to pop out at him like 3-D images in an old film. All at once this dingy little strip-mall on Witcham Street had become wonderland, and although Ralph was looking right at it, he was not sure what he was looking at, only that it was rich and gorgeous and fabulously strange.

The only things he *could* isolate were the auras surrounding the people going in and out of stores, stowing packages in their trunks, or getting in their cars and driving away. Some of these auras were brighter than others, but even the dimmest were a hundred times brighter than his first glimpses of the phenomenon.

But it's what Wyzer was talking about, no doubt of that. It's hyper-reality, and what you're looking at is no more there than the hallucinations of people who are under the influence of LSD. What you're seeing is just another symptom of your insomnia, no more and no less. Look at it, Ralph, and marvel over it as much as you want – it is *marvellous – just don't believe it.*

He didn't need to tell himself to marvel, however – there were marvels everywhere. A bakery truck was backing out of a slot in front of Day Break, Sun Down, and a bright maroon substance – it was almost the color of dried blood – came from its tailpipe. It was neither smoke nor vapor but had some of the characteristics of each. This brightness rose in gradually attenuating spikes, like the lines of an EEG read-out. Ralph looked down at the pavement and saw the tread of the van's tires printed on the concrete in that same maroon shade. The van speeded up as it left the parking lot, and the ghostly graph-trail emerging with its exhaust turned the bright red of arterial blood as it did.

There were similar oddities everywhere, phenomena which intersected in slanting paths and made Ralph think again of how the light had come slanting through the cracks in the roof and walls of that long-ago barn. But the real wonder was the people, and it was around them that the auras seemed most clearly defined and real.

A bagboy came out of the supermarket, pushing a cartload of groceries and walking in a nimbus of such brilliant white that it was like a travelling spotlight. The aura of the woman beside him was dingy by comparison, the gray-green of cheese which has begun to mould.

A young girl called to the bagboy from the open window of a Subaru and waved; her left hand left bright contrails, as pink as cotton candy, in the air as it moved. They began to fade almost as soon as they appeared. The bagboy grinned and waved back; his hand left a fantail of yellowish-white behind. To Ralph it looked like the fin of a tropical fish. This also began to fade, but more slowly.

Ralph's fear at this confused, shining vision was considerable, but for the time being, at least, fear had taken a back seat to wonder, awe, and simple amazement. It was more beautiful than anything he had ever seen in his life. *But it's not real,* he cautioned himself. *Remember that, Ralph.* He promised himself he would try, but for the time being that cautioning voice seemed very far away.

Now he noticed something else: there was a line of that lucid brightness emerging from the head of every person he could see. It trailed upward like a ribbon of bunting or brightly colored crepe paper until it attenuated and disappeared. For some people the point of disappearance was five feet above the head; for others it was ten or fifteen. In most cases the color of the bright, ascending line matched the rest of the aura – bright white for the bagboy, gray-green in the case of the female customer beside him, for instance – but there were some striking exceptions. Ralph saw a rust-red line rising from a middle-aged man who was striding along in the middle of a dark-blue aura, and a woman with a light-gray aura whose ascending line was an amazing (and slightly alarming) shade of magenta. In some cases – two or three, not a lot – the rising lines were almost black. Ralph didn't like those, and he noticed that the people to whom these 'balloon-strings' (they were named just that simply and quickly in his mind) belonged invariably looked unwell.

Of course they do. The balloon-strings are an indicator of health . . . and ill-health, in some cases. Like the Kirlian auras people were so fascinated with back in the late sixties and early seventies.

Ralph, another voice warned, *you are* not *really seeing these things, okay? I mean, I hate to be a bore, but—*

But wasn't it at least possible that the phenomenon *was* real? That his persistent insomnia, coupled with the stabilizing influence of his lucid, coherent dreams, had afforded him a glimpse of a fabulous dimension just beyond the reach of ordinary perception?

Quit it, Ralph, and right now. You have to do better than that, or you'll end up in the same boat as poor old Ed Deepneau.

Thinking of Ed kicked off some association – something he'd

said on the day he'd been arrested for beating his wife – but before Ralph could isolate it, a voice spoke almost at his left elbow.

'Mom? Mommy? Can we get the Honey Nut Cheerios again?'

'We'll see once we get inside, hon.'

A young woman and a little boy passed in front of him, walking hand-in-hand. It was the boy, who looked to be four or five, who had spoken. His mother was walking in an envelope of almost blinding white. The 'balloon-string' rising out of her blonde hair was also white and very wide – more like the ribbon on a fancy gift box than a string. It rose to a height of at least twenty feet and floated out slightly behind her as she walked. It made Ralph think of things bridal – trains, veils, gauzy billows of skirt.

Her son's aura was a healthy dark blue verging on violet, and as the two of them walked past, Ralph saw a fascinating thing. Tendrils of aura were also rising from their clasped hands: white from the woman, dark blue from the boy. They twined in a pigtail as they rose, faded, and disappeared.

Mother-and-son, mother-and-son, Ralph thought. There was something perfectly, simply symbolic about those bands, which were wrapped around each other like woodbine climbing a garden stake. Looking at them made his heart rejoice – corny, but it was exactly how he felt. *Mother-and-son, white-and-blue, mother-and—*

'Mom, what's that man looking at?'

The blonde woman's glance at Ralph was brief, but he saw the way her lips thinned down and pressed together before she turned away. More importantly, he saw the brilliant aura which surrounded her suddenly darken, close in, and pick up spiraling tints of dark red.

That's the color of fright, Ralph thought. *Or maybe anger.*

'I don't know, Tim. Come on, stop dawdling.' She began to move him along faster, her ponytailed hair flipping back and forth and leaving small fans of gray tinged with red in the air. To Ralph they looked like the arcs that wipers sometimes left on dirty windshields.

'Hey, Mom, get a life! Quit *pull*-ing!' The little boy had to trot in order to keep up.

That's my fault, Ralph thought, and an image of how he must have looked to the young mother flashed into his mind: old guy, tired face, big purplish pouches under his eyes. He's

standing – *hunching* – by the mailbox outside the Rite Aid
Pharmacy, staring at her and her little boy as if they were the
most remarkable things in the world.

Which you just about are, ma'am, if you but knew it.

To her he must have looked like the biggest pervo of all time.
He had to get rid of this. Real or hallucination, it didn't matter
– he had to make it quit. If he didn't somebody was going to
call either the cops or the men with the butterfly nets. For
all he knew, the pretty mother could be making the bank of
pay-phones just inside the market's main doors her first stop.

He was just asking himself how one thought away something which was all in one's mind to begin with when he
realized it had already happened. Psychic phenomenon or
sensory hallucination, it had simply disappeared while he'd
been thinking about how awful he must have looked to the
pretty young mother. The day had gone back to its previous
Indian summery brilliance, which was wonderful but still a
long way from that pellucid, all-pervading glow. The people
crisscrossing the parking lot of the strip-mall were just people
again: no auras, no balloon-strings, no fireworks. Just people
on their way to buy groceries in the Shop 'n Save, or to pick
up their last batch of summer pictures at Photo-Mat, or to grab
a take-out coffee from Day Break, Sun Down. Some of them
might even be ducking into the Rite Aid for a box of Trojans
or, God bless us and keep us, a SLEEPING AID.

Just your ordinary, everyday citizens of Derry going about
their ordinary, everyday business.

Ralph released pent-up breath in a gusty sigh and braced
himself for a wave of relief. Relief *did* come, but not in the tidal
wave he had expected. There was no sense of having drawn
back from the brink of madness in the nick of time; no sense
of having been close to *any* sort of brink. Yet he understood
perfectly well that he couldn't live for long in a world that
bright and wonderful without endangering his sanity; it would
be like having an orgasm which lasted for hours. That might
be how geniuses and great artists experienced things, but it was
not for him; so much juice would blow his fuses in short order,
and when the men with the butterfly nets rolled up to give him a
shot and take him away, he would probably be happy to go.

The most readily identifiable emotion he was feeling just
now wasn't relief but a species of pleasant melancholy which
he remembered sometimes experiencing after sex when he was
a very young man. This melancholy was not deep but it was

wide, seeming to fill the empty places of his body and mind the way a receding flood leaves a scrim of loose, rich topsoil. He wondered if he would ever have such an alarming, exhilarating moment of epiphany again. He thought the chances were fairly good . . . at least until next month, when James Roy Hong got his needles into him, or perhaps until Anthony Forbes started swinging his gold pocket watch in front of his eyes and telling him he was getting . . . very . . . sleepy. It was possible that neither Hong nor Forbes would have any success in curing his insomnia, but if one of them did, Ralph guessed he would stop seeing auras and balloon-strings after his first good night's sleep. And, after a month or so of restful nights, he would probably forget this had ever happened. As far as he was concerned, that was a perfectly good reason to feel a touch of melancholy.

You better get moving, buddy – if your new friend happens to look out the drugstore window and sees you still standing here like a dope, he'll probably send for the men with the nets himself.

'Call Dr Litchfield, more like it,' Ralph muttered, and cut across the parking lot toward Harris Avenue.

5

He poked his head through Lois's front door and called, 'Yo! Anybody home?'

'Come on in, Ralph!' Lois called back. 'We're in the living room!'

Ralph had always imagined a hobbit-hole would be a lot like Lois Chasse's little house half a block or so down the hill from the Red Apple – neat and crowded, a little too dark, perhaps, but scrupulously clean. And he guessed a hobbit like Bilbo Baggins, whose interest in his ancestors was eclipsed only by his interest in what might be for dinner, would have been enchanted by the tiny living room, where relatives looked down from every wall. The place of honor, on top of the television, was held by a tinted studio photograph of the man Lois always referred to as 'Mr Chasse'.

McGovern was sitting hunched forward on the couch with a plate of macaroni and cheese balanced on his bony knees. The television was on and a game-show was clattering through the bonus round.

'What does she mean, *we're* in the living room?' Ralph asked, but before McGovern could answer, Lois came in with a steaming plate in her hands.

'Here,' she said. 'Sit down, eat. I talked with Simone, and she said it'll probably be on *News at Noon*.'

'Gee, Lois, you didn't have to do this,' he said, taking the plate, but his stomach demurred strongly when he got his first smell of onions and mellow cheddar. He glanced at the clock on the wall – just visible between photos of a man in a raccoon coat and a woman who looked as if *vo-do-dee-oh-do* might have been in her vocabulary – and was astounded to see it was five minutes of twelve.

'I didn't do anything but stick some leftovers into the microwave,' she said. 'Someday, Ralph, I'll *cook* for you. Now sit down.'

'Not on my hat, though,' McGovern said, without taking his eyes from the bonus round. He picked the fedora up off the couch, dropped it on the floor beside him, and went back to his own portion of the casserole, which was disappearing rapidly. 'This is very tasty, Lois.'

'Thank you.' She paused long enough to watch one of the contestants bag a trip to Barbados and a new car, then hurried back into the kitchen. The screaming winner faded out and was replaced by a man in wrinkled pajamas, tossing and turning in bed. He sat up and looked at the clock on the nightstand. It said 3:18 a.m., a time of day with which Ralph had become very familiar.

'Can't sleep?' an announcer asked sympathetically. 'Tired of lying awake night after night?' A small glowing pill came gliding in through the insomniac's bedroom window. To Ralph it looked like the world's smallest flying saucer, and he wasn't surprised to see that it was blue.

Ralph sat down beside McGovern. Although both men were quite slim (*scrawny* might actually have described Bill better), between them they used up most of the couch.

Lois came in with her own plate and sat down in the rocker by the window. Over the canned music and studio applause that marked the end of the game-show, a woman's voice said, 'This is Lisette Benson. Topping our *News at Noon*, a well-known women's rights advocate agrees to speak in Derry, sparking a protest – and six arrests – at a local clinic. We'll also have Chris Altoberg's weather and Bob McClanahan on sports. Stay tuned.'

Ralph forked a bite of macaroni and cheese into his mouth, looked up, and saw Lois watching him. 'All right?' she asked.

'Delicious,' he said, and it was, but he thought that right now a big helping of Franco-American spaghetti served cold right out of the can would have tasted just as good. He wasn't just hungry; he was ravenous. Seeing auras apparently burned a lot of calories.

'What happened, very briefly, was this,' McGovern said, swallowing the last of his own lunch and putting the plate down next to his hat. 'About eighteen people showed up outside WomanCare at eight-thirty this morning, while people were arriving for work. Lois's friend Simone says they're calling themselves The Friends of Life, but the core group are the assorted fruits and nuts that used to go by the name of Daily Bread. She said one of them was Charles Pickering, the guy the cops caught apparently getting ready to firebomb the joint late last year. Simone's niece said the police only arrested four people. It looks like she was a little low.'

'Was Ed really with them?' Ralph asked.

'Yes,' Lois said, 'and he got arrested, too. At least no one got Maced. That was just a rumor. No one got hurt at all.'

'*This* time,' McGovern added darkly.

The *News at Noon* logo appeared on Lois's hobbit-sized color TV, then dissolved into Lisette Benson. 'Good afternoon,' she said. 'Topping our news on this beautiful late-summer day, prominent writer and controversial women's rights advocate Susan Day agrees to speak at the Civic Center next month, and the announcement of her speech sparks a demonstration at WomanCare, the Derry women's resource center and abortion clinic which has so polarized—'

'There they go with that abortion clinic stuff again!' McGovern exclaimed. 'Jesus!'

'Hush!' Lois said in a peremptory tone not much like her usual tentative murmur. McGovern gave her a surprised look and hushed.

'– John Kirkland at WomanCare, with the first of two reports,' Lisette Benson was finishing, and the picture switched to a reporter doing a stand-up outside a long, low brick building. A super at the bottom of the screen informed viewers that this was a LIVE-EYE REPORT. A strip of windows ran along one side of WomanCare. Two of them were broken, and several others were smeared with red stuff that looked like blood. Yellow police-line tape had been strung between the reporter and the building; three uniformed Derry cops and one plainclothesman stood in a little group on the far side of it. Ralph was not very surprised to recognize the detective as John Leydecker.

'They call themselves The Friends of Life, Lisette, and they claim their demonstration this morning was a spontaneous out-pouring of indignation prompted by the news that Susan Day – the woman radical pro-life groups nationwide call "America's Number One Baby-Killer" – is coming to Derry next month to speak at the Civic Center. At least one Derry police officer believes that's not quite the way it was, however.'

Kirkland's report went to tape, beginning with a close-up of Leydecker, who seemed resigned to the microphone in his face.

'There was no spontaneity about this,' he said. 'Clearly a lot of preparation went into it. They've probably been sitting on advance word of Susan Day's decision to come here and speak for most of the week, just getting ready and waiting for the news to break in the paper, which it did this morning.'

The camera went to a two-shot. Kirkland was giving Leydecker his most penetrating Geraldo look. 'What do you mean "a lot of preparation"?' he asked.

'Most of the signs they were carrying had Ms Day's name on them. Also, there were over a dozen of *these*.'

A surprisingly human emotion slipped through Leydecker's policeman-being-interviewed mask; Ralph thought it was dis-taste. He raised a large plastic evidence bag, and for one horrified instant Ralph was positive that there was a mangled and bloody baby inside. Then he realized that, whatever the red stuff might be, the body in the evidence bag was a doll's body.

'They didn't buy these at Kmart,' Leydecker told the TV reporter. 'I guarantee you that.'

The next shot was a long-lens close-up of the smeared and broken windows. The camera panned them slowly. The stuff on the smeared ones looked more like blood than ever, and Ralph decided he didn't want the last two or three bites of his macaroni and cheese.

'The demonstrators came with baby-dolls whose soft bodies had been injected with what police believe to be a mixture of Karo syrup and red food-coloring,' Kirkland said in voice-over. 'They flung the dolls at the side of the building as they chanted anti-Susan Day slogans. Two windows were broken, but there was no major damage.'

The camera stopped, centering on a gruesomely smeared pane of glass.

'Most of the dolls split open,' Kirkland was saying, 'splattering a substance that looked enough like blood to badly frighten the employees who witnessed the bombardment.'

The shot of the red-smeared window was replaced by one of a lovely dark-haired woman in slacks and a pullover.

'Oooh, look, it's Barbie!' Lois cried. 'Golly, I hope Simone's watching! Maybe I ought to—'

It was McGovern's turn to say hush.

'I was terrified,' Barbara Richards told Kirkland. 'At first I thought they were really throwing dead babies, or maybe fetuses they'd gotten hold of somehow. Even after Dr Warper ran through, yelling they were only dolls, I still wasn't sure.'

'You said they were chanting?' Kirkland asked.

'Yes. What I heard most clearly was "Keep the Angel of Death out of Derry."'

The report now reverted to Kirkland in his live stand-up mode. 'The demonstrators were ferried from WomanCare to Derry Police Headquarters on Main Street around nine o'clock this morning, Lisette. I understand that twelve were questioned and released; six others were arrested on charges of malicious mischief, a misdemeanor. So it seems that another shot in Derry's continuing war over abortion has been fired. This is John Kirkland, Channel Four news.'

'"Another shot in —"' McGovern began, and threw up his hands.

Lisette Benson was back on the screen. 'We now go to Anne Rivers, who talked less than an hour ago to two of the so-called Friends of Life who *were* arrested in this morning's demonstration.'

Anne Rivers was standing on the steps of the Main Street cop-shop with Ed Deepneau on one side and a tall, sallow, goateed individual on the other. Ed was looking natty and downright handsome in a gray tweed jacket and navy slacks. The tall man with the goatee was dressed as only a liberal with daydreams of what he might think of as 'the Maine proletariat' could dress: faded jeans, faded blue workshirt, wide red fireman's suspenders. It took Ralph only a second to place him. It was Dan Dalton, owner of Secondhand Rose, Secondhand Clothes. The last time Ralph had seen him, he had been standing behind the hanging guitars and bird-cages in his shop window, flapping his hands at Ham

Davenport in a gesture that said *Who gives a shit what you think?*

But it was Ed his eyes were drawn back to, of course, Ed who looked natty and put together in more ways than one.

McGovern apparently felt the same. 'My God, I can't believe it's the same man,' he murmured.

'Lisette,' the good-looking blonde was saying, 'with me I have Edward Deepneau and Daniel Dalton, both of Derry, two of those arrested in this morning's demonstration. That's correct, gentlemen? You were arrested?'

They nodded, Ed with the barest twinkle of humor, Dalton with dour, jut-jawed determination. The gaze the latter fixed on Anne Rivers made him look – to Ralph, at least – as if he were trying to remember which abortion clinic he had seen her hurrying into, head down and shoulders hunched.

'Have you been released on bail?'

'We were released on our own recognizance,' Ed answered. 'The charges were minor. It was not our intention to hurt anyone, and no one *was* hurt.'

'We were arrested only because the Godless entrenched power-structure in this town wants to make an example of us,' Dalton said, and Ralph thought he saw a minute wince momentarily tighten Ed's face. A there-he-goes-again expression.

Anne Rivers swung the mike back to Ed.

'The major issue here isn't philosophical but practical,' he said. 'Although the people who run WomanCare like to concentrate on their counselling services, therapy services, free mammograms and other such admirable functions, there's another side to the place. Rivers of blood run out of WomanCare—'

'*Innocent* blood!' Dalton cried. His eyes glowed in his long, lean face, and Ralph had a disturbing insight: all over eastern Maine, people were watching this and deciding that the man in the red suspenders was crazy, while his partner seemed like a pretty reasonable fellow. It was almost funny.

Ed treated Dalton's interjection as the pro-life equivalent of *Hallelujah,* giving it a single respectful beat before speaking again.

'The slaughter at WomanCare has been going on for nearly eight years now,' Ed told her. 'Many people – especially radical feminists like Dr Roberta Warper, WomanCare's chief administrator – like to gild the lily with phrases like "early termination", but what she's talking about is abortion, the ultimate act of abuse against women by a sexist society.'

'But is lobbing dolls loaded with fake blood against the windows of a private clinic the way to put your views before the public, Mr Deepneau?'

For a moment – just a moment, there and gone – the twinkle of good humor in Ed's eyes was replaced by a flash of something much harder and colder. For that one moment Ralph was again looking at the Ed Deepneau who had been ready to take on a truck-driver who outweighed him by a hundred pounds. Ralph forgot that what he was watching had been taped an hour ago and was afraid for the slim blonde, who was almost as pretty as the woman to whom her interview subject was still married. *Be careful, young lady,* Ralph thought. *Be careful and be afraid. You're standing next to a very dangerous man.*

Then the flash was gone and the man in the tweed coat was once more just an earnest young fellow who had followed his conscience to jail. Once more it was Dalton, now nervously snapping his suspenders like big red rubber bands, who looked a few sandwiches shy of a picnic.

'What we're doing is what the so-called good Germans failed to do in the thirties,' Ed was saying. He spoke in the patient, lecturely tones of a man who has been forced to point this out over and over . . . mostly to those who should already know it. 'They were silent and six million Jews died. In this country a similar holocaust—'

'Over a thousand babies every day,' Dalton said. His former shrillness had departed. He sounded horrified and desperately tired. 'Many of them are ripped from the wombs of their mothers in pieces, with their little arms waving in protest even as they die.'

'Oh good God,' McGovern said. 'That's the most ridiculous thing I have ever—'

'Hush, Bill!' Lois said.

'– purpose of this protest?' Rivers was asking Dalton.

'As you probably know,' Dalton said, 'the City Council has agreed to re-examine the zoning regulations that allow WomanCare to operate where it does and how it does. They could vote on the issue as early as November. The abortion rights people are afraid the Council might throw sand in the gears of their death-machine, so they've summoned Susan Day, this country's most notorious pro-abortion advocate, to try and keep the machine running. We are marshalling our forces—'

The pendulum of the microphone swung back to Ed. 'Will there be more protests, Mr Deepneau?' she asked, and Ralph suddenly had an idea she might be interested in him in a way which was not strictly professional. Hey, why not? Ed was a good-looking guy, and Ms Rivers could hardly know that he believed the Crimson King and his Centurions were in Derry, joining forces with the baby-killers at WomanCare.

'Until the legal aberration which opened the door to this slaughter has been corrected, the protests will continue,' Ed replied. 'And we'll go on hoping that the histories of the next century will record that not all Americans were good Nazis during this dark period of our history.'

'*Violent* protests?'

'It's violence we oppose.' The two of them were now maintaining strong eye contact, and Ralph thought Anne Rivers had what Carolyn would have called a case of hot thighs. Dan Dalton was standing off to one side of the screen, all but forgotten.

'And when Susan Day comes to Derry next month, can you guarantee her safety?'

Ed smiled, and in his mind's eye Ralph saw him as he had been on that hot August afternoon less than a month ago – kneeling with one hand planted on either side of Ralph's shoulders and breathing *They burn the fetuses over in Newport* into his face. Ralph shivered.

'In a country where thousands of children are sucked from the wombs of their mothers by the medical equivalent of industrial vacuum cleaners, I don't believe anyone can guarantee anything,' Ed replied.

Anne Rivers looked at him uncertainly for a moment, as if deciding whether or not she wanted to ask another question (maybe for his telephone number), and then turned back to face the camera. 'This is Anne Rivers, at Derry Police Headquarters,' she said.

Lisette Benson reappeared, and something in the bemused cast of her mouth made Ralph think that perhaps he hadn't been the only one to sense the attraction between interviewer and interviewee. 'We'll be following this story all day,' she said. 'Be sure to tune in at six for further updates. In Augusta, Governor Greta Powers responded to charges that she may have—'

Lois got up and pushed the Off button on the TV. She simply stared at the darkening screen for a moment, then sighed heavily and sat down. 'I have blueberry compote,' she said, 'but after that, do either of you want any?'

Both men shook their heads. McGovern looked at Ralph and said, 'That was scary.'

Ralph nodded. He kept thinking of how Ed had gone striding back and forth through the spray thrown by the lawn-sprinkler, breaking the rainbows with his body, pounding his fist into his open palm.

'How could they let him out on bail and then interview him on the news as if he was a normal human being?' Lois asked indignantly. 'After what he did to poor Helen? My God, that Anne Rivers looked ready to invite him home to dinner!'

'Or to eat crackers in bed with her,' Ralph said dryly.

'The assault charge and this stuff today are entirely different matters,' McGovern said, 'and you can bet your boots the lawyer or lawyers these yo-yos have got on retainer will be sure to keep it that way.'

'And even the assault charge was only a misdemeanor,' Ralph reminded her.

'How can assault be a misdemeanor?' Lois asked. 'I'm sorry, but I never *did* understand that part.'

'It's a misdemeanor when you only do it to your wife,' McGovern said, hoisting his satiric eyebrow. 'It's the American way, Lo.'

She twisted her hands together restlessly, took Mr Chasse down from the television, looked at him for a moment, then put him back and resumed twisting her hands. 'Well, the law's one thing,' she said, 'and I'd be the first to admit that I don't understand it all. But somebody ought to tell them he's crazy. That he's a wife-beater and he's crazy.'

'You don't know *how* crazy,' Ralph said, and for the first time he told them the story of what had happened the previous summer, out by the airport. It took about ten minutes. When he finished, neither of them said anything – they only looked at him with wide eyes.

'What?' Ralph asked uneasily. 'You don't believe me? You think I imagined it?'

'Of course I believe it,' Lois said. 'I was just . . . well . . . stunned. And frightened.'

'Ralph, I think maybe you ought to pass that story on to John Leydecker,' McGovern said. 'I don't think he can do a goddam thing with it, but considering Ed's new playmates, I think it's information he should have.'

Ralph thought it over carefully, then nodded and pushed himself to his feet. 'No time like the present,' he said. 'Want to come, Lois?'

She thought it over, then shook her head. 'I'm tired out,' she said. 'And a little – what do the kids call it these days? – a little freaked. I think I'll put my feet up for a bit. Take a nap.'

'You do that,' Ralph said. 'You do look a little tuckered. And thanks for feeding us.' Impulsively, he bent over her and kissed the corner of her mouth. Lois looked up at him with startled gratitude.

6

Ralph turned off his own television a little over six hours later, as Lisette Benson finished the evening news and handed off to the sports guy. The demonstration at WomanCare had been bumped to the number two slot – the evening's big story was the continuing allegations that Governor Greta Powers had used cocaine as a grad student – and there was nothing new, except that Dan Dalton was now being identified as the head of the Friends of Life. Ralph thought *figurehead* was probably a better word. Was Ed actually in charge yet? If he wasn't, Ralph guessed he would be before long – Christmas at the latest. A potentially more interesting question was what Ed's employers thought about Ed's legal adventures up the road in Derry. Ralph had an idea they would be a lot less comfortable with what had gone on today than with last month's domestic abuse charge; he had read only recently that Hawking Labs would soon become the fifth such research center in the Northeast to be working with fetal tissue. They probably wouldn't applaud the information that one of their research chemists had been arrested for chucking dolls filled with fake blood at the side of a clinic that did abortions. And if they knew how crazy he really was—

Who's going to tell them, Ralph? You?

No. That was a step further than he was willing to go, at least for the time being. Unlike going down to the police station with McGovern to talk to John Leydecker about the incident last summer, it felt like persecution. Like writing KILL

THIS CUNT beside a picture of a woman with whose views you didn't agree.

That's bullshit, and you know it.

'I don't know anything,' he said, getting up and going to the window. 'I'm too *tired* to know anything.' But as he stood there, looking across the street at two men coming out of the Red Apple with a six-pack apiece, he suddenly *did* know something, remembered something that drew a cold line up his back.

This morning, when he had come out of the Rite Aid and been overwhelmed by the auras – and a sense of having stepped up to some new level of awareness – he had reminded himself again and again to enjoy but not to believe; that if he failed to make that crucial distinction, he was apt to end up in the same boat as Ed Deepneau. That thought had almost opened the door on some associative memory, but the shifting auras in the parking lot had pulled him away from it before it had been able to kick all the way in. Now it came to him: *Ed* had said something about seeing auras, hadn't he?

No – he might have meant *auras, but the word he actually used was* colors. *I'm almost positive of that. It was right after he talked about seeing the corpses of babies everyplace, even on the roofs. He said—*

Ralph watched the two men get into a beat-up old van and thought that he would never be able to remember Ed's words exactly; he was just too tired. Then, as the van drove off trailing a cloud of exhaust that reminded him of the bright maroon stuff he'd seen coming from the tailpipe of the bakery truck that noon, another door opened and the memory *did* come.

'He said that sometimes the world is full of colors,' Ralph told his empty apartment, 'but that at some point they all started turning black. I *think* that was it.'

It was close, but was it everything? Ralph thought there had been at least a little more to Ed's spiel, but he couldn't remember what. And did it matter, anyway? His nerves suggested strongly that it did – the cold line up his back had both widened and deepened.

Behind him, the telephone rang. Ralph turned and saw it sitting in a bath of baleful red light, dark red, the color of nosebleeds and

(*cocks fighting cocks*)

rooster-combs.

No, part of his mind moaned. *Oh no, Ralph, don't get going on this again—*

Each time the phone rang, the envelope of light got brighter. During the intervals of silence, it darkened. It was like looking at a ghostly heart with a telephone inside it.

Ralph closed his eyes tightly, and when he opened them again, the red aura around the telephone was gone.

No, you just can't see it right now. I'm not sure, but I think you might have willed it away. Like something in a lucid dream.

As he crossed the room to the telephone, he told himself – and in no uncertain terms – that that idea was as crazy as seeing the auras in the first place. Except it wasn't, and he *knew* it wasn't. Because if it was crazy, how come it had taken only one look at that rooster-red halo of light to make him sure that it was Ed Deepneau calling?

That's crap, Ralph. You think it's Ed because Ed's on your mind . . . and because you're so tired your head's getting funny. Go on, pick it up, you'll see. It's not the tell-tale heart, not even the tell-tale phone. It's probably some guy wanting to sell you subscriptions or the lady at the blood-bank, wondering why you haven't been in lately.

Except he knew better.

Ralph picked up the phone and said hello.

7

No answer. But *someone* was there; Ralph could hear breathing.

'Hello?' he asked again.

There was still no immediate answer, and he was about to say *I'm hanging up now* when Ed Deepneau said, 'I called about your mouth, Ralph. It's trying to get you in trouble.'

The line of cold between his shoulderblades was no longer a line; now it was a thin plate of ice covering him from the nape of his neck to the small of his back.

'Hello, Ed. I saw you on the news today.' It was the only thing he could think of to say. His hand did not seem to be holding the phone so much as to be cramped around it.

'Never mind that, old boy. Just pay attention. I've had a visit from that wide detective who arrested me last month – Leydecker. He just left, in fact.'

Ralph's heart sank, but not as far as he might have feared. After all, Leydecker's going to see Ed wasn't that surprising, was it? He had been very interested in Ralph's story of the airport confrontation in the summer of '92. Very interested indeed.

'Did he?' Ralph asked evenly.

'Detective Leydecker has the idea that I think people – or possibly supernatural beings of some sort – are trucking fetuses out of town in flatbeds and pickup trucks. What a scream, huh?'

Ralph stood beside the sofa, pulling the telephone cord restlessly through his fingers and realizing that he could see dull red light creeping out of the wire like sweat. The light pulsed with the rhythms of Ed's speech.

'You've been telling tales out of school, old boy.'

Ralph was silent.

'Calling the police after I gave that bitch the lesson she so richly deserved didn't bother me,' Ed told him. 'I put it down to . . . well, grandfatherly concern. Or maybe you thought that if she was grateful enough, she might actually spare you a mercy-fuck. After all, you're old but not exactly ready for Jurassic Park yet. You might have thought she'd let you get a finger into her at the very least.'

Ralph said nothing.

'Right, old boy?'

Ralph said nothing.

'You think you're going to rattle me with the silent treatment? Forget it.' But Ed *did* sound rattled, thrown off his stride. It was as if he had made the call with a certain script in his head and Ralph was refusing to read his lines. 'You can't . . . you better not . . .'

'My calling the police after you beat Helen didn't upset you, but your conversation with Leydecker today obviously did. Why's that, Ed? Are you finally starting to have some questions about your behavior? And your thinking, maybe?'

It was Ed's turn to be silent. At last he whispered harshly, 'If you don't take this seriously, Ralph, it would be the worst mistake—'

'Oh, I take it seriously,' Ralph said. 'I saw what you did today, I saw what you did to your wife last month . . . and I saw what you did out by the airport a year ago. Now the police know. I listened to you, Ed, now you listen to me. You're ill. You've had some sort of mental breakdown, you're having delusions—'

'*I don't have to listen to your crap!*' Ed nearly screamed.

'No, you don't. You can hang up. It's your dime, after

all. But until you do, I'm going to keep hammering away. Because I liked you, Ed, and I want to like you again. You're a bright guy, delusions or no delusions, and I think you can understand me: Leydecker knows, and Leydecker is going to be watching y—'

'Are you seeing the colors yet?' Ed asked. His voice had become calm again. At the same instant, the red glow around the telephone wire popped out of existence.

'What colors?' Ralph asked at last.

Ed ignored the question. 'You said you liked me. Well, I like you, too. I've *always* liked you. So I'm going to give you some very valuable advice. You're drifting into deep water, and there are things swimming around in the undertow you can't even *conceive* of. You think I'm crazy, but I want to tell you that you don't know what madness is. You don't have the slightest idea. You will, though, if you keep on meddling in things that don't concern you. Take my word for it.'

'What things?' Ralph asked. He tried to keep his voice light, but he was still squeezing the telephone receiver tight enough to make his fingers throb.

'Forces,' Ed replied. 'There are forces at work in Derry that you don't want to know about. There are . . . well, let's just say there are *entities*. They haven't really noticed you yet, but if you keep fooling with me, they will. And you don't want that. Believe me, you don't.'

Forces. Entities.

'You asked me how I found out about all this stuff. Who brought me into the picture. Do you remember that, Ralph?'

'Yes.' He did, too. Now. That had been the last thing Ed had said to him before turning on the big game-show grin and going over to greet the cops. *I've seen the colors since* he *came and told me . . . we'll talk about it later.*

'The doctor told me. The little bald doctor. I think it's him you'll have to answer to if you try to mind my business again. And then God help you.'

'The little bald doctor, uh-huh,' Ralph said. 'Yes, I see. First the Crimson King and the Centurions, now the little bald doctor. I suppose next it'll be—'

'Spare me your sarcasm, Ralph. Just stay away from me and my interests, do you hear? *Stay away.*'

There was a click and Ed was gone. Ralph looked at the telephone in his hand for a long time, then slowly hung it up.

Just stay away from me and my interests.

Yes, and why not? He had plenty of his own fish to fry.

Ralph walked slowly into the kitchen, stuck a TV dinner (filet of haddock, as a matter of fact) into the oven, and tried to put abortion protests, auras, Ed Deepneau, and the Crimson King out of his mind.

It was easier than he would have expected.

Chapter Six

1

Summer slipped away as it does in Maine, almost unnoticed. Ralph's premature waking continued, and by the time the fall colors had begun to burn in the trees along Harris Avenue, he was opening his eyes around two-fifteen each morning. That was lousy, but he had his appointment with James Roy Hong to look forward to and there had been no repeat of the weird fireworks show he had been treated to after his first meeting with Joe Wyzer. There were occasional flickers around the edges of things, but Ralph found that if he squeezed his eyes shut and counted to five, the flickers were gone when he opened them again.

Well . . . *usually* gone.

Susan Day's speech was scheduled for Friday, the eighth of October, and as September drew toward its conclusion, the protests and the public abortion-on-demand debate sharpened and began to focus more and more on her appearance. Ralph saw Ed on the TV news many times, sometimes in the company of Dan Dalton but more and more frequently on his own, speaking swiftly, cogently, and often with that little gleam of humor not only in his eyes but in his voice.

People liked him, and The Friends of Life was apparently attracting the large membership to which Daily Bread, its political progenitor, had only been able to aspire. There were no more doll-throwing parties or other violent demonstrations, but there were plenty of marches and counter-marches, plenty of name-calling and fist-shaking and angry letters to the editor. Preachers promised damnation; teachers urged moderation and education; half a dozen young women calling themselves The

Gay Lesbo Babes for Jesus were arrested for parading in front of The First Baptist Church of Derry with signs which read GET THE FUCK OUT OF MY BODY. A nameless policeman was quoted in the Derry *News* as saying that he hoped Susan Day would come down with the flu or something and have to cancel her appearance.

Ralph received no further communications from Ed, but on September twenty-first he received a postcard from Helen with fourteen jubilant words scrawled across the back: *'Hooray, a job! Derry Public Library! I start next month! See you soon – Helen.'*

Feeling more cheered than he had since the night Helen had called him from the hospital, Ralph went downstairs to show the card to McGovern, but the door of the downstairs apartment was shut and locked.

Lois, then . . . except that Lois was also gone, probably off to one of her card-parties or maybe downtown shopping for yarn and plotting another afghan.

Mildly chagrined and musing on how the people you most wanted to share good news with were hardly ever around when you were all but bursting with it, Ralph wandered down to Strawford Park. And it was there that he found Bill McGovern, sitting on a bench near the softball field and crying.

2

Crying was perhaps too strong a word; *leaking* might have been better. McGovern sat with a handkerchief sticking out of one gnarled fist, watching a mother and her young son play roll-toss along the first-base line of the diamond where the last big softball event of the season – the Intramural City Tournament – had concluded just two days before.

Every now and then he would raise the fist with the handkerchief in it to his face and swipe at his eyes. Ralph, who had never seen McGovern weep – not even at Carolyn's funeral – loitered near the playground for a few moments, wondering if he should approach McGovern or just go back the way he had come.

At last he gathered up his courage and walked over to the park bench. ''Lo, Bill,' he said.

McGovern looked up with eyes that were red, watery, and a trifle embarrassed. He wiped them again and tried a smile. 'Hi, Ralph. You caught me snivelling. Sorry.'

'It's okay,' Ralph said, sitting down. 'I've done my share of it. What's wrong?'

McGovern shrugged, then dabbed at his eyes again. 'Nothing much. I'm suffering the effects of a paradox, that's all.'

'What paradox is that?'

'Something good is happening to one of my oldest friends – the man who hired me for my first teaching position, in fact. He's dying.'

Ralph raised his eyebrows but said nothing.

'He's got pneumonia. His niece will probably haul him off to the hospital today or tomorrow, and they'll put him on a ventilator, at least for awhile, but he's almost certainly dying. I'll celebrate his death when it comes, and I suppose it's that more than anything else that's depressing the shit out of me.' McGovern paused. 'You don't understand a thing I'm saying, do you?'

'Nope,' Ralph said. 'But that's all right.'

McGovern looked into his face, did a doubletake, then snorted. The sound was harsh and thick with his tears, but Ralph thought it was a real laugh just the same, and risked a small return smile.

'Did I say something funny?'

'No,' McGovern said, and clapped him lightly on the shoulder. 'I was just looking at your face, so earnest and sincere – you're really an open book, Ralph – and thinking how much I like you. Sometimes I wish I could *be* you.'

'Not at three in the morning, you wouldn't,' Ralph said quietly.

McGovern sighed and nodded. 'The insomnia.'

'That's right. The insomnia.'

'I'm sorry I laughed, but—'

'No apology necessary, Bill.'

'– but please believe me when I say it was an *admiring* laugh.'

'Who's your friend, and why's it a good thing that he's dying?' Ralph asked. He already had a guess as to what lay at the root of McGovern's paradox; he was not quite as goodheartedly dense as Bill sometimes seemed to think.

'His name's Bob Polhurst, and his pneumonia is good news because he's suffered from Alzheimer's since the summer of '88.'

It was what Ralph had thought . . . although AIDS had crossed his mind, as well. He wondered if that would shock

McGovern, and felt a small ripple of amusement at the idea. Then he looked at the man and felt ashamed of his amusement. He knew that when it came to gloom McGovern was at least a semi-pro, but he didn't believe that made his obvious grief over his old friend any less genuine.

'Bob was head of the History Department at Derry High from 1948, when he couldn't have been more than twenty-five, until 1981 or '82. He was a great teacher, one of those fiercely bright people you sometimes find out in the sticks, hiding their lights under bushels. They usually end up heading their departments and running half a dozen extra-curricular activities on the side because they simply don't know how to say no. Bob sure didn't.'

The mother was now leading her little boy past them and toward the little snackbar that would be closing up for the season very soon now. The kid's face had an extraordinary translucence, a beauty that was enhanced by the rose-colored aura Ralph saw revolving about his head and moving across his small, lively face in calm waves.

'Can we go home, Mommy?' he asked. 'I want to use my Play-Doh now. I want to make the Clay Family.'

'Let's get something to eat first, big boy – 'kay? Mommy's hungry.'

'Okay.'

There was a hook-shaped scar across the bridge of the boy's nose, and here the rosy glow of his aura deepened to scarlet.

Fell out of his crib when he was eight months old, Ralph thought. *Reaching for the butterflies on the mobile his mom hung from the ceiling. It scared her to death when she ran in and saw all the blood; she thought the poor kid was dying. Patrick, that's his name. She calls him Pat. He's named after his grandfather, and—*

He closed his eyes tightly for a moment. His stomach was fluttering lightly just below his Adam's apple and he was suddenly sure he was going to vomit.

'Ralph?' McGovern asked. 'Are you all right?'

He opened his eyes. No aura, rose-colored or otherwise; just a mother and son heading over to the snackbar for a cold drink, and there was no way, absolutely no way that he could tell she didn't want to take Pat home because Pat's father was drinking again after almost six months on the wagon, and when he drank he got mean—

Stop it, for God's sake stop it.

'I'm okay,' he told McGovern. 'Got a speck in my eye is all. Go on. Finish telling me about your friend.'

'Not much to tell. He was a genius, but over the years I've become convinced that genius is a vastly overrated commodity. I think this country is *full* of geniuses, guys and gals so bright they make your average card-carrying MENSA member look like Fucko the Clown. And I think that most of them are teachers, living and working in small-town obscurity because that's the way they like it. It was certainly the way Bob Polhurst liked it.

'He saw into people in a way that seemed scary to me . . . at first, anyway. After awhile you found out you didn't have to be scared, because Bob was kind, but at first he inspired a sense of dread. You sometimes wondered if it was an ordinary pair of eyes he was using to look at you, or some kind of X-ray machine.'

At the snackbar, the woman was bending down with a small paper cup of soda. The kid reached up for it with both hands, grinning, and took it. He drank thirstily. The rosy glow pulsed briefly into existence around him again as he did, and Ralph knew he had been right: the kid's name was Patrick, and his mother didn't want to take him home. There was no way he could know such things, but he did just the same.

'In those days,' McGovern said, 'if you were from central Maine and not one hundred per cent heterosexual, you tried like hell to *pass* for it. That was the only choice there was, outside of moving to Greenwich Village and wearing a beret and spending Saturday nights in the kind of jazz clubs where they used to applaud by snapping their fingers. Back then, the idea of "coming out of the closet" was ridiculous. For most of us the closet was all there was. Unless you wanted a pack of liquored-up fraternity boys sitting on you in an alley and trying to pull your face off, the *world* was your closet.'

Pat finished his drink and tossed his paper cup on the ground. His mother told him to pick it up and put it in the litter basket, a task he performed with immense good cheer. Then she took his hand and they began to walk slowly out of the park. Ralph watched them go with a feeling of trepidation, hoping the woman's fears and worries would turn out to be unjustified, fearing that they wouldn't be.

'When I applied for a job in the Derry High history department – this was in 1951 – I was fresh from two years teaching in the sticks, way to hell and gone in Lubec, and I figured if I could get along up there with no questions being asked, I could get along anywhere. But Bob took one look at me – hell, *inside* me – with those X-ray eyes of his and just knew. And he wasn't shy, either. "If I decide to offer you this job and you decide to take it, Mr McGovern, may I be assured that there will never be so much as an iota of trouble over the matter of your sexual preference?"

'*Sexual preference,* Ralph! Man, oh man! I'd never even *dreamed* of such a phrase before that day, but it came sliding out of his mouth slicker than a ball-bearing coated with Crisco. I started to get up on my high horse, tell him I didn't have the slightest idea what he was talking about but I resented the hell out of it just the same – on general principles, you might say – and then I took another look at him and decided to save my energy. I might have fooled some people up in Lubec, but I wasn't fooling Bob Polhurst. He wasn't thirty himself yet, probably hadn't been south of Kittery more than a dozen times in his whole life, but he knew everything that mattered about me, and all it had taken him to find it out was one twenty-minute interview.

'"No, sir, not an iota," I said, just as meek as Mary's little lamb.'

McGovern dabbed at his eyes with the handkerchief again, but Ralph had an idea that this time the gesture was mostly theatrical.

'In the twenty-three years before I went off to teach at Derry Community College, Bob taught me everything I know about teaching history and playing chess. He was a brilliant player . . . he certainly would have given that windbag Faye Chapin some hard bark to chew on, I can tell you that. I only beat him once, and that was after the Alzheimer's started to take hold. I never played him again after that.

'And there were other things. He never forgot a joke. He never forgot the birthdays or anniversaries of the people who were close to him – he didn't send cards or give gifts, but he always offered congratulations and good wishes, and no one ever doubted his sincerity. He published over sixty articles on teaching history and on the Civil War, which was his specialty. In 1967 and 1968 he wrote a book called *Later That Summer,* about what happened in the months following Gettysburg. He let me read the manuscript ten years ago, and I think it's the best book on the Civil War I've ever read – the only one that even comes close is a novel called *The Killer Angels,* by Michael

Shaara. Bob wouldn't hear of publishing it, though. When I asked him why, he said that I of all people should understand his reasons.'

McGovern paused briefly, looking out across the park, which was filled with green-gold light and black interlacings of shadow which moved and shifted with each breath of wind.

'He said he had a fear of exposure.'

'Okay,' Ralph said. 'I get it.'

'Maybe this sums him up best of all: he used to do the big *Sunday New York Times* crossword puzzle in ink. I poked him about that once – accused him of *hubris*. He gave me a grin and said, "There's a big difference between pride and optimism, Bill – I'm an optimist, that's all."

'Anyway, you get the picture. A kind man, a good teacher, a brilliant mind. His specialty was the Civil War, and now he doesn't even know what a civil war is, let alone who won ours. Hell, he doesn't even know his own name, and at some point soon – the sooner the better, actually – he's going to die without any idea that he ever lived.'

A middle-aged man in a University of Maine tee-shirt and a pair of ragged blue jeans came shuffling through the playground, carrying a crumpled paper shopping bag under one arm. He stopped beside the snackbar to examine the contents of the waste-barrel, hoping for a returnable or two. As he bent over, Ralph saw the dark green envelope which surrounded him and the lighter green balloon-string which rose, wavering, from the crown of his head. And suddenly he was too tired to close his eyes, too tired to wish it away.

He turned to McGovern and said, 'Ever since last month I've been seeing stuff that—'

'I guess I'm in mourning,' McGovern said, giving his eyes another theatrical wipe, 'although I don't know if it's for Bob or for me. Isn't that a hoot? But if you could have seen how bright he was in those days . . . how goddam scary-bright . . .'

'Bill? You see that guy over there by the snackbar? The one rooting through the trash barrel? I see—'

'Yeah, those guys are all over the place now,' McGovern said, giving the wino (who had found two empty Budweiser cans and tucked them into his bag) a cursory glance before turning to Ralph again. 'I hate being old – I guess maybe that's all it really comes down to. I mean big-time.'

The wino approached their bench in a bent-kneed shuffle, the breeze heralding his arrival with a smell which was not English

Leather. His aura – a sprightly and energetic green that made Ralph think of Saint Patrick's Day decorations – went oddly with his subservient posture and sickly grin.

'Say, you guys! How you doon?'

'We've been better,' McGovern said, hoisting the satiric eyebrow, 'and I expect we'll be better again once you shove off.'

The wino looked at McGovern uncertainly, seemed to decide he was a lost cause, and shifted his gaze to Ralph. 'You got a bitta spare change, mister? I gotta get to Dexter. My uncle call me out dere at the Shelter on Neibolt Street, say I can have my old job back at the mill, but only if I—'

'Get lost, chum,' McGovern said.

The wino gave him a brief, anxious glance, and then his bloodshot brown eyes rolled back to Ralph again. 'Dass a good job, you know? I could have it back, but on'y if I get dere today. Dere's a bus—'

Ralph reached into his pocket, found a quarter and a dime, and dropped them into the outstretched hand. The wino grinned. The aura surrounding him brightened, then suddenly disappeared. Ralph found that a great relief.

'Hey, great! Thank you, mister!'

'Don't mention it,' Ralph said.

The wino lurched off in the direction of the Shop 'n Save, where such brands as Night Train, Old Duke, and Silver Satin were always on sale.

Oh shit, Ralph, would it hurt you to be a little charitable in your head, as well? he asked himself. *Go another half a mile in that direction, you come to the bus station.*

True, but Ralph had lived long enough to know there was a world of difference between charitable thinking and illusions. If the wino with the dark green aura was going to the bus station, then Ralph was going to Washington to be Secretary of State.

'You shouldn't do that, Ralph,' McGovern said reprovingly. 'It just encourages them.'

'I suppose,' Ralph said wearily.

'What were you saying when we were so rudely interrupted?'

The idea of telling McGovern about the auras now seemed an incredibly bad one, and he could not for the life of him imagine how he had gotten so close to doing it. The insomnia, of course – that was the only answer. It had done a number on his judgement as well as his short-term memory and sense of perception.

'That I got something in the mail this morning,' Ralph said. 'I thought it might cheer you up.' He passed Helen's postcard over to McGovern, who read it and then reread it. The second time through, his long, horsey face broke into a broad grin. The combination of relief and honest pleasure in that expression made Ralph forgive McGovern his self-indulgent bathos at once. It was easy to forget that Bill could be generous as well as pompous.

'Say, this is great, isn't it? A job!'

'It sure is. Want to celebrate with some lunch? There's a nice little diner two doors down from the Rite Aid – Day Break, Sun Down, it's called. Maybe a little ferny, but—'

'Thanks, but I promised Bob's niece I'd go over and sit with him awhile. Of course he's doesn't have the slightest idea of who I am, but that doesn't matter, because *I* know who *he* is. You *capisce*?'

'Yep,' Ralph said. 'A raincheck, then?'

'You got it.' McGovern scanned the message on the post-card again, still grinning. 'This is the berries – the absolute berries!'

Ralph laughed at this winsome old expression. 'I thought so, too.'

'I would have bet you five bucks she was going to walk right back into her marriage to that weirdo, and pushing the baby in front of her in its damn stroller . . . but I would have been glad to lose the money. I suppose that sounds crazy.'

'A little,' Ralph said, but only because he knew it was what McGovern expected to hear. What he really thought was that Bill McGovern had just summed up his own character and world-view more succinctly than Ralph ever could have done himself.

'Nice to know someone's getting better instead of worse, huh?'

'You bet.'

'Has Lois seen that yet?'

Ralph shook his head. 'She's not home. I'll show it to her when I see her, though.'

'You do that. Are you sleeping any better, Ralph?'

'I'm doing okay, I guess.'

'Good. You look a little better. A little stronger. We can't give in, Ralph, that's the important thing. Am I right?'

'I guess you are,' Ralph said, and sighed. 'I guess you are, at that.'

3

Two days later Ralph sat at his kitchen table, slowly eating a bowl of bran flakes he didn't really want (but supposed in some vague way to be good for him) and looking at the front page of the Derry *News*. He had skimmed the lead story quickly, but it was the photo that kept drawing his eye back; it seemed to express all the bad feelings he had been living with over the last month without really explaining any of them.

Ralph thought the headline over the photograph – WOMAN-CARE DEMONSTRATION SPARKS VIOLENCE – didn't reflect the story which followed, but that didn't surprise him; he had been reading the *News* for years and had gotten used to its biases, which included a firm anti-abortion stance. Still, the paper had been careful to distance itself from The Friends of Life in that day's tut-tut, now-you-boys-just-stop-it editorial, and Ralph wasn't surprised. The Friends had gathered in the parking lot adjacent to both WomanCare and Derry Home Hospital, waiting for a group of about two hundred pro-choice marchers who were walking across town from the Civic Center. Most of the marchers were carrying signs with pictures of Susan Day and the slogan CHOICE, NOT FEAR on them.

The marchers' idea was to gather supporters as they went, like a snowball rolling downhill. At WomanCare there would be a short rally – intended to pump people up for the coming Susan Day speech – followed by refreshments. The rally never happened. As the pro-choice marchers approached the parking lot, the Friends of Life people rushed out and blocked the road, holding their own signs (MURDER IS MURDER, SUSAN DAY STAY AWAY, STOP THE SLAUGHTER OF THE INNOCENTS) in front of them like shields.

The marchers had been escorted by police, but no one had been prepared for the speed with which the heckling and angry words escalated into kicks and punches. It had begun with one of The Friends of Life recognizing her own daughter among the pro-choice people. The older woman had dropped her sign and charged the younger. The daughter's boyfriend had caught the older woman and tried to restrain her. When Mom opened his face with her finger-nails, the young man had thrown her to the ground. That had ignited a ten-minute mêlée and provoked more than thirty arrests, split roughly half and half between the two groups.

The picture on the front page of this morning's *News* featured Hamilton Davenport and Dan Dalton. The photographer had caught Davenport in a snarl which was entirely unlike his usual look of calm self-satisfaction. One fist was raised over his head in a primitive gesture of triumph. Facing him – and wearing Ham's CHOICE, NOT FEAR sign around the top of his head like a surreal cardboard halo – was The Friends of Life's *grand fromage*. Dalton's eyes were dazed, his mouth slack. The high-contrast black and white photo made the blood flowing from his nostrils look like chocolate sauce.

Ralph would look away from this for awhile, try to concentrate on finishing his cereal, and then he would remember the day last summer when he had first seen one of the pseudo 'wanted' posters that were now pasted up all over Derry – the day he had nearly fainted outside Strawford Park. Mostly it was their faces his mind fixed on: Davenport's full of angry intensity as he peered into the dusty show window of Secondhand Rose, Secondhand Clothes, Dalton's wearing a small, disdainful smile that seemed to suggest that an ape like Hamilton Davenport could not be expected to understand the higher morality of the abortion issue, and they both knew it.

Ralph would think of those two expressions and the distance between the men who wore them, and after awhile his dismayed eyes would wander back to the news photo. Two men stood close behind Dalton, both carrying pro-life signs and watching the confrontation intently. Ralph didn't recognize the skinny man with the hornrimmed glasses and the cloud of receding gray hair, but he knew the man beside him. It was Ed Deepneau. Yet in this context, Ed seemed almost not to matter. What drew Ralph – and frightened him – were the faces of the two men who had done business next door to each other on Lower Witcham Street for years – Davenport with his caveman's snarl and clenched fist, Dalton with his dazed eyes and bloody nose.

He thought, *If you're not careful with your passions, this is where they get you. But this is where things had better stop, because—*

'Because if those two had had guns, they'd've shot each other,' he muttered, and at that moment the doorbell rang – the one down on the front porch. Ralph got up, looked at the picture again, and felt a kind of vertigo sweep through him.

With it came an odd, dismal surety: it was Ed down there, and God knew what he might want.

Don't answer it then, Ralph!

He stood by the kitchen table for a long undecided moment, wishing bitterly that he could cut through the fog that seemed to have taken up permanent residence in his head this year. Then the doorbell chimed again and he found he *had* decided. It didn't matter if that was Saddam Hussein down there; this was *his* place, and he wasn't going to cower in it like a whipped cur.

Ralph crossed the living room, opened the door to the hall, and went down the shadowy front stairs.

4

Halfway down he relaxed a little. The top half of the door which gave on the front porch was composed of heavy glass panes. They distorted the view, but not so much that Ralph could not see that his two visitors were both women. He guessed at once who one of them must be and hurried the rest of the way down, running one hand lightly over the banister. He threw the door open and there was Helen Deepneau with a tote-bag (BABY FIRST-AID STATION was printed on the side) slung over one shoulder and Natalie peering over the other, her eyes as bright as the eyes of a cartoon mouse. Helen was smiling hopefully and a little nervously.

Natalie's face suddenly lit up and she began to bounce up and down in the Papoose carrier Helen was wearing, waving her arms excitedly in Ralph's direction.

She remembers me, Ralph thought. *How about that.* And as he reached out and let one of the waving hands grasp his right index finger, his eyes flooded with tears.

'Ralph?' Helen asked. 'Are you okay?'

He smiled, nodded, stepped forward, and hugged her. He felt Helen lock her own arms around his neck. For a moment he was dizzy with the smell of her perfume, mingled with the milky smell of healthy baby, and then she gave his ear a dazzling smack and let him go.

'You *are* okay, aren't you?' she asked. There were tears in her eyes, too, but Ralph barely noticed them; he was too busy taking inventory, wanting to make sure that no signs of the beating remained. So far as he could see, none did. She looked flawless.

'Better right now than in weeks,' he said. 'You are *such* a sight for sore eyes. You too, Nat.' He kissed the small, chubby hand that was still wrapped around his finger, and was not entirely surprised to see the ghostly gray-blue lip-print his mouth left behind. It faded almost as soon as he had noted it and he hugged Helen again, mostly to make sure that she was really there.

'Dear Ralph,' she murmured in his ear. 'Dear, sweet Ralph.'

He felt a stirring in his groin, apparently brought on by the combination of her light perfume and the gentle puffs her words made against the cup of his ear . . . and then he remembered another voice in his ear. Ed's voice. *I called about your mouth, Ralph. It's trying to get you in trouble.*

Ralph let her go and held her at arm's length, still smiling. 'You're a sight for sore eyes, Helen. I'll be damned if you're not.'

'You are, too. I'd like you to meet a friend of mine. Ralph Roberts, Gretchen Tillbury. Gretchen, Ralph.'

Ralph turned toward the other woman and took his first good look at her as he carefully folded his large, gnarled hand over her slim white one. She was the kind of woman that made a man (even one who had left his sixties behind) want to stand up straight and suck in his gut. She was very tall, perhaps six feet, and she was blonde, but that wasn't it. There was something else – something that was like a smell, or a vibration, or

(*an aura*)

yes, all right, like an aura. She was, quite simply, a woman you couldn't not look at, couldn't not think about, couldn't not speculate about.

Ralph remembered Helen's telling him that Gretchen's husband had cut her leg open with a kitchen knife and left her to bleed to death. He wondered how any man could do such a thing; how any man could touch a creature such as this with anything but awe.

Also a little lust, maybe, once he got beyond the 'She walks in beauty like the night' stage. And just by the way, Ralph, this might be a really good time to reel your eyes back into their sockets.

'Very pleased to meet you,' he said, letting go of her hand. 'Helen told me about how you came to see her in the hospital. Thank you for helping her.'

'Helen was a pleasure to help,' Gretchen said, and gave him a dazzling smile. 'She's the kind of woman that makes it all worthwhile, actually . . . but I have an idea you already know that.'

'I guess I might at that,' Ralph said. 'Have you got time for a cup of coffee? Please say yes.'

Gretchen glanced at Helen, who nodded.

'That would be fine,' Helen said. 'Because . . . well . . .'

'This isn't entirely a social call, is it?' Ralph asked, looking from Helen to Gretchen Tillbury and then back to Helen again.

'No,' Helen said. 'There's something we need to talk to you about, Ralph.'

5

As soon as they had reached the top of the gloomy front stairs, Natalie began to wriggle impatiently around in the Papoose carrier and to talk in that imperious baby pig Latin that would all too soon be replaced by actual words.

'Can I hold her?' Ralph asked.

'All right,' Helen said. 'If she cries, I'll take her right back. Promise.'

'Deal.'

But the Exalted & Revered Baby didn't cry. As soon as Ralph had hoisted her out of the Papoose, she slung an arm companionably around his neck and cozied her bottom into the crook of his right arm as if it were her own private easy-chair.

'Wow,' Gretchen said. 'I'm impressed.'

'Blig!' Natalie said, seizing Ralph's lower lip and pulling it out like a windowshade. 'Ganna-wig! Andoo-sis!'

'I think she just said something about the Andrews Sisters,' Ralph said. Helen threw her head back and laughed her hearty laugh, the one that seemed to come all the way up from her heels. Ralph didn't realize how much he had missed it until he heard it.

Natalie let Ralph's lower lip snap back as he led them into the kitchen, the sunniest room of the house at this time of day. He saw Helen looking around curiously as he turned on the Bunn, and realized she hadn't been here for a long time. Too long. She picked up the picture of Carolyn that stood on the kitchen table and looked at it closely, a little smile playing about the corners of her lips. The sun lit the tips of her hair, which had been cropped short, making a kind of corona around her head,

154

and Ralph had a sudden revelation: he loved Helen in large part because Carolyn had loved her – they had both been allowed into the deeper ranges of Carolyn's heart and mind.

'She was so pretty,' Helen murmured. 'Wasn't she, Ralph?'

'Yes,' he said, putting out cups (and being careful to set them beyond the reach of Natalie's restless, interested hands). 'That was taken just a month or two before the headaches started. I suppose it's eccentric to keep a framed studio portrait on the kitchen table in front of the sugar-bowl, but this is the room where I seem to spend most of my time lately, so . . .'

'I think it's a lovely place for it,' Gretchen said. Her voice was low, sweetly husky. Ralph thought, *If she'd been the one to whisper in my ear, I bet the old trouser-mouse would have done a little more than just turn over in its sleep.*

'I do, too,' Helen said. She gave him a fragile, not-quite-eye-contact smile, then slipped the pink tote-bag off her shoulder and set it on the counter. Natalie began to gabble impatiently and hold her hands out again as soon as she saw the plastic shell of the Playtex Nurser. Ralph had a vivid but mercifully brief flash of memory: Helen staggering toward the Red Apple, one eye puffed shut, her cheek lashed with beads of blood, carrying Nat on one hip, the way a teenager might carry a textbook.

'Want to give it a try, old fella?' Helen asked. Her smile had strengthened a little and she was meeting his eye again.

'Sure, why not? But the coffee—'

'I'll take care of the coffee, Daddy-O,' Gretchen said. 'Made a million cups in my time. Is there half-and-half?'

'In the fridge.' Ralph sat down at the table, letting Natalie rest the back of her head in the hollow of his shoulder and grasp the bottle with her tiny, fascinating hands. This she did with complete assurance, guiding the nipple into her mouth and beginning to suck at once. Ralph grinned up at Helen and pretended not to see that she had begun to cry a little again. 'They learn fast, don't they?'

'Yes,' she said, and pulled a paper towel off the roll mounted on the wall by the sink. She wiped her eyes with it. 'I can't get over how easy she is with you, Ralph – she wasn't that way before, was she?'

'I don't really remember,' he lied. She hadn't been. Not standoffish, no, but a long way from this comfortable.

'Keep pushing up on the plastic liner inside the bottle, okay? Otherwise she'll swallow a lot of air and get all gassy.'

'Roger.' He glanced over at Gretchen. 'Doing okay?'

'Fine. How do you take it, Ralph?'

'Just in a cup's fine.'

She laughed and put the cup on the table out of Natalie's reach. When she sat down and crossed her legs, Ralph checked – he was helpless not to. When he looked up again, Gretchen was wearing a small, ironic smile.

What the hell, Ralph thought. *No goat like an old goat, I guess. Even an old goat that can't manage much more than two or two and a half hours' worth of sleep a night.*

'Tell me about your job,' he said as Helen sat down and sipped her coffee.

'Well, I think they ought to make Mike Hanlon's birthday a national holiday – does that tell you anything?'

'A little, yes,' Ralph said, smiling.

'I was all but positive I'd have to leave Derry. I sent away for applications to libraries as far south as Portsmouth, but I felt sick doing it. I'm going on thirty-one and I've only lived here for six of those years, but Derry feels like home – I can't explain it, but it's the truth.'

'You don't have to explain it, Helen. I think home's just one of those things that happens to a person, like their complexion or the color of their eyes.'

Gretchen was nodding. 'Yes,' she said. 'Just like that.'

'Mike called Monday and told me the assistant's position in the Children's Library had opened up. I could hardly believe it. I mean, I've been walking around all week just pinching myself. Haven't I, Gretchen?'

'Well, you've been very happy,' Gretchen said, 'and that's been very good to see.'

She smiled at Helen, and for Ralph that smile was a revelation. He suddenly understood that he could look at Gretchen Tillbury all he wanted, and it wouldn't make any difference. If the only man in this room had been Tom Cruise, it still would have made no difference. He wondered if Helen knew, and then scolded himself for his foolishness. Helen was many things, but stupid wasn't one of them.

'When do you start?' he asked her.

'Columbus Day week,' she said. 'The twelfth. Afternoons and evenings. The salary's not exactly a king's ransom, but it'll be enough to keep us through the winter no matter how the . . . the rest of my situation works out. Isn't it great, Ralph?'

'Yes,' he said. 'Very great.'

The baby had drunk half the bottle and now showed signs of

losing interest. The nipple popped halfway out of her mouth, and a little rill of milk ran down from the corner of her lips toward her chin. Ralph reached to wipe it away, and his fingers left a series of delicate gray-blue lines in the air.

Baby Natalie snatched at them, then laughed as they dissolved in her fist. Ralph's breath caught in his throat.

She sees. The baby sees what I see.

That's nuts, Ralph. That's nuts and you know it.

Except he knew no such thing. He had just *seen* it – had seen Nat try to grab the aural contrails his fingers left behind.

'Ralph?' Helen asked. 'Are you all right?'

'Sure.' He looked up and saw that Helen was now surrounded by a luxurious ivory-colored aura. It had the satiny look of an expensive slip. The balloon-string floating up from it was an identical shade of ivory, and as broad and flat as the ribbon on a wedding present. The aura surrounding Gretchen Tillbury was a dark orange shading to yellow at the edges. 'Will you be moving back into the house?'

Helen and Gretchen exchanged another of those glances, but Ralph barely noticed. He didn't need to observe their faces or gestures or body language to read their feelings, he discovered; he only had to look at their auras. The lemony tints at the edges of Gretchen's now darkened, so that the whole was a uniform orange. Helen's, meanwhile, simultaneously pulled in and brightened until it was hard to look at. Helen was afraid to go back. Gretchen knew it, and was infuriated by it.

And her own helplessness, Ralph thought. *That infuriates her even more.*

'I'm going to stay at High Ridge awhile longer,' Helen was saying. 'Maybe until winter. Nat and I will move back into town eventually, I imagine, but the house is going up for sale. If someone actually buys it – and with the real estate market the way it is that looks like a pretty big question mark – the money goes into an escrow account. That account will be divided according to the decree. You know – the divorce decree.'

Her lower lip was trembling. Her aura had grown still tighter; it now fit her body almost like a second skin, and Ralph could see minute red flashes skimming through it. They looked like sparks dancing over an incinerator. He reached out across the table, took her hand, squeezed it. She smiled at him gratefully.

'You're telling me two things,' he said. 'That you're going ahead with the divorce and that you're still scared of him.'

'She's been regularly battered and abused for the last two years of her marriage,' Gretchen said. 'Of *course* she's still scared of him.' She spoke quietly, calmly, reasonably, but looking at her aura now was like looking through the small isinglass window you used to find in the doors of coal-furnaces.

He looked down at the baby and saw her now surrounded in her own gauzy, brilliant cloud of wedding-satin. It was smaller than her mother's, but otherwise identical . . . like her blue eyes and auburn hair. Natalie's balloon-string rose from the top of her head in a pure white ribbon that floated all the way to the ceiling and then actually coiled there in an ethereal heap beside the light-fixture. When a breath of breeze puffed in through the open window by the stove, he saw the wide white band bell and ripple. He glanced up and saw Helen's and Gretchen's balloon-strings were also rippling.

And if I could see my own, it would be doing the same thing, he thought. *It's real – whatever that two-and-two-make-four part of my mind may think, the auras are real. They're real and I'm seeing them.*

He waited for the inevitable demurral, but this time none came.

'I feel like I'm spending most of my time in an emotional washing-machine these days,' Helen said. 'My mom's mad at me . . . she's done everything but call me a quitter outright . . . and sometimes I *feel* like a quitter . . . ashamed . . .'

'You have nothing to be ashamed of,' Ralph said. He glanced up at Natalie's balloon-string again, wavering in the breeze. It was beautiful, but he felt no urge to touch it; some deep instinct told him that might be dangerous for both of them.

'I guess I know that,' Helen said, 'but girls go through a lot of indoctrination. It's like, "Here's your Barbie, here's your Ken, here's your Hostess Play Kitchen. Learn well, because when the real stuff comes along it'll be your job to take care of it, and if any of it gets broken, you'll get the blame." And I think I could have gone down the line with that – I really do. Except no one told me that in some marriages Ken goes nuts. Does that sound self-indulgent?'

'No. That's pretty much what happened, so far as I can see.'

Helen laughed – a jagged, bitter, guilty sound. 'Don't try to tell my mother that. She refuses to believe Ed ever did anything more than give me a husbandly swat on the fanny once in awhile . . . just to get me moving in the right direction

158

again if I happened to slip off-course. She thinks I imagined the rest. She doesn't come right out and say it, but I hear it in her voice every time we talk on the phone.'

'*I* don't think you imagined it,' Ralph said. 'I saw you, remember? And I was there when you begged me not to call the police.'

He felt his thigh squeezed beneath the table and looked up, startled. Gretchen Tillbury gave him a very slight nod and another squeeze – this one more emphatic.

'Yes,' Helen said. 'You *were* there, weren't you?' She smiled a little, which was good, but what was happening to her aura was better – those tiny red flickers were fading, and the aura itself was spreading out again.

No, he thought. *Not spreading out. Loosening. Relaxing.*

Helen got up and came around the table. 'Nat's bailing out on you – better let me take her.'

Ralph looked down and saw Nat looking across the room with heavy, fascinated eyes. He followed her gaze and saw the little vase standing on the windowsill beside the sink. He had filled it with fall flowers less than two hours ago and now a low green mist was sizzling off the stems and surrounding the blooms with a faint, misty glow.

I'm watching them breathe their last, Ralph thought. *Oh my God, I'm never going to pick another flower in my life. I promise.*

Helen took the baby gently from his arms. Nat went tractably enough, although her eyes never left the sizzling flowers as her mother went back around the table, sat down, and nestled her in the crook of her arm.

Gretchen tapped the face of her watch lightly. 'If we're going to make that meeting at noon—'

'Yes, of course,' Helen said, a little apologetically. 'We're on the official Susan Day Welcoming Committee,' she told Ralph, 'and in this case that's not quite as Junior League as it sounds. Our main job really isn't to welcome her but to help protect her.'

'Is that going to be a problem, do you think?'

'It'll be tense, let's put it that way,' Gretchen said. 'She's got half a dozen of her own security people, and they've been sending us turn-around faxes of all the Derry-related threats she's received. It's standard operating procedure with them – she's been in a lot of people's faces for a lot of years. They're keeping us in the picture, but they're also making sure we understand that, because we're the inviting group, her safety is WomanCare's responsibility as well as theirs.'

Ralph opened his mouth to ask if there had been many threats, but he supposed he already knew the answer to that question. He'd lived in Derry for seventy years, off and on, and he knew it was a dangerous machine – there were a lot of sharp points and cutting edges just below the surface. That was true of a lot of cities, of course, but in Derry there had always seemed to be an extra dimension to the ugliness. Helen had called it home, and it was his home, too, but—

He found himself remembering something which had happened almost ten years ago, shortly after the annual Canal Days Festival had ended. Three boys had thrown an unassuming and inoffensive young gay man named Adrian Mellon into the Kenduskeag after repeatedly biting and stabbing him; it was rumored they had stood there on the bridge behind the Falcon Tavern and watched him die. They'd told the police they hadn't liked the hat he was wearing. That was also Derry, and only a fool would ignore the fact.

As if this memory had led him to it (perhaps it had), Ralph looked at the photo on the front page of today's paper again – Ham Davenport with his upraised fist, Dan Dalton with his bloody nose and dazed eyes, wearing Ham's sign on his head.

'How many threats?' he asked. 'Over a dozen?'

'About thirty,' Gretchen said. 'Of those, her security people take half a dozen seriously. Two are threats to blow up the Civic Center if she doesn't cancel. One – this is a real honey – is from someone who says he's got a Big Squirt water-gun filled with battery acid. "If I make a direct hit, not even your dyke friends will be able to look at you without throwing up," that one says.'

'Nice,' Ralph said.

'It brings us to the point, anyway,' Gretchen said. She rummaged in her bag, brought out a small can with a red top, and put it on the table. 'A little present from all your grateful friends at WomanCare.'

Ralph picked the can up. On one side was a picture of a woman spraying a cloud of gas at a man wearing a slouch hat and a Beagle Boys-type eye-mask. On the other was a single word in bright red capital letters:

BODYGUARD

'What is this?' he asked, shocked in spite of himself. 'Mace?'

'No,' Gretchen said. 'Mace is a risky proposition in Maine, legally speaking. This stuff is much milder . . . but if you give somebody a faceful, they won't even think of hassling you for at least a couple of minutes. It numbs the skin, irritates the eyes, and causes nausea.'

Ralph took the cap off the can, looked at the red aerosol nozzle beneath, then replaced the cap. 'Good Christ, woman, why would I want to lug around a can of this stuff?'

'Because you've been officially designated a Centurion,' Gretchen said.

'A *what*?' Ralph asked.

'A Centurion,' Helen repeated. Nat was fast asleep in her arms, and Ralph realized the auras were gone again. 'It's what The Friends of Life call their major enemies – the ringleaders of the opposition.'

'Okay,' Ralph said, 'I've got it now. Ed talked about people he called Centurions on the day he . . . assaulted you. He talked about a lot of things that day, though, and all of them were crazy.'

'Yes, Ed's at the bottom of it, and he *is* crazy,' Helen said. 'We don't think he's mentioned this Centurion business except to a small inner circle – people who are almost as gonzo as he is. The rest of The Friends of Life . . . I don't think they have any idea. I mean, did you? Until last month, did *you* have any idea that he was crazy?'

Ralph shook his head.

'Hawking Labs finally fired him,' Helen said. 'Yesterday. They held onto him as long as they could – he's great at what he does, and they had a lot invested in him – but in the end they had to let him go. Three months' severance pay in lieu of notice . . . not bad for a guy who beats up his wife and throws dolls loaded with fake blood at the windows of the local women's clinic.' She tapped the newspaper. 'This last demonstration was the final straw. It's the third or fourth time he's been arrested since he got involved with The Friends of Life.'

'You have someone inside, don't you?' Ralph said. 'That's how you know all this.'

Gretchen smiled. 'We're not the only ones who've got someone at least partway inside; we have a running joke that there really *are* no Friends of Life, just a bunch of double agents. Derry PD's got someone; the State Police do, too. And those are just the ones our . . . our *person* . . . knows about. Hell, the FBI could be monitoring them, as well. The Friends of Life are eminently infiltratable, Ralph, because they're convinced that, deep down, *everyone* is on their side. But we believe that our person is the only one who's gotten in toward the middle, and this person says that Dan Dalton is just the tail Ed Deepneau wags.'

'I guessed that the first time I saw them together on the TV news,' Ralph said.

Gretchen got up, gathered the coffee cups, took them over to the sink, and began to rinse them. 'I've been active in the women's movement for thirteen years now, and I've seen a lot of crazy shit, but I've never seen anything like this. He's got these dopes believing that women in Derry are undergoing involuntary abortions, that half of them haven't even realized they're pregnant before the Centurions come in the night and take their babies.'

'Has he told them about the incinerator over in Newport?' Ralph asked. 'The one that's really a baby crematorium?'

Gretchen turned from the sink, her eyes wide. 'How did *you* know about that?'

'Oh, I got the lowdown from Ed himself, up close and in person. Starting in July of '92.' He hesitated for just a moment, then gave them an account of the day he had met Ed out by the airport, and how Ed had accused the man in the pickup of hauling dead babies in the barrels marked WEED-GO. Helen listened silently, her eyes growing steadily wider and rounder. 'He was going on about the same stuff on the day he beat you up,' Ralph finished, 'but he'd embellished it considerably by then.'

'That probably explains why he's fixated on you,' Gretchen said, 'but in a very real sense, the why doesn't matter. The fact is, he's given his nuttier friends a list of these so-called Centurions. We don't know everyone who's on it, but I am, and Helen is, and Susan Day, of course . . . and you.'

Why me? Ralph almost asked, then recognized it as another pointless question. Maybe Ed had targeted him because he had called the cops after Ed had beaten Helen; more likely it had happened for no understandable reason at all. Ralph remembered reading somewhere that David Berkowitz – also known as the Son of Sam – claimed to have killed on some occasions under instructions from his dog.

'What do you expect them to try?' Ralph asked. 'Armed assault, like in a Chuck Norris movie?'

He smiled, but Gretchen did not answer it. 'The thing is, we don't know *what* they might try,' she said. 'The most likely answer is nothing at all. Then again, Ed or one of the others might take it into his head to try and push you out your own kitchen window. The spray is basically nothing but watered-down teargas. A little insurance policy, that's all.'

'Insurance,' he said thoughtfully.

'You're in very select company,' Helen said with a wan smile. 'The only other male Centurion on their list – that we know about, anyway – is Mayor Cohen.'

'Did you give him one of these?' Ralph asked, picking up the aerosol can. It looked no more dangerous than the free samples of shaving cream he got in the mail from time to time.

'We didn't need to,' Gretchen said. She looked at her watch again. Helen saw the gesture and stood up with the sleeping baby in her arms. 'He's got a license to carry a concealed weapon.'

'How would you know a thing like that?' Ralph asked.

'We checked the files at City Hall,' she said, and grinned. 'Gun permits are a matter of public record.'

'Oh.' A thought occurred to him. 'What about Ed? Did you check on him? Does he have one?'

'Nope,' she said. 'But guys like Ed don't necessarily apply for weapons permits once they get past a certain point . . . you know that, don't you?'

'Yes,' Ralph replied, also getting up. 'I suppose I do. What about you guys? Are you watching out?'

'You bet, Daddy-O. You bet we are.'

He nodded, but wasn't entirely satisfied. There was a faintly patronizing tone in her voice that he didn't like, as if the very question were a silly one. But it *wasn't* silly, and if she didn't know that, she and her friends could be in trouble down the line. Bad trouble.

'I hope so,' he said. 'I really do. Can I carry Nat downstairs for you, Helen?'

'Better not – you'd wake her.' She looked at him gravely. 'Would you carry that spray for me, Ralph? I can't stand the thought of you being hurt just because you tried to help me and he's got some crazy bee in his bonnet.'

'I'll think about it very seriously. Will that do?'

'I guess it will have to.' She looked at him closely, her eyes searching his face. 'You look much better than the last time I saw you – you're sleeping again, aren't you?'

He grinned. 'Well, to tell you the truth, I'm still having my problems, but I *must* be getting better, because people keep telling me that.'

She stood on tiptoe and kissed the corner of his mouth. 'We'll be in touch, won't we? I mean, we'll *stay* in touch.'

'I'll do my part if you'll do yours, sweetie.'

She smiled. 'You can count on that, Ralph – you're the nicest male Centurion I know.'

They all laughed at that, so hard that Natalie woke up and looked around at them in sleepy surprise.

6

After he had seen the women off (I'M PRO-CHOICE, AND I *VOTE!* read the sticker on the rear bumper of Gretchen Tillbury's Accord fastback), Ralph climbed slowly up to the second floor again. Weariness dragged at his heels like invisible weights. Once in the kitchen he looked first at the vase of flowers, trying to see that strange and gorgeous green mist rising from the stems. Nothing. Then he picked up the aerosol and re-examined the cartoon on the side of the can. One Menaced Woman, heroically warding off her attacker; one Bad Man, complete with eye-mask and slouch hat. No shades of gray here; just a case of go ahead, punk, make my day.

It occurred to Ralph that Ed's madness was catching. There were women all over Derry – Gretchen Tillbury and his own sweet Helen among them – walking around with these little spray-cans in their purses, and all the cans really said the same thing: *I'm afraid. The bad men in the masks and the slouch hats have arrived in Derry and I'm afraid.*

Ralph wanted no part of it. Standing on tiptoe, he put the can of Bodyguard on top of the kitchen cabinet beside the sink, then shrugged into his old gray leather jacket. He would go up to the picnic area near the airport and see if he could find a game of chess. Lacking that, maybe a few rounds of cribbage.

He paused in the kitchen doorway, looking fixedly at the flowers, trying to *make* that sizzling green mist come. Nothing happened.

But it was there. You saw it; Natalie did, too.

But had she? Had she really? Babies were always goggling at stuff, *everything* amazed them, so how could he know for sure?

'I just do,' he said to the empty apartment. Correct. The green mist rising from the stems of the flowers had been there, *all* the auras had been there, and . . .

'And they're *still* there,' he said, and did not know if he should be relieved or appalled by the firmness he heard in his own voice.

For right now, why don't you try being neither, sweetheart?

His thought, Carolyn's voice, good advice.

Ralph locked up his apartment and went out into the Derry of the Old Crocks, looking for a game of chess.

Chapter Seven

1

When Ralph came walking up Harris Avenue to his apartment on October 2nd, with a couple of recycled Elmer Kelton Westerns from Back Pages in one hand, he saw that someone was sitting on the porch steps with his own book. The visitor wasn't reading, however; he was watching with dreamy intensity as the warm wind which had been blowing all day harvested the yellow and gold leaves from the oaks and the three surviving elms across the street.

Ralph came closer, observing the thin white hair flying around the skull of the man on the porch, and the way all his bulk seemed to have run into his belly, hips, and bottom. That wide center section, coupled with the scrawny neck, narrow chest, and spindly legs clad in old green flannel pants, gave him the look of a man wearing an inner tube beneath his clothes. Even from a hundred and fifty yards away, there was really no question about who the visitor was: Dorrance Marstellar.

Sighing, Ralph walked the rest of the way up to his building. Dorrance, seemingly hypnotized by the bright falling leaves, did not look around until Ralph's shadow dropped across him. Then he turned, craned his neck, and smiled his sweet, strangely vulnerable smile.

Faye Chapin, Don Veazie, and some of the other old-timers who hung out at the picnic area up by Runway 3 (they would retire to the Jackson Street Billiard Emporium once Indian summer broke and the weather turned cold) saw that smile as just another indicator that Old Dor, poetry books or no poetry books, was essentially brainless. Don Veazie, nobody's idea of Mr Sensitivity, had fallen into the habit of calling Dorrance

167

Old Chief Dumbhead, and Faye had once told Ralph that he, Faye, wasn't in the least surprised that Old Dor had lived to the age of half-past ninety. 'People who don't have any furniture on their upper storey *always* live the longest,' he had explained to Ralph earlier that year. 'They don't have anything to worry about. That keeps their blood-pressure down and they ain't so likely to blow a valve or throw a rod.'

Ralph, however, was not so sure. The sweetness in Dorrance's smile did not make the old man look empty-headed to him; it made him look somehow ethereal and knowing at the same time . . . sort of like a small-town Merlin. None the less, he could have done without a visit from Dor today; this morning he had set a new record, waking at 1:58 a.m., and he was exhausted. He only wanted to sit in his own living room, drink coffee, and try to read one of the Westerns he had picked up downtown. Maybe later on he would take another stab at napping.

'Hello,' Dorrance said. The book he was holding was a paperback – *Cemetery Nights,* by a man named Stephen Dobyns.

'Hello, Dor,' he said. 'Good book?'

Dorrance looked down at the book as if he'd forgotten he had one, then smiled and nodded. 'Yes, very good. He writes poems that are like stories. I don't always like that, but sometimes I do.'

'That's good. Listen, Dor, it's great to see you, but the walk up the hill kind of tired me out, so maybe we could visit another t—'

'Oh, that's all right,' Dorrance said, standing up. There was a faint cinnamony smell about him that always made Ralph think of Egyptian mummies kept behind red velvet ropes in shadowy museums. His face was almost without lines except for the tiny sprays of crow's feet around his eyes, but his age was unmistakable (and a little scary): his blue eyes were faded to the watery gray of an April sky and his skin had a translucent clarity that reminded Ralph of Nat's skin. His lips were loose and almost lavender in color. They made little smacking sounds when he spoke. 'That's all right, I didn't come to visit; I came to give you a message.'

'What message? From who?'

'I don't know who it's *from*,' Dorrance said, giving Ralph a look that suggested he thought Ralph was either being foolish or playing dumb. 'I don't mess in with long-time business. I told *you* not to, either, don't you remember?'

Ralph *did* remember something, but he was damned if he knew exactly what. Nor did he care. He was tired, and he had already had to listen to a fair amount of tiresome proselytizing on the subject of Susan Day from Ham Davenport. He had no urge to go round and round with Dorrance Marstellar on top of that, no matter how beautiful this Saturday morning was. 'Well then, just give me the message,' he said, 'and I'll toddle along upstairs – how would that be?'

'Oh, sure, good, fine.' But then Dorrance stopped, looking across the street as a fresh gust of wind sent a funnel of leaves storming into the bright October sky. His faded eyes were wide, and something in them made Ralph think of the Exalted & Revered Baby again – of the way she had snatched at the gray-blue marks left by his fingers, and the way she had looked at the flowers sizzling in the vase by the sink. Ralph had seen Dor stand watching airplanes take off and land on Runway 3 with that same slack-jawed expression, sometimes for an hour or more.

'Dor?' he prompted.

Dorrance's sparse eyelashes fluttered. 'Oh! Right! The message! The message is . . .' He frowned slightly and looked down at the book which he was now bending back and forth in his hands. Then his face cleared and he looked up at Ralph again. 'The message is, "Cancel the appointment."'

It was Ralph's turn to frown. 'What appointment?'

'You shouldn't have messed in,' Dorrance repeated, then heaved a big sigh. 'But it's too late now. Done-bun-can't-be-undone. Just cancel the appointment. Don't let that fellow stick any pins in you.'

Ralph had been turning to the porch steps; now he turned back to Dorrance. 'Hong? Are you talking about *Hong*?'

'How would I know?' Dorrance asked in an irritated tone of voice. 'I don't mess in, I told you that. Every now and then I carry a message, is all, like now. I was supposed to tell you to cancel the appointment with the pin-sticker man, and I done it. The rest is up to you.'

Dorrance was looking up at the trees across the street again, his odd, lineless face wearing an expression of mild exaltation. The strong fall wind rippled his hair like seaweed. When Ralph touched his shoulder the old man turned to him willingly enough, and Ralph suddenly realized that what Faye Chapin and the others saw as foolishness might actually be joy. If so, the mistake probably said more about them than it did about Old Dor.

'Dorrance?'

'What, Ralph?'

'This message – who gave it to you?'

Dorrance thought it over – or perhaps only appeared to think it over – and then held out his copy of *Cemetery Nights*. 'Take it.'

'No, I'll pass,' Ralph said. 'I'm not much on poetry, Dor.'

'You'll like these. They're like stories—'

Ralph restrained a strong urge to reach out and shake the old man until his bones rattled like castanets. 'I just picked up a couple oat operas downtown, at Back Pages. What I want to know is who gave you the message about—'

Dorrance thrust the book of poems into Ralph's right hand – the one not holding the Westerns – with surprising force. 'One of them starts, "Each thing I do I rush through so I can do something else."'

And before Ralph could say another word, Old Dor cut across the lawn to the sidewalk. He turned left and started toward the Extension with his face turned dreamily up to the blue sky where the leaves flew wildly, as if to some rendezvous over the horizon.

'Dorrance!' Ralph shouted, suddenly infuriated. Across the street at the Red Apple, Sue was sweeping fallen leaves off the hot-top in front of the door. At the sound of Ralph's voice she stopped and looked curiously over at him. Feeling stupid – feeling *old* – Ralph manufactured what he hoped looked like a big, cheerful grin and waved to her. Sue waved back and resumed her sweeping. Dorrance, meanwhile, had continued serenely on his way. He was now almost half a block up the street.

Ralph decided to let him go.

2

He climbed the steps to the porch, switching the book Dorrance had given him to his left hand so he could grope for his key-ring, and then saw he didn't have to bother – the door was not only unlocked but standing ajar. Ralph had scolded McGovern repeatedly for his carelessness about locking the front door, and had thought he was finally having some success in getting the message through his downstairs tenant's thick skull. Now, however, it seemed that McGovern had backslid.

'Dammit, Bill,' he said under his breath, pushing his way into the shadowy lower hall and looking nervously up the stairs. It was all too easy to imagine Ed Deepneau lurking up there, broad daylight or not. Still, he could not stay here in the foyer all day. He turned the thumb-bolt on the front door and started up the stairs.

There was nothing to worry about, of course. He had one bad moment when he thought he saw someone standing in the far corner of the living room, but it was only his own old gray jacket. He had actually hung it on the coat-tree for a change instead of just slinging it onto a chair or draping it over the arm of the sofa; no wonder it had given him a turn.

He went into the kitchen and, with his hands poked into his back pockets, stood looking at the calendar. Monday was circled, and within the circle he had scrawled HONG – 10:00.

I was supposed to tell you to cancel the appointment with the pin-sticker man, and I done it. The rest is up to you.

For a moment Ralph felt himself step back from his life so he was able to look at the latest section of the mural it made instead of just the detail which was this day. What he saw frightened him: an unknown road heading into a lightless tunnel where anything might be waiting. Anything at all.

Then turn back, Ralph!

But he had an idea he couldn't do that. He had an idea he was for the tunnel, whether he wanted to go in there or not. The feeling was not one of being led so much as it was one of being shoved forward by powerful, invisible hands.

'Never mind,' he muttered, rubbing his temples nervously with the tips of his fingers and still looking at the circled date – two days from now – on the calendar. 'It's the insomnia. That's when things really started to . . .'

Really started to *what*?

'To get weird,' he told the empty apartment. 'That's when things started to get really weird.'

Yes, weird. Lots of weird things, but the auras he was seeing were clearly the weirdest of them all. Cold gray light – it had looked like living frost – creeping over the man reading the paper in Day Break, Sun Down. The mother and son walking toward the supermarket, their entwined auras rising from their clasped hands like a pigtail. Helen and Nat buried in gorgeous clouds of ivory light; Natalie snatching at the marks left by his moving fingers, ghostly contrails which only she and Ralph had been able to see.

And now Old Dor, turning up on his doorstep like some peculiar Old Testament prophet . . . only instead of telling him to repent, Dor had told him to cancel his appointment with the acupuncturist Joe Wyzer had recommended. It should have been funny, but it wasn't.

The mouth of that tunnel. Looming closer every day. *Was there really a tunnel? And if so, where did it lead?*

I'm more interested in what might be waiting for me in there, Ralph thought. *Waiting in the dark.*

You shouldn't have messed in, Dorrance had said. *Anyway, it's too late now.*

'Done-bun-can't-be-undone,' Ralph murmured, and suddenly decided he didn't want to take the wide view anymore; it was unsettling. Better to move in close again and consider things a detail at a time, beginning with his appointment for acupuncture treatment. Was he going to keep it, or follow the advice of Old Dor, alias the Ghost of Hamlet's Father?

It really wasn't a question that needed much thought, Ralph decided. Joe Wyzer had sweet-talked Hong's secretary into finding him an appointment in early October, and Ralph intended to keep it. If there was a path out of this thicket, starting to sleep through the night was probably it. And that made Hong the next logical step.

'Done-bun-can't-be-undone,' he repeated, and went into the living room to read one of his Westerns.

Instead he found himself paging through the book of poetry Dorrance had given him – *Cemetery Nights,* by Stephen Dobyns. Dorrance had been right on both counts: the majority of the poems *were* like stories, and Ralph discovered that he liked them just fine. The poem from which Old Dor had quoted was called 'Pursuit', and it began:

> *Each thing I do I rush through so I can do*
> *something else. In such a way do the days pass –*
> *a blend of stock car racing and the never*
> *ending building of a gothic cathedral.*
> *Through the windows of my speeding car, I see*
> *all that I love falling away: books unread,*
> *jokes untold, landscapes unvisited . . .*

Ralph read the poem twice, completely absorbed, thinking he would have to read it to Carolyn. Carolyn would like it, which was good, and she would like him (who usually stuck to westerns and historical novels) even more for finding it and bringing it to her like a bouquet of flowers. He was actually getting up to find a scrap of paper he could mark the page with when he remembered that Carolyn had been dead for half a year now and burst into tears. He sat in the wing-chair for almost fifteen minutes, holding *Cemetery Nights* in his lap and wiping at his eyes with the heel of his left hand. At last he went into the bedroom, lay down, and tried to sleep. After an hour of staring at the ceiling, he got up, made himself a cup of coffee, and found a college football game on TV.

3

The Public Library was open on Sunday afternoons from one until six, and on the day after Dorrance's visit, Ralph went down there, mostly because he had nothing better to do. The high-ceilinged reading room would ordinarily have contained a scattering of other old men like himself, most of them leafing through the various Sunday papers they now had time to read, but when Ralph emerged from the stacks where he had spent forty minutes browsing, he discovered he had the whole room to himself. Yesterday's gorgeous blue skies had been replaced by driving rain that pasted the new-fallen leaves to the sidewalks or sent them flooding down the gutters and into Derry's peculiar and unpleasantly tangled system of storm-drains. The wind was still blowing, but it had shifted into the north and now had a nasty cutting edge. Old folks with any sense (or any luck) were at home where it was warm, possibly watching the last game of another dismal Red Sox season, possibly playing Old Maid or Candyland with the grandkids, possibly napping off a big chicken dinner.

Ralph, on the other hand, did not care for the Red Sox, had no children or grandchildren, and seemed to have completely lost any capacity for napping he might once have had. So he had taken the one o'clock Green Route bus down to the library, and here he was, wishing he had worn something heavier than his old scuffed gray jacket – the reading room was chilly. Gloomy, as well. The fireplace was empty, and the clankless radiators

173

strongly suggested that the furnace had yet to be fired up. The Sunday librarian hadn't bothered flipping the switches that turned on the hanging overhead globes, either. The light which did manage to find its way in here seemed to fall dead on the floor, and the corners were full of shadows. The loggers and soldiers and drummers and Indians in the old paintings on the walls looked like malevolent ghosts. Cold rain sighed and gusted against the windows.

I should have stayed home, Ralph thought, but didn't really believe it; these days the apartment was even worse. Besides, he had found an interesting new book in what he had come to think of as the Mr Sandman Section of the stacks: *Patterns of Dreaming,* by James A. Hall, MD. He turned on the overheads, rendering the room marginally less gruesome, sat down at one of the four long, empty tables, and was soon absorbed in his reading.

> *Prior to the realization that REM sleep and NREM sleep were distinct states* [Hall wrote], *studies concerned with total deprivation of a particular stage of sleep led to Dement's suggestion (1960) that deprivation . . . causes disorganization of the waking personality . . .*

Boy, you got that *right, my friend,* Ralph thought. *Can't even find a fucking Cup-A-Soup packet when you want one.*

> *. . . early dream-deprivation studies also raised the exciting specu-lation that schizophrenia might be a disorder in which deprivation of dreaming at night led to a breakthrough of the dream process into everyday waking life.*

Ralph hunched over the book, elbows on the table, fisted hands pressed against his temples, forehead lined and eyebrows drawn together in a clench of concentration. He wondered if Hall could be talking about the auras, maybe without even knowing it. Except he was still *having* dreams, dammit – very vivid ones, for the most part. Just last night he'd had one in which he was dancing at the old Derry Pavilion (gone now; destroyed in the big storm which had wiped out most of the downtown area eight years before) with Lois Chasse. He seemed to have taken her out with the intention of proposing to her, but Trigger Vachon, of all people, had kept trying to cut in.

He rubbed his eyes with his knuckles, tried to focus his

attention, and began to read again. He did not see the man in the baggy gray sweatshirt materialize in the doorway of the reading room and stand there, silently watching him. After about three minutes of this, the man reached beneath the sweatshirt (Charlie Brown's dog Snoopy was on the front, wearing his Joe Cool glasses) and produced a hunting knife from the scabbard on his belt. The hanging overhead globes threw a thread of light along the knife's serrated blade as the man turned it this way and that, admiring the edge. Then he moved forward toward the table where Ralph was sitting with his head propped on his hands. He sat down beside Ralph, who noticed that someone was there only in the faintest, most distant way.

> *Tolerance to sleep loss varies somewhat with the age of the subject. Younger subjects show an earlier onset of disturbance and more physical reactions, while older subjects—*

A hand closed lightly on Ralph's shoulder, startling him out of the book.

'I wonder what they'll look like?' an ecstatic voice whispered in his ear, the words flowing on a tide of what smelled like spoiled bacon cooking slowly in a bath of garlic and rancid butter. 'Your guts, I mean. I wonder what they'll look like when I let them out all over the floor. What do you think, you Godless baby-killing Centurion? Do you think they'll be yellow or black or red or what?'

Something hard and sharp pressed into Ralph's left side and then slowly traced its way down along his ribs.

'I can't wait to find out,' the ecstatic voice whispered. 'I can't *wait*.'

4

Ralph turned his head very slowly, hearing the tendons in his neck creak. He didn't know the name of the man with the bad breath – the man who was sticking something that felt too much like a knife not to be one into his side – but he recognized him at once. The hornrimmed glasses helped, but the zany gray hair, standing up in clumps that reminded Ralph simultaneously of Don King and Albert Einstein, was the clincher. It was the man who had been standing with Ed Deepneau in the background of the newspaper photo that had showed Ham Davenport with his fist raised and Dan Dalton wearing Davenport's CHOICE, NOT FEAR sign for a hat. Ralph thought he had seen this same guy in some of the TV news stories about the continuing abortion demonstrations. Just another sign-waving, chanting face in the crowd; just another spear-carrier. Except it now seemed that this particular spear-carrier intended to kill him.

'What do you think?' the man in the Snoopy sweatshirt asked, still in that ecstatic whisper. The sound of his voice frightened Ralph more than the blade as it slid slowly up and then back down his leather jacket, seeming to map the vulnerable organs on the left side of his body: lung, heart, kidney, intestines. 'What color?'

His breath was nauseating, but Ralph was afraid to pull back or turn his head, afraid that any gesture might cause the knife to stop tracking and plunge. Now it was moving back up his side again. Behind the thick lenses of his hornrims, the man's brown eyes floated like strange fish. The expression in them was disconnected and oddly frightened, Ralph thought. The eyes of a man who would see signs in the sky and perhaps hear voices whispering from deep in the closet late at night.

'I don't know,' Ralph said. 'I don't know why you'd want to hurt me in the first place.' He shot his eyes quickly around, still not moving his head, hoping to see someone, anyone, but the reading room remained empty. Outside, the wind gusted and rain racketed against the windows.

'Because you're a fucking *Centurion*!' the gray-haired man spat. 'A fucking *baby-killer*! Stealing the *fetal unborn*! Selling them to the *highest bidder*! I know all about you!'

Ralph dropped his right hand slowly from the side of his head. He was right-handed, and all the stuff he happened to pick up in the course of the day generally went into the handiest righthand pocket of whatever he was wearing. The old gray jacket had big flap pockets, but he was afraid that even if he could sneak his hand in there unnoticed, the most lethal thing he would find was apt to be a crumpled-up Dentyne wrapper. He doubted that he even had a nail-clipper.

'Ed Deepneau told you that, didn't he?' Ralph asked, then grunted as the knife poked painfully into his side just below the place where his ribs stopped.

'Don't speak his name,' the man in the Snoopy sweatshirt whispered. 'Don't you even speak his *name*! Stealer of infants!

Cowardly murderer! *Centurion!*' He thrust forward with the blade again, and this time there was real pain as the tip punched through the leather jacket. Ralph didn't think he was cut – yet, anyway – but he was quite sure the nut had already applied enough pressure to leave a nasty bruise. That was okay, though; if he got out of this with no more than a bruise, he would count himself lucky.

'All right,' he said. 'I won't mention his name.'

'Say you're sorry!' the man in the Snoopy sweatshirt hissed, prodding with the knife again. This time it went through Ralph's shirt, and he felt the first warm trickle of blood down his side. *What's under the point of the blade right now?* he wondered. *Liver? Gall bladder? What's under there on the lefthand side?*

He either couldn't remember or didn't want to. A picture had come into his mind, and it was trying to get in the way of any organized thought – a deer hung head-down from a set of scales outside some country store during hunting season. Glazed eyes, lolling tongue, and a dark slit up the belly where a man with a knife – a knife just like this one – had opened it up and yanked its works out, leaving just head, meat, and hide.

'I'm sorry,' Ralph said in a voice which was no longer steady. 'I am, really.'

'Yeah, right! You ought to be, but you aren't! You *aren't!*'

Another prod. A bright lance of pain. More wet heat trickling down his side. And suddenly the room was brighter, as if two or three of the camera crews which had been wandering around Derry since the abortion protests began had crowded in here and turned on the floods they mounted over their videocams. There were no cameras, of course; the lights had gone on inside of *him*.

He turned toward the man with the knife – the man who was actually pressing the blade into him now – and saw he was surrounded by a shifting green and black aura that made Ralph think of

(*swampfire*)

the dim phosphorescence he had sometimes seen in marshy woods after dark. Twisting through it were spiky brambles of purest black. He looked at his assailant's aura with mounting dismay, hardly feeling the tip of the knife sink a sixteenth of an inch deeper into him. He was distantly aware that blood was puddling at the bottom of his shirt, along the line of his belt, but that was all.

He's crazy, and he really does mean to kill me – it isn't just talk. He's not quite ready to do it yet, he hasn't quite worked himself up to it, but he's almost there. And if I try to run – if I try to move even an inch away from the knife he's got in me – he'll do it right away. I think he's hoping I will decide to move . . . then he can tell himself I brought it on myself, that it was my own fault.

'You and your kind, oh boy,' the man with the zany shock of gray hair was saying. 'We know all about *you*.'

Ralph's hand had reached the right pocket . . . and felt a largish something inside he didn't recognize or remember putting there. Not that that meant much; when you could no longer remember if the last four digits of the cinema center phone number were 1317 or 1713, anything was possible.

'You guys, oh boy!' the man with the zany hair said. 'Ohboy ohboy *ohboy*!' This time Ralph had no trouble feeling the pain when the man pushed with the knife; the tip spread a thin red net all the way across the curve of his chest wall and up the nape of his neck. He uttered a low moan, and his right hand clamped tight on the gray jacket's right-hand pocket, moulding the leather to the curved side of the object inside.

'Don't scream,' the man with the zany hair said in that low, ecstatic whisper. 'Oh jeepers jeezly crow, you don't want to do *that*!' His brown eyes peered at Ralph's face, and the lenses of his glasses so magnified them that the tiny flakes of dandruff caught in his lashes looked almost as big as pebbles. Ralph could see the man's aura even in his eyes – it went sliding across his pupils like green smoke across black water. The snakelike twists running through the green light were thicker now, twining together, and Ralph understood that when the knife sank all the way in, the part of this man's personality which was generating those black swirls would be what pushed it. The green was confusion and paranoia; the black was something else. Something

(*from outside*)

much worse.

'No,' he gasped. 'I won't. I won't scream.'

'Good. I can feel your heart, you know. It's coming right up the blade of the knife and into the palm of my hand. It must be beating really hard.' The man's mouth pulled up in a jerky, humorless smile. Flecks of spittle clung to the corners of his lips. 'Maybe you'll just keel over and die of a heart attack, save me the trouble of killing you.' Another gust of that sickening breath washed over Ralph's face. 'You're awful old.'

Blood was now running down his side in what felt like two

streams, maybe even three. The pain of the knife-point gouging into him was maddening – like the stinger of a gigantic bee.

Or a pin, Ralph thought, and discovered that this idea was funny in spite of the fix he was in . . . or perhaps because of it. This was the *real* pin-sticker man; James Roy Hong could be only a pale imitation.

And I never had a chance to cancel this appointment, Ralph thought. But then again, he had an idea that nuts like the guy in the Snoopy sweatshirt didn't take cancellations. Nuts like this had their own agenda and they stuck to it, come hell or high water.

Whatever else might happen, Ralph knew he couldn't stand that knife-tip boring into him much longer. He used his thumb to lift the flap of his coat pocket and slipped his hand inside. He knew what the object was the minute his fingertips touched it: the aerosol can Gretchen had taken out of her purse and put on his kitchen table. *A little present from all your grateful friends at WomanCare,* she had said.

Ralph had no idea how it had gotten from the top of the kitchen cabinet where he had put it into the pocket of his battered old fall jacket, and he didn't care. His hand closed around it, and he used his thumb again, this time to pop off the can's plastic top. He never took his eyes away from the twitching, frightened, exhilarated face of the man with the zany hair as he did this.

'I know something,' Ralph said. 'If you promise not to kill me, I'll tell you.'

'What?' the man with the zany hair asked. 'Jeepers, what could a scum like *you* know?'

What could *a scum like me know?* Ralph asked himself, and the answer came at once, popping into his mind like jackpot bars in the windows of a slot machine. He forced himself to lean into the green aura swirling around the man, into the terrible cloud of stink coming from his disturbed guts. At the same time he eased the small can from his pocket, held it against his thigh, and settled his index finger on the button which triggered the spray.

'I know who the Crimson King is,' he murmured.

The eyes widened behind the dirty hornrims – not just in surprise but in shock – and the man with the zany hair recoiled a little. For a moment the terrible pressure high on Ralph's left side eased. It was his chance, the only one he was apt to have, and he took it, throwing himself to the right, falling off his chair and tumbling to the floor. The back of his head smacked the tiles, but the pain seemed distant and unimportant compared to the relief at the removal of the knife-point.

The man with the zany hair squawked – a sound of mingled rage and resignation, as if he had become used to such setbacks over his long and difficult life. He leaned over Ralph's now-empty chair, his twitching face thrust forward, his eyes looking like the sort of fantastic, glowing creatures which live in the ocean's deepest trenches. Ralph raised the spray-can and had just a moment to realize he hadn't had time to check which direction the pinhole in the nozzle was pointing – he might very well succeed only in giving himself a faceful of Bodyguard.

No time to worry about that now.

He pressed the nozzle as the man with the zany hair thrust his knife forward. The man's face was enveloped in a thin haze of droplets that looked like the stuff that came out of the pine-scented air-freshener Ralph kept on the bathroom toilet tank. The lenses of his glasses fogged over.

The result was immediate and all Ralph could have wished for. The man with the zany hair screamed in pain, dropped his knife (it landed on Ralph's left knee and came to rest between his legs), and clutched at his face, pulling his glasses off. They landed on the table. At the same time the thin, somehow greasy aura around him flashed a brilliant red and then winked out – out of Ralph's view, at least.

'*I'm blind!*' the man with the zany hair cried in a high, shrieky voice. '*I'm blind, I'm blind!*'

'No, you're not,' Ralph said, getting shakily to his feet. 'You're just—'

The man with the zany hair screamed again and fell to the floor. He rolled back and forth on the black and white tiles with his hands over his face, howling like a child who has gotten his hand caught in a door. Ralph could see little pie-wedges of cheeks between his splayed fingers. The skin there was turning an alarming shade of red.

Ralph told himself to leave the guy alone, that he was crazy as a loon and dangerous as a rattlesnake, but he found himself too horrified and ashamed of what he had done to take this no doubt excellent advice. The idea that it had been a matter of survival, of disabling his assailant or dying, had already begun to seem unreal. He bent down and put a tentative hand on the man's arm. The nut rolled away from him and began to drum his dirty low-top sneakers on the floor like a child having a tantrum. '*Oh you son of a bitch!*' he was screaming. 'You shot me with something!' And then, incredibly: '*I'll sue the pants off you!*'

'You'll have to explain about the knife before you're able to progress much with your lawsuit, I think,' Ralph said. He saw the knife lying on the floor, reached for it, then thought again. It would be better if his fingerprints weren't on it. As he straightened, a wave of dizziness rushed through his head and for a moment the rain beating against the window sounded hollow and distant. He kicked the knife away, then tottered on his feet and had to grab the back of the chair he'd been sitting in to keep from falling over. Things steadied again. He heard approaching footsteps from the main lobby and murmuring, questioning voices.

Now *you come,* Ralph thought wearily. *Where were you three minutes ago, when this guy was on the verge of popping my left lung like a balloon?*

Mike Hanlon, looking slim and no more than thirty despite his tight cap of gray hair, appeared in the doorway. Behind him was the teenage boy Ralph recognized as the weekend desk assistant, and behind the teenager were four or five gawkers, probably from the periodicals room.

'Mr Roberts!' Mike exclaimed. 'Christ, how bad are you hurt?'

'I'm fine, it's *him* that's hurt,' Ralph said. But he happened to look down at himself as he pointed at the man on the floor and saw he *wasn't* fine. His coat had pulled up when he pointed, and the left side of the plaid shirt beneath had gone a deep, sodden red in a teardrop shape that started just below the armpit and spread out from there. 'Shit,' he said faintly, and sat down in his chair again. He bumped the hornrimmed glasses with his elbow and they skittered almost all the way across the table. The mist of droplets on their lenses made them look like eyes which had been blinded by cataracts.

'*He shot me with acid!*' the man on the floor screamed. '*I can't see and my skin is melting! I can feel it melting!*' To Ralph, he sounded like an almost conscious parody of the Wicked Witch of the West.

Mike tossed a quick glance at the man on the floor, then sat down in the chair next to Ralph. 'What happened?'

'Well, it sure wasn't acid,' Ralph said, and held up the can of Bodyguard. He set it on the table beside *Patterns of Dreaming*.

'The lady who gave it to me said it's not as strong as Mace, it just irritates your eyes and makes you sick to your—'

'It's not what's wrong with *him* that I'm worried about,' Mike said impatiently. 'Anyone who can yell that loud probably isn't going to die in the next three minutes. It's you I'm worried about, Mr Roberts – any idea how bad he stabbed you?'

'He didn't actually stab me at all,' Ralph said. 'He . . . sort of poked me. With that.' He pointed at the knife lying on the tile floor. At the sight of the red tip, he felt another wave of faintness track through his head. It felt like an express train made of feather pillows. That was stupid, of course, made no sense at all, but he wasn't in a very sensible frame of mind.

The assistant was looking cautiously down at the man on the floor. 'Uh-oh,' he said. 'We know this guy, Mike – it's Charlie Pickering.'

'Goodness-gracious, great balls of fire,' Mike said. 'Now why aren't I surprised?' He looked at the teenage assistant and sighed. 'Better call the cops, Justin. It looks like we've got us a situation here.'

5

'Am I in trouble for using that?' Ralph asked an hour later, and pointed to one of the two sealed plastic bags sitting on the cluttered surface of the desk in Mike Hanlon's office. A strip of yellow tape, marked EVIDENCE aerosol can DATE 3 October 93 and SITE Derry Public Library ran across the front.

'Not as much as our old pal Charlie's going to be in for using this,' John Leydecker said, and pointed to the other sealed bag. The hunting knife was inside, the blood on the tip now dried to a tacky maroon. Leydecker was wearing a University of Maine football sweater today. It made him look approximately the size of a dairy barn. 'We still pretty much believe in the concept of self-defense out here in the sticks. We don't talk it up much, though – it's sort of like admitting you believe the world is flat.'

Mike Hanlon, who was leaning in the doorway, laughed.

Ralph hoped his face didn't show how deeply relieved he

felt. As a paramedic (one of the guys who had run Helen Deepneau to the hospital back in August, for all he knew) worked on him – first photographing, then disinfecting, finally butterfly-clamping and bandaging – he had sat with his teeth gritted, imagining a judge sentencing him to six months in the county clink for assault with a semi-deadly weapon. *Hopefully, Mr Roberts, this will serve as an example and a warning to any other old farts in this vicinity who may feel justified in carrying around spray-cans of disabling nerve gas . . .*

Leydecker looked once more at the six Polaroid photographs lined up along the side of Hanlon's computer terminal. The fresh-faced emergency medical technician had taken the first three before patching Ralph up. These showed a small dark circle – it looked like the sort of oversized period made by children just learning to print – low down on Ralph's side. The EMT had taken the second set of three after applying the butterfly clamp and getting Ralph's signature on a form attesting to the fact that he had been offered hospital service and had refused it. In this latter group of photographs, the beginnings of what was going to be an absolutely spectacular bruise could be seen.

'God bless Edwin Land and Richard Polaroid,' Leydecker said, putting the photographs into another EVIDENCE Baggie.

'I don't think there ever was a Richard Polaroid,' Mike Hanlon said from his spot in the doorway.

'Probably not, but God bless him just the same. No jury who got a look at these photos would do anything but give you a medal, Ralph, and not even Clarence Darrow could keep em out of evidence.' He looked back at Mike. 'Charlie Pickering.'

Mike nodded. 'Charlie Pickering.'

'Fuckhead.'

Mike nodded again. 'Fuckhead deluxe.'

The two of them looked at each other solemnly, then burst into gales of laughter at the same moment. Ralph understood exactly how they felt – it was funny because it was awful and awful because it was funny – and he had to bite his lips savagely to keep from joining them. The last thing in the world he wanted to do right now was get laughing; it would hurt like a bastard.

Leydecker took a handkerchief out of his back pocket, mopped his streaming eyes with it, and began to get himself under control.

'Pickering's one of the right-to-lifers, isn't he?' Ralph asked. He was remembering how Pickering had looked when Hanlon's teenage assistant had helped him sit up. Without his glasses, the man had looked about as dangerous as a bunny in a petshop window.

'You could say that,' Mike agreed dryly. 'He's the one they caught last year in the parking garage that services the hospital and WomanCare. He had a can of gasoline in his hand and a knapsack filled with empty bottles on his back.'

'Also strips of sheeting, don't forget those,' Leydecker said. 'Those were going to be his fuses. That was back when Charlie was a member in good standing of Daily Bread.'

'How close did he come to lighting the place up?' Ralph asked curiously.

Leydecker shrugged. 'Not very. Someone in the group apparently decided firebombing the local women's clinic might be a little closer to terrorism than politics and made an anonymous phone call to your local police authority.'

'Good deal,' Mike said. He snorted another little chuckle, then crossed his arms as if to hold any further outburst inside.

'Yeah,' Leydecker said. He laced his fingers together, stretched out his arms, and popped his knuckles. 'Instead of prison, a thoughtful, caring judge sent Charlie to Juniper Hill for six months' worth of treatment and therapy, and they must have decided he was okay, because he's been back in town since July or so.'

'Yep,' Mike agreed. 'He's down here just about every day. Kind of improving the tone of the place. Buttonholes everyone who comes in, practically, and gives them his little peptalk on how any woman who has an abortion is going to perish in brimstone, and how the real baddies like Susan Day are going to burn forever in a lake of fire. But I can't figure out why he'd take after you, Mr Roberts.'

'Just lucky, I guess.'

'Are you okay, Ralph?' Leydecker asked. 'You look pale.'

'I'm fine,' Ralph said, although he did not feel fine; in fact, he had begun to feel very queasy.

'I don't know about fine, but you're sure lucky. Lucky those women gave you that can of pepper-gas, lucky you had it with you, and luckiest of all that Pickering didn't just walk up behind you and stick that knife of his into the nape of your neck. Do you feel like coming down to the station and making a formal statement now, or—'

Ralph abruptly lunged out of Mike Hanlon's ancient swivel chair, bolted across the room with his left hand over his mouth, and clawed open the door in the rear right corner of the office, praying it wasn't a closet. If it was, he was probably going to fill up Mike's galoshes with a partially processed grilled cheese sandwich and some slightly used tomato soup.

It turned out to be the room he needed. Ralph dropped to his knees in front of the toilet and vomited with his eyes closed and his left arm clamped tightly against the hole Pickering had made in his side. The pain as his muscles first locked and then pushed was still enormous.

'I take it that's a no,' Mike Hanlon said from behind him, and then put a comforting hand on the back of Ralph's neck. 'Are you okay? Did you get that thing bleeding again?'

'I don't think so,' Ralph said. He started to unbutton his shirt, then paused and clamped his arm tight against his side again as his stomach gave another lurch before quieting once more. He raised his arm and looked at the dressing. It was pristine. 'I appear to be okay.'

'Good,' Leydecker said. He was standing just behind the librarian. 'You done?'

'I think so, yes.' Ralph looked at Mike shamefacedly. 'I apologize for that.'

'Don't be a goof.' Mike helped Ralph to his feet.

'Come on,' Leydecker said, 'I'll give you a ride home. Tomorrow will be time enough for the statement. What you need is to put your feet up the rest of today, and a good night's sleep tonight.'

'Nothing like a good night's sleep,' Ralph agreed. They had reached the office door. 'You want to let go of my arm now, Detective Leydecker? We're not going steady just yet, are we?'

Leydecker looked startled, then dropped Ralph's arm. Mike started to laugh again. '"Not going –" That's pretty good, Mr Roberts.'

Leydecker was smiling. 'I guess we're not, but you can call me Jack, if you want. Or John. Just not Johnny. Since my mother died, the only one who calls me Johnny is old Prof McGovern.'

Old Prof McGovern, Ralph thought. *How strange that sounds.*

'Okay – John it is. And both of you guys can call me Ralph. As far as I'm concerned, *Mr Roberts* is always going to be a Broadway play starring Henry Fonda.'

'You got it,' Mike Hanlon said. 'And take care of yourself.'

'I'll try,' he said, then stopped in his tracks. 'Listen, I have something to thank you for, quite apart from your help today.'

Mike raised his eyebrows. 'Oh?'

'Yes. You hired Helen Deepneau. She's one of my favorite people, and she desperately needed the job. So thanks.'

Mike smiled and nodded. 'I'll be happy to accept the bouquets, but she's the one who did me the favor, really. She's actually over-qualified for the job, but I think she wants to stay in town.'

'So do I, and you've helped make it possible. So thanks again.'

Mike grinned. 'My pleasure.'

6

As Ralph and Leydecker stepped out behind the circulation desk, Leydecker said: 'I guess that honeycomb must have really turned the trick, huh?'

Ralph at first had absolutely no idea what the big detective was talking about – he might as well have asked a question in Esperanto.

'Your insomnia,' Leydecker said patiently. 'You got past it, right? Must have – you look a gajillion times better than on the day I first met you.'

'I was a little stressed that day,' Ralph said. He found himself remembering the old Billy Crystal routine about Fernando – the one that went, *Listen, dahling, don't be a schnook; it's not how you feel, it's how you* look! *And you . . . look . . . MAHVELLOUS!*

'And you're not today? C'mon, Ralph, this is me. So give – was it the honeycomb?'

Ralph appeared to think this over, then nodded. 'Yes, I guess that must have been what did it.'

'Fantastic! Didn't I tell you?' Leydecker said cheerfully as they pushed their way out into the rainy afternoon.

They were waiting for the light at the top of Up-Mile Hill when Ralph turned to Leydecker and asked what the chances were of nailing Ed as Charlie Pickering's accomplice. 'Because Ed put him up to it,' he said. 'I know that as well as I know that's Strawford Park over there.'

'You're probably right,' Leydecker replied, 'but don't kid yourself – the chances of nailing him as an accomplice are shitty. They wouldn't be very good even if the County Prosecutor wasn't as conservative as Dale Cox.'

'Why not?'

'First of all, I doubt if we'll be able to show any deep connection between the two men. Second, guys like Pickering tend to be fiercely loyal to the people they identify as "friends", because they have so few of them – their worlds are mostly made up of enemies. Under interrogation I don't think Pickering will repeat much or any of what he told you while he was tickling your ribs with his hunting knife. Third, Ed Deepneau is no fool. Crazy, yes – maybe crazier than Pickering, when you get right down to it – but not a fool. He won't admit anything.'

Ralph nodded. It was exactly his opinion of Ed.

'If Pickering *did* say that Deepneau ordered him to find you and waste you – on the grounds that you were one of these baby-killing, fetus-snatching Centurions – Ed would just smile at us and nod and say he was sure that poor Charlie had told us that, that poor Charlie might even *believe* that, but that didn't make it true.'

The light turned green. Leydecker drove through the intersection, then bent left onto Harris Avenue. The windshield wipers thumped and flapped. Strawford Park, on Ralph's right, looked like a wavery mirage through the rain streaming down the passenger window.

'And what could we say to that?' Leydecker asked. 'The fact is, Charlie Pickering has got a *long* history of mental instability – when it comes to nuthatches, he's made the grand tour: Juniper Hill, Acadia Hospital, Bangor Mental Health Institute . . . if it's a place where they have free electrical treatments and jackets that button up the back, Charlie's most likely been there. These days his hobby-horse is abortion. Back in the late sixties he had a bug up his ass about Margaret Chase Smith. He wrote letters to everyone – Derry PD, the State Police, the FBI – claiming she was a Russian spy. He had the evidence, he said.'

'Good God, that's incredible.'

'Nope; that's Charlie Pickering, and I bet there's a dozen like him in every city this size in the United States. Hell, all over the world.'

Ralph's hand crept to his left side and touched the square of bandage there. His fingers traced the butterfly shape beneath the gauze. What he kept remembering was Pickering's magnified brown eyes – how they had looked terrified and ecstatic at the same time. He was already having trouble believing the man to whom those eyes belonged had almost killed him, and he was afraid that by tomorrow the whole thing would seem like one of the so-called 'breakthrough dreams' James A. Hall's book talked about.

'The bitch of it is, Ralph, a nut like Charlie Pickering makes the perfect tool for a guy like Deepneau. Right now our little wife-beating buddy has got about a ton of deniability.'

Leydecker turned into the driveway next to Ralph's building and parked behind a large Oldsmobile with blotches of rust on the trunk lid and a very old sticker – DUKAKIS '88 – on the bumper.

'Who's *that* brontosaurus belong to? The Prof?'

'No,' Ralph said. 'That's my brontosaurus.'

Leydecker gave him an unbelieving look as he shoved the gearshift lever of his stripped-to-the-bone Police Department Chevy into Park. 'If you own a car, how come you're out standing around the bus stop in the pouring rain? Doesn't it run?'

'It runs,' Ralph said a little stiffly, not wanting to add that he could be wrong about that; he hadn't had the Olds on the road in over two months. 'And I wasn't standing around in the pouring rain; it's a bus *shelter,* not a bus *stop.* It has a roof. Even a bench inside. No cable TV, true, but wait till next year.'

'Still . . .' Leydecker said, gazing doubtfully at the Olds.

'I spent the last fifteen years of my working life driving a desk, but before that I was a salesman. For twenty-five years or so I averaged eight hundred miles a week. By the time I settled in at the printshop, I didn't care if I ever sat behind the wheel of a car again. And since my wife died, there hardly ever seems to be any reason to drive. The bus does me just fine for most things.'

All true enough; Ralph saw no need to add that he had

increasingly come to mistrust both his reflexes and his short vision. A year ago, a kid of about seven had chased his football out into Harris Avenue as Ralph was coming back from the movies, and although he had been going only twenty miles an hour, Ralph had thought for two endless, horrifying seconds that he was going to run the little boy down. He hadn't, of course – it hadn't even been close, not really – but since then he thought he could count the number of times he'd driven the Olds on both hands.

He saw no need to tell John that, either.

'Well, whatever does it for you,' Leydecker said, giving the Olds a vague wave. 'How does one o'clock tomorrow afternoon sound for that statement, Ralph? I come on at noon, so I could kind of look over your shoulder. Buy you a coffee, if you wanted one.'

'That sounds fine. And thanks for the ride home.'

'No problem. One other thing . . .'

Ralph had started to open the car door. Now he closed it again and turned back to Leydecker, eyebrows raised.

Leydecker looked down at his hands, shifted uncomfortably behind the wheel, cleared his throat, then looked up again. 'I just wanted to say that I think you're a class act,' Leydecker said. 'Lots of guys forty years younger than you would have finished today's little adventure in the hospital. Or the morgue.'

'My guardian angel was looking out for me, I guess,' Ralph said, thinking of how surprised he had been when he realized what the round shape in his jacket pocket was.

'Well, maybe that was it, but you still want to be sure to lock your door tonight. You hear what I'm saying?'

Ralph smiled and nodded. Warranted or not, Leydecker's praise had made a warm spot in his chest. 'I will, and if I can just get McGovern to cooperate, everything will be hunky-dory.'

Also, he thought, *I can always go down and double-check the lock myself when I wake up. That should be just about two and a half hours after I fall asleep, the way things are going.*

'Everything *is* going to be hunky-dory,' Leydecker said. 'No one down where I work was very pleased when Deepneau more or less co-opted The Friends of Life, but I can't say we were surprised – he's an attractive, charismatic guy. If, that is, you happen to catch him on a day when he hasn't been using his wife for a punching-bag.'

Ralph nodded.

'On the other hand, we've seen guys like him before, and

they have a way of self-destructing. That process has already started with Deepneau. He's lost his wife, he's lost his job . . . did you know that?'

'Uh-huh. Helen told me.'

'Now he's losing his more moderate followers. They're peeling off like jet fighters heading back to base because they're running out of fuel. Not Ed, though – he's going on come hell or high water. I imagine he'll keep at least some of them with him until the Susan Day speech, but after that I think it's gonna be a case of the cheese stands alone.'

'Has it occurred to you that he might try something Friday? That he might try to hurt Susan Day?'

'Oh yes,' Leydecker said. 'It's occurred to us, all right. It certainly has.'

8

Ralph was extremely happy to find the porch door locked this time. He unlocked it just long enough to let himself in, then trudged up the front stairs, which seemed longer and gloomier than ever this afternoon.

The apartment seemed too silent in spite of the steady beat of the rain on the roof, and the air seemed to smell of too many sleepless nights. Ralph took one of the chairs from the kitchen table over to the counter, stood on it, and looked at the top of the cabinet closest to the sink. It was as if he expected to find another can of Bodyguard – the *original* can, the one he'd put up here after seeing Helen and her friend Gretchen off – on top of that cabinet, and part of him actually did expect that. There was nothing up there, however, but a toothpick, an old Buss fuse, and a lot of dust.

He got carefully down off the chair, saw he had left muddy footprints on the seat, and used a swatch of paper towels to wipe them away. Then he replaced the chair at the table and went into the living room. He stood there, letting his eyes run from the couch with its dingy floral coverlet to the wing-chair to the old television sitting on its oak table between the two windows looking out on Harris Avenue. From the TV his gaze moved into the far corner. When he had come into the apartment yesterday, still a little on edge from finding the porch door unlatched, Ralph had briefly mistaken his jacket hanging on the coat-tree in that corner for an intruder. Well, no need to be coy; he had thought for a moment that Ed had decided to pay him a visit.

I never hang my coat up, though. *It was one of the things about me — one of the few, I think — that used to genuinely irritate Carolyn. And if I never managed to get in the habit of hanging it up when she was alive, I sure as shit haven't since she died. No, I'm not the one who hung this jacket up.*

Ralph crossed the room, rummaging in the pockets of the gray leather jacket and putting the stuff he found on top of the television. Nothing in the left but an old roll of Life Savers with lint clinging to the top one, but the righthand pocket was a treasure-trove even with the aerosol can gone. There was a lemon Tootsie Pop, still in its wrapper; a crumpled advertising circular from the Derry House of Pizza; a double-A battery; a small empty carton that had once contained an apple pie from McDonald's; his discount card from Dave's Video Stop, just four punches away from a free rental (the card had been MIA for over two weeks and Ralph had been sure it was lost); a book of matches; various scraps of tinfoil . . . and a folded piece of lined blue paper.

Ralph unfolded it and read a single sentence, written in a scrawling, slightly unsteady old man's script: *Each thing I do I rush through so I can do something else.*

That was all there was, but it was enough to confirm for his brain what his heart already knew: Dorrance Marstellar had been on the porch steps when Ralph had returned from Back Pages with his paperbacks, but he'd had other stuff to do before sitting down to wait. He had gone up to Ralph's apartment, taken the aerosol can from the top of the kitchen shelf, and put it in the righthand pocket of Ralph's old gray jacket. He had even left his calling-card: a bit of poetry scrawled on a piece of paper probably torn from the battered notebook in which he sometimes recorded arrivals and departures along Runway 3. Then, instead of returning the jacket to wherever Ralph had left it, Old Dor had hung it neatly on the coat-tree. With that accomplished

(*done-bun-can't-be-undone*)

he had returned to the porch to wait.

Last night Ralph had given McGovern a scolding for leaving the front door unlocked again, and McGovern had borne it as patiently as Ralph himself had borne Carolyn's scoldings about tossing his jacket onto the nearest chair when he came in instead of hanging it up, but now Ralph found himself wondering if he hadn't accused Bill unjustly. Perhaps Old Dor had picked the lock . . . or witched it. Under the circumstances, witchery seemed the more likely choice. Because . . .

'Because look,' Ralph said in a low voice, mechanically scooping his pocket litter up from the top of the TV and dumping it back into his pockets. 'It isn't just like he knew I'd need the stuff; he knew where to find it, and *he knew where to put it.*'

A chill zig-zagged up his back at that, and his mind tried to gavel the whole idea down – to label it mad, illogical, just the sort of thing a man with a grade-A case of insomnia would think up. Maybe so. But that didn't explain the scrap of paper, did it?

He looked at the scrawled words on the blue-lined sheet again – *Each thing I do I rush through so I can do something else.* That wasn't his handwriting any more than *Cemetery Nights* was his book.

'Except it is now; Dor gave it to me,' Ralph said, and the chill raced up his back again, jagged as a crack in a windshield.

And what other explanation comes to mind? That can didn't just fly into your pocket. The sheet of notepaper, either.

That sense of being pushed by invisible hands toward the maw of some dark tunnel had returned. Feeling like a man in a dream, Ralph walked back toward the kitchen. On the way he slipped out of the gray jacket and tossed it over the arm of the couch without even thinking about it. He stood in the doorway for some time, looking fixedly at the calendar with its picture of two laughing boys carving a jack-o-lantern. Looking at tomorrow's date, which was circled.

Cancel the appointment with the pin-sticker man, Dorrance had said; that was the message, and today the knife-sticker man had more or less underlined it. Hell, lit it in neon.

Ralph hunted out a number in the Yellow Pages and dialed it.

'You have reached the office of Dr James Roy Hong,' a pleasant female voice informed him. 'There is no one available to take your call right now, so please leave a message at the sound of the tone. We will get back to you just as soon as possible.'

The answering machine beeped. In a voice which surprised him with its steadiness, Ralph said: 'This is Ralph Roberts. I'm scheduled to come in tomorrow at ten o'clock. I'm sorry, but

I won't be able to make it. Something has come up. Thank you.' He paused, then added: 'I'll pay for the appointment, of course.'

He shut his eyes and groped the phone back into the cradle. Then he leaned his forehead against the wall.

What are you doing, Ralph? What in God's name do you think you're doing?

'It's a long walk back to Eden, sweetheart.'

You can't seriously think whatever you're thinking . . . can you?

'. . . a long walk, so don't sweat the small stuff.'

What exactly are *you thinking, Ralph?*

He didn't know; he didn't have the slightest idea. Something about fate, he supposed, and appointments in Samarra. He only knew for sure that rings of pain were spreading out from the little hole in his left side, the hole the knife-sticker man had made. The EMT had given him half a dozen pain-pills and he supposed he should take one, but just now he felt too tired to go to the sink and draw a glass of water . . . and if he was too tired to cross one shitty little room, how the hell would he ever make the long walk back to Eden?

Ralph didn't know, and for the time being he didn't care. He only wanted to stand where he was, with his forehead against the wall and his eyes shut so he wouldn't have to look at anything.

Chapter Eight

1

The beach was a long white edging, like a flirt of silk slip at the hem of the bright blue sea, and it was totally empty except for a round object about seventy yards away. This round object was about the size of a basketball, and it filled Ralph with a fear that was both deep and – for the moment, at least – groundless.

Don't go near it, he told himself. *There's something bad about it. Something* really *bad. It's a black dog barking at a blue moon, blood in the sink, a raven perched on a bust of Pallas just inside my chamber door. You don't want to go near it, Ralph, and you don't* need *to go near it, because this is one of Joe Wyzer's lucid dreams. You can just turn and cruise away, if you want.*

Except his feet began to carry him forward anyway, so maybe this wasn't a lucid dream. Not pleasant, either, not at all. Because the closer he got to that object on the beach, the less it looked like a basketball.

It was by far the most realistic dream Ralph had ever experienced, and the fact that he knew he was dreaming actually seemed to heighten that sense of realism. Of lucidity. He could feel the fine, loose sand under his bare feet, warm but not hot; he could hear the grinding, rock-throated roar of the incoming waves as they lost their balance and sprawled their way up the lower beach, where the sand glistened like wet tanned skin; could smell salt and drying seaweed, a strong and tearful smell that reminded him of summer vacations spent at Old Orchard Beach when he was a child.

Hey, old buddy, if you can't change this dream, I think maybe you ought to hit the ejection switch and bail out of it – wake yourself up, in other words, and right away.

He had closed half the distance to the object on the beach and there was no longer any question about what it was – not a basketball but a head. Someone had buried a human being up to the chin in the sand . . . and, Ralph suddenly realized, the tide was coming in.

He didn't bail out; he began to run. As he did, the frothy edge of a wave touched the head. It opened its mouth and began to scream. Even raised in a shriek, Ralph knew that voice at once. It was Carolyn's voice.

The froth of another wave ran up the beach and backwashed the hair which had been clinging to the head's wet cheeks. Ralph began to run faster, knowing he was almost certainly going to be too late. The tide was coming in fast. It would drown her long before he could free her buried body from the sand.

You don't have to save her, Ralph. Carolyn's already dead, and it didn't happen on some deserted beach. It happened in Room 317 of Derry Home Hospital. You were with her at the end, and the sound you heard wasn't surf but sleet hitting the window. Remember?

He remembered, but he ran faster nevertheless, sending puffs of sugary sand out behind him.

You won't ever get to her, though; you know how it is in dreams, don't you? Each thing you rush toward turns into something else.

No, *that* wasn't how the poem went . . . or was it? Ralph couldn't be sure. All he clearly remembered now was that it had ended with the narrator running blindly from something deadly

(*Glancing over my shoulder I see its shape*)

which was hunting him through the woods . . . hunting him and closing in.

Yet he *was* getting closer to the dark shape on the sand. It wasn't changing into anything else, either, and when he fell on his knees before Carolyn, he understood at once why he had not been able to recognize his wife of forty-five years, even from a distance: something was terribly wrong with her aura. It clung to her skin like a filthy dry-cleaning bag. When Ralph's shadow fell on her, Carolyn's eyes rolled up like the eyes of a horse that has shattered its leg going over a high fence. She was breathing in rapid, frightened gasps, and each expulsion of air sent jets of gray-black aura from her nostrils.

The tattered balloon-string straggling up from the crown of her head was the purple-black of a festering wound. When she opened her mouth to scream again, an unpleasant glowing substance flew from her lips in gummy strings which disappeared almost as soon as his eyes had registered their existence.

I'll save you, Carol! he shouted. He fell on his knees and began digging at the sand around her like a dog digging up a bone . . . and as the thought occurred to him, he realized that Rosalie, the early morning scavenger of Harris Avenue, was sitting tiredly behind his screaming wife. It was as if the dog had been summoned by the thought. Rosalie, he saw, was also surrounded by one of those filthy black auras. She had Bill McGovern's missing Panama hat between her paws, and it looked as though she had enjoyed many a good chew on it since it had come into her possession.

So that's where the damn hat went, Ralph thought, then turned back to Carolyn and began to dig even faster. So far he hadn't managed to uncover so much as a single shoulder.

Never mind me! Carolyn screamed at him. *I'm already dead, remember? Watch for the white-man tracks, Ralph! The—*

A wave, glassy green on the bottom and the curdled white of soapsuds on top, broke less than ten feet from the beach. It ran up the sand toward them, freezing Ralph's balls with cold water and burying Carolyn's head momentarily in a grit-filled surge of foam. When the wave retreated, Ralph raised his own horror-filled shriek to the indifferent blue sky. The retreating wave had done in seconds what it had taken the radiation treatments almost a month to do; took her hair, washed her bald. And the crown of her head had begun to bulge at the spot where the blackish balloon-string was attached.

Carolyn, no! he howled, digging even faster. The sand was now dank and unpleasantly heavy.

Never mind, she said. Gray-black puffs came from her mouth with each word, like dirty vapor from an industrial smokestack. *It's just the tumor, and it's inoperable, so don't lose any sleep over* that *part of the show. What the hell, it's a long walk back to Eden, so don't sweat the small stuff, right? But you have to keep an eye out for those tracks . . .*

Carolyn, I don't know what you're talking about!

Another wave came, wetting Ralph to the waist and inundating Carolyn again. When it withdrew, the swelling on the crown of her head was beginning to split open.

You'll find out soon enough, Carolyn replied, and then the swelling on her head popped with a sound like a hammer striking a slab of meat. A haze of blood flew into the clear, salt-smelling air, and a horde of black bugs the size of cockroaches were pouring out of her. Ralph had never seen anything like them before – not even in a dream – and they filled him with an almost hysterical loathing. He would have fled, Carolyn or not, but he was frozen in place, too stunned to move a single finger, let alone get up and run.

Some of the black bugs ran back into Carolyn by way of her screaming mouth, but most of them hurried down her cheek and shoulder to the wet sand. Their accusing, alien eyes never left Ralph as they went. *All this is your fault,* the eyes seemed to say. *You could have saved her, Ralph, and a better man would have saved her.*

Carolyn! he screamed. He put his hands out to her, then pulled them back, terrified of the black bugs, which were still spewing out of her head. Behind her, Rosalie sat in her own small pocket of darkness, looking gravely at him and now holding McGovern's misplaced *chapeau* in her mouth.

One of Carolyn's eyes popped out and lay on the wet sand like a blob of blueberry jelly. Bugs vomited from the now-empty socket.

Carolyn! he screamed. *Carolyn! Carolyn! Car—*

2

'– olyn! Carolyn! Car—'

Suddenly, in the same instant that he knew the dream was over, Ralph was falling. He barely registered the fact before he thumped to the bedroom floor. He managed to break his fall with one outstretched hand, probably saving himself a nasty rap on the head but provoking a howl of pain from beneath the butterfly bandage taped high up on his left side. For the moment, at least, he barely registered the pain. What he felt was fear, revulsion, a horrible, aching grief . . . and most of all an overwhelming sense of gratitude. The bad dream – surely the worst dream he'd ever had – was over, and he was in the world of real things again.

He pulled back his mostly unbuttoned pajama top, checked the bandage for bleeding, saw none, and then sat up. Just doing that much seemed to exhaust him; the thought of getting up, even long enough to fall back into bed, seemed out of the question for the time being. Maybe after his panicky, racing heart slowed down a little.

Can people die of bad dreams? he wondered, and in answer he heard Joe Wyzer's voice: *You bet they can, Ralph, although the medical examiner usually ends up writing* suicide *on the cause-of-death line.*

In the shaky aftermath of his nightmare, sitting on the floor and hugging his knees with his right arm, Ralph had no real doubt that some dreams *were* powerful enough to kill. The details of this one were fading out now, but he could still remember the climax all too well: that thudding sound, like a hammer hitting a thick cut of beef, and the vile spew of bugs from Carolyn's head. Plump they had been, plump and lively, and why not? They had been feasting on his dead wife's brain.

Ralph uttered a low, watery moan and swiped at his face with his left hand, provoking another jolt from beneath the bandage. His palm came away slick with sweat.

What, exactly, had she been telling him to watch out for? White-man traps? No – *tracks,* not traps. White-man *tracks,* whatever they were. Had there been more? Maybe, maybe not. He couldn't remember for sure, and so what? It had been a dream, for Christ's sake, just a *dream,* and outside of the fantasy world described in the tabloid newspapers, dreams meant nothing and proved nothing. When a person went to sleep, his mind seemed to turn into a kind of rathouse bargain hunter, sifting through the discount bins of mostly worthless short-term memories, looking not for items which were valuable or even useful but only for things that were still bright and shiny. These it put together in freakshow collages which were often striking but had, for the most part, all the sense of Natalie Deepneau's conversation. Rosalie the dog had turned up, even Bill's missing Panama had made a cameo appearance, but it all meant nothing . . . except tomorrow night he would not take one of the pain-pills the EMT had given him even if his arm felt like it was falling off. Not only had the one he'd taken during the late news failed to keep him under, as he had hoped and half-expected; it had probably played its own part in causing the nightmare.

Ralph managed to get up off the floor and sit on the edge of the bed. A wave of faintness floated through his head like parachute silk, and he shut his eyes until the feeling passed. While he was sitting there with his head down and his eyes closed, he groped for the lamp on the bedside table and turned it on. When he opened his eyes, the area of the bedroom lit by its warm yellow glow looked very bright and very real.

He looked at the clock beside the lamp: 1:48 a.m., and he felt totally awake and totally alert, pain-pill or no pain-pill. He got up, walked slowly into the kitchen, and put on the teakettle. Then he leaned against the counter, absently massaging the bandage beneath his left armpit, trying to quiet the throbbing his most recent adventures had awakened there. When the kettle steamed, he poured hot water over a bag of Sleepytime – *there was a joke for you* – and then took the cup into the living room. He plopped into the wing-back chair without bothering to turn on a light; the streetlamps and the dim glow coming from the bedroom provided all he needed.

Well, he thought, *here I am again, front row center. Let the play begin.*

Time passed, just how much he could not have said, but the throbbing beneath his arm had eased and the tea had gone from hot to barely lukewarm when he registered movement at the corner of his eye. Ralph turned his head, expecting to see Rosalie, but it wasn't Rosalie. It was two men stepping out onto the stoop of a house on the other side of Harris Avenue. Ralph couldn't make out the colors of the house – the orange arc-sodiums the city had installed several years ago provided great visibility but made any perception of true colors almost impossible – yet he could see that the color of the trim was radically different from the color of the rest. That, coupled with its location, made Ralph almost positive it was May Locher's house.

The two men on May Locher's stoop were very short, probably no more than four feet tall. They appeared to be surrounded by greenish auras. They were dressed in identical white smocks, which looked to Ralph like the ones worn by actors in those old TV doc-operas – black and white melodramas like *Ben Casey* and *Dr Kildare*. One of them had something in his hand. Ralph squinted. He couldn't make it out, but it had a sharp and hungry look. He could not have sworn under oath that it was a knife, but he thought it might be. Yes, it might very well be a knife.

His first clear evaluative thought about this experience was that the men over there looked like aliens in a movie about UFO abductions – *Communion*, perhaps, or *Fire in the Sky*. His second was that he had fallen asleep again, right here in his wing-chair, without even noticing.

That's right, Ralph – it's just a little more rummage-sale action, probably brought on by the stress of being stabbed and helped along by that frigging pain-pill.

He sensed nothing frightening about the two figures on May Locher's stoop other than the long, sharp-looking thing one of them was holding. Ralph supposed that not even your dreaming mind could do much with a couple of short bald guys wearing white tunics which looked left over from Central Casting. Also, there was nothing frightening about their behaviour – nothing furtive, nothing menacing. They stood on the stoop as if they had every right to be there in the darkest, stillest hour of the morning. They were facing each other, the attitudes of their bodies and large bald heads suggesting two old friends having a sober, civilized conversation. They looked thoughtful and intelligent – the kind of space-travellers who would be more apt to say 'We come in peace' than kidnap you, stick a probe up your ass, and then take notes on your reaction.

All right, so maybe this new dream's not an out-and-out nightmare. After the last one, are you complaining?

No, of course he wasn't. Winding up on the floor once a night was plenty, thanks. Yet there was something very disquieting about this dream just the same; it felt real in a way that his dream of Carolyn had not. This was his own living room, after all, not some weird, deserted beach he had never seen before. He was sitting in the same wing-back chair where he sat every morning, holding a cup of tea which was now almost cold in his left hand, and when he raised the fingers of his right hand to his nose, as he was doing now, he could still smell a faint whiff of soap beneath the nails . . . the Irish Spring he liked to use in the shower . . .

Ralph suddenly reached beneath his left armpit and pressed his fingers to the bandage there. The pain was immediate and intense . . . but the two small bald men in the white tunics stayed right where they were, on May Locher's doorstep.

It doesn't matter what you think you feel, Ralph. It can't *matter, because—*

'Fuck you!' Ralph said in a hoarse, low voice. He rose from the wing-chair, putting his cup down on the little table beside it as he did. Sleepytime slopped onto the *TV Guide* there. 'Fuck you, *this is no dream!*'

3

He hurried across the living room to the kitchen, pajamas flapping, old worn slippers scuffing and thumping, the place where Charlie Pickering had stuck him sending out hot little bursts of pain. He grabbed a chair and took it into the apartment's small foyer. There was a closet here. Ralph opened its door, snapped on the light just inside, positioned the chair so he would be able to reach the closet's top shelf, and then stood on it.

The shelf was a clutter of lost or forgotten items, most of which had belonged to Carolyn. These were small things, little more than scraps, but looking at them drove away the last lingering conviction that this had to be a dream. There was an ancient bag of M&M's – her secret snack-food, her comfort-food. There was a lace heart, a single discarded white satin pump with a broken heel, a photo album. These things hurt a lot more than the knife-prick under his arm, but he had no time to hurt just now.

Ralph leaned forward, placing his left hand on the high, dusty shelf to balance his weight, then began to shuffle through the junk with his right hand, all the while praying that the kitchen chair wouldn't take a notion to scoot out from under him. The wound below his armpit was now throbbing outrageously, and he knew he was going to get it bleeding again if he didn't stop the athletics soon, but . . .

I'm sure they're up here somewhere . . . well . . . almost sure . . .

He pushed aside his old fly-box and his wicker creel. There was a stack of magazines behind the creel. The one on top was an issue of *Look* with Andy Williams on the cover. Ralph shoved them aside with the heel of his hand, sending up a flurry of dust. The old bag of M&M's fell to the floor and split open, spraying brightly colored bits of candy in every direction. Ralph leaned even farther forward, now almost on his toes. He supposed it was his imagination, but he thought he could sense the kitchen chair he was on getting ready to be evil.

The thought had no more than crossed his mind when the chair squawked and began to slide slowly backward on the hardwood floor. Ralph ignored that, ignored his throbbing side, and ignored the voice telling him he ought to stop this, he really ought to, because he was dreaming awake, just as the Hall book said many insomniacs eventually did, and although those little fellows across the street didn't really exist, he could really be standing here on this slowly sliding chair, and he could really break his hip when it went out from under him, and just how the hell was he going to explain what had happened when some smartass doctor in the Emergency Room of Derry Home asked him?

Grunting, he reached all the way back, pushed aside a carton from which half a Christmas tree star protruded like a strange spiky periscope (knocking the heel-less evening pump to the floor in the process), and saw what he wanted in the far lefthand corner of the shelf: the case which contained his old Zeiss-Ikon binoculars.

Ralph stepped off the chair just before it could slide all the way out from under him, moved it closer in, then got up on it again. He couldn't reach all the way into the corner where the binocular case stood, so he grabbed the trout-net which had been lying up here next to his creel and fly-box for lo these many years and succeeded in bagging the case on his second try. He dragged it forward until he could grab the strap, stepped off the chair, and came down on the fallen evening pump. His ankle twisted painfully. Ralph staggered, flailed his arms for balance, and managed to avoid going face-first into the wall. As he started back into the living room, however, he felt liquid warmth beneath the bandage on his side. He had managed to open the knife-wound again after all. Wonderful. Just a wonderful night *chez* Roberts . . . and how long had he been away from the window? He didn't know, but it felt like a long time, and he was sure the little bald doctors would be gone when he got back there. The street would be empty, and—

He stopped dead, the binocular case dangling at the end of its strap and tracking a long slow trapezoidal shadow back and forth across the floor where the orange glow of the streetlights lay like an ugly coat of paint.

Little bald doctors? Was that how he had just thought of them? Yes, of course, because that was what *they* called them – the folks who claimed to have been abducted by them . . . examined by them . . . operated on by them in some cases. They were physicians from space, proctologists from the great beyond. But that wasn't the big deal. The big deal was—

Ed used the phrase, Ralph thought. *He used it the night he called me and warned me to stay away from him and his interests. He said it was the doctor who told him about the Crimson King and the Centurions and all the rest.*

'Yes,' Ralph whispered. His back was prickling madly with gooseflesh. 'Yes, that's what he said. "The doctor told me. The little bald doctor." '

When he reached the window, he saw that the strangers were still out there, although they had moved from May Locher's stoop to the sidewalk while he had been fishing for the binoculars. They were standing directly beneath one of those damned orange streetlights, in fact. Ralph's feeling that Harris Avenue looked like a deserted stage set after the evening performance returned with weird, declamatory force . . . but with a different significance. For one thing, the set was no longer deserted, was it? Some ominous, long-past-midnight play had commenced in what the two odd creatures below no doubt assumed was a totally empty theater.

What would they do if they knew they had an audience? Ralph wondered. *What would they do to me?*

The bald doctors now had the shared demeanor of men who have nearly reached agreement. In that instant they did not look like doctors at all to Ralph, in spite of their smocks – they looked like blue-collar workers coming offshift at some plant or factory. These two guys, clearly buddies, have stopped outside the main gate for a moment or two to finish off some subject that can't wait even long enough for them to walk down the block to the nearest bar, knowing it will only take a minute or so in any case; total agreement is only a conversational exchange or two away.

Ralph uncased the binoculars, raised them to his eyes, and wasted a moment or two in puzzled fiddling with the focus knob before realizing he had forgotten to take off the lens caps. He did so, then raised the glasses again. This time the two figures standing under the streetlamp jumped into his field of vision at once, large and perfectly lit, but fuzzed out. He turned the little knob between the barrels again, and the two men popped into focus almost immediately. Ralph's breath stopped in his throat.

The look he got was extremely brief; no more than three seconds passed before one of the men (if they were men) nodded and clapped a hand on his companion's shoulder. Then they both turned away, leaving Ralph with nothing to look at but their bald heads and smooth, white-clad backs. Only three seconds at most, but Ralph saw enough in that brief space of time to make him profoundly uneasy.

He had run to get the binoculars for two reasons, both predicated on his inability to go on believing that this was a dream. First, he wanted to be sure he could identify the two men if he was ever called upon to do so. Second (this one was less admissible to his conscious mind but every bit as urgent), he had wanted to dispel the unsettling notion that he was having his own close encounter of the third kind.

Instead of dispelling it, his brief look through the binoculars intensified it. The little bald doctors did not actually seem to *have* features. They had *faces*, yes – eyes, noses, mouths – but they seemed as interchangeable as the chrome trim on the same make and model of a car. They could have been identical twins, but that wasn't the impression Ralph got, either. To him they looked more like department store mannequins with their Arnel wigs whisked off for the night, their eerie resemblance not the result of genetics but of mass production.

The only peculiar quality he could isolate and name was the preternaturally smooth quality of their skin – neither of them had so much as a single visible line or wrinkle. No moles, blotches, or scars, either, although Ralph supposed those were things you might miss with even a great pair of binoculars. Beyond the smooth and strangely line-free quality of their skin, everything became subjective. And his only look had been so goddam *brief*! If he had been able to get to the binoculars more quickly, without the rigmarole of the chair and the fishing net, and if he had realized that the lens caps were on right away instead of wasting more time fiddling with the focusing knob, he might have saved himself some or all of the unease he was now feeling.

They look sketched, he thought in the instant before they turned their backs on him. *That's what's really bothering me, I think. Not the identical bald heads, the identical white smocks, or even the lack of wrinkles. It's how they look sketched – the eyes just circles, the small pink ears just squiggles made with a felt-tip pen, the mouths a pair of quick, almost careless strokes of pale pink watercolor. They don't really look like* either *people or aliens; they look like hasty representations of . . . well, of I don't know what.*

He was sure of one thing: Docs #1 and #2 were both immersed in bright auras which in the binoculars appeared to be green-gold and filled with deep reddish-orange flecks that looked like sparks swirling up from a campfire. These auras conveyed a feeling of power and vitality to Ralph that their featureless, uninteresting faces did not.

The faces? I'm not sure I could pick them out again even if someone held a gun to my head. It's as if they were made to be forgotten. If they were still bald, sure – no problem. But if they were wearing wigs and maybe sitting down, so I couldn't see how short they are? Maybe . . . the lack of lines might do the trick . . . but then again, maybe not. The auras, though . . . those green-gold auras with the red flecks swirling through them . . . I'd know them anywhere. But there's something wrong with them, isn't there? What is it?

The answer popped into Ralph's mind as suddenly and easily as the two creatures had popped into view when he had finally remembered to remove the lens caps from the binoculars. Both of the little doctors were swaddled in brilliant auras . . . but neither had a balloon-string floating up from his hairless head. Not even a sign of one.

They went strolling down Harris Avenue in the direction of Strawford Park, moving with the ease of two friends out for a Sunday stroll. Just before they left the bright circle of light thrown by the streetlamp in front of May Locher's house, Ralph dropped the angle of the binoculars so they picked up the item in Doc #1's right hand. It wasn't a knife, as he had surmised, but it still wasn't the sort of object you felt comfortable seeing in the hand of a departing stranger in the wee hours of the morning.

It was a pair of long-bladed, stainless-steel scissors.

4

That sense of being pushed relentlessly toward the mouth of a tunnel where all sorts of unpleasant things were waiting was with him again, only now it was accompanied by a feeling of panic, because it seemed that the latest big shove had taken place while he had been asleep and dreaming of his dead wife. Something inside him wanted to shriek with terror, and Ralph understood that if he didn't do something to soothe it immediately, he would soon be shrieking out loud. He closed his eyes and began to take deep breaths, trying to picture a different item of food with each one: a tomato, a potato, an ice-cream sandwich, a Brussels sprout. Dr Jamal had taught Carolyn this simple relaxation technique, and it had frequently staved off her headaches before they could get up a full head of steam – even in the last six weeks, when the tumor had been out of control, the technique had sometimes worked, and it controlled Ralph's panic now. His heartbeat began to slow, and that feeling that he needed to scream began to pass.

Continuing to take deep breaths and to think

(*apple   pear   slice of lemon pie*)

of food, Ralph carefully snapped the lens caps back on the binoculars. His hands were still trembling, but not so badly he couldn't use them. Once the binoculars were capped and returned to their case, Ralph gingerly raised his left arm and looked at the bandage. There was a red spot in the center of it the size of an aspirin tablet, but it did not appear to be spreading. Good.

There isn't anything good about this, Ralph.

Fair enough, but that wasn't going to help him decide exactly what had happened, or what he was going to do about it. Step one was to push his dreadful dream of Carolyn to one side for the time being and decide what had actually happened.

'I've been awake ever since I hit the floor,' Ralph told the empty room. 'I know that, and I know I saw those men.'

Yes. He had really seen them, and the green-gold auras around them. He wasn't alone, either; Ed Deepneau had seen at least one of them, too. Ralph would have bet the farm on it, if he'd had a farm to bet. It didn't ease his mind much, however, to know that he and the wife-beating paranoid from up the street were seeing the same little bald guys.

And the auras, Ralph – didn't he say something about those, too?

Well, he hadn't used that exact word, but Ralph was quite sure he had spoken of the auras at least twice, just the same. *Ralph, sometimes the world is full of colors.* That had been August, shortly before John Leydecker had arrested Ed on a charge of domestic abuse, a misdemeanor. Then, almost a month later, when he had called Ralph on the phone: *Are you seeing the colors yet?*

First the colors, now the little bald doctors; surely the Crimson King himself would be along any time. And all that aside, what was he supposed to do about what he had just seen?

The answer came in an unexpected but welcome burst of clarity. The issue, he saw, was not his own sanity, not the auras, not the little bald doctors, but May Locher. He had just seen two strangers step out of Mrs Locher's house in the dead of night . . . and one of them had been carrying a potentially lethal weapon.

Ralph reached past the cased binoculars, took the telephone, and dialed 911.

5

'This is Officer Hagen.' A woman's voice. 'How may I help you?'

'By listening carefully and acting fast,' Ralph said crisply. The look of dazed indecision which he had worn so frequently since midsummer was gone now; sitting erect in the wing-back chair with the phone in his lap he looked not seventy but a healthy and capable fifty-five. 'You may be able to save a woman's life.'

'Sir, would you please give me your name and—'

'Don't interrupt me, please, Officer Hagen,' said the man who could no longer remember the last four digits of the Derry Cinema Center. 'I woke up a short time ago, couldn't go back to sleep, and decided to sit up for a while. My living room looks out on upper Harris Avenue. I just saw—'

Here Ralph paused for the barest moment, thinking not about what he had seen but what he wanted to tell Officer Hagen he had seen. The answer came as quickly and effortlessly as the decision to call 911 in the first place.

'I saw two men coming out of a house up the street from the Red Apple store. The house belongs to a woman named May Locher. That's L-O-C-H-E-R, first letter L as in Lexington. Mrs Locher is severely ill. I've never seen these two men before.' He paused again, but this time consciously, wanting to achieve maximum effect. 'One of them had a pair of scissors in his hand.'

'Site address?' Officer Hagen asked. She was calm enough, but Ralph sensed he had turned on a lot of her lights.

'I don't know,' he said. 'Get it out of the phone book, Officer Hagen, or just tell the responding officers to look for the yellow house with the pink trim half a block or so up from the Red Apple. They'll probably have to use a flashlight to pick it out because of the damned orange streetlights, but they'll find it.'

'Yes, sir, I'm sure they will, but I still need your name and telephone number for our rec—'

Ralph replaced the phone gently in its cradle. He sat looking at it for almost a full minute, expecting it to ring. When it didn't, he decided they either didn't have the fancy traceback equipment he saw on the TV true-crime shows, or it hadn't been turned on. That was good. It didn't solve the problem of what he was going to do or say if they hauled May Locher out of her hideous yellow-and-pink house in pieces, but it *did* buy a little more thinking time.

Below, Harris Avenue remained still and silent, lit only by the hi-intensity lamps which marched off in both directions like some surrealist dream of perspective. The play – short, but full of drama – appeared to be over. The stage was empty again. It—

No, not quite empty after all. Rosalie came limping out of the alley between the Red Apple and the True-Value Hardware next door. The faded bandanna flapped around her neck. This wasn't a Thursday, there were no garbage cans set out for Rosalie to investigate, and she moved briskly up the sidewalk until she got to May Locher's house. There she stopped and lowered her nose (looking at that long and rather pretty nose, Ralph had thought on occasion that there must be a collie somewhere in Rosalie's woodpile).

Something was glimmering there, Ralph realized.

He got the binoculars out of their case once more and trained them on Rosalie. As he did, he found his mind returning to September 10th again – this time to his meeting with Bill and Lois just outside the entrance to Strawford Park. He remembered how Bill had put his arm around Lois's waist and led her up the street; how the two of them together had made Ralph think of Ginger Rogers and Fred Astaire. Most of all he remembered the spectral tracks the two of them had left behind. Lois's had been gray; Bill's olive green. Hallucinations, he had thought them at the time, back in the good old days before he'd started attracting the attention of nuts like Charlie Pickering and seeing little bald doctors in the middle of the night.

Rosalie was sniffing at a similar track. It was the same green-gold as the auras which had surrounded Bald Doc #1 and Bald Doc #2. Ralph panned the binoculars slowly away from the dog and saw more tracks, two sets of them, leading down the sidewalk in the direction of the park. They were fading – he could almost see them fading as he looked at them – but they were there.

Ralph panned the binoculars back to Rosalie, suddenly feeling an enormous wave of affection for the mangy old stray . . . and why not? If he had needed final, absolute proof that he had actually seen the things he *thought* he had seen, Rosalie was it.

If baby Natalie was here, she'd see them too, Ralph thought . . . and then all his doubts tried to crowd back in. Would she? Would she really? He thought he had seen the baby grab at the faint auras left by his fingers, and he had been sure she was gawking at the spectral green smoke sizzling off the flowers in the kitchen, but how could he be sure? How could anyone be sure what a baby was looking at or reaching for?

But Rosalie . . . look, right down there, see her?

The only trouble with that, Ralph realized, was that he hadn't seen the tracks until Rosalie had begun to sniff the sidewalk. Maybe she was sniffing at an entrancing remnant of leftover postman, and what he was seeing had been created by nothing more than his tired, sleep-starved mind . . . like the little bald doctors themselves.

In the magnified field of the binoculars, Rosalie now began to make her way down Harris Avenue with her nose to the sidewalk and her ragged tail waving slowly back and forth. She was moving from the green-gold tracks left by Doc #1 to those left by Doc #2, and then back to Doc #1's trail again.

So now why don't you tell me what that stray bitch is following, Ralph? Do you think it's possible for a dog to track a fucking hallucination? It's not *a hallucination; it's tracks. Real tracks. The white-man tracks that Carolyn told you to watch out for. You know that. You see that.*

'It's crazy, though,' he told himself. 'Crazy!'

But was it? Was it really? The dream might have been more than a dream. If there was such a thing as hyper-reality – and he could now testify that there was – then maybe there was such a thing as precognition, too. Or ghosts which came in dreams and foretold the future. Who knew? It was as if a door in the wall of reality had come ajar . . . and now all sorts of unwelcome things were flying through.

Of one thing he was sure: the tracks *were* really there. He saw them, Rosalie smelled them, and that was all there was to it. Ralph had discovered a number of strange and interesting things during his six months of premature waking, and one of them was that a human being's capacity for self-deception seemed to be at its lowest ebb between three and six in the morning, and it was now . . .

Ralph leaned forward so he could see the clock on the kitchen wall. Just past three-thirty. Uh-huh.

He raised the binoculars again and saw Rosalie still moving up the bald docs' backtrail. If someone came strolling along Harris Avenue right now – unlikely, given the hour, but not impossible – they would see nothing but a stray mutt with a dirty coat, sniffing at the sidewalk in the aimless fashion of untrained, unowned dogs everywhere. But Ralph could see what Rosalie was sniffing *at,* and had finally given himself permission to believe his eyes. It was a permission he might revoke once the sun was up, but for now he knew exactly what he was seeing.

Rosalie's head came up suddenly. Her ears cocked forward. For one moment she was almost beautiful, the way a hunting dog on point is beautiful. Then, moments before the headlights of a car approaching the Harris Avenue–Witcham Street intersection splashed the street, she was gone back the way she had come, running in a corkscrewing, limping gait that made Ralph feel sorry for her. When you came right down to it, what was Rosalie but another Harris Avenue Old Crock, one that didn't even have the comfort of the occasional game of gin rummy or penny-ante poker with others of her kind? She darted back into the alley between the Red Apple and the hardware store an instant before a Derry police cruiser turned the corner and floated slowly up the street. Its siren was off, but the revolving flashers were on. They painted the sleeping houses and small businesses ranged along this part of Harris Avenue with alternating pulses of red and blue light.

Ralph put the binoculars back in his lap and leaned forward in the wing-chair, forearms on his thighs, watching intently. His heart was beating hard enough for him to be able to feel it in his temples.

The cruiser slowed to a crawl as it passed the Red Apple. The spotlight mounted on its righthand side snapped on, and the beam began to slide across the fronts of the sleeping houses on the far side of the street. In most cases it also slid across the street numbers mounted beside doors or on porch columns. When it lit on the number of May Locher's house (86, Ralph saw, and he didn't need the binoculars to read it, either), the cruiser's tail-lights flashed and the car came to a stop.

Two uniformed policemen got out and approached the walk leading up to the house, oblivious of both the man watching from a darkened second-floor window across the street and the fading green-gold footprints over which they were walking. They conferred, and Ralph raised the binoculars again to get a closer look. He was almost positive that the younger of the two men was the uniformed cop who had shown up with Leydecker at Ed's house on the day Ed had been arrested. Knoll? Had that been his name?

'No,' Ralph murmured. 'Nell. Chris Nell. Or maybe it was Jess.'

Nell and his partner seemed to be having a serious discussion about something – much more serious than the one the little bald doctors had been having before they strolled away. This one ended with the cops drawing their sidearms and then climbing the narrow steps to Mrs Locher's stoop in single file, with Nell in front. He pressed the doorbell, waited, then pressed it again. This time he leaned on the button for a good five seconds. They waited a little more, and then the second cop brushed past Nell and had a go at the button himself.

Maybe that one knows The Secret Art of Doorbell-Ringing, Ralph thought. *Probably learned it by answering a Rosicrucians ad.*

If so, the technique failed him this time. There was still no response, and Ralph wasn't surprised. Strange bald men with scissors notwithstanding, he doubted May Locher could even get out of bed.

But if she's bedridden, she might have a companion, someone to get her her meals, help her to the toilet or give her the bedpan—

Chris Nell – or maybe it was Jess – stepped up to the plate again. This time he forwent the doorbell in favor of the old wham-wham-wham, open-in-the-name-of-the-law technique.

He used his left fist to do this. He was still holding his gun in his right, the barrel pressed against the leg of his uniform pants.

A terrible image, every bit as clear and persuasive as the auras he had been seeing, suddenly filled Ralph's mind. He saw a woman with a clear plastic oxygen mask over her mouth and nose lying in bed. Above the mask, her glazed eyes bulged sightlessly from their sockets. Below it, her throat had been opened in a wide, ragged smile. The bedclothes and the bosom of the woman's nightgown were drenched with blood. Not far away, lying on the floor, was the facedown corpse of another woman – the companion. Marching up the back of this second woman's pink flannel nightgown were half a dozen stab-wounds made by the points of Doc #1's scissors. And, Ralph knew, if you raised the nightgown for a closer look, each would look a lot like the wound under his own arm . . . like the sort of oversized period made by children just learning to print.

Ralph tried to blink the grisly vision away. It wouldn't go. He felt dull pain in his hands and saw he had closed them into tight fists; the nails were digging into his palms. He forced his hands open and clamped them on his thighs. Now the eye in his mind saw the woman in the pink nightgown twitching slightly – she was still alive. But maybe not for long. Almost certainly not for long unless these two oafs decided to try something a little more productive than just standing on the stoop and taking turns knocking or jazzing the doorbell.

'Come on, you guys,' Ralph said, squeezing at his thighs. 'Come on, come on, let's get with it, what do you say?'

You know the things you're seeing are all in your head, don't you? he asked himself uneasily. *I mean, there might be a couple of women lying dead over there, sure, there* might *be, but you don't* know *that, right? It's not like the auras, or the tracks . . .*

No, it wasn't like the auras or the tracks, and yes, he *did* know that. He also knew that no one was answering the door over there at 86 Harris Avenue, and that did not bode well for Bill McGovern's old Cardville schoolmate. He hadn't seen any blood on the scissors in Doc #1's hand, but given the iffy quality of the old Zeiss-Ikon binocs, that didn't prove much. Also, the guy could have wiped them clean before leaving the house. The thought had no more than crossed Ralph's mind before his imagination added a bloody handtowel lying beside the dead companion in the pink nightgown.

'Come *on*, you two!' Ralph cried in a low voice. 'Jesus Christ, you gonna stand there all *night?*'

More headlights splashed up Harris Avenue. The new arrival was an unmarked Ford sedan with a flashing red dashboard bubble. The man who got out was wearing plain clothes – gray poplin windbreaker and blue knitted watchcap. Ralph had maintained momentary hopes that the newcomer would turn out to be John Leydecker, even though Leydecker had told him he wouldn't be coming on until noon, but he didn't have to check with the binoculars to make sure it wasn't. This man was much slimmer, and wearing a dark mustache. Cop #2 went down the walk to meet him while Chris-or-Jess Nell went around the corner of Mrs Locher's house.

One of those pauses which the movies so conveniently edit out then ensued. Cop #2 reholstered his gun. He and the newly arrived detective stood at the foot of Mrs Locher's stoop, apparently talking and glancing at the closed door every now and then. Once the uniformed cop took a step or two in the direction Nell had gone. The detective reached out, grasped his arm, detained him. They talked some more. Ralph clutched his upper thighs tighter and made a small, frustrated noise in his throat.

A few minutes crawled by, and then everything happened at once in that confusing, overlapping, inconclusive way with which emergency situations seem to develop. Another police car arrived (Mrs Locher's house and those neighboring it on the right and left were now bathed in streaks of conflicting red and yellow light). Two more uniformed cops got out of it, opened the trunk, and removed a bulky contraption that looked to Ralph like a portable torture device. He believed this gadget was known as the Jaws of Life. Following the huge storm in the spring of 1985, a storm which had resulted in the deaths of more than two hundred people – many of whom had been trapped and drowned in their cars – Derry's schoolchildren had mounted a penny-drive to buy one.

As the two new cops were carrying the Jaws of Life across the sidewalk, the front door of the house on the uphill side of Mrs Locher's opened and the Eberlys, Stan and Georgina, stepped out onto *their* stoop. They wore matching his 'n hers bathrobes, and Stan's gray hair was standing up in wild tufts that made Ralph think of Charlie Pickering. He raised the binoculars, scanned their curious, excited faces briefly, then put them back in his lap again.

The next vehicle to appear was an ambulance from Derry Home Hospital. Like the police cars which had already arrived, its howler was off in deference to the hour, but it had a full roofrack of red lights, and they were strobing wildly. To Ralph, the developments across the street looked like a scene from one of his beloved *Dirty Harry* movies, only with the sound turned off.

The two cops got the Jaws of Life halfway across the lawn and then dropped it. The detective in the windbreaker and the watchcap turned to them and raised his hands to shoulder-level, palms out, as if to say *What did you think you were going to do with* that *thing? Break down the goddam door with it?* At the same second, Officer Nell came back around the house. He was shaking his head.

The detective in the watchcap abruptly turned, brushed past Nell and his partner, mounted the steps, raised one foot, and kicked in May Locher's front door. He paused to unzip his jacket, probably to free access to his gun, and then walked in without looking back.

Ralph felt like applauding.

Nell and his partner looked at each other uncertainly, then followed the detective up the steps and through the door. Ralph leaned forward even farther in his chair, now close enough to the window for his nostrils to make little fog-roses on the glass. Three men, their white hospital pants looking orange in the glare of the hi-intensity streetlamps, got out of the ambulance. One of them opened the rear doors and then all three of them simply stood there, hands in jacket pockets, waiting to see if they would be needed. The two cops who had carried the Jaws of Life halfway across Mrs Locher's lawn looked at each other, shrugged, picked it up, and began carrying it back toward their cruiser again. There were several large divots in the lawn where they had dropped it.

Just let her be okay, that's all, Ralph thought. *Just let her – and anyone who was in the house with her – be okay.*

The detective appeared in the doorway again, and Ralph's heart sank as he motioned to the men standing at the rear of the ambulance. Two of them removed a stretcher with a collapsible undercarriage; the third remained where he was. The men with the stretcher went up the walk and into the house at a smart pace, but they did not run, and when the orderly who had remained behind produced a pack of cigarettes and lit one, Ralph knew – suddenly, completely, and with no doubts – that May Locher was dead.

6

Stan and Georgina Eberly walked to the low line of hedge which separated their front yard from Mrs Locher's. They had put their arms around each other's waists, and to Ralph they looked like the Bobbsey Twins grown old and fat and frightened.

Other neighbors were also coming out, either awakened by the silent convergence of emergency lights or because the telephone network along this little stretch of Harris Avenue was already beginning to operate. Most of the people Ralph saw were old ('We golden-agers', Bill McGovern liked to call them . . . always with that small satirical lift of the eyebrow, of course), men and women whose rest was fragile and easily broken at the best of times. He suddenly realized that Ed, Helen, and Baby Natalie had been the youngest people between here and the Extension . . . and now the Deepneaus were gone.

I could go down there, he thought. *I'd fit right in. Just another one of Bill's golden-agers.*

Except he couldn't. His legs felt like bunches of teabags held together by weak twists of string, and he was quite sure that if he tried to get up, he would go flopping bonelessly to the floor. So he sat and watched from his window, watched the play develop below him on the stage which had always been empty at this hour before . . . except for the occasional walk-through by Rosalie, that was. It was a play he had produced himself, with a single anonymous telephone call. He watched the orderlies re-emerge with the stretcher, this time moving more slowly because of the sheeted figure which had been strapped to it. Warring streaks of blue and red light flickered over that sheet, and the shapes of legs, hips, arms, neck, and head beneath it.

Ralph was suddenly plunged back into his dream. He saw his wife under the sheet – not May Locher but Carolyn Roberts, and at any moment her head would split open and the black bugs, the ones which had grown fat on the meat of her diseased brain, would begin to boil out.

216

Ralph raised the heels of his palms to his eyes. Some sound – some inarticulate sound of grief and rage, horror and weariness – escaped him. He sat that way for a long time, wishing he had never seen any of this and hoping blindly that if there really *was* a tunnel, he would not be required to enter it after all. The auras were strange and beautiful, but there was not enough beauty in all of them to make up for one moment of that terrible dream in which he had discovered his wife buried below the high-tide line, not enough beauty to make up for the dreary horror of his lost, wakeful nights, or the sight of that sheeted figure being rolled out of the house across the street.

It was a lot more than just wishing that the play was over; as he sat there with the heels of his palms pressing against the lids of his closed eyes, he wanted *all* of it to be over – all of it. For the first time in his twenty-five thousand days of life, Ralph Roberts found himself wishing he were dead.

Chapter Nine

1

There was a movie poster, probably picked up at one of the local video stores for a buck or three, on the wall of the cubbyhole which served Detective John Leydecker as an office. It showed Dumbo the elephant cruising along with his magical ears outstretched. A headshot of Susan Day had been pasted over Dumbo's face, carefully cut to allow for the trunk. On the cartoon landscape below, someone had drawn a signpost which read DERRY 250.

'Oh, charming,' Ralph said.

Leydecker laughed. 'Not very politically correct, is it?'

'I think that's an understatement,' Ralph said, wondering what Carolyn would have made of the poster – wondering what Helen would make of it, for that matter. It was quarter of two on an overcast, chilly Monday afternoon, and he and Leydecker had just come across from the Derry County Courthouse, where Ralph had given his statement about his encounter with Charlie Pickering the day before. He had been questioned by an assistant district attorney who looked to Ralph as if he might be ready to start shaving in another year or two.

Leydecker had accompanied him as promised, sitting in the corner of the assistant DA's office and saying nothing. His promise to buy Ralph a cup of coffee turned out to be mostly a figure of speech – the evil-looking brew had come from the Silex in the corner of the cluttered second-floor Police Department dayroom. Ralph sipped cautiously at his and was relieved to find it tasted a little better than it looked.

'Sugar? Cream?' Leydecker asked. 'Gun to shoot it with?'

Ralph smiled and shook his head. 'Tastes fine . . . although it'd probably be a mistake to trust my judgement. I cut back to two cups a day last summer, and now it all tastes pretty good to me.'

'Like me with cigarettes – the less I smoke, the better they taste. Sin's a bitch.' Leydecker took out his little tube of toothpicks, shook one out, and stuck it in the corner of his mouth. Then he put his own cup on top of his computer terminal, went over to the Dumbo poster, and began to lever out the thumbtacks which held the corners.

'Don't do it on my account,' Ralph said. 'It's *your* office.'

'Wrong.' Leydecker pulled the carefully scissored photo of Susan Day off the poster, balled it up, tossed it in the wastebasket. Then he began to roll the poster itself into a tight little cylinder.

'Oh? Then how come your name's on the door?'

'It's my name, but the office belongs to you and your fellow taxpayers, Ralph. Also to any news vidiot with a Minicam who happens to wander in here, and if this poster happened to show up on *News at Noon*, I'd be in a world of hurt. I forgot to take it down when I left Friday night, and I had most of the weekend off – a rare occurrence around here, let me tell you.'

'You didn't put it up, I take it.' Ralph moved some papers off the tiny office's one extra chair and sat down.

'Nope. Some of the fellows had a party for me Friday afternoon. Complete with cake, ice cream, and presents.' Leydecker rummaged in his desk and came up with a rubber band. He slipped it around the poster so it wouldn't spring open again, peeked one amused eye through it at Ralph, then tossed it into the wastebasket. 'I got a set of those days-of-the-week panties with the crotches snipped out, a can of strawberry-scented vaginal douche, a packet of Friends of Life anti-abortion literature – said literature including a comic-book called *Denise's Unwanted Pregnancy* – and that poster.'

'I guess it wasn't a birthday party, huh?'

'Nope.' Leydecker cracked his knuckles and sighed at the ceiling. 'The boys were celebrating my appointment to a special detail.'

Ralph could see faint flickers of blue aura around Leydecker's face and shoulders, but in this case he didn't have to try and read them. 'It's Susan Day, isn't it? You got the job of protecting her while she's in town.'

'Hole in one. Of course the State Police will be around, but they stick pretty much to traffic control in situations like this.

There may be some FBI, too, but what they do mostly is hang back, take pictures, and give each other the secret Club Sign.'

'She's got her own security people, doesn't she?'

'Yes, but I don't know how many or how good. I talked to the head guy this morning and he's at least coherent, but we have to put in our own guys. Five of them, according to the orders I got on Friday. That's me plus four guys who'll volunteer as soon as I tell em to. The object is . . . wait a minute . . . you'll like this . . .' Leydecker shuffled through the papers on his desk, found the one he was looking for, and held it up. '". . . to maintain a strong presence and high visibility".'

He dropped the paper again and grinned at Ralph. The grin did not have a lot of humor in it.

'In other words, if someone tries to shoot the bitch or give her an acid shampoo, we want Lisette Benson and the other vidiots to at least record the fact that we were there.' Leydecker looked at the rolled-up poster leaning in his wastebasket and flipped it the bird.

'How can you dislike someone so much when you've never even met her?'

'I don't just *dislike* her, Ralph; I fucking *hate* her. Listen – I'm a Catholic, my lovin mother was a Catholic, my kids – if I ever have any – are all gonna be altarboys at St Joe's. Great. Being a Catholic's great. They even let you eat meat on Fridays now. But if you think being Catholic means I'm in favor of making abortions illegal again, you got the wrong puppy. See, I'm the Catholic who gets to question the guys who beat their kids with rubber hoses or push them downstairs after a night of drinking good Irish whiskey and getting all sentimental about their mothers.'

Leydecker fished inside his shirt and brought out a small gold medallion. He placed it on his fingers and tilted it toward Ralph.

'Mary, mother of Jesus. I've worn this since I was thirteen. Five years ago I arrested a man wearing one just like it. He had just boiled his two-year-old stepson. This is a true thing I'm telling you. Guy put on a great big pot of water, and when it was boiling, he picked the kid up by the ankles and dropped him into the pot like he was a lobster. Why? Because the kid wouldn't stop wetting the bed, he told us. I saw the body, and I'll tell you what, after you've seen something like that, the photos the right-to-life assholes like to show of vacuum abortions don't look so bad.'

221

Leydecker's voice had picked up a slight tremor.

'What I remember most of all is how the guy was crying, and how he kept holding onto that Mary medallion around his neck and saying he wanted to go to confession. Made me proud to be a Catholic, Ralph, let me tell you . . . and as far as the Pope goes, I don't think he should be allowed to have an opinion until he's had a kid himself, or at least spent a year or so taking care of crack-babies.'

'Okay,' Ralph said. 'What's your problem with Susan Day?'

'She's stirring the motherfucking *pot!*' Leydecker cried. 'She comes into my town and I have to protect her. Fine. I've got good men, and with just a pinch of luck, I think we can probably see her out of town with her head still on and her tits pointing the right way, but what about what happens before? And what happens after? Do you think she cares about any of that? Do you think the people who run WomanCare give much of a shit about the side-effects, as far as that goes?'

'I don't know.'

'The WomanCare advocates are a little less prone to violence than The Friends of Life, but in terms of the all-important ass-ache quotient, they're not much different. Do you know what this was all about when it started?'

Ralph cast his memory back to his first conversation about Susan Day, the one he'd had with Ham Davenport. For a moment he almost had it, but then it squiggled away. The insomnia had won again. He shook his head.

'Zoning,' Leydecker said, and laughed with disgusted amazement. 'Plain old garden-variety zoning regulations. Great, huh? Early this summer, two of our more conservative City Councillors, George Tandy and Emma Wheaton, petitioned the Zoning Committee to reconsider the zone with WomanCare in it, the idea being to kind of gerrymander the place out of existence. I doubt if that's exactly the right word, but you get the gist, don't you?'

'Sure.'

'Uh-huh. So the pro-choicers ask Susan Day to come to town and make a speech, help them to raise a war-chest to combat the pro-life grinches. The only problem is, the grinches never had a chance of rezoning District 7, *and the WomanCare people knew it!* Hell, one of their directors, June Halliday, is *on* the City Council. She and the Wheaton bitch just about spit at each other when they pass in the hall.

'Rezoning District 7 was a pipe-dream from the start, because

WomanCare is technically a hospital, just like Derry Home, which is only a stone's throw away. If you change the zoning laws to make WomanCare illegal, you do the same to one of only three hospitals in Derry County – the third-largest county in the state of Maine. So it was never going to happen, but that's okay, because it was never about that in the first place. It was about being pissy and in-your-face. About being an ass-ache. And for most of the pro-choicers – one of the guys I work with calls em the Whale People – it's about being *right*.'

'Right? I don't get you.'

'It isn't enough that a woman can walk in there and get rid of the troublesome little fishie growing inside her any time she wants; the pro-choicers want the argument to *end*. What they want, down deep, is for people like Dan Dalton to admit they're right, and that'll never happen. It's more likely that the Arabs and the Jews will decide it was all a mistake and throw down their weapons. I support the right of a woman to have an abortion if she really needs to have one, but the pro-choicers' holier-than-thou attitude makes me want to puke. They're the new Puritans, as far as I'm concerned, people who believe that if you don't think the way they do, you're going to hell . . . only their version is a place where all you get on the radio is hillbilly music and all you can find to eat is chicken-fried steak.'

'You sound pretty bitter.'

'Try sitting on a powderkeg for three months and see how it makes *you* feel. Tell me this – do you think Pickering would have stuck a knife in your armpit yesterday if it hadn't been for WomanCare, The Friends of Life, and Susan Leave-My-Sacred-Twat-Alone Day?'

Ralph appeared to give the question serious thought, but what he was really doing was watching John Leydecker's aura. It was a healthy dark blue, but the edges were tinged with rapidly shifting greenish light. It was this edging which interested Ralph; he had an idea he knew what it meant.

Finally he said, 'No. I guess not.'

'Me either. You got wounded in a war that's already been decided, Ralph, and you won't be the last. But if you went to the Whale People – or to Susan Day – and opened your shirt and pointed at the bandage and said "This is partly your fault, so own the part that's yours," they'd raise their hands and say, "Oh no, goodness no, we're sorry you got hurt, Ralph, we whale watchers *abhor* violence, but it wasn't *our* fault, we have to keep WomanCare open, we have to man and woman the barricades, and if a little spilled blood is what it takes to do that, then so be it." But it's not *about* WomanCare, and that's what drives me absolutely bugfuck. It's about—'

'– abortion.'

'Shit, no! Abortion rights are safe in Maine and in Derry, no matter what Susan Day says at the Civic Center Friday night. This is about whose team is the best team. About whose side God's on. It's about who's *right*. I wish they'd all just sing "We Are the Champions" and go get drunk.'

Ralph threw back his head and laughed. Leydecker laughed with him.

'So they're assholes,' he finished with a shrug. 'But they're *our* assholes. Does that sounds like I'm joking? I'm not. WomanCare, Friends of Life, Body Watch, Daily Bread . . . they're *our* assholes, *Derry* assholes, and I really don't mind watching out for our own. That's why I took this job, and why I stay with it. But you'll have to forgive me if I'm less than crazy about being tapped to watch out for some long-stemmed American Beauty from New York who's going to fly in here and give an incendiary speech and then fly out with a few more press-clippings and enough material for chapter five of her new book.

'To our faces she'll talk about what a wonderful little grassroots community we are, and when she gets back to her duplex on Park Avenue, she'll tell her friends about how she hasn't managed to shampoo the stink of our paper mills out of her hair yet. She is woman, hear her roar . . . and if we're lucky, the whole thing will quiet down with no one dead or disabled.'

Ralph had become sure of what those greenish flickers meant. 'But you're scared, aren't you?' he asked.

Leydecker looked at him, surprised. 'Shows, does it?'

'Only a little,' Ralph said, and thought: *Just in your aura, John, that's all. Just in your aura.*

'Yeah, I'm scared. On a personal level I'm scared of fucking up the assignment, which has absolutely no upside to compensate for all the things that can go wrong. On a professional level I'm scared of something happening to her on my watch. On a community level I'm fucking *terrified* of what happens if there's some sort of confrontation and the genie comes out of the bottle . . . more coffee, Ralph?'

'I'll pass. I ought to be going soon, anyway. What's going to happen to Pickering?'

He didn't actually care much about Charlie Pickering's fate, but the big cop would probably think it strange if he asked about May Locher before he asked about Pickering. Suspicious, maybe.

'Steve Anderson – the ADA who questioned you – and Pickering's court-appointed attorney are probably horse-trading even as we speak. Pickering's guy will be saying he might be able to get his client – the thought of Charlie Pickering being *anyone's* client, for *anything,* sort of blows my mind, by the way – to plead out to second-degree assault. Anderson will say the time has come to put Pickering away for good and he's going for attempted murder. Pickering's lawyer will pretend to be shocked, and tomorrow your buddy is going to be charged with first-degree assault with a deadly weapon and bound over for trial. Then, possibly in December but more likely early next year, you'll be called as the star witness.'

'Bail?'

'It'll probably be set in the forty-thousand-dollar range. You can get out on ten per cent if the rest can be secured in event of flight, but Charlie Pickering doesn't have a house, a car, or even a Timex watch. In the end, he's liable to go back to Juniper Hill, but that's really not the object of the game. We're going to be able to keep him off the street for quite awhile this time, and with people like Charlie, *that's* the object of the game.'

'Any chance The Friends of Life might go his bail?'

'Nah. Ed Deepneau spent a lot of last week with him, the two of them drinking coffee in the Bagel Shop. I imagine Ed was giving Charlie the lowdown on the Centurions and the King of Diamonds—'

'Crimson King is what Ed—'

'Whatever,' Leydecker agreed, waving a hand. 'But most of all I imagine he spent the time explaining how you were the devil's righthand man and how only a smart, brave, and dedicated fellow like Charlie Pickering could take you out of the picture.'

'You make him sound like such a calculating shit,' Ralph said. He was remembering the Ed Deepneau he'd played chess with before Carolyn had fallen ill. That Ed had been an intelligent, well-spoken, civilized man with a deep capacity for kindness. Ralph still found it all but impossible to reconcile that Ed with the one he'd first glimpsed in July of 1992. He had come to think of the more recent arrival as 'rooster Ed'.

'Not just a calculating shit, a *dangerous* calculating shit,'

Leydecker said. 'For him Charlie was just a tool, like a paring knife you'd use to peel an apple with. If the blade snaps off a paring knife, you don't run to the knife-grinder's to get a new one put on; that's too much trouble. You toss it in the wastebasket and get a new paring knife instead. That's the way guys like Ed treat guys like Charlie, and since Ed *is* The Friends of Life – for the time being, at least – I don't think you have to worry about Charlie making bail. In the next few days, he's going to be lonelier than a Maytag repairman. Okay?'

'Okay,' Ralph said. He was a little appalled to realize he felt sorry for Pickering. 'I want to thank you for keeping my name out of the paper, too . . . if you were the one who did it, that is.'

There had been a brief mention of the incident in the Derry *News*'s Police Beat column, but it said only that Charles H. Pickering had been arrested on 'a weapons charge' at the Derry Public Library.

'Sometimes we ask them for a favor, sometimes they ask us for one,' Leydecker said, standing up. 'It's how things work in the real world. If the nuts in The Friends of Life and the prigs in The Friends of WomanCare ever discover that, my job is going to get a lot easier.'

Ralph plucked the rolled-up Dumbo poster from the waste-basket, then stood up on his side of Leydecker's desk. 'Could I have this? I know a little girl who might really like it, in a year or so.'

Leydecker held out his hands expansively. 'Be my guest – think of it as a little premium for being a good citizen. Just don't ask for my crotchless panties.'

Ralph laughed. 'Wouldn't think of it.'

'Seriously, I appreciate you coming in. Thanks, Ralph.'

'No problem.' He reached across the desk, shook Leydecker's hand, then headed for the door. He felt absurdly like Lieutenant Columbo on TV – all he needed was the cigar and the ratty trenchcoat. He put his hand on the knob, then paused and turned back. 'Can I ask you about something totally unrelated to Charlie Pickering?'

'Fire away.'

'This morning in the Red Apple Store I heard that Mrs Locher, my neighbor up the street, died in the night. Nothing so surprising about that; she had emphysema. But there are police-line tapes up between the sidewalk and her front yard, plus a sign on the door saying the site has been sealed by the Derry PD. Do you know what it's about?'

Leydecker looked at him so long and hard that Ralph would have felt acutely uncomfortable . . . if not for the man's aura. There was nothing in it which communicated suspicion.

God, Ralph, you're taking these things a little too seriously, aren't you?

Well, maybe yes and maybe no. Either way he was glad that the green flickers at the edges of Leydecker's aura had not reappeared.

'Why are you looking at me that way?' Ralph asked. 'If I presumed or spoke out of turn, I'm sorry.'

'Not at all,' Leydecker said. 'It's a little weird, that's all. If I tell you about it, can you keep it quiet?'

'Yes.'

'It's your downstairs tenant I'm chiefly worried about. When the word discretion is mentioned, it's *not* the Prof I think of.'

Ralph laughed heartily. 'I won't say a word to him – Scout's Honor – but it's interesting you'd mention him; Bill went to school with Mrs Locher, way back when. *Grammar* school.'

'Man, I can't imagine the Prof in grammar school,' Leydecker said. 'Can you?'

'Sort of,' Ralph said, but the picture which rose in his mind was an exceedingly peculiar one: Bill McGovern looking like a cross between Little Lord Fauntleroy and Tom Sawyer in a pair of knickers, long white socks . . . and a Panama hat.

'We're not sure *what* happened to Mrs Locher,' Leydecker said. 'What we do know is that shortly after three a.m., 911 logged an anonymous call from someone – a male – who claimed to have just seen two men, one carrying a pair of scissors, come out of Mrs Locher's house.'

'She was killed?' Ralph exclaimed, realizing two things simultaneously: that he sounded more believable than he ever would have expected, and that he had just crossed a bridge. He hadn't burned it behind him – not yet, anyway – but he would not be able to go back to the other side without a lot of explanations.

Leydecker turned his hands palms up and shrugged. 'If she was, it wasn't with a pair of scissors or any other sharp object. There wasn't a mark on her.'

That, at least, was something of a relief.

'On the other hand, it's possible to scare someone to death – especially someone who's old and sick – during the commission

227

of a crime,' Leydecker said. 'Anyway, this'll be easier to explain if you let me just tell you what I know. It won't take long, believe me.'

'Of course. Sorry.'

'Want to hear something funny? The first person I thought of when I looked over the 911 call-sheet was you.'

'Because of the insomnia, right?' Ralph asked. His voice was steady.

'That and the fact that the caller claimed to have seen these men from his living room. *Your* living room looks out on the Avenue, doesn't it?'

'Yes.'

'Uh-huh. I even thought of listening to the tape, then I remembered that you were coming in today . . . and that you're sleeping through again. That's right, isn't it?'

Without an instant of pause or consideration, Ralph set fire to the bridge he had just crossed. 'Well, I'm not sleeping like I did when I was sixteen and working two after-school jobs, I won't kid you about that, but if I was the guy who called 911 last night, I did it in my sleep.'

'Exactly what I figured. Besides, if you saw something a little off-kilter on the street, why would you make the call anonymously?'

'I don't know,' Ralph said, and thought, *But suppose it was a little more than off-kilter, John? Suppose it was completely unbelievable?*

'Me, neither,' Leydecker said. 'Your place has a view of Harris Avenue, yes, but so do about three dozen others . . . and just because the guy who made the call *said* he was inside, that doesn't mean he really was, does it?'

'I guess not. There's a pay-phone outside the Red Apple he could have called from, plus one outside the liquor store. A couple in Strawford Park, too, if they work.'

'Actually there are four in the park, and they all work. We checked.'

'Why would he lie about where he was calling from?'

'The most likely reason is because he was lying about the rest of what he had to say, too. Anyway, Donna Hagen said the guy sounded very young and sure of himself.' The words were barely out of his mouth before Leydecker winced and put a hand on top of his head. 'That didn't come out just the way I meant it, Ralph. Sorry.'

'It's okay – the idea that I sound like an old fart on a pension is not exactly a new concept to me. I *am* an old fart on a pension. Go on.'

'Chris Nell was the responding officer – first on the scene. Do you remember him from the day we arrested Ed?'

'I remember the name.'

'Uh-huh. Steve Utterback was the responding detective and the OIC – officer in charge. He's a good man.'

The guy in the watchcap, Ralph thought.

'The lady was dead in bed, but there was no sign of violence. Nothing obvious taken, either, although old ladies like May Locher aren't usually into a lot of real hockable stuff – no VCR, no big fancy stereo, nothing like that. She *did* have one of those Bose Waves, though, and two or three pretty nice pieces of jewelry. This is not to say that there wasn't other jewelry as nice or nicer, but—'

'But why would a burglar take some and not all?'

'Exactly. What's more interesting in this case is that the front door – the one the 911 caller said he saw the two men coming out of – was locked from the inside. Not just a spring-lock, either; there was a thumb-bolt and a chain. Same with the back door, by the way. So if the 911 caller was on the up and up, and if May Locher was dead when the two guys left, who locked the doors?'

Maybe it was the Crimson King, Ralph thought . . . and to his horror, almost said aloud.

'I don't know. What about the windows?'

'Locked. Thumb-latches turned. And, just in case that's not Agatha Christie enough for you, Steve says the storms were on. One of the neighbors told him Mrs Locher hired a kid to put them on just last week.'

'Sure she did,' Ralph said. 'Pete Sullivan, the same kid who delivers the newspaper. Now that I think of it, I saw him doing it.'

'Mystery-novel bullshit,' Leydecker said, but Ralph thought Leydecker would have swapped Susan Day for May Locher in about three seconds. 'The prelim medical came in just before I left for the courthouse to meet you. I had a glance at it. Myocardial this, thrombosis that . . . heart-failure's what it comes down to. Right now we're treating the 911 call as a crank – we get em all the time, all cities do – and the lady's death as a heart-attack brought on by her emphysema.'

'Just a coincidence, in other words.' That conclusion might

save him a lot of trouble – if it flew, that was – but Ralph could hear the disbelief in his own voice.

'Yeah, I don't like it, either. Neither does Steve, which is why the house has been sealed. State Forensics will give it a complete top-to-bottom, probably starting tomorrow morning. Meanwhile, Mrs Locher has taken a little ride down to Augusta for a more comprehensive postmortem. Who knows what it'll show? Sometimes they *do* show things. You'd be surprised.'

'I suppose I would,' Ralph said.

Leydecker tossed his toothpick into the trash, appeared to brood for a moment, then brightened up. 'Hey, here's an idea – maybe I'll get someone in clerical to make a dupe of that 911 call. I could bring it over and play it for you. Maybe you'll recognize the voice. Who knows? Stranger things have happened.'

'I suppose they have,' Ralph said, smiling uneasily.

'Anyway, it's Utterback's case. Come on, I'll see you out.'

In the hall, Leydecker gave Ralph another searching look. This one made Ralph feel a good deal more uncomfortable, because he had no idea what it meant. The auras had disappeared again.

He tried on a smile that felt lame. 'Something hanging out of my nose that shouldn't be?'

'Nope. I'm just amazed at how good you look for someone who went through what you did yesterday. And compared to how you looked last summer . . . if that's what honeycomb can do, I'm going to buy myself a beehive.'

Ralph laughed as though this were the funniest thing he had ever heard.

2

1:42 a.m., Tuesday morning.

Ralph sat in the wing-chair, watching wheels of fine mist revolve around the streetlights. Up the street, the police-line tapes hung dispiritedly in front of May Locher's house.

Barely two hours' sleep tonight, and he found himself again thinking that dead might be better. No more insomnia then. No more long waits for dawn in this hateful chair. No more days when he seemed to be looking at the world through the Gardol

Invisible Shield they used to prattle about on the toothpaste commercials. Back when TV had been almost brand-new, that had been, in the days when he had yet to find the first strands of gray in his hair and he was always asleep five minutes after he and Carol had finished making love.

And people keep talking about how good I look. That's the weirdest part of it.

Except it wasn't. Considering some of the things he'd seen just lately, a few people saying he looked like a new man was far, far down on his list of oddities.

Ralph's eyes returned to May Locher's house. The place had been locked up, according to Leydecker, but Ralph had seen the two little bald doctors come out the front door, he had *seen* them, goddammit—

But had he?

Had he really?

Ralph cast his mind back to the previous morning. Sitting down in this same chair with a cup of tea and thinking *Let the play begin.* And then he had seen those two little bald bastards come out, damn it, *he had seen them come out of May Locher's house!*

Except maybe that was wrong, because he hadn't really been looking at Mrs Locher's house; he had been pointed more in the direction of the Red Apple. He'd thought the flicker of movement in the corner of his eye was probably Rosalie, and had turned his head to check. *That* was when he'd seen the little bald doctors on the stoop of May Locher's house. He was no longer entirely sure he had seen the front door open; maybe he had just assumed that part, and why not? They sure as hell hadn't come up Mrs Locher's walk.

You can't be sure of that, Ralph.

Except he could. At three in the morning, Harris Avenue was as still as the mountains of the moon – the slightest movement anywhere within the range of his vision registered.

Had Doc #1 and Doc #2 come out the front door? The longer Ralph thought about it, the more he doubted it.

Then what happened, Ralph? Did they maybe step out from behind the Gardol Invisible Shield? Or – how's this? – maybe they walked through *the door, like those ghosts that used to haunt Cosmo Topper in that old TV show!*

And the craziest thing of all was that felt just about right.

What? That they walked through the fucking DOOR? *Oh, Ralph, you need help. You need to talk to someone about what's happening to you.*

Yes. That was the one thing of which he was sure: he needed to spill all this to someone before it drove him crazy. But who? Carolyn would have been best, but she was dead. Leydecker? The problem there was that Ralph had already lied to him about the 911 call. Why? Because the truth would have sounded insane. It would have sounded, in fact, as if he had caught Ed Deepneau's paranoia like a cold. And wasn't that really the most likely explanation, when you looked at the situation dead on?

'But that's not it,' he whispered. 'They were real. The auras, too.'

It's a long walk back to Eden, sweetheart . . . and watch out for those green-gold white-man tracks while you're on the way.

Tell someone. Lay it all out. Yes. And he ought to do it before John Leydecker listened to that 911 tape and showed up asking for an explanation. Wanting to know, basically, why Ralph had lied, and what Ralph actually knew about the death of May Locher.

Tell someone. Lay it all out.

But Carolyn was dead, Leydecker was still too new, Helen was lying low at the WomanCare shelter somewhere out in the willywags, and Lois Chasse might gossip to her girlfriends. Who did that leave?

The answer became clear once he put it to himself that way, but Ralph still felt a surprising reluctance to talk to McGovern about the things which had been happening to him. He remembered the day he had found Bill sitting on a bench by the softball field, crying over his old friend and mentor, Bob Polhurst. Ralph had tried to tell Bill about the auras, and it had been as if McGovern couldn't hear him; he had been too busy running through his well-thumbed script on the subject of how shitty it was to grow old.

Ralph thought of the satiric raised eyebrow. The unfailing cynicism. The long face, always so gloomy. The literary allusions, which usually made Ralph smile but often left him feeling a tad inferior, as well. And then there was McGovern's attitude toward Lois: condescending, even a touch cruel.

Yet this was a long way from being fair, and Ralph knew it. Bill McGovern *was* capable of kindness, and – perhaps far more important in this case – understanding. He and Ralph had known each other for over twenty years; for the last ten of those years they had lived in the same building. He had been one of Carolyn's pallbearers, and if Ralph couldn't talk to Bill about what had been happening to him, who *could* he talk to?

The answer seemed to be no one.

Chapter Ten

1

The misty rings around the streetlamps were gone by the time daylight began to brighten the sky in the east, and by nine o'clock the day was clear and warm – the beginning of Indian summer's final brief passage, perhaps. Ralph went downstairs as soon as *Good Morning America* was over, determined to tell McGovern what had been happening to him (or as much as he dared, anyway) before he could lose his nerve. Standing outside the door of the downstairs apartment, however, he could hear the shower running and the mercifully distant sound of William D. McGovern singing 'I Left My Heart in San Francisco'.

Ralph went out to the porch, stuck his hands in his back pockets, and read the day like a catalogue. There was nothing, he reflected, really nothing in the world like October sunshine; he could almost feel his night-miseries draining away. They would undoubtedly be back, but for now he felt all right – tired and muzzy-headed, yes, but still pretty much all right. The day was more than pretty; it was downright gorgeous, and Ralph doubted if there would be another as good before next May. He decided he would be a fool not to take advantage of it. A walk up to the Harris Avenue Extension and back again would take half an hour, forty-five minutes if there happened to be someone up there worth batting a little breeze with, and by then Bill would be showered, shaved, combed, and dressed. Also ready to lend a sympathetic ear, if Ralph was lucky.

He walked as far as the picnic area outside the County Airport fence without quite admitting to himself that he was hoping to come across Old Dor. If he did, perhaps the two of them could talk a little poetry – Stephen Dobyns, for instance – or maybe even a bit of philosophy. They might start that part of their conversation with Dorrance explaining what 'long-time business' was, and why he believed Ralph shouldn't 'mess in' with it.

Except Dorrance wasn't at the picnic area; no one was there but Don Veazie, who wanted to explain to Ralph why Bill Clinton was doing such a horrible job as President, and why it would have been better for the good old US of A if the American people had elected that fiscal genius Ross Perot. Ralph (who had voted for Clinton and actually thought the man was doing a pretty good job) listened long enough to be polite, then said he had an appointment to have his hair cut. It was the only thing he could think of on short notice.

'Something else, too!' Don blared after him. 'That uppity wife of his! Woman's a lesbian! I can always tell! You know how? I look at their shoes! Shoes is like a secret code with em! They always wear those ones with the square toes and—'

'See you, Don!' Ralph called back, and beat a hasty retreat.

He had gone about a quarter of a mile back down the hill when the day exploded silently all around him.

2

He was opposite May Locher's house when it happened. He stopped dead in his tracks, staring down Harris Avenue with wide, unbelieving eyes. His right hand was pressed against the base of his throat and his mouth hung open. He looked like a man having a heart attack, and while his heart seemed all right – for the time being, anyway – he certainly felt as if he were having *some* kind of an attack. Nothing he had seen this fall had prepared him for this. Ralph didn't think *anything* could have prepared him for this.

That other world – the secret world of auras – had come into view again, and this time there was more of it than Ralph had ever dreamed . . . so much that he wondered fleetingly if it was possible for a person to die of perceptual overload. Upper Harris Avenue was a fiercely glowing wonderland filled with overlapping spheres and cones and crescents of color. The trees, which were still a week or more away from the climax of their fall transformation, none the less burned like torches in Ralph's eyes and mind. The sky had gone past color; it was a vast blue sonic boom.

The telephone lines on Derry's west side were still above ground, and Ralph stared fixedly at them, vaguely aware that he had stopped breathing and should probably start again soon if he didn't want to pass out. Jagged yellow spirals were running briskly up and down the black wires, reminding Ralph of how barber-poles had looked when he was a kid. Every now and then this bumblebee pattern was broken by a spiky red vertical stroke or a green flash that seemed to spread both ways at once, obliterating the yellow rings for a moment before fading out.

You're watching people talk, he thought numbly. *Do you know that, Ralph? Aunt Sadie in Dallas is chatting with her favorite nephew, who lives in Derry; a farmer in Haven is jawing with the dealer he buys his tractor parts from; a minister is trying to help a troubled parishioner. Those are* voices, *and I think the bright strokes and flashes are coming from people in the grip of some strong emotion – love or hate, happiness or jealousy.*

And Ralph sensed that all he was seeing and all he was feeling was *not* all; that there was a whole world still waiting just beyond the current reach of his senses. Enough, perhaps, to make even what he was seeing now seem faint and faded. And if there *was* more, how could he possibly bear it without going mad? Not even putting his eyes out would help; he understood somehow that his sense of 'seeing' these things came mostly from his lifelong acceptance of sight as his primary sense. But there was, in fact, a lot more than seeing going on here.

In order to prove this to himself he closed his eyes . . . and went right on seeing Harris Avenue. It was as if his eyelids had turned to glass. The only difference was that all the usual colors had reversed themselves, creating a world that looked like the negative of a color photograph. The trees were no longer orange and yellow but the bright, unnatural green of lime Gatorade. The surface of Harris Avenue, repaved with fresh asphalt in June, had become a great white way, and the sky was an amazing red lake. He opened his eyes again, almost positive that the auras would be gone, but they weren't; the world still boomed and rolled with color and movement and deep, resonating sound.

When do I start seeing them? Ralph wondered as he began to walk slowly down the hill again. *When do the little bald doctors start coming out of the woodwork?*

There were no doctors in evidence, however, bald or otherwise; no angels in the architecture; no devils peering up from the sewer gratings. There was only—

'Look out, Roberts, watch where you're going, can't you?'

The words, harsh and a little alarmed, seemed to have actual physical texture; it was like running a hand over oak panelling in some ancient abbey or ancestral hall. Ralph stopped short and saw Mrs Perrine from down the street. She had stepped off the sidewalk into the gutter to keep from being bowled over like a tenpin, and now she stood ankle-deep in fallen leaves, holding her net shopping bag in one hand and glaring at Ralph from beneath her thick salt-and-pepper eyebrows. The aura which surrounded her was the firm, no-nonsense gray of a West Point uniform.

'Are you drunk, Roberts?' she asked in a clipped voice, and suddenly the riot of color and sensation fell out of the world and it was just Harris Avenue again, drowsing its way through a lovely weekday morning in mid-autumn.

'Drunk? Me? Not at all. Sober as a judge, honest.'

He held out his hand to her. Mrs Perrine, over eighty but not giving in to it so much as a single inch, looked at it as if she believed Ralph might have a joy-buzzer hidden in his palm. *Wouldn't put it past you, Roberts,* her cool gray eyes said. *Wouldn't put it past you at all.* She stepped back onto the sidewalk without Ralph's aid.

'I'm sorry, Mrs Perrine. I wasn't watching where I was going.'

'No, you certainly weren't. Lollygagging along with your mouth hanging open is what you were doing. You looked like the village idiot.'

'Sorry,' he repeated, and then had to bite his tongue to stifle a bray of laughter.

'Hmmp.' Mrs Perrine looked him slowly up and down, like a Marine drill-sergeant inspecting a raw recruit. 'There's a rip under the arm of that shirt, Roberts.'

Ralph raised his left arm and looked. There was indeed a large rip in his favorite plaid shirt. He could look through it and see the bandage with its dried spot of blood; also an unsightly tangle of old-man armpit hair. He lowered his arm hurriedly, feeling a blush rising in his cheeks.

'Hmmp,' Mrs Perrine said again, expressing everything she needed to express on the subject of Ralph Roberts without recourse to a single vowel. 'Drop it off at the house, if you like. Any other mending you might have, as well. I can still run a needle, you know.'

'Oh yes, I'll bet you can, Mrs Perrine.'

Mrs Perrine now gave him a look which said, *You're a dried-up old asskisser, Ralph Roberts, but I suppose you can't help it.*

'Not in the afternoon,' she said. 'I help make dinner at the homeless shelter in the afternoons, and help serve it out at five. It's God's work.'

'Yes, I'm sure it—'

'There'll be no homeless in heaven, Roberts. You can count on that. No ripped shirts, either, I'm sure. But while we're here, we have to get along and make do. It's our job.' *And I, for one, am doing spectacularly well at it,* Mrs Perrine's face proclaimed. 'Bring your mending in the morning or in the evening, Roberts. Don't stand on ceremony, but don't you show up on my doorstep after eight-thirty. I go to bed at nine.'

'That's very kind of you, Mrs Perrine,' Ralph said, and had to bite his tongue again. He was aware that very soon this trick would cease to work; soon it was going to be a case of laugh or die.

'Not at all. Christian duty. Also, Carolyn was a friend of mine.'

'Thank you,' Ralph said. 'Terrible about May Locher, wasn't it?'

'No,' Mrs Perrine said. 'God's mercy.' And she glided upon her way before Ralph could say another word. Her spine was so excruciatingly straight that it hurt him to look at it.

He walked on a dozen steps, then could hold it no longer. He leaned a forearm against a telephone pole, pressed his mouth to his arm, and laughed as quietly as he could – laughed until tears poured down his cheeks. When the fit (and that was what it really felt like; a kind of hysterical seizure) had passed, Ralph raised his head and looked around with attentive, curious, slightly teary eyes. He saw nothing that anyone else couldn't see as well, and that was a relief.

But it will come back, Ralph. You know it will. All of it.

Yes, he supposed he *did* know it, but that was for later. Right now he had some talking to do.

3

When Ralph finally arrived back from his amazing journey up the street, McGovern was sitting in his chair on the porch and idling through the morning paper. As Ralph turned up the walk, he came to a sudden decision. He would tell Bill a lot, but not everything. One of the things he would definitely leave out was how much the two guys he'd seen coming out of Mrs Locher's house had looked like the aliens in the tabloids for sale at the Red Apple.

McGovern looked up as he climbed the steps. 'Hello, Ralph.'

'Hi, Bill. Can I talk to you about something?'

'Of course.' He closed the paper and folded it carefully. 'They finally took my old friend Bob Polhurst to the hospital yesterday.'

'Oh? I thought you expected that to happen sooner.'

'I did. *Everybody* did. He fooled us. In fact, he seemed to be getting better – of the pneumonia, at least – and then he relapsed. He had a breathing arrest yesterday around noon, and his niece thought he was going to die before the ambulance got there. He didn't, though, and now he seems to have stabilized again.' McGovern looked up the street and sighed. 'May Locher pops off in the middle of the night and Bob just keeps chugging along. What a world, huh?'

'I guess so.'

'What did you want to talk about? Have you finally decided to pop the question to Lois? Want a little fatherly advice on how to handle it?'

'I need advice, all right, but not about my love-life.'

'Spill it,' McGovern said tersely.

Ralph did, gratified and more than a little relieved by McGovern's silent attentiveness. He began by sketching in things Bill already knew about – the incident between Ed and the truck-driver in the summer of '92, and how similar Ed's rantings on that occasion had been to the things he had said on the day he had beaten Helen for signing the petition. As Ralph spoke, he began to feel more strongly than ever that there were connections between all the odd things which had been happening to him, connections he could almost see.

He told McGovern about the auras, although not about the

silent cataclysm he had experienced less than half an hour before – that was also further than he was willing to go, at least for the time being. McGovern knew about Charlie Pickering's attack on Ralph, of course, and that Ralph had averted a much more serious injury by using the spray Helen and her friend had given him, but now Ralph told him something he had held back on Sunday night, when he'd told McGovern about the attack over a scratch dinner: how the spray-can had magically appeared in his jacket pocket. Except, he said, he suspected that the magician had been Old Dor.

'Holy shit!' McGovern exclaimed. 'You've been living dangerously, Ralph!'

'I guess so.'

'How much of this have you told Johnny Leydecker?'

Very little, Ralph started to say, then realized that even that would be an exaggeration. 'Almost none of it. And there's something else I haven't told him. Something a lot more . . . well, a lot more substantive, I guess. To do with what happened up there.' He pointed toward May Locher's house, where a couple of blue and white vans had just pulled up. MAINE STATE POLICE was written on the sides. Ralph assumed they were the forensics people Leydecker had mentioned.

'May?' McGovern leaned a little further forward in his chair. 'You know something about what happened to May?'

'I think I do.' Speaking carefully, moving from word to word like a man using stepping-stones to cross a treacherous brook, Ralph told McGovern about waking up, going into the living room, and seeing two men come out of Mrs Locher's house. He recounted his successful rummage for the binoculars, and told McGovern about the scissors he had seen one of the men carrying. He did not mention his nightmare of Carolyn or the glowing tracks, and he most certainly did not mention his belated impression that the two men might have come right through the door; that would have finished off any remaining tatters of credibility he might still possess. He ended with his anonymous call to 911 and then sat in his chair, looking at McGovern anxiously.

McGovern shook his head as if to clear it. 'Auras, oracles, mysterious housebreakers with scissors . . . you *have* been living dangerously.'

'What do you think, Bill?'

McGovern sat quietly for several moments. He had rolled his newspaper up while Ralph was talking, and now he began to tap it absently against his leg. Ralph felt an urge to phrase his question even more bluntly – *Do you think I'm crazy, Bill?* – and quashed it. Did he really believe that was the sort of question to which people gave honest answers . . . at least without a healthy shot of sodium pentothal first? That Bill might say *Oh yes, I think you're just as crazy as a bedbug, Ralphie-baby, so why don't we call Juniper Hill right away and see if they have a bed for you?* Not very likely . . . and since any answer Bill gave would mean nothing, it was better to forgo the question.

'I don't exactly *know* what I think,' Bill said at last. 'Not yet, at least. What did they look like?'

'Their faces were hard to make out, even with the binoculars,' Ralph said. His voice was as steady as it had been yesterday, when he had denied making the 911 call.

'You probably don't have any idea of how old they were, either?'

'No.'

'Could either of them have been our old pal from up the street?'

'Ed Deepneau?' Ralph looked at McGovern in surprise. 'No, neither one was Ed.'

'What about Pickering?'

'No. Not Ed, not Charlie Pickering. I would have known either of them. What are you driving at? That my mind just sort of buckled and put the two guys who've caused me the most stress in the last few months on May Locher's front stoop?'

'Of course not,' McGovern replied, but the steady tap-tap-tap of the newspaper against his leg paused and his eyes flickered. Ralph felt a sinking in the pit of his stomach. Yes; that was in fact *exactly* what McGovern had been driving at, and it wasn't really so surprising, was it?

Maybe not, but it didn't change that sinking feeling.

'And Johnny said all the doors were locked.'

'Yes.'

'From the inside.'

'Uh-huh, but—'

McGovern got up from his chair so suddenly that for one crazy moment Ralph had the idea that he was going to run away, perhaps screaming *Watch out for Roberts! He's gone crazy!* as he went. But instead of bolting down the steps, he turned toward the door leading back into the house. In some ways Ralph found this even more alarming.

'What are you going to do?'

'Call Larry Perrault,' McGovern said. 'May's younger brother. He still lives out in Cardville. She'll be buried in Cardville, I imagine.' McGovern gave Ralph a strange, speculative look. 'What did you *think* I was going to do?'

'I don't know,' Ralph said uneasily. 'For a second there I thought you were going to run away like the Gingerbread Man.'

'Nope.' McGovern reached out and patted him on the shoulder, but to Ralph the gesture felt cold and comfortless. Perfunctory.

'What does Mrs Locher's brother have to do with any of this?'

'Johnny said they sent May's body down to Augusta for a more comprehensive autopsy, right?'

'Well, I think the word he actually used was postmortem—'

McGovern waved this away. 'Same difference, believe me. If anything odd *does* crop up – anything suggesting that she was murdered – Larry would have to be informed. He's her only close living relative.'

'Yes, but won't he wonder what your interest is?'

'Oh, I don't think we have to worry about that,' McGovern said, speaking in a soothing tone Ralph didn't care for at all. 'I'll say the police have sealed off the house and that the old Harris Avenue rumor mill is turning briskly. He knows May and I were school chums, and that I visited her regularly over the last couple of years. Larry and I aren't crazy about each other, but we get along reasonably well. He'll tell me what I want to know if for no other reason than that we're both Cardville survivors. Get it?'

'I guess so, but—'

'I *hope* so,' McGovern said, and suddenly he looked like a very old and very ugly reptile – a gila monster, or perhaps a basilisk lizard. He pointed a finger at Ralph. 'I'm not a stupid man, and I *do* know how to respect a confidence. Your face just now said you weren't sure about that, and I resent it. I resent the hell out of it.'

'I'm sorry,' Ralph said. He was stunned by McGovern's outburst.

McGovern looked at him a moment longer with his leathery lips pulled back against his too-large dentures, then nodded. 'Yeah, okay, apology accepted. You've been sleeping like shit, I have to factor that into the equation, and as for me, I can't seem to get Bob Polhurst off my mind.' He heaved one of his weightiest poor-old-Bill sighs. 'Listen – if you'd prefer me not to try calling May's brother—'

'No, no,' Ralph said, thinking that what he'd like to do was roll the clock back ten minutes or so and cancel this entire conversation. And then a sentiment he was sure Bill McGovern would appreciate floated into his mind, fully constructed and ready for use. 'I'm sorry if I impugned your discretion.'

McGovern smiled, reluctantly at first and then with his whole face. 'Now I know what keeps you awake – thinking up crap like that. Sit still, Ralph, and think good thoughts about a hippopotamus, as my mother used to say. I'll be right back. Probably won't even catch him in, you know; funeral arrangements and all that. Want to look at the paper while you wait?'

'Sure. Thanks.'

McGovern handed him the paper, which still retained the tube shape into which it had been rolled, then went inside. Ralph glanced at the front page. The headline read PRO-CHOICE, PRO–LIFE ADVOCATES READY FOR ACTIVIST'S ARRIVAL. The story was flanked by two news photographs. One showed half a dozen young women making signs which said things like OUR BODIES, OUR CHOICE and IT'S A BRAND-NEW DAY IN DERRY! The other showed picketers marching in front of WomanCare. They carried no signs and needed none; the hooded black robes they wore and the scythes they carried said it all.

Ralph heaved a sigh of his own, dropped the paper onto the seat of the rocking chair beside him, and watched Tuesday morning unfold along Harris Avenue. It occurred to him that McGovern might well be on the phone with John Leydecker rather than Larry Perrault, and that the two of them might at this very moment be having a little student-teacher conference about that nutty old insomniac Ralph Roberts.

Just thought you'd like to know who really made that 911 call, Johnny.

Thanks, Prof. We were pretty sure, anyway, but it's good to get confirmation. I imagine he's harmless. I actually sort of like him.

Ralph pushed away his speculations about who Bill might or might not be calling. It was easier just to sit here and not think at all, not even good thoughts about a hippopotamus. Easier to watch the Budweiser truck lumber into the Red Apple parking lot, pausing to give courtesy to the Magazines Incorporated van which had dropped off this week's ration of tabloids, magazines, and paperbacks and was now leaving. Easier to watch old Harriet Bennigan, who made Mrs Perrine look like a spring chicken, bent over her walker in her bright red fall coat, out for her morning lurch. Easier to watch the young girl, who was wearing jeans, an oversized white tee-shirt, and a man's hat about four sizes too big for her, jumping rope in the weedy vacant lot between Frank's Bakery and Vicky Moon's Tanning Saloon (Body Wraps Our Specialty). Easier to watch the girl's small hands penduluming up and down. Easier to listen as she chanted her endless, shuttling rhyme.

Three-six-nine, the goose drank wine . . .

Some distant part of Ralph's mind realized, with great astonishment, that he was on the verge of going to sleep as he sat here on the porch steps. At the same time this was happening, the auras were creeping into the world again, filling it with fabulous colors and motions. It was wonderful, but . . .

. . . but something was wrong with it. *Something.* What?

The girl jumping rope in the vacant lot. *She* was wrong. Her denim-clad legs pumped up and down like the bobbin of a sewing machine. Her shadow jumped next to her on the jumbled pavement of an ancient alley overgrown with weeds and sunflowers. The rope whirled up and down . . . all around . . . up and down and all around . . .

Not an oversized tee-shirt, though, he'd been wrong about that. The figure was wearing a smock. A white smock, like the kind worn by actors in the old TV doc-operas.

Three-six-nine, hon, the goose drank wine,
The monkey chewed tobacco on the streetcar line . . .

A cloud blocked the sun and a grim green light sailed across the day, driving it underwater. Ralph's skin first chilled, then broke out in goosebumps. The girl's pumping shadow disappeared. She looked up at Ralph and he saw she wasn't a little girl at all. The creature looking at him was a man about four feet tall. Ralph had first taken the hat-shadowed face for that of a child because it was utterly smooth, unmarked by so much as a single line. And yet despite that, it conveyed a clear feeling to Ralph – a sense of evil, of malignity beyond the comprehension of a sane mind.

That's it, Ralph thought numbly, staring at the skipping

creature. *That's exactly it. Whatever the thing over there is, it's insane. Totally gone.*

The creature might have read Ralph's thought, for at that moment its lips skinned back in a grin that was both coy and nasty, as if the two of them shared some unpleasant secret. And he was sure – yes, quite sure, almost positive – that it was somehow chanting through its grin, doing it without moving its lips in the slightest:

[*The line* BROKE! *The monkey got* CHOKED! *And they all died together in a little row-*BOAT!]

It was neither of the two little bald doctors Ralph had seen coming out of Mrs Locher's, he was almost positive of that. *Related* to them, maybe, but not the same. It was—

The creature threw its jump-rope away. The rope turned first yellow and then red, seeming to give off sparks as it flew through the air. The small figure – Doc #3 – stared at Ralph, grinning, and Ralph suddenly realized something else, something which filled him with horror. He finally recognized the hat the creature was wearing.

It was Bill McGovern's missing Panama.

4

Again it was as if the creature had read his mind. It dragged the hat from its head, revealing the round, hairless skull beneath, and waved McGovern's Panama in the air as if it were a cowpoke astride a bucking bronco. It continued to grin its unspeakable grin as it waved the hat.

Suddenly it pointed at Ralph, as if marking him. Then it clapped the hat back on its head and darted into the narrow, weed-choked opening between the tanning salon and the bakery. The sun sailed free of the cloud which had covered it, and the shifting brightness of the auras began to fade once more. A moment or two after the creature had disappeared it was just Harris Avenue in front of him again – boring old Harris Avenue, the same as always.

Ralph pulled a shuddering breath, remembering the madness in that small, grinning face. Remembering the way it had pointed

(*the monkey got* CHOKED)

at him, as if

(they all died together in a little row-BOAT!)
marking him.

'Tell me I fell asleep,' he whispered hoarsely. 'Tell me I fell asleep and dreamed that little bugger.'

The door opened behind him. 'Oh my, talking to yourself,' McGovern said. 'Must have money in the bank, Ralphie.'

'Yeah, about enough to cover my burial expenses,' Ralph said. To himself he sounded like a man who has just suffered a terrible shock and is still trying to cope with the residual fright; he half expected Bill to dart forward, face filling with concern (or maybe just suspicion), to ask what was wrong.

McGovern did nothing of the sort. He plumped into the rocking chair, crossed his arms over his narrow chest in a brooding X, and looked out at Harris Avenue, the stage upon which he and Ralph and Lois and Dorrance Marstellar and so many other old folks – we golden-agers, in McGovern-ese – were destined to play out their often boring and sometimes painful last acts.

Suppose I told him about his hat? Ralph thought. *Suppose I just opened the conversation by saying, 'Bill, I also know what happened to your Panama. Some badass relation to the guys I saw last night has got it. He wears it when he jumps rope between the bakery and the tanning salon.'*

If Bill had any lingering doubts about his sanity, *that* little newsflash would certainly set them to rest. Yep.

Ralph kept his mouth shut.

'Sorry I was gone so long,' McGovern said. 'Larry claimed I just caught him going out the door to the funeral parlor, but before I could ask my questions and get away he'd rehashed half of May's life and damned near all of his own. Talked nonstop for forty-five minutes.'

Positive this was an exaggeration – McGovern had surely been gone five minutes, tops – Ralph glanced at his watch and was astounded to see it was eleven-fifteen. He looked up the street and saw that Mrs Bennigan had disappeared. So had the Budweiser truck. *Had* he been asleep? It seemed that he must have been . . . but he could not for the life of him find the break in his conscious perceptions.

Oh, come on, don't be dense. You were sleeping when you saw the little bald guy. Dreamed *the little bald guy.*

That made perfect sense. Even the fact that it had been wearing Bill's Panama made sense. The same hat had shown up in his nightmare about Carolyn. It had been between Rosalie's paws in that one.

Except this time he hadn't been dreaming. He was sure of it.

Well . . . *almost* sure.

'Aren't you going to ask me what May's brother said?' McGovern sounded slightly piqued.

'Sorry,' Ralph said. 'I was woolgathering, I guess.'

'Forgiven, my son . . . provided you listen closely from here on out, that is. The detective in charge of the case, Funderburke—'

'I'm pretty sure it's Utterback. Steve Utterback.'

McGovern waved his hand airily, his most common response to being corrected on some point. 'Whatever. Anyway, he called Larry and said the autopsy showed nothing but natural causes. The thing they were most concerned about, in light of your call, was that May had been scared into a heart attack – literally frightened to death – by housebreakers. The doors being locked from the inside and the lack of missing valuables militated against that, of course, but they took your call seriously enough to investigate the possibility.'

His half-reproachful tone – as if Ralph had wantonly poured glue into the gears of some usually smooth-running machine – made Ralph feel impatient. 'Of *course* they took it seriously. I saw two guys leaving her house and reported it to the authorities. When they got there, they found the lady dead. How could they *not* take it seriously?'

'Why didn't you give your name when you made the call?'

'I don't know. What difference does it make? And how in God's name can they be sure she *wasn't* scared into a heart attack?'

'I don't know if they *can* be a hundred per cent sure,' McGovern said, now sounding a bit testy himself, 'but I guess it must be close to that if they're turning May's body over to her brother for burial. It's probably a blood-test of some kind. All I know is that this guy Funderburke—'

'Utterback—'

'—told Larry that May probably died in her sleep.'

McGovern crossed his legs, fiddled with the creases in his blue slacks, then gave Ralph a clear and piercing look.

'I'm going to give you some advice, so listen up. Go to the doctor. Now. Today. Do not pass Go, do not collect two hundred dollars, go directly to Litchfield. This is getting heavy.'

The ones I saw coming out of Mrs Locher's didn't see me, but this one did, Ralph thought. *It saw me and it pointed at me. For all I know, it might actually have been* looking *for me.*

Now *there* was a nice paranoid thought.

'Ralph? Did you hear what I said?'

'Yes. I take it you don't believe I actually saw anyone coming out of Mrs Locher's house.'

'You take it right. I saw the look on your face just now when I told you I'd been gone forty-five minutes, and I also saw the way you looked at your watch. You didn't believe so much time had passed, did you? And the *reason* you didn't believe it is because you dozed off without even being aware of it. Had yourself a little pocket nap. That's probably what happened to you the other night, Ralph. Only the other night you dreamed up those two guys, and the dream was so real you called 911 when you woke up. Doesn't that make sense?'

Three-six-nine, Ralph thought. *The goose drank wine.*

'What about the binoculars?' he asked. 'They're still sitting on the table beside my chair in the living room. Don't they prove I was awake?'

'I don't see how. Maybe you were sleepwalking, have you thought of that? You say you saw these intruders, but you can't really describe them.'

'Those orange hi-intensity lights—'

'All the doors locked from the inside—'

'Just the same I—'

'And these auras you talked about. The insomnia is causing them – I'm almost sure of it. Still, it *could* be more serious than that.'

Ralph got up, walked down the porch steps, and stood at the head of the walk with his back to McGovern. There was a throbbing at his temples and his heart was beating hard. Too hard.

He didn't just point. I was right the first time, the little sonofabitch marked me. And he was no dream. Neither were the ones I saw coming out of Mrs Locher's. I'm sure of it.

Of course you are, Ralph, another voice replied. *Crazy people are always sure of the crazy things they see and hear. That's what makes them crazy, not the hallucinations themselves. If you really saw what you saw, what happened to Mrs Bennigan? What happened to the Budweiser truck? How did you lose the forty-five minutes McGovern spent on the phone with Larry Perrault?*

'You're experiencing very serious symptoms,' McGovern said from behind him, and Ralph thought he heard something terrible in the man's voice. Satisfaction? Could it possibly be satisfaction?

'One of them had a pair of scissors,' Ralph said without turning around. 'I saw them.'

'Oh, come on, Ralph! Think! Use that brain of yours and *think*! On Sunday afternoon, less than twenty-four hours before you're due to have acupuncture treatment, a lunatic nearly sticks a knife into you. Is it any wonder that your mind serves up a nightmare featuring a sharp object that night? Hong's pins and Pickering's hunting knife become scissors, that's all. Don't you see that this hypothesis covers all the bases while what you claim to have seen covers none of them?'

'And I was sleepwalking when I got the binoculars? That's what you think?'

'It's possible. Even likely.'

'Same thing with the spray-can in my jacket pocket, right? Old Dor didn't have a thing to do with it.'

'I don't care about the spray-can or Old Dor!' McGovern cried. 'I care about *you*! You've been suffering from insomnia since April or May, you've been depressed and disturbed ever since Carolyn died—'

'I have *not* been depressed!' Ralph shouted. Across the street, the mailman paused and looked in their direction before going on down the block toward the park.

'Have it your own way,' McGovern said. 'You haven't been depressed. You also haven't been sleeping, you're seeing auras, guys creeping out of locked houses in the middle of the night . . .' And then, in a deceptively light voice, McGovern said the thing Ralph had been dreading all along: 'You want to watch out, old son. You're starting to sound too much like Ed Deepneau for comfort.'

Ralph turned around. Dull hot blood pounded behind his face. 'Why are you being this way? Why are you taking after me this way?'

'I'm not taking after you, Ralph, I'm trying to *help* you. To be your friend.'

'That's not how it feels.'

'Well, sometimes the truth hurts a little,' McGovern said calmly. 'You need to at least consider the idea that your mind and body are trying to tell you something. Let me ask you a question – is this the *only* disturbing dream you've had lately?'

Ralph thought fleetingly of Carol, buried up to her neck in the sand and screaming about white-man tracks. Thought of the bugs which had flooded out of her head. 'I haven't had *any* bad dreams lately,' he said stiffly. 'I suppose you don't believe that because it doesn't fit into the little scenario you've created.'

'Ralph—'

'Let me ask *you* something. Do you really believe that my seeing those two men and May Locher turning up dead was just a coincidence?'

'Maybe not. Maybe your physical and emotional upset created conditions favorable to a brief but perfectly genuine psychic event.'

Ralph was silenced.

'I believe such things do happen from time to time,' McGovern said, standing up. 'Probably sounds funny, coming from a rational old bird like me, but I do. I'm not out-and-out saying that *is* what happened here, but it *could* have been. What I *am* sure of is that the two men you think you saw did not in fact exist in the real world.'

Ralph stood looking up at McGovern with his hands jammed deep into his pockets and clenched into fists so hard and tight they felt like rocks. He could feel the muscles in his arms thrumming.

McGovern came down the porch steps and took him by the arm, gently, just above the elbow. 'I only think—'

Ralph pulled his arm away so sharply that McGovern grunted with surprise and stumbled a little on his feet. 'I *know* what you think.'

'You're not hearing what I—'

'Oh, I've heard plenty. More than enough. Believe me. And excuse me – I think I'm going for another walk. I need to clear my head.' He could feel dull hot blood pounding away in his cheeks and brow. He tried to throw his brain into some forward gear that would allow it to leave this senseless, impotent rage behind and couldn't do it. He felt a lot as he had when he had awakened from the dream of Carolyn; his thoughts roared with terror and confusion, and as he started his legs moving the sense he got was not one of walking but of falling, as he had fallen out of bed yesterday morning. Still, he kept going. Sometimes that was all you could do.

'Ralph, you need to see a doctor!' McGovern called after him, and Ralph could no longer tell himself that he didn't hear a weird, shrewish pleasure in McGovern's voice. The concern which overlaid it was probably genuine enough but it was like sweet icing on a sour cake.

'Not a pharmacist, not a hypnotist, not an acupuncturist! You need to see *your own family doctor!*'

Yeah, the guy who buried my wife below the high-tide line! he thought in a kind of mental scream. *The guy who stuck her in sand up to her neck and then told her she didn't have to worry about drowning as long as she kept taking her Valium and Tylenol-3!*

Aloud he said, 'I need to take a *walk!* That's what I need and that's *all* I need.' His heartbeat was now slamming into his temples like the short, hard blows of a sledgehammer, and it occurred to him that this was how strokes must happen; if he didn't control himself soon, he was apt to fall down with what his father had called 'a bad-temper apoplexy'.

He could hear McGovern coming down the walk after him. *Don't touch me, Bill,* Ralph thought. *Don't even put your hand on my shoulder, because I'm probably going to turn around and slug you if you do.*

'I'm trying to *help* you, don't you see that?' McGovern shouted. The mailman on the other side of the street had stopped again to watch them, and outside the Red Apple, Karl, the guy who worked mornings, and Sue, the young woman who worked afternoons, were gawking frankly across the street at them. Karl, he saw, had a bag of hamburger buns in one hand. It was really sort of amazing, the things you saw at a time like this . . . although not as amazing as some of the things he had already seen that morning.

The things you thought *you saw, Ralph,* a traitor voice whispered softly from deep inside his head.

'Walk,' Ralph muttered desperately. 'Just a damn *walk.*' A mind-movie had begun to play in his head. It was an unpleasant one, the sort of film he rarely went to see even if he had seen everything else that was playing at the cinema center. The soundtrack to this mental horror flick seemed to be 'Pop Goes the Weasel', of all things.

'*Let me tell you something, Ralph – at our age, mental illness is common! At our age it's common as hell, so* GO SEE YOUR DOCTOR!'

Mrs Bennigan was now standing on her stoop, her walker abandoned at the foot of the front steps. She was still wearing her bright red fall coat, and her mouth appeared to be hanging open as she stared down the street at them.

'*Do you hear me, Ralph? I hope you do! I just hope you do!*'

Ralph walked faster, hunching his shoulders as if against a cold wind. *Suppose he just keeps on yelling, louder and louder? Suppose he follows me right up the street?*

If he does that, people will think he's *the one who's gone crazy,*
he told himself, but this idea had no power to soothe him. In
his mind he continued to hear a piano playing a children's tune
– no, not really *playing*; picking it out in nursery-school plinks
and plonks:

> *All around the mulberry bush*
> *The monkey chased the weasel,*
> *The monkey thought 'twas all in fun,*
> *Pop! Goes the weasel!*

And now Ralph began to see the old people of Harris Avenue,
the ones who bought their insurance from companies that
advertised on cable TV, the ones with the gallstones and
the skin tumors, the ones whose memories were diminishing
even as their prostates enlarged, the ones who were living on
Social Security and peering at the world through thickening
cataracts instead of rose-colored glasses. These were the people
who now read all the mail which came addressed to Occupant
and scanned the supermarket advertising circulars for specials
on canned goods and generic frozen dinners. He saw them
dressed in grotesque short pants and fluffy short skirts, saw
them wearing beanies and tee-shirts which showcased such
characters as Beavis and Butt-Head and Rude Dog. He saw
them, in short, as the world's oldest pre-schoolers. They were
marching around a double row of chairs as a small bald man
in a white smock played 'Pop Goes the Weasel' on the piano.
Another baldy filched the chairs one by one, and when the
music stopped and everyone sat down, one person – this
time it had been May Locher, next time it would probably
be McGovern's old department head – was left standing. That
person would have to leave the room, of course. And Ralph
heard McGovern laughing. Laughing because *he'd* found a seat
again. Maybe May Locher was dead, Bob Polhurst dying,
Ralph Roberts losing his marbles, but *he* was still all right,
William D. McGovern, Esq was still fine, still dandy, still
vertical and taking nourishment, still able to find a chair when
the music stopped.

Ralph walked faster still, shoulders hunched even higher,
anticipating another fusillade of advice and admonition. He
thought it unlikely that McGovern would actually follow him
up the street, but not entirely out of the question. If McGovern
was angry enough he might do just that – remonstrating, telling

Ralph to stop fooling around and go to the doctor, reminding him that the piano could stop anytime, any old time at all, and if he didn't find a chair while the finding was good, he might be out of luck forever.

No more shouts came, however. He thought of looking back to see where McGovern was, then thought better of it. If he saw Ralph looking back, it might set him off all over again. Best to just keep going. So Ralph lengthened his stride, heading back in the direction of the airport again without even thinking about it, walking with his head down, trying not to hear the relentless piano, trying not to see the old children marching around the chairs, trying not to see the terrified eyes above their make-believe smiles.

It came to him as he walked that his hopes had been denied. He had been pushed into the tunnel after all, and the dark was all around him.

PART II

The Secret City

Old men ought to be explorers.
T.S. Eliot
Four Quartets

Chapter Eleven

1

The Derry of the Old Crocks was not the only secret city existing quietly within the place Ralph Roberts had always thought of as home; as a boy growing up in Mary Mead, where the various Old Cape housing developments stood today, Ralph had discovered there was, in addition to the Derry that belonged to the grownups, one that belonged strictly to the children. There were the abandoned hobo jungles near the railroad depot on Neibolt Street, where one could sometimes find tomato soup cans half-full of mulligatawny stew and bottles with a swallow or two of beer left in them; there was the alley behind the Aladdin Theater, where Bull Durham cigarettes were smoked and Black Cat firecrackers sometimes set off; there was the big old elm which overhung the river, where scores of boys and girls had learned to dive; there were the hundred (or perhaps it was closer to two hundred) tangled trails winding through the Barrens, an overgrown valley which slashed through the center of town like a badly healed scar.

These secret streets and highways in hiding were all below the adult plane of vision and were consequently overlooked by them . . . although there *had* been exceptions. One of them had been a cop named Aloysius Nell – Mr Nell to generations of Derry children – and it was only now, as he walked up toward the picnic area near the place where Harris Avenue became the Harris Avenue Extension, that it occurred to Ralph that Chris Nell was probably old Mr Nell's son . . . except that couldn't be quite right, because the cop Ralph had first seen in the company of John Leydecker wasn't old enough to be old Mr Nell's son. Grandson, more like it.

Ralph had become aware of a second secret city – one that belonged to the old folks – around the time he retired, but he hadn't fully realized that he himself was a citizen of it until after Carol's death. What he had discovered then was a submerged geography eerily similar to the one he had known as a child, a place largely ignored by the hurry-to-work, hurry-to-play world which thumped and hustled all around it. The Derry of the Old Crocks overlapped yet a third secret city: the Derry of the Damned, a terrible place inhabited mostly by winos, runaways, and lunatics who could not be kept locked up.

It was in the picnic area that Lafayette Chapin had introduced Ralph to one of life's most important considerations . . . once you'd become a bona fide Old Crock, that was. This consideration had to do with one's 'real life'. The subject had come up while the two men were just getting to know one another. Ralph had asked Faye what he had done before he started coming out to the picnic area.

'Well, in my real life I was a carpenter n fancy cabinet-maker,' Chapin had replied, exposing his remaining teeth in a wide grin, 'but all that ended almost ten year ago.' As if, Ralph remembered thinking, retirement was something like a vampire's kiss, pulling those who survived it into the world of the undead. And when you got right down to cases, was that really so far off the mark?

2

Now, with McGovern safely behind him (at least he hoped so), Ralph stepped through the screen of mixed oak and maple which shielded the picnic area from the Extension. He saw that eight or nine people had drifted in since his earlier walk, most with bag lunches or Coffee Pot sandwiches. The Eberlys and Zells were playing hearts with the greasy deck of Top Hole cards which was kept stashed in a knothole of a nearby oak; Faye and Doc Mulhare, a retired vet, were playing chess; a couple of kibbitzers wandered back and forth between the two games.

Games were what the picnic area was about – what *most* of the places in the Derry of the Old Crocks were about – but Ralph thought the games were really just framework. What people actually came here for was to touch base, to report in, to confirm (if only to themselves) that they were still living *some* kind of life, real or otherwise.

Ralph sat on an empty bench near the Cyclone fence and traced one finger absently over the engraved carvings – names, initials, lots of FUCK YOUS – as he watched planes land at orderly two-minute intervals: a Cessna, a Piper, an Apache, a Twin Bonanza, the eleven forty-five Air Express out of Boston. He kept one ear cocked to the ebb and flow of conversation behind him. May Locher's name was mentioned more than once. She had been known by several of these people, and the general opinion seemed to be Mrs Perrine's – that God had finally shown mercy and ended her suffering. Most of the talk today, however, concerned the impending visit of Susan Day. As a rule, politics wasn't much of a conversational draw with the Old Crocks, who preferred a good bowel cancer or stroke any day, but even out here the abortion issue exercised its singular ability to engage, inflame, and divide.

'She picked a bad town to come to, and the hell of it is, I doubt she knows it,' Doc Mulhare said, watching the chessboard with glum concentration as Faye Chapin blitzkrieged his king's remaining defenders. 'Things have a way of happening here. Remember the fire at the Black Spot, Faye?'

Faye grunted and captured the doc's remaining bishop.

'What *I* don't understand is *these* cootie-bugs,' Lisa Zell said, picking up the front section of the *News* from the picnic table and slapping the photograph of the hooded figures marching in front of WomanCare. 'It's like they want to go back to the days when women gave themselves abortions with coathangers.'

'That's what they *do* want,' Georgina Eberly said. 'They figure if a woman's scared enough of dying, she'll have the baby. It never seems to cross their minds that a woman can be more scared of having a kid than using a coathanger to get rid of it.'

'What does bein afraid have to do with it?' one of the kibbitzers – a shovel-faced oldster named Pedersen – asked truculently. 'Murder is murder whether the baby's inside or outside, that's the way I look at it. Even when they're so small you need a microscope to see em, it's still murder. Because they'd *be* kids if you let em alone.'

'I guess that just about makes you Adolf Eichmann every time you jerk off,' Faye said, and moved his queen. 'Check.'

'La-fay-*ette Cha*-pin!' Lisa Zell cried.

'Playin with yourself ain't the same at all,' Pedersen said, glowering.

'Oh no? Wasn't there some guy in the Bible got cursed by God for hammerin the old haddock?' the other kibbitzer asked.

'You're probably thinking of Onan,' said a voice from behind Ralph. He turned, startled, and saw Old Dor standing there. In one hand he held a paperback with a large number 5 on the cover. *Where the hell did* you *come from?* Ralph wondered. He could almost have sworn there had been no one standing behind him a minute or so before.

'Onan, Shmonan,' Pedersen said. 'Those sperms aren't the same as a baby—'

'No?' Faye asked. 'Then why ain't the Catholic Church sellin rubbers at Bingo games? Tell me that.'

'That's just ignorant,' Pedersen said. 'And if you don't see—'

'But it wasn't masturbation Onan was punished for,' Dorrance said in his high, penetrating old man's voice. 'He was punished for refusing to impregnate his brother's widow, so his brother's line could continue. There's a poem, by Allen Ginsberg, I think—'

'Shut up, you old fool!' Pedersen yelled, and then glowered at Faye Chapin. 'And if you don't see that there's a big difference between a man beating his meat and a woman flushing the baby God put in her belly down the toilet, you're as big a fool as he is.'

'This is a *disgusting* conversation,' Lisa Zell said, sounding more fascinated than disgusted. Ralph looked over her shoulder and saw a section of chainlink fencing had been torn loose from its post and bent backward, probably by the kids who took this place over at night. That solved one mystery, anyway. He hadn't noticed Dorrance because the old man hadn't been in the picnic area at all; he'd been wandering around the airport grounds.

It occurred to Ralph that this was his chance to grab Dorrance and maybe get some answers out of him . . . except that Ralph would likely end up more confused than ever. Old Dor was too much like the Cheshire Cat in *Alice in Wonderland* – more smile than substance.

'Big difference, huh?' Faye was asking Pedersen.

'Yeah!' Red patches glowered in Pedersen's chapped cheeks.

Doc Mulhare shifted uneasily on his seat. 'Look, let's just forget it and finish the game, Faye, all right?'

Faye took no notice; his attention was still fixed on Pedersen.

'Maybe you ought to think again about all the little spermies that died in the palm of your hand every time you sat on the toilet seat thinkin about how nice it'd be to have Marilyn Monroe cop your—'

Pedersen reached out and slapped the remaining chess-pieces off the board. Doc Mulhare winced backward, mouth trembling, eyes wide and frightened behind pink-rimmed glasses which had been mended in two places with electrical tape.

'Yeah, good!' Faye shouted. 'That's a very reasonable fuckin argument, you geek!'

Pedersen raised his fists in an exaggerated John L. Sullivan pose. 'Want to do somethin about it?' he asked. 'Come on, let's go!'

Faye got slowly to his feet. He stood easily a foot taller than the shovel-faced Pedersen and outweighed him by at least sixty pounds.

Ralph could hardly believe what he was seeing. And if the poison had seeped this far, what about the rest of the city? It seemed to him that Doc Mulhare was right; Susan Day must not have the slightest idea of how bad an idea bringing her act to Derry really was. In some ways – in a lot of ways, actually – Derry wasn't like other places.

He was moving before he was consciously aware of what he meant to do, and he was relieved to see Stan Eberly doing the same thing. They exchanged a glance as they approached the two men standing nose to nose, and Stan nodded slightly. Ralph slipped an arm around Faye's shoulders a bare second before Stan gripped Pedersen's upper left arm.

'You ain't doing none of that,' Stan said, speaking directly into one of Pedersen's tufted ears. 'We'll end up taking the both of you over to Derry Home with heart attacks, and you don't need another one of those, Harley – you had two already. Or is it three?'

'I ain't letting him make jokes about wimmin murderin babies!' Pedersen said, and Ralph saw there were tears rolling down the man's cheeks. 'My wife *died* havin our second daughter! Sepsis carried her off back in '46! So I ain't havin that talk about murderin babies!'

'Christ,' Faye said in a different voice. 'I didn't know that, Harley. I'm sorry—'

'Ah, *frig* your sorry!' Pedersen cried, and ripped his arm out of Stan Eberly's grip. He lunged toward Faye, who raised his fists and then lowered them again as Pedersen went blundering past without looking at him. He took the path through the trees which led back out to the Extension and was gone. What followed his departure was thirty seconds of pure shocked silence, broken only by the wasp-whine of an incoming Piper Cub.

3

'Jesus,' Faye said at last. 'You see a guy every few days over five, ten years, and you start to think you know everything. Christ, Ralphie, *I* didn't know how his wife died. I feel like a fool.'

'Don't let it get you down,' Stan said. 'He's prob'ly just havin his monthlies.'

'Shut up,' Georgina said. 'We've had enough dirty talk for one morning.'

'I'll be glad when that Day woman comes n goes n things can get back to normal,' Fred Zell said.

Doc Mulhare was down on his hands and knees, collecting chess-pieces. 'Do you want to finish, Faye?' he asked. 'I think I remember where they all were.'

'No,' Faye said. His voice, which had remained steady during the confrontation with Pedersen, now sounded trembly. 'Think I've had enough for awhile. Maybe Ralph'll give you a little tourney prelim.'

'Think I'm going to pass,' Ralph said. He was looking around for Dorrance, and at last spotted him. He had gone back through the hole in the fence. He was standing in knee-high grass at the edge of the service road over there, bending his book back and forth in his hands as he watched the Piper Cub taxi toward the General Aviation terminal. Ralph found himself remembering how Ed had come tearing along that service road in his old brown Datsun, and how he had sworn

(*Hurry up! Hurry up and lick shit!*)

at the slowness of the gate. For the first time in over a year he found himself wondering what Ed had been doing in there to begin with.

'– than you did.'

'Huh?' He made an effort and focused on Faye again.

'I said you must be sleepin again, because you look a hell of a lot better than you did. But now your hearin's goin to hell, I guess.'

'I guess so,' Ralph said, and tried a little smile. 'Think I'll go grab myself a little lunch. You want to come, Faye? My treat.'

'Nah, I already had a Coffee Pot,' Faye said. 'It's sittin in my gut like a piece of lead right now, to tell you the truth. Cheez, Ralph, the old fart was *crying,* did you see that?'

'Yes, but I wouldn't make it into a big deal if I were you,' Ralph said. He started walking toward the Extension, and Faye ambled along beside him. With his broad shoulders slumped and his head lowered, Faye looked quite a lot like a trained bear in a man-suit. 'Guys our age cry over just about anything. You know that.'

'I spose.' He gave Ralph a grateful smile. 'Anyway, thanks for stoppin me before I could make it worse. You know how I am, sometimes.'

I only wish someone had been there when Bill and I got into it, Ralph thought. Out loud he said, 'No problem. It's me that should be thanking you, actually. It's something else to put on my résumé when I apply for that high-paying job at the UN.'

Faye laughed, delighted, and clapped Ralph on the shoulder. 'Yeah, Secretary-General! Peacemaker Number One! You could do it, Ralph, no shit!'

'No question about it. Take care of yourself, Faye.'

He started to turn away and Faye touched his arm. 'You're still up for the tournament next week, aren't you? The Runway 3 Classic?'

It took a moment for Ralph to figure out what he was talking about, although it had been the retired carpenter's main topic of conversation ever since the leaves had begun to show color. Faye had been putting on the chess tournament he called The Runway 3 Classic ever since the end of his 'real life' in 1984. The trophy was an oversized chrome hubcap with a fancy crown and scepter engraved on it. Faye, easily the best player among the Old Crocks (on the west side of town, at least), had awarded the trophy to himself on six of the nine occasions it had been given out, and Ralph had a suspicion that he had gone in the tank the other three times, just to keep the rest of the tourney participants interested. Ralph hadn't thought much about chess this fall; he'd had other things on his mind.

'Sure,' he said, 'I guess I'll be playing.'

Faye grinned. 'Good. We should have had it last weekend – that was the schedule – but I was hopin that if I put it off, Jimmy V would be able to play. He's still in the hospital, though, and if I put it off much longer it'll be too cold to play outdoor and we'll end up in the back of Duffy Sprague's barber shop, like we did in '90.'

'What's wrong with Jimmy V?'

'Cancer come back on him again,' Faye said, then added in a lower tone: 'I don't think he's got a snowball's chance in hell of beatin it this time.'

Ralph felt a sudden and surprisingly sharp pang of sorrow at this news. He and Jimmy Vandermeer had known each other well during their own 'real lives'. Both had been on the road back then, Jimmy in candy and greeting cards, Ralph in printing supplies and paper products, and the two of them had gotten on well enough to team up on several New England tours, splitting the driving and sharing rather more luxurious accommodations than either could have afforded alone.

They had also shared the lonely, unremarkable secrets of travelling men. Jimmy told Ralph about the whore who'd stolen his wallet in 1958, and how he'd lied to his wife about it, telling her that a hitchhiker had robbed him. Ralph told Jimmy about his realization, at the age of forty-three, that he had become a terpin hydrate junkie, and about his painful, ultimately successful struggle to kick the habit. He had no more told Carolyn about his bizarre cough-syrup addiction than Jimmy V had told his wife about his last B-girl.

A lot of trips; a lot of changed tires; a lot of jokes about the travelling salesman and the farmer's beautiful daughter; a lot of late-night talks which had gone on until the small hours of the morning. Sometimes it was God they had talked about, sometimes the IRS. All in all, Jimmy Vandermeer had been a damned good pal. Then Ralph had gotten his desk-job with the printing company and fallen out of touch with Jimmy. He'd only begun to reconnect out here, and at a few of the other dim landmarks which dotted the Derry of the Old Crocks – the library, the pool-hall, the back room of Duffy Sprague's barber shop, four or five others. When Jimmy told him shortly after Carolyn's death that he had come through a bout with cancer a lung shy but otherwise okay, what Ralph had remembered was the man talking baseball or fishing as he fed smoldering Camel stubs into the slipstream rushing by the wing-window of the car, one after another.

I got lucky was what he had said. *Me and the Duke, we both got lucky.* Except neither of them had stayed lucky, it seemed. Not that anyone did, in the end.

'Oh, man,' Ralph said. 'I'm sorry to hear that.'

'He's been in Derry Home almost three weeks now,' Faye said. 'Havin those radiation treatments and gettin injects of poison that's supposed to kill the cancer while it's half killing you. I'm surprised you didn't know, Ralph.'

I suppose you are, but I'm not. The insomnia keeps swallowing stuff, you see. One day it's the last Cup-A-Soup envelope you lose track of; next day it's your sense of time; the day after that it's your old friends.

Faye shook his head. 'Fucking cancer. It's spooky, how it waits.'

Ralph nodded, now thinking of Carolyn. 'What room's Jimmy in, do you know? Maybe I'll go visit him.'

'Just so happens I do. 315. Think you can remember it?'

Ralph grinned. 'For awhile, anyway.'

'Go see him if you can, sure – they got him pretty doped up, but he still knows who comes in, and I bet he'd love to see you. Him and you had a lot of high old times together, he told me once.'

'Well, you know,' Ralph said. 'Couple of guys on the road, that's all. If we flipped for the check in some diner, Jimmy V always called tails.' Suddenly he felt like crying.

'Lousy, isn't it?' Faye said quietly.

'Yes.'

'Well, you go see him. He'll be glad, and you'll feel better. That's how it's supposed to work, anyway. And don't you go and forget the damn chess tournament!' Faye finished, straightening up and making a heroic effort to look and sound cheerful. 'If you step out now you'll fuck up the seedings.'

'I'll do my best.'

'Yeah, I know you will.' He made a fist and punched Ralph's upper arm lightly. 'And thanks again for stopping me before I could do something I'd, you know, feel bad about later.'

'Sure. Peacemaker Number One, that's me.' Ralph started

down the path which led to the Extension, then turned back. 'You see that service road over there? The one that goes from General Aviation out to the street?' He pointed. A catering truck was currently driving away from the private terminal, its windshield reflecting bright darts of sunlight into their eyes. The truck stopped just short of the gate, breaking the electric-eye beam. The gate began to trundle open.

'Sure I do,' Faye said.

'Last summer I saw Ed Deepneau using that road, which means he had a key-card to the gate. Any idea how he would have come by a thing like that?'

'You mean The Friends of Life guy? Lab scientist who did a little research in wife-beating last summer?'

Ralph nodded. 'But it's the summer of '92 I'm talking about. He was driving an old brown Datsun.'

Faye laughed. 'I wouldn't know a Datsun from a Toyota from a Honda, Ralph – I stopped bein able to tell cars apart around the time Chevrolet gave up the gullwing tailfins. But I can tell you who mostly uses that road: caterers, mechanics, pilots, crew, and flight controllers. Some passengers have key-cards, I think, if they fly private a lot. The only scientists over there are the ones who work at the air-testing station. Is that the kind of scientist he is?'

'Nope, a chemist. He worked at Hawking Labs until just a little while ago.'

'Played with the white rats, did he? Well there aren't any rats over at the airport – that I know of, anyway – but now that I think of it, there *is* one other bunch of people who use that gate.'

'Oh? Who?'

Faye pointed at a prefab building with a corrugated roof standing about seventy yards from the General Aviation terminal. 'See that building? That's SoloTech.'

'What's SoloTech?'

'A school,' Faye said. 'They teach people to fly.'

4

Ralph walked back down Harris Avenue with his big hands stuffed into his pockets and his head lowered so he did not see much more than the cracks in the sidewalk passing beneath his sneakers. His mind was fixed on Ed Deepneau again . . . and on SoloTech. He had no way of knowing if SoloTech was the reason Ed had been out at the airport on the day he had run into Mr West Side Gardeners, but all of a sudden that was a question to which Ralph very much wanted an answer. He was also curious as to just where Ed was living these days. He wondered if John Leydecker might share his curiosity on these two points, and decided to find out.

He was passing the unpretentious double storefront which housed George Lyford, CPA, on one side and Maritime Jewelry (WE BUY YOUR OLD GOLD AT TOP PRICES) on the other, when he was pulled out of his thoughts by a short, strangled bark. He looked up and saw Rosalie sitting on the sidewalk just outside the upper entrance to Strawford Park. The old dog was panting rapidly; saliva drizzled off her lolling tongue, building up a dark puddle on the concrete between her paws. Her fur was stuck together in dark clumps, as if she had been running, and the faded blue bandanna around her neck seemed to shiver with her rapid respiration. As Ralph looked at her, she gave another bark, this one closer to a yelp.

He glanced across the street to see what she was barking at and saw nothing but the Buffy-Buffy Laundromat. There were a few women moving around inside, but Ralph found it impossible to believe Rosalie was barking at them. No one at all was currently passing on the sidewalk in front of the coin-op laundry.

Ralph looked back and suddenly realized that Rosalie wasn't just sitting on the sidewalk but crouching there . . . *cowering* there. She looked scared almost to death.

Until that moment, Ralph had never thought much about how eerily human the expressions and body language of dogs were: they grinned when they were happy, hung their heads when they were ashamed, registered anxiety in their eyes and tension in the set of their shoulders – all things that people did. And, like people, they registered abject, total fear in every quivering line of the body.

He looked across the street again, at the spot where Rosalie's attention seemed focused, and once again saw nothing but the laundry and the empty sidewalk in front of it. Then, suddenly, he remembered Natalie, the Exalted & Revered Baby, snatching at the gray-blue contrails his fingers left behind as he reached out with them to wipe the milk from her chin. To anyone else she would have looked as if she were grabbing at nothing, the way babies always appeared to be grabbing at nothing . . . but Ralph had known better.

He had *seen* better.

Rosalie uttered a string of panicky yelps that grated on Ralph's ear like the sound of unoiled hinges.

So far it's only happened on its own . . . but maybe I can make it happen. Maybe I make myself see—

See what?

Well, the auras. Them, of course. And maybe whatever Rosalie

(*three-six-nine hon*)

was looking at, as well. Ralph already had a pretty good idea

(*the goose drank wine*)

of what it was, but he wanted to be sure. The question was how to do it.

How does a person see in the first place?

By looking, of course.

Ralph looked at Rosalie. Looked at her carefully, trying to see everything there was to see: the faded pattern on the blue bandanna which served as her collar, the dusty clumps and tangles in her uncared-for coat, the sprinkle of gray around her long muzzle. After a few moments of this she seemed to feel his gaze, for she turned, looked at him, and whined uneasily.

As she did, Ralph felt something turn over in his mind – it felt like the starter-motor of a car. There was a brief but very clear sense of being suddenly *lighter,* and then brightness flooded into the day. He had found his way back into that more vivid, more deeply textured world. He saw a murky membrane – it made him think of spoiled eggwhite – swim into existence around Rosalie, and saw a dark gray balloon-string rising from her. Its point or origin wasn't the skull, however, as had been the case in all the people Ralph had seen while in this heightened state of awareness; Rosalie's balloon-string rose from her muzzle.

Now you know the most essential difference between dogs and men, he thought. *Their souls reside in different places.*

[*Doggy! Here, doggy, c'mere!*]

Ralph winced and drew back from that voice, which was like chalk squeaking on a blackboard. The heels of his palms rose most of the way to his ears before he realized that wouldn't help; he wasn't really hearing it with his ears, and the part that the voice hurt the worst was deep inside his head, where his hands couldn't reach.

[*Hey, you fucking flea suitcase! You think I've got all day? Get your raggedy ass over here!*]

Rosalie whined and switched her gaze from Ralph back toward whatever she had been looking at before. She started to get up, then shrank back down on her haunches again. The bandanna she wore was shaking harder than ever, and Ralph saw a dark crescent begin to spread around her left flank as her bladder let go.

He looked across the street and there was Doc #3, standing between the laundromat and the elderly apartment house next door, Doc #3 in his white smock (it was badly stained, Ralph noticed, as if he had been wearing it for a long time) and his midget-sized blue jeans. He still had McGovern's Panama on his head. The hat now appeared to balance on the creature's ears; it was so big for him that the top half of his head seemed submerged in it. He was grinning ferociously at the dog, and Ralph saw a double row of pointed white teeth – the teeth of a cannibal. In his left hand he was holding something which was either an old scalpel or a straight-razor. Part of Ralph's mind tried to convince him that it was blood he saw on the blade, but he was pretty sure it was just rust.

Doc #3 slipped the first two fingers of his right hand into the corners of his mouth and blew a piercing whistle that went through Ralph's head like a drillbit. Down the sidewalk, Rosalie flinched backward and then voiced a brief howl.

[*Get your fucking ass over, Rover! Do it now!*]

Rosalie got up, tail between her legs, and began to slink toward the street. She whined as she went, and her fear had worsened her limp to the point where she was barely able to stagger; her hindquarters threatened to slide out from under her at each reluctant, lurching step.

[*'Hey!'*]

Ralph only realized that he had yelled when he saw the small blue cloud float up in front of his face. It was etched with gossamer silver lines that made it look like a snowflake.

The bald dwarf wheeled toward the sound of Ralph's shout,

instinctively raising the weapon he held as he did. His expression was one of snarling surprise. Rosalie had stopped with her front paws in the gutter and was looking at Ralph with wide, anxious brown eyes.

[*What do* you *want, Shorts?*]

There was fury at being interrupted in that voice, fury at being challenged . . . but Ralph thought there were other emotions underneath. Fear? He wished he could believe it. Perplexity and surprise seemed surer bets. Whatever this creature was, it wasn't used to being seen by the likes of Ralph, let alone challenged.

[*What's the matter, Short-Time, cat got your tongue? Or have you already forgotten what you wanted?*]

['*I want you to leave that dog alone!*']

Ralph heard himself in two different ways. He was fairly sure he was speaking aloud, but the sound of his actual voice was distant and tinny, like music drifting up from a pair of Walkman headphones which have been temporarily laid aside. Someone standing right beside him might have heard what he said, but Ralph knew the words would have sounded like a weak, out-of-breath gasp – talk from a man who has just been gutpunched. Inside his head, however, he sounded as he hadn't in years – young, strong, and confident.

Doc #3 must have heard it that second way, for he recoiled momentarily, again raising his weapon (Ralph was now almost certain it was a scalpel) for a moment, as if in self-defense. Then he seemed to regroup. He left the sidewalk and strode to the edge of Harris Avenue, standing on the leaf-drifted strip of grass between the sidewalk and the street. He hitched at the waistband of his jeans, yanking it through the dirty smock, and stared grimly at Ralph for several moments. Then he raised the rusty scalpel in the air and made an unpleasantly suggestive sawing gesture with it.

[*You can see me – big deal! Don't poke your nose into what doesn't concern you, Short-Time! The mutt belongs to me!*]

The bald doc turned back to the cringing dog.

[*I'm done fooling with you, Rover! Get over here! Right now!*]

Rosalie gave Ralph a beseeching, despairing look and then began to cross the street.

I don't mess in with long-time business, Old Dor had told him on the day he'd given him the book of Stephen Dobyns poems. *I told* you *not to, either.*

Yes, he had, yes indeed, but Ralph had a feeling it was too late now. Even if it wasn't, he had no intention of leaving Rosalie to the unpleasant little gnome standing in front of the coin-op laundry across the street. Not if he could help it, that was.

[*'Rosalie! Over here, girl! Heel!'*]

Rosalie gave a single bark and trotted over to where Ralph stood. She placed herself behind his right leg and then sat down, panting and looking up at him. And here was another expression Ralph found he could read with ease: one part relief, two parts gratitude.

The face of Doc #3 was twisted into a grimace of hate so severe it was almost a cartoon.

[*Better send her across, Shorts! I'm warning you!*]

[*'No.'*]

[*I'll fuck you over, Shorts. I'll fuck you over big-time. And I'll fuck your friends over. Do you get me? Do you—*]

Ralph suddenly raised one hand to shoulder height with the palm turned inward toward the side of his head, as if he meant to administer a karate chop. He brought it down and watched, amazed, as a tight blue wedge of light flew off the tips of his fingers and sliced across the street like a thrown spear. Doc #3 ducked just in time, clapping one hand to McGovern's Panama to keep it from flying off. The blue wedge skimmed two or three inches over that small, clutching hand and struck the front window of the Buffy-Buffy. There it spread like some supernatural liquid, and for a moment the dusty glass became the brilliant, perfect blue of today's sky. It faded after only a moment and Ralph could see the women inside the laundromat again, folding their clothes and loading their washers exactly as if nothing had happened.

The bald dwarf straightened, rolled his hands into fists, and shook them at Ralph. Then he snatched McGovern's hat off his head, stuck the brim in his mouth, and tore a bite out of it. As he performed this bizarre equivalent of a child's tantrum, the sun struck splinters of fire from the lobes of his small, neatly made ears. He spat out the chunk of splintery straw and then clapped the hat back on his head.

[*That dog was mine, Shorts! I was gonna play with her! I guess maybe I'll have to play with you instead, huh? You and your asshole friends!*]

[*'Get out of here.'*]

[*Cuntlicker! Fucked your mother and licked her cunt!*]

Ralph knew where he had heard *that* charming sentiment before: Ed Deepneau, out at the airport, in the summer of '92.

It wasn't the sort of thing you forgot, and all at once he was terrified. What in God's name had he stumbled into?

5

Ralph lifted his hand to the side of his head again, but something inside had changed. He could bring it down in that chopping gesture again, but he was almost positive that this time no bright blue flying wedge would result.

The doc apparently didn't know he was being threatened with an empty gun, however. He shrank back, raising the hand holding the scalpel in a shielding gesture. The grotesquely bitten hat slipped down over his eyes, and for a moment he looked like a stage-melodrama version of Jack the Ripper . . . one who might have been working out pathologic inadequacies caused by extreme shortness.

[*Gonna get you for this, Shorts! You wait! You just wait! No Short-Timer runs the game on me!*]

But for the time being, the little bald doctor had had enough. He wheeled around and ran into the weedy lane between the laundromat and the apartment house with his dirty, too-long smock flapping and snapping at the legs of his jeans. The brightness slipped out of the day with him. Ralph marked its passage to a large extent with senses he had never before even suspected. He felt totally awake, totally energized, and almost exploding with delighted excitement.

I drove it off, by God! I drove the little sonofawhore off!

He had no idea what the creature in the white smock really was, but he knew he had saved Rosalie from it, and for now that was enough. Nagging questions about his sanity might creep back tomorrow morning as he sat in the wing-chair looking down at the deserted street below . . . but for the time being, he felt like a million bucks.

'You saw him, didn't you, Rosalie? You saw the nasty little—'

He looked down, saw that Rosalie was no longer sitting by his heel, and looked up in time to see her limping into the park, head down, right leg slueing stiffly off to the side with every pained stride.

'Rosalie!' he shouted. 'Hey, girl!' And, without really knowing why – except that they had just gone through something extraordinary together – Ralph started after her, first just jogging, then running, finally sprinting all out.

He didn't sprint for long. A stitch that felt like a hot chrome needle buried itself in his left side, then spread rapidly across the left half of his chest wall. He stopped just inside the park, standing bent over at the intersection of two paths, hands clamped on his legs just above the knees. Sweat ran into his eyes and stung like tears. He panted harshly, wondering if it was just the ordinary sort of stitch he remembered from the last lap of the mile run in high-school track, or if this was how the onset of a fatal heart attack felt.

After thirty or forty seconds the pain began to abate, so maybe it had just been a stitch, after all. Still, it went a good piece toward supporting McGovern's thesis, didn't it? *Let me tell you something, Ralph – at our age, mental illness is common! At our age it's common as hell!* Ralph didn't know if that was true or not, but he did know that the year he had made All-State Track was now over half a century in the past, and sprinting after Rosalie the way he'd done was stupid and probably dangerous. If his heart *had* seized up, he supposed he wouldn't have been the first old guy to be punished with a coronary thrombosis for getting excited and forgetting that when eighteen went, it went forever.

The pain was almost gone and he was getting his wind back, but his legs still felt untrustworthy, as if they might unlock at the knees and spill him onto the gravel path without the slightest warning. Ralph lifted his head, looking for the nearest park bench, and saw something that made him forget stray dogs, shaky legs, even possible heart attacks. The nearest bench was forty feet farther along the left-hand path, at the top of a gentle, sloping hill. Lois Chasse was sitting on that bench in her good blue fall coat. Her gloved hands were folded together in her lap, and she was sobbing as if her heart would break.

Chapter Twelve

1

'What's wrong, Lois?'

She looked up at him, and the first thought to cross Ralph's mind was actually a memory: a play he had taken Carolyn to see at the Penobscot Theater in Bangor eight or nine years ago. Some of the characters in it had supposedly been dead, and their makeup had consisted of clown-white greasepaint with dark circles around the eyes to give the impression of huge empty sockets.

His second thought was much simpler: *Raccoon.*

She either saw some of his thoughts on his face or simply realized how she must look, because she turned away, fumbled briefly at the clasp of her purse, then simply raised her hands and used them to shield her face from his view.

'Go away, Ralph, would you?' she asked in a thick, choked voice. 'I don't feel very well today.'

Under ordinary circumstances, Ralph would have done as she asked, hurrying away without looking back, feeling nothing but a vague shame at having come across her with her mascara smeared and her defenses down. But these weren't ordinary circumstances, and Ralph decided he wasn't leaving – not yet, anyway. He still retained some of that strange lightness, and still felt that other world, that other Derry, was very close. And there was something else, something perfectly simple and straightforward. He hated to see Lois, whose happy nature he had never even questioned, sitting here by herself and bawling her eyes out.

'What's the matter, Lois?'

'I just don't feel well!' she cried. 'Can't you leave me alone?'

Lois buried her face in her gloved hands. Her back shook, the sleeves of her blue coat trembled, and Ralph thought of how Rosalie had looked when the bald doctor had been yelling at her to get her ass across the street: miserable, scared to death.

Ralph sat down next to Lois on the bench, slipped an arm around her, and pulled her to him. She came, but stiffly . . . as if her body were full of wires.

'Don't you look at me!' she cried in that same wild voice. 'Don't you *dare*! My makeup's a mess! I put it on special for my son and daughter-in-law . . . they came for breakfast . . . we were going to spend the morning . . . "We'll have a nice time, Ma," Harold said . . . but the *reason* they came . . . you see, the real reason . . .'

Communication broke down in a fresh spate of weeping. Ralph groped in his back pocket, came up with a handkerchief which was wrinkled but clean, and put it in one of Lois's hands. She took it without looking at him.

'Go on,' he said. 'Scrub up a little if you want, although you don't look bad, Lois; honest you don't.'

A little raccoony is all, he thought. He began to smile, and then the smile died. He remembered the day in September when he had set off for the Rite Aid to check out the over-the-counter sleep aids and had encountered Bill and Lois standing outside the park, talking about the doll-throwing demonstration which Ed had orchestrated at WomanCare. She had been clearly distressed that day – Ralph remembered thinking that she looked tired in spite of her excitement and concern – but she had also been close to beautiful: her considerable bosom heaving, her eyes flashing, her cheeks flushed with a maid's high color. That all but irresistible beauty was hardly more than a memory today; in her melting mascara Lois Chasse looked like a sad and elderly clown, and Ralph felt a quick hot spark of fury for whatever or whoever had wrought the change.

'I look *horrible*!' Lois said, applying Ralph's handkerchief vigorously. 'I'm a *fright*!'

'No, ma'am. Just a little smeary.'

Lois at last turned to face him. It clearly took a lot of effort with her rouge and eye makeup now mostly on Ralph's handkerchief. 'How bad am I?' she breathed. 'Tell the truth, Ralph Roberts, or your eyes'll cross.'

He bent forward and kissed one moist cheek. 'Only lovely, Lois. You'll have to save ethereal for another day, I guess.'

She gave him an uncertain smile, and the upward movement of her face caused two fresh tears to spill from her eyes. Ralph took the crumpled handkerchief from her and gently wiped them away.

'I'm so glad it was you who came along and not Bill,' she told him. 'I would have died of shame if Bill had seen me crying in public.'

Ralph looked around. He saw Rosalie, safe and sound at the bottom of the hill – she was lying between the two Portosans that stood down there, her muzzle resting on one paw – but otherwise this part of the park was empty. 'I think we've got the place pretty much to ourselves, at least for now,' he said.

'Thank God for small favors.' Lois took the handkerchief back and went to work on her makeup again, this time in a rather more businesslike manner. 'Speaking of Bill, I stopped into the Red Apple on my way down here – that was before I got feeling sorry for myself and started to bawl my silly head off – and Sue said you two had a big argument just a little while ago. Yelling and everything, right out in your front yard.'

'Nah, not that big,' Ralph said, smiling uneasily.

'Can I be nosy and ask what it was about?'

'Chess,' Ralph said. It was the first thing to pop into his mind. 'The Runway 3 Tournament Faye Chapin has every year. Only it really wasn't about anything. You know how it is – sometimes people get out of bed on the wrong side and just grab the first excuse.'

'I wish that was all it was with me,' Lois said. She opened her purse, managing the clasp effortlessly this time, and took out her compact. Then she sighed and stuffed it back into the bag again without opening it. 'I can't. I know I'm being a baby, but I just *can't*.'

Ralph darted his hand into her purse before she could close it, removed the compact, opened it, and held the mirror up in front of her. 'See? That's not so bad, is it?'

She averted her face like a vampire turning away from a crucifix. 'Ugh,' she said. 'Put it away.'

'If you promise to tell me what happened.'

'Anything, just put it away.'

He did. For a little while Lois said nothing but only sat and watched her hands fiddle restlessly with the clasp of her purse. He was about to prod her when she looked up at him with a pitiful expression of defiance.

'It just so happens you're not the *only* one who can't get a decent night's sleep, Ralph.'

'What are you talking ab—'

'*Insomnia!*' she snapped. 'I go to sleep at about the same time I always did, but I don't sleep through anymore. And it's worse than that. I wake up earlier every morning, it seems.'

Ralph tried to remember if he had told Lois about that aspect of his own problem. He didn't think he had.

'Why are you looking so surprised?' Lois asked. 'You didn't really think you were the only person in the world to ever have a sleepless night, did you?'

'Of course not!' Ralph responded with some indignation . . . but hadn't it often felt as if he were the only person in the world to have that particular *kind* of sleepless night? Standing helplessly by as his good sleep-time was eroded minute by minute and quarter hour by quarter hour? It was like a weird variant of the Chinese water-torture.

'When did yours start?' he asked.

'A month or two before Carol died.'

'How much sleep are you getting?'

'Barely an hour a night since the start of October.' Her voice was calm, but Ralph heard a tremor which might have been panic just below the surface. 'The way things are going, I'll have entirely quit sleeping by Christmas, and if that really happens, I don't know how I'll survive it. I'm barely surviving now.'

Ralph struggled for speech and asked the first question to come into his mind: 'How come I've never seen your light?'

'For the same reason I hardly ever see yours, I imagine,' she said. 'I've been living in the same place for almost thirty-five years, and I don't need to turn on the lights to find my way around. Also, I like to keep my troubles to myself. You keep turning on the lights at two in the morning and sooner or later someone sees them. It gets around, and then the nosybirds start asking questions. I don't like nosybird questions, and I'm not one of those people who feel like they have to take an ad out in the paper every time they have a little constipation.'

Ralph burst out laughing. Lois looked at him in round-eyed perplexity for a moment, then joined in. His arm was still around her (or had it crept back on its own after he had taken it away? Ralph didn't know and didn't really care), and he hugged her tightly. This time she pressed against him easily; those stiff little wires had gone out of her body. Ralph was glad.

'You're not laughing at me, are you, Ralph?'

'Nope. Absolutely not.'

She nodded, still smiling. '*That's* all right, then. You never even saw me moving around in my living room, did you?'

'No.'

'That's because there's no streetlamp in front of my house. But there's one in front of *yours*. I've seen you in that ratty old wing-chair of yours many times, sitting and looking out and drinking tea.'

I always assumed I was the only one, he thought, and suddenly a question – both comic and embarrassing – popped into his head. How many times had she seen him sitting there and picking his nose? Or picking at his crotch?

Either reading his mind or the color in his cheeks, Lois said, 'I really couldn't make out much more than your shape, you know, and you were always wearing your robe, perfectly decent. So you don't have to worry about *that*. Also, I hope you know that if you'd ever started doing anything you wouldn't want people to *see* you doing, I wouldn't have looked. I wasn't exactly raised in a barn, you know.'

He smiled and patted her hand. 'I *do* know that, Lois. It's just . . . you know, a surprise. To find out that while I was sitting there and watching the street, somebody was watching *me*.'

She fixed him with an enigmatic smile that might have said, *Don't worry, Ralph – you were just another part of the scenery to me.*

He considered this smile for a moment, then groped his way back to the main point. 'So what happened, Lois? Why were you sitting here and crying? Just sleeplessness? If that's what it was, I certainly sympathize. There's really no just about it, is there?'

Her smile slipped away. Her gloved hands folded together again in her lap and she looked somberly down at them. 'There are worse things than insomnia. Betrayal, for instance. Especially when the people doing the betraying are the people you love.'

2

She fell quiet. Ralph didn't prompt her. He was looking down the hill at Rosalie, who appeared to be looking up at him. At both of them, maybe.

'Did you know we share the same doctor as well as the same problem, Ralph?'

'You go to Litchfield, too?'

'*Used* to go to Litchfield. He was Carolyn's recommendation. I'll never go to him again, though. He and I are quits.' Her upper lip drew back. 'Double-crossing son of a *bitch*!'

'What happened?'

'I went along for the best part of a year, waiting for things to get better by themselves – for nature to take her course, as they say. Not that I didn't try to help nature along every now and then. We probably tried a lot of the same things.'

'Honeycomb?' Ralph asked, smiling again. He couldn't help it. *What an amazing day this has been,* he thought. *What a perfectly amazing day . . . and it's not even one in the afternoon yet.*

'Honeycomb? What about it? Does that help?'

'No,' Ralph said, grinning more widely than ever, 'doesn't help a bit, but it tastes *wonderful.*'

She laughed and squeezed his bare left hand in both of her gloved ones. Ralph squeezed back.

'You never went to see Dr Litchfield about it, did you, Ralph?'

'Nope. Made an appointment once, but cancelled it.'

'Did you put it off because you didn't trust him? Because you felt he missed the boat on Carolyn?'

Ralph looked at her, surprised.

'Never mind,' Lois said. 'I had no right to ask that.'

'No, it's okay. I guess I'm just surprised to hear the idea from someone else. That he . . . you know . . . that he might have misdiagnosed her.'

'Huh!' Lois's pretty eyes flashed. 'It crossed *all* our minds! Bill used to say he couldn't believe you didn't have that fumble-fingered bastard in district court the day after Carolyn's funeral. Of course back then I was on the other side of the fence, defending Litchfield like mad. *Did* you ever think of suing him?'

'No. I'm seventy, and I don't want to spend whatever time

I have left flogging a malpractice suit. Besides – would it bring Carol back?'

She shook her head.

Ralph said, 'What happened to Carolyn *was* the reason I didn't go see him, though. I guess it was, at least. I just couldn't seem to trust him, or maybe . . . I don't know . . .'

No, he didn't really know, that was the devil of it. All he knew for sure was that he had cancelled the appointment with Dr Litchfield, as he had cancelled his appointment with James Roy Hong, known in some quarters as the pin-sticker man. That latter appointment had been scratched on the advice of a ninety-two- or -three-year-old man who could probably no longer remember his own middle name. His mind slipped to the book Old Dor had given him, and to the poem Old Dor had quoted from – 'Pursuit', it had been called, and Ralph couldn't seem to get it out of his head . . . especially the part where the poet talked about all the things he saw falling away behind him: the unread books, the untold jokes, the trips that would never be taken.

'Ralph? Are you there?'

'Yeah – just thinking about Litchfield. Wondering why I cancelled that appointment.'

She patted his hand. 'Just be glad you did. I kept mine.'

'Tell me.'

Lois shrugged. 'When it got so bad I felt I couldn't stand it anymore, I went to him and told him everything. I thought he'd give me a prescription for sleeping pills, but he said he couldn't even do that – I sometimes have an irregular heartbeat, and sleeping pills can make that worse.'

'When did you see him?'

'Early last week. Then, yesterday, my son Harold called me out of a clear blue sky and said he and Janet wanted to take me out to breakfast. Nonsense, I said. I can still get around the kitchen. If you're coming all the way down from Bangor, I said, I'll get up a nice little feed for you, and that's the end of it. Then, after, if you want to take me out – I was thinking of the mall, because I always like to go out there – why, that would be fine. That's just what I said.'

She turned to Ralph with a smile that was small and bitter and fierce.

'It never occurred to me to wonder why *both* of them were coming to see me on a weekday, when both of them have jobs – and they must really love those jobs, because they're about all they ever talk about. I just thought how *sweet* of them it was . . . how *thoughtful* . . . and I put out a special effort to look nice and do everything right so Janet wouldn't suspect I was having a problem. I think *that* rankles most of all. Silly old Lois, "Our Lois", as Bill always says . . . don't look so surprised, Ralph! Of course I knew about that; did you think I fell off a stump just yesterday? And he's right. I *am* foolish, I *am* silly, but that doesn't mean I don't hurt just like anyone else when I'm taken advantage of . . .' She was beginning to cry again.

'Of course it doesn't,' Ralph said, and patted her hand.

'You would have laughed if you'd seen me,' she said, 'baking fresh squash muffins at four o'clock in the morning and slicing mushrooms for an Italian omelette at four-fifteen and starting in with the makeup at four-thirty just to be *sure,* absolutely *sure* that Jan wouldn't get going with that "Are you sure you feel all right, Mother Lois?" stuff. I *hate* it when she starts in with that crap. And do you know what, Ralph? She knew what was wrong with me all the time. They *both* did. So I guess the laugh was on me, wasn't it?'

Ralph thought he had been following closely, but apparently he had lost her on one of the turns. 'Knew? How could they know?'

'*Because Litchfield told them!*' she shouted. Her face twisted again, but this time it was not hurt or sorrow Ralph saw there but a terrible rueful rage. '*That tattling son of a bitch called my son on the telephone and* TOLD HIM EVERYTHING!'

Ralph was dumbfounded.

'Lois, they can't do that,' he said when he finally found his voice again. 'The doctor–patient relationship is . . . well, it's privileged. Your son would know all about it, because he's a lawyer, and the same thing applies to them. Doctors can't tell *anyone* what their patients tell them unless the patient—'

'Oh Jesus,' Lois said, rolling her eyes. 'Crippled wheelchair Jesus. What world are you living in, Ralph? Fellows like Litchfield do whatever they think is right. I guess I knew that all along, which makes me double-stupid for going to him at all. Carl Litchfield is a vain, arrogant man who cares more about how he looks in his suspenders and designer shirts than he does about his patients.'

'That's awfully cynical.'

'And awfully true, that's the sad part. You know what? He's thirty-five or thirty-six, and he's somehow gotten the idea that when he hits forty, he's just going to . . . stop. Stay forty for as long as he wants to. He's got an idea that people are old once they get to be sixty, and that even the best of them are pretty much in their dotage by the age of sixty-eight or so, and that once you're past eighty, it'd be a mercy if your relatives would turn you over to that Dr Kevorkian. Children don't have any rights of confidentiality from their parents, and as far as Litchfield is concerned, old poops like us don't have any rights of confidentiality from our kids. It wouldn't be in our best interests, you see.

'What Carl Litchfield did practically the minute I was out of his examining room was to phone Harold in Bangor. He said I wasn't sleeping, that I was suffering from depression, and that I was having the sort of sensory problems that accompany a premature decline in cognition. And then he said, "You have to remember that your mother is getting on in years, Mr Chasse, and if I were you I'd think very seriously about her situation down here in Derry."'

'He didn't!' Ralph cried, amazed and horrified. 'I mean . . . did he?'

Lois was nodding grimly. 'He said it to Harold and Harold said it to me and now I'm saying it to you. Silly old me, I didn't even know what "a premature decline in cognition" meant, and neither of them wanted to tell me. I looked up "cognition" in the dictionary, and do you know what it means?'

'Thinking,' Ralph said. 'Cognition is thinking.'

'Right. My doctor called my son to tell him I was going senile!' Lois laughed angrily and used Ralph's handkerchief to wipe fresh tears off her cheeks.

'I can't believe it,' Ralph said, but the hell of it was he could. Ever since Carolyn's death he had been aware that the naïveté with which he had regarded the world up until the age of eighteen or so had apparently not departed forever when he crossed the threshold between childhood and manhood; that peculiar innocence seemed to be returning as he stepped over the threshold between manhood and *old* manhood. Things kept surprising him . . . except surprise was really too mild a word. What a lot of them did was knock him ass over teakettle.

The little bottles under the Kissing Bridge, for instance. He had taken a long walk out to Bassey Park one day in July and had gone under the bridge to rest out of the afternoon sun for awhile. He had barely gotten comfortable before noticing a little pile of broken glass in the weeds by the stream that trickled beneath the bridge. He had swept at the high grass with a length of broken branch and discovered six or eight small bottles. One had some crusty white stuff in the bottom. Ralph had picked it up, and as he turned it curiously before his eyes, he realized he was looking at the remains of a crack-party. He had dropped the bottle as if it were hot. He could still remember the numbed shock he had felt, his unsuccessful attempt to convince himself that he was nuts, that it *couldn't* be what he thought it was, not in this hick town two hundred and fifty miles north of Boston. It was that emerging naïf which had been shocked, of course; that part of him seemed to believe (or had until he had discovered the little bottles under the Kissing Bridge) that all those news stories about the cocaine epidemic had just been make-believe, no more real than a TV crime show or a Jean-Claude Van Damme movie.

He felt a similar sensation of shock now.

'Harold said they wanted to "run me up to Bangor" and show me the place,' Lois was saying. 'He never takes me for rides these days; he just runs me places. Like I'm an errand. They had lots of brochures, and when Harold gave Janet the nod, she whipped them out so fast—'

'Whoa, slow down. What place? What brochures?'

'I'm sorry, I'm getting ahead of myself, aren't I? It's a place in Bangor called Riverview Estates.'

Ralph knew the name; had gotten a brochure himself, as a matter of fact. One of those mass mailing things, this one targeted at people sixty-five and over. He and McGovern had shared a laugh about it . . . but the laugh had been just a touch uneasy – like kids whistling past the grave-yard.

'Shit, Lois – that's a retirement home, isn't it?'

'No, *sir*!' she said, widening her eyes innocently. 'That's what *I* said, but Harold and Janet set me straight. No, Ralph, Riverview Estates is *a condominium development site for community-oriented senior citizens*! When Harold said that I said, "Is that so? Well, let me tell you both something – you can put a fruit pie from McDonald's in a sterling-silver chafing dish and call it a French tart, but it's still just a fruit pie from McDonald's, as far as I am concerned."

'When I said that, Harold started to sputter and get red in the face, but Jan just gave me that sweet little smile of hers, the one she saves up for special occasions because she knows it drives me crazy. She says, "Well, why don't we look at the brochures anyway, Mother Lois? You'll do *that* much, won't you, after we both took Personal Days from work and drove all the way down here to see you?"'

'Like Derry was in the heart of Africa,' Ralph muttered.

Lois took his hand and said something that made him laugh. 'Oh, to her it is!'

'Was this before or after you found out Litchfield had tattled?' Ralph asked. He used the same word Lois had on purpose; it seemed to fit this situation better than a fancier word or phrase would have done. "Committed a breach of confidentiality" was far too dignified for this nasty bit of work. Litchfield had run and tattled, simple as that.

'Before. I thought I might as well look at the brochures; after all, they'd come forty miles, and it wouldn't exactly kill me. So I looked while they ate the food I'd fixed – there wasn't any that had to be scraped into the swill later on, either – and drank coffee.

'That's quite a place, that Riverview. They have their own medical staff on duty twenty-four hours a day, and their own kitchen. When you move in they give you a complete physical and decide what you can have to eat. There's a Red Diet Plan, a Blue Diet Plan, a Green Diet Plan, and a Yellow Diet Plan. There were three or four other colors as well. I can't remember what all of them were, but Yellow is for diabetics and Blue is for fatties.'

Ralph thought of eating three scientifically balanced meals a day for the rest of his life – no more sausage pizzas from Gambino's, no more Coffee Pot sandwiches, no more chiliburgers from Mexico Milt's – and found the prospect almost unbearably grim.

'Also,' Lois said brightly, 'they have a pneumatic-tube system that delivers your daily pills right to your kitchen. Isn't that a marvellous idea, Ralph?'

'I guess so,' Ralph said.

'Oh, yes, it is. It's marvellous, the wave of the future. There's a computer to oversee everything, and I bet it never has a decline in cognition. There's a special bus that takes the Riverview people to places of scenic or cultural interest twice a week, and it also takes them shopping. You have to take the bus, because Riverview people aren't allowed to have cars.'

'Good idea,' he said, giving her hand a little squeeze. 'What are a few drunks on Saturday night compared to an old fogey with a slippery cognition on the loose in a Buick sedan?'

She didn't smile, as he had hoped she would. 'The pictures

in those brochures turned my blood. Old ladies playing canasta. Old men throwing horseshoes. Both flavors together in this big pine-panelled room they call the River Hall, square-dancing. Although that *is* sort of a nice name, don't you think? River Hall?'

'I guess it's okay.'

'I think it sounds like the kind of room you'd find in an enchanted castle. But I've visited quite a few old friends in Strawberry Fields – that's the geriatrics' home in Skowhegan – and I know an old folks' rec room when I see one. It doesn't matter how pretty a name you give it, there's still a cabinet full of board games in the corner and jigsaw puzzles with five or six pieces missing from each one and the TV's always tuned to something like *Family Feud* and never to the kind of movies where good-looking young people take off their clothes and roll around on the floor together in front of the fireplace. Those rooms always smell of paste . . . and piss . . . and the five-and-dime watercolors that come in a long tin box . . . and despair.'

Lois looked at him with her dark eyes.

'I'm only sixty-eight, Ralph. I know that sixty-eight doesn't seem like only *anything* to Dr Fountain of Youth, but it does to me, because my mother was ninety-two when she died last year and my dad lived to be eighty-six. In my family, dying at eighty is dying young . . . and if I had to spend twelve years living in a place where they announce dinner over the loudspeaker, I'd go crazy.'

'I would, too.'

'I looked, though. I wanted to be polite. When I was finished, I made a neat little pile of them and handed them back to Jan. I said they were very interesting and thanked her. She nodded and smiled and put them back in her purse. I thought that was going to be the end of it and good riddance, but then Harold said, "Put your coat on, Ma."

'For a second I was so scared I couldn't breathe. I thought they'd already signed me up! And I had an idea that if I said I wasn't going, Harold would open the door and there would be two or three men in white coats outside, and one of them would smile and say, "Don't worry, Mrs Chasse; once you get that first handful of pills delivered direct to your kitchen, you'll never want to live anywhere else."

' "I don't *want* to put my coat on," I told Harold, and I tried to sound the way I used to when he was only ten and always tracking mud into the kitchen, but my heart was beating so hard I could hear it tapping in my voice. "I've changed my mind about going out. I forgot how much I had to do today." And then Jan gave the laugh I hate even more than her syrupy little smile and said, "Why, Mother Lois, what would you have to do that's so important you can't go up to Bangor with *us* after we've taken time off to come down to Derry and see *you?*"

'That woman always gets my back hair up, and I guess I do the same to her. I must, because I've never in my life known one woman to smile that much at another without hating her guts. Anyway, I told her I had to wash the kitchen floor, to start with. "Just look at it," I said. "Dirty as the devil."

'"Huh!" Harold says. "I can't believe you're going to send us back to the city empty-handed after we came all the way down here, Ma."

'"Well I'm not moving into that place no matter how far you came," I said back, "so you can get *that* idea right out of your head. I've been living in Derry for thirty-five years, half my life. All my friends are here, and I'm not moving."

'They looked at each other the way parents do when they've got a kid who's stopped being cute and started being a pain in the tail. Janet patted my shoulder and said, "Now don't get all upset, Mother Lois – we only want you to come and *look.*" Like it was the brochures again, and all I had to do was be polite. Just the same, her saying it was just to look set my mind at ease a little. I should have known they couldn't *make* me live there, or even afford it on their own. It's Mr Chasse's money they're counting on to swing it – his pension and the railroad insurance I got because he died on the job.

'It turned out they had an appointment all made for eleven o'clock, and a man lined up to show me around and give me the whole pitch. I was mostly over being scared by the time I got all that straight in my mind, but I was hurt by the high-handed way they were treating me, and mad at how every other thing out of Janet's mouth was Personal Days this and Personal Days that. It was pretty clear that she could think of a lot better ways to spend a day off than coming to Derry to see her fat old bag of a mother-in-law.

'"Stop fluttering and come on, Mother," she says after a little more back-and-forth, like I was so pleased with the whole idea I couldn't even decide which hat to wear. "Hop into your coat. I'll help you clean up the breakfast things when we get back."

'"You didn't hear me," I said. "I'm not going anywhere. Why waste a beautiful fall day like this touring a place I'll never live in? And what gives you the right to drive down here and give me this kind of bum's rush in the first place? Why didn't one of you at least call and say, 'We have an idea, Mom, want to hear it?' Isn't that how you would have treated one of your friends?"

'And when I said that, they traded another glance . . .'

Lois sighed, wiped her eyes a final time, and gave back Ralph's handkerchief, damper but otherwise none the worse for wear.

'Well, I knew from that look that we hadn't reached bottom yet. Mostly it was the way Harold looked – like he did when he'd just hooked a handful of chocolate bits out of the bag in the pantry. And Janet . . . she gave him back the expression I dislike most of all. Her bulldozer look, I call it. And then she asked him if he wanted to tell me what the doctor had said, or if she should do it.

'In the end they both told it, and by the time they were done I was so mad and scared that I felt like yanking my hair out by the roots. The thing I just couldn't seem to get over no matter how hard I tried was the thought of Carl Litchfield telling Harold all the things I thought were private. Just calling him and *telling* him, like there was nothing in the world wrong with it.

'"So you think I'm senile?" I asked Harold. "Is that what it comes down to? You and Jan think I've gone soft in the attic at the advanced age of sixty-eight?"

'Harold got red in the face and started shuffling his feet under his chair and muttering under his breath. Something about how he didn't think any such thing, but he had to consider my safety, just like I'd always considered his when he was growing up. And all the time Janet was sitting at the counter, nibbling a muffin and giving him a look I could have killed her for – as if she thought he was just a cockroach that had learned to talk like a lawyer. Then she got up and asked if she could "use the facility". I told her to go ahead, and managed to keep from saying it would be a relief to have her out of the room for two minutes.

'"Thanks, Mother Lois," she says. "I won't be long. Harry and I have to leave soon. If you feel you can't come with us and keep your appointment, then I guess there's nothing more to say."'

'What a peach,' Ralph said.

'Well, that was the end of it for me; I'd had enough. "I keep my appointments, Janet Chasse," I said, "but only the ones I make for myself. I don't give a fart in a high wind for the ones other people make for me."

'She tossed up her hands like I was the most unreasonable woman who ever walked the face of the earth, and left me with Harold. He was looking at me with those big brown eyes of his, like he expected me to apologize. I almost felt like I *should* apologize, too, if only to get that cocker spaniel look off his face, but I didn't. *I wouldn't.* I just looked back at him, and after awhile he couldn't stand it anymore and told me I ought to stop being mad. He said he was just worried about me down here all by myself, that he was only trying to be a good son and Janet was only trying to be a good daughter.

'"I guess I understand that," I said, "but you should know that sneaking around behind a person's back is no way to express love and concern." He got all stiff then, and said he and Jan didn't see it as sneaking around. He cut his eyes toward the bathroom for a second or two when he said it, and I pretty much got the idea that what he meant was *Jan* didn't see it as sneaking around. Then he told me it wasn't the way I was making it out to be – that *Litchfield* had called *him*, not the other way around.

'"All right," I said back, "but what kept you from hanging up once you realized what he'd called to talk to you *about*? That was just plain *wrong,* Harry. What in God's good name got into you?"

'He started to flutter and flap around – I think he might even have been starting to apologize – when Jan came back and the you-know-what really hit the fan. She asked where my diamond earrings were, the ones they'd given me for Christmas. It was such a change of direction that at first I could only sputter, and I suppose I sounded like I *was* going senile. But finally I managed to say they were in the little china dish on my bedroom bureau, same as always. I have a jewelry box, but I keep those earrings and two or three other nice pieces out because they are so pretty that looking at them always cheers me up. Besides, they're only clusters of diamond chips – it's not like anyone would want to break in just to steal *those*. Same with my engagement ring and my ivory cameo, which are the other two pieces I keep in that dish.'

Lois gave Ralph an intense, pleading look. He squeezed her hand again.

She smiled and took a deep breath. 'This is very hard for me.'

'If you want to stop—'

'No, I want to finish . . . except that, past a certain point, I can't remember what happened, anyway. It was all so horrible. You see, Janet said she *knew* where I kept them, but they weren't there. My engagement ring was, and the cameo, but not my Christmas earrings. I went in to check myself, and she was right. We turned the place upside down, looked everywhere, but we didn't find them. They're *gone*.'

Lois was now gripping Ralph's hands in both of her own, and seemed to be talking mostly to the zipper of his jacket.

'We took all the clothes out of the bureau . . . Harold pulled the bureau itself out from the wall and looked behind it . . . under the bed and the sofa cushions . . . and it seemed like every time I looked at Janet, she was looking back at *me,* giving me that sweet, wide-eyed look of hers. Sweet as melting butter, it is – except in the eyes, anyway – and she didn't have to come right out and say what she was thinking, because I already knew. "You see? You see how right Dr Litchfield was to call us, and how right *we* were to make that appointment? And how pigheaded *you're* being? Because you *need* to be in a place like Riverview Estates, and this just proves it. You've lost the lovely earrings we gave you for Christmas, you're having a *serious* decline in cognition, and this just proves it. It won't be long before you're leaving the stove-burners on . . . or the bathroom heater . . ."'

She began to cry again, and these tears made Ralph's heart hurt – they were the deep, scouring sobs of someone who has been shamed to the deepest level of her being. Lois hid her face against his jacket. He tightened his arm around her. *Lois,* he thought. *Our Lois.* But no; he didn't like the sound of that anymore, if he ever had.

My Lois, he thought, and at that instant, as if some greater power had approved, the day began to fill with light again. Sounds took on a new resonance. He looked down at his hands and Lois's, entwined on her lap, and saw a lovely blue-gray nimbus around them, the color of cigarette smoke. The auras had returned.

3

'You should have sent them away the minute you realized the earrings were gone,' he heard himself say, and each word was separate and gorgeously unique, like a crystal thunderclap. 'The very second.'

'Oh, I know that now,' Lois said. 'She was just waiting for me to stick my foot in my mouth, and of course I obliged. But I was so *upset* – first the argument about whether or not I was going to Bangor with them to look at Riverview Estates, then hearing my doctor had told them things he had no right to tell them, and on top of all that, finding out I'd lost one of my most treasured possessions. And do you know what the cherry on top was? Having *her* be the one to discover those earrings were gone! Do you blame me for not knowing what to do?'

'No,' he said, and lifted her gloved hands to his mouth. The sound of them passing through the air was like the hoarse whisper of a palm sliding down a wool blanket, and for a moment he clearly saw the shape of his lips on the back of her right glove, printed there in a blue kiss.

Lois smiled. 'Thank you, Ralph.'

'Welcome.'

'I suppose you have a pretty good idea of how things turned out, don't you? Jan said, "You really *should* take better care, Mother Lois, only Dr Litchfield says you've come to a time of life when you really *can't* take better care, and that's why we've been thinking about Riverview Estates. I'm sorry we ruffled your feathers, but it seemed important to move quickly. Now you see why."'

Ralph looked up. Overhead, the sky was a cataract of green-blue fire filled with clouds that looked like chrome airboats. He looked down the hill and saw Rosalie still lying between the Portosans. The dark gray balloon-string rose from her snout, wavering in the cool October breeze.

'I got really mad, then –' She broke off and smiled. Ralph thought it was the first smile he'd seen from her today which expressed real humor instead of some less pleasant and more complicated emotion. 'No – that's not right. I did more than just get mad. If my great-nephew had been there, he would have said, "Nana went nuclear."'

Ralph laughed and Lois laughed with him, but her half sounded a trifle forced.

'What galls me is that Janet knew I would,' she said. 'She *wanted* me to go nuclear, I think, because she knew how guilty I'd feel later on. And God knows I *do*. I screamed at them to get the hell out. Harold looked like he wanted to sink right through the floorboards – shouting has always made him so embarrassed – but Jan just sat there with her hands folded in her lap, smiling and actually *nodding her head,* as if to say "That's right, Mother Lois, you go on and get all that nasty old poison out of your system, and when it's gone, maybe you'll be ready to hear sense." '

Lois took a deep breath.

'Then something happened. I'm not sure just what. This wasn't the first time, either, but it was the *worst* time. I'm afraid it was some kind of . . . well . . . some kind of seizure. Anyway, I started to see Janet in a really funny way . . . a really *scary* way. And I said something that finally got to her. I can't remember what it was, and I'm not sure I want to know, but it certainly wiped that sweety-sweety-sweet smile I hate so much off her face. In fact, she just about *dragged* Harold out. The last thing I remember her saying is that one of them would call me when I wasn't so hysterical that I couldn't help making ugly accusations about the people who loved me.

'I stayed in my house for a little while after they were gone, and then I came out to sit in the park. Sometimes just sitting in the sun makes a body feel better. I stopped in the Red Apple for a snack, and that's when I heard you and Bill had a fight. Are you and he really on the outs, do you think?'

Ralph shook his head. 'Nah – we'll make it up. I really like Bill, but—'

'– but you have to be careful what you say with him,' she finished. 'Also, Ralph, may I add that you can't take what he says back to you too seriously?'

This time it was Ralph who gave their linked hands a squeeze. 'That might be good advice for you, too, Lois – you shouldn't take what happened this morning too seriously.'

She sighed. 'Maybe, but it's hard not to. I said some terrible things at the end, Ralph. *Terrible.* That awful smile of hers . . .'

A rainbow of understanding suddenly hit Ralph's consciousness. In its glow he saw a very large thing, so large it seemed both unquestionable and preordained. He fully faced Lois for the first time since the auras had returned to him . . . or since he had returned to them. She sat in a capsule of translucent gray light as bright as fog on a summer morning which is about to turn sunny. It transformed the woman Bill McGovern called 'Our Lois' into a creature of great dignity . . . and almost unbearable beauty.

She looks like Eos, he thought. *Goddess of the dawn.*

Lois stirred uneasily on the bench. 'Ralph? Why are you looking at me that way?'

Because you're beautiful, and because I've fallen in love with you, Ralph thought, amazed. *Right now I'm so in love with you that I feel as if I'm drowning, and the dying's fine.*

'Because you remember *exactly* what you said.'

She began to play nervously with the clasp of her purse again. 'No, I—'

'Yes you do. You told your daughter-in-law that *she* took your earrings. She did it because she realized you were going to stick to your guns about not going with them, and not getting what she wants makes your daughter-in-law crazy . . . it makes her go nuclear. She did it because you pissed her off. Isn't that about the size of it?'

Lois was looking at him with round, frightened eyes. 'How do you know that, Ralph? *How do you know that about her?*'

'I know it because *you* know it, and you know it because you saw it.'

'Oh, no,' she whispered. 'No, I didn't see anything. I was in the kitchen with Harold the whole time.'

'Not *then,* not when she did it, but when she came back. You saw it in her and all around her.'

As he himself now saw Harold Chasse's wife in Lois, as if the woman sitting beside him on the bench had become a lens. Janet Chasse was tall, fair-skinned, and long-waisted. Her cheeks were spattered with freckles she covered with makeup, and her hair was a vivid, gingery shade of red. This morning she had come to Derry with that fabulous hair lying over one shoulder in a bulky braid like a sheaf of copper wire. What else did he know about this woman he had never met?

Everything, everything.

She coveres her freckles with pancake because she thinks they make her look childish; that people don't take women with freckles seriously. Her legs are beautiful and she knows it. She wears short skirts to work, but today when she came to see

(the old bitch)

Mother Lois, she was wearing a cardigan and an old pair of jeans. Derry dress-downs. Her period is overdue. She's reached that time of life when it doesn't come as regular as clockwork anymore, and during that uneasy two- or three-day pause she suffers through every month, a pause when the whole world seems made of glass and everyone in it seems either stupid or wicked, her behavior and her moods have become erratic. That's probably the real reason she did what she did.

Ralph saw her coming out of Lois's tiny bathroom. Saw her shoot an intense, furious glance toward the kitchen door – there is no sign of the sweety-sweety-sweet smile on that narrow, intense face now – and then scoop the earrings out of the china dish. Saw her cram them into the left front pocket of her jeans.

No, Lois had not actually witnessed this small, ugly theft, but it had changed the color of Jan Chasse's aura from pale green to a complex, layered pattern of browns and reds which Lois had seen and understood at once, probably without the slightest idea of what was really happening to her.

'She took them, all right,' Ralph said. He could see a gray mist drifting dreamily across the pupils of Lois's wide eyes. He could have looked at it for the rest of the day.

'Yes, but—'

'If you'd agreed to keep the appointment at Riverview Estates after all, I bet you would have found them again after her next visit . . . or *she* would have found them, I guess that's more likely. Just a lucky accident – "Oh, Mother Lois, come see what *I* found!" Under the bathroom sink, or in a closet, or lying in some dark corner.'

'Yes.' She was looking into his face now, fascinated, almost hypnotized. 'She must feel terrible . . . and she won't dare bring them back, will she? Not after the things I said. Ralph, how did you *know*?'

'The same way you did. How long have you been seeing the auras, Lois?'

4

'Auras? I don't know what you mean.' Except she did.

'Litchfield told your son about the insomnia, but I doubt if that alone would have been enough to get even Litchfield to . . . you know, tattle. The other thing – what you said he called sensory problems – went right by me. I was too amazed by the idea of anyone thinking you could possibly be prematurely senile, I guess, even though I've been having my own sensory problems lately.'

'*You!*'

'Yes, ma'am. Then, just a little bit ago, you said something even more interesting. You said you started to see Janet in a really funny way. A really *scary* way. You couldn't remember what you *said* just before the two of them walked out, but you knew exactly how you *felt*. You're seeing the other part of the world – the *rest* of the world. Shapes around things, shapes *inside* things, sounds within sounds. I call it the world of auras, and that's what you're experiencing. Isn't it, Lois?'

She looked at him silently for a moment, then put her hands over her face. 'I thought I was losing my mind,' she said, and then said it again: 'Oh Ralph, I thought I was losing my mind.'

5

He hugged her, then let her go and tilted her chin up. 'No more tears,' he said. 'I didn't bring a spare hanky.'

'No more tears,' she agreed, but her eyes were already brimming again. 'Ralph, if you only knew how awful it's been—'

'I *do* know.'

She smiled radiantly. 'Yes . . . you do, don't you?'

'What made that idiot Litchfield decide you were slipping into senility – except Alzheimer's is probably what he had in mind – wasn't just insomnia but insomnia accompanied by something else . . . something he decided were hallucinations. Right?'

'I guess, but he didn't say anything like that at the time. When I told him about the things I'd been seeing – the colors and all – he seemed very understanding.'

'Uh-huh, and the minute you were out the door he called your son and told him to get the hell down to Derry and do something about old Mom, who's started seeing people walking around in colored envelopes with long balloon-strings floating up from their heads.'

'You see those, too? Ralph, *you see those, too?*'

'Me too,' he said, and laughed. It sounded a bit loonlike, and he wasn't surprised. There were a hundred things he wanted to ask her; he felt crazed with impatience. And there was something else, something so unexpected he hadn't even been able to identify it at first: he was horny. Not just interested; actually horny.

Lois was crying again. Her tears were the color of mist on a still lake, and they smoked a little as they slipped down her cheeks. Ralph knew they would taste dark and mossy, like fiddleheads in spring.

'Ralph . . . this . . . this is . . . oh *my!*'

'Bigger than Michael Jackson at the SuperBowl, isn't it?'

She laughed weakly. 'Well, just . . . you know, just a little.'

'There's a name for what's happening to us, Lois, and it's not insomnia or senility or Alzheimer's Disease. It's hyper-reality.'

'Hyper-reality,' she murmured. 'God, what an exotic word!'

'Yes, it is. A pharmacist down the street at Rite Aid, Joe Wyzer, told it to me. Only there's a lot more to it than he knew. More than anyone in their right minds would guess.'

'Yes, like telepathy . . . if it's really happening, that is. Ralph, *are* we in our right minds?'

'Did your daughter-in-law take your earrings?'

'I . . . she . . . yes.' Lois straightened. 'Yes, she did.'

'No doubts?'

'No.'

'Then you've answered your own question. We're sane, all right . . . but I think you're wrong about the telepathy part. It isn't *minds* we read, but *auras*. Listen, Lois, there's all sorts of things I want to ask you, but I have an idea that right now there's only one thing I really have to know. Have you seen –' He stopped abruptly, wondering if he really wanted to say what was on the tip of his tongue.

'Have I seen what?'

'Okay. This is going to sound crazier than anything you've told me, but I'm not crazy. Do you believe that? I'm *not.*'

'I believe you,' she said simply, and Ralph felt a vast weight slip from his heart. She was telling the truth. There was no question about it; her belief shone all around her.

'Okay, listen. Since this started happening to you, have you seen certain people who don't look like they belong on Harris

Avenue? People who don't look like they belong *anywhere* in the ordinary world?'

Lois was looking at him with puzzled incomprehension.

'They're bald, they're very short, they wear white smock tops, and what they look like more than anything are the drawings of space aliens they sometimes have on the front pages of those tabloid newspapers they sell in the Red Apple. You haven't seen anyone like that when you've been having one of these hyper-reality attacks?'

'No, no one.'

He banged a fist on his leg in frustration, thought for a moment, then looked up again. 'Monday morning,' he said. 'Before the cops showed up at Mrs Locher's . . . did you see me?'

Very slowly, Lois nodded her head. Her aura had darkened slightly, and spirals of scarlet, thin as threads, began to twist slowly up through it on a diagonal.

'I imagine you have a pretty good idea of who called the police, then,' Ralph said. 'Don't you?'

'Oh, I know it was you,' Lois said in a small voice. 'I suspected before, but I wasn't sure until just now. Until I saw it . . . you know, in your colors.'

In my colors, he thought. It was what Ed had called them, too.

'But you didn't see two pint-sized versions of Mr Clean come out of her house?'

'No,' she said, 'but that doesn't mean anything. I can't even *see* Mrs Locher's house from my bedroom window. The Red Apple's roof is in the way.'

Ralph laced his hands together on top of his head. Of *course* it was, and he should have known it.

'The reason I thought you called the police is that just before I went to take a shower, I saw you looking at something through a pair of binoculars. I never saw you do that before, but I thought maybe you just wanted a better look at the stray dog who raids the garbage cans on Thursday mornings.' She pointed down the hill. *'Him.'*

Ralph grinned. 'That's no him, that's the gorgeous Rosalie.'

'Oh. Anyway, I was in the shower a long time, because there's a special rinse I put in my hair. Not *color,*' she said sharply, as if he had accused her of this, 'just proteins and things that are supposed to keep it looking a little thicker. When I came out, the police were flocking all around. I looked over your way once, but I couldn't see you anymore. You'd either gone into a different room or kind of scrunched back in your chair. You do that, sometimes.'

Ralph shook his head as if to clear it. He hadn't been in an empty theater on all those nights, after all; someone else had been there, too. They had just been in separate boxes.

'Lois, the fight Bill and I had wasn't really about chess. It—'

Down the hill, Rosalie voiced a rusty bark and began struggling to her feet. Ralph looked in that direction and felt an icicle slip into his belly. Although the two of them had been sitting here for going on half an hour and no one had even come near the comfort stations at the bottom of the hill, the pressed plastic door of the Portosan marked MEN was now slowly opening.

Doc #3 emerged from it. McGovern's hat, the Panama with the crescent bitten in the brim, was cocked back on his head, making him look weirdly as McGovern had on the day Ralph had first seen him in his brown fedora – like an enquiring newshawk in a forties crime drama.

Upraised in one hand the bald stranger held the rusty scalpel.

Chapter Thirteen

1

'Lois?' To Ralph's own ears, his voice seemed to be an echo winding down a long, deep canyon. 'Lois, do you see that?'

'I don't –' Her voice broke off. 'Did the wind blow that bathroom door open? It didn't, did it? Is someone there? Is that why the dog's making that racket?'

Rosalie backed slowly away from the bald man, her ragged ears laid back, her muzzle wrinkled to expose teeth so badly eroded that they were not much more menacing than hard rubber pegs. She uttered a cracked volley of barks, then began to whine desperately.

'Yes! Don't you *see* him, Lois? Look! He's *right there*!'

Ralph got to his feet. Lois got up with him, shielding her eyes with one hand. She peered down the slope with desperate intensity. 'I see a shimmer, that's all. Like the air over an incinerator.'

'*I told you to leave her alone!*' Ralph shouted down the hill. '*Quit it! Get the hell out!*'

The bald man looked in Ralph's direction, but there was no surprise in the glance this time; it was casual, dismissive. He raised the middle finger of his right hand, flicked it at Ralph in the ancient salute, then bared his own teeth – much sharper and much more menacing than Rosalie's – in a silent laugh.

Rosalie cringed as the little man in the dirty smock began to walk toward her again, then actually raised a paw and put it on her own head, a cartoonish gesture that should have been funny and was horribly expressive of her terror instead.

'What can't I see, Ralph?' Lois moaned. 'I see *something*, but—'

'Get AWAY *from her!*' Ralph shouted, and raised his hand in that karate-chop gesture again. The hand inside – the hand which earlier had produced that wedge of tight blue light – still felt like an unloaded gun, however, and this time the bald doc seemed to know it. He glanced in Ralph's direction and offered a small, jeering wave.

[*Aw, quit it, Shorts – sit back, shut up, and enjoy the show.*]

The creature at the foot of the hill returned his attention to Rosalie, who sat huddled at the base of an old pine. The tree was emitting a thin green fog from the cracks in its bark. The bald doctor bent over Rosalie, one hand outstretched in a gesture of solicitude that went very badly with the scalpel curled into his left fist.

Rosalie whined . . . then stretched her neck forward and humbly licked the bald creature's palm.

Ralph looked down at his own hands, sensing something in them – not the power he'd had before, nothing like that, but *something*. Suddenly there were snaps of clear white light dancing just above his nails. It was as if his fingers had been turned into sparkplugs.

Lois was grabbing frantically at him now. 'What's wrong with the dog? *Ralph, what's wrong with it?*'

With no thought about what he was doing or why, Ralph put his hands over Lois's eyes, like someone playing Guess Who with a loved one. His fingers flashed a momentary white so bright it was almost blinding. *Must be the white they're always talking about in the detergent commercials,* he thought.

Lois screamed. Her hands flew to his wrists, clamped on them, then loosened. 'My God, Ralph, what did you do to me?'

He took his hands away and saw a glowing figure-eight surrounding her eyes; it was as if she had just taken off a pair of goggles which had been dipped in confectioner's sugar. The white began to dim almost as soon as his hands were gone . . . except . . .

It's not dimming, he thought. *It's sinking in.*

'Never mind,' he said, and pointed. 'Look!'

The widening of her eyes told him what he needed to know. Doc #3, completely unmoved by Rosalie's desperate effort to make friends, shoved her muzzle aside with the hand holding the scalpel. He seized the old bandanna hanging around her neck in his other hand and yanked her head up. Rosalie howled miserably. Slobber ran back along the sides of her face. The bald man voiced a scabrous chuckle that made Ralph's flesh crawl.

[*'Hi! Leave off! Leave off teasing that dog!'*]

The bald man's head snapped around. The grin ran off his face and he snarled at Lois, sounding a little like a dog himself.

[*Yahh, go fuck yourself, you fat old Short-Time cunt! Dog's mine, just like I already told your limpdick boyfriend!*]

The bald man had let go of the blue bandanna when Lois shouted at him, and Rosalie was now cringing back against the pine again, her eyes rolling, curds of foam dripping from the sides of her muzzle. Ralph had never seen such a completely terrified creature in his life.

'*Run!*' Ralph screamed. '*Get away!*'

She seemed not to hear him, and after a moment Ralph realized she *wasn't* hearing him, because Rosalie was no longer entirely *there*. The bald doctor had done something to her already – had pulled her at least partway out of ordinary reality like a farmer using his tractor and a length of chain to pull a stump.

Ralph tried once more, anyway.

[*'Run, Rosalie! Run away!'*]

This time her laid-back ears cocked forward and her head began to turn in Ralph's direction. He didn't know if she would have obeyed him or not, because the bald man renewed his hold on the bandanna before she could even begin to move. He yanked her head up again.

'*He's going to kill it!*' Lois screamed. '*He's going to cut its throat with that thing he has! Don't let him, Ralph! Make him stop!*'

'I can't! Maybe you can! Shoot him! Shoot your hand at him!'

She looked at him, not understanding. Ralph made frantic wood-chopping gestures with his right hand, but before Lois could respond, Rosalie gave a dreadful lost howl. The bald doc raised the scalpel and brought it down, but it wasn't Rosalie's throat he cut.

He cut her balloon-string.

2

A thread emerged from each of Rosalie's nostrils and floated upward. They twined together about six inches above her snout, making a delicate pigtail, and it was at this point that Baldy #3's scalpel did its work. Ralph watched, frozen with horror, as the severed pigtail rose into the sky like the string of a released helium balloon. It was unravelling as it went. He thought it would tangle in the branches of the old pine, but it didn't. When the ascending balloon-string finally did meet one of the branches, it simply passed through.

Of course, Ralph thought. *The same way this guy's buddies walked through May Locher's locked front door after they finished doing the same thing to her.*

This idea was followed by a thought too simple and gruesomely logical not to be believed: not space-aliens, not little bald doctors, but Centurions. Ed Deepneau's Centurions. They didn't look like the Roman soldiers you saw in tin-pants epics like *Spartacus* and *Ben Hur,* true, but they *had* to be Centurions . . . didn't they?

Sixteen or twenty feet above the ground, Rosalie's balloon-string simply faded away to nothingness.

Ralph looked back down in time to see the bald dwarf pull the faded blue bandanna off over the dog's head and then push her down at the base of the tree. Ralph looked at her more closely and felt all his flesh shrink closer to his bones. His dream of Carolyn recurred with cruel intensity, and he found himself struggling to bottle up a shriek of terror.

That's right, Ralph, don't scream. You don't want to do that because once you start, you might not be able to stop – you might just go on doing it until your throat bursts. Remember Lois, because she's in this now, too. Remember Lois and don't start screaming.

Ah, but it was hard not to, because the dream-bugs which had come spewing out of Carolyn's head were now pouring from Rosalie's nostrils in writhing black streams.

Those aren't bugs. I don't know what they are, but they are not bugs.

No, not bugs – just another kind of aura. Nightmarish black stuff, neither liquid nor gas, was pumping out of Rosalie with each exhaled breath. It did not float away but instead began to surround her in slow, nasty coils of anti-light. That blackness should have hidden her from view, but it didn't. Ralph could see her pleading, terrified eyes as the darkness gathered around her head and then began to ooze down her back and sides and legs.

It was a deathbag, a *real* deathbag this time, and he was watching as Rosalie, her balloon-string now cut, wove it relentlessly about herself like a poisonous placental sac. This metaphor triggered the voice of Ed Deepneau inside his head, Ed saying that the Centurions were ripping babies from the wombs of their mothers and taking them away in covered trucks.

Ever wonder what was under most of those tarps? Ed had asked.

Doc #3 stood grinning down at Rosalie. Then he united the knot in her bandanna and put it around his own neck, tying it in a big, loose knot, making it look like a bohemian artist's necktie. This done, he looked up at Ralph and Lois with an expression of loathsome complacency. *There!* his look said. *I took care of my business after all, and there wasn't a damned thing you could do about it, was there?*

['*Do something, Ralph! Please do something! Make him stop!*']

Too late for that, but maybe not too late to send him packing before he could enjoy the sight of Rosalie dropping dead at the foot of the tree. He was pretty sure Lois couldn't produce a karate-chop of blue light as he had done, but maybe she could do something else.

Yes — she can shoot him in her own way.

He didn't know why he was so sure of that, but suddenly he was. He grabbed Lois by the shoulders to make her look at him, then raised his right hand. He cocked his thumb and pointed his forefinger at the bald man. He looked like a small child playing cops and robbers.

Lois responded with a look of dismay and incomprehension. Ralph grabbed her hand and stripped off her glove.

['*You! You, Lois!*']

She got the idea, raised her own hand, extended her forefinger, and made the child's shooting gesture: Pow! Pow!

Two compact lozenge shapes, their gray-blue shade identical to Lois's aura but much brighter, flew from the end of her finger and streaked down the hill.

Doc #3 screeched and leaped upward, fisted hands held at shoulder height, the heels of his black shoes clipping against his buttocks, as the first of these 'bullets' went under him. It struck the ground, rebounded like a flat stone skipped across

the surface of a pond, and hit the Portosan marked WOMEN.
For a moment the entire front of it glowed fiercely, as the
window of the Buffy-Buffy had done.

The second blue-gray pellet clipped the baldy's left hip and
ricocheted up into the sky. He screamed – a high, chattery
sound that seemed to twist like a worm in the middle of
Ralph's head. Ralph raised his hands to his ears even though
it could do no good, and saw Lois doing the same thing. He
felt sure that if that scream went on for long, it would burst
his head open just as surely as high C shatters fine crystal.

Doc #3 fell to the needle-carpeted ground beside Rosalie and
rolled back and forth, howling and holding his hip the way a
small child will hold the place he banged when he tumbled off
his tricycle. After a few moments of this, his cries began to
diminish and he scrambled to his feet. His eyes blazed at them
from below the white expanse of his brow. Bill's Panama was
tilted far back on his head now, and the left side of his smock
was black and smoking.

[*I'll get you! I'll get you both! Goddam interfering Short-Time
fucks! I'LL GET YOU BOTH!*]

He whirled and bounded down the path which led to the
playground and the tennis courts, running in big flying leaps
like an astronaut on the moon. Lois's shot didn't appear to have
done any real damage, judging by his speed afoot.

Lois seized Ralph's shoulder and shook him. As she did, the
auras began to fade again.

[*'The children! It's going toward the child*   ]

She was fading out, and that seemed to make perfect sense,
because he suddenly saw that Lois wasn't really talking at all,
only staring at him fixedly with her dark eyes as she clutched
his shoulder.

'I can't hear you!' he yelled. 'Lois, I can't hear you!'

'What's wrong, are you deaf? It's going toward the playground! Toward the children! *We can't let it hurt the children!*'

Ralph let out a deep, shuddering sigh. 'It won't.'

'How can you be sure?'

'I don't know. I just am.'

'I shot it.' She turned her finger toward her face, for a
moment looking like a woman who mimes suicide. 'I shot it
with my finger.'

'Uh-huh. It stung him, too. Hard, from the way he looked.'

'I can't see the colors anymore, Ralph.'

He nodded. 'They come and go, like radio stations at night.'

'I don't know how I feel . . . I don't even know how I *want* to feel!' She wailed this last, and Ralph folded her into his arms. In spite of everything that was going on in his life right now, one fact registered very clearly: it was wonderful to be holding a woman again.

'That's okay,' he told her, and pressed his face against the top of her head. Her hair smelled sweet, with none of the underlying murk of beauty-shop chemicals he'd gotten used to in Carolyn's hair over the last ten or fifteen years of their life together. 'Let go of it for now, okay?'

She looked at him. He could no longer see the faint mist drifting across her pupils, but felt sure it was still there. And besides, they were very pretty eyes even without the extra added attraction. 'What's it for, Ralph? Do you know what it's *for*?'

He shook his head. His mind was whirling with jigsaw pieces – hats, docs, bugs, protest signs, dolls that exploded in splatters of fake blood – that would not fit together. And for the time being, at least, the thing that seemed to recur with the most resonance was Old Dor's nonsense saying: *Done-bun-can't-be-undone.*

Ralph had an idea that was nothing but the truth.

3

A sad little whine came to his ears and Ralph looked down the hill. Rosalie was lying at the base of the big pine, trying to get up. Ralph could no longer see the black bag around her, but he was sure it was still there.

'Oh Ralph, the poor thing! What can we do?'

There was nothing they could do. Ralph was sure of it. He took Lois's right hand in both of his and waited for Rosalie to lie back and die.

Instead of that, she gave a whole-body lurch that sent her so strongly to her feet that she almost toppled over the other way. She stood still for a moment, her head held so low her muzzle was almost on the ground, and then sneezed three or four times. With that out of the way, she shook herself and looked up at Ralph and Lois. She yapped at them once, a short, brisk sound. To Ralph it sounded as if she were telling them to quit worrying. Then she turned and made off through a little grove of pine trees toward the park's lower entrance. Before Ralph lost sight of her, she had achieved the limping yet insouciant trot which was her trademark. The bum leg was no better than it had been before Doc #3's interference, but it seemed no worse. Clearly old but seemingly a long way from dead (*Just like the rest of the Harris Avenue Old Crocks,* Ralph thought), she disappeared into the trees.

'I thought that thing was going to kill her,' Lois said. 'In fact, I thought it *had* killed her.'

'Me too,' Ralph said.

'Ralph, did all that really happen? It did, didn't it?'

'Yes.'

'The balloon-strings . . . do you think they're lifelines?'

He nodded slowly. 'Yes. Like umbilical cords. And Rosalie . . .'

He thought back to his first real experience with the auras, of how he'd stood outside the Rite Aid with his back to the blue mailbox and his jaw hanging down almost to his breastbone. Of the sixty or seventy people he had observed before the auras faded again, only a few had been walking inside the dark envelopes he now thought of as deathbags, and the one Rosalie had knitted around herself just now had been blacker by far than any he had seen that day. Still, those people in the parking lot whose auras had been dingy-dark had invariably looked unwell . . . like Rosalie, whose aura had been the color of old sweatsocks even before Baldy #3 started messing with her.

Maybe he just hurried up what may otherwise be a perfectly natural process, he thought.

'Ralph?' Lois asked. 'What about Rosalie?'

'I think my old friend Rosalie is living on borrowed time now,' Ralph said.

Lois considered this, looking down the hill and into the sun-dusty grove where Rosalie had disappeared. At last she turned to Ralph again. 'That midget with the scalpel was one of the men you saw coming out of May Locher's house, wasn't he?'

'No. Those were two other ones.'

'Have you seen more?'

'No.'

'Do you think there *are* more?'

'I don't know.'

He had an idea that next she'd ask if Ralph had noticed that the creature had been wearing Bill's Panama, but she didn't. Ralph supposed it was possible she hadn't recognized it. Too much weirdness swirling around, and besides, there hadn't been a chunk bitten out of the brim the last time she'd seen Bill wearing it. *Retired history teachers just aren't the hat-biting type,* he reflected, and grinned.

'This has been quite a morning, Ralph.' Lois met his gaze frankly, eye to eye. 'I think we need to talk about this, don't you? I really need to know what's going on.'

Ralph remembered this morning – a thousand years ago, now – walking back down the street from the picnic area, running over his short list of acquaintances, trying to decide whom he should talk to. He had crossed Lois off that mental list on the grounds that she might gossip to her girlfriends, and he was now embarrassed by that facile judgement, which had been based more on McGovern's picture of Lois than on his own. It turned out that the only person Lois had spoken to about the auras before today was the one person she should have been able to trust to keep her secret.

He nodded at her. 'You're right. We need to talk.'

'Would you like to come back to my house for a little late lunch? I make a pretty mean stir-fry for an old gal who can't keep track of her earrings.'

'I'd love to. I'll tell you what I know, but it's going to take awhile. When I talked to Bill this morning, I gave him the *Reader's Digest* version.'

'So,' Lois said. 'The fight was about chess, was it?'

'Well, maybe not,' Ralph said, smiling down at his hands. 'Maybe it was actually more like the fight you had with your son and your daughter-in-law. And I didn't even tell him the craziest parts.'

'But you'll tell me?'

'Yes,' he said, and started to get up. 'I'll bet you're a hell of a good cook, too. In fact—' He stopped suddenly and clapped one hand to his chest. He sat back down on the bench, heavily, his eyes wide and his mouth ajar.

'Ralph? Are you all right?'

Her alarmed voice seemed to be coming from a great distance. In his mind's eye he was seeing Baldy #3 again, standing between the Buffy-Buffy and the apartment house next door. Baldy #3 trying to get Rosalie to cross Harris Avenue so he could cut her balloon-string. He'd failed then, but he'd gotten the job done

(*I was gonna play with her!*)

before the morning was out.

Maybe the fact that Bill McGovern isn't the hat-biting type wasn't the only reason Lois didn't notice whose hat Baldy #3 was wearing, Ralph old buddy. Maybe she didn't notice because she didn't want to notice. Maybe there are a couple of pieces here that fit together, and if you're right about that, the implications are wide-ranging. You see that, don't you?

'Ralph? What's wrong?'

He saw the dwarf snatching a bite from the brim of the Panama and then clapping it back on his head. Heard him saying he guessed he would have to play with Ralph instead.

But not just me. Me and my friends, he said. Me and my asshole friends.

Now, thinking back on it, he saw something else, as well. He saw the sun striking splinters of fire from the lobes of Doc #3's ears as he – or it – chomped into the brim of McGovern's hat. The memory was too clear to deny, and so were those implications.

Those wide-ranging implications.

Take it easy – you don't know a thing for sure, and the funny-farm is just over the horizon, my friend. I think you need to remember that, maybe use it as an anchor. I don't care if Lois is also seeing all this stuff or not. The other men in the white coats, not the pint-sized baldies but the muscular guys with the butterfly nets and the Thorazine shots, can show up at any time. Any old time at all.

But still.

Still.

'Ralph! Jesus Christ, *talk* to me!' Lois was shaking him now and shaking hard, like a wife trying to rouse a husband who is going to be late for work.

He looked around at her and tried to manufacture a smile. It felt false from the inside but must have looked all right to Lois, because she relaxed. A little, anyway. 'Sorry,' he said. 'For a few seconds there it all just sort of . . . you know, ganged up on me.'

'Don't you scare me like that! The way you grabbed your chest, my God!'

'I'm fine,' Ralph said, and forced his false smile even wider. He felt like a kid pulling a wad of Silly Putty, seeing how far he could stretch it before it thinned enough to tear. 'And if you're still cookin, I'm still eatin.'

Three-six-nine, hon, the goose drank wine.

Lois took a close look at him and then relaxed. 'Good. That would be fun. I haven't cooked for anyone but Simone and

Mina – they're my girlfriends, you know – in a long time.'
Then she laughed. 'Except that isn't what I mean. That isn't
why it would be, you know, fun.'

'What *do* you mean?'

'That I haven't cooked for a *man* in a long time. I hope I
haven't forgotten how.'

'Well, there was the day Bill and I came in to watch the news
with you – we had macaroni and cheese. It was good, too.'

She made a dismissive gesture. 'Reheated. Not the same.'

*The monkey chewed tobacco on the streetcar line. The line
broke—*

Smiling wider than ever. Waiting for the rips to start. 'I'm
sure you haven't forgotten how, Lois.'

'Mr Chasse had a *very* hearty appetite. All sorts of hearty
appetites, in fact. But then he started having his liver trouble,
and . . .' She sighed, then reached for Ralph's arm and took it
with a mixture of timidity and resolution he found completely
endearing. 'Never mind. I'm tired of snivelling and moaning
about the past. I'll leave that to Bill. Let's go.'

He stood up, linked his arm through hers, and walked her
down the hill and toward the lower entrance to the park. Lois
beamed blindingly at the young mothers in the playground as
she and Ralph passed them. Ralph was glad for the distraction.
He could tell himself to withhold judgement, he could remind
himself over and over again that he didn't know enough about
what was happening to him and Lois to even kid himself that
he could think logically about it, but he kept jumping at that
conclusion anyway. The conclusion felt right to his heart, and
he had already come a long way toward believing that, in the
world of auras, feeling and knowing were close to identical.

*I don't know about the other two, but #3 is one crazy medic . . .
and he takes souvenirs. Takes them the way some of the crazies in
Vietnam took ears.*

That Lois's daughter-in-law had given in to an evil impulse,
scooping the diamond earrings from the china dish and putting
them in the pocket of her jeans, he had no doubt. But Janet
Chasse no longer had them; even now she was no doubt
reproaching herself bitterly for having lost them and wondering
why she had ever taken them in the first place.

Ralph knew the shrimp with the scalpel had McGovern's hat
even if Lois had failed to recognize it, and they had both seen
him take Rosalie's bandanna. What Ralph had realized as he
started to get up from the bench was that those splinters of light

he had seen reflected from the bald creature's earlobes almost certainly meant that Doc #3 had Lois's earrings, as well.

4

The late Mr Chasse's rocking chair stood on faded linoleum by the door to the back porch. Lois led Ralph to it and admonished him to 'stay out from underfoot'. Ralph thought this was an assignment he could handle. Strong light, mid-afternoon light, fell across his lap as he sat and rocked. Ralph wasn't sure how it had gotten so late so fast, but somehow it had. *Maybe I fell asleep,* he thought. *Maybe I'm asleep right now, and dreaming all this.* He watched as Lois took down a wok (definitely hobbit-sized) from an overhead cupboard. Five minutes later, savory smells began to fill the kitchen.

'I *told* you I'd cook for you someday,' Lois said, adding vegetables from the fridge crisper and spices from one of the overhead cabinets. 'That was the same day I gave you and Bill the leftover macaroni and cheese. Do you remember?'

'I believe I do,' Ralph said, smiling.

'There's a jug of fresh cider in the milk-box on the front porch – cider always keeps best outside. Would you get it? You can pour out, too. My good glasses are in the cupboard over the sink, the one I can't reach without dragging over a chair. You're tall enough to do without the chair, I judge. What are you, Ralph, about six-two?'

'Six-three. At least I was; I guess maybe I've lost an inch or two in the last ten years. Your spine settles, or something. And you don't have to go putting on the dog just for me. Honest.'

She looked at him levelly, hands on hips, the spoon with which she had been stirring the contents of the wok jutting from one of them. Her severity was offset by a trace of a smile. 'I said my *good* glasses, Ralph Roberts, not my *best* glasses.'

'Yes, ma'am,' he said, grinning, then added: 'From the way that smells, I guess you still remember how to cook for a man.'

'The proof of the pudding is in the eating,' Lois replied, but Ralph thought she looked pleased as she turned back to the wok.

310

5

The food was good, and they didn't talk about what had happened in the park as they applied themselves to it. Ralph's appetite had become uncertain, out more often than in, since his insomnia had really begun to bite, but today he ate heartily and chased Lois's spicy stir-fry with three glasses of apple cider (hoping uneasily as he finished the last one that the rest of the day's activities wouldn't take him too far from a toilet). When they had finished, Lois got up, went to the sink, and began to draw hot water for dishes. As she did, she resumed their earlier conversation as if it were a half-finished piece of knitting which had been temporarily laid aside for some other, more pressing, chore.

'What did you do to me?' she asked him. 'What did you do to make the colors come back?'

'I don't know.'

'It was as if I was on the edge of that world, and when you put your hands over my eyes, you pushed me into it.'

He nodded, remembering how she'd looked in the first few seconds after he'd removed his hands – as if she'd just taken off a pair of goggles which had been dipped in powdered sugar. 'It was pure instinct. And you're right, it *is* like a world. I keep thinking of it just that way, as the world of auras.'

'It's wonderful, isn't it? I mean, it's scary, and when it first started to happen to me – back in late July or early August, this was – I was sure I was going crazy, but even then I liked it, too. I couldn't help liking it.'

Ralph gazed at her, startled. Had he once upon a time thought of Lois as transparent? Gossipy? Unable to keep a secret?

No, I'm afraid it was a little worse than that, old buddy. You thought she was shallow. You saw her pretty much through Bill's eyes, as a matter of fact: as 'our Lois'. No less . . . but not much more.

'What?' she asked, a little uneasily. 'Why are you looking at me like that?'

'You've been seeing these auras since *summer*? That long?'

'Yes – brighter and brighter. Also more often. That's why I finally went to see the tattletale. Did I really shoot that thing with my finger, Ralph? The more time goes by, the less I can believe that part of it.'

'You did. I did something like it myself shortly before I ran into you.'

He told her about his earlier confrontation with Doc #3, and about how he had banished the dwarf . . . temporarily, at least. He raised his hand to his shoulder and brought it swiftly down. 'That's all I did – like a kid pretending to be Chuck Norris or Steven Seagal. But it sent this incredible bolt of blue light at him, and he scurried in a hurry. Which was probably for the best, because I couldn't have done it again. I don't know how I did *that,* either. Could you have shot your finger again?'

Lois giggled, turned toward him, and cocked her finger in his general direction. 'Want to find out? Kapow! Kablam!'

'Don't point dat ding at me, lady,' Ralph told her. He smiled as he said it, but wasn't entirely sure he was joking.

Lois lowered her finger and squirted Joy into the sink. As she began to stir the water around with one hand, puffing up the suds, she asked what Ralph thought of as the Big Questions: 'Where did this power come from, Ralph? And what's it for?'

He shook his head as he got up and walked over to the dish-drainer. 'I don't know and I don't know. How's that for helpful? Where do you keep your dish-wipers, Lois?'

'Never mind where I keep my dish-wipers. Go sit down. Please tell me you're not one of these modern men, Ralph – the ones that are always hugging each other and bawling.'

Ralph laughed and shook his head. 'Nope. I was just well trained, that's all.'

'Okay. As long as you don't start going on about how sensitive you are. There are *some* things a girl likes to find out for herself.' She opened the cupboard under the sink and tossed him a faded but scrupulously clean dishtowel. 'Just dry them and put them on the counter. I'll put them away myself. While you're working, you can tell me your story. The unabridged version.'

'You got a deal.'

He was still wondering where to begin when his mouth opened, seemingly of its own accord, and began for him. 'When I finally started to get it through my head that Carolyn was going to die, I went for a lot of walks. And one day, while I was out on the Extension . . .'

6

He told her everything, beginning with his intervention between Ed and the fat man wearing the West Side Gardeners gimme-cap and ending with Bill telling him that he'd better go see his doctor, because at their age mental illness was common, at their age it was common as hell. He had to double back several times to pick up dropped stitches – the way Old Dor had showed up in the middle of his efforts to keep Ed from going at the man from West Side Gardeners, for instance – but he didn't mind doing that, and Lois didn't seem to have any trouble keeping his narrative straight, either. The overall feeling Ralph was conscious of as he wound his way through his tale was a relief so deep it was nearly painful. It was as if someone had stacked bricks on his heart and mind and he was now removing them, one by one.

By the time he was finished, the dishes were done and they had left the kitchen in favor of the living room with its dozens of framed photographs, presided over by Mr Chasse from his place on the TV.

'So?' Ralph said. 'How much of it do you believe?'

'All of it, of course,' she said, and either did not notice the expression of relief of Ralph's face or chose to ignore it. 'After what we saw this morning – not to mention what you knew about my wonderful daughter-in-law – I can't very well not believe. That's my advantage over Bill.'

Not your only one, Ralph thought but didn't say.

'None of this stuff is coincidental, is it?' she asked him.

Ralph shook his head. 'No, I don't think so.'

'When I was seventeen,' she said, 'my mother hired this boy from down the road – Richard Henderson, his name was – to do chores around our place. There were a lot of boys she could have hired, but she hired Richie because she liked him . . . and she liked him for *me,* if you understand what I mean.'

'Of course I do. She was matchmaking.'

'Uh-huh, but at least she wasn't doing it in a big, gruesome, embarrassing way. Thank God, because I didn't care a fig for Richie – at least not like that. Still, Mother gave it her very best. If I was studying my books at the kitchen table, she'd have him loading the woodbox even though it was May and already hot. If I was feeding the chickens, she'd have Richie

313

cutting side-hay next to the dooryard. She wanted me to see him around . . . to get used to him . . . and if we got to like each other's company and he asked me to a dance or the town fair, that would have been just fine with her. It was gentle, but it was there. A push. And that's what this is like.'

'The pushes don't feel all that gentle to me,' Ralph said. His hand went involuntarily to the place where Charlie Pickering had pricked him with the point of his knife.

'No, of course they don't. Having a man stick a knife in your ribs like that must have been horrible. Thank God you had that spray-can. Do you suppose Old Dor sees the auras, too? That something from that world *told* him to put the can in your pocket?'

Ralph gave a helpless shrug. What she was suggesting had crossed his mind, but once you got beyond it, the ground really started to slope away. Because if Dorrance had done that, it suggested that some

(*entity*)

force or being had known that Ralph would need help. Nor was that all. That force – or being – would also have had to know that (a) Ralph would be going out on Sunday afternoon, that (b) the weather, quite nice up until then, would turn nasty enough to require a jacket, and (c) which jacket he would wear. You were talking, in other words, about something that could foretell the future. The idea that he had been noticed by such a force frankly scared the hell out of him. He recognized that in the case of the aerosol can, at least, the intervention had probably saved his life, but it still scared the hell out of him.

'Maybe,' he said. 'Maybe something *did* use Dorrance as an errand-boy. But why?'

'And what do we do now?' she added.

Ralph could only shake his head.

She glanced up at the clock squeezed in between the picture of the man in the raccoon coat and the young woman who looked ready to say *Twenty-three skidoo* any old time, then reached for the phone. 'Almost three-thirty! My goodness!'

Ralph touched her hand. 'Who are you calling?'

'Simone Castonguay. I'd made plans to go over to Ludlow with her and Mina this afternoon – there's a card-party at the Grange – but I can't go after all this. I'd lose my shirt.' She laughed, then colored prettily. 'Just a figure of speech.'

Ralph put his hand over hers before she could lift the receiver. 'Go on to your card-party, Lois.'

'Really?' She looked both doubtful and a little disappointed.

'Yes.' He was still unclear about what was going on here, but he sensed that was about to change. Lois had spoken of being pushed, but to Ralph it felt more as if he were being *carried,* the way a river carries a man in a small boat. But he couldn't see where he was going; heavy mist shrouded the banks, and now, as the current began to grow swifter, he could hear the rumble of rapids somewhere up ahead.

Still, there are shapes, Ralph. Shapes in the mist.

Yes. Not very comforting ones, either. They might be trees that only looked like clutching fingers . . . but on the other hand, they might be clutching fingers trying to look like trees. Until Ralph knew which was the case, he liked the idea of Lois being out of town just fine. He had a strong intuition – or perhaps it was only hope masquerading as intuition – that Doc #3 couldn't follow her to Ludlow, that he might not even be able to follow her across the Barrens to the east side.

You can't know any such thing, Ralph.

Maybe not, but it *felt* right, and he was still convinced that in the world of the auras, feeling and knowing were pretty nearly the same thing. One thing he *did* know was that Doc #3 hadn't cut Lois's balloon-string yet; that Ralph had seen for himself, along with the joyously healthy gray glow of her aura. Yet Ralph could not escape a growing certainty that Doc #3 – Crazy Doc – *intended* to cut it, and that, no matter how lively Rosalie had looked when she went trotting away from Strawford Park, the severing of that cord was a mortal, murderous act.

Let's say you're right, Ralph; let's say he can't get at her this afternoon if she's playing nickel-in, dime-or-out in Ludlow. What about tonight? Tomorrow? Next week? What's the solution? Does she call up her son and her bitch of a daughter-in-law, tell them she's changed her mind about Riverview Estates and wants to go there after all?

He didn't know. But he knew he needed time to think, and he also knew that constructive thinking would be hard to do until he was fairly sure that Lois was safe, at least for awhile.

'Ralph? You're getting that moogy look again.'

'That *what* look?'

'Moogy.' She tossed her hair pertly. 'That's a word I made up to describe how Mr Chasse looked when he was pretending to listen to me but was actually thinking about his coin collection. I know a moogy look when I see one, Ralph. What are you thinking about?'

'I was wondering what time you think you'll get back from your card-game.'

'That depends.'

'On what?'

'On whether or not we stop at Tubby's for chocolate frappés.' She spoke with the air of a woman revealing a secret vice.

'Suppose you come straight back.'

'Seven o'clock. Maybe seven-thirty.'

'Call me as soon as you get home. Would you do that?'

'Yes. You *want* me out of town, don't you? That's what that moogy look really means.'

'Well . . .'

'You think that nasty bald thing means to hurt me, don't you?'

'I think it's a possibility.'

'Well, he might hurt you, too!'

'Yes, but . . .'

But so far as I can tell, Lois, he's not wearing any of my *fashion accessories.*

'But *what*?'

'I'm going to be okay until you get back, that's all.' He remembered her deprecating remark about modern men hugging each other and bawling and tried for a masterful frown. 'Go play cards and leave this business to me, at least for the time being. That's an order.'

Carolyn would have either laughed or gotten angry at such comic-opera macho posturing. Lois, who belonged to an entirely different school of feminine thought, only nodded and looked grateful to have the decision taken out of her hands. 'All right.' She tilted his chin down so she could look directly into his eyes. 'Do you know what you're doing, Ralph?'

'Nope. Not yet, anyway.'

'All right. Just as long as you admit it.' She placed a hand on his forearm and a soft, open-mouthed kiss on the corner of his mouth. Ralph felt an entirely welcome prickle of heat in his groin. 'I'll go to Ludlow and win five dollars playing poker with those silly women who are always trying to fill their inside straights. Tonight we'll talk about what to do next. Okay?'

'Yes.'

Her small smile – a thing more in the eyes than of the mouth

– suggested that they might do a little more than just talk, if Ralph was bold . . . and at that moment he felt quite bold, indeed. Not even Mr Chasse's stern gaze from his place atop the TV affected that feeling very much.

Chapter Fourteen

1

It was quarter to four by the time Ralph crossed the street and walked the short distance back up the hill to his own building. Weariness was stealing over him again; he felt as if he had been up for roughly three centuries. Yet at the same time he felt better than he had since Carolyn had died. More together. More *himself.*

Or is that maybe just what you want to believe? That a person can't feel this miserable without some sort of positive payback? It's a lovely idea, Ralph, but not very realistic.

All right, he thought, *so maybe I'm a little confused right now.*

Indeed he was. Also frightened, exhilarated, disoriented, and a touch horny. Yet one clear idea came through this mix of emotions, one thing he needed to do before he did anything else: he had to make up with Bill. If that meant apologizing, he could do that. Maybe an apology was even in order. Bill, after all, hadn't come to *him,* saying, 'Gee, old buddy, you look terrible, tell me all about it.' No, *he* had gone to *Bill.* He had done so with misgivings, true, but that didn't change the fact, and—

Ah, Ralph, jeez, what am I going to do with you? It was Carolyn's amused voice, speaking to him as clearly as it had during the weeks following her death, when he'd handled the worst of his grief by discussing everything with her inside his head . . . and sometimes aloud, if he happened to be alone in the apartment. *Bill was the one who blew his top, sweetie, not you. I see you're just as determined to be hard on yourself now as you were when I was alive. I guess some things never change.*

Ralph smiled a little. Yeah, okay, maybe some things never

did change, and maybe the argument *had* been more Bill's fault than his. The question was whether or not he wanted to cut himself off from Bill's companionship over a stupid quarrel and a lot of stiff-necked horseshit about who had been right and who had been wrong. Ralph didn't think he did, and if that meant making an apology Bill didn't really deserve, what was so awful about that? So far as he knew, there were no bones in the three little syllables that made up *I'm sorry*.

The Carolyn inside his head responded to this idea with wordless incredulity.

Never mind, he told her as he started up the walk. *I'm doing this for me, not for him. Or for you, as far as that goes.*

He was amazed and amused to discover how guilty that last thought made him feel – almost as if he had committed an act of sacrilege. But that didn't make the thought any less true.

He was feeling around in his pocket for his latchkey when he saw a note thumbtacked to the door. Ralph felt for his glasses, but he had left them upstairs on the kitchen table. He leaned back, squinting to read Bill's scrawling hand:

Dear Ralph/Lois/Faye/Whoever,
 I expect to be spending most of the day at Derry Home. Bob Polhurst's niece called and told me that this time it's almost certainly the real thing; the poor man has almost finished his struggle. Room 313 in Derry Home ICU is about the last place on earth I want to be on a beautiful day in October, but I guess I'd better see this through to the end.
 Ralph, I'm sorry I gave you such a hard time this morning. You came to me for help and I damned near clawed your face off instead. All I can say by way of apology is that this thing with Bob has completely wrecked my nerves. Okay? I think I owe you a dinner . . . if you still want to eat with the likes of me, that is.
 Faye, please please PLEASE *quit bugging me about your damned chess tournament. I promised I'd play, and I keep my promises.*
 Goodbye, cruel world,
 Bill

Ralph straightened up with a feeling of relief and gratitude. If only everything else that had been happening to him lately could straighten itself out as easily as this part had done!

He went upstairs, shook the teakettle, and was filling it at the sink when the telephone rang. It was John Leydecker. 'Boy,

I'm glad I finally got hold of you,' he said. 'I was getting a little worried, old buddy.'

'Why?' Ralph asked. 'What's wrong?'

'Maybe nothing, maybe something. Charlie Pickering made bail after all.'

'You told me that wouldn't happen.'

'I was wrong, okay?' Leydecker said, clearly irritated. 'It wasn't the only thing I was wrong about, either. I told you the judge'd probably set bail in the forty-thousand-dollar range, but I didn't know Pickering was going to draw Judge Steadman, who has been known to say that he doesn't even *believe* in insanity. Steadman set bail at eighty grand. Pickering's court-appointed bellowed like a calf in the moonlight, but it didn't make any difference.'

Ralph looked down and saw he was still holding the teakettle in one hand. He put it on the table. 'And he *still* made bail?'

'Yep. Remember me telling you that Ed would throw him away like a paring knife with a broken blade?'

'Yes.'

'Well, score it as another strikeout for John Leydecker. Ed marched into the bailiff's office at eleven o'clock this morning with a briefcase full of money.'

'Eight thousand dollars?' Ralph asked.

'I said briefcase, not envelope,' Leydecker replied. 'Not eight but eighty. They're still buzzing down at the courthouse. Hell, they'll be buzzing about it even after the Christmas tinsel comes down.'

Ralph tried to imagine Ed Deepneau in one of his baggy old sweaters and a pair of worn corduroys – Ed's mad-scientist outfits, Carolyn had called them – pulling banded stacks of twenties and fifties out of his briefcase and couldn't do it. 'I thought you said ten per cent was enough to get out.'

'It is, if you can also escrow something – a house or a piece of property, for instance – that stacks up somewhere near the total bail amount. Apparently Ed couldn't do that, but he *did* have a little rainy-day cash under the mattress. Either that or he gave the tooth-fairy one hell of a blowjob.'

Ralph found himself remembering the letter he had gotten from Helen about a week after she had left the hospital and moved out to High Ridge. She had mentioned a check she'd gotten from Ed – seven hundred and fifty dollars. *It seems to indicate he understands his responsibilities,* she had written. Ralph wondered if Helen would still feel that way if she knew that Ed had walked into the Derry County Courthouse with enough money to send his daughter sailing through the first fifteen years of her life . . . and pledged it to free a crazy guy who liked to play with knives and Molotov cocktails.

'Where in God's name *did* he get it?' he asked Leydecker.

'Don't know.'

'And he isn't required to say?'

'Nope. It's a free country. I understand he said something about cashing in some stocks.'

Ralph thought back to the old days – the good old days before Carolyn had gotten sick and died and Ed had just gotten sick. Thought back to meals the four of them had had together once every two weeks or so, take-out pizza at the Deepneaus' or maybe Carol's chicken pot-pie in the Robertses' kitchen, and remembered Ed saying on one occasion that he was going to treat them all to prime rib at the Red Lion in Bangor when his stock accounts matured. *That's right,* Helen had replied, smiling at Ed fondly. She had been pregnant then, just beginning to show, and looking all of fourteen with her hair pulled back in a ponytail and wearing a checkered smock that was still yards too big for her. *Which do you think will mature first, Edward? The two thousand shares of United Toejam or the six thousand of Amalgamated Sourballs?* And he had growled at her, a growl that had made them all laugh because Ed Deepneau didn't have a mean bone in his body, anyone who had known him more than two weeks knew that Ed wouldn't hurt a fly. Except Helen might have known a little different – even back then Helen had almost surely known a little different, fond look or no fond look.

'Ralph?' Leydecker asked. 'Are you still there?'

'Ed didn't have any stocks,' Ralph said. 'He was a research chemist, for Christ's sake, and his father was foreman in a bottling plant in some crazy place like Plaster Rock, Pennsylvania. No dough there.'

'Well, he got it somewhere, and I'd be lying if I said I liked it.'

'From the other Friends of Life, do you think?'

'No, I don't. First, we're not talking rich folks here – most of the people who belong to The Friends are blue-collar types, working-class heroes. They give what they can, but this much? No. They could have gotten together enough property deeds among them to spring Pickering, I suppose, but they didn't. Most of them wouldn't, even if Ed had asked. Ed's all but *persona non grata* with them now, and I imagine they wish they'd never heard of Charlie Pickering. Dan Dalton's taken back the leadership of The Friends of Life, and to most of them, that's a big relief. Ed and Charlie and two other people – a man named Frank Felton and a woman named Sandra McKay – seem to be operating very much on their own hook now. Felton I don't know anything about and there's no jacket on him, but the McKay woman has toured some of the same fine institutions as Charlie. She's unmissable, too – pasty complexion, lots of acne, glasses so thick they make her eyes look like poached eggs, goes about three hundred pounds.'

'You joking?'

'No. She favors stretch pants from Kmart and can usually be observed travelling in the company of assorted Ding-Dongs, Funny Bones, and Hostess Twinkies. She often wears a big sweatshirt with the words BABY FACTORY on the front. Claims to have given birth to fifteen children. She's never actually had any, and probably can't.'

'Why are you telling me all this?'

'Because I want you to watch out for these people,' Leydecker said. He spoke patiently, as if to a child. 'They may be dangerous. Charlie is for sure, that you know without me telling you, and Charlie is out. Where Ed got the money to spring him is secondary – he got it, that's what matters. I wouldn't be a bit surprised if he came after you again. Him, or Ed, or the others.'

'What about Helen and Natalie?'

'They're with their friends – friends who are very hip to the dangers posed by screwloose hubbies. I filled Mike Hanlon in, and he'll also keep an eye on her. The library is being watched very closely by our men. We don't think Helen's in any real danger at the present time – she's still staying at High Ridge – but we're doing what we can.'

'Thank you, John. I appreciate that, and I appreciate the call.'

'I appreciate that you appreciate it, but I'm not quite done yet. You need to remember who Ed called and threatened, my friend – not Helen but *you*. She doesn't seem to be much of a concern to him anymore, but you linger on his mind, Ralph. I asked Chief Johnson if I could assign a man – Chris Nell would be my pick – to keep an eye on you, at least until after WomanCare's Rent-A-Bitch has come and gone. I was turned down. Too much going on this week, he said . . . but the *way* I was turned down suggests to me that if *you* asked, you'd get someone to watch your back. So what do you say?'

Police protection, Ralph thought. *That's what they call it on the TV cop shows and that's what he's talking about – police protection.*

He tried to consider the idea, but too many other things got in the way; they danced in his head like weird sugarplums. Hats, docs, smocks, spray-cans. Not to mention knives, scalpels, and a pair of scissors glimpsed in the dusty lenses of his old binoculars. *Each thing I do I rush through so I can do something else,* Ralph thought, and on the heels of that: *It's a long walk back to Eden, sweetheart, so don't sweat the small stuff.*

'No,' he said.

'What?'

Ralph closed his eyes and saw himself picking up this same phone and calling to cancel his appointment with the pin-sticker man. This was the same thing all over again, wasn't it? Yes. He could get police protection from the Pickerings and the McKays and the Feltons, but that wasn't the way this was supposed to go. He knew that, felt it in every beat of his heart and pulse of his blood.

'You heard me,' he said. 'I don't want police protection.'

'For God's sake, *why?*'

'I can take care of myself,' Ralph said, and grimaced a little at the pompous absurdity of this sentiment, which he had heard expressed in John Wayne Westerns without number.

'Ralph, I hate to be the one to break the news to you, but you're old. You got lucky on Sunday. You might not get lucky again.'

I didn't just get lucky, Ralph thought. *I've got friends in high places. Or maybe I should say entities in high places.*

'I'll be okay,' he said.

Leydecker sighed. 'If you change your mind, will you call me?'

'Yes.'

'And if you see either Pickering or a large lady with thick glasses and stringy blonde hair hanging around—'

'I'll call you.'

'Ralph, please think this over. Just a guy parked down the street is all I'm talking about.'

'Done-bun-can't-be-undone,' Ralph said.

'Huh?'

'I said I appreciate it, but no. I'll be talking to you.'

Ralph gently replaced the telephone in its cradle. Probably John was right, he thought, probably he was crazy, yet he had never felt so completely sane in his life.

'Tired,' he told his sunny, empty kitchen, 'but sane.' He paused, then added: 'Also halfway to being in love, maybe.'

That made him grin, and he was still grinning when he finally put the kettle on to heat.

2

He was on his second cup of tea when he remembered what Bill had said in his note about owing him a meal. He decided on the spur of the moment to ask Bill to meet him at Day Break, Sun Down for a little supper. They could start over.

I think we have to start over, he thought, *because that little psycho has got his hat, and I'm pretty sure that means he's in trouble.*

Well, no time like the present. He picked up the phone and dialed a number he had no trouble remembering: 941–5000. The number of Derry Home Hospital.

3

The hospital receptionist connected him with Room 313. The clearly tired woman who answered the phone was Denise Polhurst, the dying man's niece. Bill wasn't there, she told him. Four other teachers from what she termed 'Unc's glory days' had shown up around one, and Bill had proposed lunch. Ralph even knew how his downstairs tenant would have put it: better belated than never. It was one of his favorites. When Ralph asked her if she expected him back soon, Denise Polhurst said she did.

'He's been so faithful. I don't know what I would have done without him, Mr Robbins.'

'Roberts,' he said. 'Bill made Mr Polhurst sound like a wonderful man.'

'Yes, they all feel that way. But of course the bills won't be coming to his *fan club,* will they?'

'No,' Ralph said uncomfortably. 'I suppose not. Bill's note said your uncle is very low.'

'Yes. The doctor says he probably won't last the day, let alone the night, but I've heard *that* song before. God forgive me, but sometimes it's like Uncle Bob's one of those ads from Publishers Clearing House – always promising, never delivering. I suppose that sounds awful, but I'm too tired to care. They turned off the life-support stuff this morning – I couldn't have taken the responsibility all by myself, but I called Bill and he said it was what Unc would have wanted. "It's time for Bob to explore the next world," he said. "He's mapped this one to a nicety." Isn't that poetic, Mr Robbins?'

'Yes. It's *Roberts,* Ms Polhurst. Will you tell Bill that Ralph Roberts called and would like him to call ba—'

'So we turned it off and I was all prepared – nerved up, I guess you'd say – and then he didn't die. I can't understand it. He's ready, *I'm* ready, his life's work is done . . . so why won't he die?'

'I don't know.'

'Death is very stupid,' she said, speaking in the nagging and unlovely voice which only the very tired and the deeply heartsick seem to employ. 'An obstetrician this slow in cutting a baby's umbilical cord would be fired for malpractice.'

Ralph's mind had a tendency to drift these days, but this time it snapped back in a hurry. 'What did you say?'

'Beg your pardon?' She sounded startled, as if her own mind had been drifting.

'You said something about cutting the cord.'

'I didn't *mean* anything,' she said. That nagging tone had grown stronger . . . except it wasn't nagging, Ralph realized; it was whining, and it was frightened. Something was wrong here. His heartbeat suddenly speeded up. 'I didn't mean any-thing at *all*,' she insisted, and suddenly the phone Ralph was holding turned a deep and sinister shade of blue in his hand.

She's been thinking about killing him, and not just idly, either – she's been thinking about putting a pillow over his face and smothering him with it. It wouldn't take long, *she thinks.* A mercy, *she thinks.* Over at last, *she thinks.*

Ralph pulled the phone away from his ear. Blue light, cold as a February sky, rose in pencil-thin rays from the holes in the earpiece.

Murder is blue, Ralph thought, holding the phone at arm's length and staring with wide-eyed unbelief as the blue rays began to bend and drip toward the floor. He could hear, very faintly, the quacking, anxious voice of Denise Polhurst. *It*

*wasn't anything I ever wanted to know, but I guess I know it
anyway: murder is blue.*

He brought the handset toward his mouth again, cocking
it to keep the top half, with its freight of icicle aura, away
from him. He was afraid that if that end of the handset got
too close to his ear, it might deafen him with her cold and
furious desperation.

'Tell Bill that Ralph called,' he said. '*Roberts, not Robbins.*'
He hung up without waiting for a reply. The blue rays shattered
away from the phone's earpiece and tumbled toward the floor.
Ralph was again reminded of icicles; this time of how they fell in
a neat row when you ran your gloved hand along the underside
of an eave after a warm winter day. They disappeared before
they hit the linoleum. He glanced around. Nothing in the room
glowed, shimmered, or vibrated. The auras were gone again.
He began to let out a sigh of relief and then, from outside on
Harris Avenue, a car backfired.

In the empty second-floor apartment, Ralph Roberts screamed.

4

He didn't want any more tea, but he was still thirsty. He found
half a Diet Pepsi – flat but wet – in the back of the fridge, poured
it into a plastic cup with a faded Red Apple logo on it, and took
it outside. He could no longer stand to be in the apartment,
which seemed to smell of unhappy wakefulness. Especially not
after what had happened with the phone.

The day had become even more beautiful, if that was
possible; a strong, mild wind had developed, rolling bands of
light and shadow across the west side of Derry and combing the
leaves from the trees. These the wind sent hurrying along the
sidewalks in rattling dervishes of orange and yellow and red.

Ralph turned left not because he had any conscious desire to
revisit the picnic area up by the airport but only because he
wanted the wind at his back. Nevertheless, he found himself
entering the little clearing again some ten minutes later. This
time it was empty, and he wasn't surprised. There was no edge
in the wind that had sprung up, nothing to make old men and
women scurry indoors, but it was hard work keeping cards on
the table or chess-pieces on the board when the puckish wind
kept trying to snatch them away. As Ralph approached the

small trestle table where Faye Chapin usually held court, he was not exactly surprised to see a note held down by a rock, and he had a good idea what the subject would be even before he put down his plastic Red Apple cup and picked it up.

Two walks; two sightings of the bald doc with the scalpel; two old people suffering insomnia and seeing brightly colored visions; two notes. It's like Noah leading the animals onto the ark, not one by one but in pairs . . . and is another hard rain going to fall? Well, what do you think, old man?

He didn't know what he thought . . . but Bill's note had been a kind of obituary-in-progress, and he had absolutely no doubt that Faye's was the same thing. That sense of being carried forward, effortlessly and without hesitation, was simply too strong to doubt; it was like awakening on some alien stage to find oneself speaking lines (or stumbling through them, anyway) in a drama for which one could not remember having rehearsed, or seeing a coherent shape in what had up until then looked like complete nonsense, or discovering . . .

Discovering what?

'Another secret city, that's what,' he murmured. 'The Derry of Auras.' Then he bent over Faye's note and read it while the wind played prankishly with his thinning hair.

5

Those of you who want to pay your final respects to Jimmy Vandermeer are advised to do so by tomorrow at the very latest. Father Coughlin came by this noon and told me the poor old guy is sinking fast. He CAN have visitors, tho. He is in Derry Home ICU, Room 315.

Faye

PS Remember that time is short.

Ralph read the note twice, put it back on the table with the rock on top to weight it down for the next Old Crock to happen along, then simply stood there with his hands in his pockets and his head down, gazing out at Runway 3 from beneath the bushy tangle of his brows. A crisp leaf, orange as one of the Halloween pumpkins which would soon decorate the street, came flipping down from the deep blue sky and landed in his sparse hair. Ralph brushed it away absently and thought of two hospital rooms on Home's ICU floor, two rooms side by side. Bob Polhurst in one, Jimmy V in the other. And the next room up the hall? That one was 317, the room in which his wife had died.

'This is not a coincidence,' he said softly.

But what was it? Shapes in the mist? A secret city? Evocative phrases, both of them, but they answered no questions.

Ralph sat on top of the picnic table next to the one upon which Faye had left his note, took off his shoes, and crossed his legs. The wind gusted, ruffling his hair. He sat there amid the falling leaves with his head slightly bent and his brow furrowed in thought. He looked like a Winslow Homer version of Buddha as he meditated with his hands cupping his kneecaps, carefully reviewing his impressions of Doc #1 and Doc #2 . . . and then contrasting these impressions with those he'd gotten of Doc #3.

First impression: all three docs had reminded him of the aliens in tabloids like *Inside View,* and pictures which were always labelled 'artist's conceptions'. Ralph knew that these bald-headed, dark-eyed images of mysterious visitors from space went back a good many years; people had been reporting contacts with short baldies – the so-called little doctors – for a long time, maybe for as long as people had been reporting UFOs. He was quite sure that he had read at least one such account way back in the sixties.

'Okay, so say there are quite a few of these fellows around,' Ralph told a sparrow which had just lit on the picnic area's litter barrel. 'Not just three docs but three hundred. Or three thousand. Lois and I aren't the only ones who've seen them. And . . .'

And didn't most of the people who gave accounts of such meetings also mention sharp objects?

Yes, but not scissors or scalpels – at least Ralph didn't think so. Most of the people who claimed to have been abducted by the little bald doctors talked about probes, didn't they?

The sparrow flew off. Ralph didn't notice. He was thinking about the little bald docs who had visited May Locher on the night of her death. What else did he know of them? What else had he seen? They had been dressed in white smocks, like the ones worn by TV-show doctors in the fifties and sixties, like the ones pharmacists still wore. Only *their* smocks, unlike the one worn by Doc #3, had been clean. #3 had been toting a rusty scalpel; if there had been any rust on the scissors Doc #1 had been holding in his right hand, Ralph hadn't noticed it. Not even after he'd trained the binoculars on them.

Something else – probably not important, but at least you noticed it. Scissors-Toting Doc was right-handed, at least judging from the way he held his weapon. Scalpel-Wielding Doc is a southpaw.

No, probably not important, but something about it – another of those shapes in the mist, this a small one – tugged at him just the same. Something about the dichotomy of left and right.

'Go to the left and you'll be right,' Ralph muttered, repeating the punchline of some joke he no longer even remembered. 'Go to the right and you'll be left.'

Never mind. What else did he know about the docs?

Well, they had been surrounded by auras, of course – rather lovely greenish-gold ones – and they had left those

(*white-man tracks*)

Arthur Murray dance-diagrams behind them. And although their features had struck him as perfectly anonymous, their auras had conveyed feelings of power . . . and sobriety . . . and . . .

'And *dignity,* goddammit,' Ralph said. The wind gusted again and more leaves blew down from the trees. Some fifty yards from the picnic area, not far from the old train tracks, a twisted, half-uprooted tree seemed to reach in Ralph's direction, stretching branches that actually *did* look a little like clutching hands.

It suddenly occurred to Ralph that he had seen quite a lot that night for an old guy who was supposed to be living on the edge of the last age of man, the one Shakespeare (and Bill McGovern) called 'the slippered pantaloon'. And none of it – not one single thing – suggested danger or evil intent. That Ralph had *inferred* evil intent wasn't very surprising. They were physically freakish strangers; he had observed them coming out of a sick woman's house at a time of night when visitors seldom if ever called; he had seen them only minutes after waking from a nightmare of epic proportions.

Now, however, recollecting what he had seen, other things

recurred. The way they had stood on Mrs Locher's stoop, for instance, as if they had every right to be there; the sense he had gotten of two old friends indulging themselves in a bit of conversation before going on their way. Two old buddies talking it over one more time before heading home after a long night's work.

That was your impression, yes, but that doesn't mean you can trust it, Ralph.

But Ralph thought he *could* trust it. Old friends, long-time colleagues, done for the night. May Locher's had been their last stop.

All right, so Docs #1 and #2 were as different from the third one as day is from night. They were clean while he was dirty, they were invested with auras while he had none (none that Ralph had seen, at least), they carried scissors while he carried a scalpel, they seemed as sane and sober as a couple of respected village elders while #3 seemed as crazy as a shithouse rat.

One thing is perfectly clear, though, isn't it? Your playmates are supernatural beings, and other than Lois, the only person who seems to know they're there is Ed Deepneau. Want to bet on how much sleep Ed is getting just lately?

'No,' Ralph said. He raised his hands from his knees and held them in front of his eyes. They were shaking a little. Ed had mentioned bald docs, and there *were* bald docs. Was it the docs he'd been talking about when he talked about Centurions? Ralph didn't know. He almost hoped so, because that word – Centurions – had begun to call up a much more terrible image in his mind each time it occurred to him: the Ringwraiths from Tolkien's fantasy trilogy. Hooded figures astride skeletal, red-eyed horses, bearing down on a small party of cowering hobbits outside the Prancing Pony Tavern in Bree.

Thinking of hobbits made him think of Lois, and the trembling in his hands grew worse.

Carolyn: *It's a long walk back to Eden, sweetheart, so don't sweat the small stuff.*

Lois: *In my family, dying at eighty is dying young.*

Joe Wyzer: *The medical examiner usually ends up writing suicide on the cause-of-death line rather than insomnia.*

Bill: *His specialty was the Civil War, and now he doesn't even know what a civil war is, let alone who won ours.*

Denise Polhurst: *Death is very stupid. An obstetrician this slow in cutting a baby's umbilical cord—*

It was as if someone had suddenly clicked on a bright

searchlight inside his head, and Ralph cried out into the sunny autumn afternoon. Not even the Delta 727 settling in for a landing on Runway 3 could entirely drown that cry.

6

He spent the rest of the afternoon sitting on the porch of the house he shared with McGovern, waiting impatiently for Lois to come back from her card-game. He could have tried McGovern again at the hospital, but didn't. The need to speak to McGovern had passed. Ralph didn't understand everything yet, but he thought he understood a great deal more than he had, and if his sudden flash of insight at the picnic area had any validity at all, telling McGovern what had happened to his Panama would serve absolutely no purpose even if Bill believed him.

I have to get the hat back, Ralph thought. *And I have to get Lois's earrings back, too.*

It was an amazing late afternoon and early evening. On the one hand, nothing happened. On the other hand, *everything* happened. The world of auras came and went around him like the stately progression of cloud-shadows across the west side. Ralph sat and watched, rapt, breaking off only to eat a little and make a trip to the bathroom. He saw old Mrs Bennigan standing on her front porch in her bright red coat, clutching her walker and taking inventory of her fall flowers. He saw the aura surrounding her – the scrubbed and healthy pink of a freshly bathed infant – and hoped Mrs B didn't have a lot of relatives waiting around for her to die. He saw a young man of no more than twenty bopping along the other side of the street toward the Red Apple. He was the picture of health in his faded jeans and sleeveless Celtics jersey, but Ralph could see a deathbag clinging to him like an oilslick, and a balloon-string rising from the crown of his head that looked like a decaying drape-pull in a haunted house.

He saw no little bald doctors, but shortly after five-thirty he observed a startling shaft of purple light erupt from a manhole cover in the middle of Harris Avenue; it rose into the sky like a special effect in a Cecil B. DeMille Bible epic for perhaps three minutes, then simply winked out. He also saw a huge bird that looked like a prehistoric hawk go floating between the chimneys of the old dairy building around the corner on Howard Street, and alternating red and blue thermals twisting over Strawford Park in long, lazy ribbons.

When soccer practice at Fairmount Grammar let out at quarter to six, a dozen or so kids came swarming into the parking lot of the Red Apple, where they would buy tons of pre-supper candy and bales of trading cards – football cards by this time of year, Ralph supposed. Two of them stopped to argue about something, and their auras, one green and the other a vibrant shade of burnt orange, intensified, drew in, and began to gleam with rising spirals of scarlet thread.

Look out! Ralph shouted mentally at the boy within the orange envelope of light, just a moment before Green Boy dropped his schoolbooks and socked the other in the mouth. The two of them grappled, spun around in a clumsy, aggressive dance, then tumbled to the sidewalk. A little circle of yelling, cheering kids formed around them. A purplish-red dome like a thunderhead began to build up around and above the fight. Ralph found this shape, which was circulating in a slow counter-clockwise movement, both terrible and beautiful, and he wondered what the aura above a full-scale military battle would look like. He decided that was a question to which he didn't really want an answer. Just as Orange Boy climbed on top of Green Boy and began to pummel him in earnest, Sue came out of the store and hollered at them to quit fighting in the damned parking lot.

Orange Boy dismounted reluctantly. The combatants rose to their feet, looking at each other warily. Then Green Boy, trying to appear nonchalant, turned and went into the store. Only his quick glance back over his shoulder to make sure his opponent was not pursuing, spoiled the effect.

The spectators were either following Green Boy into the store for their post-practice supplies or clustered around Orange Boy, congratulating him. Above them, unseen, that virulent red-purple toadstool was breaking up like a cloudbank before a strong wind. Pieces of it tattered, unravelled, and disappeared.

The street is a carnival of energy, Ralph thought. *The juice thrown off by those two boys during the ninety seconds they were mixing it up looked like enough to light Derry for a week, and if a person could tap the energy the* watchers *generated – the energy inside that mushroom cloud – you could probably light the whole state of Maine for a month. Can you imagine what it would be like to enter*

*the world of auras in Times Square at two minutes to midnight on
New Year's Eve?*

He couldn't and didn't want to. He suspected he had
glimpsed the leading edge of a force so huge and so vital
that it made all the nuclear weapons created since 1945 seem
about as powerful as a child's cap-pistol fired into an empty
peach can. Enough force to destroy the universe, perhaps . . .
or to create a new one.

7

Ralph went upstairs, dumped a can of beans into one pot and
a couple of hotdogs into another, and walked impatiently
back and forth through the flat, snapping his fingers and
occasionally running his fingers through his hair, as he waited
for this impromptu bachelor's supper to cook. The bone-deep
weariness which had hung on him like invisible weights ever
since midsummer was, for the time being, at least, entirely
gone; he felt filled with manic, antic energy, absolutely *stuffed*
with it. He supposed this was why people liked Benzedrine and
cocaine, only he had an idea that this was a much better high,
that when it departed it would not leave him feeling plundered
and mistreated, more used than user.

Ralph Roberts, unaware that the hair his fingers were
combing through had grown thicker, and that threads of black
were visible in it for the first time in five years, jive-toured his
apartment, walking on the balls of his feet, first humming and
then singing an old rock-and-roll tune from the early sixties:
'Hey, pretty bay-bee, you can't sit down . . . you gotta slop,
bop, slip, slop, flip top *alll* about . . .'

The beans were bubbling in their pot, the hotdogs boiling
in theirs – only it looked to Ralph almost as if they were
dancing in there, doing the Bristol Stomp to the old Dovells
tune. Still singing at the top of his lungs ('When you hear the
hippie with the backbeat, you can't sit down'), Ralph cut the
hotdogs into the beans, dumped in half a pint of ketchup, added
some chili sauce, then stirred everything vigorously together
and headed for the door. He carried his supper, still in the
pot, in one hand. He ran down the stairs as nimbly as a kid
who's running late on the first day of school. He hooked
a baggy old cardigan sweater – McGovern's, but what the

hell – out of the front hall closet, and then went back out on the porch.

The auras were gone, but Ralph wasn't dismayed; for the time being he was more interested in the smell of food. He couldn't remember the last time he'd felt as flat-out hungry as he did at that moment. He sat on the top step with his long thighs and bony knees sticking out on either side of him, looking decidedly Ichabod Crane-ish, and began to eat. The first few bites burned his lips and tongue, but instead of being deterred, Ralph ate faster, almost gobbling.

He paused with half the pot of beans and franks consumed. The animal in his stomach hadn't gone back to sleep – not yet – but it had been pacified a bit. Ralph belched unselfconsciously and looked out at Harris Avenue with a feeling of contentment he hadn't known in years. Under the current circumstances, that feeling made no sense at all, but that didn't change it in the slightest. When was the last time he had felt this good? Maybe not since the morning he'd awakened in that barn somewhere between Derry, Maine and Poughkeepsie, New York, amazed by the conflicting rays of light – thousands of them, it had seemed – which crisscrossed the warm, sweet-smelling place where he lay.

Or maybe never.

Yes, or maybe never.

He spied Mrs Perrine coming up the street, probably returning from A Safe Place, the combination soup-kitchen and homeless shelter down by the canal. Ralph once again found himself fascinated by her strange, gliding walk, which she achieved without the aid of a cane and seemingly without any side-to-side movement of her hips. Her hair, still more black than gray, was now held – or perhaps subdued was the word – by the hairnet she wore on the serving line. Thick support hose the color of cotton candy rose from her spotless white nurse's shoes . . . not that Ralph could see much of either them or the legs they covered; this evening Mrs Perrine wore a man's wool overcoat, and the hem came almost to her ankles. She seemed to depend almost entirely on her upper legs to move her along – a sign of some chronic back problem, Ralph guessed – and this mode of locomotion, coupled with the overcoat, gave Esther Perrine a somewhat surreal aspect as she approached. She looked like the black queen on a chessboard, a piece that was either being guided by an invisible hand or moving all by itself.

As she neared the place where Ralph sat – still wearing the ripped shirt and now eating his supper directly from the pot in the bargain – the auras began to steal back into the world again. The streetlights had already come on, and now Ralph saw delicate lavender arcs hung over each. He could also see a red haze hovering above some roofs, a yellow haze above others, a pale cerise above still others. In the east, where night was now gathering itself, the horizon flocked with dim green speckles.

Closer to hand, he watched as Mrs Perrine's aura sprang to life around her – that firm gray that reminded him of a West Point cadet's uniform. A few darker spots, like phantom buttons, shimmered above her bosom (Ralph assumed there *was* a bosom hidden somewhere beneath the overcoat). He was not sure, but thought these might be signs of impending ill health.

'Good evening, Mrs Perrine,' he said politely, and watched as the words rose in front of his eyes in snowflake shapes.

She gave him a penetrating glance, flicking her eyes up and down, seeming to simultaneously sum him up and dismiss him in a single look. 'I see you're still wearing that same shirt, Roberts,' she said.

What she didn't say – but what Ralph was sure she was thinking – was *I also see you sitting there and eating beans right out of the pot, like some ragged street-person who never learned any better . . . and I have a way of remembering what I see, Roberts.*

'So I am,' Ralph said. 'I guess I forgot to change it.'

'Hmmp,' said Mrs Perrine, and now he thought it was his underwear she was considering. *When was the last time it occurred to you to change that? I shudder to think, Roberts.*

'Lovely evening, isn't it, Mrs Perrine?'

Another of those quick, birdlike glances, this time up at the sky. Then back to Ralph. 'It's going to turn cold.'

'Do you think so?'

'Oh, yes – Indian summer's over. My back isn't good for much besides weather forecasting these days, but at that it does very well.' She paused. 'I believe that's Bill McGovern's sweater.'

'I guess it is,' Ralph agreed, wondering if she would ask him next if Bill knew he had it. He wouldn't have put it past her.

Instead, she told him to button it up. 'You don't want to be a candidate for pneumonia, do you?' she asked, and the tucked set of her mouth added, *As well as for the nuthouse?*

'Absolutely not,' Ralph said. He set the pot aside, reached for the sweater buttons, then stopped. He was still wearing a quilted stove-glove on his left hand. He hadn't noticed it until now.

'It will be easier if you take that off,' Mrs Perrine said. There might have been the faintest gleam in her eyes.

'I suppose so,' Ralph said humbly. He shook off the glove and buttoned McGovern's sweater.

'My offer holds good, Roberts.'

'Beg your pardon?'

'My offer to mend your shirt. If you can bring yourself to part with it for a day or so, that is.' She paused. 'You *do* have another shirt, I assume? One you could wear while I mend the one you have on?'

'Oh, yes,' Ralph said. 'You bet. Quite a few of them.'

'Choosing among them each day must be challenging for you. There's bean juice on your chin, Roberts.' With this pronouncement, Mrs Perrine's eyes flicked forward and she began to march once more.

What Ralph did then he did with no forethought or understanding; it was as instinctive as the chopping gesture he had made earlier to scare Doc #3 away from Rosalie. He raised the hand which had been wearing the thermal glove and curled it into a tube around his mouth. Then he inhaled sharply, producing a faint, whispery whistle.

The results were amazing. A pencil of gray light poked out of Mrs Perrine's aura like the quill of a porcupine. It lengthened rapidly, angling backward as the lady herself moved forward, until it had crossed the leaf-littered lawn and darted into the tube formed by Ralph's curled fingers. He felt it enter him as he inhaled and it was like swallowing pure energy. He suddenly felt lit up, like a neon sign or the marquee of a big-city movie theater. An explosive sense of force – a feeling of *Pow!* – ran through his chest and stomach, then raced down his legs all the way to the tips of his toes. At the same time it rocketed upward into his head, threatening to blow off the top of his skull as if it were the thin concrete roof of a missile silo.

He could see rays of light, as gray as electrified fog, smoking out from between his fingers. A terrible, joyous sense of power lit up his thoughts, but only for a moment. It was followed by shame and amazed horror.

What are you doing, Ralph? Whatever that stuff is, it doesn't belong to you. Would you reach into her purse and take some of her money while she wasn't looking?

He felt his face flush. He lowered his cupped hand and shut his mouth. As his lips and teeth came together, he clearly heard – and actually *felt* – something crunch crisply inside. It was the sound you heard when you were chomping off a bite of fresh rhubarb.

Mrs Perrine stopped, and Ralph watched apprehensively as she made a half-turn and looked out at Harris Avenue. *I didn't mean to,* he thought at her. *Honest I didn't, Mrs P – I'm still learning my way around this thing.*

'Roberts?'

'Yes?'

'Did you hear something? It sounded almost like a gunshot.'

Ralph could feel his ears throbbing with hot blood as he shook his head. 'No . . . but my ears aren't what they—'

'Probably just a backfire over on Kansas Street,' she said, dismissing his weak-sister excuses out of hand. 'It made my heart miss a beat, though, I can tell you.'

She started off again in her odd, gliding, chess-queen walk, then stopped once more and looked back at him. Her aura had begun to fade out of Ralph's view, but he had no trouble seeing her eyes – they were as sharp as a kestrel's.

'You look different, Roberts,' she said. 'Younger, some-how.'

Ralph, who had expected something else (*Give me back what you stole, Roberts, and right this minute,* for instance), could only flounder. 'Do you think . . . that's very . . . I mean to say thank y—'

She flapped an impatient oh-shut-up hand at him. 'Probably the light. I advise you not to dribble on that sweater, Roberts. My impression of Mr McGovern is that he is a man who takes care of his things.'

'He should have taken better care of his hat,' Ralph said.

Those bright eyes, which had begun once more to shift away from him, shifted back. 'I beg your pardon?'

'His Panama,' Ralph said. 'He lost it somewhere.'

Mrs Perrine held this up to the light of her intellect for a moment, then cast it aside with another *Hmmp*. 'Go inside, Roberts. If you stay out here much longer, you'll catch your death of cold.' And then she slid upon her way, not visibly the worse for wear as a result of Ralph's thoughtless act of thievery.

Thievery? I'm pretty sure that's the wrong word, Ralph. What you did just now was a lot closer to—

'Vampirism,' Ralph said bleakly. He put the pot of beans aside and began to slowly rub his hands together. He felt ashamed . . . guilty . . . and all but exploding with energy.

You stole some of her life-force instead of her blood, but a vampire is a vampire, Ralph.

Yes indeed. And it suddenly occurred to Ralph that this must not have been the first time he had done such a thing.

You look different, Roberts. Younger, somehow. That was what Mrs Perrine had said tonight, but people had been making similar comments to him ever since the end of the summer, hadn't they? The main reason his friends hadn't hectored him into going to the doctor was because he didn't *look* like anything was wrong with him. He complained of insomnia, but he apparently looked like the picture of health. *I guess that honeycomb must have really turned the trick,* Johnny Leydecker had said just before the two of them had left the library on Sunday – back in the Iron Age, that felt like now. And when Ralph had asked him what he was talking about, Leydecker had said he was talking about Ralph's insomnia. *You look a gajillion times better than on the day I first met you.*

And Leydecker hadn't been the only one. Ralph had been more or less dragging himself through the days, feeling folded, spindled, and mutilated . . . but people kept telling him how *good* he looked, how *refreshed* he looked, how *young* he looked. Helen . . . McGovern . . . even Faye Chapin had said something a week or two ago, although Ralph couldn't remember exactly what—

'Sure I do,' he said in a low, dismayed voice. 'He asked me if I was using wrinkle cream. *Wrinkle* cream, for God's sake!'

Had he been stealing from the life-force of others even back then? Stealing without even knowing it?

'I must have been,' he said in that same low voice. 'Dear Jesus, I'm a vampire.'

But was that the right word? he wondered suddenly. Wasn't it at least possible that, in the world of auras, a life-stealer was called a Centurion?

Ed's pallid, frantic face rose before him like a ghost which returns to accuse its murderer, and Ralph, suddenly terrified, wrapped his arms around his knees and lowered his head to rest upon them.

Chapter Fifteen

1

At twenty minutes past seven, a perfectly maintained Lincoln Town Car of late seventies vintage drew up to the curb in front of Lois's house. Ralph – who had spent the last hour showering, shaving, and trying to get himself calmed down – stood on the porch and watched Lois get out of the back seat. Goodbyes were said and girlish, sprightly laughter drifted across to him on the breeze.

The Lincoln pulled away and Lois started up her walk. Halfway along it, she stopped and turned. For a long moment the two of them regarded each other from their opposite sides of Harris Avenue, seeing perfectly well in spite of the deepening darkness and the two hundred yards which separated them. They burned for each other in that darkness like secret torches.

Lois pointed a finger at him. It was very close to the hand gesture she'd made before shooting at Doc #3, but this didn't upset Ralph in the least.

Intent, he thought. *Everything lies in·intent. There are few mistakes in this world . . . and once you get to know your way around, maybe there are no mistakes at all.*

A narrow, gray-glistening beam of force appeared at the end of Lois's finger and began to extend itself across the deepening shadows of Harris Avenue. A passing car drove blithely through it. The car's windows flashed a momentary bright, blind gray and its headlights seemed to flicker briefly, but that was all.

Ralph raised his own finger, and a blue beam grew from it. These two narrowcasts of light met in the center of

Harris Avenue and twined together like woodbine. Higher and higher the interwoven pigtail rose, paling slightly as it went. Then Ralph curled his finger, and his half of the love-knot in the middle of Harris Avenue winked out of existence. A moment later, Lois's half also disappeared. Ralph slowly descended the porch steps and began to cross his lawn. Lois came toward him. They met in the middle of the street . . . where, in a very real sense, they had met already.

Ralph put his arms around her waist and kissed her.

2

You look different, Roberts. Younger, somehow.

Those words kept running through his head – recycling themselves like an endless tape-loop – as Ralph sat in Lois's kitchen, drinking coffee. He was unable to take his eyes off her. She looked easily ten years younger and ten pounds lighter than the Lois he'd gotten used to seeing over the last few years. Had she looked this young and pretty in the park this morning? Ralph didn't think so, but of course she had been upset this morning, upset and crying, and he supposed that made a difference.

Still . . .

Yes, still. The tiny networks of wrinkles around the corners of her mouth were gone. So were the incipient turkey-wattles beneath her neck and the sag of flesh which had begun to hang from her upper arms. She had been crying this morning and was radiantly happy tonight, but Ralph knew that couldn't account for all the changes he saw.

'I know what you're looking at,' Lois said. 'It's spooky, isn't it? I mean, it solves the question of whether or not all this has just been in our minds, but it's still spooky. We've found the Fountain of Youth. Forget Florida; it was right here in Derry, all along.'

'*We've* found it?'

For a moment she only looked surprised . . . and a little wary, as if she suspected he was teasing her, having her on. Of treating her as 'our Lois'. Then she reached across the table and squeezed his hand. 'Go in the bathroom. Take a look at yourself.'

342

'I know what I look like. Hell, I just finished shaving. Took my time over it, too.'

She nodded. 'You did a fine job, Ralph . . . but this isn't about your five o'clock shadow. Just *look* at yourself.'

'Are you serious?'

'Yes,' she said firmly. 'I am.'

He had almost gotten to the door when she said, 'You didn't just shave; you changed your shirt, too. That's good. I didn't like to say anything, but that plaid one was ripped.'

'Was it?' Ralph asked. His back was to her, so she couldn't see his smile. 'I didn't notice.'

3

He stood with his hands braced on the bathroom sink, looking into his own face, for a good two minutes. It took him that long to admit to himself that he was really seeing what he thought he was seeing. The streaks of black, lustrous as crow feathers, which had returned to his hair were amazing, and so was the disappearance of the ugly pouches beneath his eyes, but the thing he could not seem to take his eyes away from was the way the lines and deep cracks had disappeared from his lips. It was a small thing . . . but it was also an enormous thing. It was the mouth of a young man. And . . .

Abruptly, Ralph ran a finger into his mouth, along the righthand line of his lower teeth. He couldn't be entirely positive, but it seemed to him that they were longer, as if some of the wear had been rolled back.

'Holy shit,' Ralph murmured, and his mind returned to that sweltering day last summer when he had confronted Ed Deepneau on his lawn. Ed had first told him to drag up a rock and then confided in him that Derry had been invaded by sinister, baby-killing creatures. *Life-stealing* creatures. *All lines of force have begun to converge here,* Ed had told him. *I know how difficult that is to believe, but it's true.*

Ralph was finding it less difficult to believe all the time. What was getting harder to believe was the idea that Ed was mad.

'If this doesn't stop,' Lois said from the doorway, startling him, 'we're going to have to get married and leave town, Ralph. Simone and Mina could not – literally *could not* – take their eyes off me. I made a lot of glib talk about some new makeup I'd gotten out at the mall, but they didn't swallow it. A man would, but a woman knows what makeup can do. And what it can't.'

They walked back to the kitchen, and although the auras were gone again for the time being, Ralph discovered he could see one anyway: a blush rising out of the collar of Lois's white silk blouse.

'Finally I told them the only thing they *would* believe.'

'What was that?' Ralph asked.

'I said I'd met a man.' She hesitated, and then, as the rising blood reached her cheeks and stained them pink, she plunged. 'And had fallen in love with him.'

He touched her arm and turned her toward him. He looked at the small, clean crease in the bend of her elbow and thought how much he would like to touch it with his mouth. Or the tip of his tongue, perhaps. Then he raised his eyes to look at her. 'And was it true?'

She looked back with eyes that were all hope and candor. 'I *think* so,' she said in a small, clear voice, 'but everything's so strange now. All I know for sure is that I *want* it to be true. I want a friend. I've been frightened and unhappy and lonely for quite awhile now. The loneliness is the worst part of getting old, I think – not the aches and pains, not the cranky bowels or the way you lose your breath after climbing a flight of stairs you could have just about *flown* up when you were twenty – but being lonely.'

'Yes,' Ralph said. 'That *is* the worst.'

'No one talks to you anymore – oh, they talk *at* you, sometimes, but that's not the same – and mostly it's like people don't even *see* you. Have you ever felt that way?'

Ralph thought of the Derry of the Old Crocks, a city mostly ignored by the hurry-to-work, hurry-to-play world which surrounded it, and nodded.

'Ralph, would you hug me?'

'My pleasure,' he said, and pulled her gently into the circle of his arms.

4

Some time later, rumpled and dazed but happy, Ralph and Lois sat together on the living-room couch, a piece of furniture so stringently hobbit-sized it was really not much more than a love-seat. Neither of them minded. Ralph's arm was around Lois's shoulders. She had let her hair down and he twined a lock of it in his fingers, musing upon how easy it was to forget the feel of a woman's hair, so marvellously different from the feel of a man's. She had told him about her card-game and Ralph had listened closely, amazed but not, he discovered, much surprised.

There were a dozen or so of them who played every week or so at the Ludlow Grange for small stakes. It was possible to go home a five-buck loser or a ten-buck winner, but the most likely result was finishing a dollar ahead or a handful of change behind. Although there were a couple of good players and a couple of *shlumps* (Lois counted herself among the former), it was mostly just a fun way to spend an afternoon – the Lady Old Crock version of chess tournaments and marathon gin-rummy games.

'Only this afternoon I just couldn't lose. I should have come home completely broke, what with all of them asking what kind of vitamins I was taking and where I'd gotten my last facial and all the rest of it. Who can concentrate on a silly game like Deuces and Jacks, Man with the Axe, Natural Sevens Take All when you have to keep telling new lies and trying not to trip over the ones you've already told?'

'Must have been hard,' Ralph said, trying not to grin.

'It *was*. *Very* hard! But instead of losing, I just kept raking it in. And do you know why, Ralph?'

He did, but shook his head so she would tell him. He liked listening to her.

'It was their auras. I didn't always know the exact cards they were holding, but a lot of times I did. Even when I didn't, I could get a pretty clear idea of how good their hands were. The auras weren't always there, you know how they come and go, but even when they were gone I played better than I ever have in my life. During the last hour, I began to lose on purpose just so they wouldn't all *hate* me. And do you know something? Even *losing on purpose* was hard.' She looked down at her hands, which had begun to twine together nervously in her lap. 'And on the way back, I did something I'm ashamed of.'

Ralph began to glimpse her aura again, a dim gray ghost in which unformed blobs of dark blue swirled. 'Before you tell me,' he said, 'listen to this and see if it sounds familiar.'

He related how Mrs Perrine had approached while he was sitting on the porch, eating and waiting for Lois to get back. As he told her what he had done to the old lady, he dropped his eyes and felt his ears heating up again.

'Yes,' she said when he was finished. 'It's the same thing *I* did . . . but I didn't *mean* to, Ralph . . . at least, I don't *think* I meant to. I was sitting in the back seat with Mina, and she was starting to go on and on again about how *different* I looked, how *young* I looked, and I thought – I'm embarrassed to say it right out loud, but I guess I better – I thought, I'll shut you up, you snoopy, envious old thing. Because it *was* envy, Ralph. I could see it in her aura. Big, jagged spikes the exact color of a cat's eyes. No wonder they call jealousy the green-eyed monster! Anyway, I pointed out the window and said "Oooh, Mina, isn't that the *dearest* little house?" And when she turned to look, I . . . I did what you did, Ralph. Only I didn't curl up my hand. I just kind of puckered my lips . . . like this . . .' She demonstrated, looking so kissable that Ralph felt moved (almost compelled, in fact) to take advantage of the expression. '. . . and I breathed in a big cloud of her stuff.'

'What happened?' Ralph asked, fascinated and afraid.

Lois laughed ruefully. 'To me or her?'

'Both of you.'

'Mina jumped and slapped the back of her neck. "There's a bug on me!" she said. "It bit me! Get it off, Lo! Please get it off!" Of course there was no bug on her – *I* was the bug – but I brushed at her neck just the same, then opened the window and told her it was gone, it flew away. She was lucky I didn't knock her brains out instead of just brushing her neck – that's how full of pep I was. I felt like I could have opened the car door and run all the way home.'

Ralph nodded.

'It was wonderful . . . *too* wonderful. It's like the stories about drugs you see on TV, how they take you to heaven at first and then lock you in hell. What if we start doing this and can't stop?'

'Yeah,' Ralph said. 'And what if it hurts people? I keep thinking about vampires.'

'Do you know what *I* keep thinking about?' Lois's voice had dropped to a whisper. 'Those things you said Ed Deepneau talked about. Those Centurions. What if they're us, Ralph? What if they're *us*?'

He hugged her and kissed the top of her head. Hearing his worst fear coming from her mouth made it less heavy on his own heart, and that made him think of what Lois had said about loneliness being the worst part of getting old.

'I know,' he said. 'And what I did to Mrs Perrine was totally spur-of-the-moment – I don't remember thinking about it at all, just doing it. Was it that way with you?'

'Yes. Just like that.' She laid her head against his shoulder.

'We can't do it anymore,' he said. 'Because it really might be addictive. Anything that feels that good just about *has* to be addictive, don't you think? We've got to try and build up some safeguards against doing it unconsciously, too. Because I think I *have* been. That could be why—'

A scream of brakes and sliding, wailing tires cut him off. They stared at each other, wide-eyed, as outside on the street that sound went on and on, grief seeming to search for a point of impact.

There was a muffled thud from the street as the scream of the brakes and tires silenced. It was followed by a brief cry uttered by either a woman or a child, Ralph could not tell which. Someone else shouted, 'What happened?' and then, 'Oh, *cripe!*' There was a rattle of running footsteps on pavement.

'Stay on the couch,' Ralph said, and hurried to the living room window. When he ran up the shade Lois was standing right beside him, and Ralph felt a flash of approval. It was what Carolyn would have done under similar circumstances.

They looked out on a night-time world that pulsed with strange color and fabulous motion. Ralph knew it was Bill they were going to see, *knew* it – Bill hit by a car and lying dead in the street, his Panama with the crescent bitten out of the brim lying near one outstretched hand. He slipped an arm around Lois and she gripped his hand.

But it wasn't McGovern in the fan of headlights thrown by the Ford which was slued around in the middle of Harris Avenue; it was Rosalie. Her early-morning shopping expeditions were at an end. She lay on her side in a spreading pool of blood, her back bunched and twisted in several places. As the driver of the car which had struck her knelt beside the old stray, the pitiless glare of the nearest streetlamp illuminated his face. It was Joe Wyzer, the Rite Aid druggist, his orange-yellow aura now swirling with confused eddies of red and blue. He stroked the old dog's side, and each time his hand slipped into the vile black aura which clung to Rosalie, it disappeared.

Dreamy of terror washed through Ralph, dropping his temperature and shrivelling his testicles until they felt like hard little peach-pits. Suddenly it was July of 1992 again, Carolyn dying, the deathwatch ticking, and something weird had happened to Ed Deepneau. Ed had freaked out, and Ralph had found himself trying to keep Helen's normally good-natured husband from springing at the man in the West Side Gardeners cap and attempting to rip his throat out. Then – the cherry on the *Charlotte russe*, Carol would have said – Dorrance Marstellar had arrived. Old Dor. And what had he said?

I wouldn't touch him anymore . . . I can't see your hands.

I can't see your hands.

'Oh my God,' Ralph whispered.

5

He was brought back to the here and now by the feeling of Lois swaying against him, as if she were on the edge of a faint.

'Lois!' he said sharply, gripping her arm. 'Lois, are you okay?'

'I think so . . . but Ralph . . . do you see . . .'

'Yes, it's Rosalie. I guess she—'

'I don't mean *her*; I mean *him*!' She pointed to the right.

Doc #3 was leaning against the trunk of Joe Wyzer's Ford, McGovern's Panama tipped jauntily back on his bald skull. He looked toward Ralph and Lois, grinned insolently, then slowly raised his thumb to his nose and waggled his small fingers at them.

'*You bastard!*' Ralph bellowed, and slammed his fist against the wall beside the window in frustration.

Half a dozen people were running toward the scene of the accident, but there was nothing they could do; Rosalie would be dead before even the closest of them arrived at the place where she lay in the glare of the car's headlights. The black aura was solidifying, becoming something which looked almost like soot-darkened brick. It encased her like a form-fitting shroud, and Wyzer's hand disappeared up to the wrist every time it slipped through that terrible garment.

Now Doc #3 raised his hand with the forefinger sticking up and cocked his head – a teacherly pantomime so good that it almost said *Pay attention, please!* right out loud. He tiptoed forward – unnecessary, as he couldn't be seen by the people out there, but good theater – and reached toward Joe Wyzer's back pocket. He glanced around at Ralph and Lois, as if to ask them if they were still paying attention. Then he began to tiptoe forward again, reaching out with his left hand.

'Stop him, Ralph,' Lois moaned. 'Oh please stop him.'

Slowly, like a man who has been drugged, Ralph raised his hand and then chopped it down. A blue wedge of light flew from his fingertips, but it diffused as it passed through the windowglass. A pastel fog spread out a little distance from Lois's house and then disappeared. The bald doctor shook his finger in an infuriating pantomime – *Oh, you naughty boy,* it said.

Doc #3 reached out again, and plucked something from Wyzer's back pocket as he knelt in the street, mourning the dog. Ralph couldn't tell for sure what it was until the creature in the dirty smock swept McGovern's hat from his head and pretended to use it on his own nonexistent hair. He had taken a black pocket-comb, the kind you could buy in any convenience store for a buck twenty-nine. Then he leaped into the air, clicking his heels like a malignant elf.

Rosalie had raised her head at the bald doctor's approach. Now she lowered it back to the pavement and died. The aura surrounding her disappeared at once, not fading but simply winking out of existence like a soapbubble. Wyzer got to his feet, turned to a man standing on the curb, and began to tell him what had happened, gesturing with his hands to indicate how the dog had run out in front of his car. Ralph found he could actually read a string of six words as they came off Wyzer's lips: *seemed to come out of nowhere.*

And when Ralph shifted his gaze back down to the side of Wyzer's car, he saw that was the place to which the little bald doctor had returned.

Chapter Sixteen

1

Ralph was able to get his rustbucket Oldsmobile started, but it still took him twenty minutes to get them across town to Derry Home on the east side. Carolyn had understood his increasing worries about his driving and had tried to be sympathetic, but she'd had an impatient, hurry-up streak in her nature, and the years had not mellowed it much. On trips longer than half a mile or so, she was almost always unable to keep from lapsing into reproof. She would stew in silence for awhile, thinking, then begin her critique. If she was particularly exasperated with their progress – or lack of it – she might ask him if he thought an enema would help him get the lead out of his ass. She was a sweetheart, but there had always been an edge to her tongue.

Following such remarks, Ralph would always offer – and always without rancor – to pull over and let her drive. Such offers Carol had always declined. Her belief was that, on short hops, at least, it was the husband's job to drive and the wife's to offer constructive criticism.

He kept waiting for Lois to comment on either his speed or his sloppy driving habits (he didn't think he would be able to remember his blinkers with any consistency these days even if someone put a gun to his head), but she said nothing – only sat where Carolyn had sat on five thousand rides or more, holding her purse on her lap exactly as Carolyn had always held hers. Wedges of light – store neon, traffic signals, streetlights – ran like rainbows across Lois's cheeks and brows. Her dark eyes were distant and thoughtful. She had cried after Rosalie died, cried hard, and made Ralph pull down the shade again.

Ralph almost hadn't done that. His first impulse had been to bolt out into the street before Joe Wyzer could get away. To tell Joe he had to be very careful. To tell him that when he emptied his pants pockets tonight, he was going to be missing a cheap comb, no big deal, people were always losing combs, except this time it *was* a big deal, and next time it might be Rite Aid pharmacist Joe Wyzer lying at the end of the skid. *Listen to me, Joe, and listen closely. You have to be very careful, because there's all sorts of news from the Hyper-Reality Zone, and in your case all of it comes inside black borders.*

There were problems with that, however. The biggest was that Joe Wyzer, sympathetic as he had been on the day he had gotten Ralph an appointment with the acupuncturist, would think Ralph was crazy. Besides, how did one defend oneself against a creature one couldn't even see?

So he had pulled the shade . . . but before he did, he took one last hard look at the man who had told him he used to be Joe Wyze but was now older and Wyzer. The auras were still there, and he could see Wyzer's balloon-string, a bright orange-yellow, rising intact from the top of his head. So he was still all right.

For now, at least.

Ralph had led Lois into the kitchen and poured her another cup of coffee – black, with lots of sugar.

'He killed her, didn't he?' she asked as she raised the cup to her lips with both hands. 'The little beast killed her.'

'Yes. But I don't think he did it tonight. I think he really did it this morning.'

'Why? *Why?*'

'Because he could,' Ralph said grimly. 'I think that's the only reason he needs. Just because he could.'

Lois had given him a long, appraising look, and an expression of relief had slowly crept into her eyes. 'You've figured it out, haven't you? I should have known it the minute I saw you this evening. I *would* have known, if I hadn't had so many other things rolling around in what passes for my mind.'

'Figured it out? I'm miles from that, but I have had some ideas. Lois, do you feel up to a trip to Derry Home with me?'

'I suppose so. Do you want to see Bill?'

'I'm not sure exactly *who* I want to see. It *might* be Bill, but it might be Bill's friend, Bob Polhurst. Maybe even Jimmy Vandermeer – do you know him?'

'Jimmy V? Of *course* I know him! I knew his wife even better. In fact, she used to play poker with us until she died. It was a heart attack, and so sudden –' She broke off suddenly, looking at Ralph with her dark Spanish eyes. 'Jimmy's in the hospital? Oh God, it's the cancer, isn't it? The cancer came back.'

'Yes. He's in the room right next to Bill's friend.' Ralph told her about the conversation he'd had with Faye that morning and the note he'd found on the picnic table that afternoon. He pointed out the odd conjunction of rooms and residents – Polhurst, Jimmy V, Carolyn – and asked Lois if she thought it was just a coincidence.

'No. I'm sure it isn't.' She had glanced at the clock. 'Come on – regular visiting hours over there finish at nine-thirty, I think. If we're going to get there before then, we'd better wiggle.'

2

Now, as he turned onto Hospital Drive (*Forgot your damned turnblinker again, sweetheart,* Carolyn commented), he glanced at Lois – Lois sitting there with her hands clasped on her purse and her aura invisible for the time being – and asked if she was all right.

She nodded. 'Yes. Not great, but okay. Don't worry about me.'

But I do worry, Lois, Ralph thought. *A lot. And by the way, did you see Doc #3 take the comb out of Joe Wyzer's pocket?*

That was a stupid question. Of course she'd seen. The bald midget had *wanted* her to see. Had wanted *both* of them to see. The real question was how much significance she had attached to it.

How much do you really know, Lois? How many connections have you made? I have to wonder, because they're not really that hard to see. I wonder . . . but I'm afraid to ask.

There was a low brick building about a quarter of a mile farther down the feeder road – WomanCare. A number of spotlights (new additions, he was quite sure) threw fans of illumination across its lawn, and Ralph could see two men walking back and forth at the end of grotesquely elongated shadows . . . rent-a-cops, he supposed. Another new wrinkle; another straw flying in an evil wind.

He turned left (this time remembering the blinker, at least) and eased the Olds carefully up the chute which led into the multilevel hospital parking garage. At the top, an orange barrier-arm blocked the way. PLEASE STOP & TAKE TICKET, read the sign next to it. Ralph could recall a time when there used to be actual people in places like this, rendering them a little less eerie. *Those were the days, my friend, we thought they'd never end,* he thought as he unrolled his window and took a ticket from the automated dispenser.

'Ralph?'

'Hmmm?' He was concentrating on avoiding the back bumpers of the cars slant-parked on both sides of the ascending aisles. He knew that the aisles were much too wide for the bumpers of those other cars to be an actual impediment to his progress – *intellectually* he knew it – but what his guts knew was something else. *How Carolyn would bitch and moan about the way I'm driving,* he thought with a certain distracted fondness.

'*Do* you know what we're doing here, or are we just winging it?'

'Just another minute – let me get this damned thing parked.'

He passed several slots big enough for the Olds on the first level, but none with enough buffer-zone to make him feel comfortable. On the third level he found three spaces side by side (together they were big enough to hold a Sherman tank comfortably) and babied the Olds into the one in the middle. He killed the motor and turned to face Lois. Other engines idled above and below them, their locations impossible to pinpoint because of the echo. Orange light – that persistent, penetrating tone-glow now common to all such facilities as this, it seemed – lay upon their skins like thin toxic paint. Lois looked back at him steadily. He could see traces of the tears she had cried for Rosalie in her puffy, swollen lids, but the eyes themselves were calm and sure. He was struck by how much she had changed just since that morning, when he had found her sitting slump-shouldered on a park bench and weeping. *Lois,* he thought, *if your son and daughter-in-law could see you tonight, I think they might run away screaming at the top of their lungs. Not because you look scary, but because the woman they came to bulldoze into moving to Riverview Estates is gone.*

'Well?' she asked with just a hint of a smile. 'Are you going to talk to me or just look at me?'

Ralph, ordinarily a cautious sort of man, recklessly said the first thing to come into his head. 'What I'd *like* to do, I think, is eat you like ice-cream.'

Her smile deepened enough to make dimples at the corners of her mouth. 'Maybe later we'll see how much of an appetite for ice-cream you really have, Ralph. For now, just tell me why you brought me here. And don't tell me you don't know, because I think you do.'

Ralph closed his eyes, drew in a deep breath, and opened them again. 'I guess we're here to find the other two bald guys. The ones I saw coming out of May Locher's. If anyone can explain what's going on, it'll be them.'

'What makes you think you'll find them here?'

'I think they've got work to do . . . two men, Jimmy V and Bill's friend, dying side by side. I should have known what the bald doctors are – what they *do* – from the minute I saw the ambulance guys bring Mrs Locher out strapped to a stretcher and with a sheet over her face. I *would* have known, if I hadn't been so damned tired. The scissors should have been enough. Instead, it took me until this afternoon, and I only got it then because of something Mr Polhurst's niece said.'

'What was it?'

'That death was stupid. That if an obstetrician took as much time cutting the umbilical cord, he'd be sued for malpractice. It made me think of a myth I read when I was in grade-school and couldn't get enough of gods and goddesses and Trojan horses. The story was about three sisters – the Greek Sisters, maybe, or maybe it was the Weird Sisters. Shit, don't ask me; I can't even remember to use my damned turnblinkers half the time. Anyway, these sisters were responsible for the course of all human life. One of them spun the thread, one of them decided how long it would be . . . is any of this ringing a bell, Lois?'

'Of course it is!' she nearly shouted. 'The balloon-strings!'

Ralph nodded. 'Yes. The balloon-strings. I don't remember the names of the first two sisters, but I never forgot the name of the last one – Atropos. And according to the story, her job is to cut the thread the first one spins and the second one measures. You could argue with her, you could beg, but it never made any difference. When she decided it was time to cut, she cut.'

Lois was nodding. 'Yes, I remember that story. I don't know if I read it or someone told it to me when I was a kid. You believe it's actually true, Ralph, don't you? Only it turns out to be the Bald Brothers instead of the Weird Sisters.'

'Yes and no. As I remember the story, the sisters were all on the same side – a team. And that's the feeling I got about the two men who came out of Mrs Locher's house, that they were long-time partners with *immense* respect for each other. But the other guy, the one we saw again tonight, isn't like them. I think Doc #3's a rogue.'

Lois shivered, a theatrical gesture that became real at the last moment. 'He's awful, Ralph. I hate him.'

'I don't blame you.'

He reached for the doorhandle, but Lois stopped him with a touch. 'I saw him do something.'

Ralph turned and looked at her. The tendons in his neck creaked rustily. He had a pretty good idea what she was going to say.

'He picked the pocket of the man who hit Rosalie,' she said. 'While he was kneeling beside her in the street, the bald man picked his pocket. Except all he took was a comb. And the hat that bald man was wearing . . . I'm pretty sure I recognized it.'

Ralph went on looking at her, fervently hoping that Lois's memory of Doc #3's apparel did not extend any further.

'It was Bill's, wasn't it? Bill's Panama.'

Ralph nodded. 'Sure it was.'

Lois closed her eyes. 'Oh, Lord.'

'What do you say, Lois? Are you still game?'

'Yes.' She opened her door and swung her legs out. 'But let's get going right away, before I lose my nerve.'

'Tell me about it,' said Ralph Roberts.

3

As they approached the main doors of Derry Home, Ralph leaned toward Lois's ear and murmured, 'Is it happening to you?'

'Yes.' Her eyes were very wide. 'God, yes. It's strong this time, isn't it?'

As they broke the electric-eye beam and the doors to the hospital lobby swung open before them, the surface of the world suddenly peeled back, disclosing another world, one that simmered with unseen colors and shifted with unseen shapes. Overhead, on the wall-to-wall mural depicting Derry as it had been during its halcyon lumbering days at the turn of the century, dark brown arrow-shapes chased each other, growing closer and closer together until they touched. When that happened, they flashed a momentary dark green and changed direction. A bright silver funnel that looked like either a waterspout or a toy cyclone was descending the curved staircase which led up to the second-floor meeting rooms, cafeteria, and auditorium. Its wide top end nodded back and forth as it moved from step to step, and to Ralph it felt distinctly *friendly*, like an anthropomorphic character in a Disney cartoon. As Ralph watched, two men with briefcases hurried up the stairs, and one of them passed directly through the silver funnel. He never paused in what he was saying to his companion, but when he emerged on the other side, Ralph saw he was absently using his free hand to smooth back his hair . . . although not a strand was out of place.

The funnel reached the bottom of the stairs, raced around the center of the lobby in a tight, exuberant figure-eight, and then popped out of existence, leaving only a faint, rosy mist behind. This quickly dissipated.

Lois dug her elbow into Ralph's side, started to point toward an area beyond the Central Information booth, realized there were people all around them, and settled for lifting her chin in that direction instead. Earlier, Ralph had seen a shape in the sky which had looked like a prehistoric bird. Now he saw something which looked like a long translucent snake. It was essing its way across the ceiling above a sign which read PLEASE WAIT HERE FOR BLOOD-TESTING.

'Is it *alive*?' Lois whispered with some alarm.

Ralph looked more closely and realized the thing had no head . . . no discernible tail, either. It was all body. He supposed it *was* alive – he had an idea *all* the auras were alive in some fashion – but he didn't think it was really a snake, and he doubted that it was dangerous, at least to the likes of them.

'Don't sweat the small stuff, sweetheart,' he whispered back to her as they joined the short line at Central Information, and as he said it, the snake-thing seemed to melt into the ceiling and disappear.

Ralph didn't know how important such things as the bird and the cyclone were in the secret world's scheme of things, but he was positive that people were still the main show. The lobby of Derry Home Hospital was like a gorgeous Fourth of July fireworks display, a display in which the parts of the Roman candles and Chinese fountains were being played by human beings.

Lois hooked a finger into his collar to make him bend his head toward her. 'You'll have to do the talking, Ralph,' she said in a strengthless, amazed little voice. 'I'm having all I can do not to wee in my pants.'

The man ahead of them left the booth and Ralph stepped forward. As he did, a clear, sweetly nostalgic memory of Jimmy V surfaced in his mind. They'd been on the road someplace in Rhode Island – Kingston, maybe – and had decided on the spur of the moment that they wanted to attend the tent revival going on in a nearby hayfield. They had both been drunk as fleas in a gin-bottle, of course. A pair of well-scrubbed young ladies had been standing outside the turned-back flaps of the tent, handing out tracts, and as he and Jimmy neared them, they began to admonish each other in aromatic whispers to act sober, dammit, to just act sober. Had they gotten in that day? Or—

'Help you?' the woman in the Central Information booth asked, her tone saying she was doing Ralph a real favor just by speaking to him. He looked through the glass at her and saw a woman buried inside a troubled orange aura that looked like a burning bramble-bush. *Here's a lady who loves the fine print and stands on all the ceremony she can,* he thought, and on the heels of that, Ralph remembered that the two young women flanking the entrance to the tent had gotten one whiff of him and Jimmy V and turned them politely but firmly away. They had ended up spending the evening in a Central Falls juke-joint, as he recalled, and had probably been lucky not to get rolled when they staggered out after last call.

'Sir?' the woman in the glass booth asked impatiently. 'Can I *help* you?'

Ralph came back to the present with a thud he could almost feel. 'Yes, ma'am. My wife and I would like to visit Jimmy Vandermeer on the third floor, if—'

'That's ICU!' she snapped. 'Can't go up to ICU without a special pass.' Orange hooks began to poke their way out of the glow around her head, and her aura began to look like barbed wire strung across some ghostly no-man's-land.

'I know,' Ralph said, more humbly than ever, 'but my friend, Lafayette Chapin, he said—'

'Gosh!' the woman in the booth interrupted. 'It's wonderful, the way everyone's got a friend. Really *wonderful*.' She rolled a satiric eye toward the ceiling.

'Faye said Jimmy could have visitors, though. You see, he has cancer and he's not expected to live much l—'

'Well, I'll check the files,' the woman in the booth said with the grudging air of one who knows she is being sent upon a fool's errand, 'but the computer is very slow tonight, so it's going to take awhile. Give me your name, then you and your wife go sit over there. I'll page you as soon as—'

Ralph decided that he had eaten enough humble pie in front of this bureaucratic guard dog. It wasn't as if he wanted an exit visa from Albania, after all; just a goddam ICU pass would do.

There was a slot in the base of the glass booth. Ralph reached through it and grasped the woman's wrist before she could pull it away. There was a sensation, painless but very clear, of those orange hooks passing directly through his flesh without finding anything to catch on. Ralph squeezed gently and felt a small burst of force – something that would have been no bigger than a pellet if it had been seen – pass from him to the woman. Suddenly the officious orange aura around her left arm and side turned the faded turquoise of Ralph's aura. She gasped and jerked forward on her chair, as if someone had just dumped a paper cup filled with ice-cubes down the back of her uniform.

[*'Never mind the computer. Just give me a couple of passes, please. Right away.'*]

'Yes, sir,' she said at once, and Ralph let go of her wrist so she could reach beneath her desk. The turquoise glow around her arm was turning orange again, the change in color creeping down from her shoulder toward her wrist.

But I could have turned her all *blue,* Ralph thought. *Taken her over. Run her around the room like a wind-up toy.*

He suddenly remembered Ed quoting Matthew's Gospel – *Then Herod, when he saw that he was mocked, was exceeding wroth* – and a mixture of fright and shame filled him. Thoughts of vampirism recurred as well, and a snatch from a famous old Pogo comic strip: *We have met the enemy and he is us.* Yes, he could probably do almost anything he wanted with this orange-haloed grump; his batteries were fully charged. The only problem was that the juice in those batteries – and in Lois's, as well – was stolen goods.

When the information-lady's hand emerged from beneath the desk, it was holding two pink laminated badges marked INTENSIVE CARE/VISITOR. 'Here you are, sir,' she said in a courteous voice utterly unlike the tone in which she had first addressed him. 'Enjoy your visit and thank you for waiting.'

'Thank *you*,' Ralph said. He took the badges and grasped Lois's hand. 'Come on, dear. We ought to

['*Ralph, what did you* DO *to her?*']
['*Nothing, I guess – I think she's all right.*']
get upstairs and make our visit before it gets too late.'

Lois glanced back at the woman in the information booth. She was dealing with her next customer, but slowly, as if she'd just been granted some moderately amazing revelation and had to think it over. The blue glow was now visible only at the very tips of her fingers, and as Lois watched, that disappeared as well.

Lois looked up at Ralph again and smiled.

['*Yes . . . she* IS *all right. So stop beating up on yourself.*']
['*Was that what I was doing?*']
['*I think so, yes . . . we're talking that way again, Ralph.*']
['*I know.*']
['*Ralph?*']
['*Yes?*']
['*This is all pretty wonderful, isn't it?*']
['*Yes.*']

Ralph tried to hide the rest of what he was thinking from her: that when the price for something which felt this wonderful came due, they were apt to discover it was very high.

4

['*Stop staring at that baby, Ralph. You're making its mother nervous.*']

Ralph glanced at the woman in whose arms the baby slept and saw that Lois was right . . . but it was hard *not* to look. The baby, no more than three months old, lay within a capsule of violently shifting yellow-gray aura. This powerful but disquieting thunderlight circled the tiny body with the idiot speed of the atmosphere surrounding a gas giant – Jupiter, say, or Saturn.

['*Jesus, Lois, that's brain-damage, isn't it?*']
['*Yes. The woman says there was a car accident.*']
['*Says? Have you been talking to her?*']
['*No. It's - - - - -.*']
['*I don't understand.*']
['*Join the club.*']

The oversized hospital elevator labored slowly upward. Those inside – the lame, the halt, the guilty few in good

health – didn't speak but either turned their eyes up to the
floor-indicator over the doors or down to inspect their own
shoes. The only exception to this was the woman with the
thunderstruck baby. She was watching Ralph with distrust and
alarm, as if she expected him to leap forward at any moment
and try to rip her infant from her arms.

It's not just that I was looking, Ralph thought. *At least I don't
think so. She felt me thinking about her baby. Felt me . . . sensed
me . . . heard me . . . some damned thing, anyway.*

The elevator stopped on the second floor and the doors
wheezed open. The woman with the baby turned to Ralph.
The infant shifted slightly as she did, and Ralph got a look at
the crown of its head. There was a deep crease in the tiny skull.
A red scar ran the length of it. To Ralph it looked like a rill
of tainted water standing at the bottom of a ditch. The ugly
and confused yellow-gray aura which surrounded the baby was
emerging from this scar like steam from a crack in the earth.
The baby's balloon-string was the same color as its aura, and
it was unlike any other balloon-string Ralph had seen so far
– not unhealthy in appearance but short, ugly, and no more
than a stub.

'Didn't your mother ever teach you any manners?' the baby's
mother asked Ralph, and what cut him wasn't so much the
admonition as the way she made it. He had scared her badly.

'Madam, I assure you—'

'Yeah, go on and assure my fanny,' she said, and stepped
out of the car. The elevator doors started to slide closed. Ralph
glanced at Lois and the two of them exchanged a moment of
brief but total understanding. Lois shook her finger at the doors
as if scolding them, and a gray, meshlike substance fanned out
from its tip. The doors struck this and then slid back into their
slots, as they were programmed to do upon encountering any
barrier to their progress.

[*'Madam!'*]

The woman stopped and turned around, clearly confused.
She shot suspicious glances about her, trying to identify who
had spoken. Her aura was a dark, buttery yellow with faint
tints of orange spoking out from its inner edges. Ralph fixed
her eyes with his.

[*'I'm sorry if I offended you. This is all very new to my friend and
me. We're like children at a formal dinner. I apologize.'*]

['- - - - - - - - - - - - -.']

He didn't know just what she was trying to communicate –

it was like watching someone talk inside a soundproof booth – but he sensed relief and deep unease . . . the sort of unease people feel when they think they may have been observed doing something they shouldn't. Her doubtful eyes remained on his face a moment or two longer, then she turned and began to walk rapidly down the corridor in the direction of a sign reading NEUROLOGICAL SURVEY. The gray mesh Lois had cast at the door was thinning, and when the doors tried to close again, they cut neatly through it. The car continued its slow upward journey.

[*'Ralph . . . Ralph, I think I know what happened to that baby.'*]

She reached toward his face with her right hand and slipped it between his nose and mouth with her palm down. She pressed the pad of her thumb lightly against one of his cheekbones and the pad of her index finger lightly against the other. It was done so quickly and confidently that no one else in the elevator noticed. If one of the three other riders *had* noticed, he or she would have seen something that looked like a neatness-minded wife smoothing away a blot of skin lotion or a dollop of leftover shaving cream.

Ralph felt as if someone had pulled a high-voltage switch inside his brain, one that turned on whole banks of blazing stadium lights. In their raw, momentary glow, he saw a terrible image: hands clad in a violent brownish-purple aura reaching into a crib and snatching up the baby they had just seen. He was shaken back and forth, head snapping and rolling on the thin stalk of neck like the head of a Raggedy Andy doll—

– and *thrown*—

The lights in his head went black then, and Ralph let out a harsh, shuddery sigh of relief. He thought of the pro-life protestors he'd seen on the evening news just last night, men and women waving signs with Susan Day's picture and WANTED FOR MURDER on them, men and women in Grim Reaper robes, men and women carrying a banner which read LIFE, WHAT A BEAUTIFUL CHOICE.

He wondered if the thunderstruck baby might have a differing opinion on that last one. He met Lois's amazed, agonized eyes with his own, and groped out to take her hands.

[*'Father did it, right? Threw the kid against the wall?'*]

[*'Yes. The baby wouldn't stop crying.'*]

[*'And she knows. She knows, but she hasn't told anyone.'*]

[*'No . . . but she might, Ralph. She's thinking about it.'*]

[*'She might also wait until he does it again. And next time he might finish the job.'*]

A terrible thought occurred to Ralph then; it shot across his mind like a meteor scratching momentary fire across a midnight summer sky: it might be better if he *did* finish the job. The thunderstruck baby's balloon-string had only been a stump, but it had been a *healthy* stump. The child might live for years, not knowing who he was or where he was, let alone *why* he was, watching people come and go like trees in the mist . . .

Lois was standing with her shoulders slumped, looking at the floor of the elevator car and radiating a sadness that squeezed Ralph's heart. He reached out, put a finger under her chin, and watched a delicate blue rose spin itself out of the place where his aura touched hers. He tilted her head up and was not surprised to see tears in her eyes.

'Do you still think it's all pretty wonderful, Lois?' he asked softly, and to this he received no answer, either with his ears or in his mind.

5

They were the only two to get out on the third floor, where the silence was as thick as the dust under library shelves. A pair of nurses stood halfway up the hall, clipboards held to white-clad bosoms, talking in low whispers. Anyone else standing by the elevators might have looked at them and surmised a conversation dealing with life, death, and heroic measures; Ralph and Lois, however, took one look at their overlapping auras and knew that the subject currently under discussion was where to go for a drink when their shift ended.

Ralph saw this and at the same time he didn't, the way a deeply preoccupied man sees and obeys traffic signals without really seeing them. Most of his mind was occupied with a deadly sense of *déjà vu* which had washed over him the moment he and Lois stepped out of the elevator and into this world where the faint squeak of the nurses' shoes on the linoleum sounded almost exactly like the faint beep of the life-support equipment.

Even-numbered rooms on your left; odd-numbered rooms on your right, he thought, *and 317, where Carolyn died, is up by the nurses' station. It was 317, all right – I remember. Now that I'm here I remember* everything. *How someone was always sticking her chart in the little pocket on the back of the door upside down. How the light from the window fell across the bed in a kind of crooked rectangle on sunny days. How you could sit in the visitor's chair and look out at the desk-nurse, whose job it is to monitor vital signs, incoming telephone calls, and outgoing pizza orders.*

The same. All the same. It was early March again, the gloomy end of a leaden, overcast day, sleet beginning to spick-spack off the one window of Room 317, and he had been sitting in the visitor's chair with an unopened copy of Shirer's *Rise and Fall of the Third Reich* in his lap since early morning. Sitting there, not wanting to get up even long enough to use the bathroom because the deathwatch had almost run down by then, each tick was a lurch and the gap between each tick and the next was a lifetime; his long-time companion had a train to catch and he wanted to be on the platform to see her off. There would only be one chance to do it right.

It was very easy to hear the sleet as it picked up speed and velocity, because the life-support equipment had been turned off. Ralph had given up during the last week of February; it had taken Carolyn, who had never given up in her life, a little longer to get the message. And what, exactly, was that message? Why that, in a hard-fought ten-round match pitting Carolyn Roberts against Cancer, the winner was Cancer, that all-time heavyweight champeen, by a TKO.

He had sat in the visitor's chair, watching and waiting as her respiration grew more and more pronounced – the long, sighing exhale, the flat, moveless chest, the growing certainty that the last breath had indeed been the last breath, that the watch had run down, the train arrived in the station to take on its single passenger . . . and then another huge, unconscious gasp would come as she tore the next lungful out of the unfriendly air, no longer breathing in any normal sense but only lunging reflexively along from one gasp to the next like a drunk lurching down a long dark corridor in a cheap hotel.

Spickle-spickle-spackle-spackle: the sleet had gone on rapping invisible fingernails against the window as the dirty March day drew down to dirty March dark and Carolyn went on fighting the last half of her last round. By then she had been running completely on autopilot, of course; the brain which had once existed within that finely made skull was gone. It had been replaced by a mutant – a stupid gray-black delinquent that could not think or feel but only eat and eat and eat until it had gorged itself to death.

Spickle-spickle-spackle-spackle, and he had seen that the T-shaped breathing apparatus in her nose had come askew. He waited for her to tear one of her awful, labored breaths out of the air and then, as she exhaled, he had leaned forward and replaced the small plastic nosepiece. He had gotten a little mucus on his fingers, he remembered, and had wiped it off on a tissue from the box on the bedside table. He had sat back, waiting for the next breath, wanting to make sure the nosepiece didn't come askew again, but there *wasn't* any next breath, and he realized that the ticking sound he had heard coming from everywhere since the previous summer seemed to have stopped.

He remembered waiting as the minutes passed – one, then three, then six – unable to believe that all the good years and good times (not to mention the few bad ones) had ended in this flat and toneless fashion. Her radio, tuned to the local easy-listening station, was playing softly in the corner and he listened to Simon and Garfunkel sing 'Scarborough Fair'. They sang it all the way to the end. Wayne Newton came on next, and began to sing 'Danke Shoen'. He sang it all the way to the end. The weather report came next, but before the disc jockey could finish telling about how the weather was going to be on Ralph Roberts's first full day as a widower, all that stuff about clearing and colder and winds shifting around to the north-east, Ralph finally got it through his head. The watch had stopped ticking, the train had come, the boxing match was over. All the metaphors had fallen down, leaving only the woman in the room, silent at last. Ralph began to cry. Still crying, he had blundered over into the corner and turned off the radio. He remembered the summer they had taken a fingerpaint class, and the night they had ended up fingerpainting each other's naked bodies. This memory made him cry harder. He went to the window and leaned his head against the cold glass and cried. In that first terrible minute of understanding, he had wanted only one thing: to be dead himself. A nurse heard him crying and came in. She tried to take Carolyn's pulse. Ralph told her to stop being a goddam fool. She came over to Ralph and for a moment he thought she was going to try to take *his* pulse. Instead, she had put her arms around him. She—

['*Ralph? Ralph, are you all right?*']

He looked around at Lois, started to say he was fine, and

then remembered there was precious little he could hide from her while they were in this state.

['*Feeling sad. Too many memories in here. Not good ones.*']

['*I understand . . . but look down, Ralph! Look on the floor!*']

He did, and his eyes widened. The floor was covered with an overlay of multicolored tracks, some fresh, most fading to invisibility. Two sets stood out clearly from the rest, as brilliant as diamonds in a litter of paste imitations. They were a deep green-gold in which a few tiny reddish flecks still swam.

['*Do they belong to the ones we're looking for, Ralph?*']

['*Yes – the docs are here.*']

Ralph took Lois's hand – it felt very cold – and began to lead her slowly up the hall.

Chapter Seventeen

1

They hadn't gone far when something very strange and rather frightening happened. For a moment the world bled white in front of them. The doors to the rooms ranged along the hall, barely visible in this bright white haze, expanded to the size of warehouse loading bays. The corridor itself seemed to simultaneously elongate and grow taller. Ralph felt the bottom go out of his stomach the way it often had back when he was a teenager, and a frequent customer on the Dust Devil roller coaster at Old Orchard Beach. He heard Lois moan, and she squeezed his hand with panicky tightness.

The whiteout lasted only a second, and when the colors swarmed back into the world, they were brighter and crisper than they had been a moment before. Normal perspective returned, but objects looked *thicker*, somehow. The auras were still there, but they appeared both thinner and paler – pastel coronas instead of spray-painted primary colors. At the same time Ralph realized he could see every crack and pore in the Sheetrocked wall to his left . . . and then he realized he could see the pipes, wires, and insulation *behind* the walls, if he wanted to; all he had to do was look.

Oh my God, he thought. *Is this really happening? Can this really be happening?*

Sounds were everywhere: hushed bells, a toilet being flushed, muted laughter. Sounds a person normally took for granted, as part of everyday life, but not now. Not here. Like the visible reality of things, the sounds seemed to have an extra-ordinarily sensuous texture, like thin overlapping scallops of silk and steel.

Nor were all the sounds ordinary; there were a great many exotic ones weaving their way through the mix. He heard a fly buzzing deep in a heating duct. The fine-grain sandpaper sound of a nurse adjusting her pantyhose in the staff bathroom. Beating hearts. Circulating blood. The soft tidal flow of respiration. Each sound was perfect on its own; fitted into the others, they made a beautiful and complicated auditory ballet – a hidden *Swan Lake* of gurgling stomachs, humming power outlets, hurricane hairdryers, whispering wheels on hospital gurneys. Ralph could hear a TV at the end of the hall beyond the nurses' station. It was coming from Room 340, where Mr Thomas Wren, a kidney patient, was watching Kirk Douglas and Lana Turner in *The Bad and the Beautiful*. 'If you team up with me, baby, we'll turn this town on its ear,' Kirk was saying, and Ralph knew from the aura which surrounded the words that Mr Douglas had been suffering a toothache on the day that particular scene was filmed. Nor was that all; he knew he could go

(*higher? deeper? wider?*)

if he wanted. Ralph most definitely did *not* want. This was the forest of Arden, and a man could get lost in its thickets.

Or eaten by tigers.

[*'Jesus! It's another level – it must be, Lois! A whole other level!'*]

[*'I know.'*]

[*'Are you okay with this?'*]

[*'I think I am, Ralph . . . are you?'*]

[*'I guess so, for now . . . but if the bottom drops out again, I don't know. Come on.'*]

But before they could begin following the green-gold tracks again, Bill McGovern and a man Ralph didn't know came out of Room 313. They were in deep conversation.

Lois turned a horror-struck face toward Ralph.

[*'Oh, no! Oh God, no! Do you see, Ralph? Do you see?'*]

Ralph gripped her hand more tightly. He saw, all right. McGovern's friend was surrounded by a plum-colored aura. It didn't look especially healthy, but Ralph didn't think the man was seriously ill, either; it was just a lot of chronic stuff like rheumatism and kidney gravel. A balloon-string of the same mottled purple shade rose from the top of the man's aura, wavering hesitantly back and forth like a diver's air-hose in a mild current.

McGovern's aura, however, was totally black. The stump

of what had once been a balloon-string jutted stiffly up from it. The thunderstruck baby's balloon-string had been short but healthy; what they were looking at now was the decaying remnant of a crude amputation. Ralph had a momentary image, so strong it was almost a hallucination, of McGovern's eyes first bulging and then popping out of their sockets, knocked loose by a flood of black bugs. He had to close his own eyes for a moment to keep from screaming, and when he opened them again, Lois was no longer at his side.

2

McGovern and his friend were walking in the direction of the nurses' station, probably bound for the water-fountain. Lois was in hot pursuit, trotting up the corridor, bosom heaving. Her aura flashed with twizzling pinkish sparks that looked like neon-flavored asterisks. Ralph bolted after her. He didn't know what would happen if she caught McGovern's attention, and didn't really want to find out. He thought he was probably going to, however.

[*'Lois! Lois, don't do that!'*]

She ignored him.

[*'Bill, stop! You have to listen to me! Something's wrong with you!'*]

McGovern paid no attention to her; he was talking about Bob Polhurst's manuscript, *Later That Summer.* 'Best damned book on the Civil War I ever read,' he told the man inside the plum-colored aura, 'but when I suggested that he publish, he told me that was out of the question. Can you believe it? A possible Pulitzer Prize winner, but—'

[*'Lois, come back! Don't go near him!'*]

[*'Bill! Bill! B—'*]

Lois reached McGovern just before Ralph was able to reach her. She put out her hand to grab his shoulder. Ralph saw her fingers plunge into the murk which surrounded him . . . and then slide *into* him.

Her aura changed at once, from a gray-blue shot with those pinkish sparks to a red as bright as the side of a fire engine. Jagged flocks of black shot through it like clouds of tiny swarming insects. Lois screamed and pulled her hand back. The expression on her face was a mixture of terror and loathing.

She held her hand up in front of her eyes and screamed again, although Ralph could see nothing on it. Narrow black stripes were now whirring giddily around the outer edges of her aura; to Ralph they looked like planetary orbits marked on a map of the solar system. She turned to flee. Ralph grabbed her by the upper arms and she beat at him blindly.

McGovern and his friend, meanwhile, continued their placid amble up the hall to the drinking fountain, completely unaware of the shrieking, struggling woman not ten feet behind them. 'When I asked Bob why he wouldn't publish the book,' McGovern was continuing, 'he said that I of all people should understand his reasons. I told him . . .'

Lois drowned him out, shrieking like a firebell.

[*'!!! - - - - - - - !!! - - - - - - - - - - - !!!'*]

[*'Quit it, Lois! Quit it right now! Whatever happened to you is over now! It's over and you're all right!'*]

But Lois continued to struggle, dinning those inarticulate screams into his head, trying to tell him how awful it had been, how he'd been *rotting,* that there were things inside him, *eating him alive,* and that was bad enough, but it wasn't the worst. Those things were *aware,* she said, they were *bad,* and *they had known she was there.*

[*'Lois, you're with me! You're with me and it's all r—'*]

One of her flying fists clipped the side of his jaw and Ralph saw stars. He understood that they had passed to a plane of reality where physical contact with others was impossible – hadn't he seen Lois's hand pass directly into McGovern, like the hand of a ghost? – but they were obviously still real enough to each other; he had the bruised jaw to prove it.

He slipped his arms around her and hugged her against him, imprisoning her fists between her breasts and his chest. Her cries

[*'!!! - - - - - - - - - !!! - - - - - - - - !!!'*]

continued to rant and blast in his head, however. He locked his hands together between her shoulderblades and squeezed. He felt the power leap out of him again, as it had that morning, only this time it felt entirely different. Blue light spilled through Lois's turbulent red–black aura, soothing it. Her struggles slowed and then ceased. He felt her draw a shuddering breath. Above and around her, the blue glow was expanding and fading. The black bands disappeared from her aura, one after the other, from the bottom up, and then that alarming shade of infected red also began to fade. She put her head against his arm.

[*'I'm sorry, Ralph – I went nuclear again, didn't I?'*]

[*'I suppose so, but never mind. You're okay now. That's the important thing.'*]

[*'If you knew how horrible that was . . . touching him that way . . .'*]

[*'You put it across very well, Lois.'*]

She glanced down the corridor, where McGovern's friend was now getting a drink. McGovern lounged against the wall next to him, talking about how the Exalted & Revered Bob Polhurst had always done the *Sunday New York Times* crossword puzzle in ink. 'He used to tell me that wasn't pride but optimism,' McGovern said, and the deathbag swirled sluggishly around him as he spoke, flowing in and out of his mouth and between the fingers of his gesturing, eloquent hand.

[*'We can't help him, can we, Ralph? There's not a thing in the world we can do.'*]

Ralph gave her a brief, strong hug. Her aura, he saw, had entirely returned to normal.

McGovern and his friend were walking back down the corridor toward them. Acting on impulse, Ralph disengaged himself from Lois and stepped directly in front of Mr Plum, who was listening to McGovern hold forth on the tragedy of old age and nodding in the right places.

[*'Ralph, don't do that!'*]

[*'It's okay, don't worry.'*]

But all at once he wasn't so sure it *was* okay. He might have stepped back, given another second. Before he could, however, Mr Plum glanced unseeingly into his face and walked right through him. The sensation that swept through Ralph's body at his passage was perfectly familiar; it was the pins-and-needles feeling one gets when a sleeping limb starts to wake up. For one moment his aura and Mr Plum's mingled, and Ralph knew everything about the man that there was to know, including the dreams he'd had in his mother's womb.

Mr Plum stopped short.

'Something wrong?' McGovern asked.

'I guess not, but . . . did you hear a bang someplace? Like a firecracker, or a car backfire?'

'Can't say I did, but my hearing isn't what it used to be.' McGovern chuckled. 'If something *did* blow up, I certainly hope it wasn't in one of the radiation labs.'

'I don't hear anything now. Probably just my imagination.'
They turned into Bob Polhurst's room.

Ralph thought, *Mrs Perrine said it sounded like a gunshot. Lois's friend thought there was a bug on her, maybe biting her. Just a difference in touch, maybe, the way different piano-players have different touches. Either way, they feel it when we mess with them. They may not know what it is, but they sure do feel it.*

Lois took his hand and led him to the door of Room 313. They stood in the hall, looking in as McGovern seated himself in a plastic contour chair at the foot of the bed. There were at least eight people crammed into the room and Ralph couldn't see Bob Polhurst clearly, but he could see one thing: although he was deep within his own deathbag, Polhurst's balloon-string was still intact. It was as filthy as a rusty exhaust pipe, peeling in some places and cracked in others . . . but it was still intact. He turned to Lois.

[*'These people may have longer to wait than they think.'*]

Lois nodded, then pointed down at the greeny-gold foot-prints – the white-man tracks. They bypassed 313, Ralph saw, but turned in at the next doorway – 315, Jimmy V's room.

He and Lois walked up together and stood looking in. Jimmy V had three visitors, and the one sitting beside the bed thought he was all alone. That one was Faye Chapin, idly looking through the double stack of get-well cards on Jimmy's bedside table. The other two were the little bald doctors Ralph had seen for the first time on May Locher's stoop. They stood at the foot of Jimmy V's bed, solemn in their clean white tunics, and now that he stood close to them, Ralph could see that there were worlds of character in those unlined, almost identical faces; it just wasn't the sort of thing one could see through a pair of binoculars – or maybe not until you slid up the ladder of perception a little way. Most of it was in the eyes, which were dark, pupil-less, and flecked with deep golden glints. Those eyes shone with intelligence and lively awareness. Their auras gleamed and flashed around them like the robes of emperors . . .

. . . or perhaps of Centurions on a visit of state.

They looked over at Ralph and Lois, who stood holding hands in the doorway like children who have lost their way in a fairy-tale wood, and smiled at them.

[*Hello, woman.*]

That was Doc #1. He was holding the scissors in his right hand. The blades were very long, and the points looked very sharp. Doc #2 took a step toward them and made a funny little half-bow.

[*Hello, man. We've been waiting for you.*]

3

Ralph felt Lois's hand tighten on his own, then loosen as she decided they were in no immediate danger. She took a small step forward, looking from Doc #1 to Doc #2 and then back to #1 again.

[*'Who are you?'*]

Doc #1 crossed his arms over his small chest. The long blades of his scissors lay the entire length of his white-clad left forearm.

[*We don't have names, not the way Short-Timers do – but you may call us after the fates in the story this man has already told you. That these names originally belonged to women means little to us, since we are creatures with no sexual dimension. I will be Clotho, although I spin no thread, and my colleague and old friend will be Lachesis, although he shakes no rods and has never thrown the coins. Come in, both of you – please!*]

They came in and stood warily between the visitor's chair and the bed. Ralph didn't think the docs meant them any harm – for now, at least – but he still didn't want to get too close. Their auras, so bright and fabulous compared to those of ordinary people, intimidated him, and he could see from Lois's wide eyes and half-open mouth that she felt the same. She sensed him looking at her, turned toward him, and tried to smile. *My Lois,* Ralph thought. He put an arm around her shoulders and hugged her briefly.

Lachesis: [*We've given you our names – names you may use, at any rate; won't you give us yours?*]

Lois: [*'You mean you don't already know? Pardon me, but I find that hard to believe.'*]

Lachesis: [*We could know, but choose not to. We like to observe the rules of common Short-Time politeness wherever we can. We find them lovely, for they are passed on by your kind from large hand to small and create the illusion of long lives.*]

[*'I don't understand.'*]

Ralph didn't, either, and wasn't sure he wanted to. He found something faintly patronizing in the tone of the one who called himself Lachesis, something that reminded him of McGovern when he was in a mood to lecture or pontificate.

Lachesis: [*It doesn't matter. We felt sure you would come. We know that you were watching us on Monday morning, man, at the home of*]

At this point there was a queer overlapping in Lachesis's speech. He seemed to say two things at exactly the same time, the terms rolling together like a snake with its own tail in its mouth:

[*May Locher.*]   [*the finished woman.*]

Lois took a hesitant step forward.

[*'My name is Lois Chasse. My friend is Ralph Roberts. And now that we've all been properly introduced, maybe you two fellows will tell us what's going on around here.'*]

Lachesis: [*There is another to be named.*]

Clotho: [*Ralph Roberts has already named him.*]

Lois looked at Ralph, who was nodding his head.

[*'They're talking about Doc #3. Right, guys?'*]

Clotho and Lachesis nodded. They were wearing identical approving smiles. Ralph supposed he should have been flattered, but he wasn't. Instead he was afraid, and very angry – they had been neatly manipulated, every step down the line. This was no chance meeting; it had been a setup from the word go. Clotho and Lachesis, just a couple of little bald doctors with time on their hands, standing around in Jimmy V's room waiting for the Short-Timers to arrive, ho-hum.

Ralph glanced over at Faye and saw he had taken a book called *50 Classic Chess Problems* out of his back pocket. He was reading and picking his nose in ruminative fashion as he did so. After a few preliminary explorations, Faye dove deep and hooked a big one. He examined it, then parked it on the underside of the bedside table. Ralph looked away, embarrassed, and a saying of his grandmother's popped into his mind: *Peek not through a keyhole, lest ye be vexed.* He had lived to be seventy without fully understanding that; at last he thought he did. Meanwhile, another question had occurred to him.

[*'Why doesn't Faye see us? Why didn't Bill and his friend see us, for that matter? And how could that man walk right through me? Or did I just imagine that?'*]

Clotho smiled.

[*You didn't imagine it. Try to think of life as a kind of building, Ralph – what you would call a skyscraper.*]

Except that wasn't quite what Clotho was thinking of, Ralph

discovered. For one flickering moment he seemed to catch an image from the mind of the other, one he found both exciting and disturbing: an enormous tower constructed of dark and sooty stone, standing in a field of red roses. Slit windows twisted up its sides in a brooding spiral.

Then it was gone.

[*You and Lois and all the other Short-Time creatures live on the first two floors of this structure. Of course there are elevators—*]

No, Ralph thought. *Not in the tower I saw in your mind, my little friend. In that building – if such a building actually exists – there are no elevators, only a narrow staircase festooned with cobwebs and doorways leading to God knows what.*

Lachesis was looking at him with a strange, almost suspicious curiosity, and Ralph decided he didn't much care for that look. He turned back to Clotho and motioned for him to go on.

Clotho: [*As I was saying, there are elevators, but Short-Timers are not allowed to use them under ordinary circumstances. You are not*
[*ready*]   [*prepared*]   [- - - - - - - - -.]

The last explanation was clearly the best, but it danced away from Ralph just before he could grasp it. He looked at Lois, who shook her head, and then back at Clotho and Lachesis again. He was beginning to feel angrier than ever. All the long, endless nights sitting in the wing-chair and waiting for dawn; all the days he'd spent feeling like a ghost inside his own skin; the inability to remember a sentence unless he read it three times; the phone numbers, once carried in his head, which he now had to look up—

A memory came then, one which simultaneously summed up and justified the anger he felt as he looked at these bald creatures with their darkly golden eyes and almost blinding auras. He saw himself peering into the cupboard over his kitchen counter, looking for the powdered soup his tired, overstrained mind insisted must be in there someplace. He saw himself poking, pausing, then poking some more. He saw the expression on his face – a look of distant perplexity that could easily have been mistaken for mild mental retardation but which was really simple exhaustion. Then he saw himself drop his hands and simply stand there, as if he expected the packet to jump out on its own.

Not until now, at this moment and at this memory, did he realize how totally horrible the last few months had been. Looking back at them was like looking into a wasteland painted in desolate maroons and grays.

[*'So you took us onto the elevator . . . or maybe that wasn't good enough for the likes of us and you just trotted us up the fire stairs. Got us acclimated a little at a time so we wouldn't strip our gears completely, I imagine. And it was easy. All you had to do was rob us of our sleep until we were half-crazy. Lois's son and daughter-in-law want to put her in a theme-park for geriatrics, did you know that? And my friend Bill McGovern thinks I'm ready for Juniper Hill. Meanwhile, you little angels—'*]

Clotho offered just a trace of his former wide smile.

[*We're no angels, Ralph.*]

[*'Ralph, please don't shout at them.'*]

Yes, he *had* been shouting, and at least some of it seemed to have gotten through to Faye; he had closed his chess book, stopped picking his nose, and was now sitting bolt upright in his chair, looking uneasily about the room.

Ralph looked from Clotho (who took a step backward, losing what was left of his smile) to Lachesis.

[*'Your friend says you're not angels. So where are they? Playing poker six or eight floors farther up? And I suppose God's in the penthouse and the devil's stoking coal in the boiler room.'*]

No reply. Clotho and Lachesis glanced doubtfully at each other. Lois plucked at Ralph's sleeve, but he ignored her.

[*'So what are we supposed to do, guys? Track down your little bald version of Hannibal Lecter and take his scalpel away? Well, fuck you.'*]

Ralph would have turned on his heel and walked out then (he had seen a lot of movies, and he knew a good exit-line when he heard one), but Lois burst into shocked, frightened tears, and that held him where he was. The look of bewildered reproach in her eyes made him regret his outburst at least a little. He slipped his arm back around Lois's shoulders, and looked at the two bald men defiantly.

They exchanged another glance and something – some communication just above his and Lois's ability to hear or understand – passed between them. When Lachesis turned to them again, he was smiling . . . but his eyes were grave.

[*I hear your anger, Ralph, but it is not justified. You do not believe that now, but perhaps you may. For the time being, we must set your questions and our answers – such answers as we may give – aside.*]

[*'Why?'*]

[*Because the time of severing has come for this man. Watch closely, that you may learn and know.*]

Clotho stepped to the left side of the bed. Lachesis approached from the right, walking through Faye Chapin as he went. Faye bent over, afflicted with a sudden coughing-fit, and then opened his book of chess problems again as it eased.

[*'Ralph, I can't watch this! I can't watch them do it!'*]

But Ralph thought she would. He thought they both would. He held her tighter as Clotho and Lachesis bent over Jimmy V. Their faces were lit with love and caring and gentleness; they made Ralph think of the faces he had once seen in a Rembrandt painting – *The Night Watch,* he thought it had been called. Their auras mingled and overlapped above Jimmy's chest, and suddenly the man in the bed opened his eyes. He looked through the two little bald doctors at the ceiling for a moment, his expression vague and puzzled, and then his gaze shifted toward the door and he smiled.

'Hey! Look who's here!' Jimmy V exclaimed. His voice was rusty and choked, but Ralph could still hear his South Boston wiseguy accent, where *here* came out *heah*. Faye jumped. The book of chess problems tumbled out of his lap and fell on the floor. He leaned over and took Jimmy's hand, but Jimmy ignored him and kept looking across the room at Ralph and Lois. 'It's Ralph Roberts! And Paul Chasse's wife widdim! Say, Ralphie, do you remember the day we tried to get into that tent revival so we could hear em sing "Amazing Grace"?'

[*'I remember, Jimmy.'*]

Jimmy appeared to smile, and then his eyes slipped closed again. Lachesis placed his hands against the dying man's cheeks and moved his head a bit, like a barber getting ready to shave a customer. At the same moment Clotho leaned even closer, opened his scissors, and slid them forward so that the long blades held Jimmy V's black balloon-string. As Clotho closed the scissors, Lachesis leaned forward and kissed Jimmy's forehead.

[*Go in peace, friend.*]

There was a small, unimportant *snick!* sound. The segment of the balloon-string above the scissors drifted up toward the ceiling and disappeared. The deathbag in which Jimmy V lay turned a momentary bright white, then winked out of existence just as Rosalie's had done earlier that evening. Jimmy opened his eyes again and looked at Faye. He started to smile, Ralph thought, and then his gaze turned fixed and distant. The dimples which had begun to form at the corners of his mouth smoothed out.

'Jimmy?' Faye shook Jimmy V's shoulder, running his hand

through Lachesis's side to do it. 'You all right, Jimmy? . . . Oh shit.'

Faye got up and left the room, not quite running.

Clotho: [*Do you see and understand that what we do we do with love and respect? That we are, in fact, the physicians of last resort? It is vital to our dealings with you, Ralph and Lois, that you understand that.*]

['*Yes.*']

['*Yes.*']

Ralph hadn't intended to agree with anything either one of them said, but that phrase – the physicians of last resort – sliced cleanly and effortlessly through his anger. It felt true. They had freed Jimmy V from a world where there was nothing left for him but pain. Yes, they had undoubtedly stood in Room 317 with Ralph on a sleety afternoon some seven months ago and given Carolyn the same release. And yes, they went about their work with love and respect – any doubts he might have had on that score had been laid to rest when Lachesis kissed Jimmy V's forehead. But did love and respect give them the right to put him – and Lois, too – through hell and then send them after a supernatural being that had gone off the rails? Did it give them the right to even *dream* that two ordinary people, neither of them young anymore, could deal with such a creature?

Lachesis: [*Let us move on from this place. It's going to fill up with people, and we need to talk.*]

['*Do we have any choice?*']

Their answers

[*Yes, of course!*]   [*There is always a choice!*]

came back quickly, colored with overtones of surprise.

Clotho and Lachesis walked toward the door; Ralph and Lois shrank back to let them pass. The auras of the little bald doctors swept over them for a moment, however, and Ralph registered them in taste and texture: the taste of sweet apples, the texture of dry, light bark.

As they left, side by side, speaking gravely and respectfully to each other, Faye came back in, now accompanied by a pair of nurses. These newcomers passed through Lachesis and Clotho, then through Ralph and Lois, without slowing or seeming to notice anything untoward.

In the hall outside, life went on at its usual muted pace. No buzzers went off, no lights flashed, no orderlies came sprinting down the hallway, pushing the crash-wagon ahead of them. No one cried 'Stat!' over the loudspeaker. Death was too common a visitor here for such things. Ralph guessed that it was not welcome, even under such circumstances as these, but it was familiar and accepted. He also guessed that Jimmy V would have been happy enough with his exit from the third floor of Derry Home – he had done it with no fuss or bother, and he hadn't had to show anyone either his driver's license or his Blue Cross Major Medical card. He had died with the dignity that simple, expected things often hold. One or two moments of consciousness, accompanied by a slightly wider perception of what was going on around him, and then poof. Pack up all my care and woe, blackbird, bye-bye.

4

They joined the bald docs in the hallway outside Bob Polhurst's room. Through the open door, they could see the deathwatch continuing around the old teacher's bed.

Lois: [*'The man closest to the bed is Bill McGovern, a friend of ours. There's something wrong with him. Something awful. If we do what you want, could you— ?'*]

But Lachesis and Clotho were shaking their heads in unison.

Clotho: [*Nothing can be changed.*]

Yes, Ralph thought. *Dorrance knew: done-bun-can't-be-undone.*

Lois: [*'When will it happen?'*]

Clotho: [*Your friend belongs to the other, to the third. To the one Ralph has already named Atropos. But Atropos could tell you the exact hour of the man's death no more than we could. He cannot even tell whom he will take next. Atropos is an agent of the Random.*]

This phrase sent a chill through Ralph's heart.

Lachesis: [*But this is no place for us to talk. Come.*]

Lachesis took one of Clotho's hands, then held out his free hand to Ralph. At the same time, Clotho reached toward Lois. She hesitated, then looked at Ralph.

Ralph, in his turn, looked grimly at Lachesis.

[*'You better not hurt her.'*]

[*Neither of you will be hurt, Ralph. Take my hand.*]

I'm a stranger in paradise, Ralph's mind finished. Then he sighed through his teeth, nodded to Lois, and gripped Lachesis's outstretched hand. That shock of recognition, as deep and pleasant as an unexpected encounter with an old and valued friend, washed over him again. Apples and bark; memories of orchards he had walked through as a kid. He was somehow aware, without actually seeing it, that his aura had changed color and become – at least for a little while – the gold-flecked green of Clotho and Lachesis.

Lois took Clotho's hand, inhaled a sharp little gasp over her teeth, then smiled hesitantly.

Clotho: [*Complete the circle, Ralph and Lois. Don't be afraid. All is well.*]

Boy, do I ever disagree with that, Ralph thought, but when Lois reached for his hand, he grasped her fingers. The taste of apples and the texture of dry bark was joined by some dark and unknowable spice. Ralph inhaled its aroma deeply and then smiled at Lois. She smiled back – no hesitation in that smile – and Ralph felt a dim, far-off confusion. How *could* you be afraid? How could you even hesitate when what they brought felt this good and seemed this right?

I sympathize, Ralph, but hesitate anyway, a voice counseled.

[*'Ralph? Ralph!'*]

She sounded alarmed and giddy at the same time. Ralph looked around just in time to see the top of the door of Room 315 descending past her shoulders . . . except it wasn't the door going down; it was Lois going up. *All* of them going up, still holding hands in a circle.

Ralph had just gotten this through his head when momentary darkness, sharp as a knife-edge, crossed his vision like a shadow thrown by the slat of a venetian blind. He had a brief glimpse of narrow pipes that were probably part of the hospital's sprinkler system, surrounded by tufted pink pads of insulation. Then he was looking down a long tiled corridor. A gurney cart was rolling straight at his head . . . which, he suddenly realized, had surfaced like a periscope in one of the fourth-floor corridors.

He heard Lois cry out and felt her grip on his hand tighten. Ralph closed his eyes instinctively and waited for the approaching gurney to flatten his skull.

Clotho: [*Be calm! Please, be calm! Remember that these things exist on a different level of reality from the one where you are now!*]

Ralph opened his eyes. The gurney was gone, although he could hear its receding wheels. The sound was coming from behind him now. The gurney, like McGovern's friend, had passed right through him. The four of them were now levitating slowly into the corridor of what had to be the pediatrics wing – fairy-tale creatures pranced and gambolled up and down the walls, and characters from Disney's *Aladdin* and *The Little Mermaid* were decaled onto the windows of a large, brightly lighted play area. A doctor and a nurse strolled toward them, discussing a case.

'– further tests seem indicated, but only if we can make at least ninety per cent sure that—'

The doctor walked through Ralph and as he did Ralph understood that he had started smoking again on the sly after five years off the weed and was feeling guilty as hell about it. Then they were gone. Ralph looked down just in time to see his feet emerge from the tiled floor. He turned to Lois, smiling tentatively.

['*It sure beats the elevator, doesn't it?*']

She nodded. Her grip on his hand was still very tight.

They rose through the fifth floor, surfaced in a doctor's lounge on the sixth (two doctors – the full-sized kind – present, one watching an old *F Troop* rerun and the other snoring on the hideous Swedish Modern sofa), and then they were on the roof.

The night was clear, moonless, gorgeous. Stars glittered across the arc of the sky in an extravagant, misty sprawl of light. The wind was blowing hard, and he thought of Mrs Perrine saying Indian summer was over, he could mark her words. Ralph could hear the wind but not feel it . . . although he had an idea he *could* feel it, if he wanted to. It was just a matter of concentrating in the right way . . .

Even as this thought came, he sensed some minor, momentary change in his body, something that felt like a blink. Suddenly his hair was blowing back from his forehead, and he could hear his pants cuffs flapping around his shins. He shivered. Mrs Perrine's back had been right about the weather changing. Ralph gave another interior blink and the push of the wind was gone. He looked over at Lachesis.

['*Can I let go of your hand now?*']

Lachesis nodded and dropped his own grip. Clotho released Lois's hand. Ralph looked across town to the west and saw the pulsing blue runway lights of the airport. Beyond them was the gridwork of orange arc sodiums that marked Cape Green, one of the new housing developments on the far side of the Barrens.

And someplace, in the sprinkle of lights just east of the airport, was Harris Avenue.

[*'It's beautiful, isn't it, Ralph?'*]

He nodded and thought that standing there and seeing the city spread out in the dark like this was worth everything he had been through since the insomnia had started. Everything and then some. But that wasn't a thought he entirely trusted.

He turned to Lachesis and Clotho.

[*'All right, explain. Who are you, who is he, and what do you want us to do?'*]

The two bald docs were standing between two rapidly turning heat ventilators which were spraying brownish–purple fans of effluent into the air. They glanced nervously at each other, and Lachesis gave Clotho an almost imperceptible nod. Clotho stepped forward, looked from Ralph to Lois, and seemed to gather his thoughts.

[*Very well. First, you must understand that the things which are happening, while unexpected and distressing, are not precisely unnatural. My colleague and I do what we were made to do; Atropos does what he was made to do; and you, my Short-Time friends, will do what you were made to do.*]

Ralph favored him with a bright, bitter smile.

[*'There goes freedom of choice, I guess.'*]

Lachesis: [*You mustn't think so! It's simply that what you call freedom of choice is part of what we call* ka, *the great wheel of being.*]

Lois: [*'We see now through a glass darkly . . . is that what you mean?'*]

Clotho, smiling his somehow youthful smile: [*The Bible, I believe. And a very good way of putting it.*]

Ralph: [*'Also pretty convenient for guys like you, but let's pass on that for now. We have a saying that isn't from the Bible, gentlemen, but it's a pretty good one, just the same: Don't gild the lily. I hope you'll keep it in mind.'*]

Ralph had an idea, however, that that might be a little too much to ask.

5

Clotho began to speak then, and he went on for a fair length of time. Ralph had no idea how long, exactly, because time was different on this level – compressed, somehow. At times there were no words at all in what he said; verbal terms were replaced with simple bright images like those in a child's rebus puzzle. Ralph supposed this was telepathy, and thus pretty amazing, but while it was happening it felt as natural as breath.

Sometimes both words and images were lost, interrupted by puzzling breaks

[- - - - - - - - - - - -]

in communication. Yet even then Ralph was usually able to get some idea of what Clotho was trying to convey, and he had an idea Lois was understanding what was hidden in those lapses even more clearly than he was himself.

[*First, know that there are only four constants in that area of existence where your lives and ours, the lives of the*

[- - - - - - - - - -

[*overlap. These four constants are Life, Death, the Purpose, and the Random. All these words have meaning for you, but you now have a slightly different concept of Life and Death, do you not?*]

Ralph and Lois nodded hesitantly.

[*Lachesis and I are agents of Death. This makes us figures of dread to most Short-Timers; even those who pretend to accept us and our function are usually afraid. In pictures we are sometimes shown as a fearsome skeleton or a hooded figure whose face cannot be seen.*]

Clotho put his tiny hands on his white-clad shoulders and pretended to shudder. The burlesque was good enough to make Ralph grin.

[*But we are not only agents of death, Ralph and Lois; we are also agents of the Purpose. And now you must listen closely, for I would not be misunderstood. There are those of your kind who feel that everything happens by design, and there are those who feel all events are simply a matter of luck or chance. The truth is that life is both random and on purpose, although not in equal measure. Life is like*]

Here Clotho formed a circle with his arms, like a small child trying to show the shape of the earth, and within it Ralph saw a brilliant and evocative image: thousands (or perhaps it was millions) of playing cards fanned out in a flickering rainbow of hearts and spades and clubs and diamonds. He also saw a great many jokers in this huge pack; not so many as to make up a suit of their own, but clearly a lot more, proportionally speaking, than the two or three found in the usual deck. Every one of them was grinning, and every one was wearing a battered Panama with a crescent bitten out of the brim.

Every one carried a rusty scalpel.

Ralph looked at Clotho with widening eyes. Clotho nodded.

[*Yes. I don't know exactly what you saw, but I know you saw what I was trying to convey. Lois? What about you?*]

Lois, who loved playing cards, nodded palely.

[*'Atropos is the joker in the deck – that's what you mean.'*]

[*He is an agent of the Random. We, Lachesis and I, serve that other force, the one which accounts for most events in both individual lives and in life's wider stream. On your level of the building, Ralph and Lois, every creature is a Short-Time creature, and has an appointed span. This isn't to say that a child pops out of its mother's womb with a sign around its neck reading* CUT CORD @ 84 YEARS, 11 MONTHS, 9 DAYS, 6 HOURS, 4 MINUTES, AND 21 SECONDS. *That idea is ridiculous. Yet time passages are usually set, and as both of you have seen, one of the many functions the Short-Time aura serves is as a clock.*]

Lois stirred, and as Ralph turned to look at her, he saw an amazing thing: the sky overhead was growing pale. He guessed it must be five in the morning. They had arrived at the hospital at around nine o'clock on Tuesday evening, and now all at once it was Wednesday, October 6th. Ralph had heard of time flying, but this was ridiculous.

Lois: [*'Your job is what we call natural death, isn't it?'*]

Her aura flickered with confused, incomplete images. A man (the late Mr Chasse, Ralph was quite sure) lying in an oxygen tent. Jimmy V opening his eyes to look at Ralph and Lois in the instant before Clotho cut his balloon-string. The obituary page from the Derry *News,* peppered with photographs, most not much bigger than postage stamps, of the weekly harvest from the local hospitals and nursing homes.

Both Clotho and Lachesis shook their heads.

Lachesis: [*There is no such thing as natural death, not really. Our job is* purposeful *death. We take the old and the sick, but we take others, as well. Just yesterday, for instance, we took a young man of twenty-eight. A carpenter. Two Short-Time weeks ago, he fell from a scaffold and fractured his skull. During those two weeks his aura was*]

Ralph got a fractured image of a thunderstruck aura like the one which had surrounded the baby in the elevator.

Clotho: [*At last the change came – the turning of the aura. We knew it would come, but not* when *it would come. When it did, we went to him and sent him on.*]

[*'Sent him on to where?'*]

It was Lois who asked the question, broaching the touchy subject of the afterlife almost by accident. Ralph grabbed for his mental safety belt, almost hoping for one of those peculiar blanks, but when their overlapped answers came, they were perfectly clear.

Clotho: [*To everywhere.*]

Lachesis: [*To other worlds than these.*]

Ralph felt a mixture of relief and disappointment.

[*'That sounds very poetic, but I think what it means – correct me if I'm wrong – is that the afterlife is as much a mystery to you guys as it is to us.'*]

Lachesis, sounding a bit stiff: [*On another occasion we might have time to discuss such things, but not now – as you have no doubt already noticed, time passes faster on this level of the building.*]

Ralph looked around and saw the morning had already brightened considerably.

[*'Sorry.'*]

Clotho, smiling: [*Not at all – we enjoy your questions, and find them refreshing. Curiosity exists everywhere along life's continuum, but nowhere is it as abundant as here. But what you call the afterlife has no place in the four constants – Life and Death, the Random and the Purpose – which concern us now.*

[*The approach of almost every death which serves the Purpose takes a course with which we are very familiar. The auras of those who will die Purposeful deaths turn gray as the time of finishing approaches. This gray deepens steadily to black. We are called when the aura*
[- - - - - - - - - - - -,

[*and we come exactly as you saw last night. We give release to those who suffer, peace to those in terror, rest to those who cannot find rest. Most Purposeful deaths are expected, even welcomed, but not all. We are sometimes called to take men, women, and children who are in the best of health . . . yet their auras turn suddenly and their time of finishing has come.*]

Ralph remembered the young man in the sleeveless Celtics jersey he'd seen bopping into the Red Apple yesterday afternoon. He had been the picture of health and vitality . . . except for the spectral oil-slick surrounding him, that was.

Ralph opened his mouth, perhaps to mention this young man (or to ask about his fate), then closed it again. The sun was directly overhead now, and a bizarre certainty suddenly came to him: that he and Lois had become the subject of lecherous discussion in the secret city of the Old Crocks.

Anybody seen em? . . . No? . . . Think they run off together? . . . Eloped, maybe? . . . Naw, not at their age, but they might be shacked up . . . I dunno if Ralphie's got any live rounds left in the old ammo dump, but she's always looked like a hot ticket to me . . . Yeah, walks like she knows what to do with it, don't she?

The image of his oversized rustbucket waiting patiently behind one of the ivy-covered units of the Derry Cabins while the springs boinged and sproinged salaciously inside came to Ralph, and he grinned. He couldn't help it. A moment later the alarming idea that he might be broadcasting his thoughts on his aura came to him, and he slammed the door on the picture at once. Yet wasn't Lois looking at him with a certain amused speculation?

Ralph turned his attention hastily back to Clotho.

[*Atropos serves the Random. Not all deaths of the sort Short-Timers call 'senseless' and 'unnecessary' and 'tragic' are his work, but most are. When a dozen old men and women die in a fire at a retirement hotel, the chances are good that Atropos has been there, taking souvenirs and cutting cords. When an infant dies in his crib for no apparent reason, the cause, more often than not, is Atropos and his rusty scalpel. When a dog — yes, even a dog, for the destinies of almost all living things in the Short-Time world fall among either the Random or the Purpose — is run over in the road because the driver of the car that hit him picked the wrong moment to glance at his watch—*]

Lois: [*'Is that what happened to Rosalie?'*]

Clotho: [Atropos *is what happened to Rosalie. Ralph's friend Joe Wyzer was only what we call 'fulfilling circumstance'.*]

Lachesis: [*And Atropos is also what happened to your friend, the late Mr McGovern.*]

Lois looked the way Ralph felt: dismayed but not really surprised. It was now late afternoon, perhaps as many as eighteen Short-Time hours had passed since they had last seen Bill, and Ralph had known the man's time was extremely short even last night. Lois, who had inadvertently put her hand inside him, probably knew it even better.

Ralph: [*'When did it happen? How long after we saw him?'*]

Lachesis: [*Not long. While he was leaving the hospital. I'm sorry for your loss, and for giving you the news in such clumsy fashion. We*

*speak to Short-Timers so infrequently that we forget how. I didn't
mean to hurt you, Ralph and Lois.*]

Lois told him it was all right, that she quite understood,
but tears were trickling down her cheeks, and Ralph felt them
burning in his own eyes. The idea that Bill could be gone – that
the little shithead in the dirty smock had gotten him – was hard
to grasp. Was he to believe McGovern would never hoist that
satiric, bristly eyebrow of his again? Never bitch about how
cruddy it was to get old again? Impossible. He turned suddenly
to Clotho.

[*'Show us.'*]

Clotho, surprised, almost dithering: [*I . . . I don't think—*]

Ralph: [*'Seeing is believing to us Short-Time schmoes. Didn't
you guys ever hear that one?'*]

Lois spoke up unexpectedly.

[*'Yes – show us. But only enough so we can know it and accept
it. Try not to make us feel any worse than we already do.'*]

Clotho and Lachesis looked at each other, then seemed
to shrug without actually moving their narrow shoulders.
Lachesis flicked the first two fingers of his right hand upward,
creating a blue-green peacock's fan of light. In it Ralph saw
a small, eerily perfect representation of the ICU corridor. A
nurse pushing a pharmacy cart came into this arc and crossed
it. At the far side of the viewing area, she actually seemed to
curve for a moment before passing out of view.

Lois, delighted in spite of the circumstances: [*'It's like watching
a movie in a soapbubble!'*]

Now McGovern and Mr Plum stepped out of Bob Polhurst's
room. McGovern had put on an old Derry High letter sweater
and his friend was zipping up a jacket; they were clearly
giving up the deathwatch for another night. McGovern was
walking slowly, lagging behind Mr Plum. Ralph could see
that his downstairs neighbor and sometime friend didn't look
good at all.

He felt Lois's hand slip into his upper arm and grip hard. He
put his hand over hers.

Halfway to the elevator, McGovern stopped, braced himself
against the wall with one hand, and lowered his head. He
looked like a totally blown runner at the end of a marathon.
For a moment Mr Plum went on walking. Ralph could see his
mouth moving and thought, *He doesn't know he's talking to thin
air – not yet, at least.*

Suddenly Ralph didn't want to see any more.

Inside the blue-green arc, McGovern put one hand to his chest. The other went to his throat and began to rub, as if he were checking for wattles. Ralph couldn't tell for sure, but he thought his downstairs neighbor's eyes looked frightened. He remembered the grimace of hate on Doc #3's face when he realized a Short-Timer had presumed to step into his business with one of the local strays. What had he said?

[*I'll fuck you over, Shorts. I'll fuck you over big-time. And I'll fuck your friends over. Do you get me?*]

A terrible idea, almost a certainty, dawned in Ralph's mind as he watched Bill McGovern crumple slowly to the floor.

Lois: [*'Make it go away – please make it go away!'*]

She buried her face against Ralph's shoulder. Clotho and Lachesis exchanged uneasy looks, and Ralph realized he had already begun to revise his mental picture of them as omniscient and all-powerful. They might be supernatural creatures, but Dr Joyce Brothers they were not. He had an idea they weren't much shakes at predicting the future, either; fellows with really efficient crystal balls probably wouldn't have a look like that in their entire repertoire.

They're feeling their way along, just like the rest of us, Ralph thought, and he felt a certain reluctant sympathy for Mr C and Mr L.

The blue-green arc of light floating in front of Lachesis – and the images trapped inside it – suddenly disappeared.

Clotho, sounding defensive: [*Please remember that it was your choice to see, Ralph and Lois. We did not show you that willingly.*]

Ralph barely heard this. His terrible idea was still developing, like a photograph one does not wish to see but cannot turn away from. He was thinking of Bill's hat . . . Rosalie's faded blue bandanna . . . and Lois's missing diamond earrings.

[*I'll fuck your friends over, Shorts – do you get me? I hope so. I most certainly do.*]

He looked from Clotho to Lachesis, his sympathy for them disappearing. What replaced it was a dull pulse of anger. Lachesis had said there was no such thing as accidental death, and that included McGovern's. Ralph had no doubt that Atropos had taken McGovern when he had for one simple reason: he'd wanted to hurt Ralph, to punish Ralph for messing into . . . what had Dorrance called it? Long-time business.

Old Dor had suggested he not do that – a good policy, no doubt, but he, Ralph, had really had no choice . . . because these two bald half-pints had messed in with *him*. They had, in a very real sense, gotten Bill McGovern killed.

Clotho and Lachesis saw his anger and took a step backward (although they seemed to do it without actually moving their feet), their faces becoming more uneasy than ever.

[*'You two are the reason Bill McGovern's dead. That's the truth of it, isn't it?'*]

Clotho: [*Please . . . if you'll just let us finish explaining—*]

Lois was staring at Ralph, worried and scared.

[*'Ralph? What's wrong? Why are you angry?'*]

[*'Don't you get it? This little setup of theirs cost Bill McGovern his life. We're here because Atropos has either done something these guys don't like or is getting ready to—'*]

Lachesis: [*You're jumping to conclusions, Ralph—*]

[*'– but there's one very basic problem: he* knows *we see him!* Atropos KNOWS we see him!']

Lois's eyes widened with terror . . . and with understanding.

Chapter Eighteen

1

A small white hand fell on Ralph's shoulder and lay there like smoke.

[*Please . . . if you'll only let us explain—*]

He felt that change – that *blink* – happen in his body even before he was fully aware he had willed it. He could feel the wind again, coming out of the dark like the blade of a cold knife, and shivered. The touch of Clotho's hand was now no more than a phantom vibration just below the surface of his skin. He could see all three of them, but now they were milky and faint. Now they were ghosts.

I've stepped down. Not all the way back down to where we started, but at least down to a level where they can have almost no physical contact with me. My aura, my balloon-string . . . yes, I'm sure they could get at those things, but the physical part of me that lives my real life in the Short-Time world? No way, José.

Lois's voice, as distant as a fading echo: ['*Ralph! What are you doing to your*]

He looked at the ghostly images of Clotho and Lachesis. Now they looked not just uneasy or slightly guilty but downright scared. Their faces were distorted and hard to see, but their fear was none the less unmistakable.

Clotho, his voice distant but audible: [*Come back, Ralph! Please come back!*]

'If I do, will you quit playing games and be straight with us?'

Lachesis, fading, disappearing: [*Yes! Yes!*]

Ralph made that interior blink happen again. The three of them came back into focus. At the same time, color once more

391

filled up the spaces of the world and time resumed its former sprint – he observed the waning moon sliding down the far side of the sky like a dollop of glowing mercury. Lois threw her arms around his neck, and for a moment he wasn't sure if she was hugging him or trying to strangle him.

[*'Thank God! I thought you were going to leave me!'*]

Ralph kissed her and for a moment his head was filled with a pleasant jumble of sensory input: the taste of fresh honey, a texture like combed wool, and the smell of apples. A thought blipped across his mind

(*what would it be like to make love up here?*)

and he banished it at once. He needed to think and speak very carefully in the next few

(*minutes? hours? days?*)

and thinking about stuff like that would only make it that much harder. He turned to the little bald doctors and measured them with his eyes.

[*'I hope you mean it. Because if you don't, I think we'd better call this horserace off right now and go our separate ways.'*]

Clotho and Lachesis didn't bother with the exchanged glance this time; they both nodded eagerly. Lachesis spoke, and he did so in a defensive tone of voice. These fellows, Ralph suspected, were a lot more pleasant to deal with than Atropos, but no more used to being questioned – to being put on their mettle, Ralph's mother would have said – than he was.

[*Everything we told you was true, Ralph and Lois. We may have left out the possibility that Atropos has a slightly greater understanding of the situation than we would really like, but—*]

Ralph: [*'What if we refuse to listen to any more of this nonsense? What if we just turn and walk away?'*]

Neither replied, but Ralph thought he saw a dismaying thing in their eyes: they knew that Atropos had Lois's earrings, and they knew *he* knew. The only one who didn't know – he hoped – was Lois herself.

She was now tugging his arm.

[*'Don't do that, Ralph – please don't. We need to hear them out.'*]

He turned back to them and made a curt motion for them to go on.

Lachesis: [*Under ordinary circumstances, we don't interfere with Atropos, nor he with us. We* couldn't *interfere with him even if we wanted to; the Random and the Purpose are like the red and black squares on a checkerboard, defining each other by contrast. But Atropos* does *want to interfere with the way things operate – interfering is, in a very real sense, what he was made to do – and on rare occasions, the opportunity to do so in a really big way presents itself. Efforts to stop his meddling are rare—*]

Clotho: [*The truth is actually a little stronger, Ralph and Lois; never in our experience has an effort been made to check or bar him.*]

Lachesis: [*– and are made only if the situation into which he intends to meddle is a very delicate one, where many serious matters are balanced and counterbalanced. This is one of those situations. Atropos has severed a life-cord he would have done well to leave alone. This will cause terrible problems on all levels, not to mention a serious imbalance between the Random and the Purpose, unless the situation is rectified. We cannot deal with what's happening; the situation has passed far beyond our skills. We can no longer see clearly, let alone act. Yet in this case our inability to see hardly matters, because in the end, only Short-Timers can oppose the will of Atropos. That is why you two are here.*]

Ralph: [*'Are you saying that Atropos cut the cord of someone who was supposed to die a natural death . . . or a Purposeful death?'*]

Clotho: [*Not exactly. Some lives – a very few – bear no clear designation. When Atropos touches such lives, trouble is always likely. 'All bets are off,' you say. Such undesignated lives are like—*]

Clotho drew his hands apart and an image – playing cards again – flashed between them. A row of seven cards that were swiftly turned over, one after another, by an unseen hand. An ace; a deuce; a joker; a trey; a seven; a queen. The last card the invisible hand flipped over was blank.

Clotho: [*Does this picture help?*]

Ralph's brow furrowed. He didn't know if it did or not. Somewhere out there was a person who was neither a regular playing card nor a joker in the deck. A person who was perfectly blank, up for grabs by either side. Atropos had slashed this guy's metaphysical air-hose, and now somebody – or some*thing* – had called a time-out.

Lois: [*'It's Ed you're talking about, isn't it?'*]

Ralph wheeled around and stared at her sharply, but she was looking at Lachesis.

[*'Ed Deepneau is the blank card.'*]

Lachesis was nodding.

[*'How did you know that, Lois?'*]

[*'Who else could it be?'*]

She wasn't smiling at him, precisely, but Ralph felt the *sense* of a smile. He turned back to Clotho and Lachesis.

['*Okay, at last we're getting somewhere. So who flashed the red light on this deal? I don't think it was you guys – I have an idea that on this one, at least, you two aren't much more than the hired help.*']

They put their heads together for a moment and murmured, but Ralph saw a faint ocher tinge appear like a seam at the place where their green–gold auras overlapped and knew he was right. At last the two of them faced Ralph and Lois again.

Lachesis: [*Yes, that is basically the case. You have a way of putting things in perspective, Ralph. We haven't had a conversation like this in a thousand years—*]

Clotho: [*If ever.*]

Ralph: ['*All you have to do is tell the truth, boys.*']

Lachesis, as plaintively as a child: [*We have been!*]

Ralph: ['*The* whole *truth.*']

Lachesis: [*All right; the whole truth. Yes, it is Ed Deepneau's cord Atropos cut. We don't know this because we have seen it – we've passed beyond our ability to see clearly, as I said – but because it is the only logical conclusion. Deepneau is undesignated, neither of the Random nor of the Purpose, that we* do *know, and his must have been some sort of master-cord to have caused all this uproar and concern. The very fact that he has lived so long after his life-cord was severed indicates his power and importance. When Atropos severed this cord, he set a terrible chain of events in motion.*]

Lois shivered and stepped closer to Ralph.

Lachesis: [*You called us hired help. You were more right than you knew. We are, in this case, simply messengers. Our job is to make you and Lois aware of what has happened and what is expected of you, and that job is now almost done. As to who 'flashed the red light', we can't answer that question because we don't really know.*]

['*I don't believe you.*']

But he heard the lack of conviction in his own voice (if it *was* a voice).

Clotho: [*Don't be silly – of course you do! Would you expect the directors of a large automobile company to invite a lowly worker up to the boardroom so they could explain the reasons behind all the company's policies? Or perhaps give him the details on why they decided to close one plant and leave another one open?*]

Lachesis: [*We're a little more highly placed than the men who work on automobile assembly lines, but we're still what you would call 'working joes', Ralph – no more and no less.*]

Clotho: [*Be content with this: beyond the Short-Time levels of existence and the Long-Time levels on which Lachesis, Atropos, and I exist, there are yet other levels. These are inhabited by creatures we could call All-Timers, beings which are either eternal or so close to it as to make no difference. Short-Timers and Long-Timers live in overlapping spheres of existence – on connected floors of the same building, if you like – ruled by the Random and the Purpose. Above these floors, inaccessible to us but very much a part of the same tower of existence, live other beings. Some of them are marvellous and wonderful; others are hideous beyond our ability to comprehend, let alone yours. These beings might be called the Higher Purpose and the Higher Random . . . or perhaps there is no Random beyond a certain level; we suspect that may be the case, but we have no real way of telling. We do know that it is something from one of these higher levels that has interested itself in Ed, and that something else from up there made a countermove. That countermove is you, Ralph and Lois.*]

Lois gave Ralph a dismayed look that he hardly noticed. The idea that something was moving them around like chess-pieces in Faye Chapin's beloved Runway 3 Classic – an idea that would have infuriated him under other circumstances – went right by him for the time being. He was remembering the night Ed had called him on the telephone. *You're drifting into deep water,* he'd said, *and there are things swimming around in the undertow you can't even* conceive *of.*

Entities, in other words.

Beings too hideous to comprehend, according to Mr C, and Mr C was a gentleman who dealt death for a living.

They haven't really noticed you yet, Ed had told him that night, *but if you keep fooling with me, they will. And you don't want that. Believe me, you don't.*

Lois: [*'How did you get us up to this level in the first place? It was the insomnia, wasn't it?'*]

Lachesis, cautiously: [*Essentially, yes. We're able to make certain small changes in Short-Time auras. These adjustments caused a rather special form of insomnia that altered the way you dream and the way you perceive the waking world. Adjusting Short-Term auras is delicate, frightening work. Madness is always a danger.*]

Clotho: [*At times you may have felt that you were going mad, but neither of you was ever even close. You're much tougher, both of you, than you give yourself credit for.*]

These assholes actually think they're being comforting, Ralph marvelled, and then pushed his anger away again. He simply had no time to be angry now. Later, maybe, he could make up for that. He hoped so. For now he simply patted Lois's hands, then turned to Clotho and Lachesis again.

[*'Last summer, after he beat his wife up, Ed spoke to me of a being he called the Crimson King. Does that mean anything to you fellows?'*]

Clotho and Lachesis exchanged another look, one which Ralph at first mistook for solemnity.

Clotho: [*Ralph, you must remember that Ed is insane, existing in a delusional state—*]

[*'Yeah, tell me about it.'*]

[*– but we believe that his 'Crimson King' does exist in one form or another, and that when Atropos cut his life-cord, Ed Deepneau fell directly under this being's influence.*]

The two little bald doctors looked at each other again, and this time Ralph saw the shared expression for what it really was: not solemnity but terror.

2

A new day had dawned – Thursday – and was now brightening its way toward noon. Ralph couldn't tell for sure, but he thought the speed with which the hours were passing down there on the Short-Time level was increasing; if they didn't wrap this thing up soon, Bill McGovern wouldn't be the only one of their friends they outlived.

Clotho: [*Atropos knew that the Higher Purpose would send someone to try to change what he has set in motion, and now he knows who. But you must not allow yourselves to be sidetracked by Atropos; you must remember that he is little more than a pawn on this board. It is not Atropos who really opposes you.*]

He paused and looked doubtfully at his colleague. Lachesis nodded for him to go on, and he did so confidently enough, but Ralph felt his heart sink a little, just the same. He was sure the two bald doctors had the best of intentions, but they were pretty clearly flying on instruments, just the same.

Clotho: [*You must not approach Atropos directly, either. I cannot emphasize that enough. He has been surrounded by forces much greater than himself, forces that are malignant and powerful, forces that are conscious and will stop at nothing to stop you. Yet we think that, if you stay away from Atropos, you may be able to block the terrible*] *thing which is about to happen . . . which is, in a very real sense, happening already.*]

Ralph didn't much care for the unspoken assumption that he and Lois were going to do whatever it was these two happy gauchos wanted, but this didn't seem like exactly the right time to say so.

Lois: [*'What is about to happen? What is it you want from us? Are we supposed to find Ed and talk him out of doing something bad?'*]

Clotho and Lachesis looked at her with identical expressions of shocked horror.

[*Haven't you been listening to—*]

[*– you mustn't even think of—*]

They stopped, and Clotho motioned Lachesis to go ahead.

[*If you didn't hear us before, Lois, hear us now:* stay away from Ed Deepneau! *Like Atropos, this unusual situation has temporarily invested him with great power. To even go near him would be to risk a visit from the entity he thinks of as the Crimson King . . . and besides, he is no longer in Derry.*]

Lachesis glanced out over the roof, where lights were coming on in the dusk of Thursday evening, then looked back at Ralph and Lois again.

[*He has left for*

[- -.]

No words, but Ralph caught a clear sensory impression which was part smell (oil, grease, exhaust, sea-salt), part feel and sound (the wind snapping at something – perhaps a flag), and part sight (a large rusty building with a huge door standing open on a steel track).

[*'He's on the coast, isn't he? Or going there.'*]

Clotho and Lachesis nodded, and their faces suggested that the coast, eighty miles from Derry, was a very good place for Ed Deepneau.

Lois tugged his hand again, and Ralph glanced at her.

[*'Did you see the building, Ralph?'*]

He nodded.

Lois: [*'It's not Hawking Labs, but it's near there. I think it might even be a place I know—'*]

Lachesis, speaking rapidly, as if to change the subject: [*Where he is or what he might be planning really doesn't matter. Your task lies elsewhere, in safer waters, but you still may need to use all of your considerable Short-Time powers to accomplish it, and there still may be great danger.*]

Lois looked nervously at Ralph.

[*'Tell them we won't hurt anybody, Ralph – we might agree to help them if we can, but we won't hurt anybody, no matter what.'*]

Ralph, however, told them no such thing. He was thinking of how the diamond chips had glittered at Atropos's earlobes, and meditating on how perfectly he had been trapped – and Lois along with him, of course. Yes, he would hurt someone to get the earrings back. That wasn't even a question. But just how far would he go? Would he perhaps kill to get them back?

Not wanting to tackle that issue – not wanting to even look at Lois, at least for the time being – Ralph turned back to Clotho and Lachesis. He opened his mouth to speak, but she got there first.

[*'There's one other thing I want to know before we go any further.'*]

It was Clotho who replied, sounding slightly amused – sounding, in fact, remarkably like Bill McGovern. Ralph didn't care for it much.

[*What is that, Lois?*]

[*'Is Ralph in danger, too? Does Atropos have something of Ralph's we need to take back later on? Something like Bill's hat?'*]

Lachesis and Clotho exchanged a quick, apprehensive glance. Ralph didn't think Lois caught it, but he did. *She's getting too close for comfort,* that look said. Then it was gone. Their faces were smooth again as they turned their attention back to Lois.

Lachesis: [*No. Atropos has taken nothing from Ralph because, up until now, doing so would not help him in any way.*]

Ralph: [*'What do you mean, "up until now"?'*]

Clotho: [*You have spent your life as part of the Purpose, Ralph, but that has changed.*]

Lois: [*'When did it change? It happened when we started seeing the auras, didn't it?'*]

They looked at each other, then at Lois, then – nervously – at Ralph. They said nothing, and an interesting idea occurred to Ralph: like the boy George Washington of the cherry tree myth, Clotho and Lachesis could not tell a lie . . . and at moments like this they probably regretted it. The only alternative was the one they were employing: keeping their lips zipped and hoping the conversation would move on to safer areas. Ralph decided he didn't want it to move on – at least not yet – even though they were dangerously close to allowing Lois to find out where her earrings had gone . . . always assuming she didn't know that already, a possibility that did not strike him as at all remote.

An old carny pitchman's line occurred to him: *Step right up,
gentlemen . . . but if you want to* play, *you have to* pay.

[*'Oh no, Lois – the change didn't happen when I started to see the
auras. I think a lot of people catch a glimpse into the Long-Time
world of auras every now and again, and nothing bad happens to
them. I don't think I got knocked out of my nice safe place in the
Purpose until we started to talk to these two fine fellows. What do you
say, fine fellows? You did everything but leave a trail of breadcrumbs,
even though you knew perfectly well what was going to happen. Isn't
that about the size of it?'*]

They looked down at their feet, then slowly, reluctantly,
back up at Ralph. It was Lachesis who answered.

[*Yes, Ralph. We drew you to us even though we knew it would
alter your* ka. *It's unfortunate, but the situation demanded it.*]

Now Lois will ask about herself, Ralph thought. *Now she
must ask.*

But she didn't. She only looked at the two little bald doctors
with an inscrutable expression completely unlike any of her
usual *Our Lois* looks. Ralph wondered again how much she
knew or guessed, marvelled again that he didn't have the
slightest clue . . . and then these speculations were swallowed
in a fresh wave of anger.

[*'You guys . . . man oh man, you guys . . .'*]

He didn't finish, although he might have, if Lois hadn't been
standing beside him: *You guys have done quite a bit more than just
mess with our sleep, haven't you? I don't know about Lois, but I had a
nice little niche in the Purpose . . . which means that you deliberately
made me an exception to the very rules you've spent your whole lives
upholding. In a way, I've become as much a blank as this guy we're
supposed to find. How did Clotho put it? 'All bets are off.' How very
fucking true.*

Lois: [*'You talked about using our powers. What* powers*?'*]

Lachesis turned to her, clearly delighted at the change of
subject. He pressed his hands together, palm to palm, then
opened them in a curiously Oriental gesture. What appeared
between them were two swift images: Ralph's hand producing
a bolt of cold blue fire as it cut the air in a karate chop, and
Lois's forefinger producing bright blue-gray pellets of light that
looked like nuclear cough-drops.

Ralph: [*'Yes, all right, we have* something, *but it isn't reliable.
It's like—'*]

He concentrated and created an image of his own: hands
opening the back of a radio and removing a pair of AA batteries

encrusted with blue-gray crud. Clotho and Lachesis frowned at him, not getting it.

Lois: [*'He's trying to say we can't always do that, and when we can, we can't do it for long. Our batteries go flat, you see.'*]

Understanding mixed with amused incredulity broke over their features.

Ralph: [*'What's so damned funny?'*]

Clotho: [*Nothing . . . everything. You have no concept of how strange you and Lois seem to us – incredibly wise and perceptive at one moment, incredibly naïve at the next. Your batteries, as you call them, need never go flat, because the two of you are standing next to a bottomless reservoir of power. We assumed that, since you have both already drunk from it, you must surely know about it.*]

Ralph: [*'What in the world are you talking about?'*]

Lachesis made that curiously Oriental hand-opening gesture again. This time Ralph saw Mrs Perrine, walking stiffly upright within an aura the color of a West Pointer's dress uniform. Saw a shaft of gray brilliance, as thin and straight as the quill of a porcupine, poke out of this aura.

This image was overlaid by one of a skinny woman encased in a smoggy brown aura. She was looking out a car window. A voice – Lois's – spoke: *Oooh, Mina, isn't that the* dearest *little house?* A moment later there was a soft, indrawn whistle and a narrow ray of the woman's aura poked out from behind her neck.

This was followed by a third image, brief but strong: Ralph reaching through the slot in the bottom of the information booth and gripping the wrist of the woman with the brambly orange aura . . . except that all at once the aura around her left arm no longer *was* orange. All at once it was the faded turquoise he now thought of as Ralph Roberts Blue.

The image faded. Lachesis and Clotho stared at Ralph and Lois; they stared back, shocked.

Lois: [*'Oh, no! We can't do that! It's like—'*]

Image: Two men in striped prison suits and little black masks tiptoeing out of a bank vault, carrying bulging sacks with the $ symbol printed on the sides.

Ralph: [*'No, even worse. It's like—'*]

Image: A bat flies in through an open casement window, makes two swooping circles in a silvery shaft of moonlight, then turns into Ralph Lugosi in a cape and old-fashioned tuxedo. He approaches a sleeping woman – not a young, rosy

virgin but old Mrs Perrine in a sensible flannel nightgown –
and bends over to suck her aura.

When Ralph looked back at Clotho and Lachesis, both of
them were shaking their heads vehemently.

Lachesis: [*No! No, no, no! You couldn't be more wrong! Have
you not wondered why you are Short-Timers, marking the spans of
your lives in decades rather than in centuries? Your lives are short
because you burn like bonfires! When you draw energy from your
fellow Short-Timers, it's like*—]

Image: A child at the seashore, a lovely little girl with
golden ringlets bouncing on her shoulders, runs down the
beach to where the waves break. In one hand she carries a red
plastic bucket. She kneels and fills it from the vast gray–blue
Atlantic.

Clotho: [*You are like that child, Ralph and Lois – your fellow
Short-Timers are like the sea. Do you understand now?*]

Ralph: [*'There's really that much of this aural energy in the
human race?'*]

Lachesis: [*You still don't understand. That's how much there
is*—]

Lois broke in. Her voice was trembling, although whether
with fear or ecstasy, Ralph could not tell.

[*'That's how much there is* in each one of us, Ralph. *That's how
much there is in every human being on the face of the earth!'*]

Ralph whistled softly and looked from Lachesis to Clotho.
They were nodding confirmation.

[*'You're saying we can stock up on this energy from whoever
happens to be handy? That it's safe for the people we take it from?'*]

Clotho: [*Yes. You could no more hurt them than you could empty
the Atlantic with a child's beach-pail.*]

Ralph hoped that was so, because he had an idea that he
and Lois had been unconsciously borrowing energy like mad
– it was the only explanation he could think of for all the
compliments he had been getting. People telling him that he
looked great. People telling him that he must be over his
insomnia, had to be, because he looked so rested and healthy.
That he looked younger.

Hell, he thought, *I am younger.*

The moon had set again, and Ralph realized with a start that
the sun would soon be coming up on Friday morning. It was
high time they got back to the central issue of this discussion.

[*'Let's cut to the chase here, fellows. Why have you gone to all this
trouble? What is it we're supposed to stop?'*]

And then, before either of them could reply, he was struck by a flash of insight too strong and bright to be questioned or denied.

[*'It's Susan Day, isn't it? He means to kill Susan Day. To assassinate her.'*]

Clotho: [*Yes, but—*]

Lachesis: [*– but that isn't what matters—*]

Ralph: [*'Come on, you guys – don't you think the time has come to lay the rest of your cards on the table?'*]

Lachesis: [*Yes, Ralph. That time has come.*]

There had been little or no touching among them since they had formed the circle and risen through the intervening hospital floors to the roof, but now Lachesis put a gentle, feather-light arm around Ralph's shoulders and Clotho took Lois by the arm, as a gentleman of a bygone age might have led a lady onto a dance-floor.

Scent of apples, taste of honey, texture of wool . . . but this time Ralph's delight in that mingled sensory input could not mask the deep disquiet he felt as Lachesis turned him to the left and then walked with him toward the edge of the flat hospital roof.

Like many larger and more important cities, Derry seemed to have been built in the most geographically unsuitable place the original settlers could find. The downtown area existed on the steep sides of a valley; the Kenduskeag River flowed sluggishly through the overgrown tangle of the Barrens at this valley's lowest level. From their vantage point atop the hospital, Derry looked like a town whose heart had been pierced by a narrow green dagger . . . except in the darkness, the dagger was black.

One side of the valley was Old Cape, site of a seedy postwar housing development and a glossy, flossy new mall. The other side contained most of what people meant when they talked about 'downtown'. Derry's downtown centered around Up-Mile Hill. Witcham Street took the most direct course up this hill, rising steeply before branching off into the tangle of streets (Harris Avenue was one of them) that made up the west side. Main Street diverged from Witcham halfway up the hill and headed southwest along the valley's shallower side. This area of town was known both as Main Street Hill and as Bassey Park. And, near the very top of Main Street's rise—

Lois, almost moaning: [*'Dear God, what is it?'*]

Ralph tried to say something comforting and produced

nothing but a feeble croak. Near the top of Main Street Hill, a huge black umbrella-shape floated above the ground, blotting out stars which had begun to pale toward morning. Ralph tried to tell himself at first that it was only smoke, that one of the warehouses out that way had caught on fire . . . perhaps even the abandoned railroad depot at the end of Neibolt Street. But the warehouses were farther south, the old depot was farther west, and if that evil-looking toadstool had really been smoke, the prevailing wind would be driving it across the sky in plumes and banners. That wasn't happening. Instead of dissipating, the silent blotch in the sky simply hung there, darker than the darkness.

And no one sees it, Ralph thought. *No one but me . . . and Lois . . . and the little bald doctors. The goddam little bald doctors.*

He squinted to make out the shape within the giant deathbag, although he didn't really need to; he had lived in Derry most of his life, and could almost have navigated its streets with his eyes closed (as long as he did not have to do so behind the wheel of his car, that was). Nevertheless, he *could* make out the building inside the deathbag, especially now that daylight was beginning to seep over the horizon. The flat circular roof which sat atop the curving glass-and-brick facade was a dead giveaway. This throwback to the 1950s, designed very much tongue-in-cheek by the famous architect (and one-time Derry resident) Benjamin Hanscom, was the new Derry Civic Center, a replacement for the one destroyed in the flood of '85.

Clotho turned Ralph to look at him.

[*You see, Ralph, you were right – he does mean to assassinate Susan Day . . . but not just Susan Day.*]

He paused, glanced at Lois, then turned his grave face back to Ralph.

[*That cloud – what you two quite correctly call a deathbag – means that in a sense he has already done what Atropos has set him on to do. There will be more than two thousand people there tonight . . . and Ed Deepneau means to kill them all. If the course of events is not changed, he* will *kill them all.*]

Lachesis stepped forward to join his colleague.

[*You, Ralph and Lois, are the only ones who can stop that from happening.*]

3

In his mind's eye Ralph saw the poster of Susan Day which had been propped in the empty storefront between the Rite Aid Pharmacy and Day Break, Sun Down. He remembered the words written in the dust on the outside of the window: KILL THIS CUNT. And something like that might well happen in Derry, that was the thing. Derry was not precisely *like* other places. It seemed to Ralph that the city's atmosphere had improved a great deal since the big flood eight years before, but it was still not precisely like other places. There was a mean streak in Derry, and when its residents got wrought up, they had been known to do some exceedingly ugly things.

He wiped at his lips and was momentarily distracted by the silky, distant feel of his hand on his mouth. He kept being reminded in different ways that his state of being had changed radically.

Lois, horrified: [*'How are we supposed to do it? If we can't go near Atropos or Ed, how are we supposed to stop it from happening?'*]

Ralph realized he could see her face quite clearly now; the day was brightening with the speed of stop-motion photography in an old Disney nature film.

[*'We'll phone in a bomb-threat, Lois. That should work.'*]

Clotho looked dismayed at this; Lachesis actually smacked his forehead with the heel of his hand before glancing nervously at the brightening sky. When he looked back at Ralph, his small face was full of something that might have been carefully muzzled panic.

[*That* won't *work, Ralph. Now listen to me, both of you, and listen carefully: whatever you do in the next fourteen hours or so, you must not underestimate the power of the forces Atropos unleashed when he first discovered Ed and then slashed his life-cord.*]

Ralph: [*'Why won't it work?'*]

Lachesis, sounding both angry and frightened: [*We can't just go on and on answering your questions, Ralph – from here on you're going to have to take things on trust. You know how fast time passes on this level; if we stay up here much longer, your chance to stop what is going to happen tonight at the Civic Center will be lost. You and Lois must step down again. You* must!]

Clotho held up a hand to his colleague, then turned back to Ralph and Lois.

[*I'll answer this one last question, although I'm sure that with a little thought you could answer it yourself. There have already been* twenty-three *bomb-threats regarding Susan Day's speech tonight. The police have explosives-sniffing dogs at the Civic Center, for the last forty-eight hours they have been X-raying all packages and deliveries which have come into the building, and they have been conducting spot searches, as well. They* expected *bomb-threats, and they take them seriously, but their assumption in this case is that they are being made by pro-life advocates who are trying to keep Ms Day from speaking.*]

Lois, dully: ['*Oh God – the little boy who cried wolf.*']

Clotho: [*Correct, Lois.*]

Ralph: ['*Has he planted a bomb? He has, hasn't he?*']

Bright light washed across the roof, stretching the shadows of the twirling heat–ventilators like taffy. Clotho and Lachesis looked at these shadows and then to the east, where the sun's top arc had broken over the horizon, with identical expressions of dismay.

Lachesis: [*We don't know, and it doesn't matter. You must stop the speech from happening, and there is only one way to do that: you must convince the women in charge to cancel Susan Day's appearance. Do you understand? She must not appear in the Civic Center tonight! You can't stop Ed, and you daren't try to approach Atropos, so you must stop Susan Day.*]

Ralph: ['*But—*']

It wasn't the strengthening sunlight that shut his mouth, or the growing look of harried fear on the faces of the little bald docs. It was Lois. She put a hand on his cheek and gave a small but decisive shake of the head.

['*No more. We have to go down, Ralph. Now.*']

Questions were circling in his mind like mosquitoes, but if she said there was no more time, there was no more time. He glanced at the sun, saw it had entirely cleared the horizon, and nodded. He slipped his arm around her waist.

Clotho, anxiously: [*Do not fail us, Ralph and Lois.*]

Ralph: ['*Save the pep-talk, short stuff. This isn't a football game.*']

Before either of them could reply, Ralph closed his eyes and concentrated on dropping back down to the Short-Time world.

Chapter Nineteen

1

There was that sensation of *blink!* and a chill morning breeze struck his face. Ralph opened his eyes and looked at the woman beside him. For just a moment he could see her aura wisping away behind her like the gauzy overskirt of a lady's ball-gown and then it was just Lois, looking twenty years younger than she had the week before . . . and also looking extremely out of place, in her light fall coat and good visiting-the-sick dress, here on the tar-and-gravel hospital roof.

Ralph hugged her tighter as she began to shiver. Of Lachesis and Clotho there was no sign.

Although they could be standing right beside us, Ralph thought. *Probably are, as a matter of fact.*

He suddenly thought of that old carny pitchman's line again, the one about how you had to pay if you wanted to play, so step right up, gentlemen, and lay your money down. But more often than not you were played instead of playing. Played for what? A sucker, of course. And why did he have that feeling now?

Because there were a lot of things you never found out, Carolyn said from inside his head. *They led you down a lot of interesting sidetracks and kept you away from the main point until it was too late for you to ask the questions they might not have wanted to answer . . . and I don't think something like that happens by accident, do you?*

No. He didn't.

That feeling of being pushed by invisible hands into some dark tunnel where anything might be waiting was stronger now. That sense of being manipulated. He felt small . . . and vulnerable . . . and pissed off.

407

'W-Well, we're b-b-back,' Lois said through her briskly chattering teeth. 'What time is it, do you think?'

It felt like about six o'clock, but when Ralph glanced down at his watch, he wasn't surprised to see it had stopped. He couldn't remember when he had last wound it. Tuesday morning, probably.

He followed Lois's gaze to the southwest and saw the Civic Center standing like an island in the middle of a parking-lot ocean. With the early morning sunlight kicking bright sheets of reflection from its curved banks of windows, it looked like an oversized version of the office building George Jetson worked in. The vast deathbag which had surrounded it only moments before was gone.

Oh, no it's not. Don't kid yourself, buddy. You may not be able to see it right now, but it's there, all right.

'Early,' he said, pulling her more tightly against him as the wind gusted, blowing his hair – hair that now had almost as much black in it as white – back from his forehead. 'But it's going to get late fast, I think.'

She took his meaning and nodded. 'Where are L-Lachesis and C-C—'

'On a level where the wind doesn't freeze your ass off, I imagine. Come on. Let's find a door and get the hell off this roof.'

She stayed where she was a moment longer, though, shivering and looking across town. 'What has he done?' she asked in a small voice. 'If he hasn't planted a bomb in there, what *can* he have done?'

'Maybe he *has* planted a bomb and the dogs with the educated noses just haven't found it yet. Or maybe it's something the dogs aren't trained to find. A canister stuck up in the rafters, say – a little something nasty Ed whipped up in the bathtub. Chemistry is what he did for a living, after all . . . at least until he gave up his job to become a full-time psycho. He could be planning to gas them like rats.'

'Oh Jesus, Ralph!' She put her hand to her chest just above the swell of her bosom and looked at him with wide, dismayed eyes.

'Come on, Lois. Let's get off this damned roof.'

This time she came willingly enough. Ralph led her toward the roof door . . . which, he fervently hoped, they would find unlocked.

'Two thousand people,' she almost moaned as they reached

the door. Ralph was relieved when the knob turned under his hand, but Lois seized his wrist with chilly fingers before he could pull the door open. Her uptilted face was full of frantic hope. 'Maybe those little men were lying, Ralph – maybe they've got their own axe to grind, something we couldn't even *hope* to understand, and they were lying.'

'I don't think they *can* lie,' he said slowly. 'That's the hell of it, Lois – I don't think they *can*. And then there's that.' He pointed at the Civic Center, at the dirty membrane they couldn't see but which both knew was still there. Lois would not turn to look at it. She put her cold hand over his instead, pulled the roof door open, and started down the stairs.

2

Ralph opened the door at the foot of the stairs, peeped into the sixth-floor corridor, saw that it was empty, and drew Lois out of the stairwell. They headed for the elevators, then stopped together outside an open door with DOCTOR'S LOUNGE printed on the wall beside it in bright red letters. Inside was the room they had seen on their way up to the roof with Clotho and Lachesis – Winslow Homer prints hanging crooked on the walls, a Silex standing on a hotplate, hideous Swedish Modern furniture. No one was in the room right now, but the TV bolted to the wall was playing nevertheless, and their old friend Lisette Benson was reading the morning news. Ralph remembered the day he and Lois and Bill had sat in Lois's living room, eating macaroni and cheese as they watched Lisette Benson report on the doll-throwing incident at WomanCare. Less than a month ago that had been. He suddenly remembered that Bill McGovern would never watch Lisette Benson again, or forget to lock the front door, and a sense of loss as fierce as a November gale swept through him. He could not completely believe it, at least not yet. How could Bill have died so quickly and so unceremoniously? *He would have hated it,* Ralph thought, *and not just because he would have considered dying of a heart attack in a hospital corridor in bad taste. He would've considered it bad theater, as well.*

But he had seen it happen, and Lois had actually felt it eating away at Bill's insides. That made Ralph think of the deathbag surrounding the Civic Center, and what was going to happen there if they didn't stop the speech. He started toward the elevator again, but Lois pulled him back. She was looking at the TV, fascinated.

'– will feel a lot of relief when tonight's speech by feminist abortion-rights advocate Susan Day is history,' Lisette Benson was saying, 'but the police aren't the *only* ones who will feel that way. Apparently both pro-life and pro-choice advocates are beginning to feel the strain of living on the edge of confrontation. John Kirkland is live at the Derry Civic Center this morning, and he has more. John?'

The pallid, unsmiling man standing next to Kirkland was Dan Dalton. The button on his shirt showed a scalpel descending toward an infant with its knees drawn up in the fetal position. This was surrounded by a red circle with a diagonal red line slashed across it. Ralph could see half a dozen police cars and two news trucks, one with the NBC logo on its side, in the background of the shot. A uniformed cop strolled across the lawn leading two dogs – a bloodhound and a German Shepherd – on leashes.

'That's right, Lisette, I'm here at the Civic Center, where the mood could be termed one of worry and quiet determination. With me is Dan Dalton, President of The Friends of Life organization which has been so vehemently opposed to Ms Day's speech. Mr Dalton, would you agree with that assessment of the situation?'

'That there's a lot of worry and determination in the air?' Dalton asked. To Ralph his smile looked both nervous and disdainful. 'Yes, I suppose you could put it that way. We're *worried* that Susan Day, one of this country's greatest unindicted criminals, will succeed in her efforts to confuse the central issue here in Derry: the murder of twelve to fourteen helpless unborn children each and every day.'

'But Mr Dalton—'

'And,' Dalton overrode him, 'we are *determined* to show a watching nation that we are not willing to be good Nazis, that we are not all cowed by the religion of political correctness – the dreaded pee-cee.'

'Mr Dalton—'

'We are also determined to show a watching nation that some of us are still capable of standing up for our beliefs, and to fulfill the sacred responsibility which a loving God has—'

'Mr Dalton, are The Friends of Life planning any sort of violent protest here?'

That shut him up for a moment and at least temporarily drained all the canned vitality from his face. With it gone, Ralph saw a dismaying thing: underneath his bluster, Dalton was scared to death.

'Violence?' he said at last. He brought the word out carefully, like something that could give his mouth a bad cut if mishandled. 'Good Lord, no. The Friends of Life reject the idea that two wrongs can ever make a right. We intend to mount a massive demonstration – we are being joined in this fight by pro-life advocates from Augusta, Portland, Portsmouth, and even Boston – but there will be no violence.'

'What about Ed Deepneau? Can you speak for him?'

Dalton's lips, already thinned down to little more than a seam, now seemed to disappear altogether. 'Mr Deepneau is no longer associated with The Friends of Life,' he said. Ralph thought he detected both fear and anger in Dalton's tone. 'Neither are Frank Felton, Sandra McKay, and Charles Pickering, in case you intended to ask.'

John Kirkland's glance at the camera was brief but telling. It said that he thought Dan Dalton was as nutty as a bag of trail-mix.

'Are you saying that Ed Deepneau and these other individuals – I'm sorry, I don't know who they are – have formed their own anti-abortion group? A kind of offshoot?'

'We are not anti-abortion, we are *pro-life*!' Dalton cried. 'There's a big difference, but you reporters seem to keep missing it!'

'So you don't know Ed Deepneau's whereabouts, or what – if anything – he might be planning?'

'I don't know where he is, I don't *care* where he is, and I don't care about his . . . *offshoots,* either.'

You're afraid, though, Ralph thought. *And if a self-righteous little prick like you is afraid, I think I'm terrified.*

Dalton started off. Kirkland, apparently deciding he wasn't wrung completely dry yet, walked after him, shaking out his microphone cord as he went.

'But isn't it true, Mr Dalton, that while he was a member of The Friends of Life, Ed Deepneau instigated *several* violence-oriented protests, including one last month where dolls soaked with artificial blood were thrown—'

'You're all the same, aren't you?' Dan Dalton asked. 'I'll pray for you, my friend.' He stalked off.

Kirkland looked after him for a moment, bemused, then

turned back to the camera. 'We tried to get hold of Mr Dalton's opposite number – Gretchen Tillbury, who has taken on the formidable job of coordinating this event for WomanCare – but she was unavailable for comment. We've heard that Ms Tillbury is at High Ridge, a women's shelter and halfway house which is owned and operated by WomanCare. Presumably, she and her associates are out there putting the finishing touches on plans for what they hope will be a safe, violence-free rally and speech at the Civic Center tonight.'

Ralph glanced at Lois and said, 'Okay – now we know where we're going, at least.'

The TV picture switched to Lisette Benson, in the studio. 'John, are there any real signs of possible violence at the Civic Center?'

Back to Kirkland, who had returned to his original location in front of the cop cars. He was holding up a small white rectangle with some printing on it in front of his tie. 'Well, the private security police on duty here found hundreds of these file-cards scattered on the Civic Center's front lawn this morning just after first light. One of the guards claims to have seen the vehicle they were dumped from. He says it was a Cadillac from the late sixties, either brown or black. He didn't get the license number, but says there was a sticker on the back bumper reading ABORTION IS MURDER, NOT CHOICE.'

Back to the studio, where Lisette Benson was looking mighty interested. 'What's on those cards, John?'

Back to Kirkland.

'I guess you'd have to say it's sort of a riddle.' He glanced down at the card. '"If you have a gun loaded with only two bullets and you're in a room with Hitler, Stalin, and an abortionist, what do you do?"' Kirkland looked back up into the camera and said, 'The answer printed on the other side, Lisette, is "Shoot the abortionist twice."'

'This is John Kirkland, reporting live from the Derry Civic Center.'

3

'I'm starving,' Lois said as Ralph carefully guided the Olds-mobile down the series of parking-garage ramps which would presumably set them free . . . if Ralph didn't miss any of the exit signs, that was. 'And if I'm exaggerating, I'm not doing it by much.'

'Me too,' Ralph said. 'And considering that we haven't eaten since Tuesday, I guess that's to be expected. We'll grab a good sit-down breakfast on the way out to High Ridge.'

'Do we have time?'

'We'll *make* time. After all, an army fights on its stomach.'

'I suppose so, although I don't feel very army-ish. Do you know where—'

'Hush a second, Lois.'

He stopped the Oldsmobile short, put the gearshift lever in Park, and listened. There was a clacking sound from under the hood that he didn't like very much. Of course the concrete walls of places like this tended to magnify sounds, but still . . .

'Ralph?' she asked nervously. 'Don't tell me something's wrong with the car. Just don't tell me that, okay?'

'I think it's fine,' he said, and began creeping toward daylight again. 'I've just kind of fallen out of touch with old Nellie here since Carol died. Forgotten what kinds of sounds she makes. You were going to ask me something, weren't you?'

'If you know where that shelter is. High Ridge.'

Ralph shook his head. 'Somewhere out near the Newport town line is all I know. I don't think they're supposed to tell men where it is. I was kind of hoping you might have heard.'

Lois shook her head. 'I never had to use a place like that, thank God. We'll have to call her. The Tillbury woman. You've met her with Helen, so you can talk to her. She'll listen to you.'

She gave him a brief glance, one that warmed his heart – *Anyone with any sense would listen to you, Ralph,* it said – but Ralph shook his head. 'I bet the only calls she's taking today are ones that come from the Civic Center or from wherever Susan Day is.' He shot her a glance. 'You know, that woman's got a lot of guts, coming here. Either that or she's donkey-dumb.'

'Probably a little of both. If Gretchen Tillbury won't take a call, how will we get in touch with her?'

'Well, I tell you what. I was a salesman for a lot of what Faye Chapin would call my real life, and I bet I can still be inventive when I need to be.' He thought of the information-lady with the orange aura and grinned. 'Persuasive, too, maybe.'

'Ralph?' Her voice was small.

'What, Lois?'

'This feels like real life to me.'

He patted her hand. 'I know what you mean.'

4

A familiar skinny face poked out of the pay-booth of the hospital parking garage; a familiar grin – one from which at least half a dozen teeth had gone AWOL – brightened it.

'Eyyyy, Ralph, dat you? Goddam if it ain't! Beauty! Beauty!'

'Trigger?' Ralph asked slowly. 'Trigger Vachon?'

'None udder!' Trigger flipped his lank brown hair out of his eyes so he could get a better look at Lois. 'And who's dis marigold here? I know her from somewhere, goddam if I don't!'

'Lois Chasse,' Ralph said, taking his parking ticket from its place over the sun-visor. 'You might have known her husband, Paul—'

'Goddam right I did!' Trigger cried. 'We was weekend warriors togedder, back in nineteen-seb'ny, maybe seb'ny-one! Closed down Nan's Tavern more'n once! My suds n body! How is Paul dese days, ma'am?'

'Mr Chasse passed on a little over two years ago,' Lois said.

'Oh, damn! I'm sorry to hear it. He was a champ of a guy, Paul Chasse. Just an all-around champ of a guy. Everybody liked him.' Trigger looked as distressed as he might have done if she had told him it had happened only that morning.

'Thank you, Mr Vachon.' Lois glanced at her watch, then looked up at Ralph. Her stomach rumbled, as if to add one final point to the argument.

Ralph handed his parking ticket through the open window of the car, and as Trigger took it, Ralph suddenly realized the stamp would show that he and Lois had been here since Tuesday night. Almost sixty hours.

'What happened to the dry-cleaning business, Trig?' he asked hastily.

'Ahhh, dey laid me off,' Trigger said. 'Didn't I tell you? Laid almos everybody off. I was downhearted at first, but I caught on here last April, and . . . eyyy! I like dis all kindsa better. I got my little TV for when it's slow, and there ain't nobody beepin their horns at me if I don't go the firs second a traffic-light turns green, or cuttin me off out dere on the Extension. Everyone in a hurry to get to the nex place, dey are, jus why I dunno. Also, I tell you what, Ralph: dat damn van was colder'n a witch's tit in the winter. Pardon me, ma'am.'

Lois did not reply. She seemed to be studying the backs of her hands with great interest. Ralph, meanwhile, watched with relief as Trigger crumpled up the parking ticket and tossed it into his wastebasket without so much as a glance at the time-and-date stamp. He punched one of the buttons on his cash-register, and $0.00 popped up on the screen in the booth's window.

'Jeez, Trig, that's really nice of you,' Ralph said.

'Eyyy, don't mention it,' Trigger said, and grandly punched another button. This one raised the barrier in front of the booth. 'Good to see you. Say, you member dat time out by the airport? Gosh! Hotter'n hell, it was, and dose two fella almos got in a punchup? Den it rained like a bugger. Hailed some, too. You was walkin and I give you a ride home. Oney seen you once or twice since den.' He took a closer look at Ralph. 'You look a hell of a lot better today than you did den, Ralphie, I'll tell you dat. Hell, you don't look a day over fifty-five. Beauty!'

Beside him, Lois's stomach rumbled again, louder this time. She went on studying the backs of her hands.

'I feel a little older than that, though,' Ralph said. 'Listen, Trig, it was good to see you, but we ought to—'

'Damn,' Trigger said, and his eyes had gone distant. 'I had sumpin to tell you, Ralph. At least I *t'ink* I did. Bout dat day. Gosh, ain't I got a dumb old head!'

Ralph waited a moment longer, uncomfortably poised between impatience and curiosity. 'Well, don't feel bad about it, Trig. That was a long time ago.'

'What the *hell* . . .?' Trigger asked himself. He gazed up at the ceiling of his little booth, as if the answer might be written there.

'Ralph, we ought to go,' Lois said. 'It's not just wanting breakfast, either.'

'Yes. You're right.' He got the Oldsmobile rolling slowly again. 'If you think of it, Trig, give me a call. I'm in the book. It was good to see you.'

Trigger Vachon ignored this completely; he no longer seemed aware of Ralph at all, in fact. 'Was it sumpin we *saw*?' he enquired of the ceiling. 'Or sumpin we *did*? Gosh!'

He was still looking up there and scratching the frizz of hair on the nape of his neck when Ralph turned left and, with a final wave, guided his Oldsmobile down Hospital Drive toward the low brick building which housed WomanCare.

5

Now that the sun was up, there was only a single security guard, and no demonstrators at all. Their absence made Ralph remember all the jungle epics he'd seen as a young man, especially the part where the native drums would stop and the hero – Jon Hall or Frank Buck – would turn to his head bearer and say he didn't like it, it was too quiet. The guard took a clipboard from under his arm, squinted at Ralph's Olds, and wrote something down – the plate number, Ralph supposed. Then he came ambling toward them along the leaf-strewn walk.

At this hour of the morning, Ralph had his pick of the ten-minute spaces across from the building. He parked, got out, then came around to open Lois's door, as he had been trained.

'How do you want to handle this?' she asked as he took her hand and helped her out.

'We'll probably have to be a little cute, but let's not get carried away. Right?'

'Right.' She ran a nervous, patting hand down the front of her coat as they crossed, then flashed a megawatt smile at the security guard. 'Good morning, officer.'

'Morning.' He glanced at his watch. 'I don't think there's anyone in there just yet but the receptionist and the cleaning woman.'

'The receptionist is who we want to see,' Lois said cheerfully. It was news to Ralph. 'Barbie Richards. Her aunt Simone has a message for her to pass along. Very important. Just say it's Lois Chasse.'

The security guard thought this over, then nodded toward the door. 'That won't be necessary. You go on right ahead, ma'am.'

Lois said, smiling more brilliantly than ever, 'We won't be two shakes, will we, Norton?'

'Shake and a half, more like it,' Ralph agreed. As they approached the building and left the security man behind he leaned toward her and murmured: 'Norton? Good God, Lois, *Norton*?'

'It was the first name that came into my head,' she replied. 'I guess I was thinking of *The Honeymooners* – Ralph and Norton, remember?'

'Yes,' he said. 'One of these days, Alice . . . pow! Right to da moon!'

Two of the three doors were locked, but the one on the far left opened and they went in. Ralph squeezed Lois's hand and felt her answering squeeze. He sensed a strong focusing of his concentration at the same moment, a narrowing and brightening of will and awareness. All around him the eye of the world seemed to first blink and then open wide. All around them both.

The reception area was almost ostentatiously plain. The posters on the walls were mostly the sort foreign tourist agencies send out for the price of postage. The only exception was to the right of the receptionist's desk: a large black-and-white photo of a young woman in a maternity smock. She was sitting on a barstool with a martini glass in one hand. WHEN YOU'RE PREGNANT, YOU NEVER DRINK ALONE, the copy beneath the photo read. There was no indication that in a room or rooms behind this pleasant, unremarkable business space, abortions were done on demand.

Well, Ralph thought, *what did you expect? An advertisement? A poster of aborted fetuses in a galvanized garbage pail between the one showing the Isle of Capri and the one of the Italian Alps? Get real, Ralph.*

To their left, a heavyset woman in her late forties or early fifties was washing the top of a glass coffee-table; there was a little cart filled with various cleaning implements parked beside her. She was buried in a dark blue aura speckled with unhealthy-looking black dots which swarmed like queer insects over the places where her heart and lungs were,

417

and she was looking at the newcomers with undisguised suspicion.

Straight ahead, another woman was watching them carefully, although without the janitor's suspicion. Ralph recognized her from the TV news report on the day of the doll-throwing incident. Simone Castonguay's niece was dark-haired, about thirty-five, and close to gorgeous even at this hour of the morning. She sat behind a severe gray metal desk that perfectly complemented her looks and within a forest-green aura which looked much healthier than the cleaning woman's. A cut-glass vase filled with fall flowers stood on one corner of her desk.

She smiled tentatively at them, showing no immediate recognition of Lois, then wiggled the tip of one finger at the clock on the wall. 'We don't open until eight,' she said, 'and I don't think we could help you today in any case. The doctors are all off – I mean, Dr Hamilton is technically covering, but I'm not even sure I could get to her. There's a lot going on – this is a big day for us.'

'I know,' Lois said, and gave Ralph's hand another squeeze before letting it go. He heard her voice in his mind for a moment, very faint – like a bad overseas telephone conversation – but audible:

[*'Stay where you are, Ralph. She's got—'*]

Lois sent him a picture which was even fainter than the thought, and gone almost as soon as Ralph glimpsed it. This sort of communication was a lot easier on the upper levels, but what he got was enough. The hand with which Barbara Richards had pointed at the clock was now resting easily on top of the desk, but the other was underneath it, where a small white button was mounted on one side of the kneehole. If either of them showed the slightest sign of odd behavior, she would push the button, summoning first their friend with the clipboard who was posted outside, and then most of the private security cops in Derry.

And I'm the one she's watching most carefully, because I'm the man, Ralph thought.

As Lois approached the reception desk, Ralph had an unsettling thought: given the current atmosphere in Derry, that sort of sex-discrimination – unconscious but very real – could get this pretty black-haired woman hurt . . . maybe even killed. He remembered Leydecker telling him that one of Ed's small cadre of co-crazies was a woman. *Pasty complexion,* he'd said,

lots of acne, glasses so thick they make her eyes look like poached eggs.
Sandra something, her name was. And if Sandra Something
had approached Ms Richards's desk as Lois was approaching it
now, first opening her purse and then reaching into it, would
the woman dressed in the forest-green aura have pushed the
hidden alarm button?

'You probably don't remember me, Barbara,' Lois was
saying, 'because I haven't seen you much since you were in
college, when you were going with the Sparkmeyer boy—'

'Oh my God, Lennie Sparkmeyer, I haven't thought of him
in years,' Barbara Richards said, and gave an embarrassed little
laugh. 'But I remember you. Lois Delancey. Aunt Simone's
poker buddy. Do you guys still play?'

'It's Chasse, not Delancey, and we still do.' Lois sounded
delighted that Barbara had remembered her, and Ralph hoped
she wouldn't lose track of what they were supposed to be doing
here. He needn't have worried. 'Anyway, Simone sent me with
a message for Gretchen Tillbury.' She brought a piece of paper
out of her purse. 'I wonder if you could give it to her?'

'I doubt very much if I'll even talk to Gretchen on the phone
today,' Richards said. 'She's as busy as the rest of us. Busier.'

'I'll bet.' Lois tinkled an amazingly genuine little laugh. 'I
guess there's no real hurry about this, though. Gretchen has got
a niece who's been granted a full scholarship at the University
of New Hampshire. Have you ever noticed how much harder
people try to get in touch when it's bad news they have to pass
on? Strange, isn't it?'

'I suppose so,' Richards said, reaching for the folded slip of
paper. 'Anyway, I'll be happy to put this in Gretchen's—'

Lois seized her wrist, and a flash of gray light – so bright
Ralph had to squint his eyes against it to keep from being
dazzled – leaped up the woman's arm, shoulder, and neck. It
spun around her head in a brief halo, then disappeared.

No, it didn't, Ralph thought. *It didn't disappear, it sank
in.*

'What was that?' the cleaning woman asked suspiciously.
'What was that bang?'

'A car backfired,' Ralph said. 'That's all.'

'Huh,' she said. 'Goshdarn men think they know everything.
Did you hear that, Barbie?'

'Yes,' Richards said. She sounded entirely normal to Ralph,
and he knew that the cleaning woman would not be able to see
the pearl gray mist which had now filled her eyes. 'I think he's

right, but would you check with Peter outside? We can't be too careful.'

'You goshdarn *bet*,' the cleaning woman said. She set her Windex bottle down, crossed to the doors (sparing Ralph a final dark look which said *You're old but I just goshdarn bet you still have a penis down there somewhere*), and went out.

As soon as she was gone, Lois leaned over the desk. 'Barbara, my friend and I have to talk to Gretchen this morning,' she said. 'Face to face.'

'She's not here. She's at High Ridge.'

'Tell us how to get there.'

Richards's gaze drifted to Ralph. He found her gray, pupil-less eyesockets profoundly unsettling. It was like looking at a piece of classic statuary which had somehow come to life. Her dark green aura had paled considerably as well.

No, he thought. *It's been temporarily overlaid by Lois's gray, that's all.*

Lois glanced briefly around, followed Barbara Richards's gaze to Ralph, then turned back to her again. 'Yes, he's a man, but this time it's okay. I promise you that. Neither one of us means any harm to Gretchen Tillbury or any of the women at High Ridge, but we have to talk to her, *so tell us how to get there.*' She touched Richards's hand again, and more gray flashed up Richards's arm.

'Don't hurt her,' Ralph said.

'I won't, but she's going to talk.' She bent closer to Richards. 'Where is it? Come on, Barbara.'

'You take Route 33 out of Derry,' she said. 'The old Newport Road. After you've gone about ten miles, there'll be a big red farmhouse on your left. There are two barns behind it. You take your first left after that—'

The cleaning woman came back in. 'Peter didn't hear –' She stopped abruptly, perhaps not liking the way Lois was bent over her friend's desk, perhaps not liking the blank look in her friend's eyes.

'Barbara? Are you all ri—'

'Be quiet,' Ralph said in a low, friendly voice. 'They're talking.' He took the cleaning woman's arm just above the elbow, feeling a brief but powerful pulse of energy as he did so. For a moment all the colors in the world brightened further. The cleaning woman's name was Rachel Anderson. She'd been married once, to a man who'd beaten her hard and often until he disappeared eight years ago. Now she had a dog and her friends at WomanCare, and that was enough.

'Oh sure,' Rachel Anderson said in a dreamy, thoughtful voice. 'They're talking, and Peter says everything's okay, so I guess I better just be quiet.'

'What a good idea,' Ralph said, still holding her upper arm lightly.

Lois took a quick look around to confirm Ralph had the situation under control, then turned back to Barbara Richards once again. 'Take a left after the red farmhouse with the two barns. Okay, I've got that. What then?'

'You'll be on a dirt road. It goes up a long hill – about a mile and a half – and then ends at a white farmhouse. That's High Ridge. It's got the most lovely view—'

'I'll bet,' Lois said. 'Barbara, it was great to see you again. Now my friend and I—'

'Great to see you, too, Lois,' Richards said in a distant, uninterested voice.

'Now my friend and I are going to leave. Everything is all right.'

'Good.'

'You won't need to remember any of this,' Lois said.

'Absolutely not.'

Lois started to turn away, then turned back and plucked up the piece of paper she had taken from her purse. It had fallen to the desk when Lois grabbed the woman's wrist.

'Why don't you go back to work, Rachel?' Ralph asked the cleaning lady. He let go of her arm carefully, ready to grab it again at once if she showed signs of needing reinforcement.

'Yes, I better go back to work,' she said, sounding much more friendly. 'I want to be done here by noon, so I can go out to High Ridge and help make signs.'

Lois joined Ralph as Rachel Anderson drifted back to her cart of cleaning supplies. Lois looked both amazed and a little shaky. 'They'll be okay, won't they, Ralph?'

'Yes, I'm sure they will be. Are *you* all right? Not going to faint or anything like that?'

'I'm okay. Can you remember the directions?'

'Of course – she's talking about the place that used to be Barrett's Orchards. Carolyn and I used to go out there every fall to pick apples and buy cider until they sold out in the early eighties. To think *that's* High Ridge.'

'Be amazed later, Ralph – I really *am* starving to death.'

'All right. What was the note, by the way? The note about the niece with the full scholarship at UNH?'

She flashed him a little smile and handed it to him. It was her light-bill for the month of September.

6

'Were you able to leave your message?' the security guard asked as they came out and started down the walk.

'Yes, thanks,' Lois said, turning on the megawatt smile again. She kept moving, though, and her hand was gripping Ralph's very tightly. He knew how she felt; he hadn't the slightest idea how long the suggestions they had given the two women would hold.

'Good,' the guard said, following them to the end of the walk. 'This is gonna be a long, long day. I'll be glad when it's over. You know how many security people we're gonna have here from noon until midnight? A dozen. And that's just *here*. They're gonna have over forty at the Civic Center – that's in addition to the local cops.'

And it won't do a damned bit of good, Ralph thought.

'And what for? So one blonde with an attitude can run her mouth.' He looked at Lois as if he expected her to accuse him of being a male sexist oinker, but Lois only renewed her smile.

'I hope everything goes well for you, Officer,' Ralph said, and then led Lois back across the street to the Oldsmobile. He started it up and turned laboriously around in the WomanCare driveway, expecting either Barbara Richards, Rachel Anderson, or maybe both of them to come rushing out through the front door, eyes wild and fingers pointing. He finally got the Olds headed in the right direction and let out a long sigh of relief. Lois looked over at him and nodded in sympathy.

'I thought I was the salesman,' Ralph said, 'but man, I've *never* seen a selling job like that.'

Lois smiled demurely and clasped her hands in her lap.

They were approaching the hospital parking garage when Trigger came rushing out of his little booth, waving his arms. Ralph's first thought was that they weren't going to make a clean getaway after all – the security guard with the clipboard had tipped to something suspicious and phoned or radioed Trigger to stop them. Then he saw the look – out of

breath but happy – and what Trigger had in his right hand.
It was a very old and very battered black wallet. It flapped
open and closed like a toothless mouth with each wave of his
right arm.

'Don't worry,' Ralph said, slowing the Olds down. 'I don't
know what he wants, but I'm pretty sure it's not trouble. At
least not yet.'

'I don't care *what* he wants. All *I* want is to get out of here
and eat some food. If he starts to show you his fishing pictures,
Ralph, I'll step on the gas pedal myself.'

'Amen,' Ralph said, knowing perfectly well that it wasn't
fishing pictures Trigger Vachon had in mind. He still wasn't
clear on everything, but one thing he knew for sure: nothing
was happening by chance. Not anymore. This was the Purpose
with a vengeance. He pulled up beside Trigger and pushed
the button that lowered his window. It went down with an
ill-tempered whine.

'Eyyy, Ralph!' Trigger cried. 'I t'ought I missed you!'

'What is it, Trig? We're in kind of a hurry—'

'Yeah, yeah, dis won't take but a secon. I got it right here
in my wallet, Ralph. Man, I keep all my paperwork in here,
and I never lose a t'ing out of it.'

He spread the old billfold's limp jaws, revealing a few
crumpled bills, a celluloid accordion of pictures (and damned if
Ralph didn't catch a glimpse of Trigger holding up a big bass in
one of them), and what looked like at least forty business cards,
most of them creased and limber with age. Trigger began to go
through these with the speed of a veteran bank-teller counting
currency.

'I never t'row dese t'ings out, me,' Trigger said. 'They're
great to write stuff on, better'n a notebook, and free. Now just
a secon . . . just a secon, oh you damn t'ing, where you be?'

Lois gave Ralph an impatient, worried look and pointed up
the road. Ralph ignored both the look and the gesture. He had
begun to feel a strange tingling in his chest. In his mind's eye
he saw himself reaching out with his index finger and drawing
something in the foggy condensate that had appeared on the
windshield of Trigger's van as a result of a summer storm
fifteen months ago – cold rain on a hot day.

'Ralph, you 'member the scarf Deepneau was wearin dat day?
White, wit some kind of red marks on it?'

'Yes, I remember,' Ralph said. *Cuntlicker,* Ed had told the
heavyset guy. *Fucked your mother and licked her cunt.* And yes,

he remembered the scarf – of course he did. But the red thing hadn't been just marks or a splotch or a meaningless bit of pattern; it had been an ideogram or ideograms. The sudden sinking in the pit of his stomach told Ralph that Trigger could quit rummaging through his old business cards right now. He knew what this was about. He knew.

'Was you in da war, Ralph?' Trigger asked. 'The big one? Number Two?'

'In a way, I guess,' Ralph said. 'I fought most of it in Texas. I went overseas in early '45, but I was rear-echelon all the way.'

Trigger nodded. 'Dat means Europe,' he said. '*Wasn't* no rear-echelon in the Pacific, not by the end.'

'England,' Ralph said. 'Then Germany.'

Trigger was still nodding, pleased. 'If you'd been in da Pacific, you woulda known the stuff on that scarf wasn't Chinese.'

'It was *Japanese*, wasn't it? Wasn't it, Trig?'

Trigger nodded. In one hand he held a business card plucked from among many. On the blank side, Ralph saw a rough approximation of the double symbol they had seen on Ed's scarf, the double symbol he himself had drawn in the windshield mist.

'What are you talking about?' Lois asked, now sounding not impatient but just plain scared.

'I should have known,' Ralph heard himself say in a faint, horrified voice. 'I still should have *known.*'

'Known *what*?' She grabbed his shoulder and shook it. 'Known *what*?'

He didn't answer. Feeling like a man in a dream, he reached out and took the card. Trigger Vachon was no longer smiling, and his dark eyes studied Ralph's face with grave consideration. 'I copied it before it could melt offa da windshield,' Trigger said, 'cause I knew I seen it before, and by the time I got home dat night, I knew where. My big brother, Marcel, fought dar las year of the war in the Pacific. One of the t'ings he brought back was a scarf with dat same two marks on it, in dat same red. I ast him, jus to be sure, and he wrote it on dat card.' Trigger pointed to the card Ralph was holding between his fingers. 'I meant to tell you as soon as I saw you again, only I forgot until today. I was glad I finally remembered, but lookin at you now, I guess it woulda been better if I'd stayed forgetful.'

'No, it's okay.'

Lois took the card from him. 'What is it? What does it mean?'

'Tell you later.' Ralph reached for the gearshift. His heart felt like a stone in his chest. Lois was looking at the symbols on the blank side of the card, allowing Ralph to see the printed side. R.H. FOSTER, WELLS & DRY-WALLS, it said. Below this, Trigger's big brother had printed a single word in black capital letters.

KAMIKAZE.

PART III

The Crimson King

We are old-timers,
each of us holds a locked razor.
Robert Lowell
'Walking in the Blue'

Chapter Twenty

1

There was only one conversational exchange between them as the Oldsmobile rolled up Hospital Drive, and it was a brief one.

'Ralph?'

He glanced over at her, then quickly back at the road. That clacking sound under the hood had begun again, but Lois hadn't mentioned it yet. He hoped she wasn't going to do so now.

'I think I know where he is. Ed, I mean. I was pretty sure, even up on the roof, that I recognized that ramshackle old building they showed us.'

'What is it? And where?'

'It's an airplane garage. A whatdoyoucallit. Hangar.'

'Oh my God,' Ralph said. 'Coastal Air, on the Bar harbor Road?'

Lois nodded. 'They have charter flights, seaplane rides, things like that. One Saturday when we were out for a drive, Mr Chasse went in and asked a man who worked there how much he'd charge to take us for a sightseeing hop over the islands. The man said forty dollars, which was much more than we could have afforded to spend on something like that, and in the summer I'm sure the man would've stuck to his guns, but it was only April, and Mr Chasse was able to dicker him down to twenty. I thought that was still too much to spend on a ride that didn't even last an hour, but I'm glad we went. It was scary, but it was beautiful.'

'Like the auras,' Ralph said.

'Yes, like . . .' Her voice wavered. Ralph looked over and saw tears trickling down her plump cheeks. '. . . like the auras.'

'Don't cry, Lois.'

She found a Kleenex in her purse and wiped her eyes. 'I can't help it. That Japanese word on the card means kamikaze, doesn't it, Ralph? Divine Wind.' She paused, lips trembling. 'Suicide pilot.'

Ralph nodded. He was gripping the wheel very tightly. 'Yes,' he said. 'That's what it means. Suicide pilot.'

2

Route 33 – known as Newport Avenue in town – passed within four blocks of Harris Avenue, but Ralph had absolutely no intention of breaking their long fast over on the west side. The reason was as simple as it was compelling: he and Lois couldn't afford to be seen by any of their old friends, not looking fifteen or twenty years younger than they had on Monday.

Had any of those old friends reported them missing to the police yet? Ralph knew it was possible, but felt he could reasonably hope that so far they had escaped much notice and concern, at least from his circle; Faye and the rest of the folks who hung out in the picnic area near the Extension would be in too much of a dither over the passing of not just one Old Crock colleague but a pair of them to spend much time wondering about where Ralph Roberts had gotten his skinny old ass off to.

Both Bill and Jimmy could have been waked, funeralled, and buried by now, he thought.

'If we've got time for breakfast, Ralph, find a place as quick as you can – I'm so hungry I could eat a horse with the hide still on!'

They were almost a mile west of the hospital now – far enough away to allow Ralph to feel reasonably safe – and he saw the Derry Diner up ahead. As he signalled and turned into the parking lot, he realized he hadn't been here since Carol had gotten sick . . . a year at least, maybe more.

'Here we are,' he told Lois. 'And we're not just going to eat, we're going to eat all we can. We may not get another chance today.'

She grinned like a schoolkid. 'You've just put your finger on one of my great talents, Ralph.' She wriggled a little on the seat. 'Also, I have to spend a penny.'

Ralph nodded. No food since Tuesday, and no bathroom stops, either. Lois could spend her penny; he intended to pop into the men's room and let go of a couple of dollars.

'Come on,' he said, turning off the motor and silencing that troublesome clacking under the hood. 'First the bathroom, then the foodquake.'

On the way to the door she told him (speaking in a voice Ralph found just a trifle too casual) that she didn't think either Mina or Simone would have reported her missing, at least not yet. When Ralph turned his head to ask her why, he was amazed and amused to see she was blushing rosy-red.

'They both know I've had a crush on you for years.'

'Are you kidding?'

'Of course not,' she said, sounding a bit put out. 'Carolyn knew, too. Some women would have minded, but she understood how harmless it was. How harmless *I* was. She was such a dear, Ralph.'

'Yes. She was.'

'Anyway, they'll probably assume that we've . . . you know . . .'

'Gone off on a little French leave?'

Lois laughed. 'Something like that.'

'Would you *like* to go off on a little French leave, Lois?'

She stood on tiptoe and nibbled briefly at his earlobe. 'If we get out of this alive, you just ask me.'

He kissed the corner of her mouth before pushing open the door. 'You can count on it, lady.'

They made for the bathrooms, and when Ralph rejoined her, Lois looked both thoughtful and a little shaken. 'I can't believe it's me,' she said in a low voice. 'I mean, I must have spent at least two minutes staring at myself in the mirror, and I still can't believe it. The crow's-feet around my eyes are all gone, and Ralph . . . my *hair* . . .' Those dark Spanish eyes of hers looked up at him, filled with brilliance and wonder. 'And *you*! My God, I doubt if you looked this good when you were forty.'

'I didn't, but you should have seen me when I was thirty. I was an *animal*.'

She giggled. 'Come on, fool, let's sit down and murder some calories.'

3

'Lois?'

She glanced up from the menu she'd plucked from a little collection of them filed between the salt and pepper shakers.

'When I was in the bathroom, I tried to make the auras come back. This time I couldn't do it.'

'Why would you *want* to, Ralph?'

He shrugged, not wanting to tell her about the feeling of paranoia that had dropped over him as he stood at the basin in the little bathroom, washing his hands and looking into his own strangely young face in the water-spotted mirror. It had suddenly occurred to him that he might not be alone in there. Worse, Lois might not be alone next door in the women's room. Atropos might be creeping up behind her, completely unseen, diamond-cluster earrings glittering from his tiny lobes . . . scalpel outstretched . . .

Then, instead of Lois's earrings or McGovern's Panama, his mind's eye had conjured the jump-rope Atropos had been using when Ralph had spotted him

(*three-six-nine, hon, the goose drank wine*)

in the vacant lot between the bakery and the tanning salon, the jump-rope which had once been the prized possession of a little girl who had stumbled during a game of apartment-tag, fallen out of a second-storey window, and died of a broken neck (*what a dreadful accident, she had her whole life ahead of her, if there's a God why does He let things like that happen,* and so on and so on, not to mention blah-blah-blah).

He had told himself to stop it, that things were bad enough without his indulging in gruesome fantasies of Atropos slashing Lois's balloon-string, but it didn't help much . . . mostly because he knew Atropos might really be here with them in the restaurant, and Atropos could do anything to them he liked. Anything at all.

Lois reached across the table and touched the back of his hand. 'Don't worry. The colors will come back. They always do.'

'I suppose.' He took a menu of his own, opened it, and cast an eye down the breakfast bill of fare. His initial impression was that he wanted one of everything.

'The first time you saw Ed acting crazy, he was coming out

of the Derry Airport,' Lois said. 'Now we know why. He was taking flying lessons, wasn't he?'

'Of course. While Trig was giving me a lift back to Harris Avenue, he even mentioned that you need a pass to come out that way, through the service gate. He asked me if I knew how Ed had gotten one, and I said I didn't. Now I do. They must give them to all the General Aviation flying students.'

'Do you think Helen knew about his hobby?' Lois asked. 'She probably didn't, did she?'

'I'm sure she didn't. I'll bet he switched over to Coastal Air right after he ran into the guy from West Side Gardeners, too. That little episode could have convinced him he was losing control, and he might do well to move his lessons a little farther away from home.'

'Or maybe it was Atropos who convinced him,' Lois said bleakly. 'Atropos or someone from even higher up.'

Ralph didn't care for the idea, but it felt right, just the same. *Entities,* he thought, and shivered. *The Crimson King.*

'They're dancing him around like a puppet on a string, aren't they?' Lois asked.

'Atropos, you mean?'

'No. Atropos is a nasty little bugger, but otherwise I think he's not much different from Mr C and Mr L – low-level help, maybe only a step above unskilled labor in the grand scheme of things.'

'Janitors.'

'Well, yes, maybe,' Lois agreed. 'Janitors and gofers. Atropos is probably the one who's done most of the actual work on Ed, and I'd bet a cookie it's work he loves, but I'd bet my *house* that his orders come from higher up. Does that sound more or less on the beam to you?'

'Yes. We'll probably never know exactly how nuts he was before this started, or exactly when Atropos cut his balloon-string, but the thing I'm most curious about at this moment is pretty mundane. I'd like to know how in the hell he went Charlie Pickering's bail and how he paid for his damned flying lessons.'

Before Lois could reply, a waitress approached them, digging an order-pad and a ballpoint pen out of the pocket of her apron. 'Help you guys?'

'I'd like a cheese and mushroom omelet,' Ralph said.

'Uh-huh.' She switched her cud from one side of her jaw to the other. 'Two-egg or three-egg, hon?'

'Four, if that's okay.'

She raised her eyebrows slightly and jotted on the pad. 'Okay by me if it's okay by you. Anything with that?'

'Yes, please. A glass of OJ, large, an order of bacon, an order of sausage, and an order of home fries. Better make that a *double* order of home fries.' He paused, thinking, then grinned. 'Oh, and do you have any Danish left?'

'I think I might have one cheese and one apple.' She glanced up at him. 'You a little hungry, hon?'

'Feel like I haven't eaten for a week,' Ralph said. 'I'll have the cheese Danish. And coffee to start. Lots of black coffee. Did you get all that?'

'Oh, I got it, hon. I just want to see what you look like when you leave.' She looked at Lois. 'How 'bout you, ma'am?'

Lois smiled sweetly. 'I'll have what he's having. *Hon.*'

4

Ralph looked past the retreating waitress to the clock on the wall. It was only ten past seven, and that was good. They could be out at Barrett's Orchards in less than half an hour, and with their mental lasers trained on Gretchen Tillbury, it was possible that the Susan Day speech could be called off – aborted, if you liked – as early as 9:00 a.m. Yet instead of relief he felt relentless, gnawing anxiety. It was like having an itch in a place your fingers cannot quite reach.

'All right,' he said. 'Let's put it together. I think we can assume that Ed's been concerned about abortion for a long time, that he's probably been a pro-life supporter for years. Then he starts to lose sleep . . . hear voices . . .'

'. . . see little bald men . . .'

'Well, one in particular,' Ralph agreed. 'Atropos becomes his guru, filling him in on the Crimson King, the Centurions, the whole nine yards. When Ed talked to me about King Herod—'

'—he was *thinking* about Susan Day,' Lois finished. 'Atropos has been . . . what do they say on TV? . . . psyching him up. Turning him into a guided missile. Where did Ed get that scarf, do you think?'

'Atropos,' Ralph said. 'Atropos has got a lot of stuff like that, I'll bet.'

'And what do you suppose he's got in the plane he'll be flying tonight?' Lois's voice was trembling. 'Explosives or poison gas?'

'Explosives would seem the more likely bet if he really is planning to get everyone; a strong wind could create problems for him if it's gas.' Ralph took a sip of his water and was interested to see that his hand was not quite steady. 'On the other hand, we don't know what goodies he might have been cooking up in his laboratory, do we?'

'No,' Lois said in a small voice.

Ralph put his water-glass down. 'What he's planning to use doesn't interest me very much.'

'What does?'

The waitress came back with fresh coffee, and the smell alone seemed to light up Ralph's nerves like neon. He and Lois grabbed their cups and began to sip as soon as she had started away. The coffee was strong and hot enough to burn Ralph's lips, but it was heaven. When he set his cup back in its saucer again, it was half empty and there was a very warm place in his midsection, as if he had swallowed a live ember. Lois was looking at him somberly over the rim of her own cup.

'What interests me,' Ralph told her, 'is *us*. You said Atropos has turned Ed into a guided missile. That's right; that's exactly what the World War II kamikaze pilots were. Hitler had his V-2s; Hirohito had his Divine Wind. The disturbing thing is that *Clotho and Lachesis have done the same thing to us*. We've been loaded up with a lot of special powers and programmed to fly out to High Ridge in my Oldsmobile and stop Susan Day. I'd just like to know why.'

'But we *do* know,' she protested. 'If we don't step in, Ed Deepneau is going to commit suicide tonight during that woman's speech and take two thousand people with him.'

'Yeah,' Ralph said, 'and we're going to do whatever we can to stop him, Lois, don't worry about that.' He finished his coffee and set the cup down again. His stomach was fully awake now, and raving for food. 'I could no more stand aside and let Ed kill all those people than I could stand in one place and not duck if someone threw a baseball at my head. It's just that we never got a chance to read the fine print at the bottom of the contract, and that scares me.' He hesitated a moment. 'It also pisses me off.'

'What are you talking about?'

'About being played for a couple of patsies. We know why

we're going to try and stop Susan Day's speech; we can't stand the thought of a lunatic killing a couple of thousand innocent people. *But we don't know why they want us to do it.* That's the part that scares me.'

'We have a chance to save two thousand lives,' she said. 'Are you telling me that's enough for us but not for them?'

'That's what I'm telling you. I don't think numbers impress these fellows very much; they clean us up not just by the tens or hundreds of thousands but by the millions. And they're used to seeing the Random or the Purpose swat us in job lots.'

'Disasters like the fire at the Cocoanut Grove,' Lois said. 'Or the flood here in Derry eight years ago.'

'Yes, but even things like that are pretty small beans compared to what can and does go on in the world every year. The Flood of '85 here in Derry killed two hundred and twenty people, something like that, but last spring there was a flood in Pakistan that killed thirty-five hundred, and the last big earthquake in Turkey killed over four thousand. And how about that nuclear reactor accident in Russia? I read someplace that you can put the floor on that one at seventy thousand dead. That's a lot of Panama hats and jump-ropes and pairs of . . . of eyeglasses, Lois.' He was horrified at how close he had come to saying *pairs of earrings*.

'Don't,' she said, and shuddered.

'I don't like thinking about it any more than you do,' he said, 'but we *have* to, if only because those two guys were so goddam anxious to keep us from doing just that. Do you see what I'm getting at yet? You must. Big tragedies have always been a part of the Random; why is this so different?'

'I don't know,' Lois said, 'but it was important enough for them to draft us, and I have an idea that was a pretty big step.'

Ralph nodded. He could feel the caffeine hitting him now, jiving up his head, jittering his fingers the tiniest bit. 'I'm sure it was. Now think back to the hospital roof. Did you ever in your entire life hear two guys explain so much without explaining anything?'

'I don't get what you mean,' Lois said, but her face suggested something else: that she didn't *want* to get what he meant.

'What I mean goes back to one central idea: *maybe they can't lie.* Suppose they can't. If you have certain information you don't want to give out but you can't tell a lie, what do you do?'

'Keep dancing away from the danger zone,' Lois said. 'Or zones.'

'Bingo. And isn't that what they did?'

'Well,' she said, 'I guess it was a dance, all right, but I thought you did a fair amount of leading, Ralph. In fact, I was impressed by all the questions you asked. I think I spent most of the time we were on that roof just trying to convince myself it was all really happening.'

'Sure, I asked questions, lots of them, but . . .' He stopped, not sure how to express the concept in his head, a concept which seemed simultaneously complex and baby-simple to him. He made another effort to go up a little, searching inside his head for that sensation of *blink*, knowing that if he could reach her mind, he could show her a picture that would be crystal clear. Nothing happened, and he drummed his fingers on the tablecloth in frustration.

'I was just as amazed as you were,' he said finally. 'If my amazement came out as questions, it's because men – those from my generation, anyway – are taught that it's very bad form to ooh and aah. That's for women who are picking out the drapes.'

'Sexist.' She smiled as she said it, but it was a smile Ralph couldn't return. He was remembering Barbie Richards. If Ralph had moved toward her, she would almost certainly have pushed the alarm button beneath her desk, but she had allowed Lois to approach because she had swallowed a little too much of the old sister-sister-sister crap.

'Yes,' he said quietly, 'I'm sexist, I'm old-fashioned, and sometimes it gets me in trouble.'

'Ralph, I didn't mean—'

'I know what you meant, and it's okay. What I'm trying to get across to you is that I was as amazed . . . as knocked out . . . as you were. So I asked questions, so what? Were they good questions? *Useful* questions?'

'I guess not, huh?'

'Well, maybe I didn't start out so badly. As I remember, the first thing I asked when we finally made it to the roof was who they were and what they wanted. They slipped those questions with a lot of philosophical blather, but I imagine they got a little sweaty on the backs of their necks for awhile, just the same. Next we got all that background on the Purpose and the Random – fascinating, but nothing we exactly needed in order to drive out to High Ridge and persuade Gretchen Tillbury to cancel Susan Day's speech. Hell, we would have done better – saved time – getting the road directions from them that we ended up getting from Simone's niece.'

Lois looked startled. 'That's true, isn't it?'

'Yeah. And all the time we were talking, time was flying by the way it does when you go up a couple of levels. They were *watching* it fly, too, you can believe that. They were timing the whole scene so that when they finished telling us the things we *did* need to know, there would be no time left to ask the questions they didn't want to answer. I think they wanted to leave us with the idea that this whole thing was a public service, that saving all those lives is what it's all about, but they couldn't come right out and say so, because—'

'Because that would be a lie, and maybe they can't lie.'

'Right. Maybe they can't lie.'

'So what *do* they want, Ralph?'

He shook his head. 'I don't have a clue, Lois. Not even a hint.'

She finished her own coffee, set the cup carefully back down in its saucer, studied her fingertips for a moment, then looked up at him. Again he was forcibly struck by her beauty – almost levelled by it.

'They were good,' she said. 'They *are* good. I felt that very strongly. Didn't you?'

'Yes,' he said, almost reluctantly. Of course he had felt it. They were everything Atropos was not.

'And you're going to try to stop Ed regardless – you said you could no more *not* try than you could not try to duck a baseball someone chucked at your head. Isn't that so?'

'Yes,' he said, more reluctantly still.

'Then you should let the rest of it go,' she said calmly, meeting his blue eyes with her dark ones. 'It's just taking up space inside your head, Ralph. Making clutter.'

He saw the truth of what she said, but still doubted if he could simply open his hand and let that part of it fly free. Maybe you had to live to be seventy before you could fully appreciate how hard it was to escape your upbringing. He was a man whose education on how to *be* a man had begun before Adolf Hitler's rise to power, and he was still a prisoner of a generation that had listened to H.V. Kaltenborn and the Andrews Sisters on the radio – a generation of men that believed in moonlight cocktails and walking a mile for a Camel. Such an upbringing almost negated such nice moral questions as who was working for the good and who was working for the bad; the important thing was not to let the bullies kick sand in your face. Not to be led by the nose.

Is that so? Carolyn asked, coolly amused. *How fascinating. But let me be the first to let you in on a little secret, Ralph: that's crap. It was crap back before Glenn Miller disappeared over the horizon and it's crap now. The idea that a man's got to do what a man's got to do, now . . . there might be a little truth to that, even in this day and age. It's a long walk back to Eden in any case, isn't it, sweetheart?*

Yes. A very long walk back to Eden.

'What are you smiling about, Ralph?'

He was saved the need to reply by the arrival of the waitress and a huge tray of food. He noticed for the first time that there was a button pinned to the frill of her apron. LIFE IS NOT A CHOICE, it read.

'Are you going to the rally at the Civic Center tonight?' Ralph asked her.

'I'll be there,' she said, setting her tray down on the unoccupied table next to theirs in order to free her hands. 'Outside. Carrying a sign. Walking roundy-round.'

'Are you a Friend of Life?' Lois asked as the waitress began to deal out omelets and side-dishes.

'Am I livin?' the waitress asked.

'Yes, you certainly appear to be,' Lois said politely.

'Well, I guess that makes me a Friend of Life, doesn't it? Killing something that could someday write a great poem or invent a drug that cures AIDS or cancer, in my book that's just flat wrong. So I'll wave my sign around and make sure the Norma Kamali feminists and Volvo liberals can see that the word on it is MURDER. They hate that word. They don't use it at their cocktail parties and fundraisers. You folks need ketchup?'

'No,' Ralph said. He could not take his eyes off her. A faint green glow had begun to spread around her – it almost seemed to come wisping up from her pores. The auras were coming back, cycling up to full brilliance.

''D I grow a second head or somethin while I wasn't lookin?' the waitress asked. She popped her gum and switched it to the other side of her mouth.

'I was staring, wasn't I?' Ralph asked. He felt blood heating his cheeks. 'Sorry.'

The waitress shrugged her beefy shoulders, setting the upper part of her aura into lazy, fascinating motion. 'I try not to get

carried away with this stuff, you know? Most days I just do
my job and keep my mouth shut. But I ain't no quitter, either.
Do you know how long I've been marchin around in front of
that brick slaughterin pen, on days hot enough to fry my butt
and nights cold enough to freeze it off?'

Ralph and Lois shook their heads.

'Since 1984. Nine long years. You know what gets me the
most about the choicers?'

'What?' Lois asked quietly.

'They're the same people who want to see guns outlawed so
people won't shoot each other with them, the same ones who
say the electric chair and the gas chamber are unconstitutional
because they're cruel and unusual punishment. They say those
things, then go out and support laws that allow doctors –
doctors! – to stick vacuum tubes into women's wombs and pull
their unborn sons and daughters to pieces. *That's* what gets me
the most.'

The waitress said all this – it had the feel of a speech she
had made many times before – without raising her voice or
displaying the slightest outward sign of anger. Ralph only
listened with half an ear; most of his attention was fixed on
the pale green aura which surrounded her. Except it wasn't *all*
pale green. A yellowish-black blotch revolved slowly over her
lower right side like a dirty wagon wheel.

Her liver, Ralph thought. *Something wrong with her liver.*

'You wouldn't *really* want anything to happen to Susan Day,
would you?' Lois asked, looking at the waitress with troubled
eyes. 'You seem like a very nice person, and I'm sure you
wouldn't want that.'

The waitress sighed through her nose, producing two jets
of fine green mist. 'I ain't as nice as I look, hon. If *God* did
something to her, I'd be the first wavin my hands around in
the air and sayin "Thy will be done," believe me. But if you're
talking about some nut, I guess that's different. Things like that
drag us all down, put us on the same level as the people we're
trying to stop. The nuts don't see it that way, though. They're
the jokers in the deck.'

'Yes,' Ralph said. 'Jokers in the deck is just what they
are.'

'I guess I really don't want anything bad to happen to that
woman,' the waitress said, 'but something could. It really
could. And the way I look at it, if something *does,* she's got
no one to blame but herself. She's running with the wolves

. . . and women who run with wolves shouldn't go acting too surprised if they get bitten.'

5

Ralph wasn't sure how much he would want to eat after that, but his appetite turned out to have survived the waitress's views on abortion and Susan Day quite nicely. The auras helped; food had never tasted this good to him, not even as a teenager, when he'd eaten five and even six meals a day, if he could get them.

Lois matched him bite for bite, at least for awhile. At last she pushed the remains of her home fries and her last two strips of bacon aside. Ralph plugged gamely on down the home stretch alone. He wrapped the last bite of toast around the last bit of sausage, pushed it into his mouth, swallowed, and sat back in his chair with a vast sigh.

'Your aura has gone two shades darker, Ralph. I don't know if that means you finally got enough to eat or that you're going to die of indigestion.'

'Could be both,' he said. 'You see them again too, huh?'

She nodded.

'You know something?' he asked. 'Of all the things in the world, the one I'd like most right now is a nap.' Yes indeed. Now that he was warm and fed, the last four months of largely sleepless nights seemed to have fallen on him like a bag filled with sashweights. His eyelids felt as if they had been dipped in cement.

'I think that would be a bad idea right now,' Lois said, sounding alarmed. 'A *very* bad idea.'

'I suppose so,' Ralph agreed.

Lois started to raise her hand for the check, then lowered it again. 'What about calling your policeman friend? Leydecker, isn't that his name? Could he help us? Would he?'

Ralph considered this as carefully as his muzzy head would allow, then reluctantly shook his head. 'I don't quite dare try it. What could we tell him that wouldn't get us committed? And that's only part of the problem. If he *did* get involved . . . but in the wrong way . . . he might make things worse instead of better.'

'Okay.' Lois waved to the waitress. 'We're going to ride out there with all the windows open, and we're going to stop at the Dunkin' Donuts out in the Old Cape for giant economy-sized coffees. My treat.'

Ralph smiled. It felt large and dopey and disconnected on his face – almost a drunken smile. 'Yes, ma'am.'

When the waitress came over and slid their check face-down in front of him, Ralph noticed that the button reading LIFE IS NOT A CHOICE was no longer pinned to the frill of her apron.

'Listen,' she said with an earnestness Ralph found almost painfully touching, 'I'm sorry if I offended you folks. You came in for breakfast, not a lecture.'

'You didn't offend us,' Ralph said. He glanced across the table at Lois, who nodded agreement.

The waitress smiled briefly. 'Thanks for saying so, but I still kinda zoomed on you. Any other day I wouldn'ta, but we're having our own rally this afternoon at four, and I'm introducing Mr Dalton. They told me I could have three minutes, and I guess that's about what I gave you.'

'That's all right,' Lois said, and patted her hand. 'Really.'

The waitress's smile was warmer and more genuine this time, but as she started to turn away, Ralph saw Lois's pleasant expression falter. She was looking at the yellow-black blob floating just above the waitress's right hip.

Ralph pulled out the pen he kept clipped to his breast pocket, turned over his paper placemat, and printed quickly on the back. When he was done, he took out his wallet and placed a five-dollar bill carefully below what he had written. When the waitress reached for the tip, she would hardly be able to avoid seeing the message.

He picked up the check and flapped it at Lois. 'Our first real date and I guess it'll have to be dutch,' he said. 'I'm three bucks short if I leave her the five. Please tell me you're not broke.'

'Who, the poker queen of Ludlow Grange? Don't be seely, dollink.' She handed him a helter-skelter fistful of bills from her purse. While he sorted through them for what he needed, she read what he had written on the placemat:

Madam:
   You are suffering from reduced liver function and should see your doctor immediately. And I strongly advise you to stay away from the Civic Center tonight.

'Pretty stupid, I know,' Ralph said.

442

She kissed the tip of his nose. 'Trying to help other people is never stupid.'

'Thanks. She won't believe it, though. She'll think we were pissed off about her button and her little speech in spite of what we said. That what I wrote is just our weird way of trying to get our own back on her.'

'Maybe there's a way to convince her otherwise.'

Lois fixed the waitress – who was standing hipshot by the kitchen pass-through and talking to the short-order cook while she drank a cup of coffee – with a look of dark concentration. As she did, Ralph saw Lois's normal blue-gray aura deepen in color and draw inward, becoming a kind of body-hugging capsule.

He wasn't exactly sure what was going on . . . but he could feel it. The hairs on the back of his neck stood at attention; his forearms broke out in gooseflesh. *She's powering up,* he thought, *flipping all the switches, turning on all the turbines, and doing it on behalf of a woman she never saw before and will probably never see again.*

After a moment the waitress felt it, too. She turned to look at them as if she had heard her name called. Lois smiled casually and twiddled her fingers in a small wave, but when she spoke to Ralph, her voice was trembling with effort. 'I've almost . . . almost got it.'

'Almost got *what?*'

'I don't know. Whatever it is I need. It'll come in a second. Her name is Zoë, with two dots over the e. Go pay the check. Distract her. Try to keep her from looking at me. It makes it harder.'

He did as she asked and was fairly successful in spite of the way Zoë kept trying to look over his shoulder at Lois. The first time she attempted to ring the check into the register, Zoë came up with a total of $234.20. She cleared the numbers with an impatient poke of her finger, and when she looked up at Ralph, her face was pale and her eyes were upset.

'What's with your wife?' she asked Ralph. 'I apologized, didn't I? So why does she keep looking at me like that?'

Ralph knew Zoë couldn't see Lois, because he was all but tap-dancing in an effort to keep his body between the two of them, but he also knew she was right – Lois *was* staring.

He attempted to smile. 'I don't know what—'

The waitress jumped and shot a startled, irritated glance back at the short-order cook. '*Quit banging those pots around!*' she shouted, although the only thing Ralph had heard from the kitchen was a radio playing elevator-music. Zoë looked back at Ralph. 'Christ, it sounds like Vietnam back there. Now if you could just tell your wife it's not polite to—'

'To stare? She's not. She's really not.' Ralph stood aside. Lois had gone to the door and was looking out at the street with her back to them. 'See?'

Zoë didn't reply for several seconds, although she kept looking at Lois. At last she turned back to Ralph. 'Sure. I see. Now why don't you and her just make yourselves scarce?'

'All right – still friends?'

'Whatever you want,' Zoë said, but she wouldn't look at him.

When Ralph rejoined Lois, he saw that her aura had gone back to its former, more diffuse state, but it was much brighter than it had been.

'Still tired, Lois?' he asked her softly.

'No. As a matter of fact, I feel fine now. Let's go.'

He started to open the door for her, then stopped. 'Got my pen?'

'Gee, no – I guess it's still on the table.'

Ralph went over to pick it up. Below his note, Lois had added a PS in rolling Palmer-method script:

In 1989 you had a baby and gave him up for adoption. Saint Anne's, in Providence, RI. Go and see your doctor before it's too late, Zoë. No joke. No trick. We know what we're talking about.

'Oh boy,' Ralph said as he rejoined her. 'That's going to scare the bejesus out of her.'

'If she gets to her doctor before her liver goes belly-up, I don't care.'

He nodded and they went out.

6

'Did you get that stuff about her kid when you dipped into her aura?' Ralph asked as they crossed the leaf-strewn parking lot.

Lois nodded. Beyond the lot, the entire east side of Derry was shimmering with bright, kaleidoscopic light. It was coming back hard now, very hard, that secret light cycling up and up. Ralph reached out and put his hand on the side of his car. Touching it was like tasting a slick, licorice-flavored cough-drop.

'I don't think I took very much of her . . . her stuff,' Lois said, 'but it was as if I swallowed *all* of her.'

Ralph remembered something he'd read in a science magazine not long ago. 'If every cell in our bodies contains a complete blueprint of how we're made,' he said, 'why shouldn't every bit of a person's aura contain a complete blueprint of what we *are*?'

'That doesn't sound very scientific, Ralph.'

'I suppose not.'

She squeezed his arm and grinned up at him. 'It *does* sound about right, though.'

He grinned back at her.

'You need to take some more, too,' she told him. 'It still feels wrong to me – like stealing – but if you don't, I think you're going to pass right out on your feet.'

'As soon as I can. Right now all I want to do is get out to High Ridge.' Yet once he got behind the wheel, his hand faltered away from the ignition key almost as soon as he touched it.

'Ralph? What is it?'

'Nothing . . . everything. I can't drive like this. I'll wrap us around a telephone pole or drive us into somebody's living room.'

He looked up at the sky and saw one of those huge birds, this one transparent, roosting atop a satellite dish on the roof of an apartment house across the way. A thin, lemon-colored haze drifted up from its folded prehistoric wings.

Are you seeing it? a part of his mind asked doubtfully. *Are you sure of that, Ralph? Are you really, really sure?*

I'm seeing it, all right. Fortunately or unfortunately, I'm seeing it all . . . but if there was ever a right time to see such things, this isn't it.

He concentrated, and felt that interior blink happen deep within his mind. The bird faded away like a ghost-image on a TV screen. The warmly glowing palette of colors spread out across the morning lost their vibrancy. He went on perceiving that other part of the world long enough to see the colors run into one another, creating the bright gray-blue haze which he'd begun seeing on the day he'd gone into Day Break, Sun Down for coffee and pie with Joe Wyzer – and then that was gone, too. Ralph felt an almost crushing need to curl up, pillow his head on his arm, and go to sleep. He began taking long, slow breaths instead, pulling each one a little deeper into his lungs, and then turned the ignition key. The engine roared into life, accompanied by that clacking sound. It was much louder now.

'What's that?' Lois asked.

'I don't know,' Ralph said, but he thought he did – either a tie-rod or a piston. In either case they would be in trouble if it let go. At last the sound began to diminish, and Ralph dropped the transmission into Drive. 'Just poke me hard if you see me starting to nod off, Lois.'

'You can count on it,' she said. 'Now let's go.'

Chapter Twenty-one

1

The Dunkin' Donuts on Newport Avenue was a jolly pink
sugarchurch in a drab neighborhood of tract houses. Most had
been built in a single year, 1946, and were now crumbling.
This was Derry's Old Cape, where elderly cars with wired-up
mufflers and cracked windshields wore bumper stickers saying
things like DON'T BLAME ME I VOTED FOR PEROT and ALL THE
WAY WITH THE NRA, where no house was complete without
at least one Fisher-Price Big Wheel trike standing on the
listless lawn, where girls were stepping dynamite at sixteen
and all too often dull-eyed, fat-bottomed mothers of three at
twenty-four.

Two boys on fluorescent bikes with extravagant ape-hanger
handlebars were doing wheelies in the parking lot, weaving in
and out of each other's paths with a dexterity that suggested
a solid background in video gaming and possible high-paying
futures as air-traffic controllers . . . if they managed to stay
away from coke and car accidents, that was. Both wore their
hats backward. Ralph wondered briefly why they weren't in
school on a Friday morning, or at least on the way, and decided
he didn't care. Probably they didn't, either.

Suddenly the two bikes, which had been avoiding each other
easily up until then, crashed together. Both boys fell to the
pavement, then got to their feet almost immediately. Ralph
was relieved to see neither was hurt; their auras did not even
flicker.

'Goddam wet end!' the one in the Nirvana tee-shirt yelled
indignantly at his friend. He was perhaps eleven. 'What the
hell's the matter with you? You ride a bike like old people fuck!'

'I heard something,' the other said, resetting his hat carefully on his dirty-blond hair. 'Great big bang. You tellin me you didn't hear it? Boo-ya!'

'I didn't hear jack shit,' Nirvana Boy said. He held out his palms, which were now dirty (or perhaps just dirtier) and oozing blood from two or three minor scratches. 'Look at this – fuckin road-rash!'

'You'll live,' his friend said.

'Yeah, but –' Nirvana Boy noticed Ralph, leaning against his rusty whale of an Oldsmobile with his hands in his pockets, watching them. 'The fuck you lookin at?'

'You and your friend,' Ralph said. 'That's all.'

'That's all, huh?'

'Yep – the whole story.'

Nirvana Boy glanced at his friend, then back at Ralph. His eyes glowered with a purity of suspicion which, in Ralph's experience, could be found only here in the Old Cape. 'You got a problem?'

'Not me,' Ralph said. He had inhaled a great deal of Nirvana Boy's russet-colored aura and now felt quite a bit like Superman on a speed trip. He also felt like a child-molester. 'I was just thinking that we didn't talk much like you and your friend when I was a kid.'

Nirvana Boy regarded him insolently. 'Yeah? What'd you talk like?'

'I can't quite remember,' Ralph said, 'but I don't think we sounded quite so much like shitheads.' He turned away from them as the screen door slammed. Lois came out of the Dunkin' Donuts with a large container of coffee in each hand. The boys, meanwhile, jumped on their fluorescent bikes and streaked off, Nirvana Boy giving Ralph one final distrustful look over his shoulder.

'Can you drink this and drive the car at the same time?' Lois asked, handing him a coffee.

'I think so,' Ralph said, 'but I don't really need it anymore. I'm fine, Lois.'

She glanced after the two boys, then nodded. 'Let's go.'

2

The world blazed all around them as they drove out Route 33 toward what had once been Barrett's Orchards, and they didn't have to slide even a single inch up the ladder of perception to see it. The city fell away and they drove through second-growth woods on fire with autumn. The sky was a blue lane above the road, and the Oldsmobile's shadow raced beside them, wavering across leaves and branches.

'God, it's so beautiful,' Lois said. 'Isn't it beautiful, Ralph?'

'Yes. It is.'

'You know what I wish? More than anything?'

He shook his head.

'That we could just pull over to the side of the road – stop the car and get out and walk into the woods a little way. Find a clearing, sit in the sun, and look up at the clouds. You'd say, "Look at that one, Lois, it looks like a horse." And I'd say, "Look over there, Ralph, it's a man with a broom." Wouldn't that be nice?'

'Yes,' Ralph said. The woods opened in a narrow aisle on their left; power-poles marched down the steep slope like soldiers. High-tension lines shone silver between them in the morning sunlight, gossamer as spiderwebs. The feet of the poles were buried in brazen drifts of red sumac, and when Ralph looked up above the slash he saw a hawk riding an air-current as invisible as the world of auras. 'Yes,' he said again. 'That would be nice. Maybe we'll even get a chance to do it sometime. But . . .'

'But what?'

' "Each thing I do I rush through so I can do something else," ' Ralph said.

She looked at him, a little startled. 'What a terrible idea!'

'Yeah. I think most true ideas *are* terrible. It's from a book of poems called *Cemetery Nights*. Dorrance Marstellar gave it to me on the same day he slipped upstairs to my apartment and put the spray-can of Bodyguard into my jacket pocket.'

He glanced up into his rear-view mirror and saw at least two miles of Route 33 laid out behind them, a strip of black running through the fiery woods. Sunlight twinkled on chrome. A car. Maybe two or three. And coming fast, from the look.

'Old Dor,' she mused.

'Yes. You know, Lois, I think he's also a part of this.'

'Maybe he is,' Lois said. 'And if Ed's a special case, maybe Dorrance is, too.'

'Yes, that thought occurred to me. The most interesting thing about him – Old Dor, I mean, not Ed – is that I don't think Clotho and Lachesis know about him. It's like he's from an entirely different neighborhood.'

'What do you mean?'

'I'm not sure. But Mr C and Mr L never *mentioned* him, and that . . . that seems . . .'

He glanced back at the rear-view. Now there was a fourth car, behind the others but moving up fast, and he could see the blue flashers atop the closer three. Police cars. Headed for Newport? No, probably headed for someplace a little closer than that.

Maybe they're after us, Ralph thought. *Maybe Lois's suggestion that the Richards woman forget we were there didn't hold.*

But would the police send four cruisers after two golden-agers in a rustbucket Oldsmobile? Ralph didn't think so. Helen's face suddenly flashed into his mind. He felt a sinking in the pit of his stomach as he guided the Olds over to the side of the road.

'Ralph? What –' Then she heard the rising howl of the sirens and turned in her seat, alarm widening her eyes. The first three police cars roared past at better than eighty miles an hour, pelting Ralph's car with grit and sending crisp fallen leaves into dancing dervishes in their wake.

'Ralph!' she nearly screamed. 'What if it's High Ridge? Helen's out there! *Helen and her baby!*'

'I know,' Ralph said, and as the fourth police car slammed by them hard enough to rock the Oldsmobile on its springs, he felt that interior blink happen again. He reached for the transmission lever, and then his hand stopped in mid-air, still three inches from it. His eyes were fixed upon the horizon. The smudge there was less spectral than the obscene black umbrella they had seen hanging over the Civic Center, but Ralph knew it was the same thing: a deathbag.

3

'Faster!' Lois shouted at him. 'Go faster, Ralph!'

'I can't,' he said. His teeth were clamped together, and the words came out sounding squeezed. 'I've got it matted.' *Also, he did not add, this is the fastest I've gone in thirty-five years, and I'm scared to death.*

The needle quivered a hair's breadth beyond the eighty mark on the speedometer; the woods slid by in a blurred mix of reds and yellows and magentas; under the hood the engine was no longer just clacking but hammering like a platoon of blacksmiths on a binge. In spite of this, the fresh trio of police cars Ralph saw in his mirror were catching up easily.

The road curved sharply right up ahead. Denying every instinct, Ralph kept his foot away from the brake pedal. He did take it off the gas as they went into the curve . . . then mashed it back to the mat again as he felt the rear end trying to break loose on the back side. He was hunched over the wheel now, upper teeth clamped tightly on his lower lip, eyes wide open and bulging beneath the salt-and-pepper tangle of his eyebrows. The sedan's rear tires howled, and Lois fell into him, scrabbling at the back of her seat for purchase. Ralph clung to the wheel with sweaty fingers and waited for the car to flip. The Olds was one of the last true Detroit road-monsters, however, wide and heavy and low. It outlasted the curve, and on the far side Ralph saw a red farmhouse on the left. There were two barns behind it.

'Ralph, there's the turn!'

'I see.'

The new batch of police cars had caught up with them and were swinging out to pass. Ralph got as far over as he could, praying that none of them would rear-end him at this speed. None did; they zipped by in close bumper-to-bumper formation, swung left, and started up the long hill which led to High Ridge.

'Hang on, Lois.'

'Oh, I am, I am,' she said.

The Olds slid almost sideways as Ralph made the left onto what he and Carolyn had always called the Orchard Road. If the narrow country lane had been tarred, the big car probably would have rolled over like a stunt vehicle in a thrill-show. It wasn't, however, and instead of going door-over-roof the Olds just skidded extravagantly, sending up dry billows of dust. Lois gave a thin, out-of-breath shriek, and Ralph snatched a quick look at her.

'Go on!' She flapped an impatient hand at the road ahead, and in that moment she looked so eerily like Carolyn that Ralph almost felt he was seeing a ghost. He wondered what Carol, who had nearly made a career out of telling him to go faster during the last five years of her life, would have made of *this* little spin in the country. 'Never mind me, just watch the road!'

More police cars were making the turn onto Orchard Road now. How many was that in all? Ralph didn't know; he'd lost count. Maybe a dozen in all. He steered the Oldsmobile over until the right two wheels were running on the edge of a nasty-looking ditch, and the reinforcements – three with DERRY POLICE printed in gold on the sides and two State Police cruisers – blew past, throwing up fresh showers of dirt and gravel. For just a moment Ralph saw a uniformed policeman leaning out of one of the Derry police cars, waving at him, and then the Olds was buried in a yellow cloud of dust. Ralph smothered a new and even stronger urge to climb on the brake by thinking of Helen and Nat. A moment later he could see again – sort of, anyway. The newest batch of police cars was already halfway up the hill.

'That cop was waving you off, wasn't he?' Lois asked.

'You bet.'

'They're not even going to let us get close.' She was looking at the black smudge on top of the hill with wide, dismayed eyes.

'We'll get as close as we need to.' Ralph checked the rear-view for more traffic and saw nothing but hanging road-dust.

'Ralph?'

'What?'

'Are you up? Do you see the colors?'

He took a quick look at her. She still looked beautiful to him, and marvellously young, but there was no sign of her aura. 'No,' he said. 'Do you?'

'I don't know. I still see *that*.' She pointed through the windshield at the dark smudge on top of the hill. 'What is it? If it's not a deathbag, what is it?'

He opened his mouth to tell her it was smoke, and there was only one thing up there likely to be on fire, but before he could get out a single word, there was a tremendous hot bang from the Oldsmobile's engine compartment. The hood jumped and even dimpled in one place, as if an angry fist had lashed up inside. The car took a single forward snap-jerk that felt like a hiccup; the red idiot-lights came on and the engine quit.

He steered the Olds toward the soft shoulder, and when the edge gave way beneath the rightside wheels and the car canted into the ditch, Ralph had a strong, clear premonition that he had just completed his last tour of duty as a motor vehicle operator. This idea was accompanied by absolutely no regret at all.

'What happened?' Lois nearly screamed.

'We blew a rod,' he said. 'Looks like it's shank's pony the rest of the way up the hill, Lois. Come on out on my side so you don't squelch in the mud.'

4

There was a brisk westerly breeze, and once they were out of the car the smell of smoke from the top of the hill was very strong. They started the last quarter-mile without talking about it, walking hand-in-hand and walking fast. By the time they saw the State Police cruiser slued sideways across the top of the road, the smoke was rising in billows above the trees and Lois was gasping for breath.

'Lois? Are you all right?'

'I'm fine,' she gasped. 'I just weigh too—'

Crack-crack-crack: pistol-shots from beyond the car blocking the road. They were followed by a hoarse, rapid coughing sound Ralph could easily identify from TV news stories about civil wars in third-world countries and drive-by shootings in third-world American cities: an automatic weapon set to rapid-fire. There were more pistol-shots, then the louder, rougher report of a shotgun. This was followed by a shriek of pain that made Ralph wince and want to cover his ears. He thought it was a woman's scream, and he suddenly remembered something which had been eluding him: the last name of the woman John Leydecker had mentioned. McKay, it had been. Sandra McKay.

That thought coming at this time filled him with unreasoning horror. He tried to tell himself that the screamer could have been anyone – even a man, sometimes men sounded like women when they had been hurt – but he knew better. It was her. It was *them*. Ed's crazies. They had mounted an assault on High Ridge.

More sirens from behind them. The smell of the smoke, thicker now. Lois, looking at him with dismayed, frightened eyes and still gasping for breath. Ralph glanced up the hill and saw a silver R.F.D. box standing at the side of the road. There was no name on it, of course; the women who ran High Ridge had done their best to keep a low profile and maintain their anonymity, much good it had done them today. The mailbox's flag was up. Somebody had a letter for the postman. That made Ralph think of the letter Helen had sent *him* from High Ridge – a cautious letter, but full of hope nevertheless.

More gunfire. The whine of a ricochet. Breaking glass. A bellow that might have been anger but was probably pain. The hungry crackle of hot flames gobbling dry wood. Warbling sirens. And Lois's dark Spanish eyes, fixed on him because he was the man and she'd been raised to believe that men knew what to do in situations like this.

Then do something! he yelled at himself. *For Christ's sweet sake, do something!*

But what? What?

'*PICKERING!*' a bullhorn-amplified voice bellowed from beyond the place where the road curved into a grove of young Christmas-tree-size spruces. Ralph could now see red sparks and licks of orange flame in the thickening smoke rising above the firs. '*PICKERING, THERE ARE WOMEN IN THERE! LET US SAVE THE WOMEN!*'

'He *knows* there are women,' Lois murmured. 'Don't they understand that he *knows* that? Are they *fools*, Ralph?'

A strange, wavering shriek answered the cop with the bullhorn, and it took Ralph a second or two to realize that this response was a species of laughter. There was another chattering burst of automatic fire. It was returned by a barrage of pistol-shots and shotgun blasts.

Lois squeezed his hand with chilly fingers. 'What do we do, Ralph? What do we do now?'

He looked at the billowing gray-black smoke rising over the trees, then back down toward the police cars racing up the hill – over half a dozen of them this time – and finally back to Lois's pale, strained face. His mind had cleared a little – not much, but enough for him to realize there was really just one answer to her question.

'We go up,' he said.

5

Blink! and the flames shooting over the grove of spruces went from orange to green. The hungry crackling sound became muffled, like the sound of firecrackers going off inside a closed box. Still holding Lois's hand, Ralph led her around the front bumper of the State Police car which had been left as a roadblock.

The newly arrived police cars were pulling up behind the roadblock. Men in blue uniforms came spilling out of them almost before they had stopped. Several were carrying riot guns and most were wearing puffy black vests. One of them sprinted through Ralph like a gust of warm wind before he could dodge aside: a young man named David Wilbert who thought his wife might be having an affair with her boss at the real-estate office where she worked as a secretary. The question of his wife had taken a back seat (at least temporarily) to David Wilbert's almost overpowering need to pee, however, and to the constant, frightened chant that wove through his thoughts like a snake:

['*You* won't *disgrace yourself, you* won't *disgrace yourself, you* won't, *you* won't, *you* won't.']

'*PICKERING!*' the amplified voice bellowed, and Ralph found he could actually taste the words in his mouth, like small silver pellets. '*YOUR FRIENDS ARE DEAD, PICKERING! THROW DOWN YOUR WEAPON AND STEP OUT INTO THE YARD! LET US SAVE THE WOMEN!*'

Ralph and Lois rounded the corner, unseen by the men running all around them, and came to a tangle of police cars parked at the place where the road became a driveway lined on both sides by pretty planter-boxes filled with bright flowers.

The woman's touch that means so much, Ralph thought.

The driveway opened into the dooryard of a rambling white farmhouse at least seventy years old. It was three storeys high, with two wings and a long porch which ran the length of the building and commanded a fabulous view toward the west, where dim blue mountains rose in the mid-morning light. This house with its peaceful view had once housed the Barrett family and their apple business and had more recently housed dozens of battered, frightened women, but one look was enough to tell Ralph that it would house no one at all come this time tomorrow morning. The south wing was in flames, and that side of the porch was catching; tongues of fire poked out the windows and licked lasciviously along the eaves, sending shingles floating upward in fiery scraps. He saw a wicker rocking chair burning at the far end of the porch. A half-knitted scarf lay over one of the rocker's arms; the needles dangling from it glowed white-hot. Somewhere a wind-chime was tinkling a mad repetitive melody.

A dead woman in green fatigues and a flak-jacket sprawled head-down on the porch steps, glaring at the sky through the blood-smeared lenses of her glasses. There was dirt in her hair, a pistol in her hand, and a ragged black hole in her midsection. A man lay draped over the railing at the north end of the porch with one booted foot propped on the lawn-glider. He was also wearing fatigues and a flak-jacket. An assault-rifle with a banana clip sticking out of it lay in a flower-bed below him. Blood ran down his fingers and dripped from his nails. To Ralph's heightened eye, the drops looked black and dead.

Felton, he thought. *If the police are still yelling at Charlie Pickering – if Pickering's inside – then that must be Frank Felton. And what about Susan Day? Ed's down the coast somewhere – Lois seemed sure of that, and I think she's right – but what if Susan Day's in there? Jesus, is that possible?*

He supposed it was, but the possibilities didn't matter – not now. Helen and Natalie were almost certainly in there, along with God knew how many other helpless, terrorized women, and that *did* matter.

There was the sound of breaking glass from inside the house, followed by a soft explosion – almost a gasp. Ralph saw new flames jump up behind the panes of the front door.

Molotov cocktails, he thought. *Charlie Pickering finally got a chance to throw a few. How wonderful for him.*

Ralph didn't know how many cops were crouched behind the cars parked at the head of the driveway – it looked like at least thirty – but he picked out the two who had busted Ed Deepneau at once. Chris Nell was crouched behind the front tire of the Derry police car closest to the house, and John Leydecker was down on one knee beside him. Nell was the one with the bullhorn, and as Ralph and Lois approached the police strongpoint, he glanced at Leydecker. Leydecker nodded, pointed at the house, then pushed his palms at Nell in a gesture Ralph read easily: *Be careful.* He read something more distressing in Chris Nell's aura – the younger man was too excited to be careful. Too stoked. And at that instant, almost as if Ralph's thought had caused it to happen, Nell's aura began changing color. It cycled from pale blue to dark gray to dead black with gruesome speed.

'*GIVE IT UP, PICKERING!*' Nell shouted, unaware that he was a dead man breathing.

The wire stock of an assault-rifle smashed through the glass of a window on the lower floor of the north wing, then disappeared back inside. At the same instant the fanlight over the front door exploded, showering the porch with glass. Flames roared out through the hole. A second later the door itself shuddered open, as if nudged by an invisible hand. Nell leaned out farther, perhaps believing the shooter had finally seen reason and intended to give himself up.

Ralph, screaming: ['*Pull him back, Johnny! PULL HIM BACK!*']

The rifle emerged again, barrel-first this time.

Leydecker reached for Nell's collar, but he was too slow. The automatic rifle hacked its series of rapid dry coughs, and Ralph heard the metallic *pank! pank! pank!* of bullets poking holes in the thin steel of the police car. Chris Nell's aura was totally black now – it had become a deathbag. He jerked sideways as a bullet caught him in the neck, breaking Leydecker's grip on his collar and sprawling into the dooryard with one foot kicking spasmodically. The bullhorn spilled from his hand with a brief squawk of feedback. A policeman behind one of the other cars cried out in surprise and horror. Lois's shriek was much louder.

More bullets stitched across the ground toward Nell and then slapped small black holes into the thighs of his blue uniform. Ralph could dimly see the man inside the deathbag which was suffocating him; he was making blind efforts to roll over and get up. There was something singularly horrible about his struggles – to Ralph it was like watching a creature caught in a net drown in shallow, filthy water.

Leydecker lunged out from behind the police car, and as his fingers disappeared into the black membrane surrounding Chris Nell, Ralph heard Old Dor say, *I wouldn't touch him anymore if I were you, Ralph – I can't see your hands.*

Lois: ['*Don't! Don't, he's dead, he's already dead!*']

The gun poking out of the window had started to move to the right. Now it swivelled unhurriedly back toward Leydecker, the man behind it undeterred – and apparently unhurt – by the hail of bullets directed at him from the other police. Ralph raised his right hand and brought it down in the karate-chop gesture again, but this time instead of a wedge of light, his fingertips produced something that looked like a large blue teardrop. It spread across Leydecker's lemon-colored aura just as the rifle sticking out of the window opened fire. Ralph saw two slugs strike the tree just to Leydecker's right, sending chips of bark flying into the air and making black holes in the fir's yellowish-white undersurface. A third struck the blue covering which had coated Leydecker's aura – Ralph saw a momentary flicker of dark red just to the left of the detective's temple and heard a low whine as the bullet either richocheted or *skipped,* the way a flat stone will skip across the surface of a pond.

Leydecker pulled Nell back behind the car, looked at him, then tore open the driver's-side door and threw himself into the front seat. Ralph could no longer see him, but could hear him screaming at someone over the radio, asking where the fuck the rescue vehicles were.

More shattering glass, and Lois was grabbing frantically at Ralph's arm, pointing at something – at a brick tumbling end over end into the dooryard. It had come through one of the low, narrow windows at the base of the north wing. These windows were almost obscured by the flower-beds which edged the house.

'*Help us!*' a voice screamed through the broken window, even as the man with the assault-rifle fired reflexively at the tumbling brick, sending up puffs of reddish dust and then breaking it into three jagged chunks. Neither Ralph nor Lois had ever heard that voice raised in a scream, but both recognized it at once, nevertheless; it was Helen Deepneau's voice. '*Help us, please! We're in the cellar! We have children! Please don't let us burn to death,* WE HAVE CHILDREN!'

Ralph and Lois exchanged a single wide-eyed glance, then ran for the house.

6

Two uniformed figures, looking more like pro football linemen than cops in their bulky Kevlar vests, charged from behind one of the cruisers, running flat-out for the porch with their riot guns held at port arms. As they crossed the dooryard on a diagonal, Charlie Pickering leaned out of his window, still laughing wildly, his gray hair zanier than ever. The volume of fire directed at him was enormous, showering him with splinters from the sides of the window and actually knocking down the rusty gutter above his head – it struck the porch with a hollow *bonk* – but not a single bullet touched him.

How can they not *be hitting him?* Ralph thought as he and Lois mounted the porch toward the lime-colored flames which were now billowing through the open front door. *Christ Jesus, it's almost point-blank range, how can they possibly* not *be hitting him?*

But he knew how . . . and why. Clotho had told them that both Atropos and Ed Deepneau had been surrounded by forces which were malignant yet protective. Was it not likely that those same forces were now taking care of Charlie Pickering, much as Ralph himself had taken care of Leydecker when he'd left the protection of the police car to drag his dying colleague back to cover?

Pickering opened up on the charging State Troopers, his weapon switched to rapid-fire. He aimed low to negate the value of the vests they were wearing and swept their legs out from under them. One of them fell in a silent heap; the other crawled back the way he had come, shrieking that he was hit, he was hit, oh fuck, he was hit bad.

'*Barbecue!*' Pickering cried out the window in his screaming, laughing voice. '*Barbecue! Barbecue! Holy cookout! Burn the bitches! God's fire! God's holy fire!*'

There were more screams now, seemingly from right under Ralph's feet, and when he looked down he saw a terrible thing: a medley of auras was seeping up from between the porch boards like steam, the variety of their colors muted by the scarlet blood-glow which was rising with them . . . and surrounding them. This blood-red shape wasn't quite the same as the thunderhead which had formed above the fight between Green Boy and Orange Boy outside the Red Apple, but Ralph thought it was closely related; the only difference was that this one had been born of fear instead of anger and aggression.

'*Barbecue!*' Charlie Pickering was screaming, and then something about killing the devil-cunts. Suddenly Ralph hated him more than he had ever hated anyone in his life.

[*'Come on, Lois – let's go get that asshole.'*]

He took her by the hand and pulled her into the burning house.

Chapter Twenty-two

1

The porch door opened on a central hallway that ran from the front of the house to the back, and the whole length of it was now engulfed in flames. To Ralph's eyes they were a bright green, and when he and Lois passed through them, they were cool – it was like passing through gauzy membranes which had been infused with Mentholatum. The crackle of the burning house was muffled; the gunfire had become as faint and unimportant as the sound of thunder to someone who is swimming underwater . . . and that was what this felt like more than anything, Ralph decided – being underwater. He and Lois were unseen beings swimming through a river of fire.

He pointed to a doorway on the right and looked questioningly at Lois. She nodded. He reached for the knob and grimaced with disgust as his fingers passed right through it. Just as well, of course; if he had actually been able to grab the damned thing, he would have left the top two layers of his fingers hanging off the brass knob in charbroiled strips.

[*We have to go through it, Ralph!*]

He looked at her assessingly, saw a great deal of fear and worry in her eyes but no panic, and nodded. They went through the door together just as the chandelier halfway down the hall fell to the floor with an unmusical crash of glass pendants and iron chain.

There was a parlor on the other side, and what they saw there made Ralph's stomach clench in horror. Two women were propped against the wall below a large poster of Susan Day in jeans and a Western-style shirt (DON'T LET HIM CALL

YOU BABY UNLESS YOU WANT HIM TO TREAT YOU LIKE ONE, the poster advised). Both had been shot in the head at point-blank range; brains, ragged flaps of scalp, and bits of bone were splattered across the flowered wallpaper and Susan Day's fancy-stitched cowgirl boots. One of the women had been pregnant. The other had been Gretchen Tillbury.

Ralph remembered the day she had come to his home with Helen to warn him and to give him a can of something called Bodyguard; on that day he had thought her beautiful . . . but of course on that day her finely made head had still been intact and half of her pretty blonde hair hadn't been roasted off by a close-range rifle-blast. Fifteen years after she had narrowly escaped being killed by her abusive husband, another man had put a gun to Gretchen Tillbury's head and blown her right out of the world. She would never tell another woman about how she had gotten the scar on her left thigh.

For one horrible moment Ralph thought he was going to faint. He concentrated and pulled himself back by thinking of Lois. Her aura had gone a dark, shocked red. Jagged black lines raced across it and through it. They looked like the EKG readout of someone suffering a fatal heart attack.

[*'Oh Ralph! Oh Ralph, dear God!'*]

Something exploded at the south end of the house with force enough to blow open the door they had just walked through. Ralph guessed it might have been a propane tank or tanks . . . not that it mattered much at this point. Flaming scraps of wallpaper came wafting in from the hall, and he saw both the room's curtains and the remaining hair on Gretchen Tillbury's head ripple toward the doorway as the fire sucked the air out of the room to feed itself. How long would it take for the fire to turn the women and children down cellar into crispy critters? Ralph didn't know, and suspected that didn't matter much, either; the people trapped down there would be dead of suffocation or smoke inhalation long before they began to burn.

Lois was staring at the dead women in horror. Tears slipped down her cheeks. The spectral gray light which rose from the tracks they left behind looked like vapor rising from dry ice. Ralph walked her across the parlor toward the closed double doors on the far side, paused before them long enough to take a deep breath, then put his arm around Lois's waist and stepped into the wood.

There was a moment of darkness in which not just his nose

but his entire body seemed suffused with the sweet aroma of sawdust, and then they were in the room beyond, the northernmost room in the house. It had perhaps once been a study, but had since been converted into a group therapy room. In the center, a dozen or so folding chairs had been set up in a circle. The walls were hung with plaques saying things like I CANNOT EXPECT RESPECT FROM ANYONE ELSE UNTIL I RESPECT MYSELF. On a blackboard at one end of the room someone had printed WE ARE FAMILY, I'VE GOT ALL MY SISTERS WITH ME in capital letters. Crouched beside it at one of the east-facing windows that overlooked the porch, wearing his own Kevlar vest over a Snoopy sweatshirt Ralph would have recognized anywhere, was Charlie Pickering.

'*Barbecue all Godless women!*' he screamed. A bullet whined past his shoulder; another buried itself in the windowframe to his right and flicked a splinter against one of the lenses of his hornrimmed glasses. The idea that he was being protected returned to Ralph, this time with the force of a conviction. '*Lesbian cookout! Give em a taste of their own medicine! Teach em how it feels!*'

['*Stay up, Lois – right up where you are now.*']

['*What are you going to do?*']

['*Take care of him.*']

['*Don't kill him, Ralph! Please don't kill him!*']

Why not? Ralph thought bitterly. *I'd be doing the world a favor.* That was undoubtedly true, but this was no time to argue.

['*All right, I won't kill him! Now stay put, Lois – there's too many goddam bullets flying around for both of us to risk going down.*']

Before she could reply, Ralph concentrated, summoned the blink, and dropped back to the Short-Time level. It happened so fast and hard this time that it left him feeling winded, as if he had jumped out of a second-storey window onto a hard patch of concrete. Some of the color drained out of the world and noise fell in to replace it: the crackle of fire, no longer muffled but sharp and close; the crump of a shotgun blast; the crack of pistol-shots fired in rapid succession. The air tasted of soot, and the room was sweltering. Something that sounded like an insect droned past Ralph's ear. He had an idea it was a .45-caliber bug.

Better hurry up, sweetheart, Carolyn advised. *When bullets hit you on this level they kill you, remember?*

He remembered.

Ralph ran bent-over toward Pickering's turned back. His feet crunched on slivers of glass and scatters of splinters, but Pickering did not turn. In addition to the automatic weapon in his hands, there was a revolver on his hip and a small green duffle-bag by his left foot. The bag was unzipped, and Ralph saw a number of wine bottles inside. Their open mouths had been stuffed with wet rags.

'*Kill the bitches!*' Pickering screamed, spraying the yard with another burst of fire. He popped the clip and raised his sweatshirt, exposing three or four more tucked under his belt. Ralph reached into the open duffel-bag, seized one of the gasoline-filled wine bottles by the neck, and swung it at the side of Pickering's head. As he did, he saw the reason Pickering hadn't heard his approach: the man was wearing shooter's plugs. Before Ralph had time to reflect upon the irony of a man on a suicide mission taking pains to protect his hearing, the bottle shattered against Pickering's temple, dousing him with amber liquid and green glass. He staggered backward, one hand going to his scalp, which was cut open in two places. Blood poured through his long fingers – *fingers that should have belonged to a pianist or a painter,* Ralph thought – and down his neck. He turned, his eyes wide and shocked behind the smeary lenses of his spectacles, his hair reaching for the sky and making him look like a cartoon of a man who has just received a huge jolt of electricity.

'*You!*' he cried. 'Devil-sent Centurion! Godless baby-killer!'

Ralph thought of the two women in the other room and was once more overwhelmed with anger . . . except that anger was too mild a word, much too mild. He felt as if his nerves were burning inside his skin. And the thought that drummed at his mind was *one of them was pregnant so who's the baby-killer, one of them was pregnant so who's the baby-killer, one of them was pregnant so who's the baby-killer.*

Another high-caliber bug droned past his face. Ralph didn't notice. Pickering was trying to lift the rifle with which he had undoubtedly killed Gretchen Tillbury and her pregnant friend. Ralph snatched it from his hands and turned it on him. Pickering shrieked with fear. The sound of it maddened Ralph even more, and he forgot the promise he had made to Lois. He raised the rifle, fully meaning to empty it into the man who was now cringing abjectly against the wall (in the heat of the moment it occurred to neither of them that there was currently no clip in the gun), but before he could pull

the trigger he was distracted by a brilliant swarm of light
bleeding into the air beside him. At first it was without
shape, a fabulous kaleidoscope whose colors had somehow
escaped the tube which was supposed to contain them, and
then it took on the form of a woman with a long, gauzy gray
ribbon rising from her head.

[*'Don't kill him*]

Ralph, please don't kill him!'

For a moment he could see the blackboard and read the
quote chalked on it right through her, and then the colors
became her clothes and hair and skin as she came all the way
down. Pickering stared at her in cross-eyed terror. He shrieked
again, and the crotch of his army fatigue pants darkened. He
stuck his fingers into his mouth, as if to stifle the sound he
was making. '*A ghose!*' he screamed through his mouthful of
fingers. '*A Hennurion anna ghose!*'

Lois ignored him and grabbed the barrel of the rifle. 'Don't
kill him, Ralph! Don't!'

Ralph was suddenly furious with her, too. 'Don't you
understand, Lois? Don't you get it? He understood what he
was doing! On some level, he *did* understand – *I saw it in his
goddam aura!*'

'It doesn't matter,' she said, still holding the barrel of the
rifle down so it pointed at the floor. 'It doesn't matter what
he did or didn't understand. We mustn't do what they do.
We mustn't be what they are.'

'But—'

'Ralph, I want to let go of this gun-barrel. It's hot. It's
burning my fingers.'

'All right,' he said, and let go at the same instant she did.
The gun fell to the floor between them, and Pickering, who
had been sliding slowly down the wall with his fingers still
in his mouth and his shining, glazed eyes still fixed on Lois,
lunged for it with the speed of a striking rattlesnake.

What Ralph did then he did without forethought and
certainly without anger – he acted purely on instinct, reaching
out for Pickering with both hands and grasping the sides of
his face. Something flashed brightly inside his mind as he did
it, something that felt like the lens of a powerful magnifying
glass. He slammed back up through the levels, for a split
second going higher than either of them had yet been. At
the height of his ascent, he felt a terrible force flash in his
head and explode down his arms. Then, as he dropped back

down, *he* heard the bang, a hollow but emphatic sound which was entirely different from the guns still firing outside.

Pickering's body jerked galvanically, and his legs shot out with such force that one of his shoes flew off. His buttocks rose and then thumped down. His teeth clamped shut on his lower lip, and blood squirted out of his mouth. For a moment Ralph was almost sure he saw tiny blue sparks snapping from the ends of his zany hair. Then they were gone and Pickering slumped back against the wall. He stared at Ralph and Lois with eyes from which all concern had fled.

Lois screamed. At first Ralph thought she was screaming because of what he had done to Pickering, and then he saw she was beating at the top of her head. A piece of burning wallpaper had landed there and her hair was on fire.

He swept an arm around her, beat at the flames with his own hand, then covered her body with his as a fresh gust of rifle- and shotgun-fire hit the north wing. Ralph's free hand was splayed out against the wall, and he saw a bullet-hole appear between the third and fourth fingers like a magic trick.

'Go up, Lois! Go up

[*right now!*']

They went up together, turning to colored smoke before Charlie Pickering's empty eyes . . . and then disappearing.

2

['*What did you do to him, Ralph? For a second you were gone – you were up – and then . . . then he . . . what did you do?*']

She was looking at Charlie Pickering with stunned horror. Pickering was sitting against the wall in almost exactly the same position as the two dead women in the next room. As Ralph watched, a large pinkish spit-bubble appeared between his slack lips, grew, then popped.

He turned to Lois, took her by the arms just above the elbows, and made a picture in his mind: the circuit-breaker box in the basement of his house on Harris Avenue. Hands opened the box, then quickly flipped all the switches from ON to OFF. He wasn't sure that this was right – it had all happened too fast for him to be sure of anything – but he thought it was close.

Lois's eyes widened a little, and then she nodded. She looked at Pickering, then at Ralph.

['*He brought it on himself, didn't he? You didn't do it on purpose.*']

Ralph nodded, and then fresh screams came up from below their feet, screams he was quite sure he was not hearing with his ears.

['*Lois?*']

['*Yes, Ralph – right now.*']

He slipped his hands down her arms and gripped her hands, as the four of them had held hands in the hospital, only this time they went down instead of up, sliding into the plank floor as if it were a pool of water. Ralph was once again aware of a knife-edge of darkness crossing his vision, and then they were in the cellar, sinking slowly down to a dirty cement floor. He saw shadowy furnace-pipes, grimy with dust, a snowblower covered with a large sheet of dirty transparent plastic, gardening equipment lined up to one side of a dim cylinder that was probably the water heater, and cartons stacked against one brick wall – soup, beans, spaghetti sauce, coffee, garbage bags, toilet-tissue. All of these things looked slightly hallucinatory, not quite there, and at first Ralph thought this was a new side-effect of having gone to the next level. Then he realized it was just smoke – the cellar was filling up with it rapidly.

There were eighteen or twenty people clustered at one end of the long, shadowy room, most of them women. Ralph also saw a little boy of about four clinging to his mother's knees (Mommy's face showed the fading bruises of what might have been an accident but was probably on purpose), a little girl a year or two older with her face pressed against her mother's stomach . . . and he saw Helen. She was holding Natalie in her arms and blowing into the baby's face, as if she could keep the air around her clear of smoke that way. Nat was coughing and screaming in choked, desperate whoops. Behind the women and children, Ralph could make out a dusty set of steps climbing up into darkness.

['*Ralph? We have to go down now, don't we?*']

He nodded, made that blink inside his head, and suddenly he was also coughing as he pulled acrid smoke into his lungs. They materialized directly in front of the group at the foot of the stairs, but only the little boy with his arms around his mother's knees reacted. In that moment, Ralph was positive he had seen this kid somewhere before, but he had no idea where – the day near the end of summer when he'd seen him playing roll-toss with his mother in Strawford Park was the furthest thing from his mind at that moment.

'Look, Mama!' the boy said, pointing and coughing. 'Angels!'

Inside his head Ralph heard Clotho saying *We're no angels, Ralph*, and then he pushed forward toward Helen through the thickening smoke, still holding Lois's hand. His eyes were stinging and tearing already, and he could hear Lois coughing. Helen was looking at him with dazed unrecognition – looking at him the way she had on that day in August when Ed had beaten her so badly.

'Helen!'

'*Ralph?*'

'Those stairs, Helen! Where do they go?'

'What are you doing here, Ralph? How did you get h –' She broke into a coughing spasm and doubled over. Natalie almost tumbled out of her arms and Lois took the screaming child before Helen could drop her.

Ralph looked at the woman to Helen's left, saw she seemed even less aware of what was going on, then grabbed Helen again and shook her. '*Where do the stairs go?*'

She glanced over her shoulder at them. 'Cellar bulkhead,' she told him. 'But that's no good. It's –' She bent over, coughing dryly. The sound was weirdly like the chatter of Charlie Pickering's automatic weapon. 'It's locked,' Helen finished. 'The fat woman locked it. She had the lock in her pocket. I saw her put it on. Why did she do that, Ralph? How did she know we'd come down here?'

Where else did you have to go? Ralph thought bitterly, then turned to Lois. 'See what you can do, will you?'

'Okay.' She handed him the screaming, coughing baby and pushed through the little crowd of women. Susan Day was not among them, so far as Ralph could see. At the far end of the cellar, a section of the floor fell in with a gush of sparks and a wave of baking heat. The girl with her face buried against her mother's stomach began to scream.

Lois climbed four of the stairs, then reached up with her palms held out, like a minister giving a benediction. In the light of the swirling sparks, Ralph could dimly see the slanting shadow that was the bulkhead. Lois put her hands against it. For a moment nothing happened, and then she flickered briefly out of existence in a rainbow-swirl of colors. Ralph heard a sharp explosion that sounded like an aerosol can exploding in a hot fire, and then Lois was back. At the same moment he thought he saw a pulse of white light from just above her head.

'What was that, Mama?' asked the little boy who had called Ralph and Lois angels. 'What was that?' Before she could reply, a stack of curtains on a card-table about twenty feet away whooshed into flame, painting the faces of the trapped women in stark Halloween shades of black and orange.

'Ralph!' Lois cried. 'Help me!'

He pushed through the dazed women and climbed the stairs. 'What?' His throat felt as if he had been gargling with kerosene. 'Can't you get it?'

'I got it, I felt the lock break – in my mind I felt it – but this boogery door is too heavy for me! You'll have to do that part. Give me the baby.'

He let her take Nat again, then reached up and tested the bulkhead. It was heavy, all right, but Ralph was running on pure adrenaline and when he put his shoulders into it and shoved, it flew open. A flood of bright light and fresh air swept down the narrow stairwell. In one of Ralph's beloved films, such moments were usually greeted by screams of triumph and relief, but at first none of the women who had been trapped down here made any sound at all. They only stood in silence, looking up with stunned faces at the rectangle of blue sky Ralph had conjured in the roof of the room most of them had accepted as their grave.

And what will they say later? he wondered. *If they really do survive this, what will they say later? That a skinny man with bushy eyebrows and a lady on the stout side (but with beautiful Spanish eyes) materialized in the cellar, broke the lock on the bulkhead door, and led them to safety?*

He looked down and saw the strangely familiar little boy looking back up at him with large, grave eyes. There was a hook-shaped scar across the bridge of the boy's nose. Ralph had an idea that this kid was the only one who had *really* seen them, even after they had dropped back down to the Short-Time level, and Ralph knew perfectly well what he would say: that angels had come, a man angel and a lady angel, and they had saved them. *Should make for an interesting sidebar on the news tonight,* Ralph thought. Yes indeed. Lisette Benson and John Kirkland would love it.

Lois slapped her hand against one of the support-posts. 'Come on, you guys! Get going before the fire gets to the furnace oil-tanks!'

The woman with the little girl moved first. She hoisted her crying child into her arms and staggered upstairs, coughing and weeping. The others began to follow. The little boy looked up at Ralph admiringly as his mother led him past. 'Cool, man,' he said.

Ralph grinned at him – he couldn't help it – then turned to Lois and pointed up the stairs. 'If I'm not all turned around in my head, that comes out behind the house. Don't let them go around to the front yet. The cops are apt to blow half of them away before they realize they're shooting the people they came to save.'

'All right,' she said – not a single question, not another word, and Ralph loved her for that. She went up the stairs at once, pausing only to shift Nat and grab one woman by the elbow when she stumbled.

Now only Ralph and Helen Deepneau were left. 'Was that Lois?' she asked him.

'Yes.'

'She had Natalie?'

'Yes.' Another large chunk of the cellar's roof fell in, more sparks whooshed up, and runners of fire went racing nimbly along the overhead beams toward the furnace.

'Are you sure?' She clutched at his shirt and looked at him with frantic, swollen eyes. 'Are you sure she had Nat?'

'Positive. Let's go now.'

Helen looked around and seemed to count in her head. She looked alarmed. 'Gretchen!' she exclaimed. 'And Merrilee! We have to get Merrilee, Ralph, she's seven months pregnant!'

'She's up there,' Ralph said, grabbing Helen's arm when she showed signs of wanting to leave the foot of the stairs and go back into the burning cellar. 'She and Gretchen both. Is that everyone else?'

'Yes, I think so.'

'Good. Come on. We're getting out of here.'

3

Ralph and Helen stepped out of the bulkhead in a cloud of dark gray smoke, looking like the conclusion of a world-class illusionist's best trick. They were indeed in back of the house, near the clotheslines. Dresses, slacks, underwear, and bed-linen flapped in the freshening breeze. As Ralph watched, a flaming shingle landed on one of the sheets and set it ablaze. More flames were billowing out of the kitchen windows. The heat was intense.

Helen sagged against him, not unconscious but simply used up for the time being. Ralph had to grab her around the waist to keep her from falling to the ground. She clawed weakly at the back of his neck, trying to say something about Natalie. Then she saw her in Lois's arms and relaxed a little. Ralph got a better grip on her and half carried, half dragged her away from the bulkhead. As he did, he saw the remains of what looked like a brand-new padlock on the ground beside the open door. It was split into two pieces and oddly twisted, as if immensely powerful hands had torn it apart.

The women were about forty feet away, huddled at the corner of the house. Lois was facing them, talking to them, keeping them from going any farther. Ralph thought that with a little preparation and a little luck they would be okay when they did – the firing from the police strongpoint hadn't stopped, but it had slackened off considerably.

'*PICKERING!*' It sounded like Leydecker, although the amplification of the bullhorn made it impossible to be sure. '*WHY DON'T YOU BE SMART FOR ONCE IN YOUR LIFE AND COME OUT WHILE YOU STILL CAN?*'

More sirens were approaching, the distinctive watery warble of an ambulance among them. Ralph led Helen to the other women. Lois handed Natalie back to her, then turned in the direction of the amplified voice and cupped her hands around her mouth. '*Hello!*' she screamed. '*Hello out there, can you –*' She stopped, coughing so hard she was nearly retching, doubled over with her hands on her knees and tears squirting from her smoke-irritated eyes.

'Lois, are you okay?' Ralph asked. From the corner of his eye he saw Helen covering the face of the Exalted & Revered Baby with kisses.

'Fine,' she said, wiping her cheeks with her fingers. ''S the damn smoke, that's all.' She cupped her hands around her mouth again. *'Can you hear me?'*

The firing had died down to a few isolated handgun pops. Still, Ralph thought, just one of those little pops in the wrong place might be enough to get an innocent woman killed.

'Leydecker!' he yelled, cupping his own hands around his mouth. *'John Leydecker!'*

There was a pause, and then the amplified voice gave a command that gladdened Ralph's heart. *'STOP FIRING!'*

One more pop, then silence except for the sound of the burning house.

'WHO'S TALKING TO ME? IDENTIFY YOURSELVES!'

But Ralph thought he had enough problems without adding that to them.

'The women are back here!' he yelled, now having to fight a need to cough himself. *'I'm sending them around to the front!'*

'NO, DON'T!' Leydecker responded. *'THERE'S A MAN WITH A GUN IN THE LAST ROOM ON THE GROUND FLOOR! HE'S SHOT SEVERAL PEOPLE ALREADY!'*

One of the women moaned at this and put her hands over her face.

Ralph cleared his burning throat as best he could – at that moment he believed he would have swapped his whole retirement fund for one ice-cold bottle of Coke – and screamed back: *'Don't worry about Pickering! Pickering's—'*

But what exactly *was* Pickering? That was a damned good question, wasn't it?

'Mr Pickering is unconscious! That's why he's stopped shooting!' Lois screamed from beside him. Ralph didn't think 'unconscious' really covered it, but it would do. *'The women are coming around the side of the house with their hands up! Don't shoot! Tell us you won't shoot!'*

There was a moment of silence. Then: *'WE WON'T, BUT I HOPE YOU KNOW WHAT YOU'RE TALKING ABOUT, LADY.'*

Ralph nodded at the mother of the little boy. 'Go on, now. You two can lead the parade.'

'Are you sure they won't hurt us?' The fading bruises on the young woman's face (a face which Ralph also found vaguely familiar) suggested that questions of who would or would not hurt her and her son formed a vital part of her life. 'Are you *sure*?'

'Yes,' Lois said, still coughing and leaking around the

eyes. 'Just put your hands up. You can do that, can't you, big boy?'

The kid shot his hands up with the enthusiasm of a veteran cops-and-robbers player, but his shining eyes never left Ralph's face.

Pink roses, Ralph thought. *If I could see his aura, that's what color it would be.* He wasn't sure if that was intuition or memory, but he knew it was so.

'What about the people inside?' another woman asked. 'What if they shoot? They had guns – what if they shoot?'

'There won't be any more shooting from in there,' Ralph said. 'Go on, now.'

The little boy's mother gave Ralph another doubtful look, then looked down at her son. 'Ready, Pat?'

'Yes!' Pat said, and grinned.

His mother nodded and raised one hand. The other she curled around his shoulders in a frail gesture of protection that touched Ralph's heart. They walked around the side of the house that way. *'Don't hurt us!'* she cried. *'Our hands are up and my little boy is with me, so don't hurt us!'*

The others waited a moment, and then the woman who had put her hands to her face went. The one with the little girl joined her (the child was in her arms now, but holding her hands obediently in the air just the same). The others followed along, most coughing, all with their empty hands held high. When Helen started to fall in at the end of the parade, Ralph touched her shoulder. She looked up at him, her reddened eyes both calm and wondering.

'That's the second time you've been there when Nat and I needed you,' she said. 'Are you our guardian angel, Ralph?'

'Maybe,' he said. 'Maybe I am. Listen, Helen – there isn't much time. Gretchen is dead.'

She nodded and began to cry. 'I knew it. I didn't want to, but somehow I did, just the same.'

'I'm very sorry.'

'We were having such a good time when they came – I mean, we were nervous, but there was also a lot of laughing and a lot of chatter. We were going to spend the day getting ready for the speech tonight. The rally and Susan Day's speech.'

'It's tonight I have to ask you about,' Ralph said, speaking as gently as he could. 'Do you think they'll still—'

'We were making breakfast when they came.' She spoke as if she hadn't heard him; Ralph supposed she hadn't.

Nat was peeking over Helen's shoulder, and although she was still coughing, she had stopped crying. Safe within the circle of her mother's arms, she looked from Ralph to Lois and then back to Ralph again with lively curiosity.

'Helen –' Lois began.

'Look! See there?' Helen pointed to an old brown Cadillac parked beside the ramshackle shed which had been the cider-press in the days when Ralph and Carolyn had occasionally come out here; it had probably served High Ridge as a garage. The Caddy was in bad shape – cracked windshield, dented rocker panels, one headlight crisscrossed with masking tape. The bumper was layered with pro-life stickers.

'That's the car they came in. They drove around to the back of the house as if they meant to put it in our garage. I think that's what fooled us. They drove right around to the back as if they *belonged* here.' She contemplated the car for a moment, then returned her smoke-reddened, unhappy eyes to Ralph and Lois. 'Somebody should have paid attention to the stickers on the damned thing.'

Ralph suddenly thought of Barbara Richards back at Woman-Care-Barbie Richards, who had relaxed when Lois approached. It hadn't mattered to her that Lois was reaching for something in her purse; what had mattered was that Lois was a woman. Sandra McKay had been driving the Cadillac; Ralph didn't need to ask Helen to know that. They had seen the woman and ignored the bumper stickers. *We are family; I've got all my sisters with me.*

'When Deanie said the people getting out of the car were dressed in army clothes and carrying guns, we thought it was a joke. All of us but Gretchen, that is. She told us to get downstairs as quick as we could. Then she went into the parlor. To call the police, I suppose. I should have stayed with her.'

'No,' Lois said, and slipped a lock of Natalie's fine-spun auburn hair through her fingers. 'You had this one to look out for, didn't you? And still do.'

'I suppose,' she said dully. 'I suppose I do. But she was my friend, Lois. My *friend*.'

'I know, dear.'

Helen's face twisted like a rag, and she began to cry.

474

Natalie looked at her mother with an expression of comical astonishment for a moment, and then she began to cry, too.

'Helen,' Ralph said. 'Helen, listen to me. I have something to ask you. It's very, very important. Are you listening?'

Helen nodded, but she went on crying. Ralph had no idea if she was really hearing him or not. He glanced at the corner of the building, wondering how long it would be before the police charged around it, then took a deep breath. 'Do you think there's any chance that they'll still hold the rally tonight? Any chance at all? You were as close to Gretchen as anybody. Tell me what you think.'

Helen stopped crying and looked at him with still, wide eyes, as if she couldn't believe what she had just heard. Then those eyes began to fill with a frightening depth of anger.

'How can you ask? How can you even *ask*?'

'Well . . . because . . .' He stopped, unable to go on. Ferocity was the last thing he had expected.

'If they stop us now, they win,' Helen said. 'Don't you see that? Gretchen's dead, Merrilee's dead, High Ridge is burning to the ground with everything some of these women own inside, and if they stop us now they win.'

One part of Ralph's mind – a deep part – now made a terrible comparison. Another part, one that loved Helen, moved to block it, but it moved too late. Her eyes looked like Charlie Pickering's eyes when Pickering had been sitting next to him in the library, and there was no reasoning with a mind that could make eyes look like that.

'If they stop us now they win!' she screamed. In her arms, Natalie began to cry harder. *'Don't you get it? Don't you fucking* GET *it? We'll* never *let that happen! Never! Never! Never!'*

Abruptly she raised the hand she wasn't using to hold the baby and went around the corner of the building. Ralph reached for her and touched the back of her blouse with his fingertips. That was all.

'Don't shoot me!' Helen was crying at the police on the other side of the house. *'Don't shoot me, I'm one of the women! I'm one of the women! I'm one of the women!'*

Ralph lunged after her – no thought, just instinct – and Lois seized him by the back of his belt. 'Better not go out there, Ralph. You're a man, and they might think—'

'Hello, Ralph! Hello, Lois!'

They both turned toward this new voice. Ralph recognized it at once, and he felt both surprised and not surprised. Standing beyond the clotheslines with their freight of flaming sheets and garments, wearing a pair of faded flannel pants and an old pair of Converse high-tops which had been mended with electrician's tape, was Dorrance Marstellar. His hair, as fine as Natalie's (but white instead of auburn), blew about his head in the October wind which combed the top of this hill. As usual, he had a book in one hand.

'Come on, you two,' he said, waving to them and smiling. 'Hurry up and hurry along. There's not much time.'

4

He led them down a weedy, little-used path that meandered away from the house in a westerly direction. It wound first through a fair-sized garden-plot from which everything had been harvested but the pumpkins and squashes, then into an orchard where the apples were just coming to full ripeness, then through a dense blackberry tangle where thorns seemed to reach out everywhere to snag their clothes. As they passed out of the blackberry brambles and into a gloomy stand of old pines and spruces, it occurred to Ralph that they must be on the Newport side of the ridge now.

Dorrance walked briskly for a man of his years, and the placid smile never left his face. The book he carried was *for Love, Poems 1950–1960*, by a man named Robert Creeley. Ralph had never heard of him, but supposed Mr Creeley had never heard of Elmore Leonard, Ernest Haycox or Louis L'Amour, either. He only tried to talk to Old Dor once, when the three of them finally reached the foot of a slope made slick and treacherous with pine-needles. Just ahead of them, a small stream foamed coldly past.

'Dorrance, what are you doing out here? How'd you *get* here, for that matter? And where the hell are we going?'

'Oh, I hardly ever answer questions,' Old Dor replied, smiling widely. He surveyed the stream, then raised one finger and pointed at the water. A small brown trout jumped into the air, flipped bright drops from its tail, and fell back into the water again. Ralph and Lois looked at each other with identical *Did I just see what I thought I saw?* expressions.

'Nope, nope,' Dor continued, stepping off the bank and onto a wet rock. 'Hardly ever. Too difficult. Too many possibilities. Too many levels . . . eh, Ralph? The world is full of levels, isn't it? How are you, Lois?'

'Fine,' she said absently, watching Dorrance cross the stream on a number of conveniently placed stones. He did it with his arms held out to either side, a posture which made him look like the world's oldest acrobat. Just as he reached the far bank, there was a violent exhalation from the ridge behind them – not quite an explosion.

There go the oil-tanks, Ralph thought.

Dor turned to face them from the other side of the brook, smiling his placid Buddha's smile. Ralph went up this time without any conscious intention of doing so, and without that sense of a blink inside his mind. Color rushed into the day, but he barely noticed; all his attention was fixed on Dorrance, and for a space of almost ten seconds, he forgot to breathe.

Ralph had seen auras of many shades in the last month or so, but none even remotely approached the splendid envelope that enclosed the old man Don Veazie had once described as 'nice as hell, but really sort of a fool'. It was as if Dorrance's aura had been strained through a prism . . . or a rainbow. He tossed off light in dazzling arcs: blue followed by magenta, magenta followed by red, red followed by pink, pink followed by the creamy yellow-white of a ripe banana.

He felt Lois's hand groping for his and enfolded it.

['*My God, Ralph, do you see? Do you see how beautiful he is?*']

['*I sure do.*']

['*What is he? Is he even human?*']

['*I don't kn—*']

['*Stop it, both of you. Come back down.*']

Dorrance was still smiling, but the voice they heard in their heads was commanding and not a bit vague. And before Ralph could consciously think himself down, he felt a push. The colors and the heightened quality of the sounds dropped out of the day at once.

477

'There's no time for that now,' Dor said. 'Why, it's noon already.'

'*Noon?*' Lois asked. 'It *can't* be! It wasn't even nine when we got here, and that can't have been half an hour ago!'

'Time goes faster when you're high,' Old Dor said. He spoke solemnly, but his eyes twinkled. 'Just ask anyone drinking beer and listening to country music on Saturday night. Come on! Hurry up! The clock is ticking! Cross the stream!'

Lois went first, stepping carefully from stone to stone with her arms held out, as Dorrance had done. Ralph followed with his hands poised to either side of her hips, ready to catch her if she showed signs of wavering, but he was the one who ended up almost tumbling in. He managed to avoid it, but only at the cost of wetting one foot all the way to the ankle. It seemed to him that someplace in the far reaches of his head, he could hear Carolyn laughing.

'Can't you tell us anything, Dor?' he asked as they reached the far side. 'We're pretty lost here.' *And not just mentally or spiritually, either,* he thought. He had never been in these woods in his life, not even hunting partridge or deer as a young man. If the path they were on petered out, or if Old Dor lost whatever passed for his bearings, what then?

'Yes,' Dor responded at once. 'I can tell you one thing, and it's absolutely for sure.'

'What?'

'These are the best poems Robert Creeley ever wrote,' Old Dor said, holding up his copy of *for Love,* and before either of them could respond to that, he turned around and once again began tracing his way along the faint path which ran west through the woods.

Ralph looked at Lois. Lois looked back at him, equally at a loss. Then she shrugged. 'Come on, old buddy,' she said. 'We better not lose him now. I forgot the breadcrumbs.'

5

They climbed another hill, and from the top of it Ralph could see that the path they were on led down to an old woods road with a strip of grass running up the middle. It dead-ended in an overgrown gravel-pit about fifty yards further along. There was a car idling just outside the entrance to the pit, a perfectly anonymous late model Ford which Ralph nevertheless felt he knew. When the door opened and the driver got out, everything fell into place. Of course he knew the car; he had last seen it from Lois's living room window on Tuesday night. Then it had been slued around in the middle of Harris Avenue with the driver kneeling in the glow of the headlights . . . kneeling beside the dying dog he had struck. Joe Wyzer heard them coming, looked up, and waved.

Chapter Twenty-three

1

'He said he wanted me to drive,' Wyzer told them as he carefully turned his car around at the entrance to the gravel-pit.

'Where to?' Lois asked. She was sitting in the back with Dorrance. Ralph was in the front seat with Joe Wyzer, who looked as if he weren't quite sure where or even who he was. Ralph had slid up – just the tiniest bit – as he shook hands with the pharmacist, wanting to get a look at Wyzer's aura. Both it and his balloon-string were there, and both looked perfectly healthy . . . but the bright yellow-orange looked slightly muted to him. Ralph had an idea that was very likely Old Dor's influence.

'Good question,' Wyzer said. He voiced a small, confused laugh. 'I don't have the slightest idea, really. This has been the *weirdest* day of my entire life. Absolutely no doubt about it.'

The woods road ended in a T-junction with a stretch of two-lane blacktop. Wyzer stopped, looked for traffic, then turned left. They passed a sign reading TO I-95 almost right away, and Ralph guessed that Wyzer would turn north as soon as they reached the turnpike. He knew where they were now – just about two miles south of Route 33. From here they could be back in Derry in less than half an hour, and Ralph had no doubt that was just where they were going.

He abruptly began to laugh. 'Well, here we are,' he said. 'Just three happy folks out for a midday drive. Make that four. Welcome to the wonderful world of hyper-reality, Joe.'

Joe gave him a sharp look, then relaxed into a grin. 'Is that what this is?' And before either Ralph or Lois could reply: 'Yeah, I suppose it is.'

'Did you read that poem?' Dorrance asked from behind Ralph. 'The one that starts "Each thing I do I rush through so I can do something else"?'

Ralph turned and saw that Dorrance was still smiling his wide, placid smile. 'Yes, I did. Dor—'

'Isn't it a crackerjack? It's *so* good. Stephen Dobyns reminds me of Hart Crane without the pretensions. Or maybe I mean *Stephen* Crane, but I don't think so. Of course he doesn't have the music of Dylan Thomas, but is that so bad? Probably not. Modern poetry is not about music. It's about *nerve* – who has it and who doesn't.'

'Oh boy,' Lois said. She rolled her eyes.

'He could probably tell us everything we need to know if we went up a few levels,' Ralph said, 'but you don't want that, do you, Dor? Because time goes faster when you're high.'

'Bingo,' Dorrance replied. The blue signs marking the north and south entrances to the turnpike glimmered up ahead. 'You'll have to go up later, I imagine, you and Lois both, and so it's very important to save as much time as you can now. Save . . . time.' He made a queerly evocative gesture, drawing a gnarled thumb and forefinger down in the air, bringing them together as he did, as if to indicate some narrowing passage.

Joe Wyzer put on his blinker, turned left, and headed down the northbound ramp to Derry.

'How did you get involved in this, Joe?' Ralph asked him. 'Of all the people on the west side, why did Dorrance draft you as chauffeur?'

Wyzer shook his head, and when the car reached the turnpike it drifted immediately over into the passing lane. Ralph reached out quickly and made a midcourse correction, reminding himself that Joe probably hadn't been getting much sleep himself just lately. He was very happy to see the highway was mostly deserted, at least this far out of town. It would save some anxiety, and God knew he would take whatever he could get in that department today.

'We are all bound together by the Purpose,' Dorrance said abruptly. 'That's *ka-tet,* which means one made of many. The way that many rhymes make up a single poem. You see?'

'No.' Ralph, Lois, and Joe said it at the same time, in perfect, unrehearsed chorus, and then laughed nervously together. *The Three Insomniacs of the Apocalypse*, Ralph thought. *Jesus save us.*

'That's okay,' Old Dor said, smiling his wide smile. 'Just

take my word for it. You and Lois . . . Helen and her little daughter . . . Bill . . . Faye Chapin . . . Trigger Vachon . . . me! All part of the Purpose.'

'That's fine, Dor,' Lois said, 'but where's the Purpose taking us now? And what are we supposed to do when we get there?'

Dorrance leaned forward and whispered in Joe Wyzer's ear, guarding his lips with one puffy, age-spotted hand. Then he sat back again, looking deeply satisfied with himself.

'He says we're going to the Civic Center,' Joe said.

'The *Civic* Center!' Lois exclaimed, sounding alarmed. 'No, that can't be right! Those two little men said—'

'Never mind them right now,' Dorrance said. 'Just remember what it's about – nerve. Who has it, and who doesn't.'

2

Silence in Joe Wyzer's Ford for almost the space of a mile. Dorrance opened his book of Robert Creeley poems and began to read one, tracing his way from line to line with the yellowed nail of one ancient finger. Ralph found himself remembering a game they had sometimes played as kids – not a very nice one. Snipe Hunt, it had been called. You got kids who were a little younger and a lot more gullible than you were, fed them a cock-and-bull story about the mythical snipe, then gave them towsacks and sent them out to spend a strenuous afternoon wandering around in the damps and the willywags, looking for nonexistent birds. This game was also called Wild Goose Chase, and he suddenly had the inescapable feeling that Clotho and Lachesis had been playing it with him and Lois up on the hospital roof.

He turned around in his seat and looked directly at Old Dor. Dorrance folded over the top corner of the page he was reading, closed his book, and looked back at Ralph with polite interest.

'They told us we weren't to go near either Ed Deepneau or Doc #3,' Ralph said. He spoke slowly and with great clarity. 'They told us very specifically that we weren't even to *think* of doing that, because the situation had invested both of them with great power and we were apt to get swatted like flies. In fact, I think Lachesis said that if we tried getting near either Ed or Atropos, we might end up having a visit from one of the upper-level honchos . . . someone Ed calls the Crimson King. Not a very nice fellow, either, by all reports.'

'Yes,' Lois said in a faint voice. 'That's what they told us on the hospital roof. They said we had to convince the women in charge to cancel Susan Day's appearance. That's why we went out to High Ridge.'

'And did you succeed in convincing them?' Wyzer asked.

'No. Ed's crazy friends came before we could get there, set the place on fire, and killed at least two of the women. Shot them. One was the woman we really wanted to talk to.'

'Gretchen Tillbury,' Ralph said.

'Yes,' Lois agreed. 'But surely we don't need to do any more – I can't believe they'll go ahead with the rally now. I mean, how could they? My God, at least four people are dead! Probably more! They'll *have* to cancel her speech or at least postpone it. Isn't that so?'

Neither Dorrance nor Joe replied. Ralph didn't reply, either – he was thinking of Helen's red-rimmed, furious eyes. *How can you even ask?* she'd said. *If they stop us now, they win.*

If they stop us now, they win.

Was there any legal way the police *could* stop them? Probably not. The City Council, then? Maybe. Maybe they could hold a special meeting and revoke WomanCare's rally permit. But *would* they? If there were two thousand angry, grief-stricken women marching around the Municipal Building and yelling *If they stop us now they win* in unison, *would* the Council revoke the permit?

Ralph began to feel a deep sinking sensation in his gut.

Helen clearly considered tonight's rally more important than ever, and she wouldn't be the only one. It was no longer just about choice and who had the right to decide what a woman did with her own body; now it was about causes important enough to die for and honoring the friends who had done just that. Now they were talking not just about politics but about a kind of secular requiem mass for the dead.

Lois had grabbed his shoulder and was shaking it hard. Ralph came back to the here and now, but slowly, like a man being shaken awake in the middle of an incredibly vivid dream.

'They *will* cancel it, won't they? And even if they don't, if for some crazy reason they don't, most people will stay away, right? After what happened at High Ridge, they'll be afraid to come!'

Ralph thought about that and then shook his head. 'Most people will think the danger's over. The news reports are going to say that two of the radicals who attacked High Ridge are dead, and the third is catatonic, or something.'

'But Ed! What about Ed?' she cried. 'He's the one who got them to attack, for heaven's sake! *He's the one who sent them out there in the first place!*'

'That may be true, probably *is* true, but how would we prove it? Do you know what I think the cops will find at wherever Charlie Pickering's been hanging his hat? A note saying it was all his idea. A note exonerating Ed completely, probably in the guise of an accusation . . . how Ed deserted them in their time of greatest need. And if they don't find a note like that in Charlie's rented room, they'll find it in Frank Felton's. Or Sandra McKay's.'

'But that . . . that's . . .' Lois stopped, biting at her lower lip. Then she looked at Wyzer with hopeful eyes. 'What about Susan Day? Where is *she*? Does anybody know? Do you? Ralph and I will call her on the telephone and—'

'She's already in Derry,' Wyzer said, 'although I doubt if even the police know for sure where she is. But what I heard on the news while the old fella and I were driving out here is that the rally is going to happen tonight . . . and that's supposedly straight from the woman herself.'

Sure, Ralph thought. *Sure it is. The show's going on, the show has to go on, and she knows it. Someone who's ridden the crest of the women's movement all these years – hell, since the Chicago convention in '68 – knows a genuine watershed moment when she sees it. She's evaluated the risks and found them acceptable. Either that or she's evaluated the situation and decided that the credibility-loss involved in walking away would be unacceptable. Maybe both. In any case, she's as much a prisoner of events – of* ka-tet *– as the rest of us.*

They were on the outskirts of Derry again. Ralph could see the Civic Center on the horizon.

Now it was Old Dor Lois turned to. 'Where is she? Do *you* know? It doesn't matter how many security people she's got around her; Ralph and I can be invisible when we want to be . . . and we're very good at changing people's minds.'

'Oh, changing Susan Day's mind wouldn't change anything,' Dor said. He still wore that broad, maddening smile. 'They'll come to the Civic Center tonight no matter what. If they come and find the doors locked, they'll break them open and go inside and have their rally just the same. To show they're not afraid.'

'Done-bun-can't-be-undone,' Ralph said dully.

'Right, Ralph!' Dor said cheerily, and patted Ralph's arm.

3

Five minutes later, Joe drove his Ford past the hideous plastic statue of Paul Bunyan which stood in front of the Civic Center and turned in at a sign which read THERE'S ALWAYS FREE PARKING AT YOUR CIVIC CENTER!

The acre of parking lot lay between the Civic Center building itself and the Bassey Park racetrack. If the event that evening had been a rock concert or a boat-show or a wrestling card, they would have had the parking lot entirely to themselves this early, but tonight's event was clearly going to be light-years from an exhibition basketball game or a monster truck-pull. There were already sixty or seventy cars in the lot, and little groups of people standing around, looking at the building. Most of them were women. Some had picnic hampers, several were crying, and almost all wore black armbands. Ralph saw a middle-aged woman with a weary, intelligent face and a great mass of gray hair passing these out from a carrybag. She was wearing a tee-shirt with Susan Day's face on it and the words WE SHALL ♀VERC♀ME.

The drive-through area in front of the Civic Center's bank of entrance doors was even busier than the parking lot. No fewer than six TV newsvans were parked there, and various tech crews stood under the triangular cement canopy in little clusters, discussing how they were going to handle tonight's event. And according to the bedsheet banner which hung down from the canopy, flapping lazily in the breeze, there *was* going to be an event. RALLY IS *ON*, it read in large, blurry spray-paint letters. 8 P.M. COME SHOW YOUR SOLIDARITY   EXPRESS YOUR OUTRAGE   COMFORT YOUR SISTERS.

Joe put the Ford in Park, then turned to Old Dor, eyebrows raised. Dor nodded, and Joe looked at Ralph. 'I guess this is where you and Lois get out, Ralph. Good luck. I'd come with you if I could – I even asked him – but he says I'm not equipped.'

'That's all right,' Ralph said. 'We appreciate everything you've done, don't we, Lois?'

'We certainly do,' Lois said.

Ralph reached for the doorhandle, then let it go again. He turned to face Dorrance. 'What's this about? Really, I mean. It's *not* about saving the two thousand or so people Clotho and Lachesis said are going to be here tonight, that's for sure. To the kind of All-Time forces *they* talked about, two thousand lives are probably just a little more grease on the bearings. So what's it all about, Alfie? Why are we here?'

Dorrance's grin had faded at last; with it gone he looked younger and strangely formidable. 'Job asked God the same question,' he said, 'and got no answer. You're not going to get one either, but I'll tell you this much: you've become the pivot-point of great events and vast forces. The work of the higher universe has almost completely come to a stop as those of both the Random and the Purpose turn to mark your progress.'

'That's great, but I don't get it,' Ralph said, more in resignation than in anger.

'Neither do I, but those two thousand lives are enough for me,' Lois said quietly. 'I could never live with myself if I didn't at least try to stop what's going to happen. I'd dream of the deathbag around that building for the rest of my life. Even if I only got an hour's sleep a night I'd dream of it.'

Ralph considered this, then nodded. He opened his door and swung one foot out. 'That's a good point. And Helen'll be there. She might even bring Nat. Maybe, for little Short-Time farts like us, that's enough.'

And maybe, he thought, *I want a rematch with Doc #3.*

Oh, Ralph, Carolyn mourned. *Clint Eastwood? Again?*

No, not Clint Eastwood. Not Sylvester Stallone or Arnold Schwarzenegger, either. Not even John Wayne. He was no big action-hero or movie-star; he was just plain old Ralph Roberts from Harris Avenue. That didn't make the grudge he bore the doc with the rusty scalpel any less real, however. And now that grudge was a lot bigger than just a stray dog and the retired history teacher who had lived downstairs for the last ten years or so. Ralph kept thinking of the parlor at High Ridge, and the women propped against the wall below the poster of Susan Day. It wasn't upon Merrilee's pregnant belly which the eye in his mind kept focusing but Gretchen Tillbury's hair – her beautiful blonde hair that had been mostly burned off by the close-range rifle-shot that had taken her life. Charlie Pickering had pulled the trigger, and maybe Ed Deepneau had put the gun in his hands, but it was Atropos Ralph blamed,

Atropos the jump-rope-thief, Atropos the hat-thief, Atropos the comb-thief.

Atropos the earring-thief.

'Come on, Lois,' he said. 'Let's—'

But she put her hand on his arm and shook her head. 'Not just yet – get back in here and shut the door.'

He looked at her carefully, then did what she said. She paused, gathering her thoughts, and when she spoke, she looked directly at Old Dor.

'I still don't understand why we were sent out to High Ridge,' she said. 'They never even came right out and said that was what we were supposed to do, but we know – don't we, Ralph? – that that was what they wanted from us. *And I want to understand.* If we're supposed to be *here*, why did we have to go out *there*? I mean, we saved some lives, and I'm glad, but I think Ralph's right – a few lives don't mean much to the people running this show.'

Silence for a moment, and then Dorrance said, 'Did Clotho and Lachesis really strike you as all-wise and all-knowing, Lois?'

'Well . . . they were smart, but I guess they weren't exactly geniuses,' she said after a moment's thought. 'At one point they called themselves working joes who were a long way down the ladder from the boardroom executives who actually made the decisions.'

Old Dor was nodding and smiling. 'Clotho and Lachesis are almost Short-Timers themselves, in the big scheme of things. They have their own fears and mental blindspots. They are also capable of making bad decisions . . . but in the end, that doesn't matter, because they also serve the Purpose. And *ka-tet*.'

'They thought we'd lose if we went head-to-head with Atropos, didn't they?' Ralph asked. 'That's why they talked themselves into believing we could accomplish what they wanted to using the back door . . . the back door being High Ridge.'

'Yes,' Dor said. 'That's it.'

'Great,' Ralph said. 'I love a vote of confidence. Especially when—'

'No,' Dor said. 'That's *not* it.'

Ralph and Lois exchanged a bewildered glance.

'What are you talking about?'

'It's both things at the same time. That's very often the way things are within the Purpose. You see . . . well . . .' He sighed.

'I *hate* all these questions. I hardly *ever* answer questions, did I tell you that?'

'Yes,' Lois said. 'You did.'

'Yes. And now, bingo! All these questions. Nasty! And useless!'

Ralph looked at Lois, and she looked back at him. Neither of them made any move to get out.

Dor heaved a sigh. 'All right . . . but this is the last thing I'm going to say, so pay attention. Clotho and Lachesis may have sent you to High Ridge for the wrong reasons, but the Purpose sent you there for the right ones. You fulfilled your task there.'

'By saving the women,' Lois said.

But Dorrance was shaking his head.

'Then what *did* we do?' she nearly shouted. '*What?* Don't we have a right to know what part of the goshdamned Purpose we fulfilled?'

'No,' Dorrance said. 'At least not yet. Because you have to do it again.'

'This is crazy,' Ralph said.

'It isn't, though,' Dorrance replied. He was holding *for Love* tightly against his chest now, bending it back and forth and looking at Ralph earnestly. '*Random* is crazy. Purpose is sane.'

All right, Ralph thought, *what did we do at High Ridge besides save the people in the cellar? And John Leydecker, of course – I think Pickering might have killed him as well as Chris Nell if I hadn't intervened. Could it be something to do with Leydecker?*

He supposed it could, but it didn't feel right.

'Dorrance,' he said, 'can't you please give us a little more information? I mean—'

'No,' Old Dor said, not unkindly. 'No more questions, no more time. We'll have a good meal together after this is over . . . if we're still around, that is.'

'You really know how to cheer a fellow up, Dor.' Ralph opened his door. Lois did the same, and they both stepped out into the parking lot. He bent down and looked at Joe Wyzer. 'Is there anything else? Anything you can think of?'

'No, I don't think—'

Dor leaned forward and whispered in his ear. Joe listened, frowning.

'Well?' Ralph asked when Dorrance sat back. 'What did he say?'

'He said not to forget my comb,' Joe said. 'I don't have

the slightest idea what he's talking about, but what else is new?'

'That's okay,' Ralph said, and smiled a little. 'It's one of the few things I *do* understand. Come on, Lois – let's check out the crowd. Mingle a little.'

4

Halfway across the parking lot, she elbowed him so hard in the side that Ralph staggered. 'Look!' she whispered. 'Right over there! Isn't that Connie Chung?'

Ralph looked. Yes; the woman in the beige coat standing between two techs with the CBS logo on their jackets was almost certainly Connie Chung. He had admired her pretty, intelligent face and pleasant smile over too many evening meals to have much doubt about it.

'Either her or her twin sister,' he said.

Lois seemed to have forgotten all about Old Dor and High Ridge and the bald docs; in that moment she was once more the woman Bill McGovern had liked to call 'our Lois'. 'I'll be darned! What's *she* doing here?'

'Well,' Ralph began, and then covered his mouth to hide a jaw-cracking yawn, 'I guess what's going on in Derry is national news now. She must be here to do a live segment in front of the Civic Center for tonight's news. In any case—'

Suddenly, with no warning at all, the auras swam back. Ralph gasped.

'*Jesus!* Lois, are you seeing this?'

But he didn't think she was. If she *had* been, Ralph didn't think Connie Chung would have rated even an honorable mention on Lois's attention-roster. This was horrible almost beyond conceiving, and for the first time Ralph fully realized that even the bright world of auras had its dark side, one that would make an ordinary person fall on his knees and thank God for his reduced perceptions.

And this isn't even stepping up the ladder, he thought. *At least, I don't think it is. I'm only* looking *at that wider world, like a man looking through a window. I'm not actually in it.*

Nor did he *want* to be in it. Just looking at something like this was almost enough to make you wish you were blind.

Lois was frowning at him. 'What, the colors? No. Should I try to? Is there something wrong with them?'

He tried to answer and couldn't. A moment later he felt her hand seize his arm in a painful pincers grip above the elbow and knew that no explanation was necessary. For better or worse, Lois was now seeing for herself.

'Oh *dear*,' she whimpered in a breathless little voice that teetered on the edge of tears. 'Oh *dear*, oh *dear*, oh jeez Louise.'

From the roof of Derry Home, the aura hanging over the Civic Center had looked like a vast, saggy umbrella – the Travelers' Insurance Company logo colored black by a child's crayon, perhaps. Standing here in the parking lot, it was like being inside a large and indescribably nasty mosquito net, one so old and badly cared-for that its gauzy walls had silted up with blackish-green mildew. The bright October sun shrank to a bleary circle of tarnished silver. The air took on a gloomy, foggy cast that made Ralph think of pictures of London at the end of the nineteenth century. They were not just looking at the Civic Center deathbag, not anymore; they were buried alive in it. Ralph could feel it pressing hungrily in on him, trying to overwhelm him with feelings of loss and despair and dismay.

Why bother? he asked himself, watching apathetically as Joe Wyzer's Ford drove back down toward Main Street with Old Dor still sitting in the back seat. *I mean hey, really, what the hell is the use? We can't change this thing, no way we can. Maybe we did something out at High Ridge, but the difference between what was going on out there and what's happening here is like the difference between a smudge and a black hole. If we try to mess in with this business, we're going to get flattened.*

He heard moaning from beside him and realized Lois was crying. Mustering his flagging energy, he slid an arm around her shoulders. 'Hold on, Lois,' he said. 'We can stand up to this.' But he wondered.

'*We're breathing it in!*' she wept. 'It's like we're sucking up death! Oh, Ralph, let's get away from here! Please let's just get away from here!'

The idea sounded as good to him as the idea of water must sound to a man dying of thirst in the desert, but he shook his head. 'Two thousand people are going to die here tonight if we don't do something. I'm pretty confused about the rest of this business but that much I can grasp with no trouble at all.'

'Okay,' she whispered. 'Just keep your arm around me so I don't crack my head open if I faint.'

It was ironic, Ralph thought. They now had the faces and bodies of people in the early years of a vigorous middle age, but they shuffled across the parking lot like a pair of old-timers whose muscles have turned to string and whose bones have turned to glass. He could hear Lois's breathing, rapid and labored, like the breathing of a woman who has just sustained some serious injury.

'I'll take you back if you want,' Ralph said, and he meant it. He would take her back to the parking lot, he would take her to the orange bus-stop bench he could see from here. And when the bus came, getting on and going back to Harris Avenue would be the simplest thing in the world.

He could feel the killer aura which surrounded this place pressing in on him, trying to smother him like a plastic dry-cleaning bag, and he found himself remembering something McGovern had said about May Locher's emphysema that it was one of those diseases that keep on giving. And now he supposed he had a pretty good idea of how May Locher had felt during her last few years. It didn't matter how hard he sucked at the black air or how deep he dragged it down; it did not satisfy. His heart and head went on pounding, making him feel as if he were suffering the worst hangover of his life.

He was opening his mouth to repeat that he'd take her back when she spoke up, talking in little out-of-breath gasps. 'I guess I can make it . . . but I hope . . . it won't take long. Ralph, how come we can feel something this bad even without being able to see the colors? Why can't *they*?' She pointed at the media people milling around the Civic Center. 'Are we Short-Timers that insensitive? I hate to think that.'

He shook his head, indicating that he didn't know, but he thought that perhaps the news crews, video technicians, and security guards clustered around the doors and beneath the spray-painted banner hanging from the canopy *did* feel something. He saw lots of hands holding styrofoam cups of coffee, but he didn't see anyone actually drinking the stuff. There was a box of doughnuts sitting on the hood of a station wagon, but the only one which had been taken out had been laid aside on a napkin with just a single bite gone. Ralph ran his eye over two dozen faces without seeing a single smile. The newspeople were going about their work – setting camera angles, marking locations from which the talking heads would do their stand-ups, laying down coaxial cable and duct-taping it to the cement – but they were doing it without the sort of excitement which Ralph would have expected to accompany a story as big as this one was turning out to be.

Connie Chung walked out from beneath the canopy with a bearded, handsome cameraman – MICHAEL ROSENBERG, the tag on his CBS jacket said – and then raised her small hands in a framing gesture, showing him how she wanted him to shoot the bedsheet banner hanging down from the canopy. Rosenberg nodded. Chung's face was pale and solemn, and at one point during her conversation with the bearded cameraman, Ralph saw her pause and raise a hand uncertainly to her temple, as if she had lost her train of thought or perhaps felt faint.

There seemed to be an underlying similarity to all the expressions he saw – a common chord – and he thought he knew what it was: they were all suffering from what had been called melancholia when he was a kid, and melancholia was just a fancy word for the blues.

Ralph found himself remembering times in his life when he'd hit the emotional equivalent of a cold spot while swimming or clear air turbulence while flying. You'd be cruising along through your day, sometimes feeling great, sometimes just feeling okay, but getting along and getting it done . . . and then, for no apparent reason at all, you'd go down in flames and crash. A sense of *What the hell's the use* would slide over you – unconnected to any real event in your life at that moment but incredibly powerful all the same – and you felt like simply creeping back to bed and pulling the covers up over your head.

Maybe this is what causes feelings like that, he thought. *Maybe it's running into something like this – some big mess of death or sorrow waiting to happen, spread out like a banquet tent made of cobwebs and tears instead of canvas and rope. We don't see it, not down on our Short-Time level, but we feel it. Oh yes, we feel it. And now . . .*

Now it was trying to suck them dry. Maybe *they* weren't vampires, as they both had feared, but *this* thing was. The deathbag had a sluggish, half-sentient life, and it would suck them dry if it could. If they let it.

Lois stumbled against him and Ralph had all he could do to keep them both from sprawling to the pavement. Then she lifted her head (slowly, as if her hair had been dipped in cement), curled a hand around her mouth, and inhaled sharply. At the same time she flickered a little. Under other circumstances, Ralph might have dismissed that flicker as a momentary glitch in his own eyes, but not now. She had slid up. Just a little. Just enough to feed.

He hadn't seen Lois dip into the waitress's aura, but this time everything happened in front of him. The auras of the newspeople were like small but brightly colored Japanese lanterns glowing bravely in a vast, gloomy cavern. Now a tight beam of violet light speared out from one of them – from Michael Rosenberg, Connie Chung's bearded cameraman, in fact. It divided in two an inch or so in front of Lois's face. The upper branch divided in two again and slipped into her nostrils; the lower branch went between her parted lips and into her mouth. He could see it glowing faintly behind her cheeks, lighting her from the inside as a candle lights a jack-o'-lantern.

Her grip on him loosened, and suddenly the leaning pressure of her weight was gone. A moment later the violet beam of light disappeared. She looked around at him. Color – not a lot, but some – was returning to her leaden cheeks.

'That's better – a *lot* better. Now you, Ralph!'

He was reluctant – it still felt like stealing – but it had to be done if he didn't want to simply collapse right here; he could almost feel the last of Nirvana Boy's borrowed energy running out through his pores. He curled his hand around his mouth now as he had in the Dunkin' Donuts parking lot that morning and turned slightly to his left, seeking a target. Connie Chung had backed several steps closer to them; she was still looking up at the bedsheet banner hanging from the canopy and talking to Rosenberg (who seemed none the worse for wear as a result of Lois's borrowing) about it. With no further thought, Ralph inhaled sharply through the curled tube of his fingers.

Chung's aura was the same lovely shade of wedding-gown ivory as those which had surrounded Helen and Nat on the day they'd come to his apartment with Gretchen Tillbury. Instead of a ray of light, something like a long, straight ribbon shot from Chung's aura. Ralph felt strength begin to fill him almost at once, banishing the aching weariness in his joints and muscles. And he could think clearly again, as if a big cloud of sludge had just been washed out of his brain.

Connie Chung broke off, looked up at the sky for a moment, then began to talk to the cameraman again. Ralph glanced around and saw Lois looking at him anxiously. 'Any better?' she whispered.

'All kinds,' he said, 'but it's still like being zipped up in a body-bag.'

'I think –' Lois began, and then her eyes fixed on something to the left of the Civic Center doors. She screamed and shrank back against Ralph, her eyes so wide it seemed they must tumble from their sockets. He followed her gaze and felt his breath stop in his throat. The planners had tried to soften the building's plain brick sides by planting evergreen bushes along them. These had either been neglected or purposely allowed to grow until they interlaced and threatened to entirely hide the narrow strip of grass between them and the concrete walk which bordered the drive-through.

Giant bugs that looked like prehistoric trilobites were squirming in and out of these evergreens in droves, crawling over each other, bumping heads, sometimes rearing up and pawing each other with their front legs like stags locking horns during mating season. They weren't transparent, like the bird on the satellite dish, but there was something ghostly and unreal about them, just the same. Their auras flickered feverishly (and brainlessly, Ralph guessed) through a whole spectrum of colors; they were so bright and yet so ephemeral that it was almost possible to think of them as weird lightning-bugs.

Except that's not what they are. You know *what they are.*

'Hey!' It was Rosenberg, Chung's cameraman, who hailed them, but most of the others in front of the building were looking. 'She okay, bud?'

'Yes,' Ralph called back. He still had his hand curled around his mouth and lowered it quickly, feeling foolish. 'She just . . .'

'I saw a mouse!' Lois called, smiling a daffy, dazed smile . . . an 'our Lois' smile if Ralph had ever seen one. He was very proud of her. She pointed toward the evergreen shrubs to the left of the door with a finger that was almost steady. 'He went right in there. Gosh, but he was a fat one! Did you see him, Norton?'

'No, Alice.'

'Stick around, lady,' Michael Rosenberg called. 'You'll see all kinds of wildlife here tonight.' There was some desultory, almost forced laughter, and then they turned back to their tasks.

'God, Ralph!' Lois whispered. 'Those . . . those *things* . . .'

He took her hand and squeezed it. 'Steady, Lois.'

'They know, don't they? That's why they're here. They're like vultures.'

Ralph nodded. As he watched, several bugs emerged from the tops of the bushes and began to ooze aimlessly up the wall. They moved with dazed sluggishness – like flies buzzing against a windowpane in November – and left slimy trails of color behind them. These quickly dimmed and faded. Other bugs crawled out from beneath the bushes and onto the small strip of lawn.

One of the local news commentators began strolling toward this infested area, and when he turned his head, Ralph saw it was John Kirkland. He was talking to a good-looking woman dressed in one of those 'power look' business outfits which Ralph found – under normal circumstances, anyway – extremely sexy. He guessed she was Kirkland's producer, and wondered if Lisette Benson's aura turned green when this woman was around.

'They're going toward those bugs!' Lois whispered fiercely at him. 'We have to stop them, Ralph – we *have* to!'

'We're not going to do a damned thing.'

'But—'

'Lois, we can't start raving about bugs nobody but us can see. We'll end up in the nuthatch if we do. Besides, the bugs aren't there for them.' He paused and added: 'I hope.'

They watched as Kirkland and his good-looking colleague walked onto the lawn . . . and into a jellylike knot of the twitching, crawling trilobites. One slid onto Kirkland's highly polished loafer, paused until he stopped moving for a second, then climbed onto his pantsleg.

'I don't give much of a shit about Susan Day, one way or the other,' Kirkland was saying. 'WomanCare's the story here, not her – crying babes wearing black armbands.'

'Watch out, John,' the woman said dryly. 'Your sensitivity is showing.'

'Is it? Goddam.' The bug on his pantsleg appeared bound for his crotch. It occurred to Ralph that if Kirkland were suddenly given the power to see what was shortly going to be crawling over his balls, he would probably go right out of his mind.

'Okay, but be sure to talk to the women who run the local power-network,' the producer was saying. 'Now that Tillbury's dead, the ones that matter are Maggie Petrowsky, Barbara Richards, and Dr Roberta Warper. Warper's going to introduce the Big Kahuna tonight, I think . . . or maybe in this case it's the Big Kahunette.' The woman took a step off the sidewalk and one of her high heels skewered a lumbering color-bug. A rainbow of guts spewed out of it, and a waxy-white substance that looked like stale mashed potatoes. Ralph had an idea the white stuff had been eggs.

Lois pressed her face against his arm.

'And keep your eyes open for a lady named Helen Deepneau,' the producer said, taking a step closer to the building. The bug stuck on the heel of her shoe flopped and twisted as she walked.

'Deepneau,' Kirkland said. He tapped his knuckles against his brow. 'Somewhere, deep inside, a bell is ringing.'

'Nah, it's just your last active brain-cell rolling around in there,' the producer said. 'She's Ed Deepneau's wife. They're separated. If you want tears, she's your best bet. She and Tillbury were good friends. Maybe *special* friends, if you know what I mean.'

Kirkland leered – an expression so foreign to his on-camera persona that Ralph felt slightly disoriented. One of the color-bugs, meanwhile, had found its way onto the toe of the woman's shoe and was working its way up her leg. Ralph watched in helpless fascination as it disappeared beneath the hem of her skirt. Watching the moving bump climb her thigh was like watching a kitten under a bathtowel. And again, it seemed that Kirkland's colleague felt *something;* as she talked to him about interviews during Day's speech, she reached down and absently scratched at the lump, which had now made it almost all the way up to her right hip. Ralph didn't hear the thick popping sound the fragile, flabby thing made when it burst, but he could imagine it. Was helpless not to, it seemed. And he could imagine its innards dripping down her nyloned leg like pus. It would remain there at least until her evening shower, unseen, unfelt, unsuspected.

Now the two of them began discussing how they should cover the scheduled pro-life rally this afternoon . . . assuming it actually happened, that was. The woman was of the opinion that not even The Friends of Life would be dumbheaded enough to show up at the Civic Center after what had happened at High Ridge. Kirkland told her it was impossible to underestimate the idiocy of fanatics; people who could wear that much polyester in public were clearly a force to be reckoned with. And all the time they were talking, exchanging quips and ideas and gossip, more of the swollen, multi-colored bugs were swarming busily up their legs and torsos. One pioneer had made it all the way up to Kirkland's red tie, and was apparently bound for his face.

Movement off to the right caught Ralph's eye. He turned toward the doors in time to see one of the techs elbowing a buddy and pointing at him and Lois. Ralph suddenly had an all-too-clear picture of what they were seeing: two people with no visible reason for being here (neither of them was wearing a black armband and they were clearly not representatives of the media) just hanging out at the edge of the parking lot. The lady, who had already screamed once, had her face buried against the gentleman's arm . . . and the gentleman in question was gaping like a fool at nothing in particular.

Ralph spoke softly and from the corner of his mouth, like an inmate discussing escape in an old Warner Bros. jailbreak epic. 'Get your head up. We're attracting more attention than we can afford.'

For a moment he really didn't believe she was going to be able to do that . . . and then she came through and lifted her head. She glanced at the shrubs growing along the wall one final time – an involuntary, horrified little peek – and then looked resolutely back at Ralph and *only* Ralph. 'Do you see any sign of Atropos, Ralph? That *is* why we're here, isn't it . . . to pick up his trail?'

'Maybe. I suppose. Haven't even looked, to tell the truth – too many other things going on. I think we ought to get a little closer to the building.' This wasn't a thing he wanted to do, but it seemed very important to do *something*. He could feel the deathbag all around them, a gloomy, suffocating presence that was passively opposed to forward motion of any kind. *That* was what they had to fight.

'All right,' she said. 'I'm going to ask for Connie Chung's autograph, and I'm going to be all giggly and silly while I do it. Can you stand that?'

'Yes.'

'Good. Because that will mean that if they're looking at anybody, they'll be looking at me.'

'Sounds good.'

He spared one last look at John Kirkland and the woman producer. They were now discussing what events might cause them to break into the evening's network feed and go live, totally unaware of the lumbering trilobites crawling back and forth on their faces. One of them was currently squirming slowly into John Kirkland's mouth.

Ralph looked away in a hurry and let Lois pull him over to where Ms Chung stood with Rosenberg, the bearded cameraman. He saw the two of them glance first at Lois and then at each other. The shared look was one part amusement and three parts resignation – *here comes one of them* – and then Lois gave his hand a hard little squeeze that said, *Never mind me, Ralph, you take care of your business and I'll take care of mine.*

'Pardon me, but aren't you Connie Chung?' Lois asked in her gushiest isn't-this-the-living-end voice. 'I saw you over there and at first I said to Norton, "Is that the lady who's on with Dan Rather, or am I crazy?" And then—'

'I *am* Connie Chung, and it's very nice to meet you, but I'm getting ready for tonight's news, so if you could excuse me—'

'Oh, of course, I wouldn't *dream* of bothering you, I only want an autograph – just a quick little scribble would do – because I'm your number one fan, at least in Maine.'

Ms Chung glanced at Rosenberg. He was already holding a pen out in one hand, much as a good OR nurse has the instrument the doctor will want next even before he calls for it. Ralph turned his attention to the area in front of the Civic Center and slid his perceptions up the tiniest bit.

What he saw in front of the doors was a semi-transparent, blackish substance that puzzled him at first. It was about two inches deep and looked almost like some sort of geological formation. That couldn't be, though . . . could it? If what he was looking at was real (the way objects in the Short-Time world were real, at least), the stuff would have blocked the doors from opening, and it wasn't doing that. As Ralph watched, two TV techs strolled ankle-deep through the stuff as if it were no more substantial than low-lying groundmist.

Ralph remembered the aural footprints people left behind – the ones that looked like Arthur Murray learn-to-dance diagrams – and suddenly thought he understood. The tracks faded away like cigarette smoke . . . except that cigarette smoke really *didn't* go away; it left a residue on walls, on windows, and in lungs. Apparently, human auras left their own residue. It probably wasn't enough to see once the colors faded if it was only one person, but this was the biggest public meetingplace in Maine's fourth-largest city. Ralph thought of all the people who had poured in and out through these doors –

all the banquets, conventions, coin-shows, concerts, basketball tourneys – and understood that semi-transparent slag. It was the equivalent of the slight dip you sometimes saw in the middle of much-used steps.

Never mind that now, sweetheart – take care of your business.

Nearby, Connie Chung was scribbling her name on the back of Lois's light-bill for September. Ralph looked at that slaggy residue on the cement apron in front of the doors, hunting for a trace of Atropos, something which might register more as smell than sight, a nasty, meaty aroma like the alley which used to run behind Mr Huston's butcher shop when Ralph was a kid.

'Thank you!' Lois was burbling. 'I said to Norton, "She looks just like she does on TV, just like a little China doll." Those were my exact words.'

'Very welcome, I'm sure,' Chung said, 'but I really have to get back to work.'

'Of course you do. Say hello to Dan Rather for me, won't you? Tell him I said "Courage!"'

'I certainly will.' Chung smiled and nodded as she handed the pen back to Rosenberg. 'Now, if you'll excuse us—'

If it's here, it's higher up than I am, Ralph thought. *I'll have to slide up a little bit farther.*

Yes, but he'd have to be careful, and not just because time had become an extremely valuable commodity. The simple fact was that if he went up too high, he would disappear from the Short-Time world, and that was the sort of occurrence which might even distract these newspeople from the impending pro-choice rally . . . at least for awhile.

Ralph concentrated, but when the painless spasm inside his head happened this time, it didn't come as a blink but as the soft lowering of a lash. Color bloomed silently into the world; everything stood forth with exclamatory brilliance. Yet the strongest of these colors, the oppressive key-chord, was the black of the deathbag, and it was a negation of all the others. Depression and that sense of debilitating weakness fell on him again, sinking into his heart like the pointed ends of a clawhammer. He realized that if he had business to do up here, he had better do it quickly and scoot back down to the Short-Time level before he was stripped clean of life-force.

He looked at the doors again. For a moment there was still nothing but the fading auras of Short-Timers like himself . . . and then what he was looking for suddenly came clear, rising into his view as a message which has been written in lemon juice rises into sight when it is held close to a candle-flame.

He had expected something which would look and smell like the rotting guts in the bins behind Mr Huston's knacker's shop, but the reality was even worse, possibly because it was so unexpected. There were fans of a bloody, mucusy substance on the doors themselves – marks made by Atropos's restless fingers, perhaps – and a revoltingly large puddle of the same stuff sinking into the hardened residue in front of the doors. There was something so terrible about this stuff – so alien – that it made the color-bugs look almost normal by comparison. It was like a pool of vomit left by a dog suffering from some new and dangerous strain of rabies. A trail of this stuff led away from the puddle, first in drying clots and splashes, then in smaller drips like spilled paint.

Of course, Ralph thought. *That's why we had to come here. The little bastard can't stay away from the place. It's like cocaine to a dope-addict.*

He could imagine Atropos standing right here where he, Ralph, was standing now, looking . . . grinning . . . then stepping forward and putting his hands on the doors. Caressing them. Creating those filthy, filmy marks. Could imagine Atropos drawing strength and energy from the very blackness which was robbing Ralph of his own vitality.

He has other places to go and other things to do, of course – every day is undoubtedly a busy day when you're a supernatural psycho like him – but it must be hard for him to stay away from this place for long, no matter how busy he is. And how does it make him feel? Like a tight fuck on a summer afternoon, that's how.

Lois tugged his sleeve from behind and he turned to her. She was still smiling, but the feverish intensity in her eyes made the expression on her lips look suspiciously like a scream. Behind her, Connie Chung and Rosenberg were strolling back toward the building.

'You've got to get me out of here,' Lois whispered. 'I can't stand it anymore. I feel like I'm losing my mind.'

[*'Okay – no problem.'*]

'I can't hear you, Ralph – and I think I can see the sun shining through you. Jesus, I'm *sure* I can!'

[*'Oh – wait—'*]

He concentrated, and felt the world slide slightly around him. The colors faded; Lois's aura seemed to disappear back inside her skin.

'Better?'

'Well, *solider,* anyway.'

He smiled briefly. 'Good. Come on.'

He took her by the elbow and began guiding her back toward where Joe Wyzer had dropped them off. It was the same direction in which the bloody splashes led.

'Did you find what you were looking for?'

'Yes.'

She brightened at once. 'That's great! I saw you go up, you know – it was very odd, like watching you turn into a sepia-toned photograph. And then . . . thinking I could see the sun shining through you . . . that was *very* peculiar.' She looked at him severely.

'Bad, huh?'

'No . . . not *bad,* exactly. Just peculiar. Those bugs, now . . . *they* were bad. Ugh!'

'I know what you mean. But I think they're all back there.'

'Maybe, but we're still a long way from being out of the woods, aren't we?'

'Yeah – a long way from Eden, Carol would have said.'

'Just stick with me, Ralph Roberts, and don't get lost.'

'Ralph Roberts? Never heard of him. Norton's the name.'

And that, he was happy to see, made her laugh.

Chapter Twenty-four

1

They walked slowly across the asphalt parking lot with its gridwork of spray-painted yellow lines. Tonight, Ralph knew, most of these spaces would be filled. Come, look, listen, be seen . . . and, most importantly, show your city and a whole watching country beyond it that you cannot be intimidated by the Charlie Pickerings of the world. Even the minority kept away by fear would be replaced by the morbidly curious.

As they approached the racetrack, they also approached the edge of the deathbag. It was thicker here, and Ralph could see slow, swirling movement, as if the deathbag were made up of tiny specks of charred matter. It looked a bit like the air over an open incinerator, shimmering with heat and fragments of burnt paper.

And he could hear two sounds, one overlaying the other. The top one was a silvery sighing. The wind might make a sound like that, Ralph thought, if it learned how to weep. It was a creepy sound, but the one beneath it was actively unpleasant – a slobbery chewing noise, as if a gigantic toothless mouth were ingesting large amounts of soft food somewhere close by.

Lois stopped as they approached the deathbag's dark, particle-flecked skin and turned frightened, apologetic eyes up to Ralph. When she spoke, it was in a little girl's voice: 'I don't think I can go through that.' She paused, struggled, and at last brought out the rest. 'It's alive, you know. The whole thing. It sees them' – Lois jerked a thumb back over her shoulder to indicate both the people in the parking lot and the news crews closer in to the building – 'and that's bad, but it also sees *us,* and that's worse . . . because it knows that *we* see *it.* It doesn't like being seen. *Felt,* maybe, but not seen.'

Now the lower-pitched sound – the slobbery eating sound – seemed almost to be articulating words, and the longer Ralph listened, the more sure he became that that was actually the case.

[*Geddout. Fucoff. Beedit.*]

'Ralph,' Lois whispered. 'Do you hear it?'

[*Hatechew. Killyew. Eeechew.*]

He nodded and took her by the elbow again. 'Come on, Lois.'

'Come –? *Where?*'

'Down. All the way.'

For a moment she only looked at him, not understanding; then the light dawned and she nodded. Ralph felt the blink happen inside him – a little stronger than the eyelash-flutter of a few moments ago – and suddenly the day around him cleared. The swirling, smoggy barrier ahead of them melted away and was gone. Nevertheless, they closed their eyes and held their breath as they approached the place where they knew the edge of the deathbag lay. Ralph felt Lois's hand tighten on his as she hurried through the invisible barrier, and as he passed through himself, a dark node of tangled memories – the slow death of his wife, the loss of a favorite dog as a child, the sight of Bill McGovern leaning over with one hand pressed against his chest – seemed to first lightly surround his mind and then clamp down on it like a cruel hand. His ears filled with that silvery sobbing sound, so constant and so chillingly vacuous; the weeping voice of a congenital idiot.

Then they were through.

2

As soon as they had passed beneath the wooden arch on the far side of the parking lot (WE'RE OFF TO THE RACES AT BASSEY PARK! was printed along its curve), Ralph drew Lois over to a bench and made her sit down, although she insisted vehemently that she was just fine.

'Good, but I need a second or two to get myself back together.'

She brushed a lock of hair off his temple and planted a

gentle kiss in the hollow beneath. 'Take all the time you need, dear heart.'

That turned out to be about five minutes. When he felt reasonably confident that he could stand up without coming unlocked at the knees, Ralph took her hand again and they stood up together.

'Did you find it, Ralph? Did you find his trail?'

He nodded. 'In order to see it, we have to go up about two jumps. I tried going up just enough to see the auras at first, because that doesn't seem to speed everything up, but it didn't work. It has to be a little more than that.'

'All right.'

'But we have to be careful. Because when we can see—'

'We can be seen. Yes. We can't lose track of the time, either.'

'Absolutely not. Are you ready?'

'Almost. I think I need another kiss first. Just a little one will do.'

Smiling, he gave it to her.

'*Now* I'm ready.'

'Okay – here we go.'

Blink!

3

The reddish splotches of spoor led them across the packed-dirt area where the midway stood during County Fair week, then to the racetrack where the pacers ran from May to September. Lois stood at the chest-high slat fence for a moment, glanced around to make sure the grandstand was empty, and then boosted herself up. She moved with the sweet litheness of a young girl at first, but once she had swung a leg over the top and straddled the fence, she paused. On her face was an expression of mingled surprise and dismay.

['*Lois? Are you all right?*']

['*Yes, fine. It's my darned old underwear! I guess I've lost weight, because it just won't stay where it belongs! For gosh sakes!*']

Ralph realized he could see not just the frilly hem of Lois's slip but three or four inches of pink nylon. He stifled a grin as she sat astride the broad plank top of the fence, yanking at the fabric. He thought of telling her she looked cuter than kitten-britches and decided that might not be such a good idea.

['*Turn your back while I get this damned slip fixed, Ralph. And wipe the smirk off your face while you're at it.*']

He turned his back on her and looked at the Civic Center. If there *had* been a smirk on his face (he thought it more likely that she had seen one in his aura), the sight of that dark, slowly swirling deathbag took care of it in a hurry.

['*Lois, you might be happier if you just took it off.*']

['*Pardon me all to heck and back, Ralph Roberts, but I wasn't raised to take off my underwear and leave it lying around on racetracks, and if you ever knew a girl who did do things like that, I hope it was before you met Carolyn. I only wish I had a—*']

Vague image of a gleaming steel safety-pin in Ralph's head.

['*I don't suppose you have one, do you, Ralph?*']

He shook his head and sent back an image of his own: sand running through an hourglass.

['*All right, all right, I get the message. I think I've fixed it so it'll hold together at least a little longer. You can turn around now.*']

He did. She was letting herself down the other side of the board fence, and doing it with easy confidence, but her aura had paled considerably, and Ralph could see dark circles under her eyes again. The Revolt of the Foundation Garments had been quelled, however, at least for the time being.

Ralph boosted himself up, swung a leg over the fence, and dropped down on the other side. He liked the way doing it felt – it seemed to wake old, long memories in his bones.

['*We're going to need to power up again before long, Lois.*']

Lois, nodding wearily: ['*I know. Come on, let's go.*']

4

They followed the trail across the racetrack, climbed another board fence on the other side, then descended a brushy, overgrown slope to Neibolt Street. Ralph saw Lois grimly holding her slip up through the skirt of her dress as they struggled down the hill, thought again about asking if she wouldn't be happier just ditching the damned thing, and decided again to mind his own business. If it became enough of a problem to her, she would do it without any further advice on the subject from him.

Ralph's greatest worry – that Atropos's trail would simply peter out on them – initially proved groundless. The dim pink blotches led directly down the crumbling, patched surface of Neibolt Street, between paintless tenements that should have been demolished years ago. Tattered laundry flapped on sagging lines; dirty children with snotty noses watched them pass from dusty front yards. A beautiful tow-headed boy of about three gave Ralph and Lois a deeply suspicious look from his front step, then grabbed his crotch with one hand and used the other to flash them the bird.

Neibolt Street dead-ended at the old trainyards, and here Ralph and Lois momentarily lost the track. They stood by one of the sawhorses blocking off an ancient rectangular cellar-hole – all that remained of the old passenger depot – and looked around at a big semicircle of waste ground. Rusty-red siding tracks glowered from deep within tangles of sunflowers and thorny weeds; shards from a hundred broken bottles twinkled in the afternoon sun. Spray-painted in hot pink letters across the splintery side of the old diesel shed were the words SUZY SUCKT MY BIG FAT ONE. This sentimental declaration stood within a border of dancing swastikas.

Ralph: [*'Where the hell did it go?'*]

[*'Down there, Ralph – see?'*]

She was pointing along what had been the main line until 1963, the only line until 1983, and was now just another pair of rusty, overgrown steel tracks on the way to nowhere. Even most of the ties were gone, burned as evening campfires either by local winos or vags passing through on their way to the potato fields of Aroostook County or the apple orchards and fishing smacks of the Maritimes. On one of the few remaining crossties, Ralph saw splashes of pink spoor. They looked fresher than the ones they had followed down Neibolt Street.

He stared along the half-hidden course of the tracks, trying to recall. If memory served, this line skirted the Municipal Golf Course on its way back to . . . well, on its way back to the west side. Ralph thought this must be the same set of defunct tracks which ran along the edge of the airport and past the picnic area where Faye Chapin might even now be brooding over the seedings in the upcoming Runway 3 Classic.

It's all been one big loop, he thought. *It's taken us damned near three days, but I think in the end we're going to be right back where we started . . . not Eden, but Harris Avenue.*

'Say, you guys! How you doon?'

It was a voice Ralph almost thought he recognized, and that feeling was reinforced by his first look at the man it came from. He was standing behind them, at the point where the Neibolt Street sidewalk finally gave up the ghost. He looked fifty or so, but Ralph guessed he might actually be five or even ten years younger than that. He was wearing a sweatshirt and old ragged jeans. The aura surrounding him was as green as a glass of Saint Patrick's Day beer. That was finally what turned the trick for Ralph. It was the wino who had approached him and Bill on the day he had found Bill in Strawford Park, bawling over his old pal Bob Polhurst . . . who, as it had turned out, had outlived him. Life was funnier than Groucho Marx sometimes.

A queer sense of fatalism was creeping over Ralph, and with it an intuitive understanding of the forces which now surrounded them. It was one he could have done without. It hardly mattered if those forces were beneficent or malign, Random or Purpose; they were *gigantic,* that was what mattered, and they made the things Clotho and Lachesis had said about choice and free will seem like a joke. He flet as if he and Lois were roped to the spokes of a gigantic wheel – a wheel which kept rolling them back to where they had come from even as it took them deeper and deeper into this horrible tunnel.

'You got a bitta the old spare change, mister?'

Ralph slid down a little so the wino would be sure to hear him when he talked.

'I'll bet your uncle called you from Dexter,' Ralph said.

'Told you you could have your old job back at the mill . . . but only if you got there today. Is that about right?'

The wino blinked at him in cautious surprise. 'Well . . . yeah. Sumpin like that.' He felt for the story – one he probably believed in more fully than anyone he told it to these days – and found its tattered thread again. 'Dass a good job, you know? And I could have it back. There's a Bangor n Aroostook bus at two o'clock, but the fare's five-fifty and so far I got only toon a quarter . . .'

'Seventy-six cents is what you've got,' Lois said. 'Two quarters, two dimes, one nickel, and a penny. But considering how much you drink, your aura looks extremely healthy, I'll say that much for you. You must have the constitution of an ox.'

The wino gave her a puzzled look, then took a step backward and wiped his nose with the palm of one hand.

'Don't worry,' Ralph reassured him, 'my wife sees auras everywhere. She's a very spiritual person.'

'Izzat so, now?'

'Uh-huh. She's also very generous, and I think she'll do quite a bit better by you than a little spare change. Won't you, Alice?'

'He'll just drink it up,' she said. 'There's no job in Dexter.'

'No, probably not,' Ralph said, fixing her with his eyes, 'but his aura does look extremely healthy. *Extremely*.'

'You kinda got your own spiritual side, I guess,' the wino said. His eyes were still shifting cautiously back and forth between Ralph and Lois, but there was a guarded flicker of hope in them.

'You know, that's true,' Ralph said. 'And just lately it's really come to the fore.' He pursed his lips as if an interesting thought had just occurred to him, and inhaled. A bright green ray shot out of the panhandler's aura, crossed the ten feet separating him from Ralph and Lois, and entered Ralph's mouth. The taste was clear and at once identifiable: Boone's Farm Apple Wine. It was rough and lowdown, but sort of pleasant, just the same – it had a working man's sparkle to it. With the taste came that sense of returning strength, which was good, and a sharp-edged clarity of thought that was even better.

Lois, meanwhile, was holding out a twenty-dollar bill. The wino didn't immediately see it, however; he was scowling up into the sky. At that instant, another bright green ray quilled out of his aura. It shot across the weedy clearing beside the cellar-hole like a brilliant flashlight beam and into Lois's mouth and nose. The bill in her hand shook briefly.

[*'Oh, God, that's so good!'*]

'Goddam jet-jockeys from Charleston Air Force Base!' the wino cried disapprovingly. 'They ain't s'pozed to boom the soun-barrier til they get out over the ocean! I damn near wet my –' His eye fell on the bill between Lois's fingers, and his scowl deepened. 'Sa-aay, what kind of joke you think you pullin here? I ain't stupid, you know. Maybe I like a drink every now n then, but that don't make me stupid.'

Give it time, Ralph thought. *It will.*

'No one thinks you're stupid,' Lois said, 'and it's no joke. Take the money, sir.'

The bum tried to hold onto his suspicious glower, but after another close look at Lois (and a quick side-glance at Ralph), it was overwhelmed by a large and winning smile. He stepped toward Lois, putting out his hand to take the money, which he had earned without even knowing it.

Lois raised her hand just before he could close his fingers on the bill. 'Just mind you get something to eat as well as something to drink. And you might ask yourself if you're happy with the way you're living.'

'You're absolutely right!' the wino cried enthusiastically. His eyes never left the bill between Lois's fingers. 'Absolutely, ma'am! They got a program other side of the river, detox and rehab, you know. I'm thinkin about it. I really am. I think about it every damn day.' But his eyes were still tacked to the twenty, and he was almost drooling. Lois gave Ralph a brief, doubtful look, then shrugged and let the bill pass from her fingers to his. 'Thanks! Thanks, lady!' His eyes shifted to Ralph. 'Dis lady a real princess! I jus hope you know dat!'

Ralph favored Lois with a fond glance. 'As a matter of fact, I do,' he said.

5

Half an hour later, the two of them were walking between the rusty steel rails as they curved gently past the Municipal Golf Course . . . except they had drifted up a little higher above the Short-Time world after their meeting with the wino (perhaps because he had been a little high himself), and walking was not exactly what they were doing. There was little or no effort involved, for one thing, and although their feet were moving, to Ralph it felt more like gliding than walking. Nor was he entirely sure they were visible to the Short-Time world; squirrels hopped unconcernedly about their feet, busy gathering supplies for the winter ahead, and once he saw Lois duck sharply as a wren almost parted her hair. The bird veered to the left and upward, as if realizing only at the last moment that there was a human in its flight-pattern. The golfers didn't pay them any mind, either. Ralph's opinion of golfers was that they were self-absorbed to the point of obsession, but he thought this lack of interest extreme even so. If *he* had seen a couple of neatly dressed adults strolling along a defunct GS&WM spur-line in the middle of the day, he thought he might have taken a brief time-out to try and guess what they were up to and where they might be going. *I think I'd be especially curious about why the lady kept on muttering 'stay where you are, you darned old thing' and hitching at her skirt,* Ralph thought, and grinned. But the golfers didn't even spare them a glance, although a foursome bound for the ninth hole passed close enough so that Ralph could hear them worrying over a developing softness in the bond market. The idea that he and Lois had become invisible again – or at least very dim – began to seem more and more plausible to Ralph. Plausible . . . and worrisome. *Time goes faster when you're high,* Old Dor had said.

The trail became fresher as they went west, and Ralph liked the drips and splashes which made it up less and less. Where the goop had fallen on the steel rails, it had eaten away the rust like corrosive acid. The weeds it had fallen on were black and dead – even the hardiest of them had died. As Ralph and Lois passed Derry Muni's third green and entered a tangle of scrawny trees and undergrowth, Lois tugged at his sleeve. She pointed ahead. Large splotches of Atropos's spoor gleamed like sick paint on the trunks of the trees now pressing in close to the tracks, and there were pools of it in some of the sunken dips between the old rails – places where crossties had once been, Ralph supposed.

[*'We're getting close to where he lives, Ralph.'*]

[*'Yes.'*]

[*'If he comes back and finds us in his place, what will we do?'*]

Ralph shrugged. He didn't know, and wasn't sure he cared. Let the forces that were moving them around like pawns on a chessboard – the ones Mr C and Mr L had called the Higher Purpose – worry about that. If Atropos showed up, Ralph would try to yank out the little bald bugger's tongue and strangle him with it. And if that upset somebody's applecart, too goddam bad. He couldn't take responsibility for grand plans and Long-Time business; his job now was to watch out for Lois, who was at risk, and try to stop the carnage that was going to occur not far from here in just a few hours. And who knew? He might even find a little extra time along the way which he could use to try and protect his own partially rejuvenated hide. This was the stuff he had to do, and if the nasty little fuck got in Ralph's way, one of them was going down. If that didn't fit in with the big boys' plans, tough titty.

Lois was picking most of this up from his aura – he could read that in her own when she touched his arm and he turned to look at her.

[*'What does that mean, Ralph? That you'll try to kill him if he gets in our way?'*]

He considered this, then nodded.

[*'Yeah – that's* exactly *what it means.'*]

She thought about it, then nodded.

[*'Ralph?'*]

He looked at her, eyebrows raised.

[*'If it needs to be done, I'll help you do it.'*]

He was absurdly touched by this . . . and at pains to hide the rest of his thinking from her: that the only reason she was still with him at all was so that he could keep a protective eye on her. That thought led him back toward her earrings, but he pushed the image of them away, not wanting her to see – or even suspect – them in his aura.

Lois's thoughts, meanwhile, had gone on in a different, marginally safer, direction.

[*'Even if we get in and out without meeting him, he'll know someone was there, won't he? He'll probably know who it was, too.'*]

Ralph couldn't deny it, but didn't see that it mattered much; their options had been narrowed to just this one, at least temporarily. They would take it a step at a time and just keep hoping that when the sun came up tomorrow morning, they would be around to see it. *Although, given a choice, I'd probably opt to sleep in,* Ralph thought, and a small, wistful grin touched the corners of his mouth. *God, it feels like years since I slept in.* His mind flashed from there to Carolyn's favorite saying, the one about how it was a long walk back to Eden. It seemed to him right now that Eden might simply be sleeping until noon . . . or maybe a little past.

He took Lois's hand and they started forward along Atropos's trail again.

6

Forty feet east of the cyclone fence marking the edge of the airport, the rusty tracks petered out. Atropos's trail pushed on, however, although not for long; Ralph was quite sure he could see the spot where it ended, and the image of the two of them roped to the spokes of a big wheel recurred. If he was right, Atropos's den was only a stone's throw from where Ed had run into the fat man with the barrels of fertilizer in the back of his pickup truck.

The wind gusted, bringing them a sick, rotten smell from close by, and, from a little further away, the voice of Faye Chapin, haranguing someone on his favorite subject: '. . . what I *always* say! *Mah-jongg* is like chess, chess is like life, so if you can play either of those games –' The wind dropped again. Ralph could still hear Faye's voice if he strained his ears, but he had lost the individual words. That was all right, though; he had heard the lecture often enough to know pretty much how it went.

[*'Ralph, that stink is awful! It's him, isn't it?'*]

He nodded, but didn't think Lois saw him. She held his hand tightly in hers, looking straight ahead with wide eyes.

The splotchy track which had begun at the doors of the Civic Center ended at the base of a drunkenly leaning dead oak tree two hundred feet away. The cause of both the tree's death and its final leaning position was clear: one side of the venerable relic had been peeled like a banana by a glancing stroke of lightning. The cracks and crenellations and bulges of its gray bark seemed to make the shapes of half-buried, silently screaming faces, and the tree spread its nude branches against the sky like grim ideograms . . . ones which bore – at least in Ralph's imagination – an uncomfortable resemblance to the Japanese ideograms which meant *kamikaze*. The bolt which had killed the tree hadn't succeeded in knocking it over, but it had certainly done its best. The part of its extensive root-system which faced the airport had been yanked right out of the ground. These roots had extended beneath the chainlink fence and pulled a section of it upward and outward in a bell shape that made Ralph think, for the first time in years, of a childhood acquaintance named Charles Engstrom.

'Don't you play with Chuckie,' Ralph's mother used to tell him. 'He's a dirty boy.' Ralph didn't know if Chuckie was a dirty boy or not, but he was fruitcrackers, no question about that. Chuckie Engstrom liked to hide behind the tree in his front yard with a long tree-branch which he called his Peekie Wand. When a woman in a full skirt passed, Chuckie would tiptoe after her, extending the Peekie Wand under the hem and then lifting. Quite often he got to check out the color of the woman's underwear (the color of ladies' underwear held great fascination for Chuckie) before she realized what was going on and chased the wildly cackling lad back to his house, threatening to tell his mother. The airport fence, pulled out and up by the old oak's roots, reminded Ralph of the way the skirts of Chuckie's victims had looked when he started to raise them with the Peekie Wand.

['*Ralph?*']

He looked at her.

['*Who's Piggy Juan? And why are you thinking about him now?*']

Ralph burst out laughing.

['*Did you see that in my aura?*']

['*I guess so – I don't really know anymore. Who is he?*']

['*Tell you another time. Come on.*']

He took her hand and they walked slowly toward the oak tree where Atropos's trail ended, into the thickening odor of wild decay that was his scent.

Chapter Twenty-five

1

They stood at the base of the oak, looking down. Lois was gnawing obsessively on her lower lip.

[*'Do we have to go down there, Ralph? Do we really?'*]

[*Yes.*]

[*'But why? What are we supposed to do? Take something he stole? Kill him? What?'*]

Other than retrieve Joe's comb and Lois's earrings, he didn't know . . . but he felt certain he *would* know, that they both would, when the time came.

[*'I think for now we better just keep moving, Lois.'*]

The lightning had acted like a strong hand, shoving the tree violently toward the east and opening a large hole at the bottom on its western side. To a man or woman with Short-Time vision, that hole would undoubtedly look dark – and maybe a little scary, with its crumbly sides and barely glimpsed roots squirming in the deep shadows like snakes – but otherwise not very unusual.

A kid with a good imagination might see more, Ralph thought. *That dark space at the bottom of the tree might make him think of pirate treasure . . . outlaw hideouts . . . troll-holes . . .*

But Ralph didn't think even an imaginative Short-Time kid would have been able to see the dim red glow filtering up from beneath the tree, or realize that those squirming roots were actually rough rungs leading down to some unknown (and undoubtedly unpleasant) place.

No – even an imaginative kid wouldn't see those things . . . but he or she might sense *them.*

Right. And after doing so, one with any brains would turn

and run as if all the demons of hell were in hot pursuit. As would he and Lois, if they had any sense at all. Except for Lois's earrings. Except for Joe Wyzer's comb. Except for his own lost place in the Purpose. And, of course, except for Helen (and possibly Nat) and the two thousand other people who were going to be at the Civic Center tonight. Lois was right. They were supposed to do *something*, and if they backed out now, it was a something that would remain forever done-bun-undone.

And those are the ropes, he thought. *The ropes the powers that be use to tie us poor, muddled Short-Time creatures to their wheel.*

He now visualized Clotho and Lachesis through a bright lens of hate, and he thought that if the two of them had been here right now, they would have exchanged one of their uneasy looks and then taken a quick step or two away.

And they would be right to do that, he thought. *Very right.*

['*Ralph? What's wrong? Why are you so angry?*']

He raised her hand to his lips and kissed it.

['*It's nothing. Come on. Let's go before we lose our nerve.*']

She looked at him a moment longer, then nodded. And when Ralph sat down and poked his legs into the gaping, root-lined mouth at the foot of the tree, she was right beside him.

2

Ralph slid beneath the tree on his back, holding his free hand over his face to keep dirt from crumbling into his open eyes. He tried not to flinch as root-knuckles caressed the side of his neck and prodded the small of his back. The smell under the tree was a revolting monkeyhouse aroma that made his gorge rise. He was able to go on kidding himself that he would get used to it until he was all the way into the hole under the oak, and then the kidding stopped. He raised himself on one elbow, feeling smaller roots digging at his scalp and dangling flaps of bark tickling his cheeks, and ejected as much of his breakfast as still remained in the holding-tank. He could hear Lois doing the same thing on his left.

A terrible, woozy faintness went rolling through his head like a breaking wave. The stench was so thick he was almost *eating* it, and he could see the red stuff they had followed to this nightmare place under the tree all over his hands and arms. Just *looking* at this stuff had been bad; now he found himself taking a bath in it, for God's sake.

Something groped for his hand and he almost gave in to panic before realizing it was Lois. He laced his fingers through hers.

[*'Ralph, come up a little bit! It's better! You can breathe!'*]

He understood what she meant at once, and had to restrain himself, haul himself down, at the last moment. If he hadn't, he would have shot up the ladder of perception like a rocket under full thrust.

The world wavered, and suddenly there seemed to be a little more light in this stinking hole . . . and a little more room, too. The smell didn't go away, but it became bearable. Now it was like being in a small closed tent full of people with dirty feet and sweaty armpits – not nice, but something you could live with, at least for awhile.

Ralph suddenly imagined the face of a pocket-watch, complete with hands that were moving too fast. It was better without the stench trying to pour down his throat and gag him, but this was still a dangerous place to be – suppose they came out of here tomorrow morning, with nothing left of the Civic Center but a smoking hole on Main Street? And it could happen. Keeping track of time down here – short time, long time, or all-time – was impossible. He glanced at his watch, but it was meaningless. He should have set it earlier, but he had forgotten.

Let it go, Ralph – you can't do anything about it, so let it go.

He tried, and as he did it occurred to him that Old Dor had been a hundred per cent correct on the day Ed had crashed into Mr West Side Gardeners' pickup truck; it was better not to mess into Long-Time business. And yet here they were, the world's oldest Peter Pan and the world's oldest Wendy, sliding under a magic tree into some slimy underworld neither one of them wanted to see.

Lois was looking at him, her pale face lit with that sick red glow, her expressive eyes full of fright. He saw dark threads on her chin and realized it was blood. She had quit just nibbling at her lower lip and had begun taking bites out of it.

[*'Ralph, are you all right?'*]

[*'I get to crawl under an old oak tree with a pretty girl and you even have to ask? I'm fine, Lois. But I think we better hurry.'*]

[*'All right.'*]

He felt around below him and placed his foot on a gnarled root-knuckle. It took his weight and he slid down the stony slope, squeezing beneath another root and holding Lois around the waist. Her skirt skidded up to her thighs and Ralph thought again, briefly, about Chuckie Engstrom and his Peekie Wand. He was both amused and exasperated to see Lois was trying to pull the skirt back down.

[*'I know that a lady tries to keep her skirt down whenever possible, but I think the rule goes by the boards when you're sliding down troll staircases under old oak trees. Okay?'*]

She gave him an embarrassed, frightened little smile.

[*'If I'd known what we were going to be doing, I would have worn slacks. I thought we were just going to the hospital.'*]

If I'd *known what we were going to be doing,* Ralph thought, *I would have cashed in my bonds, developing softness in the market or not, and had us on a plane to Rio, my dear.*

He felt around with his other foot, very aware that if he fell, he was probably going to end up in a place far beyond the reach of Derry Rescue. Just above his eyes, a reddish worm poked out of the earth, dribbling little crumbles of dirt down on Ralph's forehead.

For what seemed like an eternity he felt nothing, and then his foot found smooth wood – not a root this time, but something like a real step. He slid down, still holding Lois around the waist, and waited to see if the thing he was standing on would hold or snap under their combined weight.

It held, and it was wide enough for both of them. Ralph looked down and saw that it was the top step of a narrow staircase which curved down into the red-tinged dark. It had been built for – and perhaps by – a creature that was a lot shorter than they were, making it necessary for them to hunch, but it was still better than the nightmare of the last few moments.

Ralph looked at the ragged wedge of daylight above them, his eyes gazing out of his dirt- and sweat-streaked face with an expression of dumb longing. Daylight had never looked so sweet or so distant. He turned back to Lois and nodded to her. She squeezed his hand and nodded back. Bending over, cringing each time a dangling root touched their necks or backs, they started down the staircase.

3

The descent seemed endless. The red light grew brighter, the stench of Atropos grew thicker, and Ralph was aware that they were both 'going up' as they went down; it was either that or be flattened by the smell. He continued telling himself that they were doing what they had to do, and that there must be a timekeeper on an operation this big – someone who would give them a poke if and when the schedule got too tight for comfort – but he kept worrying, just the same. Because there might *not* be a timekeeper, or an ump, or a team of refs in zebra-striped shirts. *All bets are off,* Clotho had said.

Just as Ralph was starting to wonder if the stairs went all the way down into hell itself, they ended. A short stone-lined corridor, no more than forty inches high and twenty feet long, led to an arched doorway. Beyond it, that red glow pulsed and flared like the reflected glow of an open oven.

['*Come on, Lois, but be ready for anything. Be ready for* him.']

She nodded, hitched at her wayward slip again, then walked beside him up the narrow passage. Ralph kicked something that wasn't a stone and bent over to pick it up. It was a red plastic cylinder, wider at one end than at the other. After a moment he realized what it was: a jump-rope handle. Three-six-nine, hon, the goose drank wine.

Don't butt into what doesn't concern you, Short-Time, Atropos had said, but he *had* butted in, and not just because of what the little bald doctors called *ka,* either. He had gotten involved because what Atropos was up to *was* his concern, whatever the little creep might think to the contrary. Derry was his town, Lois Chasse was his friend, and Ralph found within himself a sincere desire to make Doc #3 sorry he'd ever seen Lois's diamond earrings.

He flipped the jump-rope handle away and started walking again. A moment later he and Lois passed under the arch and simply stood there, staring into Atropos's underground apartment. With their wide eyes and linked hands, they looked more like children in a fairy-tale than ever – not Peter Pan and Wendy now but Hansel and Gretel, coming upon the witch's candy house after days spent wandering in the trackless forest.

4

['*Oh, Ralph. Oh my God, Ralph . . . do you see?*']
   ['*Shhh, Lois. Shhh.*']
   Directly ahead of them was a small, mean chamber which seemed to be a combination kitchen and bedroom. The room was simultaneously sordid and creepy. Standing in the center was a low round table which Ralph thought was the amputated top half of a barrel. The remains of a meal – some gray, rancid gruel that looked like liquefied brains congealing in a chipped soup tureen – stood on it. There was a single dirty folding chair. To the right of the table was a primitive commode which consisted of a rusty steel drum with a toilet-seat balanced on top of it. The smell rising from this was incredibly foul. The room's only decoration was a full-length brass-bordered mirror on one wall, its reflective surface so age-darkened that the Ralph and Lois captured within it looked as if they might have been floating in ten or twelve feet of water.
   To the left of the mirror was a stark sleeping accommodation which consisted of a filthy mattress and a burlap sack stuffed with straw or feathers. Both pillow and mattress glowed and raved with the nightsweats of the creature who used them. *The dreams inside that burlap pillow would drive me insane,* Ralph thought.
   Somewhere, God only knew how much further under the earth, water was dripping hollowly.
   On the far side of the apartment was another, higher arch, through which they could see a jumbled, surreal storage area. Ralph actually blinked two or three times to try to make sure he was really seeing what he thought he was seeing.
   This is the place, all right, he thought. *Whatever we came to find, it's here.*
   Lois began to drift toward this second arch as if hypnotized. Her mouth was quivering with dismay, but her eyes were full of helpless curiosity – it was the expression, he was quite sure, that must have been on the face of Bluebeard's wife when she had used the key which unlocked the door to her husband's forbidden room. Ralph was suddenly sure that Atropos was lurking just inside that arch with his rusty scalpel poised. He hurried after Lois and stopped her just before she could step through. He grasped her upper arm,

then put a finger to his lips and shook his head at her before she could speak.

He hunkered down with the fingers of one hand tented on the packed dirt floor, looking like a sprinter awaiting the crack of the starter's gun. Then he launched himself through the arch (relishing the eager response of his body even at this moment), hitting on his shoulder and rolling. His feet struck a cardboard box and knocked it over, spilling out a jumble of stuff: mismatched gloves and socks, a couple of old paperbacks, a pair of Bermuda shorts, a screwdriver with smears of maroon stuff – maybe paint, maybe blood – on its steel shaft.

Ralph got to his knees, looking back toward Lois, who was standing in the doorway and staring at him with her hands clasped under her chin. There was no one on either side of the archway, and really no room for anyone. More boxes were stacked on either side. Ralph read the printing on them with a kind of bemused wonder: Jack Daniel's, Gilbey's, Smirnoff, J&B. Atropos, it seemed, was as fond of liquor cartons as anyone else who couldn't bear to throw anything away.

[*'Ralph? Is it safe?'*]

The word was a joke, but he nodded his head and held out his hand. She hurried toward him, giving her slip another sharp upward yank as she came and looking about herself in growing amazement.

Standing on the other side of the arch, in Atropos's grim little apartment, this storage area had looked large. Now that they were actually in it, Ralph saw it went well beyond that; rooms this big were usually called warehouses. Aisles wandered among great, tottery piles of junk. Only the stuff by the door had actually been boxed; the rest had been piled any whichway, creating something which was two parts maze and three parts booby-trap. Ralph decided that even *warehouse* was too small a word – this was an underground suburb, and Atropos might be lurking anywhere within it . . . and if he was here, he was probably watching them.

Lois didn't ask what they were looking at; he saw by her face that she already knew. When she did speak, it was in a dreamy tone that sent a chill scampering up Ralph's back.

[*'He must be so very old, Ralph.'*]

Yes. So very old.

Twenty yards into the room, which was lit with the same sunken, sourceless red glow as the stairway, Ralph could see a large spoked wheel lying atop a cane-backed chair which was, in turn, standing on top of a splintery old clothes press. Looking at that wheel brought a deeper chill; it was as if the metaphor his mind had seized to help grasp the concept of *ka* had become real. Then he noted the rusty iron strip which circled the wheel's outer circumference and realized it had probably come from one of those Gay Nineties bikes that looked like overgrown tricycles.

It's a bicycle wheel, all right, and it's a hundred years old if it's a day, he thought. That led him to wonder how many people – how many thousands or tens of thousands – had died in and around Derry since Atropos had somehow transported this wheel down here. And of those thousands, how many had been Random deaths?

And how far back does he go? How many hundreds of years?

No way of telling, of course; maybe all the way to the beginning, whenever or however that had been. And during that time, he had taken a little something from everyone he had fucked with . . . and here it all was.

Here it all was.

['*Ralph!*']

He looked around and saw that Lois was holding out both hands. In one was a Panama hat with a crescent bitten from the brim. In the other was a black nylon pocket-comb, the kind you could buy in any convenience store for a buck twenty-nine. A ghostly glimmer of orange-yellow still clung to it, which didn't surprise Ralph much. Each time the comb's owner had used it, it must have picked up a little of that glow from both his aura and his balloon-string, like dandruff. It also didn't surprise him that the comb should have been with McGovern's hat; the last time he'd seen those two things, they'd been together. He remembered Atropos's sarcastic grin as he swept the Panama from his head and pretended to use the comb on his own bald dome.

And then he jumped up and clicked his heels together.

Lois was pointing at an old rocking chair with a broken runner.

['*The hat was right there, on the seat. The comb was underneath. It's Mr Wyzer's, isn't it?*']

['*Yes.*']

She held it out to him immediately.

['*You take it. I'm not as ditzy as Bill always thought, but sometimes I lose things. And if I lost this, I'd never forgive myself.*']

He took the comb, started to put it into his back pocket,

then thought how easily Atropos had plucked it from that same location. Easy as falling off a log, it had been. He put it into his front pants pocket instead, then looked back at Lois, who was gazing at McGovern's bitten hat with the sad wonder of Hamlet looking at the skull of his old pal Yorick. When she looked up, Ralph saw tears in her eyes.

[*'He loved this hat. He thought he looked very dashing and debonair when he had it on. He didn't – he just looked like Bill – but he thought he looked good, and that's the important part. Wouldn't you say so, Ralph?'*]

[*'Yes.'*]

She tossed the hat back into the seat of the old rocker and turned to examine a box of what looked like rummage-sale clothes. As soon as her back was to him, Ralph squatted down, peering beneath the chair, hoping to see a splintered double gleam in the darkness. If Bill's hat and Joe's comb were both here, then maybe Lois's earrings –

There was nothing beneath the rocker but dust and a pink knitted baby bootee.

Should have known that'd be too easy, Ralph thought, getting to his feet again. He suddenly felt exhausted. They had found Joe's comb with no trouble at all, and that was good, absolutely great, but Ralph was afraid it had also been a spectacular case of beginner's luck. They still had Lois's earrings to worry about . . . and doing whatever else it was they had been sent here to do, of course. And what was that? He didn't know, and if someone from upstairs was sending instructions, he wasn't receiving them.

[*'Lois, do you have any idea what—'*]

[*'Shhhh!'*]

[*'What is it? Lois, is it him?'*]

[*'No! Be quiet, Ralph! Be quiet and listen!'*]

He listened. At first he heard nothing, and then the clenching sensation – the blink – came inside his head again. This time it was very slow, very cautious. He slipped upward a little further, as lightly as a feather lifted in a draft of warm air. He became aware of a long, low groaning sound, like an endlessly creaking door. There was something familiar about it – not in the sound itself, but in its associations. It was like—

– a burglar alarm, or maybe a smoke-detector. It's telling us where it is. It's calling *us.*

Lois seized his hand with fingers that were as cold as ice.

[*'That's it, Ralph – that's what we're looking for. Do you hear it?'*]

Yes, of course he did. But whatever that sound was, it had nothing to do with Lois's earrings . . . and without Lois's earrings, he wasn't leaving this place.

[*'Come on, Ralph! Come on! We have to find it!'*]

He let her lead him deeper into the room. Atropos's souvenirs were piled at least three feet higher than their heads in most places. How a shrimp like him had managed this trick Ralph didn't know – levitation, maybe – but the result was that he quickly lost all sense of direction as they twisted, turned, and occasionally seemed to double back. All he knew for sure was that low groaning sound kept getting louder in his ears; as they began to draw near its source, it became an insectile buzzing which Ralph found increasingly unpleasant. He kept expecting to round a corner and find a giant locust staring at him with dull brownish-black eyes as big as grapefruits.

Although the separate auras of the objects which filled the storage vault had faded like the scent of flower-petals pressed between the pages of a book, they were still there beneath Atropos's stench – and at this level of perception, with all their senses exquisitely awake and attuned, it was impossible not to sense those auras and be affected by them. These mute reminders of the Random dead were both terrible and pathetic. The place was more than a museum or a packrat's lair, Ralph realized; it was a profane church where Atropos took his own version of Communion – grief for bread, tears for wine.

Their stumbling course through the narrow zigzag rows was a gruesome, almost shattering experience. Each not-quite-aimless turn presented a hundred more objects Ralph wished he had never seen and would not have to remember; each voiced its own small cry of pain and bewilderment. He did not have to wonder if Lois shared his feelings – she was sobbing steadily and quietly beside him.

Here was a child's battered Flexible Flyer sled with the knotted towrope still draped over the steering bar. The boy to whom it had belonged had died of convulsions on a crisp January day in 1953.

Here was a majorette's baton with its shaft wrapped in purple and white spirals of crepe – the colors of Grant Academy. She had been raped and bludgeoned to death with a rock in the fall of 1967. Her killer, who had never been caught, had stuffed her body into a small cave where her bones

– along with the bones of two other unlucky victims – still lay.

Here was the cameo brooch of a woman who had been struck by a falling brick while walking down Main Street to buy the new issue of *Vogue*; if she had left her home thirty seconds earlier or later, she would have been fine.

Here was the buck knife of a man who had been killed in a hunting accident in 1937.

Here was the compass of a Boy Scout who had fallen and broken his neck while hiking on Mount Katahdin.

The sneaker of a little boy named Gage Creed, run down by a speeding tanker-truck on Route 15 in Ludlow.

Rings and magazines; key-chains and umbrellas; hats and glasses; rattles and radios. They looked like different things, but Ralph thought they were really all the same thing: the faint, sorrowing voices of people who had found themselves written out of the script in the middle of the second act while they were still learning their lines for the third, people who had been unceremoniously hauled off before their work was done or their obligations fulfilled, people whose only crime had been to be born in the Random . . . and to have caught the eye of the madman with the rusty scalpel.

Lois, sobbing: [*'I hate him! I hate him so much!'*]

He knew what she meant. It was one thing to hear Clotho and Lachesis say that Atropos was also part of the big picture, that he might even serve some higher purpose himself, and quite another to see the faded Boston Bruins cap of a little boy who had fallen into an overgrown cellar-hole and died in the dark, died in agony, died with no voice left after six hours spent screaming for his mother.

Ralph reached out and briefly touched the cap. Its owner's name had been Billy Weatherbee. His final thought had been of ice-cream.

Ralph's hand tightened over Lois's.

[*'Ralph, what is it? I can hear you thinking – I'm sure I can – but it's like listening to someone whisper under his breath.'*]

[*'I was thinking that I want to bust that little bastard's chops for him, Lois. Maybe we could teach* him *what it's like to lie awake at night. What do you think?'*]

Her grip on his hand tightened. She nodded.

5

They reached a place where the narrow corridor they'd been following branched into diverging paths. That low, steady buzz was coming from the lefthand one, and not very far up it, either, by the sound. It was now impossible for them to walk side by side, and as they worked their way toward the end, the passage grew narrower still. Ralph was finally obliged to begin sidling along.

The reddish exudate Atropos left behind was very thick here, dripping down the jumbled stacks of souvenirs and making little puddles on the dirt floor. Lois was holding his hand with painful tightness now, but Ralph didn't complain.

[*'It's like the Civic Center, Ralph – he spends a lot of time here.'*]

Ralph nodded. The question was, what did Mr A come down this aisle to commune with? They were coming to the end now – it was blocked by a solid wall of junk – and he still couldn't see what was making that buzzing sound. It was now starting to drive him crazy; it was like having a horsefly trapped in the middle of your head. As they approached the end of the passage, he became more and more sure that what they were looking for was on the other side of the wall of junk which blocked it – they would either have to retrace their steps and try to find a way around, or break through. Either choice might consume more time than they could afford. Ralph felt nibbles of desperation at the back of his mind.

But the corridor did not dead-end; on the left there was a crawlspace beneath a dining room table piled high with dishes and stacks of green paper and . . .

Green paper? No, not quite. Stacks of *bills*. Tens, twenties, and fifties were piled up in random profusion on the dishes. There was a choke of hundreds in a cracked gravy-boat, and a rolled-up five hundred dollar bill poking drunkenly out of a dusty wineglass.

[*'Ralph! My God, it's a fortune!'*]

She wasn't looking at the table but at the other wall of the passageway. The last five feet had been constructed of banded gray-green bricks of currency. They were in an alleyway which was literally made of money, and Ralph realized he could now answer another of the questions that had been troubling him:

where Ed had been getting his dough. Atropos was rolling in it
. . . but Ralph had an idea that the little bald-headed sonofabitch
still had trouble getting dates.

He bent down a little to get a better look into the crawlspace
underneath the table. There appeared to be yet another chamber
on the other side, this one very small. A slow red glow waxed
and waned in there like the beating of a heart. It cast uneasy
pulses of light on their shoes.

Ralph pointed, then looked at Lois. She nodded. He dropped
to his knees and crawled beneath the money-laden table, and
into the shrine Atropos had created around the thing which
lay in the middle of the floor. It *was* what they had been sent
to find, he hadn't a single doubt about it, but he still had no
idea what it was. The object, not much bigger than the sort of
marbles children call croakers, was wrapped in a deathbag as
impenetrable as the center of a black hole.

Oh, great – lovely. Now what?

[*'Ralph! Do you hear singing? It's very faint.'*]

He looked at her dubiously, then glanced around. He had
already come to hate this cramped space, and although he was
not claustrophobic by nature, he now felt a panicky desire to get
away squeezing into his thoughts. A very distinct voice spoke
up in his head. *It's not just what I want, Ralph; it's what I need.
I'll do my best to hang in with you, but if you don't finish whatever
the hell it is you're supposed to be doing in here soon, it won't make
any difference what either of us want – I'm just going to take over
and run like hell.*

The controlled terror in that voice didn't surprise him,
because this really was a horrible place – not a room at all but the
bottom of a deep shaft whose circular walls were constructed
of rickrack and stolen goods: toasters, footstools, clock-radios,
cameras, books, crates, shoes, rakes. Dangling almost right in
front of Ralph's eyes was a battered saxophone on a frayed strap
with the word JAKE printed on it in dust-dulled rhinestones.
Ralph reached out to grab it, wanting to get the damned thing
out of his face. Then he imagined the removal of this one object
starting a landslide that would bring the walls down on them,
burying them alive. He pulled his hand back. At the same
time he opened his mind and senses as fully as he could. For
a moment he thought he *did* hear something – a faint sigh, like
the whisper of the ocean in a seashell – but then it was gone.

[*'If there are voices in here, I can't hear them, Lois – that damned
thing is drowning them out.'*]

He pointed at the object in the middle of the circle – black beyond any previously held conception of black, a deathbag which was the apotheosis of all deathbags. But Lois was shaking her head.

[*'No, not drowning them out. Sucking them dry.'*]

She looked at the screaming black thing with horror and loathing.

[*'That thing is sucking the life out of all this stuff piled up around it . . . and it's trying to suck the life out of us, too.'*]

Yes, of course it was. Now that Lois had actually said it out loud, Ralph could feel the deathbag – or the object inside it – pulling at something far down in his head, yanking at it, twisting at it, shoving at it . . . trying to pull it out like a tooth from its pink socket of gum.

Trying to suck the life out of them? Close, but no cigar. Ralph didn't think it was their lives the thing inside the deathbag wanted, nor their souls . . . at least, not exactly. It was their life-force it wanted. Their *ka*.

Lois's eyes widened as she picked up this thought . . . and then they shifted to a place just beyond his right shoulder. She leaned forward on her knees and reached out.

[*'Lois, I wouldn't do that – you could bring the whole place down around our—'*]

Too late. She yanked something free, looked at it with horrified understanding, and then held it out to him.

[*'It's still alive* – everything *that's in here is still alive. I don't know how that can be, but it is . . . somehow it is. But they're faint. Why are they so faint?'*]

What she was holding out to him was a small white sneaker that belonged to a woman or a child. As Ralph took it, he heard it singing softly in a distant voice. The sound was as lonely as November wind on an overcast afternoon, but incredibly sweet, as well – an antidote to the endless bray of the black thing on the floor.

And it was a voice he knew. He was sure it was.

There was a maroon splatter on the sneaker's toe. Ralph at first thought it was chocolate milk, then recognized it for what it really was: dried blood. In that instant he was outside the Red Apple again, grabbing Nat before Helen could drop her. He remembered how Helen's feet had tangled together; how she had stumbled backward, leaning against the Red Apple's door like a drunk against a lamppost, holding out her hands to him. *Gih me my bay-ee . . . Gih me Nah-lie.*

He knew the voice because it was Helen's voice. This sneaker had been on her foot that day, and the drops of blood on the toe had come either from Helen's smashed nose or from Helen's lacerated cheek.

It sang and sang, its voice not quite buried beneath the buzz of the thing in the deathbag, and now that Ralph's ears – or whatever passed for ears in the world of auras – were all the way open, he could hear all the other voices of all the other objects. They sang like a lost choir.

Alive. Singing.

They *could* sing, all the things lining these walls *could* sing, because their *owners* could still sing.

Their owners were still alive.

Ralph looked up again, this time noting that while some of the objects he saw were old – the battered alto sax, for instance – a great many of them were new; there were no wheels from Gay Nineties bicycles in this little alcove. He saw three clock-radios, all of them digital. A shaving kit that looked as if it had hardly been used. A lipstick that still had a Rite Aid pricetag on it.

[*'Lois, Atropos has taken this stuff from the people who'll be at the Civic Center tonight. Hasn't he?'*]

[*'Yes. I'm sure that's right.'*]

He pointed at the black cocoon shrieking on the floor, almost drowning out the songs all around it . . . drowning them out as it fed on them.

[*'And whatever's inside that deathbag has something to do with what Clotho and Lachesis called the master-cord. It's the thing that ties all these different objects – all these different* lives *– together.'*]

[*'That makes them ka-tet. Yes.'*]

Ralph handed the sneaker back to Lois.

[*'This goes with us when we go. It's Helen's.'*]

[*'I know.'*]

Lois looked at it for a moment, then did something Ralph thought extremely clever: pulled out two eyelets' worth of lacing and tied the sneaker to her left wrist like a bracelet.

He crawled closer to the small deathbag and then bent over it. Getting close was hard, and staying close was harder – it was like placing your ear next to the motor-housing of a power drill shrieking at full volume or looking into a bright light without squinting. This time there seemed to be actual words buried within that buzzing, the same ones they'd heard as they approached the edge of the deathbag around the Civic Center: *Geddout. Fucoff. Beedit.*

Ralph placed his hands over his ears for a moment, but of course that did no good. The sounds weren't coming from the outside, not really. He let his hands drop again and looked at Lois.

[*'What do you think? Any ideas on what we should do next?'*]

He didn't know exactly what he had expected of her, but it wasn't the quick, positive response he got.

[*'Cut it open and take out what's inside – and do it right away. That thing's dangerous. Also, it might be calling Atropos, have you thought of that? Tattling just like the hen tattled on Jack in the story about the magic beanstalk.'*]

Ralph actually *had* considered this possibility, although not in such vivid terms. *All right,* he thought. *Cut open the bag and take the prize. Except just how are we supposed to do that?*

He remembered the bolt of lightning he'd sent at Atropos when the little bald creep had been trying to lure Rosalie across the street. A good trick, but something like that might do more harm than good here; what if he vaporized the thing they were supposed to take?

I don't think you can do that.

All right, fair enough, as a matter of fact *he* didn't think he could do it, either . . . but when you were surrounded by the possessions of people who could all be dead when the sun came up tomorrow, taking chances seemed like a very bad idea. An *insane* idea.

What I need isn't lightning but a nice sharp pair of scissors, like the ones Clotho and Lachesis use to—

He stared at Lois, startled by the clarity of the image.

[*'I don't know what you just thought of, but hurry up and do it, whatever it is.'*]

6

Ralph looked down at his right hand – a hand from which the wrinkles and the first twists of arthritis had now disappeared, a hand which lay inside a bright blue corona of light. Feeling a little foolish, he folded his last two fingers against his palm and extended the first two, thinking of a game they'd played as kids – rock breaks scissors, scissors cut paper, paper covers rock.

Be scissors, he thought. *I need a pair of scissors. Help me out.*

Nothing. He glanced at Lois and saw her looking at him with

a serene calm which was somehow terrifying. *Oh Lois, if you only knew,* he thought, and then swept that out of his mind. Because he had felt something, hadn't he? Yes. *Something.*

This time he didn't make words in his mind but a picture: not the scissors Clotho had used to send on Jimmy V but the stainless-steel shears from his mother's sewing basket – long, slim blades tapering to a point almost as sharp as the tip of a knife. As he deepened his concentration, he could even see the two tiny words engraved on the metal just south of the pivot-point: SHEFFIELD STEEL. And now he could feel that thing in his mind again, not a blink this time but a muscle – an immensely powerful one – slowly flexing. He looked fixedly down at his fingers and made the shears in his mind open and close. As they did, he slowly opened and closed his fingers, creating a V that widened and narrowed.

Now he could feel the energy he had taken from Nirvana Boy and the bum out at the trainyards, first gathering in his head and then moving down his right arm to his fingers like a cramp.

The aura surrounding the extended first and second fingers of his right hand began to thicken . . . and to lengthen. To take on the slim shape of blades. Ralph waited until they had extended themselves about five inches out from his nails and then worked his fingers back and forth again. The blades opened and closed.

['Go, Ralph! Do it!']

Yes – he couldn't afford to wait around and run experiments. He felt like a car battery that had been called on to crank a motor much too big for it. He could feel all his energy – the stuff he'd taken as well as his own – running down his right arm and into those blades. It wouldn't last long.

He leaned forward, fingers pressed together in a pointing gesture, and sank the tip of the scissors into the deathbag. He had been concentrating so hard on first creating and then maintaining the scissors that he had stopped hearing that steady, hoarse buzz – at least with his conscious mind – but when the scissors-point sank into its black skin, the deathbag suddenly cycled up to a new, shrieking pitch of mingled pain and alarm. Ralph saw dribbles of thick, dark goo running out of the bag and across the floor. It looked like diseased snot. At the same time he felt the power-drain inside him roughly double. He could *see* it, he realized: his own aura running down his right arm and across the back of his hand in slow, peristaltic waves.

And he could sense it dimming around the rest of his body as its essential protection of him thinned out.

[*'Hurry, Ralph! Hurry!'*]

He made a tremendous effort and tore his fingers open. The shimmering blue blades also opened, making a small slit in the black egg. It screamed, and two bright, jagged flashes of red light raced across its surface. Ralph brought his fingers together and watched the shears growing from their tips snap shut, cutting through dense black stuff that was part shell and part flesh. He cried out. It was not pain he felt, exactly, but a sense of awful weariness. *This is what bleeding to death must feel like,* he thought.

Something inside the bag gleamed bright gold.

Ralph gathered all his strength and attempted to open his fingers for another cut. At first he didn't think he was going to be able to do it – they felt as if they had been stuck together with Krazy Glue – and then they drew apart, widening the slit. Now he could almost see the object inside, something small and round and shiny. *Really only one thing it* can *be,* he thought, and then his heart suddenly fluttered in his chest. The blue blades flickered.

[*'Lois! Help me!'*]

She seized his wrist. Ralph felt strength roar into him in big fresh volts. He watched, bemused, as the shears solidified again. Now only one of the blades was blue. The other was a pearly gray.

Lois, screaming inside his head: [*'Cut it! Cut it now!'*]

He brought his fingers together again, and this time the blades cut the deathbag wide open. It uttered one last wavering shriek, turned entirely red, and disappeared. The shears growing from the tips of Ralph's fingers flickered out of existence. He closed his eyes for a moment, suddenly aware that big warm drops of sweat were running down his cheeks like tears. In the dark field behind his eyelids he could see crazy afterimages that looked like dancing scissors-blades.

[*'Lois? Are you okay?'*]

[*'Yes . . . but drained. I don't have the slightest idea how I'm supposed to get back to those stairs under the tree, let alone climb them. I'm not sure I can even stand up.'*]

Ralph opened his eyes, put his hands on his thighs above the knees, and leaned forward again. Lying on the floor where the deathbag had been was a man's wedding ring. He could easily read what had been engraved on the wide inner curve: HD – ED 5–8–87.

Helen Deepneau and Edward Deepneau. Married on August 5th, 1987.

It was what they had come for. It was Ed's token. All that remained now was to pick it up . . . slip it into the watchpocket of his pants . . . find Lois's earrings . . . and get the hell out of here.

7

As he reached for the ring, a flicker of verse slipped through his mind – not Stephen Dobyns this time but J. R. R. Tolkien, who had invented the hobbits Ralph had last thought of in Lois's cozy, picture-filled living room. It had been almost thirty years since he had read Tolkien's story of Frodo and Gandalf and Sauron, the Dark Lord – a story which contained a token very similar to this one, now that he thought about it – but the lines were momentarily as clear as the scissors-blades had been only moments before:

> *One Ring to rule them all, One Ring to find them,*
> *One Ring to bring them all and in the darkness bind them*
> *In the Land of Mordor where the Shadows lie.*

I won't be able to pick it up, he thought. *It will be as tightly bound to the wheel of* ka *as Lois and I are, and I won't be able to pick it up. Either that, or it will be like grasping a live high-tension wire, and I'll be dead before I know it's happening.*

Except he didn't really believe either of those things were going to happen. If the ring was not his for the taking, why had it been protected by the deathbag? If the ring was not his for the taking, why had the forces which stood behind Clotho and Lachesis – and Dorrance, he couldn't forget Dorrance – set him and Lois upon this journey in the first place?

One Ring to rule them all, One Ring to find them, Ralph thought, and closed his fingers around Ed's wedding ring. For a moment he felt a deep, glassy pain in his hand and wrist and forearm; at the same moment, the softly singing voices of the objects which Atropos had hoarded here rose in a great, harmonic shout.

Ralph made a sound – perhaps a scream, perhaps only a moan – and lifted the ring up, clenched tightly in his right hand. A sense of victory sang in his veins like wine, or like—

[*'Ralph.'*]

He looked at her, but Lois was looking down at where Ed's ring had been, her eyes dark with a mixture of fear and confusion.

Where Ed's ring had been; where Ed's ring still was. It lay exactly as it had lain, a glimmering gold circlet with HD – ED 5–8–87 inscribed around the inner arc.

Ralph felt an instant of dizzy disorientation and controlled it with an effort. He opened his hand, half expecting the ring to be gone in spite of what his senses told him, but it still lay in the center of his palm, neatly enclosed within the fork where his loveline and his lifeline diverged, glimmering in the baleful red light of this nasty place. HD – ED 5–8–87.

The two rings were identical.

8

One in his hand; one on the floor; absolutely no difference. At least none that Ralph could see.

Lois reached for the ring which had replaced the one Ralph had picked up, hesitated, then grasped it. As they watched, ghost-gold glowed just above the chamber's floor, then solidified into a third wedding band. Like the other two, HD – ED 5–8–87 was inscribed on the inner curve.

Ralph found himself thinking of yet another story – not Tolkien's long tale of the Ring, but a story by Dr Seuss which he had read one of Carolyn's sister's kids back in the fifties. That was a long time ago, but he had never completely forgotten the story, which had been richer and darker than Dr Seuss's usual jingle-jangle nonsense about rats and bats and troublesome cats. It was called *The Five Hundred Hats of Bartholomew Cubbins,* and Ralph supposed it really wasn't any wonder that the story had come to mind now.

Poor Bartholomew was a country hayseed who had the bad luck to be in the big city when the King happened by. You were supposed to take your hat off in the presence of that august personage, and Bartholomew had certainly tried, but without any luck; each time he took his hat off, another one, identical to the last, appeared beneath it.

[*'Ralph, what's happening? What does it mean?'*]

He shook his head without answering, eyes moving from

the ring on his palm to the one in Lois's hand to the one on the floor, around and around and around. Three rings, all of them identical, just like the hats Bartholomew Cubbins had kept trying to take off. The poor kid had gone on trying to make his manners to the King, Ralph remembered, even as the executioner had led him up a curving flight of stairs to the place where he would be beheaded for the crime of disrespect . . .

Except that wasn't right, because after awhile the hats on poor Bartholomew's head *did* begin to change, to grow ever more fabulous and rococo.

And are the rings the same, Ralph? Are you sure?

No, he guessed he wasn't. When he'd picked up the first one, he had felt a deep, momentary ache spread up his arm like rheumatism, but Lois had shown no signs of pain when she picked up the second one.

And the voices – I didn't hear them shout when she picked up the one she has.

Ralph leaned forward and grasped the third ring. There was no jolt of pain and no shout from the objects which formed the walls of the room – they just kept singing softly. Meanwhile, a fourth ring materialized where the other three had been, materialized exactly like another hat on the head of hapless Bartholomew Cubbins, but Ralph barely glanced at it. He looked at the first ring, lying between the fork of his lifeline and loveline on the palm of his right hand.

One Ring to rule them all, he thought. *One Ring to bind them. And I think that's you, beautiful. I think the others are just clever counterfeits.*

And maybe there was a way to check that. Ralph held the two rings to his ears. The one in his left hand was silent; the one in his right, the one that had been inside the deathbag when he cut it open, gave off a faint, chilling echo of the deathbag's final scream.

The one in his right hand was alive.

['*Ralph?*']

Her hand on his arm, cold and urgent. Ralph looked at her, then tossed the ring in his left hand away. He held the other up and gazed at Lois's strained, strangely young face through it, as if through a telescope.

['*This is the one. The others are just place-holders, I think – like zeros in a big, complicated math problem.*']

['*You mean they don't matter?*']

He hesitated, unsure of how to reply . . . because they *did* matter, that was the thing. He just didn't know how to put his intuitive understanding of this into words. As long as the false rings kept appearing in this nasty little room, like hats on the head of Bartholomew Cubbins, the future represented by the deathbag around the Civic Center remained the one true future. But the first ring, the one which Atropos had actually stolen off Ed's finger (perhaps as he lay sleeping next to Helen in the little Cape Cod house which was now standing empty), could change all that.

The replicas were tokens which preserved the shape of *ka* just as spokes radiating out from a hub preserved the shape of a wheel. The original, however . . .

Ralph thought the original *was* the hub: One Ring to bind them.

He gripped the gold band tightly, feeling its hard curve bite into his palm and fingers. Then he slipped it into his watchpocket.

There was one thing about ka *they didn't tell us,* he thought. *It's slippery. Slippery as some nasty old fish that won't come off the hook but just keeps flopping around in your hand.*

And it was like climbing a sand dune, too – you slid one step back for every two you managed to lunge forward. They had gone out to High Ridge and accomplished *something* – just what Ralph didn't know, but Dorrance had assured them it was true; according to him, they had fulfilled their task there. Now they had come here and taken Ed's token, but it *still* wasn't enough, and why? Because *ka* was like a fish, *ka* was like a sand dune, *ka* was like a wheel that didn't want to stop but only to roll on and on, crushing whatever might happen to be in its path. A wheel of many spokes.

But most of all, perhaps, *ka* was like a ring.

Like a wedding ring.

He suddenly understood what all the talk on the hospital roof and all of Dorrance's efforts to explain hadn't been able to convey: Ed's undesignated status, coupled with Atropos's discovery of the poor, confused man, had conveyed a tremendous power upon him. A door had opened, and a demon called the Crimson King had strolled through, one that was stronger than Clotho, Lachesis, Atropos, any of them. And it didn't intend to be stopped by a Derry Old Crock like Ralph Roberts.

[*'Ralph?'*]

[*'One Ring to rule them all, Lois – One Ring to bind them.'*]

[*'What are you talking about? What do you mean?'*]

538

He patted his watchpocket, feeling the small yet momentous bulge that was Ed's ring. Then he reached out and grasped her shoulders.

[*'The replacements – the false rings – are spokes, but this one is the hub. Take away the hub, and a wheel can't turn.'*]

[*'Are you sure?'*]

He was sure, all right. He just didn't know how to do it.

[*'Yes. Now come on – let's get out of here while we still can.'*]

Ralph sent her beneath the overloaded dining room table first, then dropped to his knees and followed. He paused halfway under and looked back over his shoulder. He saw a strange and terrible thing: although the buzzing sound had not returned, the deathbag was reknitting itself around the replacement wedding ring. Already the bright gold had dimmed to a ghostly circlet.

He stared at it for several seconds, fascinated, almost hypnotized, then tore his eyes away with an effort and began to crawl after Lois.

9

Ralph was afraid they would lose valuable time trying to navigate their way back through the maze of corridors which crisscrossed Atropos's storehouse of keepsakes, but that turned out not to be a problem. Their own footprints, fading but still visible, were there to guide them.

He began to feel a little stronger as they put the terrible little room behind them, but Lois was now flagging badly. By the time they reached the archway between the storehouse and Atropos's filthy apartment, she was leaning on him. He asked if she was all right. Lois managed a shrug and a small, tired smile.

[*'Most of my problem is being in this place. It doesn't really matter how high up we go, it's still foul and I hate it. Once I get some fresh air, I think I'll be fine. Honestly.'*]

Ralph hoped she was right. As he ducked under the arch into Atropos's apartment, he was trying to think of a pretext by which he could send Lois on ahead of him. That would give him an opportunity to give the place a quick search. If that didn't turn up the earrings, he would have to assume that Atropos was still wearing them.

He noticed her slip was hanging below the hem of her dress again, opened his mouth to tell her, and saw a flicker of movement from the tail of his left eye. He realized they had been a lot less cautious on the return trip – partly because they were worn out – and now they might have to pay a high price for dropping their guard.

[*'Lois, look out!'*]

Too late. Ralph felt her arm jerked away as the snarling creature in the dirty tunic seized her about the waist and dragged her backward. Atropos's head only came to her armpit, but that was enough to allow him to hold his rusty blade over her. When Ralph made an instinctive lunge at him, Atropos brought the straight-razor down until it was touching the pearl-gray cord which drifted up from the crown of her head. He bared his teeth at Ralph in an unspeakable grin.

[*Not another step, Shorts . . . not one!*]

Well, he didn't have to worry about Lois's errant earrings anymore, at least. They glittered a murky, pinkish-red against the tiny lobes of Atropos's ears. It was more the sight of them than the shout that stopped Ralph where he was.

The scalpel drew back a little . . . but only a little.

[*Now, Shorts – you took something of mine just now, didn't you? Don't try to deny it; I know. And now you're going to give it back.*]

The scalpel returned to Lois's balloon-string; Atropos caressed it with the flat of the blade.

[*You give it back or this bitch is going to die here in front of you – you can stand there and watch the sack turn black. So what do you say, Short Stuff? Hand it over.*]

Chapter Twenty-six

1

Atropos's smile shone out, full of repulsive triumph, and full of –

Full of fear. He caught you flat-footed, he's got his scalpel to Lois's balloon-string and his hand around her throat, but he's still scared to death. Why?

[*Come on! Quit wasting time, shithead! Give me the ring!*]

Ralph reached slowly into his watchpocket and grasped the ring, wondering why Atropos hadn't killed Lois outright. Surely he didn't intend to let her – to let either of them – go.

He's afraid I might hammer him with another one of those telepathic karate-chops. And that's just for starters. I think he's also afraid of screwing up. Afraid of the thing – the entity *– that's running him. Afraid of the Crimson King. You're scared of the boss, aren't you, my filthy little friend?*

He held the ring up between the thumb and forefinger of his right hand and peeked through it again.

['*Come and get it, why don't you? Don't be shy.*']

Atropos's face knotted with rage. The expression twisted his nervy, gloating grin into a cartoon scowl.

[*I'll kill her, Shorts, didn't you hear me? Is that what you want?*]

Ralph slowly and deliberately raised his left hand. He made a sawing gesture in the air with it, and was gratified to see Atropos wince when the edge of the palm turned momentarily toward him.

['*If you even nick her with that blade, I'll hit you so hard you'll need a pocket-knife to dig your teeth out of the wall. And that's a promise.*']

[*Just give me the ring, Shorts.*]

They can't lie, Ralph thought suddenly. *I can't remember if I was actually told that or just intuited it, but I'm sure it's true – they can't lie. I can, though.*

['*I'll tell you what, Mr A – promise me it's a push and I'll give it to you.*']

Atropos gave him a narrow look in which doubt and suspicion were mingled.

[*A push? What do you mean, a push?*]

'Ralph, no!']

He glanced at her, then back at Atropos. He raised his left hand to scratch his cheek without considering how the gesture would look to the little bald doctor. The scalpel was pressed against Lois's balloon-string again in a trice, this time hard enough to dent it and create a dark splotch at the point of contact. It looked like a blood-blister. Great beads of sweat stood out on Atropos's brow, and when he spoke, his voice was a panicky shriek.

[*Don't you go throwing any of your cut-rate thunderbolts at me! The woman dies if you do!*]

Ralph lowered his hand in a hurry, then put both of them behind his back like a penitent child. Ed's wedding ring was still folded into his hand, and now, almost without thinking about it, he tucked it into the back pocket of his pants. It was only then that he was completely sure he didn't mean to give up the ring. Even if it cost Lois her life – both of them their lives – he didn't mean to give up the ring.

But perhaps it wouldn't come to that.

['*A push means we both walk away, Mr A – I give you the ring, you give me back my lady-friend. All you have to do is promise not to hurt her. What do you say?*']

['*No, Ralph, no!*']

What Atropos said was nothing. His eyes glittered at Ralph with feary, hateful impotence. If ever in his long life he'd wished for the ability to lie, Ralph supposed he must be wishing for it at that moment. All it would take was *Okay, it's a deal*, and the ball would be right back in Ralph's court. But he couldn't say that, because he couldn't *do* that.

He knows he's in a nasty corner, Ralph thought. *It really doesn't matter if he cuts her cord or lets her go – he must think I mean to flash-fry him in either case, and he's not wrong.*

How much damage can you actually do to him, sweetheart? Carolyn asked doubtfully from the place she kept inside his head. *How much juice have you got left after cutting open the deathbag around the wedding ring?*

The answer, unfortunately, was not much. Maybe enough to singe his bald head, but probably not enough to sauté it. And—

Then Ralph saw something he didn't like: the edge-of-panic quality in Atropos's grin was being replaced by cautious confidence. And he felt those mad eyes crawling avidly over him – his face, his body, but mostly his *aura*. Ralph had a sudden clear vision of a mechanic using a dipstick to find out how much oil was left in an automobile crankcase.

Do something, Lois begged him with her eyes. *Please, Ralph.*

But he didn't know what to do. He was completely out of ideas.

Atropos's smile took on a gloating, nasty edge.

[*You're unloaded, Short Stuff, ain'tcha? Gee, that's sad.*]

[*'Hurt her and you'll find out, you sawed-off piece of shit.'*]

Atropos's grin went on widening.

[*You couldn't give a rat a hotfoot with what you've got left. Why don't you just be a good boy and hand over the ring before I—*]

[*'Oh, you bastard!'*]

It was Lois. She was no longer looking at Ralph; she was looking across the room, into the mirror where Atropos no doubt checked the fit and tilt of his latest fashion accents – Rosalie's bandanna, say, or Bill McGovern's Panama. Her eyes were wide and full of fury, and Ralph knew exactly what she was seeing.

[*'Those are* MINE, *you rotten little thief!'*]

She shoved violently backward, using her greater weight to slam Atropos against the side of the archway. A startled grunt escaped him. The hand holding the scalpel flew upward; the blade dug dry scales of dirt from the wall. Lois turned toward him, her face knotted in an angry snarl – a look so un-*our Lois* that McGovern might have fainted in shock at the sight of it. Her hands clawed at the sides of his face, reaching for his ears. One of her fingers dug into his cheek. Atropos yapped like a dog whose paw has been stepped on, then grabbed her by the waist again and whirled her back around.

He turned the scalpel's blade inward, getting ready to slash. Ralph shook the forefinger of his right hand at it in a scolding gesture. A flash of light so pallid it was almost invisible shot out from the nail and struck the scalpel's tip, momentarily knocking it away from Lois's balloon-string. And that was all there was; Ralph sensed that his personal armory was now empty.

Atropos bared his teeth at him from over Lois's shoulder as she bucked and twisted in his arms. She was not trying to get away, either; she was trying to turn and attack him. Her feet flailed out as she threw all her weight against him again, trying to squash him against the wall behind them, and without having the slightest idea of what he meant to do, Ralph lunged forward and dropped to his knees with his hands out. He looked like a manic suitor making a strenuous marriage proposal, and one of Lois's thrashing feet came close to kicking him in the throat. He snatched at the hem of her slip and it came free in a slithery little rush of pink nylon. Meanwhile, Lois was still yelling.

[*'Miserable little thief! Here's something for you! How do you like it?'*]

Atropos uttered a squeal of pain, and when Ralph looked up, he saw that Lois had buried her teeth in his right wrist. His left hand, the one holding the scalpel, flailed blindly at her balloon-string, missing it by less than an inch. Ralph sprang to his feet and, still with no clear idea of what he was doing, pulled Lois's pink half-slip over Atropos's slashing hand . . . and his head.

[*'Get away from him, Lois! Run!'*]

She spat out the small white hand and stumbled toward the barrel-head table in the center of the room, wiping Atropos's blood from her mouth with atavistic loathing . . . but the dominant expression on her face was still one of anger. Atropos himself, for the moment just a bawling, writhing shape under the pink half-slip, groped after her with his free hand. Ralph slapped it away and shoved him back against the side of the archway.

[*'No you don't, my friend – not at all.'*]

[*'Let me go! Let me go, you bastard! You can't do this!'*]

And the weirdest thing of all is that he really believes that, Ralph thought. *He's had it his own way for so long that he's completely forgotten what Short-Timers can do. I can fix that, I think.*

Ralph remembered how Atropos had slashed Rosalie's balloon-string after the dog had licked his hand, and his hatred for this strutting, leering, complacently insane creature suddenly exploded in his head like a rotten-green roadflare. He grabbed one side of Lois's slip and twisted his fist twice around it in a savage winding-up gesture, pulling it so tight that Atropos's features stood out in a pink nylon deathmask.

Then, just as the blade of the scalpel popped through the fabric and began to cut it open, Ralph whirled Atropos around, using the slip as a man might use a sling to whirl a stone, and sent him flying across the archway. The damage might have been less if Atropos had fallen, but he didn't; his feet knocked against each other but never quite crossed. He hit the rock facing of the archway with a thud, voiced a muffled scream of pain, and dropped to his knees. Spots of blood bloomed on Lois's half-slip like flower-petals. The scalpel had disappeared back through the slit it had made in the cloth. Ralph sprang after Atropos just as it reappeared and lengthened the original cut, freeing the bald creature's staring, bewildered face. His nose was bleeding; so were his forehead and right temple. Before he could begin to get up, Ralph grabbed the slippery pink bulges that were his shoulders.

[*Stop it! I'm warning you, Shorts! I'll make you sorry you were ever bo*—]

Ralph ignored this pointless bluster and slammed Atropos forward, hard. The midget's arms were still tangled in the slip and he caught the floor with nothing but face. His shriek was part amazement, mostly pain. Incredibly, Ralph felt Lois in the back of his mind, telling him that enough was enough, not to really hurt him – not to hurt the pint-sized psychotic who had just tried to kill her. Atropos attempted to roll over. Ralph knee-dropped him in the middle of the back and knocked him flat again.

[*'Don't move, friend. I like you just the way you are.'*]

He looked up at Lois, and saw that her amazing fury had departed as suddenly as it had come – like some freak weather phenomenon. A tornado, perhaps, that touches down out of a clear blue sky, rips the top off a barn, and then disappears again. She was pointing at Atropos.

[*'He's got my earrings, Ralph. The nasty little thief has got my earrings. He's wearing them!'*]

[*'I know. I saw.'*]

One snarling side of Atropos's face poked out of the slit in the nylon like the face of the world's ugliest baby at the moment of its birth. Ralph could feel the muscles of the small creature's back trembling beneath his pinioning knee, and he remembered an old proverb he'd read somewhere . . . maybe at the end of a Salada teabag string: *He who takes a tiger by the tail dare not let go.* Now, in this unlikely den beneath the ground and feeling like a character in a fairy-tale concocted by a lunatic,

Ralph thought he had achieved a sort of divine understanding of that proverb. Through a combination of Lois's sudden rage and plain old shitass luck, he had wound up at least temporarily on top of the scuzzy little fuck. The question – and a fairly pressing one, at that – was what to do next.

The hand holding the scalpel lashed up, but the stroke was both weak and blind. Ralph avoided it easily. Sobbing and cursing, not afraid even now but clearly hurting and all but consumed with impotent rage, Atropos flailed up at him again.

[*Let me up, you overgrown Short-Time bastard! Silly old white-hair! Ugly wrinkle-face!*]

[*'I look a little better than that just lately, my friend. Haven't you noticed?'*]

[*Asshole! Stupid Short-Time asshole! I'll make you sorry! I'll make you so sorry!*]

Well, Ralph thought, *at least he's not begging. I almost would have expected him to start begging by now.*

Atropos continued to flail weakly with the scalpel. Ralph ducked two or three of these strokes easily, then slid one hand toward the throat of the creature lying beneath him.

[*'Ralph! No! Don't!'*]

He shook his head at her, not knowing if he was expressing annoyance, reassurance, or both. He touched Atropos's skin, and felt him shudder. The bald doc uttered a choked cry of revulsion, and Ralph knew exactly how he felt. It was sickening for both of them, but he didn't take his hand away. Instead, he tried to close it around Atropos's throat and wasn't very surprised to find he couldn't do it. Still, hadn't Lachesis said that only Short-Timers could oppose the will of Atropos? He thought so. The question was, how?

Beneath him, Atropos laughed nastily.

[*'Please, Ralph! Please just get my earrings and we'll go!'*]

Atropos rolled his eyes in her direction, then looked back at Ralph.

[*Did you think you could kill me, Shorts? Well, guess again.*]

No, he hadn't thought it, but he'd needed to find out for sure.

[*Life's a bitch, ain't it, Shorts? Why don't you just give me back the ring? I'm going to get it sooner or later, I guarantee you that.*]

[*'Fuck you, you little weasel.'*]

Tough talk, but talk was cheap. The most pressing question

was still unanswered: What the hell was he supposed to do with this monster?

Whatever it is, you won't be able to do it with Lois standing there and watching you, a cold voice that was not quite Carolyn's advised him. *She was fine when she was pissed off, but she's not pissed off now. She's too tenderhearted for whatever's going to happen next, Ralph. You have to get her out of here.*

He turned toward Lois. Her eyes were half closed. She looked ready to crumple at the base of the archway and go to sleep.

['*Lois, I want you to get out of here. Right now. Go up the stairs and wait for me under the tr—*']

The scalpel flashed up again, and this time it almost sliced off the end of Ralph's nose. He recoiled, and his knee slid on nylon. Atropos gave a mighty heave and came within a whisker of rolling out from under. At the last second, Ralph shoved the little man's head flat again with the heel of his hand – that, it seemed, was allowed by the rules – and replanted his knee.

[*Owww! Owww! Stop it! You're killing me!*]

Ralph ignored him and looked at Lois.

['*Go on, Lois! Go on up! I'll be there as soon as I can!*']

['*I don't think I can climb out on my own – I'm too tired.*']

['*Yes, you can. You have to, and you can.*']

Atropos subsided again – for the moment, at least – a small, gasping engine under Ralph's knee. But that was a long way from being enough. Time was passing topside, passing fast, and right now time was the real enemy, not Ed Deepneau.

['*My earrings—*']

['*I'll bring them when I come, Lois. I promise.*']

Making what looked like a supreme effort, Lois straightened and looked solemnly at Ralph.

['*You shouldn't hurt him, Ralph, not if you don't have to. It's not Christian.*']

No, not at all Christian, a capering little creature deep inside Ralph's head agreed. *Not Christian, but still . . . I can't wait to get started.*

['*Go on, Lois. Leave him to me.*']

She looked at him sadly.

['*It wouldn't do me any good to ask you to promise not to hurt him, would it?*']

He thought about it, then shook his head.

['*No, but I'll promise you this much: it won't be any harder than he makes it. Is that good enough?*']

Lois considered carefully, then nodded.

[*'Yes, I think that will do. And maybe I can make it back up, if I take it slow and easy . . . but what about you?'*]

[*'I'll be fine. Wait for me under the tree.'*]

[*'All right, Ralph.'*]

He watched her cross the filthy room, Helen's sneaker bobbing from one wrist. She ducked beneath the arch between the apartment and the stairway and slowly started up. Ralph waited until her feet had disappeared from view, then turned back to Atropos.

[*'Well, Chumley, here we are – two old pals reunited. What should we do? Should we play? You like to play, don't you?'*]

Atropos immediately renewed his struggles, simultaneously waving his scalpel above his head and trying to buck Ralph off.

[*Quit it! Get your hands off me, you old faggot!*]

Atropos thrashed so wildly that kneeling on him now was like kneeling on a snake. Ralph ignored the yelling, the bucking, and the blindly waving scalpel. Atropos's whole head was now sticking out of the slip, which made things a lot easier. He grabbed Lois's earrings and tugged. They stayed where they were but earned him a hearty, pained scream from Atropos. Ralph leaned forward, smiling a little.

[*'For pierced ears, aren't they, pal?'*]

[*'Yes! Yes, goddammit!'*]

[*'To quote you, life's a bitch, ain't it?'*]

Ralph seized the earrings again and ripped them free. There were two small fans of blood as the minute holes in the lobes of Atropos's ears became flaps. The bald man's scream was as sharp as a new drillbit. Ralph felt an uneasy mixture of pity and contempt.

Little bastard's used to hurting other people, but not being hurt himself. Maybe he's never been hurt himself. Well say hello to how the other half lives, pal.

[*Stop it! Stop it! You can't do this to me!*]

[*'I've got a newsflash for you, buddy . . . I am doing it. Now why don't you just get with the program?'*]

[*What do you think you're going to accomplish by this, Shorts? It'll happen anyway, you know. All those people at the Civic Center are going to go bye-bye, and taking the ring won't stop it.*]

Don't I know it, Ralph thought.

Atropos was still panting, but he had stopped thrashing. Ralph felt able to look away from him for a moment and send his eyes on a quick tour of the room. He supposed what he was really looking for was inspiration – even a small bolt would do.

['*Can I make a suggestion, Mr A? As your new little pal and playmate? I know you're busy, but you ought to find time to do something about this place. I'm not talking about getting it in* House Beautiful *or anything like that, but sheesh! What a sty!*']

Atropos, simultaneously sulky and wary: [*Do you think I give a fuck what you think, Shorts?*]

He could only think of one way to proceed. He didn't like it, but he was going to go ahead, just the same. He *had* to go ahead; there was a picture in his mind that guaranteed it. It was a picture of Ed Deepneau flying toward Derry from the coast in a light plane, one with either a crate of high explosive or a tank of nerve-gas stowed in the nose.

['*What* can *I do with you, Mr A? Any ideas?*']

The response was immediate and unequivocal.

[*Let me go. That's the answer. The* only *answer. I'll leave you alone, both of you. Leave you for the Purpose. You'll live another ten years. Hell, maybe another twenty, it's not impossible. All you and the little lady have to do is butt out. Go home. And when the big bang comes, watch it on the TV news.*]

Ralph tried to sound as if he were honestly considering this.

['*And you'd leave us alone? You'd* promise *to leave us alone?*']
[*Yes!*]

Atropos's face had taken on a hopeful look, and Ralph could see the first traces of an aura springing up around the little creep. It was the same low and nasty red as the pulsing glow which lit the apartment.

['*Do you know something, Mr A?*']

Atropos, looking more hopeful than ever: [*No, what?*]

Ralph shot one hand forward, grabbed Atropos's left wrist, and twisted it hard. Atropos shrieked in agony. His fingers loosened on the handle of the scalpel, and Ralph plucked it free with the ease of a veteran pickpocket lifting a wallet.

['*I believe you.*']

2

[*Give it back! Give it back! Give it back! Give it—*]

In his hysteria, Atropos might have gone on shrieking this for hours, so Ralph put a stop to it in the most direct way he knew. He leaned forward and slashed a shallow vertical cut down the back of the big bald head poking out of the hole in Lois's half-slip. No invisible hand tried to repel him, and his own hand moved with no trouble at all. Blood – a shocking amount of it – welled out of the line-cut. The aura around Atropos had now gone to the dark and baleful red of an infected wound. He shrieked again.

Ralph rocked forward and spoke chummily into his ear.

[*'Maybe I can't kill you, but I can certainly fuck you up, can't I? And I don't need to be loaded with psychic juice to do it, either. This little honey will do just fine.'*]

He used the scalpel to cross the first cut he'd made, making a lower-case *t* on the back of Atropos's head. Atropos shrieked and began to flail wildly. Ralph was disgusted to discover that part of him – the capering gremlin – was enjoying this enormously.

[*'If you want me to go on cutting you, go on struggling. If you want me to stop, then* you *stop.'*]

Atropos became still at once.

[*'Okay. Now I'm going to ask you a few questions. I think you'll find it in your best interest to answer them.'*]

[*Ask me anything! Whatever you want! Just don't cut me any-more!*]

[*'That's a pretty good attitude, pally, but I think there's always room for improvement, don't you? Let's see.'*]

Ralph sliced down again, this time opening a long gash in the side of Atropos's skull. A flap of skin peeled loose like badly glued wallpaper. Atropos howled. Ralph felt a cramp of revulsion in the pit of his stomach and was actually relieved . . . but when he spoke/thought at Atropos, he took great pains not to let that feeling show.

[*'Okay, that's my motivational lecture, doc. If I have to repeat it, you'll need Krazy Glue to keep the top of your head from flying off in a high wind. Do you understand me?'*]

[*Yes! Yes!*]

[*'And do you believe me?'*]

[*Yes! Rotten old white-hair,* YES!]

['*Okay, that's good. Here's my question, Mr A: if you make a promise, are you bound by it?*']

Atropos was slow in answering, an encouraging sign. Ralph laid the flat of the scalpel's blade against his cheek to hurry him up. He was rewarded with another scream and instant cooperation.

[*Yes! Yes! Just don't cut me again! Please don't cut me again!*]

Ralph took the scalpel away. The outline of the blade burned on the little creature's unlined cheek like a birthmark.

['*Okay, sunshine, listen up. I want you to promise you'll leave me and Lois alone until the rally at the Civic Center is over. No more chasing, no more slashing, no more bullshit. Promise me that.*']

[*Fuck you! Take your promise and shove it up your ass!*]

Ralph was not put out of temper by this; his smile, in fact, widened. Because Atropos hadn't said *I won't*, and even more important, Atropos hadn't said *I can't*. He had just said no. Just a little backsliding, in other words, and easily remedied.

Steeling himself, Ralph ran the scalpel straight down the middle of Atropos's back. The slip split, the dirty white tunic beneath it split, and so did the flesh beneath the tunic. Blood poured out in a sickening flood, and Atropos's tortured, wailing shriek beat at Ralph's ears.

He leaned over and murmured into the small ear again, grimacing and avoiding the blood as best he could.

['*I don't like doing this anymore, Chumley – in fact, about two more cuts and I'm going to throw up again – but I want you to know that I* can *do it and I'm going to* keep on *doing it until you either give me the promise I want or until the force that stopped me from choking you stops me again. I think if you wait for that to happen, you're going to be one hurting unit. So what do you say? Do you want to promise, or do you want me to peel you like a grape?*']

Atropos was blubbering. It was a nauseating, horrible sound.

[*You don't understand! If you succeed in stopping what's been started – the chances are slim, but it's possible that you might – I will be punished by the creature you call the Crimson King!*]

Ralph clamped his teeth together and slashed down again, his lips pressed so tightly together that his mouth looked like a long-healed scar. There was a faint tug as the scalpel's blade slid through gristle, and then Atropos's left ear tumbled to the floor. Blood poured out of the hole on the side of his bald head, and his scream this time was loud enough to hurt Ralph's ears.

They're sure a long way from being gods, aren't they? Ralph thought. He felt sick with horror and dismay. *The only real difference between them and us is that they live longer and they're a little harder to see. And I guess I'm not much of a soldier – just looking at all that blood makes me feel like passing out. Shit.*

[*All right, I promise! Just stop cutting me! No more! Please, no more!*]

[*'That's a start, but you're going to have to be more specific. I want to hear you say that you promise to stay away from me and Lois, and Ed, too, until the rally at the Civic Center is over.'*]

He expected more wiggling and weaseling, but Atropos surprised him.

[*I promise! I promise to stay away from you, and from the bitch you're running around with—*]

[*'Lois. Say her name. Lois.'*]

[*Yeah, yeah, her – Lois Chasse! I agree to stay away from her, and Deepneau, too. From all of you, just as long as you don't cut me anymore. Are you satisfied? Is it good enough, God damn you?*]

Ralph decided he *was* satisfied . . . or as satisfied as any man can be when he is deeply sickened by his own methods and actions. He didn't believe there were any trapdoors hidden in Atropos's promise; the little bald man knew he might pay a high price later for giving in now, but in the end that hadn't been able to offset the pain and terror Ralph had inflicted on him.

[*'Yes, Mr A, I think it's good enough.'*]

Ralph slid off his small victim with his stomach rolling and a sensation – it had to be false, didn't it? – that his throat was opening and closing like the valve of a clam. He looked at the blood-spattered scalpel for a moment, then cocked his arm back and threw it as hard as he could. It flew end-for-end through the arch and disappeared into the storeroom beyond.

Good riddance, Ralph thought. *At least I didn't get much on myself. There's that.* He no longer felt like vomiting. Now he felt like crying.

Atropos got slowly to his knees and looked around with the dazed eyes of a man who has survived a killer storm. He saw his ear lying on the floor and picked it up. He turned it over in his small hands and looked at the strands of gristle trailing out from the back side. Then he looked up at Ralph. His eyes swam with tears of pain and humiliation, but there was something else in them as well – a rage so deep and deadly that Ralph recoiled from it. All his precautions seemed flimsy and foolish in the face of that rage. He took a blundering step backward and pointed at Atropos with an unsteady finger.

[*'Remember your promise!'*]

Atropos bared his teeth in a gruesome grin. The dangling flap of skin on the side of his face swung back and forth like a slack sail, and the raw flesh beneath it oozed and trickled.

[*Of course I'll remember it – how could I forget? In fact, I'd like to make you another. Two for the price of one, you might say.*]

Atropos made a gesture Ralph remembered well from the hospital roof, spreading the first two fingers of his right hand in a V and then flicking them upward, creating a red arc in the air. Within it, Ralph saw a human figure. Beyond it, dimly glimpsed, as if seen though a mist of blood, was the Red Apple Store. He started to ask who that was standing in the foreground, on the curb of Harris Avenue . . . and then, suddenly, he knew. He looked up at Atropos with shocked eyes.

[*'Jesus, no! No, you can't!'*]

The grin on Atropos's face continued to widen.

[*You know, that's what I kept thinking about you, Short-Time. Only I was wrong. You are, too. Watch.*]

Atropos moved his spread fingers slightly wider. Ralph saw someone wearing a Boston Red Sox baseball cap come out of the Red Apple, and this time Ralph knew immediately whom he was looking at. This person called to the one across the street, and then something terrible began to happen. Ralph turned away, sickened, from the bloody arc of the future between Atropos's small fingers.

But he heard it when it happened.

[*The one I showed you first belongs to the Random, Shorts – to me, in other words. And here's my promise to you: if you go on getting in my way, what I've just shown you is going to happen. There's nothing you can do, no warning you can give, that will stop it from happening. But if you leave off now – if you and the woman simply stand aside and let events take their course – then I will stay my hand.*]

The vulgarities which formed so large a part of Atropos's usual discourse had been left behind like a discarded costume, and for the first time Ralph had some clear sense of how truly old and malevolently wise this being was.

[*Remember what the junkies say, Shorts: dying is easy, living is hard. It's a true saying. If anyone should know, it's me. So what do you think? Having any second thoughts?*]

Ralph stood in the filthy chamber with his head down and his fists clenched. Lois's earrings burned in one of them like small hot coals. Ed's ring also seemed to burn against him, and he knew there wasn't a thing in the world to stop him from taking it out of his pocket and throwing it into the other room after the scalpel. He remembered a story he'd read in school about a thousand years ago. 'The Lady or the Tiger?' it had been called, and now he understood what it was to be given such a terrible power . . . and such a terrible choice. On the surface it seemed easy enough; what, after all, was one life against a thousand?

But that one life— !

Yet really, it isn't as if anyone would ever have to know, he thought coldly. *No one except maybe for Lois . . . and Lois would accept my decision. Carolyn might not have done, but they're very different women.*

Yes, but did he have the right?

Atropos also read this in his aura – it was spooky, how much the creature saw.

[*Of course you do, Ralph – that's what these matters of life and death are really about: who has the right. This time it's you. So what do you say?*]

['*I don't know* what *I say. I don't know what I think. All I know is that I wish all three of you had* LEFT ME THE FUCK ALONE!']

Ralph Roberts raised his head toward the root-riddled ceiling of Atropos's den and screamed.

Chapter Twenty-seven

1

Five minutes later, Ralph's head poked out of the shadows beneath the old, leaning oak. He saw Lois at once. She was kneeling in front of him, peering anxiously through the tangle of roots at his upturned face. He raised a grimy, blood-streaked hand and she took it firmly, holding him steady as he made his way up the last few steps – gnarled roots that were actually more like ladder-rungs.

Ralph wriggled his way out from under the tree and turned over on his back, taking the sweet air in great long pulls of breath. He thought air had never in his whole life tasted so good. In spite of everything else, he was enormously grateful to be out. To be free.

['*Ralph? Are you all right?*']

He turned her hand over, kissed her palm, then put her earrings where his lips had been.

['*Yes. Fine. These are yours.*']

She looked at them curiously, as if she had never seen earrings – these or any others – before, and then put them in her dress pocket.

['*You saw them in the mirror, didn't you, Lois?*']

['*Yes, and it made me angry . . . but I don't think I was really surprised, not down deep.*']

['*Because you knew.*']

['*Yes. I guess I did. Maybe from when we first saw Atropos wearing Bill's hat. I just kept it . . . you know . . . in the back of my mind.*']

She was looking at him carefully, assessingly.

['*Never mind my earrings right now – what happened down there? How did you get away?*']

Ralph was afraid if she looked at him in that careful way for too long, she would see too much. He also had an idea that if he didn't get moving soon, he might never move again; his weariness was now so large it was like some great encrusted object – a long-sunken ocean liner, perhaps – lying inside him, calling to him, trying to drag him down. He got to his feet. He couldn't allow either of them to be dragged down, not now. The news the sky told wasn't as bad as it could have been, but it was bad enough – it was six o'clock at least. All over Derry, people who didn't give a shit one way or the other about the abortion issue (the vast majority, in other words) were sitting down to hot dinners. At the Civic Center the doors would now be open; 10-K TV lights would be bathing them, and Minicams would be transmitting live shots of early arriving pro-choice advocates driving past Dan Dalton and his sign-waving Friends of Life. Not far from here, people were chanting that old Ed Deepneau favorite, the one that went *Hey, hey, Susan Day, how many kids did you kill today?* Whatever he and Lois did, they would have to do it in the next sixty to ninety minutes. The clock was ticking.

[*'Come on, Lois. We have to get moving.'*]

[*'Are we going back to the Civic Center?'*]

[*'No, not to start with. I think that to start with, we ought to . . .'*]

Ralph discovered that he simply couldn't wait to hear what he had to say. Where *did* he think they ought to go to start with? Back to Derry Home? The Red Apple? His house? Where did you go when you needed to find a couple of well-meaning but far from all-knowing fellows who had gotten you and your few close friends into a world of hurt and trouble? Or could you reasonably expect *them* to find *you?*

They might not want *to find you, sweetheart. In fact, they might actually be hiding from you.*

[*'Ralph, are you sure you're—'*]

He suddenly thought of Rosalie, and knew.

[*'The park, Lois. Strawford Park. That's where we have to go. But we need to make a stop on the way.'*]

He led her along the Cyclone fence, and soon they heard the lazy sound of interwoven voices. Ralph could smell roasting hotdogs as well, and after the fetid stench of Atropos's den, the smell was ambrosial. A minute or two later, he and Lois stepped to the edge of the little picnic area near Runway 3.

Dorrance was there, standing at the heart of his amazing,

multicolored aura and watching as a light plane drifted down toward the runway. Behind him, Faye Chapin and Don Veazie were sitting at one of the picnic tables with a chessboard between them and a half-finished bottle of Blue Nun near to hand. Stan and Georgina Eberly were drinking beer and twiddling forks with hotdogs impaled upon them in the heat-shimmer – to Ralph that shimmer was a strangely dry pink, like coral-colored sand – above the picnic area's barbecue pit.

For a moment Ralph simply stood where he was, struck dumb by their beauty – the ephemeral, powerful beauty that was, he supposed, what Short-Time life was mostly about. A snatch of song, something at least twenty-five years old, occurred to him: *We are stardust, we are golden.* Dorrance's aura was different – fabulously different – but even the most prosaic of the others glittered like rare and infinitely desirable gemstones.

[*'Oh, Ralph, do you see? Do you see how beautiful they are?'*]

[*'Yes.'*]

[*'What a shame they don't know!'*]

But was it? In light of all that had happened, Ralph wasn't so sure. And he had an idea – a vague but strong intuition he could never have put into words – that perhaps real beauty was something unrecognized by the conscious self, a work that was always in progress, a thing of being rather than seeing.

'Come on, dumbwit, make your move,' a voice said. Ralph jerked, first thinking the voice was speaking to him, but it was Faye, talking to Don Veazie. 'You're slower'n old creepin Jesus.'

'Never mind,' Don said. 'I'm thinkin.'

'Think till hell freezes over, Slick, and it's still gonna be mate in six moves.'

Don poured some wine into a paper cup and rolled his eyes. 'Oh boogersnot!' he cried. 'I didn't realize I was playin chess with Boris Spassky! I thought it was just plain old Faye Chapin! I apologize all to hell and gone!'

'That's a riot, Don. An act like that, you could take it on the road and make a million dollars. You won't have to wait long to do it, either – you can start just six moves from now.'

'Ain't you smart,' Don said. 'You just don't know when to—'

'*Hush!*' Georgina Eberly said in a sharp tone. 'What was that? It sounded like something blew up!'

'That' was Lois, sucking a flood of vibrant rainforest green from Georgina's aura.

Ralph raised his right hand, curled it into a tube around his lips, and began to inhale a similar stream of bright blue light from Stan Eberly's aura. He felt fresh energy fill him at once; it was as if fluorescent lights were going on in his brain. But that vast sunken ship, which was really no more or less than four months' worth of mostly sleepless nights, was still there, and still trying to suck him down to the place where it was.

The decision was still right there, too – not yet made one way or the other, but only deferred.

Stan was also looking around. No matter how much of his aura Ralph took (and he had drawn off a great deal, it seemed to him), the source remained as densely bright as ever. Apparently what they had been told about the all-but-endless reservoirs of energy surrounding each human being had been the exact, literal truth.

'Well,' Stan said, 'I did hear *somethin*—'

'*I* didn't,' Faye said.

'Coss not, you're deaf as dirt,' Stan replied. 'Stop interruptin for just one minute, can'tcha? I started to say it wasn't a fuel-tank, because there ain't no fire or smoke. Can't be that Don farted, either, cause there ain't no squirrels droppin dead out of the trees with their fur burnt off. I guess it musta been one of those big Air National Guard trucks backfirin. Don't worry, darlin, I'll pertect ya.'

'Pertect this,' Georgina said, slapping one hand into the crook of her elbow and curling her fist at him. She was smiling, however.

'Oh boy,' Faye said. 'Take a peek at Old Dor.'

They all looked at Dorrance, who was smiling and waving in the direction of the Harris Avenue Extension.

'Who do you see there, old fella?' Don Veazie asked with a grin.

'Ralph and Lois,' Dorrance said, smiling radiantly. 'I see Ralph and Lois. They just came out from under the old tree!'

'Yep,' Stan said. He shaded his eyes, then pointed directly at them. This delivered a wallop to Ralph's nervous system which only abated when he realized Stan was just pointing where Dorrance was waving. 'And look! There's Glenn Miller coming out right behind em! Goddam!'

Georgina threw an elbow and Stan stepped away nimbly, grinning.

[*'Hello, Ralph! Hello, Lois!'*]

[*'Dorrance! We're going to Strawford Park! Is that right?'*]

Dorrance, grinning happily: [*'I don't know, it's all Long-Time business now, and I'm through with it. I'm going back home soon and read Walt Whitman. It's going to be a windy night, and Whitman's always best when the wind blows.'*]

Lois, sounding nearly frantic: [*'Dorrance, help us!'*]

Dor's grin faltered, and he looked at her solemnly.

[*'I can't. It's passed out of my hands. Whatever's done will have to be done by you and Ralph now.'*]

'Ugh,' Georgina said. 'I hate it when he stares that way. You could almost believe he really does see someone.' She picked up her long-handled barbecue fork and began to toast her hotdog again. '*Has* anybody seen Ralph and Lois, by the way?'

'No,' Don said.

'They're shacked up in one of those X-rated motels down the coast with a case of beer and a bottle of Johnson's Baby Oil,' Stan said. 'The giant-economy-size bottle. I toldja that yesterday.'

'Filthy old man,' Georgina said, this time throwing the elbow with a little more force and a lot more accuracy.

Ralph: [*'Dorrance, can't you give us any help at all? At least tell us if we're on the right track?'*]

For a moment he was sure Dor was going to reply. Then there was a buzzing, approaching drone from overhead and the old man looked up. His daffy, beautiful smile resurfaced. 'Look!' he cried. 'An old Grumman Yellow Bird! And a beauty!' He jogged to the chainlink fence to watch the small yellow plane land, turning his back to them.

Ralph took Lois's arm and tried to smile himself. It was hard going – he thought he had never felt quite so frightened and confused in his entire life – but he gave it the old college try.

[*'Come on, dear. Let's go.'*]

2

Ralph remembered thinking – this while they'd been making their way along the abandoned rail-line which had eventually taken them back to the airport – that walking was not exactly what they were doing; it had seemed more like gliding. They went from the picnic area at the end of Runway 3 back to Strawford Park in that same fashion, only the glide was faster and more pronounced now. It was like being carried along by an invisible conveyor belt.

As an experiment, he stopped walking. The houses and storefronts continued to flow mildly past. He looked down at his feet to make sure, and yes, they were completely still. It seemed the sidewalk was moving, not him.

Here came Mr Dugan, head of the Derry Trust's Loan Department, decked out in his customary three-piece suit and rimless eyeglasses. As always, he looked to Ralph like the only man in the history of the world to be born without an asshole. He had once rejected Ralph's application for a Bill-Payer loan, which, Ralph supposed, might account for a few of his negative feelings about the man. Now he saw that Dugan's aura was the dull, uniform gray of a corridor in a Veterans Administration hospital, and Ralph decided that didn't surprise him much. He held his nose like a man forced to swim across a polluted canal and passed directly through the banker. Dugan did not so much as twitch.

That was sort of amusing, but when Ralph glanced at Lois, his amusement faded in a hurry. He saw the worry on her face, and the questions she wanted to ask. Questions to which he had no satisfactory answers.

Ahead was Strawford Park. As Ralph looked, the street-lights came on suddenly. The little playground where he and McGovern – Lois too, more often than not – had stood watching the children play was almost deserted. Two junior-high kids were sitting side by side on the swings, smoking cigarettes and talking, but the mothers and toddlers who came here during the daylight hours were all gone now.

Ralph thought of McGovern – of his ceaseless, morbid chatter and his self-pity, so hard to see when you first got to know him, so hard to miss once you'd been around him for awhile, both of them lightened and somehow turned into something better by his irreverent wit and his surprising, impulsive acts of kindness – and felt deep sadness steal over him. Short-Timers might be stardust, and they might be golden as well, but when they were gone they were as gone as the mothers and babies who made brief playtime visits here on sunny summer afternoons.

[*'Ralph, what are we doing here? The deathbag's over the Civic Center, not Strawford Park!'*]

Ralph guided her to the park bench where he had found her several centuries ago, crying over the argument she'd had with her son and daughter-in-law . . . and over her lost earrings. Down the hill, the two Portosans glimmered in the deepening twilight.

Ralph closed his eyes. *I am going mad,* he thought, *and I'm headed there on the express rather than the local. Which is it going to be? The lady . . . or the tiger?*

[*'Ralph, we have to do something. Those lives . . . those thousands of lives . . .'*]

In the darkness behind his closed lids, Ralph saw someone coming out of the Red Apple Store. A figure in dark corduroy pants and a Red Sox cap. Soon the terrible thing would start to happen again, and because Ralph didn't want to see it, he opened his eyes and looked at the woman beside him.

[*'Every life is important, Lois, wouldn't you agree? Every single one.'*]

He didn't know what she saw in his aura, but it clearly terrified her.

[*'What happened down there after I left? What did he do or say to you? Tell me, Ralph! You tell me!'*]

So which was it going to be? The one or the many? The lady or the tiger? If he didn't choose soon, the choice would be taken out of his hands by nothing more than the simple passage of time. So which one? *Which?*

'Neither . . . or both,' he said hoarsely, unaware in his terrible agitation that he was speaking aloud, and on several different levels at once. 'I won't choose one or the other. I *won't*. Do you hear me?'

He leaped up from the bench, looking around wildly.

'*Do you hear me?*' he shouted. '*I reject this choice! I will have* BOTH *or I will have* NEITHER!'

On one of the paths north of them, a wino who had been poking through a trash-barrel, searching for returnable cans and bottles, took one look at Ralph, then turned and ran. What he had seen was a man who appeared to be on fire.

Lois stood up and grasped his face between her hands.

[*'Ralph, what is it? Who is it? Me? You? Because if it's me, if you're holding back because of me, I don't want—'*]

He took a deep, steadying breath and then put his forehead against hers, looking into her eyes.

[*'It's not you, Lois, and not me. If it was either of us, I might be able to choose. But it's not, and I'll be goddamned if I'm going to be a pawn anymore.'*]

He shook her loose and took a step away from her. His aura flashed out so brilliantly that she had to raise her hand in front of her eyes; it was as if he were somehow exploding. And when his voice came, it reverberated in her head like thunder.

[*'CLOTHO! LACHESIS! COME TO ME, DAMMIT, AND COME NOW!'*]

3

He took two or three more steps and stood looking down the hill. The two junior-high-school boys sitting on the swings were looking up at him with identical expressions of startled fear. They were up and gone the moment Ralph's eyes lit on them, running flat-out toward the lights of Witcham Street like a couple of deer, leaving their cigarettes to smolder in the foot-ditches beneath the swings.

[*'CLOTHO! LACHESIS!'*]

He was burning like an electric arc, and suddenly all the strength ran out of Lois's legs like water. She took one step backward and collapsed onto the park bench. Her head was whirling, her heart full of terror, and below everything was that vast exhaustion. Ralph saw it as a sunken ship; Lois saw it as a pit around which she was forced to walk in a gradually tightening spiral, a pit into which she must eventually fall.

[*'CLOTHO! LACHESIS! LAST CHANCE! I MEAN IT!'*]

For a moment nothing happened, and then the doors of the Portosans at the foot of the hill opened in perfect unison. Clotho stepped from the one marked MEN, Lachesis from the one marked WOMEN. Their auras, the brilliant green-gold of summer dragonflies, glimmered in the ashy light of day's end. They moved together until their auras overlapped, then walked slowly toward the top of the hill that way, with their white-clad shoulders almost touching. They looked like a pair of frightened children.

Ralph turned to Lois. His aura still blazed and burned.

[*'Stay here.'*]

[*'Yes, Ralph.'*]

She let him get partway down the hill, then gathered her courage and called after him.

[*'But I'll try to stop Ed if you won't. I mean it.'*]

Of course she did, and his heart responded to her bravery . . . but she didn't know what he knew. Hadn't seen what he had seen.

He looked back at her for a moment, then walked down to where the two little bald doctors looked at him with their luminous, frightened eyes.

4

Lachesis, nervously: [*We didn't lie to you – we didn't.*]

Clotho, even more nervously (if that were possible): [*Deepneau is on his way. You have to stop him, Ralph – you have to at least try.*]

The fact is I don't have to anything, and your faces show it, he thought. Then he turned to Lachesis, and was gratified to see the small bald man flinch from his gaze and drop his dark, pupil-less eyes.

[*'Is that so? When we were on the hospital roof you told us to stay away from Ed, Mr L. You were very emphatic about that.'*]

Lachesis shifted uncomfortably and fidgeted with his hands.

[*I . . . that is to say* we . . . *we can be wrong. This time we were.*]

Except Ralph knew that *wrong* wasn't the best word for what they had been; *self-deceived* would be better. He wanted to scold them for it – oh, tell the truth, he wanted to scold them for getting him into this shitting mess in the first place – and found he couldn't. Because, according to old Dor, even their self-deception had served the Purpose; the side-trip to High Ridge had for some reason not been a side-trip at all. He didn't understand why or how that was, but he intended to find out, if finding out was possible.

[*'Let's forget that part of it for the time being, gentlemen, and talk about why all this is happening. If you want help from me and Lois, I think you better tell me.'*]

They looked at each other with their big, frightened eyes, then back at Ralph.

Lachesis: [*Ralph, do you doubt that all those people are really going to die? Because if you do—*]

[*'No, but I'm tired of having them waved in my face. If an earthquake that served the Purpose happened to be scheduled for this area and the butcher's bill came to ten thousand instead of just two thousand and change, you'd never even bat an eye, would you? So what's so special about this situation? Tell me!'*]

Clotho: [*Ralph, we don't make the rules any more than you do. We thought you understood that.*]

Ralph sighed.

[*'You're weaseling again, and not wasting anybody's time but your own.'*]

Clotho, uneasily: [*All right, perhaps the picture we gave you wasn't completely clear, but time was short and we were frightened. And you must see that, regardless of all else, those people* will *die if you can't stop Ed Deepneau!*]

[*'Never mind all of them for now; I only want to know about* one *of them – the one who belongs to the Purpose and can't be handed over just because some undesignated* pisher *comes along with a headful of loose screws and a planeful of explosive. Who is it you feel you can't give up to the Random? Who? It's Day, isn't it? Susan Day.'*]

Lachesis: [*No. Susan Day is part of the Random. She is none of our concern, none of our worry.*]

[*'Who, then?'*]

Clotho and Lachesis exchanged another glance. Clotho nodded slightly, and then they both turned back to Ralph. Once again Lachesis flicked the first two fingers of his right hand upward, creating that peacock's fan of light. It wasn't McGovern Ralph saw this time, but a little boy with blond hair cut in bangs across his forehead and a hook-shaped scar across the bridge of his nose. Ralph placed him at once – the kid from the basement of High Ridge, the one with the bruised mother. The one who had called him and Lois angels.

And a little child shall lead them, he thought, utterly flabbergasted. *Oh my God.* He looked disbelievingly at Clotho and Lachesis.

[*'Am I understanding? All this has been about that one little boy?'*]

He expected more waffling, but the reply from Clotho was simple and direct: [*Yes, Ralph.*]

Lachesis: [*He's at the Civic Center now. His mother, whose life you and Lois also saved this morning, got a call from her babysitter less than an hour ago, saying she'd cut herself badly on a piece of glass and wouldn't be able to take care of the boy tonight after all. By then it was too late to find another sitter, of course, and this woman has been determined for weeks to see Susan Day . . . to shake her hand, even give her a hug, if possible. She idolizes the Day woman.*]

Ralph, who remembered the fading bruises on her face, supposed that was an idolatry he could understand. He understood something else even better: the babysitter's cut hand had been no accident. *Something* was determined to place the little boy with the shaggy blond bangs and the smoke-reddened eyes at the Civic Center, and was willing to move heaven and earth to do it. His mother had taken him not because she was a bad parent, but because she was as subject to human nature as anyone else. She hadn't wanted to miss her one chance at seeing Susan Day, that was all.

No, it's not all, Ralph thought. *She also took him because she thought it would be safe, with Pickering and his Daily Bread crazies all dead. It must have seemed to her that the worst she'd have to protect her son from tonight would be a bunch of sign-waving pro-lifers, that lightning couldn't possibly strike her and her son twice on the same day.*

Ralph had been gazing off toward Witcham Street. Now he turned back to Clotho and Lachesis.

['*You're* sure *he's there? Positive?*']

Clotho: [*Yes. Sitting in the upper north balcony next to his mother with a McDonald's poster to color and some storybooks. Would it surprise you to know that one of the stories is* The 500 Hats of Bartholomew Cubbins?]

Ralph shook his head. At this point, nothing would surprise him.

Lachesis: [*It's the north side of the Civic Center that Deepneau's plane will strike. This little boy will be killed instantly if steps are not taken to prevent it . . . and that can't be allowed to happen. This boy must not die before his scheduled time.*]

5

Lachesis was looking earnestly at Ralph. The fan of blue-green light between his fingers had disappeared.

[*We can't go on talking like this, Ralph – he's already in the air, less than a hundred miles from here. Soon it will be too late to stop him.*]

That made Ralph feel frantic, but he held his place just the same. Frantic, after all, was how they *wanted* him to feel. How they wanted both of them to feel.

[*'I'm telling you that none of that matters until I understand what the stakes are. I won't let it matter.'*]

Clotho: [*Listen, then. Every now and again a man or woman comes along whose life will affect not just those about him or her, or even all those who live in the Short-Time world, but those on many levels above and below the Short-Time world. These people are the Great Ones, and their lives always serve the Purpose. If they are taken too soon, everything changes. The scales cease to balance. Can you imagine, for instance, how different the world might be today if Hitler had drowned in the bathtub as a child? You may believe the world would be better for that, but I can tell you that the world would not exist at all if it had happened. Suppose Winston Churchill had died of food-poisoning before he ever became Prime Minister? Suppose Augustus Caesar had been born dead, strangled on his own umbilicus? Yet the person we want you to save is of far greater importance than any of these.*]

[*'Dammit, Lois and I already saved this kid once! Didn't that close the books, return him to the Purpose?'*]

Lachesis, patiently: [*Yes, but he is not safe from Ed Deepneau, because Deepneau has no designation in either Random or Purpose. Of all the people on earth, only Deepneau can harm him before his time comes. If Deepneau fails, the boy will be safe again – he will pass his time quietly until his moment comes and he steps upon the stage to play his brief but crucially important part.*]

[*'One life means so much, then?'*]

Lachesis: [*Yes. If the child dies, the Tower of all existence will fall, and the consequences of such a fall are beyond your comprehension. And beyond ours, as well.*]

Ralph stared down at his shoes for a moment. His head seemed to weigh a thousand pounds. There was an irony here, one he was able to grasp easily in spite of his weariness.

Atropos had apparently set Ed in motion by inflaming some sort of Messiah complex which might have been pre-existing . . . a by-product of his undesignated status, perhaps. What Ed didn't see – and would never believe if told – was that Atropos and his bosses on the upper levels intended to use him not to save the Messiah but to kill him.

He looked up again into the anxious faces of the two little bald doctors.

[*'Okay, I don't know how I'm supposed to stop Ed, but I'll give it a shot.'*]

Clotho and Lachesis looked at each other and smiled identical (and very human) broad smiles of relief. Ralph raised a cautioning finger.

[*'Wait. You haven't heard all of it.'*]

Their smiles faded.

[*'I want something back from you. One life. I'll trade the life of your four-year-old boy for—'*]

6

Lois didn't hear the end of that; his voice dropped below the range of audibility for a moment, but when she saw first Clotho and then Lachesis begin shaking their heads, her heart sank.

Lachesis: [*I understand your distress, and yes, Atropos can certainly do as he threatens. Yet you must surely comprehend that this one life is hardly as important as—*]

Ralph: [*'But I think it is, don't you see? I think it is. What you two guys need to get through your heads is that to me,* both *lives are equally—'*]

She lost him again, but had no problem hearing Clotho; in the depth of his distress he was almost wailing.

[*But this is different! This boy's life is different!*]

Now she heard Ralph clearly, speaking (if speech was what it was) with a fearless, relentless logic that made Lois think of her father.

[*'All* lives *are different. All of them matter or none matters. That's only my short-sighted, Short-Time view, of course, but I guess you boys are stuck with it, since I'm the one with the hammer. The bottom line is this: I'll trade you, even-up. The life of yours for the life of mine. All you have to do is promise, and the deal's on.'*]

Lachesis: [*Ralph, please! Please understand that we really must not!*]

There was a long moment of silence. When Ralph spoke, his voice was soft but still audible. It was, however, the last completely audible thing Lois heard in their conversation.

[*'There's a world of difference between* cannot *and* must not, *wouldn't you say?'*]

Clotho said something, but Lois caught only an isolated [*trade might possibly be*] phrase. Lachesis shook his head violently. Ralph replied and Lachesis answered by making a grim little scissoring gesture with his fingers.

Surprisingly, Ralph replied to this with a laugh and a nod.

Clotho put a hand on his colleague's arm and spoke to him earnestly before turning back to Ralph.

Lois clenched her hands in her lap, willing them to reach some sort of agreement. *Any* agreement that would keep Ed Deepneau from killing all those people while they just stood here yattering.

Suddenly the side of the hill was illuminated by brilliant white light. At first Lois thought it came down from the sky, but that was only because myth and religion had taught her to believe the sky was the source of all supernatural emanations. In reality, it seemed to come from everywhere – trees, sky, ground, even from herself, streaming out of her aura like ribbons of fog.

There was a voice, then . . . or rather a Voice. It spoke only four words, but they echoed in Lois's head like iron bells.

[*IT MAY BE SO.*]

She saw Clotho, his small face a mask of terror and awe, reach into his back pocket and bring out his scissors. He fumbled and almost dropped them, a nervous blunder that made Lois feel real kinship for him. Then he was holding them up with one handle in each hand and the blades open.

Those four words came again:

[*IT MAY BE SO.*]

This time they were followed by a glare so bright that for a moment Lois believed she must be blinded. She clapped her hands over her eyes but saw – in the last instant when she could see anything – that the light had centered on the scissors Clotho was holding up like a two-pronged lightning-rod.

There was no refuge from that light; it turned her eyelids and upraised, shielding hands to glass. The glare outlined the bones of her fingers like X-ray pencils as it streamed through her flesh. From somewhere far away she heard a woman who sounded suspiciously like Lois Chasse, screaming at the top of her mental voice:

[*'Turn it off! God, please turn it off before it kills me!'*]

And at last, when it seemed to her that she could stand no more, the light did begin to fade. When it was gone – except for a fierce blue afterimage that floated in the new darkness like a pair of phantom scissors – she slowly opened her eyes. For a moment she continued to see nothing but that brilliant blue cross and thought she had indeed been blinded. Then, as dim as a developing photograph at first, the world began to resurface. She saw Ralph, Clotho, and Lachesis lowering their own hands and peering around with the blind bewilderment of a nest of moles turned up by the blade of a harrow.

Lachesis was looking at the scissors in his colleague's hands as if he had never seen them before, and Lois was willing to bet he never *had* seen them as they were now. The blades were still shining, shedding eldritch fairy-glimmers of light in misty droplets.

Lachesis: [*Ralph! That was . . .*]

She lost the rest of it, but his tone was that of a common peasant who answers a knock at the door of his hut and finds that the Pope has stopped by for a spot of prayer and a little confession.

Clotho was still staring at the blades of the scissors. Ralph was also looking, but at last he lifted his gaze to the bald doctors.

Ralph: [*'. . . the hurt?'*]

Lachesis, speaking like a man emerging from a deep dream: [*Yes . . . won't last long, but . . . agony will be intense . . . change your mind, Ralph?*]

Lois was suddenly afraid of those shining scissors. She wanted to cry out to Ralph, tell him to never mind his one, to just give them *their* one, their little boy. She wanted to tell him to do whatever it took to get them to hide those scissors again.

But no words came from either her mouth or her mind.

Ralph: [*'. . . in the least . . . just wanted to know what to expect.'*]

Clotho: [. . . *ready?* . . . *must be* . . .]
Tell them no, Ralph! she thought at him. *Tell them* NO!
Ralph: ['. . . *ready.*']
Lachesis: [*Understand* . . . *terms he has* . . . *and the price?*]
Ralph, impatient now: ['*Yes, yes. Can we please just* . . .']
Clotho, with immense gravity: [*Very well, Ralph. It may be so.*]

Lachesis put an arm around Ralph's shoulders; he and Clotho led him a little further down the hill, to the place where the younger children started their downhill sled-runs in the winter. There was a small flat area there, circular in shape, about the size of a nightclub stage. When they reached it, Lachesis stopped Ralph, then turned him so he and Clotho were facing each other.

Lois suddenly wanted to shut her eyes and found she couldn't. She could only watch and pray that Ralph knew what he was doing.

Clotho murmured to him. Ralph nodded and slipped out of McGovern's sweater. He folded it and laid it neatly on the leaf-strewn grass. When he straightened again, Clotho took his right wrist and held his arm out straight. He then nodded to Lachesis, who unbuttoned the cuff of Ralph's shirt and rolled the sleeve to the elbow in three quick turns. With that done, Clotho rotated Ralph's arm so it was wrist-up. The fine tracery of blue veins just beneath the skin of his forearm was poignantly clear, highlighted in delicate strokes of aura. All of this was horribly familiar to Lois: it was like watching a patient on a TV doctor-show being prepped for an operation.

Except this wasn't TV.

Lachesis leaned forward and spoke again. Although she still couldn't hear the words, Lois knew he was telling Ralph this was his last chance.

Ralph nodded, and although his aura now told her that he was terrified of what was coming, he somehow even managed a smile. When he turned to Clotho and spoke, he did not seem to be seeking reassurance but rather offering a word of comfort. Clotho tried to return Ralph's smile, but without success.

Lachesis wrapped one hand around Ralph's wrist, more to steady the arm (or so it seemed to Lois) than to actually hold it immobile. He reminded her of a nurse attending a patient who must receive a painful injection. Then he looked at his partner with frightened eyes and nodded. Clotho nodded back, took a breath, and then bent over Ralph's upturned forearm with its ghostly tree of blue veins glowing beneath the skin. He paused for a moment, then slowly opened the jaws of the scissors with which he and his old friend traded life for death.

7

Lois staggered to her feet and stood swaying back and forth on legs that felt like lumber. She meant to break the paralysis which had locked her in such a cruel silence, to shout at Ralph and tell him to stop – tell him he didn't know what they meant to *do* to him.

Except he did. It was in the pallor of his face, his half-closed eyes, his painfully thinned lips. Most of all it was in the blotches of red and black which were flashing across his aura like meteors, and in the aura itself, which had tightened down to a hard blue shell.

Ralph nodded at Clotho, who brought the lower scissor-blade down until it was touching Ralph's forearm just below the fold of the elbow. For a moment the skin only dimpled, and then a smooth dark blister of blood formed where the dimple had been. The blade slid into this blister. When Clotho squeezed his fingers, bringing the razor-sharp blades together, the skin on either side of the lengthwise cut snapped back with the suddenness of windowshades. Subcutaneous fat glimmered like melting ice in the fierce blue glow of Ralph's aura. Lachesis tightened his hold on Ralph's wrist, but so far as Lois could tell, Ralph did not make even a first instinctive effort to pull back, only lowered his head and clenched his left fist in the air like a man giving a Black Power salute. She could see the cords in his neck standing out like cables. Not a single sound escaped him.

Now that this terrible business was actually begun, Clotho proceeded with a speed which was both brutal and merciful. He cut rapidly down the middle of Ralph's forearm to his wrist, using the scissors the way a man will to open a parcel which has been heavily taped, guiding the blades with the fingers and bearing down with the thumb. Inside Ralph's arm, tendons gleamed like cuts of flank steak. Blood ran in freshets, and there was a fine scarlet spray each time an artery or a vein was severed. Soon fans of backspatter decorated the white tunics of the two small men, making them look more like little doctors than ever.

When his blades had at last severed the Bracelets of Fortune at Ralph's wrist (the 'operation' took less than three seconds but seemed to last forever to Lois), Clotho removed the dripping scissors and handed them to Lachesis. Ralph's upturned arm had been cut open from elbow to wrist in a dark furrow. Clotho clamped his hands over this furrow at its point of origination and Lois thought: *Now the other one will pick up Ralph's sweater and use it as a tourniquet.* But Lachesis made no move to do that; he merely held the scissors and watched.

For a moment the blood went on flowing between Clotho's grasping fingers, and then it stopped. He slowly drew his hands down Ralph's arm, and the flesh which emerged from his grip was whole and firm, although seamed with a thick white ridge of scar-tissue.

[*Lois . . . Lo-isssss . . .*]

This voice was not coming from inside her head, nor from down the hill; it had come from behind her. A soft voice, almost cajoling. Atropos? No, not at all. She looked down and saw green and somehow sunken light flowing all around her – it rayed through the spaces between her arms and her body, between her legs, even between her fingers. It rippled her shadow ahead of her, scrawny and somehow twisted, like the shadow of a hanged woman. It caressed her with heatless fingers the color of Spanish moss.

[*Turn around, Lo-iss . . .*]

At that moment the last thing on earth Lois Chasse wanted to do was turn around and look at the source of that green light.

[*Turn around, Lo-isss . . . see me, Lo-isss . . . come into the light, Lo-isss . . . come into the light . . . see me and come into the light . . .*]

It was not a voice which could be disobeyed. Lois turned as slowly as a toy ballerina whose cogs have grown rusty, and her eyes seemed to fill up with Saint Elmo's fire.

Lois came into the light.

Chapter Twenty-eight

1

Clotho: [*You have your visible sign, Ralph – are you satis-fied?*]

Ralph looked down at his arm. Already the agony, which had swallowed him as the whale had swallowed Jonah, seemed like a dream to him, or a mirage. He supposed it was this same sort of distancing which allowed women to have lots of babies, forgetting the stark physical pain and effort of delivery each time the act was successfully accomplished. The scar looked like a length of ragged white string rippling its way over the bulges of his scant muscles.

[*'Yes. You were brave, and very quick. I thank you for both.'*]

Clotho smiled but said nothing.

Lachesis: [*Ralph, are you ready? Time is now very short.*]

[*'Yes, I'm—'*]

[*'Ralph! Ralph!'*]

It was Lois, standing at the top of the hill and waving to him. For a moment he thought her aura had changed from its usual dove-gray to some other, darker color, and then the idea, undoubtedly caused by shock and weariness, passed. He trudged up the hill to where she stood.

Lois's eyes were distant and dazed, as if she had just heard some amazing, life-changing word.

[*'Lois, what is it? What's wrong? Is it my arm? Because if that's it, don't worry. Look! Good as new!'*]

He held it out so she could see for herself, but Lois didn't look. She looked at him instead, and he saw the depth of her shock.

[*'Ralph, a green man came.'*]

A *green* man? He reached out and took her hands, instantly concerned.

[*'Green? Are you sure? It wasn't Atropos or—'*]

He didn't finish the thought. He didn't have to.

Lois shook her head slowly.

[*'It was a green man. If there are sides in this, I don't know which one this . . . this person . . . is on. He felt good, but I could be wrong. I couldn't see him. His aura was too bright. He told me to give these back to you.'*]

She held out her hand to him and tipped two small, glittering objects from her palm to his: her earrings. He could see a maroon speck on one, and supposed it was Atropos's blood. He started to close his hand over them, then winced at a tiny prick of pain.

[*'You forgot the backs, Lois.'*]

She spoke in the slow, unthoughtful tones of a woman in a dream.

[*'No, I didn't – I threw them away. The green man said to. Be careful. He felt . . . warm . . . but I don't really know, do I? Mr Chasse always said I was the most gullible woman alive, always willing to believe the best of everybody. Of anybody.'*]

She reached out slowly and grasped his wrists, looking earnestly into his face all the while.

'I just don't know.'

Vocalizing the thought seemed to wake her up, and she stood blinking at him. Ralph supposed it was possible – just barely – that she actually *had* been asleep, that she had dreamed this so-called 'green man'. But perhaps it would be wiser to just take the earrings. They might mean nothing, but then again, having Lois's earrings in his pocket couldn't hurt . . . unless he poked himself with them, that was.

Lachesis: [*Ralph, what is it? Is something wrong?*]

He and Clotho had lagged behind, and so had missed Ralph's conversation with Lois. Ralph shook his head, turning his hand to hide the earrings from them. Clotho had picked up McGovern's sweater and brushed away the few bright leaves which had been clinging to it. Now he held it out to Ralph, who unobtrusively slipped Lois's no-back earrings into one of its pockets before putting it on again.

Time to get going, and the line of warmth up the middle of his right arm – along the scar – told him how he was supposed to begin.

[*'Lois?'*]

['*Yes, dear?*']

['*I need to take from your aura, and I need to take a lot. Do you understand?*']

['*Yes.*']

['*Is it all right?*']

['*Yes, of course.*']

['*Be brave – it won't take long.*']

He put his arms on her shoulders and clasped his hands behind her neck. She copied the gesture, and they slowly leaned together until their foreheads were touching and their lips less than two inches apart. He could smell some perfume still lingering about her – coming perhaps from the dark, sweet hollows behind her ears.

['*Ready, dear?*']

He found what came in return both odd and comforting.

['*Yes, Ralph. See me. Come into the light. Come into the light and take the light.*']

Ralph pursed his lips and began to inhale. A band of smoky brilliance began to flow from her mouth and nose and into him. His aura began to brighten at once, and it continued to do so until it had become a dazzling, cloudy corona around him. And still he went on inhaling, breathing with something that was beyond breath, feeling the scar on his arm grow hotter and hotter until it was like an electric filament buried in his flesh. He could not have stopped even if he had wanted to . . . and he didn't.

She staggered once. He saw her eyes lose focus and felt her hands loosen for a moment on the back of his neck. Then her eyes, large and bright and full of trust, returned to his, and her grip firmed again. At last, as that titanic intake of breath finally began to crest, Ralph realized her aura had grown so pale he could hardly see it. Her cheeks were milk-white and the gray had come back into her hair, so much that the black was now almost gone. He had to stop it, *had* to, or he was going to kill her.

He managed to pull his left hand free of his right, and that seemed to break some sort of circuit; he was able to step back from her. Lois swayed on her feet and would have fallen, but Clotho and Lachesis, looking quite a bit like Lilliputians from *Gulliver's Travels,* grabbed her arms and lowered her carefully to the bench again.

Ralph dropped to one knee before her. He was frantic with fear and guilt, and at the same time filled with a sense of power so great that he felt as if a single hard jolt might cause him to explode, like a bottle filled with nitroglycerine. He could knock down a building with that karate-chop gesture now – maybe a whole row of them.

Still, he had hurt Lois. Perhaps badly.

[*'Lois! Lois, can you hear me? I'm sorry!'*]

She looked up at him dazedly, a woman who had blasted forward from forty to sixty in a matter of seconds . . . and then right past it and into her seventies, like a rocket overshooting its intended target. She tried a smile that didn't work very well.

[*'Lois, I'm sorry. I didn't know, and once I did, I couldn't stop.'*]

Lachesis: [*If you're to have any chance at all, Ralph, you must go now. He's almost here.*]

Lois was nodding agreement.

[*'Go on, Ralph – I'm just weak, that's all. I'll be fine. I'm just going to sit here until my strength comes back.'*]

Her eyes shifted to the left, and Ralph followed her gaze. He saw the wino they'd frightened away earlier. He had returned to inspect the litter-baskets at the top of the hill for returnable cans and bottles, and although his aura did not look as healthy as that of the fellow they had met out by the old trainyards earlier, Ralph reckoned he would do in a pinch . . . which, for Lois, this definitely was.

Clotho: [*We'll see that he wanders over this way, Ralph – we don't have much power over the physical aspects of the Short-Time world, but I think we can manage that much.*]

[*'You're sure?'*]

[*Yes.*]

[*'Okay. Good.'*]

Ralph took a quick look at the two little men, noted their anxious, frightened eyes, and nodded. Then he bent and kissed Lois's cool, wrinkled cheek. She gave him the smile of a tired old grandmother.

I did that to her, he thought. *Me.*

Then you better make sure you didn't do it for nothing, Carolyn's voice responded tartly.

Ralph gave the three of them – Clotho and Lachesis were now flanking Lois protectively on the bench – a final glance, and then began to walk down the hill again.

When he reached the toilets, he stood between them for a moment, then leaned his head against the one marked WOMEN. He heard nothing. When he tipped his head against the blue plastic wall of MEN, however, he heard a faint, droning voice raised in song:

> *Who believes that my wildest dreams*
> *And my craziest schemes will come true?*
> *You, baby, nobody but you.*

Christ, he's nuttier than a fruitcake.
This is news, sweetheart?

Ralph supposed it wasn't. He walked around to the door of the Portosan and opened it. Now he could also hear the distant, waspy buzz of an airplane engine, but there was nothing to see that he hadn't seen dozens of times before: the cracked toilet seat resting askew over the hole in the seat, a roll of toilet paper with a strange and somehow ominous *swelled* look, and, to the left, a urinal that looked like a plastic teardrop. The walls were tangles of graffiti. The largest – and most exuberant – had been printed in foot-high red letters above the urinal: TONY BOYNTON HAS GOT THE TIGHTEST LITTLE BUNS IN DERRY! A cloying pine-scented deodorizer overlay the smells of shit, piss, and lingering wino-farts like makeup on the face of a corpse. The voice he was hearing seemed to come from the hole in the center of the Portosan's bench seat, or perhaps it was seeping out of the very walls:

> *From the time I fall asleep*
> *Until the morning comes*
> *I dream about you, baby, nobody but you.*

Where is he? Ralph wondered. *And how the hell do I get to him?*

Ralph felt sudden heat against his hip; it was as if someone had slipped a warm coal into his watchpocket. He began to frown, then remembered what was in there. He reached into the scrap of a pocket with one finger, touched the gold band he had stowed there, and hooked it out. He laid it on his palm over the place where his loveline and lifeline diverged and poked at it gingerly. It had cooled again. Ralph found he wasn't very surprised.

HD – ED 5–8–87.

'One Ring to rule them all, One Ring to bind them,' Ralph murmured, and slipped Ed's wedding band onto the third finger of his own left hand. It was a perfect fit. He pushed it up until it clinked softly against the wedding ring Carolyn had put onto his own finger some forty-five years ago. Then he looked up and saw that the back wall of the Portosan had disappeared.

2

What he saw, framed by the walls which *did* remain, was a just-past-sunset sky and a swatch of Maine countryside fading into a blue-gray twilight haze. He estimated that he was looking out from a height of about ten thousand feet. He could see glimmering lakes and ponds and vast stretches of dark green woodland scrolling down toward the Portosan's bench seat and then disappearing. Far ahead – up toward the roof of the toilet cubicle – Ralph could see a glimmering nest of lights. That was probably Derry, now no more than ten minutes away. In the lower left quadrant of this vision Ralph could see part of an instrument panel. Taped over the altimeter was a small color photograph that stopped his breath. It was Helen, looking impossibly happy and impossibly beautiful. Cradled in her arms was the Exalted & Revered Baby, fast asleep and no more than four months old.

He wants them to be the last thing he sees in this world, Ralph thought. *He's been turned into a monster, but I guess even monsters don't forget how to love.*

Something on the instrument panel began to beep. A hand came into view and flicked a switch. Before it disappeared, Ralph could see the white indentation on the third finger of that hand, faint but still visible, where the wedding ring had rested for at least six years. He saw something else, as well – the aura surrounding the hand was the same as the one which had surrounded the thunderstruck baby in the hospital elevator, a turbulent, rapidly moving membrane that seemed as alien as the atmosphere of a gas giant.

Ralph looked back once and raised his hand. Clotho and Lachesis raised theirs in return. Lois blew him a kiss. Ralph made a catching gesture, then turned and stepped into the Portosan.

3

He hesitated for a moment, wondering what to do about the bench seat, then remembered the oncoming hospital gurney, which should have crushed their skulls but hadn't, and walked toward the back of the cubicle. He clenched his teeth, preparing to bark his shin – what you knew was one thing, what you believed after seventy years of bumping into stuff quite another – and then stepped through the bench seat as if it were made of smoke . . . or as if *he* were.

There was a scary sensation of weightlessness and vertigo, and for a moment he was sure he was going to vomit. This was accompanied by a feeling of *drain,* as if much of the power he had taken in from Lois was now being siphoned off. He supposed it was. This was a form of teleportation, after all, fabulous science fiction stuff, and something like that *had* to use up a lot of energy.

The vertigo passed, but it was replaced by a perception that was even worse – a feeling that he had been split at the neck somehow. He realized he now had a completely unobstructed view of a whole sprawling section of the world.

Jesus Christ, what's happened to me? What's wrong?

His senses reluctantly reported back that there was nothing wrong, exactly, it was just that he had achieved a position which should have been impossible. He was seventy-three inches tall; the cockpit of the plane was sixty inches from floor to ceiling. This meant that any pilot much bigger than Clotho and Lachesis had to slouch his way to his seat. Ralph, however, had entered the plane not only while it was in flight but while he was standing up, and he was *still* standing up, between and slightly behind the two seats in the cockpit. The reason his view was unobstructed was both simple and horrible: his head was sticking out of the top of the plane.

Ralph had a nightmare image of his old dog, Rex, who'd liked to ride with his head out the passenger window and his raggedy ears blowing back in the slipstream. He closed his eyes.

What if I fall? If I can stick my head out through the damned roof, what's to keep me from sliding right down through the floor and falling all the way to the ground? Or maybe through *the ground, and then through the very earth itself?*

But that wasn't happening, and nothing like it *would* happen, not on this level – all he had to do was remember the effortless way they'd risen through the floors of the hospital and the ease with which they'd stood on the roof. If he kept those things in mind, he would be okay. Ralph tried to center on that idea, and when he felt quite sure he had himself under control, he opened his eyes again.

Sloping out just below him was the plane's windshield. Beyond it was the nose, tipped with a quicksilver blur of propeller. The nestle of lights he had observed from the door of the Portosan was closer now.

Ralph bent his knees, and his head slid smoothly through the ceiling of the cockpit. For a moment he could taste oil in his mouth and the tiny hairs in his nose seemed to bristle as if with an electric shock, and then he was kneeling between the pilot's and co-pilot's seats.

He didn't know what he had expected to feel, seeing Ed again after all this time and under such extravagantly weird circumstances, but the pang of regret – not just pity but regret – which came was a surprise. As on the day in the summer of '92 when Ed had run into the West Side Gardeners truck, he was wearing an old tee-shirt instead of an Oxford or Arrow with buttons up the front and a fruit-loop on the back. He had lost a lot of weight – Ralph thought perhaps as much as forty pounds – and it had had an extraordinary effect, making him look not emaciated but somehow heroic, in a gothic/romantic way; Ralph was forcefully reminded of Carolyn's favorite poem, 'The Highwayman', by Alfred Noyes. Ed's skin was as pale as paper, his green eyes both dark and light (*like emeralds in moonlight,* Ralph thought) behind the small round John Lennon spectacles, his lips so red they looked as if they had been rouged. He had tied the white silk scarf with its red Japanese characters around his forehead so that the fringed ends trailed down his back. Within the thunderbolt swirls of his aura, Ed's intelligent, mobile face was filled with terrible regret and fierce determination. He was beautiful – beautiful – and Ralph felt a sense of *déjà vu* twist through him. Now he knew what he had glimpsed on the day he'd stepped between Ed and the man from West Side Gardeners; he was seeing it again. Looking at Ed, lost inside a typhoon aura from which no balloon-string floated, was like looking at a priceless Ming vase which had been thrown against a wall and shattered.

At least he can't see me, not on this level. At least, I don't think he can.

As if in response to this thought, Ed turned and glanced directly at Ralph. His eyes were wide and full of mad caution; the corners of his finely molded mouth quivered and gleamed with buds of saliva. Ralph recoiled, momentarily positive that he *was* being seen, but Ed didn't react to Ralph's sudden backward movement. He threw a suspicious glance into the empty four-seat passenger cabin behind him instead, as if he had heard the stealthy movements of a stowaway. At the same time he reached past Ralph and put his right hand on a cardboard carton which had been seatbelted into the co-pilot's chair. The hand caressed the box briefly, then went to his forehead and made some tiny adjustment to the scarf serving him as a headband. That done, he resumed singing . . . only this time it was a different song, one that sent a tremor zigzagging up Ralph's back:

> *One pill makes you bigger,*
> *One pill makes you small,*
> *And the ones that Mother gives you*
> *Don't do anything at all . . .*

Right, Ralph thought. *Go ask Alice, when she's ten feet tall.*

His heart was trip-hammering in his chest – having Ed suddenly turn around like that had scared him in a way even finding himself riding along at ten thousand feet with his head sticking out of the top of the plane hadn't been able to do. Ed didn't see him, Ralph was almost positive of that, but whoever had said that the senses of lunatics were more acute than those of the sane must have known what he was talking about, because Ed sure had an idea that *something* had changed.

The radio squawked, making both men jump. 'This is for the Cherokee over South Haven. You are on the edge of Derry airspace at an altitude which requires a filed flight-plan. Repeat, *you are about to enter controlled airspace over a municipal area.* Get your hot-dogging butt up to sixteen thousand feet, Cherokee, and come to one seventy, that's one-seven-oh. While you're doing it, please identify yourself and state—'

Ed closed his hand into a fist and began to hammer the radio with it. Glass flew; soon blood also began to fly. It spattered the instrument panel, the picture of Helen and Natalie, and Ed's clean gray tee-shirt. He went on hammering until the voice on the radio first began to fade into a rising roar of static and then quit altogether.

'Good,' he said in the low, sighing voice of a man who talks to himself a lot. '*Lots* better. I hate all those questions. They just—'

He caught sight of his bloody hand and broke off. He held it up, looked at it more closely, and then rolled it into a fist again. A large sliver of glass was sticking out of his pinky just below the third knuckle. Ed pulled it free with his teeth, spat it casually aside, then did something which chilled Ralph's heart: drew the side of his bloody fist first down his left cheek and then his right, leaving a pair of red marks. He reached into the elasticized pocket built into the wall on his left, pulled out a hand-mirror, and used it to check his makeshift warpaint. What he saw seemed to please him, because he smiled and nodded before returning the mirror to the pocket.

'Just remember what the dormouse said,' Ed advised himself in his low, sighing voice, and then pushed in on the control wheel. The Cherokee's nose dropped and the altimeter slowly began to unwind. Ralph could see Derry straight ahead now. The city looked like a handful of opals scattered across dark blue velvet.

There was a hole in the side of the carton in the co-pilot's seat. Two wires came out of it. They led into the back of a doorbell taped to the arm of Ed's seat. Ralph supposed that as soon as he had a visual on the Civic Center and actually began his kamikaze run, Ed would settle one finger on the raised white button in the middle of the plastic rectangle. And just before the plane hit, he would push it. Ding-dong, Avon calling.

Break those wires, Ralph! Break them!

An excellent idea with only one drawback: he couldn't break so much as a strand of cobweb while he was on this level. That meant dropping back down to Short-Time country, and he was preparing to do just that when a soft, familiar voice on his right spoke his name.

[*Ralph.*]

To his *right?* That was impossible. There was *nothing* on his right but the co-pilot's seat, the side of the aircraft, and leagues of twilit New England air.

The scar along his arm had begun to tingle like a filament in an electric heater.

[*Ralph!*]

Don't look. Don't pay any attention at all. Ignore it.

But he couldn't. Some great, bricklike force had come to bear on him, and his head began to turn. He fought it, aware that the airplane's angle of descent was growing steeper, but it did no good.

[*Ralph, look at me – don't be afraid.*]

He made one last effort to disobey the voice and was unable. His head went on turning, and Ralph suddenly found himself looking at his mother, who had died of lung cancer twenty-five years ago.

4

Bertha Roberts sat in her bentwood rocker about five feet beyond where the sidewall of the Cherokee's cockpit had been, knitting and rocking back and forth on thin air a mile or more above the ground. The slippers Ralph had given her for her fiftieth birthday – lined with real mink, they had been, how goofy – were on her feet. A pink shawl was thrown around her shoulders. An old political button – WIN WITH WILLKIE! it said – held the shawl closed.

That's right, Ralph thought. *She wore them as jewelry – it was her little affectation. I'd forgotten that.*

The only thing that struck a wrong note (other than that she was dead and currently rocking at six thousand feet) was the bright red piece of afghan in her lap. Ralph had never seen his mother knit, wasn't even sure she knew how, but she was knitting furiously just the same. The needles gleamed and winked as they shuttled through the stitches.

[*'Mother? Mom? Is it really you?'*]

The needles paused as she looked up from the crimson blanket in her lap. Yes, it was his mother – the version Ralph remembered from his teens, anyway. Narrow face, high scholar's brow, brown eyes, and a bun of salt-and-pepper hair rolled tightly at the nape of the neck. It was her small mouth, which looked mean and ungenerous . . . until it smiled, that was.

[*Why, Ralph Roberts! I'm surprised that you even have to ask!*]

That's not really an answer, though, is it? Ralph thought. He opened his mouth to say so and then decided it might be wiser – for the time being, at least – to keep quiet. A milky shape was now swimming in the air to her right. When Ralph looked at it, it darkened and solidified into the cherry-stained magazine stand he had made her in woodshop during his sophomore year at Derry High. It was filled with *Reader's Digests* and *Life* magazines. And now the ground far below her began to disappear into a pattern of brown and dark-red squares that spread out from the rocker in a widening ring, like a pond-ripple. Ralph recognized it at once – the kitchen linoleum of the house on Richmond Street in Mary Mead, the one where he'd grown up. At first he could see the ground through it, geometries of farmland and, not far ahead, the Kenduskeag flowing through Derry, and then it solidified. A ghostly shape like a big milkweed puff became his mom's old Angora cat, Futzy, curled up on the windowsill and looking out at the gulls circling above the old dump in the Barrens. Futzy had died around the time Dean Martin and Jerry Lewis had stopped making movies together.

[*That old man was right, boy. You've no business messing into Long-Time affairs. Pay attention to your mother and stay out of what doesn't concern you. Mind me, now.*]

Pay attention to your mother . . . mind me, now. Those words had pretty well summed up Bertha Roberts's views on the art and science of child-rearing, hadn't they? Whether it was an order to wait an hour after eating before taking a swim or to make sure that old thief Butch Bowers didn't put a lot of rotten potatoes at the bottom of the peck basket she'd sent you to fetch, the prologue (*Pay attention to your mother*) and the epilogue (*Mind me, now*) were always the same. And if you *failed* to pay attention, if you *failed* to mind her, you had to face the Wrath of Mother, and God help you then.

She picked up the needles and began to knit again, running off scarlet stitches with fingers that looked faintly red themselves. Ralph supposed that was just an illusion. Or maybe the dye wasn't completely colorfast, and some of it was coming off on his fingers.

His fingers? What a silly mistake *that* was. *Her* fingers.

Except . . .

Well, there were little bunches of whiskers at the corners of her mouth. *Long* ones. Nasty, somehow. And unfamiliar. Ralph could remember a fine down on her upper lip, but *whiskers*? No way. Those were new.

New? New? What are you thinking about? She died two days after Robert Kennedy was assassinated in Los Angeles, so what in the name of God can be new about her?

Two converging walls had bloomed on either side of Bertha Roberts, creating the kitchen corner where she had spent so much time. On one of them was a painting Ralph remembered well. It showed a family at supper – Dad, Mom, two kids. They were passing the potatoes and the corn, and looked like they were discussing their respective days. None of them noticed that there was a fifth person in the room – a white-robed man with a sandy beard and long hair. He was standing in the corner and watching them. CHRIST, THE UNSEEN VISITOR, the plaque beneath this painting read. Except the Christ Ralph remembered had looked both kind and a little embarrassed to be eavesdropping. This version, however, looked coldly thoughtful . . . evaluative . . . judgemental, perhaps. And his color was very high, almost choleric, as if he had heard something which had made him furious.

['*Mom? Are you—*']

She put the needles down again on the red blanket – that oddly *shiny* red blanket – and raised a hand to stop him.

[*Mom me no Moms, Ralph – just pay attention and mind. Stay out of this! It's too late for your muddling and meddling. You can only make things worse.*]

The voice was right, but the face was wrong and becoming wronger. Mostly it was her skin. Smooth and unlined, her skin had been Bertha Roberts's only vanity. The skin of the creature in the rocker was rough . . . more than rough, in fact. It was *scaly*. And there were two growths (or perhaps they were sores?) on the sides of her neck. At the sight of them, some terrible memory

(*get it off me Johnny oh please* GET IT OFF)

stirred far down in his mind. And—

Well, her aura. Where was her aura?

[*Never mind my aura and never mind about that fat old whore you've been running around with . . . although I'll bet Carolyn is just rolling in her grave.*]

The mouth of the woman

(*not a woman that thing is not a woman*)

in the rocker was no longer small. The lower lip had spread, puffed outward and downward. The mouth itself had developed a drooping sneer. A strangely *familiar* drooping sneer.

(*Johnny it's biting me it's* BITING ME!)

Something horridly familiar about the bunches of whiskers bristling at the corners of the mouth, too.

(*Johnny please its eyes its black eyes*)

[*Johnny can't help you, boy. He didn't help you then and he can't help you now.*]

Of course he couldn't. His older brother Johnny had died six years ago. Ralph had been a pallbearer at his funeral. Johnny had died of a heart attack, possibly as Random as the one which had felled Bill McGovern, and—

Ralph looked to the left, but the pilot's side of the cockpit had also disappeared, and Ed Deepneau with it. Ralph saw the old combination gas and woodstove on which his mother had cooked in the house on Richmond Street (a job she had resented bitterly and done badly all her life) and the arch leading into the dining room. He saw their maple dining table. A glass pitcher stood in the center of it. The pitcher had been filled with a choke of lurid red roses. Each seemed to have a face . . . a blood-red, gasping face . . .

But that's wrong, he thought. *All wrong. She never had roses in the house – she was allergic to most blooms, and roses were the worst. She used to sneeze like crazy when she was around them. The only thing I ever saw her put on the dining room table was Indian Bouquet, and that wasn't anything but autumn grasses. I see roses because—*

He looked back at the creature in the rocking chair, at red fingers which had now melted together into appendages that looked almost like fins. He regarded the scarlet mass which lay in the creature's lap, and the scar along his arm began to tingle again.

What in God's name is going on here?

But he knew, of course; he only had to look from the red thing in the rocking chair to the picture hanging on the wall, the picture of the scarlet-faced, malevolent Jesus watching the family eat their supper, to confirm it. He was not in his old house in Mary Mead, and he was not precisely in an aircraft over Derry, either.

He was in the Court of the Crimson King.

Chapter Twenty-nine

1

Without thinking about why he was doing it, Ralph slipped a hand into his sweater pocket and loosely cupped one of Lois's earrings. His hand felt far away, something which belonged to someone else. He was realizing an interesting thing: he had never been frightened in his life until now. Not once. He had *thought* he'd been frightened, of course, but it had been an illusion – the only time he'd even come close had been in the Derry Public Library, when Charlie Pickering stuck a knife into his armpit and said he was going to let Ralph's guts out all over the floor. That, however, was nothing but a mild moment of discomfort next to what he was feeling now.

A green man came . . . he felt good, but I could be wrong.

He hoped she wasn't; he most sincerely hoped she wasn't. Because the green man was about all he had left now.

The green man, and Lois's earrings.

[*Ralph! Stop woolgathering!* Look *at your mother when she's talking to you! Seventy years old and you still act like you were sixteen, with a bad case of pecker-rash!*]

He turned back to the red-finned thing slumped in the rocker. It now bore only a passing resemblance to his late mother.

[*'You're not my mother, and I'm still in the airplane.'*]

[*You're not, boy. Don't make the mistake of thinking you are. Take one step out of my kitchen and you're in for a very long fall.*]

[*'You might as well stop now. I can see what you are.'*]

The thing spoke in a bubbly, choked voice that turned Ralph's spine to a narrow line of ice.

[*You don't. You may think you do, but you don't. And you don't*

587

want to. You don't ever want to see me with my disguises laid aside. Believe me, Ralph, you don't.]

He realized with mounting horror that the mother-thing had turned into an enormous female catfish, a hungry bottom-feeder with stubby teeth gleaming between its pendulous lips and whiskers which dangled almost to the collar of the dress it still wore. The gills in its neck opened and closed like razor-cuts, revealing troubled red inner flesh. Its eyes had grown round and purplish, and as Ralph watched, the sockets began to slide away from each other. This continued until the eyes bulged from the sides rather than the front of the creature's scaly face.

[*Don't move so much as a single muscle, Ralph. You'll probably die in the explosion no matter what level you're on – the shockwaves travel here just as they do in any building – but that death will still be a great deal better than my death.*]

The catfish opened its mouth. Its teeth ringed a blood-colored maw which looked full of strange guts and tumors. It seemed to be laughing at him.

[*'Who are you? Are you the Crimson King?'*]

[*That's Ed's name for me – we ought to have our own, don't you think? Let's see. If you don't want me to be Mom Roberts, why not call me the Kingfish? You remember the Kingfish from the radio, don't you?*]

Yes, of course he did . . . but the *real* Kingfish had never been on *Amos and Andy*, and it hadn't really been a kingfish at all. The real Kingfish had been a queenfish, and it had lived in the Barrens.

2

On a summer's day during the year when Ralph Roberts was seven he had hooked an enormous catfish out of the Kenduskeag while fishing with his brother John – this had been when it was still possible to eat what you caught down in the Barrens. Ralph had asked his older brother to take the convulsively flopping thing off his hook for him and put it in the bucket of fresh water they kept on the bank beside them. Johnny had refused, loftily citing what he called the Fisherman's Creed: good fishermen tie their own flies, dig their own worms, and unhook their own catches. It was only later that Ralph realized Johnny might have been trying to hide his own fear of the huge and somehow alien creature his kid brother had reeled out of the Kenduskeag's muddy, piss-warm water that day.

Ralph had at last brought himself to grasp the catfish's pulsing body, which was at the same time slick, scaly, and prickly. As he did, Johnny had added to his terror by telling him, in a low and ominous voice, to look out for the whiskers. *They're poison. Bobby Therriault told me if one of em sticks inya, you could get paralyzed. Spend the rest of your life in a wheelchair. So be careful, Ralphie.*

Ralph had twisted the creature this way and that, trying to free the hook from its dark, wet innards without getting his hand too near its whiskers (not believing Johnny about the poison and at the same time believing him completely), exquisitely aware of the gills, the eyes, the fishy smell that seemed to shimmer its way more deeply into his lungs each time he inhaled.

At last he'd heard a gristly ripping from deep within the catfish and felt the hook start to slide free. Fresh streamlets of blood trickled from the corners of its flexing, dying mouth. Ralph gave a little sigh of relief – prematurely, as it turned out. The catfish gave a tremendous flap of its tail as the hook came out. The hand Ralph had been using to free it slipped, and all at once the catfish's bleeding mouth clamped shut on his first two fingers. How much pain had there been? A lot? Some? Maybe none at all? Ralph couldn't remember. What he *did* remember was Johnny's completely unfeigned shriek of horror and his own surety that the catfish was going to make him pay for taking its life by eating two fingers off his right hand.

He remembered screaming himself, and shaking his hand, and begging Johnny to help him, but Johnny had been backing away, his face pale, his mouth a knotted line of revulsion. Ralph shook his hand in big, swooping arcs, but the catfish hung on like death, whiskers

(*poison whiskers put me in a wheelchair for the rest of my life*)

snapping and flapping against Ralph's wrist, black eyes staring.

At last he'd struck it against a nearby tree, breaking its back. It had dropped to the grass, still flopping, and Ralph had stamped on it with one foot, provoking the final horror. A spew of guts vomited from its mouth, and from the place where Ralph's heel had smashed it open had come a gluey torrent of bloody eggs. That was when he had realized that the Kingfish had really been the Queenfish, and only a day or two from roeing.

Ralph had stared from this freakish mess to his own bloody, scale-encrusted hand, and then howled like a banshee. When Johnny touched his arm in an effort to calm him, Ralph had bolted. He hadn't stopped running until he got home, and he'd refused to come out of his room for the rest of the day. It had been almost a year before he'd eaten another piece of fish, and he'd never had anything to do with catfish again.

Until now, that was.

3

['*Ralph!*']

That was Lois's voice . . . but distant! So distant!

['*You have to do something right away! Don't let it stop you!*']

Ralph now realized that what he'd taken for an afghan in his mother's lap was actually a mat of bloody eggs in the lap of the Crimson King. It was leaning toward him over this throbbing blanket, its thick lips quivering in a parody of concern.

[*Something wrong, Ralphie? Where does it hurt? Tell Mother.*]

['*You're not my mother.*']

[*No – I be the Queenfish! I be loud and I be proud! I got the walk and I got the talk! Actually, I can be whatever I want. You may not know it, but shape-changing is a time-honored custom in Derry.*]

['*Do you know the green man Lois saw?*']

[*Of course! I know all the neighborhood folks!*]

But Ralph sensed momentary puzzlement on that scaly face.

The heat along his forearm cranked up another notch, and Ralph had a sudden realization: if Lois were here now, she would hardly be able to see him. The Queenfish was putting out a pulsing, ever-brightening glow, and it was gradually surrounding him. The glow was red instead of black, but it was still a deathbag, and now he knew what it was like to be on the inside, caught in a web woven from your sickest fears and most traumatic experiences. There was no way to retreat from it, and no way to cut through it, as he had cut through the deathbag which had surrounded Ed's wedding ring.

If I'm going to escape, Ralph thought, *I'm going to have to do it by running forward so hard and fast I rip right out the other side.*

The earring was still in his hand. Now he shifted it so that the naked prong at the back was sticking out between the two fingers a catfish had tried to swallow sixty-three years ago. Then he said a brief prayer, not to God but to Lois's green man.

4

The catfish leaned further forward, a cartoon leer spreading across its noseless face. The teeth inside that flabby grin looked longer and sharper now. Ralph saw drops of colorless fluid beading the ends of the whiskers and thought, *Poison. Spend the rest of your life in a wheelchair. Man, I'm so scared. Scared to fucking* death.

Lois, screaming far away: ['*Hurry, Ralph!* YOU HAVE TO HURRY!']

A little boy was screaming from somewhere a lot closer; screaming and waving his right hand, waving the fish clinging to the fingers buried inside the gullet of a pregnant monster that would not let go.

The catfish leaned closer yet. The dress it wore rustled. Ralph could smell his mother's perfume, Saint Elena, mixing obscenely with the fishy, garbagey aroma of bottom-feeder.

[*I intend Ed Deepneau's errand to end in success, Ralph; I intend that the boy your friends told you about should die in his mother's arms, and I want to see it happen. I've worked very hard here in Derry, and I don't feel that's too much to ask, but it means I have to finish with you right now. I—*]

Ralph took a step deeper into the thing's garbagey stink. And now he began to see a shape behind the shape of Mother, behind the shape of the Queenfish. He began to see a bright man, a *red* man with cold eyes and a merciless mouth. This man resembled the Christ he had seen only moments ago . . . but not the one which had really hung in his mother's kitchen corner.

An expression of surprise came into the lidless black eyes

of the Queenfish . . . and into the cold eyes of the red man beneath.

[*What do you think you're doing? Get away from me! Do you want to spend the rest of your life in a wheelchair?*]

['*I can think of worse things, pal – my days of playing first base are pretty definitely over.*']

The voice rose, becoming the voice of his mother when she was angry.

[*Pay attention to me, boy! Pay attention and mind me!*]

For a moment the old commands, given in a voice so eerily like his mother's, made him hesitate. Then he came on again. The Queenfish shrank back in the rocker, its tail flipping up and down below the hem of the old housedress.

[*JUST WHAT DO YOU THINK YOU'RE DOING?*]

['*I don't know; maybe I just want to give your whiskers a tug. See for myself if they're real.*']

And, exerting all of his willpower to keep from shrieking and fleeing, he reached out with his right hand. Lois's earring felt like a small, warm pebble closed within his fist. Lois herself seemed very close, and Ralph decided that wasn't surprising, considering how much of her aura he'd taken on. Perhaps she was even a part of him now. The feeling of her presence was deeply comforting.

[*No, you don't dare! You'll be paralyzed!*]

['*Catfish aren't poisonous – that was the story of a ten-year-old boy who might have been even more scared than I was.*']

Ralph reached for the whiskers with the hand concealing the metal thorn, and the massive, scaly head flinched away, as some part of him had known it would. It began to ripple and change, and its fearful red aura began to seep through. *If sickness and pain had a color,* Ralph thought, *that would be it.* And before the change could go any further, before that man he could now see – tall and coldly handsome with his blond hair and glaring red eyes – could step through the shimmer of the illusion it had cast, Ralph drove the sharp point of the earring into one black and bulging fisheye.

It made a terrible buzzing sound – like a cicada, Ralph thought – and tried to draw back. Its rapidly flipping tail produced a sound like a fan with a piece of paper caught in the blades. It slid down in the rocker, which was now changing into something that looked like a throne carved from dull orange rock. And then the tail was gone, the Queenfish was gone, and it was the Crimson King sitting there, his handsome face twisted into a snarl of pain and amazement. One of his eyes glared as red as the eye of a lynx in firelight; the other was filled with the fierce, splintered glow of diamonds.

Ralph reached into the blanket of eggs with his left hand, ripped it away, and saw nothing but blackness on the other side of the abortion. The other side of the deathbag. The way out.

[*You were warned, you Short-Time son of a bitch! You think you can pull my whiskers? Well, let's see, shall we? Let's just see!*]

The Crimson King leaned forward again on its throne, its mouth yawning, its remaining eye blazing with red light. Ralph fought the urge to yank his now-empty right hand away. Instead he pistoned it forward toward the mouth of the Crimson King, which yawned wide to engulf it, as that long-ago catfish had done that day in the Barrens.

Things – not flesh – first squirmed and jostled against his hand, then began to bite like horseflies. At the same time Ralph felt real teeth – no, *fangs* – sink into his arm. In a moment, two at the most, the Crimson King would bite through his wrist and swallow his hand whole.

Ralph closed his eyes and was at once able to find that pattern of thought and concentration which allowed movement between the levels – his pain and his fear were no bar to that. Only this time his purpose was not to *move* but to *trigger*. Clotho and Lachesis had planted a booby-trap inside his arm, and the time had come to set it off.

Ralph felt that sensation of *blink* inside his head. The scar on his arm immediately went white-hot and critical. That heat didn't burn Ralph but flew out from him in an expanding ripple of energy. He was aware of a titanic green flash, so bright that for one moment it was as if the Emerald City of Oz had exploded all around him. Something or someone was screaming. That high, jagged sound would have driven him mad if it had gone on for long, but it didn't. It was followed by a vast, hollow bang that made Ralph think of the time he had lit an M-80 firecracker and tossed it into a steel culvert.

A sudden rush of force blew past him in a fan of wind and fading green light. He caught a strange, skewed glimpse of the Crimson King, no longer handsome and no longer young but ancient and twisted and less human than the strangest creature to ever flop or hop its way along the Short-Time level of existence. Then something above them opened, revealing darkness shot through with conflicting swirls and rays of color. The wind seemed to blow the Crimson King up toward it, like a leaf in a chimney-flue. The colors began to brighten, and Ralph turned his face away, raising one hand to shield his eyes. He understood that a conduit had opened between the level where he was and the unimaginable levels stacked above it; he also understood that if he looked for long into that brightening glow, those

(*deadlights*)

swirling colors, then death would be not the worst thing that could happen to him but the best. He did not just squeeze his eyes shut; he squeezed his *mind* shut.

A moment later everything was gone – the creature which had identified itself to Ed as the Crimson King, the kitchen in the old house on Richmond Street, his mother's rocking chair. Ralph was kneeling on thin air about six feet to the right of the Cherokee's nose, his hands upraised as an oft-beaten child might raise his hands before the approach of a cruel parent, and when he looked between his knees, he saw the Civic Center and the adjacent parking lot directly below him. At first he thought his eyes were being fooled by an optical illusion, because the arc-sodiums in the parking lot seemed to be spreading apart. They almost looked like a crowd of very tall, very skinny people which is starting to break up because the excitement, whatever it was, is over. And the lot itself seemed to be . . . well . . . *expanding.*

Not expanding but getting closer, Ralph thought coldly. *He's going down. He's started his kamikaze run.*

6

For a moment Ralph was frozen in place, enchanted by the simple wonder of his position. He had become a mythical in-between creature, clearly no god (no god could be as tired and terrified as he was right now) but clearly no such earthbound creature as a man, either. This was what it was really like to fly; to see the earth from above, with no border around it. This—

['RALPH!']

Her scream was like a shotgun fired beside his ear. Ralph flinched from it, and the moment his gaze left the hypnotic sight of the ground swelling up toward him, he was able to move. He rose to his feet and walked back to the plane. He did this as easily and normally as a man walking down a hallway in his own home. No wind buffeted his face or blew his hair back from his brow, and when his left shoulder passed through the Cherokee's propeller, the whirling blade harmed him no more than it would have harmed smoke.

For a moment he saw Ed's pallid, handsome face – the face of the highwayman who'd come riding up to the old inn door in the poem which had always made Carolyn cry – and his previous feeling of mingled pity and regret was replaced by anger. It was difficult to become *really* infuriated with Ed – he was, after all, just another chess-piece being moved across the board – and yet the building he had aimed his airplane at was full of real people. *Innocent* people. Ralph saw something balky, childish, and willful about the dopey expression of disassociation on Ed's face, and as he passed through the thin skin of the cockpit wall, Ralph thought, *I think that on some level, Ed, you knew the devil had come in. I think you might even have been able to put him out again . . . didn't Mr C and Mr L say there's always a choice? If there is, you have to own a piece of this, goddam you.*

For a moment Ralph's head poked through the ceiling as it had done before, and he knelt again. Now the Civic Center filled the entire windshield of the plane and he understood that it was too late to stop Ed from doing *something*.

He had pulled the doorbell free of the tape. He was holding it in his hand.

Ralph reached into his pocket and gripped the remaining

earring, once again holding it between his fingers with the prong sticking out. He curled his other hand into a tube around the wires running between the cardboard carton and the doorbell. Then he closed his eyes and concentrated, creating that flexing sensation in the middle of his head again. There was a sudden hollow, fluttery sensation in his stomach, and he had time to think *Whoa! This is the express elevator!*

Then he was down on the Short-Time level where there were no gods or devils, no bald doctors with magic scissors and scalpels, no auras. Down where passing through walls and walking away from plane-crashes was an impossibility. Down on the Short-Time level where he could be seen . . . and Ed, Ralph realized, was doing just that.

'Ralph?' It was the drugged voice of a man just waking from his life's soundest sleep. 'Ralph Roberts? What are *you* doing here?'

'Oh, I was in the neighborhood and I thought I'd drop in,' Ralph said. 'Drag up a rock, so to speak.' And with that, he closed his curled hand into a fist and tore the wires out of the box.

7

'*No!*' Ed shrieked. '*Oh no, don't, you'll spoil everything!*'

Yes indeed, Ralph thought, then reached over Ed's lap to grab the Cherokee's control-wheel. The Civic Center was now no more than twelve hundred feet below them, perhaps less. Ralph still didn't know for sure what was in the box strapped to the co-pilot's chair, but he had an idea it was probably the *plastique* stuff the terrorists always used in the martial arts movies starring Chuck Norris and Steven Seagal. It was supposed to be fairly stable – not like the nitro in Clouzot's *Wages of Fear*, certainly – but this was hardly the time to put his trust in the Gospel of Movieland. And even a stable explosive might go off without a detonator when dropped from a height of almost two miles.

He jammed the control-wheel as far over to the left as he could. Below them, the Civic Center began to wheel sickeningly around, as if it had been mounted on the spindle of a gigantic top.

'*No, you bastard!*' Ed yelled, and something that felt like the head of a small hammer struck Ralph in the side, almost paralyzing him with pain and making it all but impossible to breathe. His hand slid off the control-wheel as Ed hammered him again, this time in the armpit. Ed seized the wheel and yanked it savagely back over. The Civic Center, which had begun to slip toward the side of the windshield, began to rotate back toward dead center.

Ralph clawed at the wheel. Ed placed the heel of his hand on Ralph's forehead and shoved him backward. 'Why couldn't you stay out of it?' he snarled. 'Why'd you have to *meddle?*' His teeth were bared, his lips pulled back in a jealous snarl. Ralph's appearance in the cockpit should have incapacitated him with shock but hadn't.

Of course not, he's nuts, Ralph thought, and suddenly raised his interior voice in a panicked yell:

['*Clotho! Lachesis! For Christ's sake, help me!*']

Nothing. It didn't feel as if his shout were going *anywhere.* And why would it? He was back down on the Short-Time level, and that meant he was on his own.

The Civic Center was only eight or nine hundred feet below them now. Ralph could see every brick, every window, every person standing outside – he could almost even tell which ones were carrying signs. They were looking up, trying to figure out what this crazy plane was doing. Ralph couldn't see the fear on their faces, not yet, but in another three or four seconds—

He launched himself at Ed again, ignoring the throb in his left side and driving his right fist forward, using his thumb to ride the prong of the earring out beyond his fingers as far as possible.

The old Earring Gag had worked on the Crimson King, but Ralph had been higher then, and he'd had the element of surprise more firmly in hand. He went for the eye this time, too, but Ed snapped his head away at the last moment. The prong drove into the side of his face just above the cheekbone. Ed swatted at it as if it were a gnat, holding on tightly to the control-wheel with his left hand as he did it.

Ralph went for the wheel again. Ed lashed out at him. His fist connected above Ralph's left eye, driving him backward. A single loud tone, pure and silvery, filled Ralph's ears. It was as if there were a large tuning fork somewhere in between them, and someone had struck it. The world went as gray and grainy as a newsprint photograph.

['*RALPH! HURRY!*']

It was Lois, and now she was in terror. He knew why; time had all but run out. He had maybe ten seconds, twenty at most. He lunged forward again, this time not at Ed but at the picture of Helen and Nat that was taped above the altimeter. He snatched it, held it up . . . and then crumpled it between his fingers. He didn't know exactly what reaction he'd hoped for, but the one he got exceeded his wildest hopes.

'*GIVE THEM BACK!*' Ed screamed. He forgot about the control wheel and groped for the picture instead. As he did, Ralph again saw the man he had glimpsed on the day Ed had beaten Helen – a man who was desperately unhappy and afraid of the forces which had been set loose within him. There were tears not just in his eyes but running down his cheeks, and Ralph thought confusedly: *Has he been crying all along?*

'*GIVE THEM BACK!*' he bawled again, but Ralph was no longer sure he was the subject of that cry; he thought his former neighbor might be addressing the being which had stepped into his life, looked around itself to make sure it would do, and then simply taken it over. Lois's earring glittered in Ed's cheek like a barbaric funerary ornament. '*GIVE THEM BACK, THEY'RE MINE!*'

Ralph held the crumpled photograph just beyond the reach of Ed's waving hands. Ed lunged, the seatbelt bit into his gut, and Ralph punched him in the throat as hard as he could, feeling an indescribable mixture of satisfaction and revulsion as the blow landed on the hard, gristly protuberance of Ed's Adam's apple. Ed fell back against the cockpit wall, eyes bulging with pain and dismay and bewilderment, hands going to his throat. A thick gagging noise came from somewhere deep inside him. It sounded like some heavy piece of machinery in the process of stripping its gears.

Ralph shoved himself forward over Ed's lap and saw the Civic Center now *leaping* up toward the airplane. He turned the wheel all the way to the left again and below him – *directly* below him – the Civic Center again began to rotate toward the side of the Cherokee's soon-to-be-defunct windshield . . . but it moved with agonizing slowness.

Ralph realized he could smell something in the cockpit – some faint aroma both sweet and familiar. Before he could think what it might be, he saw something that distracted him completely. It was the Hoodsie Ice Cream wagon that sometimes cruised along Harris Avenue, tinkling its cheery little bell.

My God, Ralph thought, more in awe than in fear. *I think I'm going to wind up in the deep freeze, along with the Creamsicles and Hoodsie Rockets.*

That sweet smell was stronger, and as hands suddenly seized his shoulders, Ralph realized it was Lois Chasse's perfume.

'Come up!' she screamed. 'Ralph, you dummy, you have to—'

He didn't think about it; he just did it. The thing in his mind clenched, the blink happened, and he heard the rest of what she had to say in that eerie, penetrating way that was more thought than speech.

[*'— come up! Push with your feet!'*]

Too late, he thought, but he did as she said nevertheless, planting his feet against the base of the radically canted instrument panel and shoving as hard as he could. He felt Lois rising up through the column of existence with him as the Cherokee shot through the last hundred feet between it and the ground, and as they zoomed upward, he felt a sudden blast of Lois-power wrap itself around him and yank him backward like a bungee cord. There was a brief, nauseating sensation of flying in two directions at the same time.

Ralph caught a final glimpse of Ed Deepneau slumped against the sidewall of the cockpit, but in a very real sense he did not see him at all. The thunderstruck yellow-gray aura was gone. Ed was also gone, buried in a deathbag as black as midnight in hell.

Then he and Lois were falling as well as flying.

Chapter Thirty

1

Just before the explosion came, Susan Day, standing in a hot white spotlight at the front of the Civic Center and now living through the last few seconds of her fabulous, provocative life, was saying: 'I haven't come to Derry to heal you, hector you, or to incite you, but to mourn with you – this is a situation which has passed far beyond political considerations. There is no right in violence, nor refuge in self-righteousness. I am here to ask that you put your positions and your rhetoric aside and help each other find a way to help each other. To turn away from the attractions of—'

The high windows lining the south side of the auditorium suddenly lit up with a brilliant white glare and then blew inward.

2

The Cherokee missed the Hoodsie wagon, but that didn't save it. The plane took one final half-turn in the air and then screwed itself into the parking lot about twenty-five feet from the fence where, earlier that day, Lois had paused to yank up her troublesome half-slip. The wings snapped off. The cockpit made a quick and violent journey back through the passenger section. The fuselage blew out with the fury of a bottle of champagne in a microwave oven. Glass flew. The tail bent over the Cherokee's body like the stinger of a dying scorpion and impaled itself in the roof of a Dodge van with the words

PROTECT WOMEN'S RIGHT TO CHOOSE! stencilled on the side.
There was a bright and bitter crunch-clang that sounded like
a dropped pile of scrap iron.

'Holy shi –' one of the cops posted on the edge of the parking
lot began, and then the C-4 inside the cardboard box flew free
like a big gray glob of phlegm and struck the remains of the
instrument panel where several 'hot' wires rammed into it like
hypo needles. The *plastique* exploded with an ear-crunching
thud, flash-frying the Bassey Park racetrack and turning the
parking lot into a hurricane of white light and shrapnel. John
Leydecker, who had been standing under the Civic Center's
cement canopy and talking to a State cop, was thrown through
one of the open doors and all the way across the lobby. He
struck the far wall and fell unconscious into the shattered glass
from the harness-racing trophy case. At that, he was luckier
than the man with whom he had been standing; the State cop
was thrown into the post between two of the open doors and
chopped in half.

The ranks of cars actually shielded the Civic Center from the
worst of the hammering, concussive blow, but that blessing
would only be counted later. Inside, over two thousand people
at first sat stunned, unsure of what they should do and even
more unsure of what most of them had just seen: America's
most famous feminist decapitated by a jagged chunk of flying
glass. Her head went flying into the sixth row like some strange
white bowling ball with a blonde wig pasted on it.

They didn't erupt into panic until the lights went out.

3

Seventy-one people were killed in the trampling, panicked rush
to the exits, and the next day's Derry *News* would trumpet the
event with a forty-eight-point scare headline, calling it a terrible
tragedy. Ralph Roberts could have told them that, all things
considered, they had gotten off lucky. Very lucky, indeed.

4

Halfway up the north balcony, a woman named Sonia Danville – a woman with the bruises of the last beating any man would ever give her still fading from her face – sat with her arms around the shoulders of her son, Patrick. Patrick's McDonald's poster, showing Ronald and Mayor McCheese and the Hamburglar dancing the Boot-Scootin' Boogie just outside a drive-thru window, was on his lap, but he had hardly done more than color the golden arches before turning the poster over to the blank side. It wasn't that he had lost interest; it was just that he'd had an idea for a picture of his own, and it had come as such ideas often did to him, with the force of a compulsion. He had spent most of the day thinking about what had happened in the cellar at High Ridge – the smoke, the heat, the frightened women, and the two angels that had come to save them – but his splendid idea banished these disturbing thoughts, and he fell to work with silent enthusiasm. Soon Patrick felt almost as if he were living in the world he was drawing with his Crayolas.

He was an amazingly competent artist already, only four years old or not ('My little genius', Sonia sometimes called him), and his picture was much better than the color-it-in poster on the other side of the sheet. What he had managed before the lights went out was work a gifted first-year art student might have been proud of. In the middle of the poster-sheet, a tower of dark, soot-colored stone rose into a blue sky dotted with fat white clouds. Surrounding it was a field of roses so red they almost seemed to clamor aloud. Standing off to one side was a man dressed in faded blue jeans. A pair of gunbelts crossed his flat middle; a holster hung below each hip. At the very top of the tower, a man in a red robe was looking down at the gunfighter with an expression of mingled hate and fear. His hands, which were curled over the parapet, also appeared to be red.

Sonia had been mesmerized by the presence of Susan Day, who was sitting behind the lectern and listening to her intro-duction, but she had happened to glance down at her son's picture just before the introduction ended. She had known for two years that Patrick was what the child psychologists called a prodigy, and she sometimes told herself she had gotten used to his sophisticated drawings and the Play-Doh sculptures he called the Clay Family. Perhaps she even had to some degree, but this particular picture gave her a strange, deep chill that she could not entirely dismiss as emotional fallout from her long and stressful day.

'Who's that?' she asked, tapping the tiny figure peering jealously down from the top of the dark tower.

'Him's the Red King,' Patrick said.

'Oh, the Red King, I see. And who's this man with the guns?'

As he opened his mouth to answer, Roberta Harper, the woman at the podium, lifted her left arm (there was a black mourning band on it) toward the woman sitting behind her. 'My friends, Ms *Susan Day!*' she cried, and Patrick Danville's answer to his mother's second question was lost in the rising storm of applause.

Him's name is Roland, Mama. I dream about him, sometimes. Him's a King, too.

5

Now the two of them sat in the dark with their ears ringing, and two thoughts ran through Sonia's mind like rats chasing each other on a treadmill: *Won't this day ever end, I knew I shouldn't have brought him, won't this day ever end, I knew I shouldn't have brought him, won't this day—*

'Mommy, you're scrunching my *picture!*' Patrick said. He sounded a little out of breath, and Sonia realized she must be scrunching him, too. She eased up a little. A tattered skein of screams, shouts, and babbled questions came from the dark pit below them, where the people rich enough to pony up fifteen-dollar 'donations' had been seated in folding chairs. A rough howl of pain cut through this babble, making Sonia jump in her seat.

The thudding crump which had followed the initial explosion had pressed in painfully on their ears and shaken the building. The blasts which were still going on – cars exploding like fire-crackers in the parking lot – sounded small and inconsequential in comparison, but Sonia felt Patrick flinch against her with each one.

'Stay calm, Pat,' she told him. 'Something bad's happened,

but I think it happened outside.' Because her eyes had been drawn to the bright glare in the windows, Sonia had mercifully missed seeing her heroine's head leaving her shoulders, but she knew that somehow lightning *had* struck in the same place

(*shouldn't have brought him, shouldn't have brought him*)

and that at least some of the people below them were panicking. If *she* panicked, she and Young Rembrandt were going to be in serious trouble.

But I'm not going to. I didn't get out of that deathbox this morning just to panic now. I'll be goddamned if I will.

She reached down and took one of Patrick's hands – the one that wasn't clutching his picture. It was very cold.

'Do you think the angels will come to save us again, Mama?' he asked in a voice that quivered slightly.

'Nah,' she said. 'I think this time we better do it ourselves. But we can do that. I mean, we're all right now, aren't we?'

'Yes,' he said, but then slumped against her. She had a terrible moment when she was sure he had fainted and she'd have to carry him from the Civic Center in her arms, but then he straightened up again. 'My books was on the floor,' he said. 'I didn't want to leave without my books, especially the one about the boy who can't take off his hat. *Are* we leaving, Mama?'

'Yes. As soon as people stop running around. There'll be lights in the halls, ones that run on batteries, even though the ones in here are out. When I say, we're going to get up and walk – *walk!* – up the steps to the door. I'm not going to carry you, but I'm going to walk right behind you with both my hands on your shoulders. Do you understand, Pat?'

'Yes, Mama.' No questions. No blubbering. Just his books, thrust into her hands for safekeeping. He held onto the picture himself. She gave him a quick hug and kissed his cheek.

They waited in their seats five minutes by her slow count to three hundred. She sensed that most of their immediate neighbors were gone before she got to a hundred and fifty, but she made herself wait. She could now see a little, enough for her to believe that something was burning fiercely outside, but on the far side of the building. That was very lucky. She could hear the warble-wail of approaching police cars, ambulances, and fire-trucks.

Sonia got to her feet. 'Come on. Keep right in front of me.'

Pat Danville stepped into the aisle with his mother's hands pressed firmly down on his shoulders. He led her up the steps toward the dim yellow lights which marked the north balcony corridor, stopping only once as the dark shape of a running man hurtled toward them. His mother's hands tightened on his shoulders as she yanked him aside.

'Goddam right-to-lifers!' the running man cried. 'Fucking self-righteous *turds*! I'd like to kill them all!'

Then he was gone and Pat began walking up the stairs again. She felt a calmness in him now, a centered lack of fear, that touched her heart with love, and with some queer darkness, as well. He was so different, her son, so special . . . but the world did not love people like that. The world tried to root them out, like tares from a garden.

They emerged at last into the corridor. A few deeply shocked people wandered back and forth, eyes dazed and mouths agape, like zombies in a horror movie. Sonia hardly glanced at them, just got Pat moving toward the stairs. Three minutes later they exited into the fireshot night perfectly unscathed, and upon all the levels of the universe, matters both Random and Purposeful resumed their ordained courses. Worlds which had trembled for a moment in their orbits now steadied, and in one of those worlds, in a desert that was the apotheosis of all deserts, a man named Roland turned over in his bedroll and slept easily once again beneath the alien constellations.

6

Across town, in Strawford Park, the door of the Portosan marked MEN blew open. Lois Chasse and Ralph Roberts came flying out backwards in a haze of smoke, clutching each other. From within came the sound of the Cherokee hitting and then the *plastique* exploding. There was a flash of white light and the toilet's blue walls bulged outward, as if some giant had hammered them with his fists. A second later they heard the explosion all over again; this time it came rolling across the open air. The second version was fainter, but somehow more real.

Lois's feet stuttered and she thumped to the grass of the lower hillside with a cry which was partly relief. Ralph landed beside her, then pushed himself up to a sitting position. He stared unbelievingly at the Civic Center, where a fist of fire was now clenched on the horizon. A purple lump the size of a doorknob was rising on his forehead, where Ed had hit him.

His left side still throbbed, but he thought maybe the ribs in there were only sprung, not broken.

[*'Lois, are you all right?'*]

She looked at him uncomprehendingly for a moment, then began to feel at her face and neck and shoulders. There was something so perfectly, sweetly *Our Lois* about this examination that Ralph laughed. He couldn't help it. Lois smiled tentatively back at him.

[*'I think I'm fine. In fact, I'm quite sure I am.'*]

[*'What were you doing there? You could have been killed!'*]

Lois, appearing somewhat rejuvenated (Ralph guessed that the handy wino had had something to do with that) looked him in the eye.

[*'I may be old-fashioned, Ralph, but if you think I'm going to spend the next twenty years or so fainting and fluttering like the heroine's best friend in those Regency romances my friend Mina's always reading, you better pick another woman to chum around with.'*]

He gaped for a moment, then pulled her to her feet and hugged her. Lois hugged back. She was incredibly warm, incredibly *there*. Ralph reflected for a moment on the similarities between loneliness and insomnia – how they were both insidious, cumulative, and divisive, the friends of despair and the enemies of love – and then he pushed those thoughts aside and kissed her.

Clotho and Lachesis, who had been standing at the top of the hill and looking as anxious as workmen who have wagered their Christmas bonuses on a prizefight underdog, now rushed down to where Ralph and Lois stood with their foreheads once more pressed together, looking into each other's eyes like lovestruck teenagers. From the far side of the Barrens, the sound of sirens rose like voices heard in uneasy dreams. The pillar of fire which marked the grave of Ed Deepneau's obsession was now too bright to look at without squinting. Ralph could hear the faint sound of cars exploding, and he thought of his car sitting abandoned somewhere out in the williwags. He decided that was okay. He was too old to drive.

7

Clotho: [*Are you both all right?*]
   Ralph: [*'We're fine. Lois reeled me in. She saved my life.'*]
   Lachesis: [*Yes. We saw her go in. It was very brave.*]
   Also very perplexing, right, Mr L? Ralph thought. *You saw it and you admire it . . . but I don't think you have any idea of how or why she could bring herself to do it. I think that, to you and your friend, the concept of rescue must seem almost as foreign as the idea of love.*

For the first time, Ralph felt a kind of pity for the little bald doctors, and understood the central irony of their lives: they were aware that the Short-Timers whose existences they had been sent to prune lived powerful inner lives, but they did not in the least comprehend the reality of those lives, the emotions which drove them, or the actions – sometimes noble, sometimes foolish – which resulted. Mr C and Mr L had studied their Short-Time charges as certain rich but timid Englishmen had studied the maps brought back by the explorers of the Victorian Age, explorers who had in many cases been funded by these same rich but timid men. With their clipped nails and soft fingers the philanthropists had traced paper rivers upon which they would never ride and paper jungles through which they would never safari. They lived in fearful perplexity and passed it off as imagination.

Clotho and Lachesis had drafted them, and had used them with a certain crude effectiveness, but they understood neither the joy of risk nor the sorrow of loss – the best they had been able to manage in the way of emotion was a nagging fear that Ralph and Lois would try to take on the Crimson King's pet research chemist directly and be swatted like elderly flies for their pains. The little bald doctors lived long lives, but Ralph suspected that, brilliant dragonfly auras notwithstanding, they were *gray* lives. He looked at their unlined, oddly childish faces from the safe haven of Lois's arms and remembered how terrified of them he had been when he had first seen them coming out of May Locher's house in the early hours of the morning. Terror, he had since discovered, could not survive mere acquaintanceship, let alone knowledge, and now he had some of both.

Clotho and Lachesis returned his gaze with an uneasiness

Ralph found he had absolutely no urge to allay. It seemed very right to him, somehow, that they should feel the way they were feeling.

Ralph: ['*Yes, she's very brave and I love her very much and I think we'll make each other very happy until—*']

He broke off, and Lois stirred in his arms. He realized with a mixture of amusement and relief that she had been half asleep.

['*Until what, Ralph?*']

['*Until you name it. I guess that there's always an* until *when you're a Short-Timer, and maybe that's okay.*']

Lachesis: [*Well, I guess this is goodbye.*]

Ralph grinned in spite of himself, reminded of *The Lone Ranger* radio program, where almost every episode had ended with some version of that line. He reached out toward Lachesis and was sourly amused to see the little man recoil from him.

Ralph: ['*Wait a minute . . . let's not be so hasty, fellas.*']

Clotho, with a tinge of apprehension: [*Is something wrong?*]

['*I don't think so, but after getting popped in the head, popped in the ribs, and then damned near roasted alive, I think I have a right to make sure that it's really over. Is it? Is your boy safe?*']

Clotho, smiling and clearly relieved: [*Yes. Can't you feel it? Eighteen years from now, just before his death, the boy is going to save the lives of two men who would otherwise die . . . and one of those men must not die, if the balance between the Random and the Purpose is to be maintained.*]

Lois: ['*Never mind all that. I just want to know if we can go back to being regular Short-Timers again.*']

Lachesis: [*Not only can, Lois, but must. If you and Ralph were to stay up here much longer, you wouldn't be able to go back down.*]

Ralph felt Lois press more tightly against him.

['*I wouldn't like that.*']

Clotho and Lachesis turned toward each other and a subtle, perplexed glance – *how could anybody* not *like it up here?* their eyes asked – passed between them before they turned back to Ralph and Lois.

Lachesis: [*We really must be going. I'm sorry, but—*]

Ralph: ['*Hold on, neighbors – you're not going anywhere yet.*']

They looked at him apprehensively while Ralph slowly pushed up the sleeve of his sweater – the cuff was now stiff with some fluid, perhaps catfish ichor, that he found he did not want to think about – and showed them the white, knotted line of scar on his forearm.

[*'Put away the constipated looks, guys. I just want to remind you that you gave me your word. Don't forget that part of it.'*]

Clotho, with obvious relief: [*You can depend on it, Ralph. What was your weapon is now our bond. The promise will not be forgotten.*]

Ralph was beginning to believe it really was over. And, crazy as it seemed, part of him regretted it. Now it was real life – life as it went on on the floors below this level – that seemed almost like a mirage, and he understood what Lachesis had meant when he told them that they would never be able to return to their normal lives if they stayed up here much longer.

Lachesis: [*We really must go. Fare you well, Ralph and Lois. We will never forget the service you have rendered us.*]

Ralph: [*'Did we ever have a choice? Did we really?'*]

Lachesis, very softly: [*We told you so, didn't we? For Short-Timers there is always a choice. We find that frightening . . . but we also find it beautiful.*]

Ralph: [*'Say – do you fellows ever shake hands?'*]

Clotho and Lachesis glanced at each other, startled, and Ralph sensed some quick dialogue flashing between them in a kind of telepathic shorthand. When they looked back at Ralph, they wore identical nervous smiles – the smiles of teenage boys who have decided that if they can't find enough courage to ride the *big* rollercoaster at the amusement park this summer, they will never truly be men.

Clotho: [*We have observed this custom many times, of course, but no – we have never shaken hands.*]

Ralph looked at Lois and saw she was smiling . . . but he thought he saw a shimmer of tears in her eyes, as well.

He offered his hand to Lachesis first, because Mr L seemed marginally less jumpy than his colleague.

[*'Put 'er there, Mr L.'*]

Lachesis looked at Ralph's hand for so long that Ralph began to think he wasn't going to be able to actually do it, although he clearly wanted to. Then, timidly, he put out his own small hand and allowed Ralph's larger one to close over it. There was a tingling vibration in Ralph's flesh as their auras first mingled, then merged . . . and in that merging he saw a series of swift, beautiful silver patterns. They reminded him of the Japanese characters on Ed's scarf.

He pumped Lachesis's hand twice, slowly and formally, then released it. Lachesis's look of apprehension had been replaced by a large goony smile. He turned to his partner.

[*His force is almost completely unguarded during this ceremony! I felt it! It's quite wonderful!*]

Clotho inched his own hand out to meet Ralph's, and in the instant before they touched, Mr C closed his eyes like a man expecting a painful injection. Lachesis, meanwhile, was shaking hands with Lois and grinning like a vaudeville hoofer taking an encore.

Clotho appeared to steel himself, then seized Ralph's hand. He flagged it once, firmly. Ralph grinned.

[*'Take her easy, Mr C.'*]

Clotho withdrew his hand. He seemed to be searching for the proper response.

[*Thank you, Ralph. I will take her any way I can get her. Correct?*]

Ralph burst out laughing. Clotho, now turning to shake hands with Lois, gave him a puzzled smile, and Ralph clapped him on the back.

[*'You got it right, Mr C – absolutely right.'*]

He slipped his arm around Lois and gave the little bald doctors a final curious look.

[*'I'll be seeing you fellows again, won't I?'*]

Clotho: [*Yes, Ralph.*]

Ralph: [*'Well, that's fine. About seventy years from now would be good for me; why don't you boys just put it down on your calendar?'*]

They responded with the smiles of politicians, which didn't surprise him much. Ralph gave them a little bow, then put his arms around Lois's shoulders and watched as Mr C and Mr L walked slowly down the hill. Lachesis opened the door of the slightly warped Portosan marked MEN; Clotho stood in the open doorway of WOMEN. Lachesis smiled and waved. Clotho lifted the long-bladed scissors in a queer sort of salute.

Ralph and Lois waved back.

The bald doctors stepped inside and closed the doors.

Lois wiped her streaming eyes and turned to Ralph.

[*'Is that it? It is, isn't it?'*]

Ralph nodded.

[*'What do we do now?'*]

He held out his arm.

[*'May I see you home, madam?'*]

Smiling, she clasped his forearm just below the elbow.

[*'Thank you, sir. You may.'*]

They left Strawford Park that way, returning to the Short-Time level as they came out on Harris Avenue, slipping back down to their normal place in the scheme of things with no fuss or bother – without, in fact, even being aware they were doing it until it was done.

8

Derry groaned with panic and sweated with excitement. Sirens wailed, people shouted from second-storey windows to friends on the sidewalks below, and on every street-corner people had clustered to watch the fire on the other side of the valley.

Ralph and Lois paid no attention to the tumult and hooraw. They walked slowly up Up-Mile Hill, increasingly aware of their exhaustion; it seemed to come piling into them like softly thrown bags of sand. The pool of white light marking the Red Apple Store's parking lot seemed an impossible distance away, although Ralph knew it was only three blocks, and short ones, at that.

To make matters worse, the temperature had dropped a good fifteen degrees since that morning, the wind was blowing hard, and neither of them was dressed for the weather. Ralph suspected this might be the leading edge of autumn's first big gale, and that in Derry, Indian summer was over.

Faye Chapin, Don Veazie, and Stan Eberly came hurrying down the hill toward them, obviously bound for Strawford Park. The field-glasses Old Dor sometimes used to watch planes taxi, land, and take off were bouncing around Faye's neck. With Don, who was balding and heavy set, in the middle, their resemblance to a more famous trio was inescapable. *The Three Stooges of the Apocalypse,* Ralph thought, and grinned.

'Ralph!' Faye exclaimed. He was breathing fast, almost panting. The wind blew his hair into his eyes and he raked it back impatiently. 'Goddam Civic Center blew up! Someone bombed it from a light plane! We heard there's a thousand people dead!'

'I heard about the same,' Ralph agreed gravely. 'In fact, Lois and I have just been down at the park, having a look. You can see straight across the valley from there, you know.'

'Christ, *I* know that, I've lived here all my damn life, haven't I? Where do you think we're going? Come on back with us!'

'Lois and I were just headed up to her house to see what they've got about it on TV. Maybe we'll join you later.'

'Okay, we – jeepers-creepers, Ralph, what'd you do to your head?'

For a moment Ralph drew a blank – what *had* he done to his head? – and then, in an instant of nightmarish recall, he saw Ed's snarling mouth and mad eyes. *Oh no, don't,* Ed had screamed at him. *You'll spoil everything.*

'We were running to get a better look and Ralph ran into a tree,' Lois said. 'He's lucky not to be in the hospital.'

Don laughed at that, but in the half-distracted manner of a fellow who has bigger fish to fry. Faye wasn't paying attention to them at all. Stan Eberly was, however, and Stan didn't laugh. He was looking at them with close, puzzled curiosity.

'Lois,' he said.

'What?'

'Did you know you've got a sneaker tied to your wrist?'

She looked down at it. Ralph looked down at it. Then Lois looked up and gave Stan a dazzling, eye-frying smile. 'Yes!' she said. 'It's an interesting look, isn't it? Sort of a . . . a life-sized charm bracelet!'

'Yeah,' Stan said. 'Sure.' But he wasn't looking at the sneaker anymore; now he was looking at Lois's face. Ralph wondered how in hell they were going to explain how they looked tomorrow, when there were no shadows between the streetlights to hide them.

'Come on!' Faye cried impatiently. 'Let's get going!'

They hurried off (Stan gave them one last doubtful glance over his shoulder as they went). Ralph listened after them, almost expecting Don Veazie to give out a *nyuck-nyuck* or two.

'Boy, that sounded so *dumb,*' Lois said, 'but I had to say something, didn't I?'

'You did fine.'

'Well, when I open my mouth, *something* always seems to fall out,' she said. 'It's one of my two great talents, the other being the ability to clean out an entire Whitman's Sampler during a two-hour TV movie.' She united Helen's sneaker and looked at it. 'She's safe, isn't she?'

'Yes,' Ralph agreed, and reached for the sneaker. As he did, he realized he already had something in his left hand. The fingers had been clamped down so long that they were creaky and reluctant to open. When they finally did, he saw the marks of his nails pressed into the flesh of his palm. The first thing he was aware of was that, while his own wedding ring was still in its accustomed place, Ed's was gone. It had seemed a perfect fit, but apparently it had slipped off his finger at some point during the last half an hour, just the same.

Maybe not, a voice whispered, and Ralph was amused to realize that it wasn't Carolyn's this time. This time the voice in his head belonged to Bill McGovern. *Maybe it just disappeared. You know, poof.*

But he didn't think so. He had an idea that Ed's wedding band might have been invested with powers that hadn't necessarily died with Ed. The Ring Bilbo Baggins had found and reluctantly given up to his grandson, Frodo, had had a way of going where it wanted to . . . and when. Perhaps Ed's ring wasn't all that different.

Before he could consider this idea further, Lois traded Helen's sneaker for the thing in his hand: a small stiff crumple of paper. She smoothed it out and looked at it. Her curiosity slowly changed to solemnity.

'I remember this picture,' she said. 'The big one was on the mantel in their living room, in a fancy gold frame. It had pride of place.'

Ralph nodded. 'This must have been the one he carried in his wallet. It was taped to the instrument panel of the plane. Until I took it, he was beating me, and not even breathing hard while he did it. Grabbing his picture was all I could think of to do. When I did, his focus switched from the Civic Center to them. The last thing I heard him say was "Give them back, they're mine."'

'And was he talking to you when he said it?'

Ralph stuck the sneaker into his back pocket and shook his head. 'Nope. Don't think so.'

'Helen was at the Civic Center tonight, wasn't she?'

'Yes.' Ralph thought of how she had looked out at High Ridge – her pale face and smoke-reddened, watering eyes. *If they stop us now, they win,* she'd said. *Don't you see that?*

And now he *did* see.

He took the picture from Lois's hand, crumpled it up again, and walked over to the litter-basket which stood on the corner of Harris Avenue and Kossuth Lane. 'We'll get another picture of them sometime, one we can keep on our own mantel. Something not quite so formal. This one, though . . . I don't want it.'

He tossed the little ball of paper at the litter-basket, an easy shot, two feet at the most, but the wind picked that moment to gust and the crumpled photo of Helen and Natalie which had been taped above the altimeter of Ed's plane flew away on its cold breath. The two of them watched it whirl up into the sky, almost hypnotized. It was Lois who looked away first. She glanced at Ralph with a trace of a smile curving her lips.

'Did I hear a backhand proposal of marriage from you, or am I just tired?' she asked.

He opened his mouth to reply and another gust of wind struck them, this one so hard it made them both wince their eyes shut. When he opened his, Lois had already started up the hill again.

'Anything's possible, Lois,' he said. 'I know that now.'

9

Five minutes later, Lois's key rattled in the lock of her front door. She led Ralph inside and shut it firmly behind them, closing out the windy, contentious night. He followed her into the living room and would have stopped there, but Lois never hesitated. Still holding his hand, not quite pulling him along (but perhaps meaning to do so if he began to lag), she showed him into her bedroom.

He looked at her. Lois looked calmly back . . . and suddenly he felt the blink happen again. He watched her aura bloom around her like a gray rose. It was still diminished, but it was already coming back, reknitting itself, healing itself.

[*'Lois, are you sure this is what you want?'*]

[*'Of course it is! Did you think I was going to give you a pat on the head and send you home after all we've been through?'*]

Suddenly she smiled – a wickedly mischievous smile.

[*'Besides, Ralph – do you really feel like getting up to dickens tonight? Tell me the truth. Better still, don't flatter me.'*]

He considered it, then laughed and drew her into his arms. Her mouth was sweet and slightly moist, like the skin of a ripe peach. That kiss seemed to tingle through his entire body, but the sensation was most concentrated in his mouth, where it felt almost like an electric shock. When their lips parted, he felt more excited than ever . . . but he also felt queerly drained.

[*'What if I say I do, Lois? What if I say I do want to get up to dickens?'*]

She stood back and looked at him critically, as if trying to decide whether he meant what he said or if it was just the usual male bluff and brag. At the same time her hands went to the buttons of her dress. As she began to slip them free, Ralph noticed a wonderful thing: she looked younger again. Not forty by any stretch of the imagination, but surely no more than fifty . . . and a *young* fifty. It had been the kiss, of course, and the really amusing thing was he didn't think she had the slightest idea that she had added a helping of Ralph to her earlier helping of wino. And what was wrong with that?

She finished her inspection, leaned forward, and kissed his cheek.

[*'I think that there'll be plenty of time for getting up to dickens later, Ralph – tonight's for sleeping.'*]

He supposed she was right. Five minutes ago he had been more than willing – he had always loved the act of physical love, and it had been a long time. For now, however, the spark was gone. Ralph didn't regret that in the least. He knew, after all, *where* it had gone.

[*'Okay, Lois – tonight's for sleeping.'*]

She went into the bathroom and the shower went on. A few minutes later, Ralph heard her brushing her teeth. It was nice to know she still had them. During the ten minutes she was gone he managed to do a certain amount of undressing, although his throbbing ribs made it slow work. He finally succeeded in wriggling McGovern's sweater off and pushing out of his shoes. His shirt came next, and he was fumbling ineffectually with the buckle of his belt when Lois came out with her hair tied back and her face shining. Ralph was stunned by her beauty, and suddenly felt much too big and stupid (not to mention old) for his own good. She was wearing a long rose-colored silk nightgown and he could smell the lotion she had used on her hands. It was a good smell.

'Let me do that,' she said, and had his belt unbuckled before he could say much, one way or the other. There was nothing erotic about it; she moved with the efficiency of a woman who had often helped her husband dress and undress during the last year of his life.

'We're down again,' he said. 'This time I didn't even feel it happening.'

'I did, while I was in the shower. I was glad, actually. Trying to wash your hair through an aura is very distracting.'

The wind gusted outside, shaking the house and blowing a long, shivering note across the mouth of a downspout. They looked toward the window, and although he was back down on the Short-Time level, Ralph was suddenly sure that Lois was sharing his own thought: Atropos was out there somewhere right now, no doubt disappointed by the way things had gone but by no means crushed, bloody but unbowed, down but not out. *From now on they can call him Old One-Ear,* Ralph thought, and shivered. He imagined Atropos swinging erratically through the scared, excited populace of the city like a rogue asteroid, peering and hiding, stealing souvenirs and slashing balloon-strings . . . taking solace in his work, in other words. Ralph found it almost impossible to believe that he had been sitting on top of that creature and slashing at him with his own scalpel not very long ago. *How did I ever find the courage?* he wondered, but he supposed he knew. The diamond earrings the little monster had been wearing had provided most of it. Did Atropos know those earrings had been his biggest mistake? Probably not. In his way, Doc #3 had proved even more ignorant of Short-Time motivations than Clotho and Lachesis.

He turned to Lois and grasped her hands. 'I lost your earrings again. This time they're gone for good, I think. I'm sorry.'

'Don't apologize. They were already lost, remember? And I'm not worried about Harold and Jan anymore, because now I've got a friend to help me when people don't treat me right, or when I just get scared. Don't I?'

'Yes. You most certainly do.'

She put her arms around him, hugged him tightly, and kissed him again. Lois had apparently not forgotten a single thing she'd ever learned about kissing, and it seemed to Ralph that she'd learned quite a lot. 'Go on and hop in the shower.' He started to say that he thought he'd fall asleep the moment he got his head under a stream of warm water, but then she added something which changed his mind in a hurry: 'Don't take offense, but there's a funny smell on you, especially on your hands. It's the way my brother Vic used to smell after he'd spent the day cleaning fish.'

Ralph was in the shower two minutes later, and in soapsuds up to his elbows.

10

When he came out, Lois was buried beneath two puffy quilts. Only her face showed, and that was visible only from the nose up. Ralph crossed the room quickly, wearing only his undershorts and painfully conscious of his spindly legs and potbelly. He tossed back the covers and slid in quickly, gasping a little as the cool sheets slid along his warm skin.

Lois slipped over to his side of the bed at once and put her arms around him. He put his face in her hair and let himself relax against her. It was very good, being with Lois under the quilts while the wind shrieked and gusted outside, sometimes hard enough to rattle the storm windows in their frames. It was, in fact, heaven.

'Thank God there's a man in my bed,' Lois said sleepily.

'Thank God it's me,' Ralph replied, and she laughed.

'Are your ribs okay? Do you want me to find you an aspirin?'

'Nope. I'm sure they'll hurt again in the morning, but right now the hot water seems to have loosened everything up.' The subject of what might or might not happen in the morning raised a question in his mind – one that had probably been waiting there all along. 'Lois?'

'Mmmmm?'

In his mind's eye Ralph could see himself snapping awake in the dark, deeply tired but not at all sleepy (it was surely one of the world's cruelest paradoxes), as the numbers on the digital clock turned wearily over from 3:47 a.m. to 3:48. F. Scott Fitzgerald's dark night of the soul, when every hour was long enough to build the Great Pyramid of Cheops.

'Do you think we'll sleep through?' he asked her.

'Yes,' she said unhesitatingly. 'I think we'll sleep just fine.'

A moment later, Lois was doing just that.

11

Ralph stayed awake for perhaps five minutes longer, holding her in his arms, smelling the wonderful interwoven scents rising from her warm skin, luxuriating in the smooth, sensuous glide of the silk under his hands, marvelling at where he was even more than the events which had brought him here. He was filled with some deep and simple emotion, one he recognized but could not immediately name, perhaps because it had been gone from his life too long.

The wind gusted and moaned outside, producing that hollow hooting sound over the top of the drainpipe again – like the world's biggest Nirvana Boy blowing over the mouth of the world's biggest pop-bottle – and it occurred to Ralph that maybe nothing in life was better than lying deep in a soft bed with a sleeping woman in your arms while the fall wind screamed outside your safe haven.

Except there *was* something better, one thing, at least, and that was the feeling of falling asleep, of going gently into that good night, slipping out into the currents of unknowing the way a canoe slips away from a dock and slides into the current of a wide, slow river on a bright summer day.

Of all the things which make up our Short-Time lives, sleep is surely the best, Ralph thought.

The wind gusted again outside (the sound of it now seeming to come from a great distance) and as he felt the tug of that great river take him, he was finally able to identify the emotion he had been feeling ever since Lois had put her arms around him and fallen asleep as easily and as trustingly as a child. It went under many different names – peace, serenity, fulfillment – but now, as the wind blew and Lois made some dark sound of sleeping contentment far back in her throat, it seemed to Ralph that it was one of those rare things which are known but essentially unnameable: a texture, an aura, perhaps a whole level of being in that column of existence. It was the smooth russet color of rest; it was the silence which follows the completion of some arduous but necessary task.

When the wind gusted again, bringing the sound of distant sirens with it, Ralph didn't hear it. He was asleep. Once he dreamed that he got up to use the bathroom, and he supposed that might not have been a dream. At another time he dreamed that he and Lois made slow, sweet love, and that might not have been a dream, either. If there were other dreams or moments of waking, he did not remember them, and this time there was no snapping awake at three or four o'clock in the morning. They slept – sometimes apart but mostly together – until just past seven o'clock on Saturday evening; about twenty-two hours, all told.

Lois made them breakfast at sunset – splendidly puffy waffles, bacon, home fries. While she cooked, Ralph tried to flex that muscle buried deep in his mind – to create that sensation of *blink*. He couldn't do it. When Lois tried, she was also unable, although Ralph could have sworn that just for a moment she flickered, and he could see the stove right through her.

'Just as well,' she said, bringing their plates to the table.

'I suppose,' Ralph agreed, but he still felt as he would have if he had lost the ring Carolyn had given him instead of the one he had taken from Atropos – as if some small but essential object had gone rolling out of his life with a wink and a gleam.

12

Following two more nights of sound, unbroken sleep, the auras had begun to fade, as well. By the following week they were gone, and Ralph began to wonder if perhaps the whole thing hadn't been some strange dream. He knew that wasn't so, but it became harder and harder to believe what he *did* know. There was the scar between the elbow and wrist of his right arm, of course, but he even began to wonder if that wasn't something he had acquired long ago, during those years of his life when there had been no white in his hair and he had still believed, deep in his heart, that old age was a myth, or a dream, or a thing reserved for people not as special as he was.

EPILOGUE:

Winding the Deathwatch (II)

Glancing over my shoulder I see its shape
and so move forward, as someone in the woods
at night might hear the sound of approaching feet
and stop to listen; then, instead of silence
he hears some creature trying to be silent.
What else can he do but run? Rushing blindly
down the path, stumbling, struck in the face by sticks;
the other ever closer, yet not really
hurrying or out of breath, teasing its kill.

Stephen Dobyns
'Pursuit'

If I had some wings, I'd fly you all around;
If I had some money, I'd buy you the goddam town;
If I had the strength, then maybe I coulda pulled you through;
If I had a lantern, I'd light the way for you,
If I had a lantern, I'd light the way for you.

Michael McDermott
'Lantern'

On January 2nd, 1994, Lois Chasse became Lois Roberts. Her son, Harold, gave her away. Harold's wife did not attend the ceremony; she was up in Bangor with what Ralph considered a highly suspect case of bronchitis. He kept his suspicions to himself, however, being far from disappointed at Jan Chasse's failure to appear. The groom's best man was Detective John Leydecker, who still wore a cast on his right arm but otherwise showed no signs of the assignment which had nearly killed him. He had spent four days in a coma, but Leydecker knew how lucky he was; in addition to the State Trooper who had been standing beside him at the time of the explosion, six cops had died, two of them members of Leydecker's handpicked team.

The bride's maid of honor was her friend Simone Castonguay, and at the reception, the first toast was made by a fellow who liked to say he used to be Joe Wyze but was now older and Wyzer. Trigger Vachon delivered a fractured but heartfelt follow-up, concluding with the wish that 'Dese two people gonna live to a hunnert and fifty and never know a day of the rheumatiz or constipations!'

When Ralph and Lois left the reception hall, their hair still full of rice thrown for the most part by Faye Chapin and the rest of the Harris Avenue Old Crocks, an old man with a book in his hand and a fine cloud of white hair floating around his head came walking up to them. He had a wide smile on his face.

'Congratulations, Ralph,' he said. 'Congratulations, Lois.'

'Thanks, Dor,' Ralph said.

'We missed you,' Lois told him. 'Didn't you get your invitation? Faye said he'd give it to you.'

'Oh, he gave it to me. Yes, oh yes, he did, but I don't go to those things if they're inside. Too stuffy. Funerals are even worse. Here, this is for you. I didn't wrap it, because the arthritis is in my fingers too bad for stuff like that now.'

Ralph took it. It was a book of poems called *Concurring Beasts*. The poet's name, Stephen Dobyns, gave him a funny little chill, but he wasn't quite sure why.

'Thanks,' he told Dorrance.

'Not as good as some of his later work, but good. Dobyns is very good.'

'We'll read them to each other on our honeymoon,' Lois said.

'That's a good time to read poetry,' Dorrance said. 'Maybe the best time. I'm sure you'll be very happy together.'

He started off, then looked back.

'You did a great thing. The Long-Timers are very pleased.'

He walked away.

Lois looked at Ralph. 'What was he talking about? Do you know?'

Ralph shook his head. He didn't, not for sure, although he felt as if he *should* know. The scar on his arm had begun to tingle as it sometimes did, a feeling which was almost like a deep-seated itch.

'Long-Timers,' she mused. 'Maybe he meant us, Ralph – after all, we're hardly spring chickens these days, are we?'

'That's probably just what he *did* mean,' Ralph agreed, but he knew better . . . and her eyes said that, somewhere deep down, so did she.

2

On that same day, and just as Ralph and Lois were saying their 'I do's, a certain wino with a bright green aura – one who actually *did* have an uncle in Dexter, although the uncle hadn't seen this ne'er-do-well nephew for five years or more – was tramping across Strawford Park, slitting his eyes against the formidable glare of sun on snow. He was looking for returnable cans and bottles. Enough to buy a pint of whiskey would be great, but a pint of Night Train wine would do.

Not far from the Portosan marked MEN, he saw a bright gleam of metal. It was probably just the sun reflecting off a bottle-cap, but such things needed to be checked out. It might be a dime . . . although to the wino, it actually seemed to have a goldy sort of gleam. It—

'Holy Judas!' he cried, snatching up the wedding ring which lay mysteriously on top of the snow. It was a broad band, almost certainly gold. He tilted it to read the engraving on the inside: HD – ED 5–8–87.

A pint? Hell, no. This little baby was going to secure him a quart. *Several* quarts. Possibly a *week's* worth of quarts.

Hurrying across the intersection of Witcham and Jackson, the one where Ralph Roberts had once almost fainted, the wino never saw the approaching Green Line bus. The driver saw him, and put on his brakes, but the bus struck a patch of ice.

The wino never knew what hit him. At one moment he was debating between Old Crow and Old Grand Dad; at the next he had passed into the darkness which awaits us all. The ring rolled down the gutter and disappeared into a sewer grate, and there it remained for a long, long time. But not forever. In Derry, things that disappear into the sewer system have a way – an often unpleasant one – of turning up.

3

Ralph and Lois didn't live happily ever after.

There really *are* no evers in the Short-Time world, happy or otherwise, a fact which Clotho and Lachesis undoubtedly knew well. They *did* live happily for quite some time, though. Neither of them liked to come right out and say these were the happiest years of all, because both remembered their first partners in marriage with love and affection, but in their hearts, both *did* consider them the happiest. Ralph wasn't sure that autumn love was the richest love, but he came firmly to believe that it was the kindest, and the most fulfilling.

Our Lois, he often said, and laughed. Lois pretended to be irritated at this, but pretending was all it ever was; she saw the look in his eyes when he said it.

On their first Christmas morning as man and wife (they had moved into Lois's tidy little house and put his own white rhino up for sale), Lois gave him a beagle puppy. 'Do you like her?' she asked apprehensively. 'I almost didn't get her, Dear Abby says you should *never* give pets as presents, but she looked so sweet in the petshop window . . . and so *sad* . . . if you don't like her, or don't want to spend the rest of the winter trying to housebreak a puppy, just say so. We'll find someone—'

'Lois,' he said, giving his eyebrow what he hoped was that special ironic Bill McGovern lift, 'you're babbling.'

'I am?'

'You am. It's something you do when you're nervous, but you can stop being nervous right now. I'm crazy 'bout dis lady.' Nor was that an exaggeration; he fell in love with the black-and-tan beagle bitch almost at once.

'What will you name her?' Lois asked. 'Any idea?'

'Sure,' Ralph said. 'Rosalie.'

4

The next four years were, by and large, good ones for Helen and Nat Deepneau, as well. They lived frugally in an apartment on the east side of town for awhile, getting along on Helen's librarian's salary but not doing much more than that. The little Cape Cod up the street from Ralph's place had sold, but that money had gone to pay outstanding bills. Then, in June of 1994, Helen received an insurance windfall . . . only the wind that blew it her way was John Leydecker.

The Great Eastern Insurance Company had originally refused to pay off on Ed Deepneau's life insurance policy, claiming he had taken his own life. Then, after a great deal of harrumphing and muttering under their corporate breath, they had offered a substantial settlement. They were persuaded to do this by a poker-buddy of John Leydecker's named Howard Hayman. When he wasn't playing lowball, five-card stud, and three-card draw, Hayman was a lawyer who enjoyed lunching on insurance companies.

Leydecker had re-met Helen at Ralph and Lois's in February of 1994, had fallen head over heels in fascination with her ('It was never quite love,' he told Ralph and Lois later, 'which was probably just as well, considering how things turned out'), and had introduced her to Hayman because he thought the insurance company was trying to screw her. 'He was *insane,* not suicidal,' Leydecker said, and stuck to that long after Helen had handed him his hat and shown him the door.

After being faced with a suit in which Howard Hayman threatened to make Great Eastern look like Snidely Whiplash tying Little Nell to the railroad tracks, Helen had received a check for seventy thousand dollars. In the late fall of 1994 she had used most of this money to buy a house on Harris Avenue, just three doors up from her old place and right across from Harriet Bennigan's.

'I was never really happy on the east side,' she told Lois one day in November of that year. They were on their way back from the park, and Natalie had been sitting slumped and fast asleep in her stroller, her presence little more than a pink nose-tip and a fog of cold breath below a large ski-hat which Lois had knitted herself. 'I used to dream about Harris Avenue. Isn't that crazy?'

'I don't think dreams are *ever* crazy,' Lois replied.

Helen and John Leydecker dated for most of that summer, but neither Ralph nor Lois was particularly surprised when the courtship abruptly ended after Labor Day, or when Helen began to wear a discreet pink triangle pin on her prim, high-necked librarian's blouses. Perhaps they were not surprised because they were old enough to have seen everything at least once, or perhaps on some deep level they were still glimpsing the auras which surround things, creating a bright gateway opening on a secret city of hidden meanings, concealed motives, and camouflaged agendas.

5

Ralph and Lois babysat Natalie frequently after Helen moved back to Harris Avenue, and they enjoyed these stints tremendously. Nat was the child their marriage might have produced if it had happened thirty years sooner, and the coldest, most overcast winter day warmed and brightened when Natalie came toddling in, looking like a midget version of the Goodyear blimp in her pink quilted snowsuit with the mittens hanging from the cuffs, and yelled exuberantly: 'Hi, Walf! Hi, Roliss! I come to bizzit you!'

In June of 1995, Helen bought a reconditioned Volvo. On the back she put a sticker which read A WOMAN NEEDS A MAN LIKE A FISH NEEDS A BICYCLE. This sentiment did not particularly surprise Ralph, either, but glimpsing that sticker always made him feel unhappy. He sometimes thought Ed's meanest legacy to his widow was summed up in its brittle, not-quite-funny sentiment, and when he saw it, Ralph often remembered how Ed had looked on that summer afternoon when he had walked up from the Red Apple Store to confront him. How Ed had been sitting, shirtless, in the spray thrown by the sprinkler. How there had been a drop of blood on one lens of his glasses. How he had leaned forward, looking at Ralph with his earnest, intelligent eyes, and said that once stupidity reached a certain level, it became hard to live with.

And after that, stuff started to happen, Ralph would sometimes think. Just what stuff was something he could no longer remember, though, and probably that was just as well. But his lapse of memory (if that was what it was) did not change his belief that Helen had been cheated in some obscure fashion . . . that some bad-tempered fate had tied a can to her tail, and she didn't even know it.

6

A month after Helen bought her Volvo, Faye Chapin suffered a heart attack while drafting a preliminary list of seeds for that fall's Runway 3 Classic. He was taken to Derry Home Hospital, where he died seven hours later. Ralph visited him shortly before the end, and when he saw the numbers on the door – 315 – a fierce sense of *déjà vu* washed over him. At first he thought it was because Carolyn had finished her last illness just up the hall, and then he remembered that Jimmy V had died in this very room. He and Lois had visited Jimmy just before the end, and Ralph thought Jimmy had recognized them both, although he couldn't be sure; his memories of the time when he had first begun to really notice Lois were mixed up and hazy in his mind. He supposed some of that was love, and probably some of it had to do with getting on in years, but probably most of it had been the insomnia – he'd gone through a really bad patch of that in the months after Carolyn's death, although it had eventually cured itself, as such things sometimes did. Still, it seemed to him that something

([*hello woman hello man we've been waiting for you*])

far out of the ordinary had happened in this room, and as he took Faye's dry, strengthless hand and smiled into Faye's frightened, confused eyes, a strange thought came to him: *They're standing right over there in the corner and watching us.*

He looked over. There was no one at all in the corner, of course, but for a moment . . . for just a moment . . .

7

Life in the years between 1993 and 1998 went on as life in places like Derry always does: the buds of April became the brittle, blowing leaves of October; Christmas trees were brought into homes in mid-December and hauled off in the backs of Dumpsters with strands of tinsel still hanging sadly from their boughs during the first week of January; babies came in through the in door and old folks went out through the out door. Sometimes people in the prime of their lives went out through the out door, too.

In Derry there were five years of haircuts and permanents, storms and senior proms, coffee and cigarettes, steak dinners at Parker's Cove and hotdogs at the Little League field. Girls and boys fell in love, drunks fell out of cars, short skirts fell out of favor. People reshingled their roofs and repaved their driveways. Old bums were voted out of office; new bums were voted in. It was life, often unsatisfying, frequently cruel, usually boring, sometimes beautiful, once in awhile exhilarating. The fundamental things continued to apply as time went by.

In the early fall of 1996, Ralph became convinced he had colon cancer. He had begun to see more than trace amounts of blood in his stool, and when he finally went to see Dr. Pickard (Dr. Litchfield's cheerful, rumpled replacement), he did so with visions of hospital beds and chemotherapy IV-drips dancing bleakly in his head. Instead of cancer, the problem turned out to be a hemorrhoid which had, in Dr. Pickard's memorable phrase, 'popped its top.' He wrote Ralph a prescription for suppositories, which Ralph took to the Rite Aid down the street. Joe Wyzer read it, then grinned cheerfully at Ralph. 'Lousy,' he said, 'but it beats the hell out of colon cancer, don't you think?'

'The thought of colon cancer never crossed my mind,' Ralph replied stiffly.

One day during the winter of 1997, Lois took it into her head to slide down her favorite hill in Strawford Park on Nat Deepneau's plastic flying-saucer sled. She went down 'faster'n a pig in a greased chute' (this was Don Veazie's phrase; he just happened to be there that day, watching the action) and crashed into the side of the Portosan marked WOMEN. She sprained her knee and twisted her back, and although Ralph knew he had no business doing so – it was unsympathetic to say the least – he laughed hilariously most of the way to the emergency room. The fact that Lois was also howling with laughter despite the pain did nothing to help Ralph regain control. He laughed until tears poured from his eyes and he thought he might have a stroke. She had just looked so goddamned *Our Lois* going down the hill on that thing, spinning around and around with her legs crossed like one of those yogis from the Mysterious East, and she had almost knocked the Portosan over when she hit it. She was completely recovered by the time spring rolled around, although that knee always ached on rainy nights and she *did* get tired of Don Veazie asking, almost every time he saw her, if she'd slid into any shithouses lately.

8

Just life, going on as it always does – which is to say mostly between the lines and outside the margins. It's what happens while we're making other plans, according to some sage or other, and if life was exceptionally good to Ralph Roberts during those years, it might have been because he had no other plans to make. He maintained friendships with Joe Wyzer and John Leydecker, but his best friend during those years was his wife. They went almost everywhere together, had no secrets, and fought so seldom one might just as well have said never. He also had Rosalie the beagle, the rocker that had once been Mr Chasse's and was now his, and almost daily visits from Natalie (who had begun calling them Ralph and Lois instead of Walf and Roliss, a change neither of them found to be an improvement). And he was healthy, which was maybe the best thing of all. It was just life, full of Short-Time rewards and setbacks, and Ralph lived it with enjoyment and serenity until mid-March of 1998, when he awoke one morning, glanced at the digital clock beside his bed, and saw it was 5:49 a.m.

He lay quietly beside Lois, not wanting to disturb her by getting up, and wondering what had awakened him.

You know what, Ralph.

No I don't.

Yes, you do. Listen.

So he listened. He listened very carefully. And after awhile he began to hear it in the walls: the low, soft ticking of the deathwatch.

9

Ralph awoke at 5:47 the following morning, and at 5:44 the morning after that. His sleep was whittled away, minute by minute, as winter slowly loosened its grip on Derry and allowed spring to find its way back in. By May he was hearing the tick of the deathwatch everywhere, but understood it was all coming from one place and simply projecting itself, as a good ventriloquist can project his voice. Before, it had been coming from Carolyn. Now it was coming from him.

He felt none of the terror that had gripped him when he'd been so sure he had developed cancer, and none of the desperation he vaguely remembered from his previous bout of insomnia. He tired more easily and began to find it more difficult to concentrate and remember even simple things, but he accepted what was happening calmly.

'Are you sleeping all right, Ralph?' Lois asked him one day. 'You're getting these big dark circles under your eyes.'

'It's the dope I take,' Ralph said.

'Very funny, you old poop.'

He took her in his arms and hugged her. 'Don't worry about me, sweetheart – I'm getting all the sleep I need.'

He awoke one morning a week later at 4:02 a.m. with a line of deep heat throbbing in his arm – throbbing in perfect sync with the sound of the deathwatch, which was, of course, nothing more or less than the beat of his own heart. But this new thing wasn't his heart, or at least Ralph didn't think it was; it felt as if an electric filament had been embedded in the flesh of his forearm.

It's the scar, he thought, and then: *No, it's the promise. The time of the promise is almost here.*

What promise, Ralph? What promise?

He didn't know.

10

One day in early June, Helen and Nat blew in to visit and tell Ralph and Lois about the trip they had taken to Boston with 'Aunt Melanie,' a bank teller with whom Helen had become close friends. Helen and Aunt Melanie had gone to some sort of feminist convention while Natalie networked with about a billion new kids in the day-care center, and then Aunt Melanie had left to do some more feminist things in New York and Washington. Helen and Nat had stayed on in Boston for a couple of days, just sightseeing.

'We went to see a movie cartoon,' Natalie said. 'It was about animals in the woods. They talked!' She pronounced this last word with Shakespearian grandiosity – *talked*.

'Movies where animals talk are neat, aren't they?' Lois asked.

'Yes! Also I got this new dress!'

'And a very pretty dress it is,' Lois said.

Helen was looking at Ralph. 'Are you okay, old chum? You look pale, and you haven't said boo.'

'Never better,' he said. 'I was just thinking how cute you two look in those caps. Did you get them at Fenway Park?'

Both Helen and Nat were wearing Boston Red Sox caps. These were common enough in New England during warm weather ('common as catdirt,' Lois would have said), but the sight of them on the heads of these two people filled Ralph with some deep, resonant feeling . . . and it was tied to a specific image, one he did not in the least understand: the front of the Red Apple Store.

Helen, meantime, had taken off her hat and was examining it. 'Yes,' she said. 'We went, but we only stayed for three innings. Men hitting balls and catching balls. I guess I just don't have much patience for men and their balls these days . . . but we like our nifty Bosox hats, don't we, Natalie?'

'Yes!' Nat agreed smartly, and when Ralph awoke the next morning at 4:01, the scar throbbed its thin line of heat inside his arm and the deathwatch seemed almost to have gained a voice, one which whispered a strange, foreign-sounding name over and over: *Atropos . . . Atropos . . . Atropos.*

I know that name.

Do you, Ralph?

Yes, he was the one with the rusty scalpel and the nasty disposition, the one who called me Shorts, the one who took . . . took . . .

Took what, Ralph?

He was getting used to these silent discussions; they seemed to come to him on some mental radio band, a pirate frequency that operated only during the little hours, the ones when he lay awake beside his sleeping wife, waiting for the sun to come up.

Took what? Do you remember?

He didn't *expect* to; the questions that voice asked him almost always went unanswered, but this time, unexpectedly, an answer came.

Bill McGovern's hat, of course. Atropos took Bill's hat, and once I made him so mad he actually took a bite out of the brim.

Who is he? Who is Atropos?

Of this he was not so sure. He only knew that Atropos had something to do with Helen, who now owned a Boston Red Sox cap of which she seemed very fond, and that he had a rusty scalpel.

Soon, thought Ralph Roberts as he lay in the dark, listening to the soft, steady tick of the deathwatch in the walls. *I'll know soon.*

11

During the third week of that baking hot June, Ralph began to see the auras again.

12

As June slipped into July, Ralph found himself bursting into tears often, usually for no discernible reason at all. It was strange; he had no sense of depression or discontent, but sometimes he would look at something – maybe only a bird winging its solitary way across the sky – and his heart would vibrate with sorrow and loss.

It's almost over, the inside voice said. It no longer belonged to Carolyn or Bill or even his own younger self; it was all its own now, the voice of a stranger, although not necessarily an unkind one. *That's why you're sad, Ralph. It's perfectly normal to be sad as things start to wind down.*

Nothing's almost over! he cried back. *Why should it be? At my last checkup, Dr Pickard said I was sound as a drum! I'm fine! Never better!*

Silence from the voice inside. But it was a *knowing* silence.

13

'Okay,' Ralph said out loud one hot afternoon near the end of July. He was sitting on a bench not far from the place where the Derry Standpipe had stood until 1985, when the big storm had come along and knocked it down. At the base of the hill, near the birdbath, a young man (a serious birdwatcher, from the binoculars he wore and the thick stack of paperbacks on the grass beside him) was making careful notes in what looked like some sort of journal. 'Okay, tell me *why* it's almost over. Just tell me that.'

There was no immediate answer, but that was all right; Ralph was willing to wait. It had been quite a stroll over here, the day was hot, and he was tired. He was now waking around three-thirty every morning. He had begun taking long walks again, but not in any hope they would help him sleep better or longer; he thought he was making pilgrimages, visiting all his favorite spots in Derry one last time. Saying goodbye.

Because the time of the promise has almost come, the voice answered, and the scar began to throb with its deep, narrow heat again. *The one that was made to you, and the one you made in return.*

'What was it?' he asked, agitated. 'Please, if I made a promise, *why can't I remember what it was?*'

The serious birdwatcher heard that and looked up the hill. What he saw was a man sitting on a park bench and apparently having a conversation with himself. The corners of the serious birdwatcher's mouth turned down in disgust and he thought, *I hope I die before I get that old. I really do.* Then he turned back to the birdbath and began making notes again.

Deep inside Ralph's head, the clenching sensation – that feeling of *blink* – suddenly came again, and although he didn't stir from the bench, Ralph felt himself propelled rapidly upward none the less . . . faster and further than ever before.

Not at all, the voice said. *Once you were* much *higher than this, Ralph – Lois, too. But you're getting there. You'll be ready soon.*

The birdwatcher, who lived all unknowing in the center of a gorgeous spun-gold aura, looked around cautiously, perhaps wanting to make sure that the senile old man on the bench at the top of the hill wasn't creeping up on him with a blunt instrument. What he saw caused the tight, prissy line of his mouth to soften in astonishment. His eyes widened. Ralph observed sudden radiating spokes of indigo in the serious birdwatcher's aura and realized he was looking at shock.

What's the matter with him? What does he see?

But that was wrong. It wasn't what the birdwatcher *saw*; it was what he *didn't* see. He didn't see *Ralph,* because Ralph had gone up high enough to disappear from this level – had become the visual equivalent of a note blown on a dog-whistle.

If they were here now, I could see them easily.

Who, Ralph? If who was here?

Clotho. Lachesis. And Atropos.

All at once the pieces began to fly together in his mind, like the pieces of a jigsaw puzzle that had looked a great deal more complicated than it actually was.

Ralph, whispering: [*'Oh my God. Oh my God. Oh my God.'*]

14

Six days later, Ralph awoke at quarter past three in the morning and knew that the time of the promise had come.

15

'I think I'll walk upstreet to the Red Apple and get an ice-cream bar,' Ralph said. It was almost ten o'clock. His heart was beating much too fast, and his thoughts were hard to find under the constant white noise of terror which now filled him. He had never felt less like ice-cream in his entire life, but it was a reasonable enough excuse for a trip to the Red Apple; it was the first week of August, and the weatherman had said the mercury would probably top ninety by early afternoon, with thunderstorms to follow in the early evening.

Ralph thought he needn't worry about the thunderstorms.

A bookcase stood on a spread of newspapers by the kitchen door. Lois had been painting it barn-red. Now she got to her feet, put her hands into the small of her back, and stretched. Ralph could hear the minute crackling sounds of her spine. 'I'll go with you. My head'll ache tonight if I don't get away from that paint for awhile. I don't know why I wanted to paint on such a muggy day in the first place.'

The last thing on earth Ralph wanted was to be accompanied up to the Red Apple by Lois. 'You don't have to, honey; I'll bring you back one of those coconut Popsicles you like. I wasn't even planning on taking Rosalie, it's so humid. Go sit on the back porch, why don't you?'

'Any Popsicle you carry back from the store on a day like this will be falling off the stick by the time you get it here,' she said. 'Come on, let's go while there's still shade on this side of the . . .'

She trailed off. The little smile she'd been wearing slipped off her face. It was replaced by a look of dismay, and the gray of her aura, which had only darkened slightly during the years Ralph hadn't been able to see it, now began to glow with flocks of reddish-pink embers.

'Ralph, what's wrong? What are you really going to do?'

'Nothing,' he said, but the scar was glowing inside his arm and the tick of the deathwatch was everywhere, loud and everywhere. It was telling him he had an appointment to keep. A *promise* to keep.

'Yes, there is, and it's been wrong for the last two or three months, maybe longer. I'm a foolish woman – I knew something was happening, but I couldn't bring myself to look at it dead-on. Because I was afraid. And I was right to be afraid, wasn't I? I was right.'

'Lois—'

She was suddenly crossing the room to him, crossing fast, almost *leaping,* the old back injury not slowing her down in the least, and before he could stop her, she had seized his right arm and was holding it out, looking at it fixedly.

The scar was glowing a fierce bright red.

Ralph had a moment to hope that it was strictly an aural glow and she wouldn't be able to see it. Then she looked up, her eyes round and full of terror. Terror, and something else. Ralph thought that something else was recognition.

'Oh my God,' she whispered. 'The men in the park. The

ones with the funny names . . . Clothes and Lashes, something like that . . . and one of them cut you. Oh Ralph, oh my God, *what are you supposed to do?*'

'Now, Lois, don't take on—'

'*Don't you dare tell me not to take on!*' she shrieked into his face. '*Don't you dare! Don't you DARE!*'

Hurry, the interior voice whispered. *You don't have time to stand around and discuss this; somewhere it's already begun to happen, and the deathwatch you hear may not be ticking just for you.*

'I have to go.' He turned and blundered toward the door. In his agitation he did not notice a certain Sherlock Holmesian circumstance attending this scene: a dog which should have barked – a dog which *always* barked her stern disapproval when voices were raised in this house – but did not. Rosalie was missing from her usual place by the screen door . . . and the door itself was standing ajar.

Rosalie was the furthest thing from Ralph's mind at that moment. He felt knee-deep in molasses, and thought he would be doing well just to make the porch, let alone the Red Apple up the street. His heart thumped and skidded in his chest; his eyes were burning.

'*No!*' Lois screamed. '*No, Ralph, please! Please don't leave me!*'

She ran after him, clutched his arm. She was still holding her paintbrush, and the fine red droplets which splattered his shirt looked like blood. Now she was crying, and her expression of utter, abject sorrow nearly broke his heart. He didn't want to leave her like this; wasn't sure he *could* leave her like this.

He turned and took her by her forearms. 'Lois, I *have* to go.'

'You haven't been sleeping,' she babbled, 'I knew that, and I knew it meant something was wrong, but it doesn't matter, we'll go away, we can leave right now, this minute, we'll just take Rosalie and our toothbrushes and go—'

He squeezed her arms and she stopped, looking up at him with her wet eyes. Her lips were trembling.

'Lois, listen to me. *I have to do this.*'

'*I lost Paul, I can't lose you, too!*' she wailed. '*I couldn't stand it! Oh Ralph, I couldn't stand it!*'

You'll be able to, he thought. *Short-Timers are a lot tougher than they look. They have to be.*

Ralph felt a couple of tears trickle down his cheeks. He suspected their source was more weariness than grief. If he could make her see that all this changed nothing, only made what he had to do harder . . .

He held her at arm's length. The scar on his arm was throbbing more fiercely than ever, and the feeling of time slipping relentlessly away had become overwhelming.

'Walk with me at least partway, if you want,' he said. 'Maybe you can even help me do what I have to do. I've *had* my life, Lois, and a fine one it was. But *she* hasn't really had anything yet, and I'll be damned if I'll let that son of a bitch have *her* just because he's got a score to settle with me.'

'What son of a bitch? Ralph, what in the world are you talking about?'

'I'm talking about Natalie Deepneau. She's supposed to die this morning, only I'm not going to let that happen.'

'*Nat?* Ralph, why would anyone want to hurt Nat?'

She looked very bewildered, very *our Lois* . . . but wasn't there something else beneath that daffy exterior? Something careful and calculating? Ralph thought the answer was yes. Ralph had an idea Lois wasn't half as bewildered as she was pretending to be. She had fooled Bill McGovern for years with that act – him, too, at least part of the time – and this was just another (and rather brilliant) variation of the same old scam.

What she was *really* trying to do was hold him here. She loved Nat deeply, but to Lois, a choice between her husband and the little girl who lived up the lane was no choice at all. She didn't consider either age or questions of fairness to have any bearing on the situation. Ralph was her man, and to Lois, that was all that mattered.

'It won't work,' he said, not unkindly. He disengaged himself and started for the door again. 'I made a promise, and I'm all out of time.'

'Break it, then!' she cried, and the mixture of terror and rage in her voice stunned him. 'I don't remember much about that time, but I remember we got involved with things that almost got us killed, and for reasons we couldn't even understand. So break it, Ralph! Better your promise than my heart!'

'And what about the kid? What about *Helen,* for that matter? Nat's all she lives for. Doesn't Helen deserve something better from me than a broken promise?'

'I don't *care* what she deserves! What *any* of them deserve!' she shouted, and then her face crumpled. 'Yes, all right, I suppose I do. But what about *us,* Ralph? Don't we count?' Her eyes, those dark and eloquent Spanish eyes of hers, pleaded with him. If he

638

looked into them too long, it would become all too easy to cry it off, so Ralph looked away.

'I mean to do it, honey. Nat's going to get what you and I have already had – another seventy years or so of days and nights.'

She looked at him helplessly, but made no attempt to stop him again. Instead, she began to cry. 'Foolish old man!' she whispered. 'Foolish, willful old man!'

'Yes, I suppose,' he said, and lifted her chin. 'But I'm a foolish, willful old man of my word. Come with me. I'd like that.'

'All right, Ralph.' She could hardly hear her own voice, and her skin was as cold as clay. Her aura had gone almost completely red. 'What is it? What's going to happen to her?'

'She's going to be hit by a green Ford sedan. Unless I take her place, she's going to be splashed all over Harris Avenue . . . and Helen's going to see it happen.'

16

As they walked up the hill toward the Red Apple (at first Lois kept falling behind, then trotting to catch up, but she quit when she saw she could not slow him with such a simple trick), Ralph told her what little more he could. She had some memory of being under the lightning-struck tree out by the Extension – a memory she had believed, at least until this morning, to be the memory of a dream – but of course she hadn't been there during Ralph's final confrontation with Atropos. Ralph told her of it now – of the random death Atropos intended Natalie to suffer if Ralph continued standing in the way of his plans. He told her of how he'd extracted a promise from Clotho and Lachesis that Atropos might in this case be overruled, and Nat saved.

'I have an idea that . . . the decision was made . . . very near the top of this crazy building . . . this Tower . . . they kept talking about. Maybe . . . at the *very* top.' He was panting out the words and his heart was beating more rapidly than ever, but he thought most of that could be attributed to the fast walk and the torrid day; his fear had subsided somewhat. Talking to Lois had done that much.

Now he could see the Red Apple. Mrs Perrine was at the bus stop half a block further up, standing straight as a general reviewing troops. Her net shopping bag hung over her arm.

There was a bus shelter nearby, and it was shady inside, but Mrs Perrine stolidly ignored its existence. Even in the dazzling sunlight he could see that her aura was the same West Point gray as it had been on that October evening in 1993. Of Helen and Nat there was as yet no sign.

17

'Of course I knew who he was,' Esther Perrine later tells the reporter from the Derry News. 'Do I look incompetent to you, young man? Or senile? I've known Ralph Roberts for over twenty years. A good man. Not cut from the same cloth as his first wife, of course – Carolyn was a Satterwaite, from the Bangor Satterwaites – but a very fine man, just the same. I recognized the driver of that green Ford auto, too, right away. Pete Sullivan delivered my paper for six years, and he did a good job. The new one, the Morrison boy, always throws it in my flower-beds or up on the porch roof. Pete was driving with his mother, on his learner's permit, I understand. I hope he won't take on too much about what happened, for he's a good lad, and it really wasn't his fault. I saw the whole thing, and I'll take my oath on it.

'I suppose you think I'm rambling. Don't bother denying it; I can read your face just like it was your own newspaper. Never mind, though – I've said most of what I have to say. I knew it was Ralph right away, but here's something you'll get wrong even if you put it in your story . . . which you probably won't. He came from nowhere to save that little girl.'

Esther Perrine fixes the respectfully silent young reporter with a formidable glance – fixes him as a lepidopterist might fix a butterfly on a pin after administering the chloroform.

'I don't mean it was like he came from nowhere, young man, although I bet that's what you'll print.'

She leans toward the reporter, her eyes never leaving his face, and says it again.

'He came from nowhere to save that little girl. Do you follow me? From nowhere.'

18

The accident made the front page of the following day's *Derry News*. Esther Perrine was sufficiently colorful in her remarks to warrant a sidebar of her own, and staff photographer Tom Matthews got a picture to go with it that made her look like Ma Joad in *The Grapes of Wrath*. The headline of the sidebar read: 'IT WAS LIKE HE CAME FROM NOWHERE,' EYEWITNESS TO TRAGEDY SAYS.

When she read it, Mrs Perrine was not at all surprised.

19

'In the end I got what I wanted,' Ralph said, 'but only because Clotho and Lachesis – and whoever it is they work for on the upper levels – were desperate to stop Ed.'

'Upper levels? What upper levels? What *building*?'

'Never mind. You've forgotten, but remembering wouldn't change anything. The point is just this, Lois: they didn't want to stop Ed because thousands of people would have died if he'd hit the Civic Center dead-on. They wanted to stop him because there was one person whose life needed to be preserved at any cost . . . in *their* reckoning, anyway. When I was finally able to make them see that I felt the same about my kid as they did about theirs, arrangements were made.'

'That's when they cut you, wasn't it? And when you made the promise. The one you used to talk about in your sleep.'

He shot her a wide-eyed, startled, and heartbreakingly boyish glance. She only looked back.

'Yes,' he said, and wiped his forehead. 'I guess so.' The air lay in his lungs like metal shavings. 'A life for a life, that was the deal – Natalie's in exchange for mine. And—'

[*Hey! Quit tryin to wiggle away! Quit it, Rover, or I'll kick your asshole square!*]

Ralph broke off at the sound of that shrill, hectoring, horridly familiar voice – a voice no human being on Harris Avenue but him could hear – and looked across the street.

'Ralph? What—'

'Shhh!'

He pulled her back against the summer-dry hedge in front of the Applebaums' house. He wasn't doing anything so polite as perspiring now; his whole body was crawling with a stinking sweat as heavy as engine oil, and he could feel every gland in his body dumping a hot load into his blood. His underwear was trying to crawl up into the crack of his ass and disappear. His tongue tasted like a blown fuse.

Lois followed the direction of his gaze. 'Rosalie!' she cried. 'Rosalie, you bad dog! What are *you* doing over there?'

The black-and-tan beagle she had given Ralph on their first Christmas was across the street, standing (except *cringing* was actually the word for what she was doing) on the sidewalk in front of the house where Helen and Nat had lived until Ed had popped his wig. For the first time in the years they'd had her, the beagle reminded Lois of Rosalie #1. Rosalie #2 appeared to be all alone over there, but that did not allay Lois's sudden terror.

Oh, what have I done? she thought. *What have I done?*

'*Rosalie!*' she screamed. '*Rosalie, get over here!*'

The dog heard, Lois could see that she did, but she didn't move.

'Ralph? What's happening over there?'

'*Shhhh!*' he said again, and then, just a little further up the street, Lois saw something which stopped her breath. Her last, unstated hope that all this was happening only in Ralph's head, that it was a kind of flashback to their previous experience, disappeared, because now their dog had company.

Holding a skip-rope looped over her right arm, six-year-old Nat Deepneau came to the end of her walk and looked down the street toward a house she didn't remember ever living in, toward a lawn where her shirtless father, an undesignated player named Ed Deepneau, had once sat among intersecting rainbows, listening to the Jefferson Airplane as a single spot of blood dried on his John Lennon spectacles. Natalie looked down the street and smiled happily at Rosalie, who was panting and watching her with miserable, frightened eyes.

20

Atropos doesn't see me, Ralph thought. *He's concentrating on Rosie . . . and on Natalie, of course . . . and he doesn't see me.*

Everything had come around with a sort of hideous perfection. The house was there, Rosalie was there, and Atropos was there, too, wearing a hat cocked back on his head and looking like a wiseacre news reporter in a 1950s B-picture – something directed by Ida Lupino, perhaps. Only this time it wasn't a Panama with a bite gone from the brim; this time it was a Boston Red Sox cap and it was too small even for Atropos because the adjustable band in the back had been pulled all the way over to the last hole. It had to be, in order to fit the head of the little girl who owned it.

All we need now is Pete the paperboy and the show would be perfect, Ralph thought. *The final scene of* Insomnia, *or,* Short-Time Life on Harris Avenue, a Tragi-Comedy in Three Acts. *Everyone takes a bow and then exits stage right.*

This dog was afraid of Atropos, just as Rosalie #1 had been, and the main reason the little bald doc hadn't seen Ralph and Lois was that he was trying to keep her from running off before he was ready. And here came Nat, headed down the sidewalk toward her favorite dog in the whole world, Ralph and Lois's Rosalie. Her jump-rope

(*three-six-nine, hon, the goose drank wine*)

was slung over her arm. She looked impossibly beautiful and impossibly fragile in her sailor shirt and blue shorts. Her pigtails bounced.

It's happening too fast, Ralph thought. *Everything is happening much too fast.*

[*Not at all, Ralph! You did splendidly five years ago; you'll do splendidly now.*]

It sounded like Clotho, but there was no time to look. A green car was coming slowly down Harris Avenue from the direction of the airport, moving with the sort of agonized care which usually meant a driver who was very old or very young. Agonized care or not, it was unquestionably *the* car; a dirty membrane hung over it like a shroud.

Life is a wheel, Ralph thought, and it occurred to him that this was not the first time the idea had occurred to him. *Sooner*

or later everything you thought you'd left behind comes around again.
For good or ill, it comes around again.

Rosie made another abortive lunge for freedom, and as Atropos yanked her back, losing his hat, Nat knelt before her and patted her. 'Are you lost, girl? Did you get out by yourself? That's okay, I'll take you home.' She gave Rosie a hug, her small arms passing through Atropos's arms, her small, beautiful face only inches from his ugly, grinning one. Then she got up. 'Come on, Rosie! Come on, sugarpie.'

Rosalie started down the sidewalk at Nat's heel, looking back once at the grinning little man and whining uneasily. On the other side of Harris Avenue, Helen came out of the Red Apple, and the last condition of the vision Atropos had shown Ralph was fulfilled. Helen had a loaf of bread in one hand. Her Red Sox hat was on her head.

Ralph swept Lois into his arms and kissed her fiercely. 'I love you with all my heart,' he said. 'Remember that, Lois.'

'I know you do,' she said calmly. 'And I love *you*. That's why I can't let you do it.'

She seized him around the neck, her arms like bands of iron, and he felt her breasts push against him hard as she drew in all the breath her lungs would hold.

'*Go away, you rotten bastard!*' she screamed. '*I can't see you, but I know you're there! Go away! Go away and leave us alone!*'

Natalie stopped dead in her tracks and looked at Lois with wide-eyed surprise. Rosalie stopped beside her, ears pricking.

'*Don't go into the street, Nat!*' Lois screamed at her. '*Don't—*'

Then her hands, which had been laced together at the back of Ralph's neck, were holding nothing; her arms, which had been locked about his shoulders in a deathgrip, were empty.

He was gone like smoke.

21

Atropos looked toward the cry of alarm and saw Ralph and Lois standing on the other side of Harris Avenue. More important, he saw Ralph seeing *him*. His eyes widened; his lips parted in a hateful snarl. One hand flew to his bald pate – it was crisscrossed with old scars, the remnants of wounds made with his own scalpel – in an instinctive gesture of defense that was five years too late.

[*Fuck you, Shorts! This little bitch is mine!*]

Ralph saw Nat, looking at Lois with uncertainty and surprise. He heard Lois shrieking at her, telling her not to go into the street. Then it was Lachesis he heard, speaking from someplace close by.

[*Come up, Ralph! As far as you can! Quickly!*]

He felt the clench in the center of his head, felt that brief swoop of vertigo in his stomach, and suddenly the whole world brightened and filled with color. He half-saw and half-felt Lois's arms and locked hands collapse inward, through the place where his body had been a moment before, and then he was drawing away from her – no, being *carried* away from her. He felt the pull of some great current and understood, in a vague way, that if there was such a thing as a Higher Purpose, he had joined it and would soon be swept downriver with it.

Natalie and Rosalie were now standing directly in front of the house which Ralph had once shared with Bill McGovern before selling up and moving into Lois's house. Nat glanced doubtfully at Lois, then waved tentatively. 'She's okay, Lois – see, she's right here.' She patted Rosalie's head. 'I'll cross her safe, don't worry.' Then, as she started into the street, she called to her mother. 'I can't find my baseball cap! I think somebody stole it!'

Rosalie was still on the sidewalk. Nat turned to her impatiently. 'Come *on*, girl!'

The green car was moving in the child's direction, but very slowly. It did not at first look like much of a danger to her. Ralph recognized the driver at once, and he did not doubt his senses or suspect he was having a hallucination. In that instant it seemed very right that the approaching sedan should be piloted by his old paperboy.

'*Natalie!*' Lois screamed. '*Natalie, no!*'

Atropos darted forward and slapped Rosalie #2 on the rump.

[*Get outta here, mutt! G'wan! Before I change my mind!*]

Atropos spared Ralph one final grimacing leer as Rosie yelped and darted into the street . . . and into the path of the Ford driven by sixteen-year-old Pete Sullivan.

Natalie didn't see the car; she was looking at Lois, whose face was all red and scary. It had finally occurred to Nat that Lois wasn't screaming about Rosie at all, but something else entirely.

Pete registered the sprinting beagle; it was the little girl he didn't see. He swerved to avoid Rosalie, a maneuver that ended with the Ford aimed directly at Natalie. Ralph could see two frightened faces behind the windshield as the car veered, and he thought Mrs Sullivan was screaming.

Atropos was leaping up and down, doing an obscenely joyful hornpipe.

[*Yahh, Short-Time! Silly white-hair! Toldja I'd fix you!*]

In slow motion Helen dropped the loaf of bread she was holding. '*Natalie,* LOOK OUUUUUUTTT!' she shrieked.

Ralph ran. Again there was that clear sensation of moving by thought alone. And as he closed in on Nat, now diving forward with his hands stretched out, aware of the car looming just beyond her, kicking bright arrows of sun through its dark deathbag and into his eyes, he clenched his mind again, bringing himself back down to the Short-Time world for the last time.

He fell into a landscape that rang with splintered screams: Helen's mingled with Lois's mingled with the ones being made by the tires of the Ford. Weaving its way through them like an outlaw vine was the sound of Atropos's jeers. Ralph got a brief glimpse of Nat's wide blue eyes, and then he shoved her in the chest and stomach as hard as he could, sending her flying backwards with her hands and feet thrust out in front of her. She landed sitting up in the gutter, bruising her tailbone on the curb but breaking nothing. From some distant place, Ralph heard Atropos squawk in fury and disbelief.

Then two tons of Ford, still travelling at twenty miles an hour, struck Ralph and the soundtrack dropped dead. He was heaved upward and backward in a low, slow arc – it *felt* slow, anyway, from inside – and went with the Ford's hood ornament imprinted on his cheek like a tattoo and one broken leg trailing behind him. There was time to see his shadow sliding along the pavement beneath him in a shape like an X; there was time to see a spray of red droplets in the air just above him and to think that Lois must have splattered more paint on him than he had thought at first. And there was time to see Natalie sitting at the side of the street, weeping but all right . . . and to sense Atropos on the sidewalk behind her, shaking his fists and dancing with rage.

I believe I did pretty damned good for an old geezer, Ralph thought, *but now I think I could really do with a nap.*

Then he came back to earth with a terrible mortal smack and rolled – skull fracturing, back breaking, lungs punctured by brittle thorns of bone as his ribcage exploded, liver turning to pulp, intestines first coming unanchored and then rupturing.

And nothing hurt.

Nothing at all.

22

Lois never forgot the awful thud that was the sound of Ralph's return to Harris Avenue, or the bloody splashmarks he left behind as he cartwheeled to a stop. She wanted to scream but dared not; some deep, true voice told her that if she did that, the combination of shock, horror, and summer heat would send her unconscious to the sidewalk, and when she came to again, Ralph would be beyond her.

She ran instead of screaming, losing one shoe, marginally aware that Pete Sullivan was getting out of the Ford, which had come to rest almost exactly where Joe Wyzer's car – also a Ford – had come to rest after Joe had hit Rosalie #1 all those years ago. She was also marginally aware that Pete was screaming.

She reached Ralph and fell on her knees beside him, seeing that his shape had somehow been changed by the green Ford, that the body beneath the familiar chino pants and paint-splattered shirt was fundamentally different from the body which had been pressed against hers less than a minute ago. But his eyes were open, and they were bright and aware.

'Ralph?'

'Yes.' His voice was clear and strong, unmarked by either confusion or pain. 'Yes, Lois, I hear you.'

She started to put her arms around him and hesitated, thinking about how you weren't supposed to move people who had been badly injured because you might hurt them even worse or kill them. Then she looked at him again, at the blood pouring from the sides of his mouth and the way his lower body seemed to have come unhinged from the upper part, and decided it would be impossible to hurt Ralph more than he had been hurt already. She hugged him, leaning close, leaning into the smells of disaster: blood and the sweet-sour acetone odor of spent adrenaline on the outrush of his breath.

'You did it this time, didn't you?' Lois asked. She kissed his cheek, his blood-soaked eyebrows, his bloody forehead where the skin had been peeled away from his skull in a flap. She began to cry. 'Look at you! Shirt torn, pants torn . . . do you think clothes grow on trees?'

'Is he all right?' Helen asked from behind her. Lois didn't

647

turn around, but she saw the shadows on the street: Helen with her arm around her weeping daughter's shoulders, and Rosie standing by Helen's right leg. 'He saved Nat's life and I didn't even see where he came from. Please, Lois, say he's all r—'

Then the shadows shifted as Helen moved to a place where she could actually see Ralph, and she pulled Nat's face against her blouse and began to wail.

Lois leaned closer to Ralph, caressing his cheeks with the palms of her hands, wanting to tell him that she had meant to come with him – she had meant to, yes, but in the end he had been too quick for her. In the end he had left her behind.

'Love you, sweetheart,' Ralph said. He reached up and copied her gesture with his own palm. He tried to raise his left hand as well, but it would only lie on the pavement and twitch.

Lois took his hand and kissed it. 'Love you, too, Ralph. Always. So much.'

'I had to do it. You see?'

'Yes.' She didn't know if she *did* see, didn't know if she would *ever* see . . . but she knew he was dying. 'Yes, I see.'

He sighed harshly – that sweet acetone smell wafted up to her again – and smiled.

'Miz Chasse? Miz Roberts, I mean?' It was Pete, speaking in hitching gasps. 'Is Mr Roberts okay? Please say I didn't hurt him!'

'Stay away, Pete,' she said without turning around. 'Ralph is fine. He just tore his pants and shirt a little . . . didn't you, Ralph?'

'Yes,' he said. 'You bet. You'll just have to hosswhip me for—'

He broke off and looked to her left. No one was there, but Ralph smiled anyway. 'Lachesis!' he said.

He put out his trembling, blood-grimy right hand, and as Lois, Helen, and Pete Sullivan watched, it rose and fell twice in the empty air. Ralph's eyes moved again, this time to the right. Slowly, very slowly, he moved his hand in that direction. When he spoke this time, his voice had begun to fade. 'Hi, Clotho. Now remember: this . . . doesn't . . . hurt. Right?'

Ralph appeared to listen, and then smiled.

'Yep,' he whispered, 'any way you can get her.'

His hand rose and fell again in the air, then dropped back to his chest. He looked up at Lois with his fading blue eyes.

'Listen,' he said, speaking with great effort. Yet his eyes blazed, would not let hers go. 'Every day I woke up next to you was like waking up young and seeing . . . everything new.' He tried to raise his hand to her cheek again, and could not. 'Every day, Lois.'

'It was like that for me, too, Ralph – like waking up young.'

'Lois?'

'What?'

'The ticking,' he said. He swallowed and then said it again, enunciating the words with great effort. 'The ticking.'

'What ticking?'

'Never mind, it's stopped,' he said, and smiled brilliantly. Then Ralph stopped, too.

23

Clotho and Lachesis stood watching Lois weep over the man who lay dead in the street. In one hand Clotho held his scissors; he raised the other to eye-level and looked at it wonderingly.

It glowed and blazed with Ralph's aura.

Clotho: [*He's here . . . in here . . . how wonderful!*]

Lachesis raised his own right hand. Like Clotho's left, it looked as if someone had pulled a blue mitten over the normal green-gold aura which swaddled it.

Lachesis: [*Yes. He was a wonderful man.*]

Clotho: [*Shall we give him to her?*]

Lachesis: [*Can we?*]

Clotho: [*There's one way to find out.*]

They approached Lois. Each placed the hand Ralph had shaken on one side of Lois's face.

24

'Mommy!' Natalie Deepnau cried. In her agitation, she had reverted to the patois of her babyhood. 'Who those wittle men? Why they touchin Roliss?'

'Shh, honey,' Helen said, and buried Nat's head against her breast again. There were no men, little or otherwise, near Lois Roberts; she was kneeling alone in the street next to the man who had saved her daughter's life.

25

Lois looked up suddenly, her eyes wide and surprised, her grief forgotten as a gorgeous feeling of
  (*light blue light*)
calmness and peace filled her. For a moment Harris Avenue was gone. She was in a dark place filled with the sweet smells of hay and cows, a dark place that was split by a hundred brilliant seams of light. She never forgot the fierce joy that leaped up in her at that moment, nor the sure sense that she was seeing a representation of a universe that Ralph wanted her to see, a universe where there was dazzling light behind the darkness . . . couldn't she see it through the cracks?

'Can you ever forgive me?' Pete was sobbing. 'Oh my God, can you ever forgive me?'

'Oh yes, I think so,' Lois said calmly.

She passed her hand down Ralph's face, closing his eyes, and then held his head in her lap and waited for the police to come. To Lois, Ralph looked as if he had gone to sleep. And, she saw, the long white scar on his right forearm was gone.

September 10, 1990 – November 10, 1993